HUMOROUS TALES
FROM
'BLACKWOOD'

First printed . . 5250 *copies*
September 1933

Reprinted . . . 3150 *copies*
December 1933

Reprinted . . . 3150 *copies*
June 1934

Reprinted . . . 3150 *copies*
April 1935

Reprinted . . . 3150 *copies*
September 1936

Reprinted . . . 3150 *copies*
November 1938

Reprinted . . . 2500 *copies*
April 1941

Reprinted . . . 2100 *copies*
February 1942

Reprinted . . . 2200 *copies*
September 1942

Humorous Tales

from

'Blackwood'

EDINBURGH AND LONDON:
WM. BLACKWOOD & SONS LTD.
1942

The paper and binding of this book conform to
the authorised economy standard.

PRINTED IN GREAT BRITAIN

CONTENTS.

'GOOD GOD, CAROLINE.'

BY EVELYNE BUXTON.

[Maga, November 1922.]

I.

WHEN General Bellowes first perceived Mr Chealey, in the early autumn of 1919, Mr Chealey was using his handkerchief, or, as he himself would have termed it, his pocket-hangkercheef, as a duster—and not without need.

General Bellowes had reached the clump of trees called Paddockclose, which ends the long level succession of fields known as the King's Mile, that lies along the edge of the King's Lodge deer-park, and still tells in its name the story of the days when King Charles coursed deer with wild Cramp Ditton in the Cotswolds long ago. Paddockclose was then the paddock whence the chase started, and the King's Mile was a mile of unbroken sward that finished in front of the King's Lodge, from the balconies and balconied roof of which king and courtiers watched the deer pulled down.

The park boundary here turning left through the Paddockclose trees, General Bellowes prepared to turn left also, but before doing so he leaned over the gate in the park hedge to take a cursory glance up and down the narrow road that ran on the other side of it, and make sure there was nothing there that needed dealing with; and in the road, a short distance away under the trees, he suddenly perceived Mr Chealey dusting himself.

Once off the chief roads of the Cotswolds, and a stranger is an event—and Mr Chealey was not only a stranger but one who, as the General instantly perceived, was evidently feeling his position as such in some depression of spirits. The white lime-dust of the blazing Cotswold uplands lay thick on his highly unsuitable shabby black coat and striped grey trousers and little bowler hat, and hung on his eyelashes in surrounding white clouds that made his pale tired eyes look paler still. He was flicking at himself with a kind of helpless and unhappy vigour, while his uncertain glance wandered down the road that went on in burning light beyond the single oasis of shadows in which he stood.

"Good day to you," said General Bellowes in a loud voice, and Mr Chealey sprang in the air.

"It's a hot day," said General Bellowes as loudly as before, and Mr Chealey sprang once more, and turned round in his spring to face the gate and the owner of the voice.

"Sorry if I startled you," said General Bellowes.

"Don't mention it, don't mention it," said Mr Chealey with a gasp.

The thoughts of General Bellowes usually travelled straight to his lips without any secondary consideration or modifying perception checking their progress *en route*. They were generally excellent thoughts, and as he seldom had more than one of them in his mind at a time, he was usually able to concentrate upon it very firmly and get it very clearly stated; and it was believed that this power of tremendous concentration on one point, and of total oblivion to all others, had very materially assisted in the success of the General's military career. He now surveyed Mr Chealey disapprovingly.

"Your nerves seem to be in a very bad state, sir," he remarked. "A man shouldn't jump like that merely because someone speaks to him on the road. You're hot, of course, and perhaps you're tired. That may be it. Come a long way?"

The thoughts of Mr Chealey, in contradistinction to those of General Bellowes, seldom travelled straight to anything. They generally met other thoughts on their way—chiefly unformed ones—and emerged, as it were, in a fighting crowd.

"Not at all—that is to say—thank you, I don't mind—you're very kind," he stammered.

"I don't know where you're going to," proceeded General Bellowes, "but as you seem a stranger to these parts, perhaps you don't know that this lane only runs into a secondary Oldwait and Southreach road, and that there are more direct routes than this to both places. As a matter of fact, it's a lane that really only exists to serve my house and a farm or two. However, if you're going on, you'll find my place about three-quarters of a mile farther along on your right. Iron gates and two appalling lodges. Go straight in and ask for a rest and a drink. That will help you on your way a bit. These are not the kind of clothes to go about the Cotswolds in. Say I sent you if I'm not back—General Bellowes. But I shall be there almost as soon as you will. I'm going round by the park. Good day to you."

He turned and tramped off, and left Mr Chealey standing helplessly in the shadows, gazing after him in bewildered agitation. When the General had quite disappeared, Mr Chealey drew a long breath and wiped his duty brow with the dustier bandanna.

"Well, if that's the owner of King's Lodge, I doubt if it's much use me going on," he said dejectedly. "You could hardly *meet* a gentleman you'd less like to put a question to!"

He looked back along the road by which he had come. The point where it ran across the main Oxford and Cheltenham road was still in sight. To go back all those weary miles to Lorton without even having tried to do what he had come to try to do—"No," said Mr Chealey, sighing. "It's got to be done somehow. It's the last time, anyway. I suppose I ought to take it as a bit of luck that I've met him and been asked in. But I wish I hadn't." He issued from the Paddockclose shadows into the blazing sunlight once more and continued on his way.

Thus it happened that when Mrs Bellowes, walking out for an early afternoon stroll, came mildly forth between the iron gates and the two appalling lodges and turned left, the first thing she perceived was Mr Chealey dusting himself busily a little way along the road between the high hedges, in preparation for what he thought must surely be by now his imminent arrival at King's Lodge.

Mrs Bellowes, not being General Bellowes, was able to perceive and pass a stranger without experiencing any very imperative desire to oblige him to become an acquaintance, and she would have floated on with no more than a passing glance and perhaps a passing reflection on the extreme unsuitability of the stranger's attire to his surroundings, had not Mr Chealey, on seeing her, ceased his anxious dusting, coughed, hesitated, raised his little bowler hat and stepped forward.

"I beg your pardon, madam," he said, "but can you tell me if I have to go much farther before I come to a house called King's Lodge?"

"You don't have to go any farther," said Mrs Bellowes, pausing graciously. "It's only the hedge that prevents your seeing it now. If you go on ten steps more you'll come to the lodges. They stand a little back from the road or you could see them too."

"Thank you, thank you, madam, I'm sure," said Mr Chealey, bowing.

"Do you want to see anybody there?" said Mrs Bellowes.

"No—that is—not exactly—perhaps—that is——" said Mr Chealey. "What I mean is, I think I met the gentleman who lives there down the road, madam—and he was so kind

—that is, he suggested—he thought it a hot day—a rest, a very brief rest, of course——"

"Do, by all means. That will have been my husband," said Mrs Bellowes.

She surveyed Mr Chealey with leisurely graciousness. She was unlike General Bellowes in that she frequently had more than one thought at a time, and unlike Mr Chealey in that she was able to decide which one of them to express. "I wonder what the queer little business can be that brings this queer little man to this part of the world," she thought. "I wonder if he's front door or back! If he goes alone, Priggles is certain to send such a meek little tired dusty sorrowful thing to the back, and he'll be put in the servants' hall and treated with condescension. I don't think I'll let him be sent to the back." The idle thoughts drifted all together through Mrs Bellowes' head, and aloud she said serenely, "Let me show you the way," and she turned and floated along beside Mr Chealey.

However unsuitable Mr Chealey's attire may have been, Mrs Bellowes' own attire, though it went most beautifully with the beauty of the country she was in and with the beauty of the weather she was enjoying, and was most delightfully suitable to both, was in other respects quite as unsuitable as Mr Chealey's. It did not in the least, for instance, go with that admirable, that unbending, that almost religious conviction on the part of the true English that there is but one kind of clothing which can possibly be considered suitable to real ladies in the country, and that no real lady would ever appear there except in tweeds, little round hats and thick nailed shoes with Indian fringes to them. Mrs Bellowes' explanation was believed to be that, not having had to marry into the class in which she lived, there was no need for her to be careful to show that she knew how to dress suitably to it, in the country or elsewhere. Anyway, she seldom did so, and on this occasion Mr Chealey's vivid and humble perception of the superior advantages possessed by nearly everybody except himself was greatly exercised by the exquisite and flower-like effect of Mrs Bellowes. He walked gingerly along the edge of the bordering grass, as one who wished to show how far he was from claiming a share with her of even so liberal a thing as a road, and accompanied their progress with earnest protests against the trouble he was giving; and thus they did the ten more steps together and came to the high wrought-iron gates and their tall stone-balled pillars, and the two appalling little lodges, much smaller than the gates, that were not only like salt-cellars but like squashed salt-cellars.

So involved in his protests and apologies was Mr Chealey that he had no leisure at first to look at anything, and they had passed the gates and the lodges and were well in the drive before he happened to glance ahead. "I do hope I am not bringing you back, madam—that is, I fear I am indeed bringing you back—what I mean is——" said Mr Chealey. Here he looked anxiously along the drive, and his face changed and he stopped dead. "My goodness," he ejaculated, quite abruptly and naturally, "it *is!*"

"Is what?" said Mrs Bellowes.

"Inigo Jones," breathed Mr Chealey, as one who sees a vision.

"Well, they *say* not, you know," said Mrs Bellowes. "I believe they think it was built by a pupil of his."

"He must have been a very good pupil!" said Mr Chealey, drawing a long breath.

Mrs Bellowes looked at her country home with her leisurely gracious gaze. Grey and square, built of the Cotswold stone—its pillars and its balconied roof, its mullions and carvings, its walls and balustrades weathered by the passing of hundreds of years—King's Lodge stood at the distant end of a long open grassed space through which a straight formal drive ran to the pillared arcade before its front door, and was set at the back of a single great half-moon of splendid beeches—high towers, on this magnificent autumn afternoon, of flaming rose and gold. They grew thick-ranked, far higher than the roof, shoulder to shoulder, and each tree a glory; and the long wings of the half-moon ran out on either side of the little grey carved house and enclosed it as in a deep three-sided court of gorgeous colour.

"Oh dear, oh dear!" said Mr Chealey, sighing. "How very pretty!"

"It *is* rather unusual, isn't it?" said Mrs Bellowes. "So odd to come upon a building like a tiny bit of a little Versailles looking out on an English country lane; isn't it! Had you heard of it before?"

"Yes—that is—I have read—that is——" said Mr Chealey, recovering from the single-mindedness of his momentary absorption and immediately recommencing to stammer.

"Are you interested in architecture?" said Mrs Bellowes.

"I—that is—it is—I have——" said Mr Chealey.

"Parts of it are not at all good *in*side," Mrs Bellowes informed him graciously. "Some of it was restored, you see, by the same generation of my husband's family that built the lodges, and even Herbert hates those. Still, of course, the best way to restore is to destroy as much as possible, and it's quite comfortable and decidedly uncommon. You can get to the second bathroom quite easily if you go completely round the house outdoors and in again by a side door; and Priggles assures us that all the best butlers are five foot three. We can't have them higher than that, you see, because the door from the back premises to the hall is five foot two. Shall we go on?"

They went on, Mr Chealey walking as one on tiptoe. They passed the lichened grey walls that stood on either side under the beeches and framed the gardens in front of the house, and Mr Chealey caught glimpses through their wrought-iron gates of the deer in the deer-park beyond. He heard the cool splashing of the fountain in the round lawn before the pillared portico. He sighed, he stammered, he plunged into abstraction, and emerged with a start. His anxious eyes and tired little face were full of nervous preoccupation.

Mrs Bellowes, who lived in these high and beech-grown solitudes, seven miles from anywhere, in the same reflective fashion in which she had always lived anywhere the General decided to put her, from a Bagdad cellar in Mesopotamia to his recently sold town house in Mayfair, and who looked at everybody she met in the world in the same detached and faintly amused fashion, glanced at Mr Chealey from time to time, but seldom interrupted, except by a gracious and encouraging smile, the spasmodic torrent of apologies, thanks and protests with which he endeavoured to express his sense of her kindness. However much he talked, Mr Chealey never seemed to get anything quite said. Whatever he wanted to say always appeared to fall over something else he wanted to say and could not—something that lay permanently on the threshold of his mind, as it were, and tripped up everything that tried to get by. The faultless kindness of Mrs Bellowes, however, remained unmoved by the constantly defeated efforts of Mr Chealey to thank her for it. She was kind as a Royalty is kind, kind as a lady is kind who has been the serene and disinterested dispenser of a public man's determined and somewhat indiscriminate hospitality in high places and low. Whether it were one chance stranger in a blue moon, as up here in the Cotswolds, or five hundred strangers in an hour, as at an official reception in Cairo, to the musing and faultless treatment by the detached Mrs Bellowes of her fellow-creatures it appeared to make very little difference.

She took Mr Chealey into the house and up the broad oak stairs and out to the great square balcony over the portico, which was as large as a room. From the outside walls of the house old carved stone faces looked down at Mr Chealey as they had once looked down on King Charles and his nobles; and over the broad top of the carved balustrade upon which the royal elbows must often have rested,

Mr Chealey looked forth at the rolling Cotswolds, disappearing to wonderful purple distances among the separated rounded assemblages of trees which here characterise the landscape. It was as lovely to look out at the open country from the heart of that red and gold court of beeches as it had been to look into it from the open country. Mr Chealey's agitation appeared to increase in an exact ratio to his perception of the beauty of the house and its situation. He gazed at the view in miserable silence.

Mrs Bellowes gave him a cushioned deck-chair to sit in, and inquired his name, and told him the names of the faraway hills, and asked him whether he would like something to drink, and had just moved back into the sitting-room that gave on to the balcony to ring the bell when there came on the stairs the sound of an echoing and ascending tramp.

"Caroline! Where are you, Caroline!" said the loud voice of General Bellowes. "Oh, here you are. Look here, Caroline, I met an extraordinary little blighter down the road just now, a suburban little blighter. Can't think what he's doing in these parts. He was so tired he jumped half out of his skin when I merely bade him good day, so I told him to come here and get a rest. He may turn up at any moment, and you'd better tell Priggles to—oh, he *has* turned up—oh, here he is. Here you are. Don't get up, don't get up. Have a drink. What'll you have?"

"Mr Chealey was just saying he thinks he would like a drink of milk," said Mrs Bellowes, as Mr Chealey achieved his exit from the low deck-chair after a desperate struggle complicated by bows.

"*Milk!*" said General Bellowes. "A drink of milk! Good God, Caroline, what use is *milk* to a tired man with a thirst on him! Have a whisky-and-soda! Have a brandy and Vichy. Have a claret and Seltzer. Have anything but milk!"

"I think—that is—I mean—I fear—alcohol," said Mr Chealey, bowing and smiling nervously.

Mrs Bellowes went through the glass balcony door into the sitting-room again, and returned with a large chunk of cake in her hand. "We always keep some handy for the birds," she said in a gracious smiling aside to Mr Chealey as she passed him, and she went to the balustrade and, leaning on it, began abstractedly to break up the cake and scatter it over the sweep below. Mr Chealey, with a suddenly arrested and concentrated gaze, followed the movements of her hands.

"No, no, no! A whisky-and-soda, *that's* the thing!" said the General, striding into the sitting-room and ringing the bell. "And I'll split one with you myself, what's more. It's a very hot day."

But when the whisky-and-soda came, borne by Mr Priggles the butler, who could never be higher than five foot three, Mr Chealey, still smiling nervously, took one sip and set it down and said how beautiful the view was, while General Bellowes obscured his entire countenance in his large tumbler and Mrs Bellowes musingly watched the birds that darted to and from the beeches.

"I think—that is—I fear—so much kindness to a stranger—a delightful rest——" said Mr Chealey.

"Why, man, you've drunk nothing," said the General as he set down his empty tumbler.

"Most kind—that is—alcohol—I fear," said Mr Chealey; and though he went on bowing and smiling more nervously than ever, and seemed overwhelmed with the kind hospitality that had been shown him, the whisky-and-soda was somehow still untouched when he finally managed to say that he thought he must be going.

"Well, we'll come down with you to the door. We generally go for a walk in the park before tea, and it's time we were starting," said General Bellowes, and they all descended the shining oak stairs together.

Mrs Bellowes had shaken hands with him graciously, and General Bellowes had shaken hands with him abruptly, and

Mr Chealey had left the front door and was out on the sweep, when he suddenly turned round and came back. With a pale face and anxious eyes gazing fixedly at General Bellowes, he approached that surprised gentleman.

" General Bellowes, sir," he said, " I suppose you wouldn't think of *letting* your house, sir, or *selling* it."

" Wouldn't think of *what*, sir!" said the astonished General Bellowes.

" Of letting your house, sir, or selling it," said Mr Chealey faintly.

Had Mr Chealey asked the question casually and lightly in the course of conversation, it is probable that the answer would have been as casual, since in itself the subject is not one to cause great emotion or excitement. But the despairing anxiety, the urgent appeal, the suddenness and the desperate earnestness of Mr Chealey's return, turned it almost into an assault. A new and unexpected thought thrust itself suddenly upon the thought that was comfortably in possession of the General's mind, and this was a sensation to which not even perpetual practice could ever quite accustom him.

" Of course I don't want to let or sell my house!" he said loudly. " What an extraordinary thing to ask! Do you mean you want to buy it?"

" Oh no, sir," said Mr Chealey, endeavouring to smile. His lips were beginning to tremble, but he still spoke without stammering. Whatever had lain on the threshold between his mind and his speech had suddenly arisen and emerged, and he spoke in the single-mindedness of one unconfused and absorbing idea. " I don't want to buy it myself," he said. " I'm afraid I'm hardly in a position to do that! But if you were thinking of selling it, sir, if you only *would*, sir, we could get you a very high price nowadays, extraordinarily high, probably more than treble what it was worth before the war; or if you wished to let we could secure you a very high rental—we could indeed, sir, almost any rental you wished to name. Moderate sized houses of this type——" He got no further in his faint and hurried speech.

"So you're a house-agent, are you!" said General Bellowes, folding his arms and surveying Mr Chealey from the porch of his home. "One of those confounded fellows whose letters I chuck by the score into the waste-paper basket every day. A man can't have a house worth looking at nowadays without being pestered to death by half a hundred agents who want to make money out of it. I suppose you came down here on purpose to get hold of me, eh? You did, eh? I thought so! I think it would have been better taste on your part if you had told me at once that you knew the place quite well, and were on your way to try and make me sell it. Well, sir, I'm afraid you've made your journey in vain. I haven't the faintest intention of either letting or selling my house. Good day to you."

For a moment longer Mr Chealey, with a white face, stared at the irritated countenance of the owner of King's Lodge. Then without a word he turned and hastened away.

So sudden, so speechless, so despairing was Mr Chealey's flight that it startled General Bellowes almost as much as Mr Chealey's equally sudden return had done. He unfolded his arms and gazed after him in amazement.

"The little blighter's mad!" he said with profound conviction.

"He's hungry," said Mrs Bellowes in her mild and indolent voice.

"*Hungry!*" repeated the General, removing his surprised gaze from Mr Chealey's fleeing little figure to contemplate in still greater surprise the faultlessly kind and faintly amused expression with which Mrs Bellowes was following the precipitate departure of their recent guest. "Why on earth should he be *hungry!*"

"How should I know, Herbert dear" said Mrs Bellowes

serenely. " But what he wanted more dreadfully than anything in the world was the cake I gave the birds."

" The cake you gave the birds ! " exclaimed the General at the top of his voice.

" The reason he wouldn't drink the whisky-and-soda," said Mrs Bellowes, " was because he was afraid it would go to his head. And so it would have, of course, with nothing inside him."

" Nothing inside him ! " exclaimed the General. " Now, how in the name of Heaven can you pretend to know, Caroline, that that little bounder had nothing inside him ! "

" Oh, well, I suppose he had *something*," conceded Mrs Bellowes, with gracious indifference. " Words, for instance. Heaps of words. Things he couldn't get said. I suppose he found it extra terrifying to get them said when it was his last chance—like striking a match when there isn't another. He couldn't bring himself to say them till he had actually turned his back to go away, and he'd been trying to the whole afternoon. Well, his match went out, poor little oddment, directly he got it struck, and, anyway, he's gone now," said Mrs Bellowes, as the far-away little Chealey shot through the distant gates and vanished. " And it's getting late. Shall we go for our walk, Herbert ? "

" Good God, Caroline ! " said the General in a loud and exasperated voice. " His last chance of *what !* "

" Dear Herbert, how should I know ! " said Mrs Bellowes mildly. " If we don't start at once we shall be late back to tea."

General Bellowes paid no heed. He stared down the empty drive. He was busy seizing a new thought. The moment he got hold of it, it got hold of him. " I'm going to see what's wrong with that miserable little beggar," he announced, and he strode across the sweep and took a short cut over the grass for a gap in the hedge at the bottom of the grounds well to the left of the gates, travelling much faster on his journey to intercept Mr Chealey than

Mr Chealey, with his shorter legs, had travelled on his journey to escape.

The gap was filled in by a low stone wall, and the General, on reaching it, looked cautiously over. He immediately perceived Mr Chealey, a little to his right, standing facing him in the road, between him and the gates. But Mr Chealey did not see the General. Trembling from head to foot, absorbed in the effort to retain his tottering self-control, he was dusting himself with all his might, and his bandanna handkerchief shook in his hand as he worked it busily round and round the rim of his little hat. Just as the General's intent countenance topped the wall, Mr Chealey addressed himself aloud, assiduously polishing the while. "Come, come, Chealey, this is *no* way to behave!" he said. "Dear me, Chealey, whatever is the matter? Come now, Chealey, *this* won't do!" adjured Mr Chealey in accents of quivering remonstrance. The heavy tears were streaming down his tired face and falling with a plop into the Cotswold dust.

Mrs Bellowes was sitting in graceful comfort against a pillar on the edge of the raised flag pavement of the portico when General Bellowes and Mr Chealey returned with great rapidity up the drive together. Such was the intensity of the thought that now possessed the General's mind, that the little feet of the bewildered and twittering Mr Chealey were barely allowed to touch the earth as he sped back to King's Lodge in the firm and enveloping grasp of its owner.

"The man's exhausted," said General Bellowes. His tones were brief and commanding, as those of one who deals with an emergency, but has been far too well accustomed to emergencies all over the world not to know exactly what to do and to insist on its being done in a calm and quiet manner. "He's ill with hunger. Waste no words, Caroline. Let there be no fuss and nonsense. We can make all inquiries later. One small cup of tea at seven in Cheltenham this morning and nothing since. What is there in the house ? Have everything there is brought in at once. Now no questions, if you please, Caroline, till the man is fed, and no noise and nonsense," said the General, sweeping Mr Chealey into the old hall that lay wide and panelled and cool beyond the glare of the sun.

"I didn't—that is—I assure you—it's only——" stammered Mr Chealey ; but the General was already roaring at the little door in the hall that led to the back premises.

"Do sit down, Mr Chealey," said Mrs Bellowes' gracious accents through the noise, as she sank into an arm-chair. "We often have tea early, and we often have it here in the hall because of this nice big table. It will be charming if you will join us."

"Priggles," roared the General at the back premises door. "Where on earth are you, Priggles ? Come here, this instant. Look here, Priggles, bring some food at once. Bring eggs, chops, sausages, bacon, anything. Bring whatever there is in the house. What *is* there in the house ? Can't *you* suggest anything, Caroline ? "

"Perhaps Priggles can," said Mrs Bellowes, her charming head resting placidly against the cushions of her chair. "This gentleman has had a long walk, Priggles, and has another long one before him, so we shall want a rather larger tea than usual."

"Thank you, madam," said Mr Priggles.

"I do assure you——" faltered Mr Chealey.

"A rather larger tea ! " said the General. "Good God, Caroline, we want an *immense* tea ! We want a *dinner !* What can we have, Priggles ! Make haste, man ! "

"If I might make a suggestion, sir," said the lofty and unmoved Mr Priggles, "a couple of poached eggs, sir, as though hunting, so to speak."

"A very good idea, Priggles," said Mrs Bellowes.

"Thank you, madam," said Mr Priggles.

"Not nearly enough, not nearly enough," said the General strongly.

"I do assure you——" faltered Mr Chealey.

"And perhaps the cold chicken-pie, sir, that was merely cast an eye on as a sideboard piece at lunch," continued Mr Priggles.

"A very good idea, Priggles," said Mrs Bellows benignly.

"Thank you, madam," said Mr Priggles.

"Then bring it, man," said the General. "Bring it at once, if that's all there is. And the eggs, and anything else you can think of. I'm afraid you'll have to make that do, Chealey. It's incomprehensible that there shouldn't be more in the house, but I'm afraid you'll have to make that do."

"I assure you, sir—I do assure you——" faltered Mr Chealey; and Mr Priggles withdrew, five foot three, and so imposing in his majesty that he was far more alarming to those outside the household than anyone else inside it, including its master.

When the meal arrived Mr Chealey drew his chair to the table in a hesitating confusion of deprecations and assurances. But at his first mouthful of poached eggs his protesting murmurs suddenly died away. He did not forget his manners. It was impossible to imagine a Mr Chealey forgetting those, even on his death-bed. But to toy with his tea as if he did not really need it, but was merely disposing of a mouthful or two as a pleasing accompaniment to the enjoyment of polite conversation—which is, of course, the only way to eat anything in high society—was more than Mr Chealey could achieve. His face changed. He became silent. With a fixed countenance he began his meal.

As for General Bellowes, he sat absorbed in Mr Chealey. He piled food upon his plate, he kept his tea-cup brimming, he cut large slices of bread for him which he coated earnestly with butter. When not thus occupied he sat back and regarded Mr Chealey strongly; while Mrs Bellowes continued to enjoy her tea in her graceful and leisurely way, and to talk in her usual gracious and conversational manner. So sustained, indeed, were both her tea and her benign conversation that it really would have been quite easy for nobody to notice that Mr Chealey was making rather an unusually large and lengthy meal, or that General Bellowes was so intent upon his doing so that he was making no conversation of any kind, either gracious or otherwise. Mr Chealey might really almost have succeeded in thinking that he was not noticing these things himself.

But—whether it was the food or the kindness or the relief, or his host's keen contemplation of him, or just a sudden realisation of his own fatigue and hopelessness—but suddenly Mr Chealey laid down his knife and fork and gazed in a strained manner at the table. Then he hurriedly took up his knife and fork again, ate a mouthful of chicken-pie, choked, put down his knife and fork once more and desperately endeavoured to get out his bandanna handkerchief in time. Too late! To the General's inexpressible horror two large tears rolled down Mr Chealey's cheeks and dropped upon the chicken-pie.

"Good God, Caroline!" said the General hurriedly. "Now, for Heaven's sake, Chealey! Come, cheer up, man! There's nothing to cry for *now*. Have some more eggs. Have some more tea. Have some more pie. Good God, Caroline, can't you do something!"

"I'm ashamed—I don't—it isn't——" sobbed Mr Chealey. "It's the first time—kindness—I haven't had much to eat for some time now—I'm so dreadfully on the rocks." He put his elbows on the table and his face in his hands, and sobbed unreservedly.

"Good God, Caroline, hadn't I better go away?" said the General, helpless before this revelation of misery and exhaustion.

"Well, you *could*, of course, Herbert," said Mrs Bellowes judicially. "Do if you like. But I don't see why you should go away because Mr Chealey wishes to cry. Do cry, Mr Chealey. There isn't the faintest reason why you shouldn't."

"Good God, Caroline!" said the General.

"Well, I don't see why he shouldn't," said Mrs Bellowes. "It's a very suitable thing for him to do. So nice for all of us not to have to pretend any longer that there isn't a good deal for him to cry about. And what I suggest," said Mrs Bellowes, with her charming, kind, encouraging smile, "is that Mr Chealey should go on crying and tell us everything."

"Yes, yes, Chealey; tell us everything," urged the General.

"While he cries," said Mrs Bellowes, as one graciously pointing out an indispensable stipulation. "If Mr Chealey waits to tell us till he's left off crying and begun to recollect the things that perhaps alarm him a little, I'm afraid he'll only try to tell us what he thinks he ought to, and then we shall none of us be much further."

"I don't know how to tell you anything," sobbed Mr Chealey. "I'm so ashamed—I don't—I can't——"

"Suppose Mr Chealey tells us to begin with if we were right in thinking him a house-agent," said Mrs Bellowes graciously, "or, if not, what he actually is."

"Yes, yes, Chealey, tell us what you actually *are*," urged the General. It gave him such strong discomfort to look at Mr Chealey's tear-disfigured face that he left off looking at it, and, leaving his seat, began to walk in a disturbed manner up and down the hall.

Mr Chealey made a great effort to regain his self-control. He sat up, drew a long breath, and wiped his eyes.

"I'm afraid I'm what you thought I was," he faltered—"a house-agent."

"Well, well, what harm is there in that!" said the General strongly. "None whatever. A very respectable thing to be."

"Go on, Mr Chealey," said Mrs Bellowes with benign serenity.

"At least it's what I'm *trying* to be," said Mr Chealey.

The barriers that had lain between him and his host were gone. His faltering uncertain little mind, harried by the fear of imperilling the appearances so essential to the success of his despairing little hopes, confused by the need of pretence, and driven back into self-consciousness by the dread of repulse after every momentary escape, let everything go now except the relief of letting go. He looked tremulously from one to the other. Neither in the absorbed countenance of the General nor in the gracious aspect of Mrs Bellowes did he see what he so shrank from seeing in the faces of his fellow-creatures. There was no repulse. There was no need to struggle back to concealment from the point of betrayal to which the flood of his breakdown had carried him. They wanted him to go on, even further, from betrayal to the infinite relief of revelation. Mr Chealey went on, with a trembling and hesitating voice and with catchings of the breath, but stammering no longer.

"It's only," he said, striving to smile apologetically through his tears, "that I don't seem somehow able to get a start. I used to be a head clerk in a big draper's office, you know. Of course it doesn't sound much to high-up gentlefolk like yourselves, but it was really quite a comfortable little position, I do assure you. But my firm had to fill up my place during the war, and when I was demobilised——"

"*Demobilised!*" said the General with a start. "Good God, Caroline, he's an ex-soldier! He would be! One of thousands flung out on the roads like this. Good God! But you didn't *join* up, I expect, Chealey," said the General, halting abruptly and in sudden hope in front of Mr Chealey. "You were probably *conscripted*, weren't you, Chealey? No fault of yours, of course, but one naturally feels more strongly about those who *joined* up, you know."

"I'm afraid I did join up, sir," said Mr Chealey, hesitatingly. "It really seemed almost my duty to do so in 1914, me being unmarried. Of course I see now——"

"Good God, Caroline, he *joined* up! He *is* another of them!" said the General.

He relinquished his last hope of not having to feel strongly, and recommenced his walk in a still more disturbed manner about the hall. The matter now, to the General, had taken on an entirely different aspect.

"It wasn't," explained Mr Chealey earnestly—"it wasn't that I didn't see quite well that I couldn't possibly ever be anything of a soldier, sir. It wasn't that I didn't see that. It wasn't——"

"Explain to Mr Chealey, Herbert," said Mrs Bellowes' irreproachably kind, indolent voice, "that there is no need for him to apologise."

"*Apologise!*" said the General, halting again in his surprise. "What's he got to apologise for?"

"It would be rather difficult to say," said Mrs Bellowes reflectively. "But perhaps he has come across that natural little feeling there seems to be in the country now that it was rather careless of people to go joining up in the way they did, and that ex-soldiers have to be explained and apologised for, though quite a large number of employers are very kind in overlooking it, I believe," added Mrs Bellowes graciously. "Still, there's no need for Mr Chealey to apologise here. Do go on, Mr Chealey. You can't have told us nearly everything yet."

"There isn't much more to tell, madam," said Mr Chealey sorrowfully. "I couldn't get a job anywhere, and I couldn't think what to do or be. I tried every agency I could hear of that was finding work for soldiers, but they couldn't find any for me."

"There *is* no work," said the General shortly. "And not nearly enough money either. I've tried them again and again myself. It's not their fault. Go on, Chealey."

"And at last," went on Mr Chealey, "I thought I'd try to be a house-agent. I've always had a fondness for buildings. I love buildings. I do indeed. And so many people seem to be letting houses and taking them just now that I thought a little work might perhaps come my way. I've always been a careful kind of man, and I had my little savings, and, of course, during the war one spent nothing, and then there was the gratuity, and so I thought I was justified in taking a little office in Cheltenham—a very little one—and I put in a few advertisements—as many as I could afford. And all—and all——" Mr Chealey stopped, and choked, and sat desperately silent.

"Go on, Mr Chealey," said Mrs Bellowes.

"It's nothing—it's nothing—I'm ashamed——" said Mr Chealey hurriedly, hoarse with the tears he was swallowing. "But all my money's gone, and nothing's come of it."

"Yet," said Mrs Bellowes graciously.

Mr Chealey gazed at her through his tears.

"What's that you say, Caroline," said the General, pausing in his perturbed walk.

"Yet," said Mrs Bellowes. "Mr Chealey says that nothing's come of it yet. Do go on, Mr Chealey. And is Cheltenham a good place for a house-agency?"

"I don't know that it is so especially good, madam," said Mr Chealey, forcing his strained voice to answer her conversational tone appropriately. "There are so many big house-agencies there already, you see. I did venture to approach one or two of them, but I don't think they quite liked a new man trying to make a beginning near them. It was bound to be like that wherever one looked. There's always somebody doing already what you want to do yourself wherever you start. And what I hoped was that with Gloucestershire such a favourite county as it is, and so much work about as there seemed to be in Cheltenham, a little of it might perhaps come my way. If I could have got just *one* house to advertise, to make a start with! But I didn't seem able to. Nobody wanted to employ an unknown beginner, and of course it was quite natural. It isn't that I don't see that. But after a bit I had to pawn my belong-ings, and then my clothes; and it's so difficult to keep as respectable-looking as you needs must if anybody's going to think well of you when you've only the one suit, and the nap of that raised so dreadfully on end, so to speak, that you can't get the dust out of it, however hard you try," said Mr Chealey apologetically; "and at last I thought—I thought——" He faltered, and stopped again.

"Yes, Mr Chealey?" said Mrs Bellowes.

"Well, at last I thought, madam," said Mr Chealey, "that I'd try going round *asking* people. Letters aren't much use, you see. Nobody takes much notice of letters. And quite right not to, and perfectly natural," added Mr Chealey hurriedly as the General emitted a brief remorseful groan. "But I thought if I went and *put* it to people—sometimes if you put a thing into people's heads they'll do it even if they haven't thought of it for themselves before, especially with the wonderful prices and rentals you can get nowadays. So I looked up some houses—though I haven't before ventured to try one as beautiful and well known as this," interpolated Mr Chealey humbly, "and I started going round asking. But it wasn't that I didn't see that it was an unpleasant kind of thing for people to have done to them, madam. It wasn't that I didn't see that all along. And when you asked me in here to rest with such kindness I could scarcely bring myself—I could hardly bring myself—it wasn't that I didn't see that people might dislike it, I do assure you."

"You see it much too plainly for success, Mr Chealey," said Mrs Bellowes with a smile. "It makes other people see it too, and become instantly filled with natural indignation."

"Why should they become instantly filled with natural indignation?" said the General strongly. "It was a most obvious thing for Chealey to do, and a very good idea."

"I thought, sir, I feared——" said Mr Chealey in faint surprise.

"And has it been any good, Mr Chealey?" said Mrs Bellowes.

Mr Chealey looked at her, trying with a smile to conceal the misery in his eyes.

"Well, no, madam, *not* very much," he said. "I can't say it has, exactly. I think perhaps, as you suggest, that I don't do it quite rightly somehow. People do mostly seem to get a little annoyed. Not that—I mean—that is—they've every reason——"

"Reason!" said the General strongly. "What reason have they to get annoyed! Most unfair and unjust!"

"Anyway, sir," said Mr Chealey, endeavouring to call up a sprightly air and rising from his chair, "this is the last time I shall do it! I haven't got any more money to spend on return-tickets, so I can't try it again. And now I must—that is—I ought—that is, I must be going. I've taken up quite enough of your time with all my little worries as it is. I can't—I shall never—I couldn't," said Mr Chealey, struggling not to give way again. "I shall never forget the kindness I have received here, not if I live to be a hundred! I'm ashamed to think of the way I've behaved. I——"

"Sit down, Mr Chealey," said Mrs Bellowes.

"Yes, sit down, Chealey," said the General, walking abstractedly about the hall. "The thing is, Chealey, the only point left is—how am I best going to help you! Now I fully realise, Chealey," said the General emphatically, coming to a stop on the other side of the table and facing Mr Chealey, "I fully realise that you don't want to be helped in that way. I fully realise that you didn't come here for that kind of help. But what I say is, in these hard times we've got to help each other, and we've got to let ourselves *be* helped. I don't speak only as man to man. I speak as soldier to soldier. I'm not going to let an ex-soldier go away from my door unhelped. It's not a thing you need think twice about, Chealey, and it won't be a gift.

It will be a loan, and you can repay me when you're on your feet again."

But a slow flush had risen to Mr Chealey's face.

"Oh, sir, I couldn't, I couldn't," he said.

"Why on earth not?" said the General strongly.

"How should I ever be able to pay you back?" said Mr Chealey agitatedly, "me that can't make enough even to pay for my own living! And where should I be when the money was gone? Just where I am now, with a debt on me into the bargain. I shouldn't be able to sleep of nights, sir, if I had a debt on me. There's two things I haven't done yet: made a debt or taken a dole——" added Mr Chealey in a quavering voice.

"But, good God, man, how else *can* I help you!" said the General loudly. "I'd do anything in the world for an ex-soldier, but I can't sell my home or let it, and go wandering all over the earth, just to start you as a house-agent! Now I put it to you! *Can* I?"

"No, no, of course not—I never—not for a moment—of course not," said Mr Chealey, horrified.

"Well, then, what *can* I do?" said the General, beginning to walk up and down again. "I could recommend you to my friends, of course, but what use is that going to be to you? It may be months before any of them happen to want a house or happen to ask me if I know of a house-agent! You might be dead of hunger months before it happened. And how else am I going to help you if you won't accept a loan?"

"Oh, but I think we can easily give Mr Chealey the letting of the house," said Mrs Bellowes gracefully.

The General stopped dead in his walk and swung round aghast.

"What?" he ejaculated.

"Easily," said Mrs Bellowes.

"Give him the letting of the house!" repeated the General dazedly; "the *letting* of it! Are you dreaming, Caroline?

But I don't *want* to let King's Lodge. I've never *thought* of letting it. Good God, Caroline, you don't mean to say you think I ought to let King's Lodge in order to help Chealey to be a house-agent!" said the General in horrified anxiety.

"Oh no," said Mrs Bellowes. "I don't mean that."

II.

On the following Saturday morning General Bellowes sat at his breakfast-table surrounded by the open sheets of several newspapers. Directly Mrs Bellowes appeared, a vision of indolent grace in a highly unsuitable pale-green gown, he addressed her briefly.

"It's out, Caroline," he said.

"Is it?" said Mrs Bellowes in her serene detached voice.

"It is," said the General. "In the 'Morning Post' and the 'Wilts. and Glos.,' and the 'Cheltenham Chronicle.' You had better read it."

He pushed one of the newspapers towards Mrs Bellowes, and she read:—

TO BE LET. Unique, celebrated and exquisite little old gentleman's house seated high in the Cotswolds. Well known as small show-place. In beautiful condition. Perfect views, splendid hunting, pillared portico, spacious rooms, panelled hall. Excellent drainage, centuries old, moderate size, easily worked by quite small staff. Lovely deer-park, central heating. King Charles' Balcony, with two bathrooms, h. and c. Deeply Interesting Historical Associations freely mingled with Every Possible Modern Improvement. All applications, without exception, to be made to

The Sole and Only Agent,

Mr CHEALEY of Cheltenham,
3 Billikin Street."

"Very nice indeed," said Mrs Bellowes, floating gracefully on to her place at the table. "And most attractive. Everyone will want to possess a deer-park with central heating, and a royal balcony upon which you can take two hot-and-

I mind waiting for it a little, because Priggles had shut up to his bedroom and was sleeping with it. As if it were a sort of wife," added Mrs Bellowes.

"I think, Caroline——" said the General.

"Oh, it was only Ambrosine's funny English," said Mrs Bellowes. "And perhaps he sometimes reads it before he sleeps with it, and if so he may have been struck yesterday by the King's Balcony and the deer-park and all the other details. Anyway, you see, he must guess *something* sooner or later, when people begin to come to see the house."

A slight frown contracted the General's brow. He perceived that a possible perplexity might be arising on his path towards the object upon which his thoughts were concentrated. He took instant steps to sweep it out of his way.

"Then tell him," he said abruptly; "tell him at once. *What* you're to tell him I don't know, but you'll have to think of something. I don't see how you can possibly tell him everything, but one thing he can understand from the first, and that is that I'll have no fuss or nonsense about it from him or anyone."

"Oh, I think it would be a great mistake to tell him *everything*," said Mrs Bellowes with graceful serenity; and Mr Priggles re-entering at that moment with the eggs and bacon, "Priggles," she said, in her friendly detached way, "we have advertised that King's Lodge is to let."

"Thank you, madam," said Mr Priggles, with a total absence of surprise which went far to confirm Mrs Bellowes' surmise that he sometimes read the 'Wilts. and Glos.' before he slept with it.

"And nobody, Priggles," continued Mrs Bellowes, "is ever to be let in to see the house without an order to view from Mr Chealey of Cheltenham."

"Certainly not," said the General strongly. "Ever."

"Thank you, madam," said Mr Priggles. "Mr Chealey. Of Cheltenham. And shall you be making any changes in the 'ouse'old, madam, if I may presoom so far?"

" Changes ! " said the General, surprised. " Why on earth should we make any changes, man ? "

" Oh no, Priggles," said Mrs Bellowes graciously.

" Thank you, madam," said Mr Priggles. " It does sometimes follow, sir, if I may presoom so far. And I 'ope it isn't for any peecooniary reason that you're thinking of letting, madam, if I may make so bold, with the natural feelings of the 'ouse'old for the family and the times what they h'are."

" Good God, no ! " said the General emphatically. " Nothing of the kind. As a matter of fact, we——"

" Oh no, Priggles, thank you," said Mrs Bellowes graciously, with her calm eyes upon the General.

" Thank you, madam," said Mr Priggles. " Then one 'ouse is much the same as another to the 'ouse'old, thank you, madam," and he retired with a majestic bow and the porridge plates.

On the following Tuesday morning the next thing happened, in the form of a letter from Mr Chealey himself. Tuesday being the first cub-hunting day of the season, and the more distant coverts of King's Lodge being the place appointed for it, the General was a vision of neatness in exactly the right apparel and a rather roused and absorbed frame of mind, owing to his natural anxiety lest everything and everybody should not combine to get him off in good time with a good breakfast inside him. But he forgot his absorption in this important aim when the post arrived and he saw the Cheltenham postmark among his letters. The General's previous absorption rushed instantly back upon his mind and eliminated every other.

" Chealey ! " he said, and opened the letter.

" Most Honoured, Most Dear Revered Respected Sir," said Mr Chealey.

" Good God, Caroline ! " said the General not unnaturally, pausing to gaze at Mrs Bellowes.

"He's almost choked with gratitude, poor little thing," said Mrs Bellowes. "Very right and nice. Go on, Herbert."

"Most Honoured, Most Dear Revered Respected Sir," read the General, "I beg your permission most humbly to inform you that I have had the great happiness of receiving, since the insertion of the advt. *re* King's Lodge, thirty-eight applications to view the same: to wit, twenty-eight letters, five telegrams, two telephonic and three personal inquiries."

"Good God, Caroline!" said the General, again pausing to gaze at Mrs Bellowes.

It must be remembered, by the way, that this was in 1919, when everybody was still taking everything they could everywhere except thought for the morrow, and when even those who had succeeded in taking a pig-sty walked chortling about it among their friends.

"Go on, Herbert," said Mrs Bellowes.

The General paid no heed. He sat gazing fixedly into space. He was perceiving a vision of undoubted horror, not before fully realised, but lying unquestionably before him on the road he meant to travel.

"Thirty-eight!" he said. "Good God! They'll be all over the place like flies."

He remained for a moment in stern contemplation of this evidently unavoidable trial—both of the resolution in possession of his mind and of his concentrated allegiance to the more than Mr Chealey that Mr Chealey stood for. Then with a determined hand he swept it out of his way, and returned unswervingly to the thought whose claim he had decided upon as sovereign.

"A very excellent thing for Chealey," he said firmly, and he picked up the letter again and went on reading.

"Have I your leave, Most Respected Sir," said Mr Chealey, "to select the more suitable and eminent of these persons and give them orders to view? I need not say I should not dream of doing this without an express and considered confirmation of the permission you have already so nobly given me. I dread, Most Honoured Sir, the trouble I may be giving you. I dread the difficulties and unpleasantnesses that may possibly arise. Dear Sir, I can see no reason why you should allow me to do it. If you have, on further consideration, as may well be the case, changed your mind with regard to the extraordinary favour you and your Honoured Lady thought in your generous kindness to bestow upon me, believe, Most Respected Sir, that I shall most fully understand and applaud your decision, and shall ever feel the better for the great goodness that prompted your first intention. I urge you, Dear Sir, to think again before you grant me permission to give these orders to view, which may cause you the utmost inconvenience.—I am, Dear Dear Sir, with the greatest respect and gratitude, your very humble, thankful and obedient servant,

"CHARLES CHEALEY."

"Mr Chealey," said Mrs Bellowes benignly, "shows people the way out of helping him with such earnestness and consideration that it's a wonder anybody ever doesn't take it. His one anxiety appears to be to enable them to travel it without a pang of self-reproach or sorrow."

"He writes a very good letter," said the General briefly, laying it down upon the table.

"Sweet," said Mrs Bellowes. "And so exactly like an ancestor's."

"And he shows a great deal of proper feeling," said the General. "I respect Chealey. I respect and like him. What's this especial difficulty and unpleasantness that he alludes to, Caroline?"

"I don't think it's anything that we can't overcome," said Mrs Bellowes serenely.

"Will the whole thirty-eight turn up at once?" said the General.

"Oh no, dear," said Mrs Bellowes benevolently. "Mr Chealey is only going to select the more suitable and eminent, and even those will only come in spots."

"Let them come," said the General shortly. "In spots or otherwise."

"Some of them, of course, may be in checks," said Mrs Bellowes; but before the General could reply a loud 'honk' sounded outside on the sweep.

"Priggles came in some little time ago, I think, to say the car was there," said Mrs Bellowes.

"Good God," said the General, suddenly recalled to the fact that he had actually forgotten that he was going cub-hunting, and he hurriedly re-attacked his half-finished breakfast.

On the following Wednesday afternoon the General was just stepping comfortably out on to the King's Balcony with the newspaper, intending there to enjoy his after-luncheon cigarette, when he suddenly stopped dead. The next thing had begun to happen, and up the straight long drive from the gates there was rolling a perfect procession of vehicles, all travelling towards the house as fast as they respectively could. First there came the Lorton Station Hotel motor-car, and then the Lorton Station Hotel fly, and then the Lorton Station Hotel motor-cycle, this last shrieking in one long unbroken yell because it was being carefully kept by the narrowness of the drive from passing the station fly. To the back of the knicker-bockered long-haired gentleman who rode the motor-cycle there was clinging, like a barnacle on a whelk, an extraordinarily short-skirted female, and the general impression the General received in the fleeting glance at it, which was all he had time for, was one of indiscriminate legs and hair, all streaming impartially together both fore and aft, as it were. He sank swiftly down into the nearest deck-chair. The broad balcony balustrade hid him completely from anyone below, but every sound came up to him and every word.

The motor-car rolled into the portico underneath the balcony, and shortly afterwards there arose a very loud noise. It appeared to take the form of a trio, in which, in increasing crescendo, two female voices sustained the high parts, while Mr Priggles supplied the bass motif in a kind of recurrent recitative.

"But we *must* see the house, we've come *miles* to see the house, why *shouldn't* we see the house?" cried the high female voices.

"Sorry, ladies. Not without an order, ladies," said the imperturbable Mr Priggles.

"We haven't *got* an order, I tell you," cried the female voices. "Take up our cards to your mistress at once. We are the Miss Belchers of Belgrave Square. Why should we be refused entrance merely because we happen to have heard of the house from another agent!"

"Sorry, ladies. Not without an order, ladies," chanted the cold tones of the unmoved Mr Priggles.

"But it's most *important* that we should see the house before anyone else does!" wailed the female voice hysterically.

"Sorry, ladies. Not without an order, ladies. From Mr Chealey. Of Cheltenham. Kindly order your motor to move on, ladies. It is blocking the h'approach."

"Good," said the General, and the motor rolled out of the portico and rushed away down the drive. The General would not have been surprised to see smoke coming out of the windows. He thought with stern satisfaction of the fury and bitterness that must be seething within from the bosoms of the thwarted Belchers of Belgrave Square, who had tried to steal a march on Mr Chealey's thirty-eight clients and had so signally failed. To two people, at any rate, the importance of Mr Chealey of Cheltenham was no longer unknown.

The motor rolled out and the fly rolled in, and to the listening General above it sounded as if a whole congregation instantly fell out of it. They all apparently had orders to view, however, for they were let in without demur. So were the cycle riders, whose machine, still emitting that ear-rending noise like a man being sick without intermission on high C, which adds so much to the beauty of the sounds of our modern countryside, had come bursting and pushing up with the fly. No words can tell how the General hated that motor-cycle. With compressed lips and a resolute air he opened his newspaper.

But he had hardly done so when he heard voices and steps ascending the stairs and entering the balcony sitting-room. He rose with a start, and the next instant three gentlemen and three ladies, all stout, poured out on to the balcony, led by the floating and unmoved Mrs Bellowes.

"Orders to view, Herbert dear," she said in graceful introduction. "From our excellent Mr Chealey of Cheltenham."

"Certainly," said the General, bowing; and the six stout orders-to-view all bowed back.

"Pretty view, isn't it?" said the General graciously.

"Lovely — topping — exquisite — topping — perfect — topping," murmured the six orders-to-view, gazing at the view in a highly embarrassed manner, as if it were somehow an improper spectacle and only to be viewed because they had orders to do so; and they all poured out again after Mrs Bellowes.

The General reseated himself in his deck-chair and reopened his newspaper with a firm countenance, but he had hardly done so when he again heard voices and steps entering the balcony sitting-room, and Mr Priggles, with incomparable stateliness, led forth upon the balcony the two cycle-riders. They had no hats and no calves, and the gentleman wore knickers like two short skirts and the lady a skirt like one short knicker, while the hairs of both hung round their heads in brief mouse-coloured curtains to their shoulders. The General rose from his chair.

"I beg your pardon, sir," said Mr Priggles with majestic apology. "I did not know you were here, sir. Orders to view, sir. From Mr Chealey. Of Cheltenham."

"Certainly," said the General, bowing; and the two orders-to-view bowed back, very low and sweetly, amid their curtains of hair.

"Pretty view, isn't it?" said the General with rigid courtesy, striving not to show his detestation.

"And how exalting," said the gentleman, flinging back his locks, advancing one enraptured step towards the landscape and waving his hand at it with an impassioned smile, "to sit thus lost before it in solemn contemplation as priests before the only God!"

"And what a perfect situation, dear Ernest," twittered his female companion in defiant if somewhat quavering tones as though she were determined not to be impressed by anything, especially Priggles, "for our unfettered life."

The disgusted and embittered countenance of Mr Priggles showed no evidence of any effort to conceal his detestation. "Kindly come this way at once," he said shortly and commandingly, leaving the balcony abruptly; and the orders-to-view bowed once more, very low and gracefully, and on coming erect departed after Mr Priggles somewhat incontinently, pushing each other through the balcony doorway.

The General sat down again, but this time he did not reopen his newspaper. He had the air of being speechless.

A short while afterwards the fly rolled forth from underneath the balcony and jig-jogged steadily away down the drive, and the motor-cycle shot out a little later in a moving cloud of appalling noise and vanished through the gates in a series of explosions; and Mrs Bellowes came out serenely on to the balcony and sank comfortably into a chair.

"They've all taken the house, Herbert dear," she announced placidly.

"*What!*" said the General, sitting up with a fearful start.

"Well," said Mrs Bellowes, "*my* party certainly has, and Priggles seems certain that his has too."

"*Taken* it!" repeated the General, gazing at his wife aghast. "Good God, Caroline! But they *can't* take it!"

"Well, they *think* they have," said Mrs Bellowes with reflective grace.

The General collected himself. "Kindly explain what has happened, Caroline," he said sternly. "I presume this development is what you expected, and that you know how to deal with it. I shall be glad to hear what we do now."

"I don't think we do anything much," said Mrs Bellowes. "You see, my party comes from Surbiton, where they made heaps of money in the war without profiteering once, they said. So clever of them. And when they decided they would take the house, I said how very sensible it was of them not to mind a bit about the old, old drains."

"The old, old drains!" said the astounded General. "Good God, Caroline, the drains are perfectly new! They're the last word in country sanitation."

"Well, the advertisement said they were centuries old, Herbert dear," said Mrs Bellowes reproachfully, as she reposed in leisurely grace among her cushions. "It's very difficult to contradict the advertisement. And anyway they aren't *main*, are they? You can't exactly call them main."

"*Main!*" exclaimed the General; "but, good God, Caroline, how on earth can they be main when there's not a main drain for twenty miles for them to be laid to!"

"No," said Mrs Bellowes, in her indolent encouraging voice; it's certainly not *your* fault, Herbert, but it seems that in Surbiton every drain is beautifully main. Anyway, the Surbitites were very grateful to me for drawing their attention to it, and they are going to ask Mr Chealey to ask you to make the drains main before they come in. I said that all negotiations must go through Mr Chealey, of course, and that even if you found you couldn't make the drains main, Mr Chealey was so clever that he would be sure to be able to find them another house quite as good as this—with all the drains main."

General Bellowes sat in silence, gazing steadfastly at his wife.

"And Priggles' party," continued Mrs Bellowes, gazing at the view, "free-loved."

"What!" said the startled General.

"Free-loved," said Mrs Bellowes. "They were Communists, you know, and Communists always free-love. You can see they'd have to. They do it with their money too, and these seemed quite rich. But Priggles hated them, poor things."

"Priggles showed his sense," said the General sternly. "Without knowing another word about that dreadful fellow, I could swear he was a conscientious objector."

"Still, I'm afraid Priggles did really harry them rather terribly through the house," said Mrs Bellowes. "The Surbitites and I were constantly getting mixed up with them in passages, and they always looked so very pale and anxious, as though they were finding it almost impossible to keep on being wonderful. However, there are going to be thirty of them all living here together, Priggles says, and they are going to put up cubicles in most of the bedrooms. Though why, if you free-love," said Mrs Bellowes, "you should want to put up——"

"Caroline——" said the General.

"So when Priggles came to tell me that his party had sent him to say they would take the house," continued Mrs Bellowes, gazing at the view, "I saw them for a moment, and said how pleased I was, and how nice it seemed that they felt they could subscribe to the clause a landowner naturally feels bound to put into the lease of a county kind of little house like this, where you have to set a good example."

"What clause, Caroline?" said the General, gazing fixedly at Mrs Bellowes.

"The one about attending church regularly twice a Sunday, Herbert dear," said Mrs Bellowes.

"Good God!" said the General.

"However, they don't seem perfectly sure about it," said Mrs Bellowes. "They said they were priests and priestesses of the worship of Nature, and sometimes experienced a little difficulty about the Ten Commandments, and I think they may be going to ask Mr Chealey to ask you not to put that clause into their lease. I said that *all* negotiations must go through Mr Chealey, of course, and that even if you found that you couldn't leave that clause out, Mr Chealey is sure to be able to find them a house in which nobody need set a good example, quite as nice as this."

The General sat in silence, gazing upon Mrs Bellowes. He had the absorbed appearance of a man upon whom an entirely new and unexpected aspect of an idea already tenaciously in possession of his mind, and supported there with unswerving determination, was slowly dawning. For an instant he sat thus. Then he shut his mouth even more grimly than before. "Very well," he said, and he took up his newspaper and plunged into the leading article.

The Communists and the Surbitites were only the first of the long succession of people who came hastening to see King's Lodge that September—and a good many of them were rather singular. That was to be expected. The singular shot up into light and air in hundreds of thousands the instant the war lifted off the earth, as flies shoot up when a lid is lifted. To the General Mr Chealey's clients appeared to arrive in hundreds, but he was not perhaps in a sufficiently disinterested position to be capable of keeping a very calm and careful count. Still, even to an impartial observer, it must have seemed certain that Mr Chealey had found it too difficult to determine which of his thirty-eight applicants were the more suitable and eminent, and had decided to send orders to them all. Mr Chealey's letters, more like those of an ancestor than ever, arrived also in great numbers.

They now invariably began, "My Revered and Honoured Patron," and were almost incoherent in his endeavours to express, generally in the same sentence, his anguished apologies for the trouble he was giving, his timid and yet implicitly trusting anxiety over the method that was being employed, his boundless gratitude to his Honoured Patrons, and his trembling happiness at his increasing hopes of ultimate success.

For the people to whom a house of the type of King's Lodge was possible after the war, and who were tumbling over each other in the little office in Billiken Street in their anxiety to secure something of a sort so rarely in the market, were not—however singular—those whom the war had exactly impoverished.

There was the lady with wonderful red hair and a beautiful slim figure and a lovely gown and a mouth like a slit and a voice like a cat's, for instance, whom someone had once told how charming and childlike it was of her to sit in an arm-chair with her feet tucked up. She lay curved exquisitely up in an arm-chair with her feet tucked sideways under her, and her hands along the arms, and said in a languid manner that King's Lodge was really quite decent, and would do quite well as a little extra place for occasional visits, and how fortunate it was that she had come across a house she could quite tolerate.

"*Most* fortunate," said Mrs Bellowes with faultless kindness, while the General sat observing this new order-to-view with immaculate courtesy and the kind of reluctant interest and firm dislike felt by all right-minded men towards red-haired ladies curled up in chairs, "and I feel sure that Mr Chealey will gladly approach my husband on your behalf with a view to his waiving his little feeling about absentee tenants."

"What's that you say, Caroline?" said the General, coming out of his trance with a slight start.

"Oh, but," said the red-haired lady languidly, "we don't

need to bother about the house-agent, do we, dear General? We'll do the bargaining with each other, won't we? You can consider the house definitely taken, for it's really quite a decent little bungalow, and I am sure you will find we are excellent tenants."

The General looked at Mrs Bellowes, not helplessly or anxiously, but with a sort of stern expectancy, as one who knows for certain that a rope will shortly descend upon him in his hole, and therefore sits in it with self-command.

"I'm sure we shall," said Mrs Bellowes graciously. "It's such a pleasure to us to feel you like our humble little villa in the country. I am sure that for your sake dear Herbert will most carefully reconsider his little feeling about our people on the estate not being left too much without anyone in the house to look after them—won't you, Herbert?—and we shall look forward with so much pleasure to hearing from you very soon through Mr Chealey."

"Oh, pray expect to hear from me without any Mr Chealey, Mrs Bellowes," said the red-haired lady with a quite nice polite little laugh. "I think agents are such silly unnecessary things between people of the same class—don't you, General?—once we know each other. And I am sure you realise that it's quite out of the question for anyone in our position, with our villa at Monte, and London and all that, to use this funny little house for anything but occasional visits, which is all we want it for. So we may consider that settled, mayn't we, General?" said the red-haired lady, smiling with perfect composure and propriety at the General out of her long sweet eyes, "and if you'll get the lease drawn up we will sign it at once."

"And if by any chance Herbert *should* find it difficult to overcome his little feeling about the estate," said Mrs Bellowes benignly, "you mustn't despair, because Mr Chealey is so extraordinary clever, so unique and lucky as a house-agent, that I'm sure he will easily find you another equally good Cotswold house, in which it won't really matter if you never stay at all."

"Oh, I promise I won't despair, Mrs Bellowes," said the red-haired lady, smiling her little careless understanding smile at the General; and she said good-bye in a languid manner and went away in her Rolls-Royce, and it was really rather sad that she wasn't understanding anything at all, of course, when she was so securely certain that she was the beautiful amused woman who did. Beauty may doubtless be often blinding to the male beholder, or at any rate he is frequently politely willing to behave as if it were; but the blindness it causes to the beholder is nothing to the cloud of little misapprehensions that so singularly often hangs round its possessor.

"But she's quite a good player," said Mrs Bellowes approvingly.

"A good what?" said the General reservedly.

"Player," said Mrs Bellowes. "She's got our languid, vacant, cold hard look so very well. You really scarcely ever find yourself wondering what back street first saw that lovely hair, or whether she came out of it in the war or after."

And there was the American gentleman who had made shells. He arrived, in spats and a large Stetson hat set sideways, when the General was away endeavouring to relieve the Windrush of some of its superfluous grayling; which was perhaps as well. Majestically conducted round by Mr Priggles, the American gentleman surveyed the whole house in an intent silence, only broken by an occasional murmur of "You don't say!" or "Do tell!" when Mr Priggles loftily conveyed to him some historical or other item calculated to establish in the mind of a foreigner a right sense of the glory of the family Mr Priggles served. But when he had seen everything, the American gentleman sent in his card to Mrs Bellowes—"Mr Gideon O. Gilkicker," with "of the United States of America" pencilled beneath it; and on being ushered in to the oak parlour, he advanced upon Mrs Bellowes, drew forth a large wad of bank-notes, and said with all the dynamic force of his progressive country driving at full pressure through his nose, "Pleased to meet you, ma'am. I would wish to deeposit upon this table the first year's rent for a twenty-year lease, and I want this house right here and nayow."

Mrs Bellowes smiled her unmoved gracious smile.

"How very nice, Mr Gilkicker," she said benevolently. "Am I to understand that you would like the General and the servants and myself to leave by the 4.15 this afternoon?"

"I sure would," said Mr Gilkicker emphatically, "and your remarks do credit to the smartness of your intelligence, ma'am. But only a sucker would look to find as much pep as all that in *this* country, I reckon. No, ma'am; I've been led to believe that it's apt to be some job to get anything done in this country under a hundred years or so, and I'm willing to make all doo allowances for your national proclivities. You clear in a week, say, and I'll make that soot if you can't git quicker. But that's the limit! Doo allowances stop right there! I'm a business man from the States, and it is my aim, ma'am, to steer clear of Versilles and Sang Germang. I want you to understand from the word go that I propose to cut the usual British neegotiations right out of this little trade."

"I *quite* understand," said Mrs Bellowes graciously. "Our slow methods must often be so very trying to your enlightened and energetic country."

"They sure are," said Mr Gilkicker with surprise and approval, "and I allow to have travelled from Noo York sorter determined that they were not going to be trying to *me*, ma'am. I'd gotta sorter hunch that it wasn't my enlightened and energetic country that was going to be tried when G. O. Gilkicker came over to do a trade in Great Britain. But I allow to have met with an exception. It appears to me that I was perhaps a trifle misled by my business friends in Amurrica concerning the obstructionist and reeactionary tackticks I should find obtaining in this island."

"You live in England, Mr Gilkicker?" said Mrs Bellowes with reflective grace.

"I don't kalkilate to live anywhere," said Mr Gilkicker. "I made my pile in the war, and I don't need to sit anywhere for keeps. This is my first visit to your shores, ma'am, and I reckon to use this little island like I do most all places, off and on as it soots with my convenience. Such being my aim, I would naturally wish to secure a right old slap-up genwine mooseum British house, and I guess this little shack of yours suttenly fills the bill. And you can feel real good and comfortable about the rent, ma'am," added Mr Gilkicker easily. "What we Amurricans want we can pay for. There's no talk in *our* country yet about repoodiating our bills—nor yet our debts."

Mrs Bellowes looked at Mr Gilkicker with the same detached and faintly amused glance with which she looked at everybody. Then she said with unimpaired serenity and graciousness, "I am so glad to think, Mr Gilkicker, that I am helping you to pay a debt. Will you let me give you a cup of tea?"

Mr Gilkicker, after a moment's slight surprise, concluded that either he had not heard the first sentence aright, or else the lady had got a trifle mixed; and he replied to the second sentence affably. "Why, suttenly, ma'am! I don't care if I do. I guess we can knock off the larst deetails of our little business over a cup of tea as slick as if we was trading over a glass of something stronger. It sure is gratifying to my feelings, ma'am, to meet with a lady who can thus rise sooperior to the proclivities of her native land."

When next observed, Mr Gilkicker was breaking the King's regulations at sixty miles an hour along the Cheltenham road, and the spirit of firm resolve in which Mr Gilkicker had travelled from New York towards his coming conflict with the business methods of the British Isles was nothing to the dynamic force of the determination with which he was now travelling to Cheltenham. He was on his way to the office of the agent who had sent him the order to view King's Lodge; and from that office it was Mr Gilkicker's intention that there should shortly burst forth upon the Cotswolds such a demonstration of American energy, will-power and hustle as should pulverise the obsolete dog-in-the-manger, fit-for-the-tomb national proclivities of old man Bellowes into dust as fine as was presumably that of that other old British back number, not more extinct than old man Bellowes himself, King Charles the Second. No long-deceased one-time tenant of King's Lodge was more entirely suited to a grave, in the opinion of Mr Gilkicker, than its present tenant, old man Bellowes, believed alive.

This swift and sudden transit of Mr Gilkicker from the King's Lodge tea-table to the Cheltenham road had been effected by scarcely more than ten minutes' conversation with the lady whose superiority to the procrastinating proclivities of her nation had so surprised and gratified him. In the first place, his attention roused by a chance remark, Mr Gilkicker had had no difficulty in skilfully eliciting from Mrs Bellowes the fact that there *were* perhaps one or two things to be said against King's Lodge, in spite of its unique charm and attractions. Its exceedingly isolated position, perhaps—great difficulties and drawbacks did certainly sometimes arise from *that*, for instance—and then its really very limited accommodation for the requirements of modern entertaining, and its undeniably rather archaic bathing arrangements—Mr Gilkicker gathered it all in and made his decision with admirable celerity. Shucks, ma'am, that did not matter the toss of a cent. It was certainly impossible for a man of his wealth, position, affairs, energy, modernity and nationality to find his activities curtailed by the limitations of the Middle Ages, and Mr Gilkicker had no intention that they should be. The spending of a few thousands of the dollars made out of shells on such simple necessities as a second telephone wire and a new wing and a palm-lounge and a macadam road and a private telegraph wire and a suite of bathrooms was sure an easy matter. Mr Gilkicker would get hold of the best man for the job right there and then that night in London, and send him down next day to make the necessary plans for the improvements. Judge of the feelings of Mr Gilkicker when the next words fell gently from the lips of Mrs Bellowes, "But I'm so much afraid, Mr Gilkicker, that my husband might object to King's Lodge being improved."

Mr Gilkicker started violently. Then for one moment he restrained himself. He would make certain that this incredible thing was true. But Mrs Bellowes remained graciously unshaken. She could only say that she was dreadfully afraid that her husband might actually refuse to allow his house to be improved, and she feared that the only course was to approach him at once through his agent, a man whom Mrs Bellowes could warmly recommend as most prompt and assiduous in the prosecution of all business, and likely to give even Mr Gilkicker entire satisfaction.

A gleam lit in Mr Gilkicker's eye. Refuse to allow a place to be improved, and the obsolete to be brought up to date, and a limited little house to be developed to a mansion! Refuse thus immensely to increase the value and smartness and size of his dwelling, even though he was not going to live in it himself, and another man's money was going to be spent on it! Mr Gilkicker's face wore the same expression as must have been seen on the countenance of the old lady who found a burglar under her bed. This was what he had expected! Here it was! Exactly! The British reactionary and obstructionist tackticks! His friends in Amurrica had *not* misled him! A few minutes later the dust of Mr Gilkicker's vanished 90-h.p. Mercedes was swirling in the empty drive of King's Lodge, and Mr Gilkicker was on his way to seize upon this Chealey of Cheltenham, through whom it would apparently be possible to deal efficiently with old man Bellowes. Old man Bellowes should learn what happened when British national proclivities came into conflict with American enlightenment and progressiveness! The tyres of the Mercedes trundled faster than ever along the Cheltenham road at the thought.

And there was the rather dreadful day when the General happened to be alone, and Mrs de Piercy-Evans, the relict of a Wesleyan Cardiff shipowner, came to see the house. She was a lady with a faint voice and a suffering face and a feeble smile, and she arrived on a day when Mr Priggles was having his afternoon out, and when Mrs Bellowes was paying a call near Burford; and as Mrs Bellowes' car turned into the drive on her return home it passed another car just coming out, in which was reclining a lady in tears. Mrs Bellowes went to look for the General when she reached the house, and found him seated in his study with a rather serious countenance reading a book, in itself a somewhat unusual occurrence. Immediately on perceiving his wife he laid the book down and said, "Did you meet her?"

"Well, I passed a lady weeping in the drive, Herbert dear," said Mrs Bellowes.

"I can only assure you, Caroline," said the General, "that I did my best."

"I am sure you did," said Mrs Bellowes. "Why was she weeping in the drive?"

"She said I was a snake," said the General.

"She can have been a person of *no* imagination," murmured Mrs Bellowes.

"Well, of course, Caroline, we can't pretend we don't see why she thought I was perhaps a snake," said the General. "But I can only assure you I did my utmost. I showed her the whole house. I showed her everything, and I told her everything, and I answered all her questions most carefully. We must have been over two hours going into everything, and I don't think you could have done it better yourself. And at the end she said she would take the house, and I said she couldn't."

"Dear Herbert," murmured Mrs Bellowes sympathetically, "and did you give her any reason why she couldn't."

"Good God, Caroline, of course I didn't," said the General. "How could I have given her a reason when the only reason was the one I couldn't give! I merely said she couldn't, and she can't. No one could have said it more kindly. I told her again and again that I was sorry she couldn't."

"And what did she do?" said Mrs Bellowes.

"She burst into tears and said I was a snake," said the General, gazing at Mrs Bellowes. "She said that instead of taking her weak heart perpetually up and down the stairs, I ought to have told her at once that I had taken a dislike to her personal appearance and never meant her to have the house from the first. You could have knocked me down with a feather. I never even *saw* her personal appearance! She wasn't the kind of woman who *had* a personal appearance."

"Oh, poor thing, Herbert dear," said Mrs Bellowes reflectively. "And did you tell her that Mr Chealey would be sure to be able to find her another house quite as nice as this?"

"How could I tell a howling woman about Chealey or anything else?" said the General with stern remonstrance. "I was far too busy trying to get her to take some brandy or tea or something. It was a most awful experience. I can't help it if I forgot Chealey. And I think, Caroline, it would be better if you arranged never to go out at all till we've seen this business through, in case this kind of thing should happen again. It was impossible to help forgetting all about Chealey, and I'm afraid that howling woman is going to be no good to him whatever."

But though it is possible that the embittered Mrs de Piercy-Evans did not again apply to the house-agent who had been the means of introducing her to a snake, the case was very different with the rest of Mr Chealey's thirty-eight orders-to-view. It can only be concluded that, on recovering from the surprise of finding that they had not taken King's Lodge—for unimpeachable reasons most apologetically and humbly conveyed to them by Mr Chealey on behalf of General Bellowes—they had felt that they could not perhaps do better than let the house-agent who wrote so earnestly and anxiously, and who had been so warmly and expressly recommended to them by the gracious and sympathetic mistress of King's Lodge, try what he could do for them. Some of them may have thought that an agent who really seemed to be almost on a footing of personal friendship with those distinguished people, the owners of King's Lodge, might be likely to know of houses not advertised by the usual channels; others again, after having once seen the Cotswolds, may have felt that they could not bear to relinquish the hope of finding a house among them, and knew no other Cotswold agent but Mr Chealey; still others may have decided that a house-agent whose leading characteristic seemed to be the most singular one of an overwhelming personal anxiety that they should get what they wanted, and who appeared never to send them to see a semi-detached villa in Eastbourne when they were looking for a manor-house in Gloucestershire, was one to be clung to at all costs and hazards. And some of the more progressive and enlightened may have been soothed by Mr Chealey's humble and vivid perception of the superior advantages enjoyed by nearly everybody except himself.

At any rate, one modest little statement had already emerged in the 'Wilts. and Glos.':—

"MR CHEALEY of Cheltenham would be glad to hear from owners of houses in Gloucestershire and neighbouring counties who are willing to let or sell, as he has several applicants for the same. 3 Billikin Street."

And one of Mr Chealey's letters had already conveyed with happy agitation the splendid news that such was the pressure of his business that he had been obliged to engage a boy to answer the door. But now there appeared, in all the local papers and a London daily, an advertisement that put the other one completely in the shade :—

"MR CHEALEY of Cheltenham, having a large number of clients of eminence, position and wealth, both American and English, who are anxious to buy or rent houses of prominence and character in the Cotswolds, would be glad to hear at once from owners who are willing to let or sell, which they may do at the present juncture at great advantage to themselves. 3 Billikin Street."

And shortly afterwards Mr Chealey, with such tremulous joy and gratitude and thankfulness that his pen was unable to convey his feelings except in broken and entirely incoherent sentences, wrote to say that the work was becoming more than he could possibly cope with alone, and that he believed he would very shortly have to engage a clerk.

And then came the Wopsleys of Wick.

They hurried in on General and Mrs Bellowes in a torrent of exclamations, waving their order-to-view; and the appalled General had only time to ejaculate *sotto voce* to his wife, "Good God, Caroline! The Wopsleys! To take the house! People we *know!*" when the Wopsleys, outstripping the indignant Mr Priggles, were upon them with outstretched hands.

"Caroline!" cried Lady Wopsley of Wick. "Dearest! Impossible! How *too* divine! When the agent in Cheltenham wrote that that advertised house was actually King's Lodge, *your* King's Lodge, I *shrieked!* We *couldn't* believe it! Are you really letting King's Lodge, the exquisite King's Lodge!"

"We have certainly advertised it to let," said Mrs Bellowes with faultless graciousness.

"Too bad, too bad, too bad!" said Lord Wopsley of Wick pityingly.

"Oh, you poor things!" cried Lady Wopsley of Wick. "The war, I suppose! Hard hit like all the rest of us!

But if you've *got* to let, it would anyhow be a comfort to let to old old friends like us, and not to strangers, *wouldn't* it ? "

Mrs Bellowes had first met and been kind to her 'old old friend' in a Brighton hotel before Miss Agatha Topp, as she then was, had succeeded in attaching herself to the industrious little solicitor, Samuel Solomons, as *he* then was, who had since succeeded in attaching himself to his party —with such well-directed moderation and lack of narrow zeal that, during an unusual dearth of even nonentities among the great men of England, he had been unanimously selected by both parties as Secretary of State for War, in the comfortable certainty that though he might have no knowledge or experience whatever that could fit him for the post, he had also not a vestige of anything strong enough to be called a political conviction. And he was now Lord Wopsley of Wick, having, with every justification, taken his title from a village near the golf-course of which he had built himself a handsome yellow brick Gothic mansion fully ten years before.

" But we must not be too precipitate ! " he now cried gaily. " We must not be premature ! We must remember that our good friends may already have promised the house to someone, Agatha ! "

" Oh, dearest Caroline, don't say so ! " cried Lady Wopsley. " Promise you won't let it to anyone else ! "

" I think we can safely promise not to let it to anyone else," said Mrs Bellowes benignly.

" And *might* we see over it ! " said Lady Wopsley, clasping her hands. " *Would* it be too much trouble, dearest Caroline ? "

So the Wopsleys of Wick saw over King's Lodge. They went over everything inside and out, and louder and louder waxed their exclamations of admiration and delight. These old friends had somehow never yet been asked to stay at King's Lodge, so all was new to them, and they sang pæans of universal praise; while Mrs Bellowes floated along unmoved and gracious, and the General brought up the rear in silence, listening to Lord Wopsley's enthusiastic comments with admirable self-command, and merely glancing at him without a word when he ecstatically expatiated upon the beauty of the lodges. The General did not love the Wopsleys, but that was the least of the reasons which kept his ears strained to catch every sentence of the conversation proceeding between the ladies in front.

They finished their inspection in the cellars where the big furnaces stood, and returned to the oak parlour for tea, and Lady Wopsley sank joyfully into a chair and looked round her with the light of possession already in her eye.

"We take it, Caroline!" she cried. "We take it on the spot! It's *exactly* what we want for a hunting-box, dear! There's no hunting round Wopsley, and though, of course, Samuel and I don't hunt, so *many* people do, and then the children—you can hardly expect a boy to live up to the traditions of his rank, *can* you, unless he has hunted in his boyhood. We'll take it on the spot! Those beautiful big furnaces have *quite* decided me! I *had* feared the house might be a little cold—so high up, you know, and these old places—I thought I felt just a little draught or two upstairs. But with all that lovely central heating——"

"Do you perhaps mean the little cold air that passed us on the landing of the stairs?" said Mrs Bellowes, in her charming indolent voice, as she poured out the tea with her usual grace. "Oh, that wasn't a draught. That was the ghost. Do you like sugar in your tea, Agatha?"

"That was the *what?*" said Lady Wopsley with a start.

"Well, it's said to be a ghost," said Mrs Bellowes, handing round the cups. "You could hardly expect an old place like this not to have ghosts, of course. It's supposed to have several. It's really quite well known in the countryside as a haunted house. Tea, Lord Wopsley?"

"*Ghosts!*" said Lady Wopsley with a gasp, staring at Mrs Bellowes. "Not *really*, Caroline!"

"Tut, tut!" said Lord Wopsley gaily. "Who believes in such nonsense nowadays? *I* felt no draught upon the stairs! And pray what kind of ghosts are they, Mrs Bellowes, that haunt you in such numbers?"

"Oh, quite nice ghosts," said Mrs Bellowes, smiling at him benignly. "There's wicked old Cramp Ditton, for instance. The people in the lodges say they often hear his coach-and-four crashing up the drive at midnight, as it used to do hundreds of years ago, to join King Charles in one of his carousals. But I don't see why he shouldn't come up the drive if he wants to. He does nobody any harm. And then there's the invisible ghost on the stairs, of course. But she matters still less. You never even hear her. Give Lord Wopsley the milk, Herbert dear."

"What *do* you do, then?" said Lady Wopsley, with an irrepressible shudder.

"Oh, really almost nothing," said Mrs Bellowes, graciously preoccupied with the wants of her guests. "At night they say you merely feel her passing near you, but in the daytime it is even less than that—no more than a little cold air suddenly blowing by. And sugar, Lord Wopsley?"

"Ha, ha, how ridiculous!" said Lady Wopsley, with a rather hollow laugh. "But—dearest Caroline—tell me—just for the interest of the thing—is this house *really* supposed to be haunted?"

"Oh yes, it's really *supposed* to be," said Mrs Bellowes, smiling her kind encouraging smile. "But then, so are nearly all old places, you know. There's nothing in that. Will you have some more cake, Agatha?"

"And do you yourself believe in all these wonderful tales, Mrs Bellowes?" said Lord Wopsley with a hearty laugh.

"Oh, *I*——" said Mrs Bellowes benevolently, "but I suppose to anyone who really did believe in them, it would perhaps be rather an uncomfortable house to live in. Do have another sandwich, Lord Wopsley. You've such a long drive before you."

"Yes, we have indeed," said Lady Wopsley, getting up rather hurriedly. "I am afraid we ought to be going almost at once, Samuel. I'm *so* sorry, dearest Caroline, but I think perhaps we ought to go now. It's such a long run up to town. *Good*-bye, and thank you *so* much for everything."

"And you will write?" said Mrs Bellowes, rising with grace to take farewell of her guests. "That is very nice. And if by any sad chance you do change your minds about the house, don't forget that Mr Chealey of Cheltenham is by far the best agent to go to. He could find you *any* kind of Cotswold house, and we should be so pleased if you employed him. He's so conscientious and honest. Quite a unique little thing among house-agents, and almost a personal friend of our own."

When the General, still with the stern and silent courtesy in which he had punctiliously carried out his duties as host all the afternoon, had finally seen the Wopsleys off the premises and shut the front door upon them, he returned to the oak parlour and stood before the fire.

"Do you mean to say," he said, "that that woman really *believes* in ghosts?—believes in them so much that she would actually be afraid to come here?"

"I don't know what Lady Wopsley of Wick believes in," said Mrs Bellowes in her detached and placid voice. "I know what Agatha Topp used to believe."

"Good God!" said the General meditatively. He added after a moment, "If she's really ass enough for that, she wouldn't stay in the house even if she *could* take it. She'd swallow every story she'd be stuffed with, and leave in a month. So *those* people needn't be on our conscience, anyway," said the General, pushing them off his with determination.

"None of them is on mine," said Mrs Bellowes with the serenity of one who has no need to push anything. "Nor ever has been. Shall we go for a turn in the park before dinner, Herbert dear?"

The gist of the subsequent outpouring of Lady Wopsley of Wick, whose tact was of a quality to be expected in Agatha Topp, may be more or less briefly repeated.

"Samuel and I feel more *dreadfully* remorseful than we can say, dearest Caroline. We can only *beg* you to forgive us. We realise how *terribly* disappointed you will be after we had raised your hopes so high. But we are afraid we should *never* be able to persuade our servants to stay, dear. Of course, to educated people like you and I the whole thing is merely *nonsense*, but the lower classes are so *terribly* superstitious. Your own servants have been with you so long that I expect they have got accustomed to living with ghosts, but really smart London servants are so different, aren't they? They would *never* put up with them, and Samuel and I are afraid we should have *endless* trouble. But we felt that the *least* we could do after disappointing you so greatly was to employ the agent you asked us to, and we were *so* anxious to please you about it, dearest Caroline, that we actually went *straight* to Cheltenham from your house and saw him! We liked him *so* much. I thought him a perfect little pet, and Samuel was so pleased with his funny old-fashioned modest manners. He says he is *sure* he can find a house for us. But we feel *so* apologetic, dearest Caroline," &c., &c.

"The lower classes are so terribly superstitious," said Mrs Bellowes benignly.

And a day or two later the following advertisement appeared in all the county newspapers:—

"MR CHEALEY of Cheltenham has been commissioned by his client, Lord Wopsley of Wick, to state that Lord Wopsley desires to lease or buy a commodious residence in the Cotswolds, preferably modern, suitable for a hunting-box. All further particulars of requirements to be obtained from Mr Chealey, 3 Billikin Street."

On the afternoon of the day after that advertisement appeared, a little figure came trudging along the Cotswold lanes and turned into the King's Lodge gates, after a brief pause by the high hedges outside them for a hurried removal of the last speck of dust from a suit the nap of which was not on end. King's Lodge lay quiet and grey between its golden beeches as the little son of a generation broken by an anguish and knowledge never dreamed of by even the stormiest of the generations that have vanished since the building of those weathered walls, came up the long drive and past the playing fountain and paused again an instant to listen to the singing voice of the water.

"When I think what I was feeling the last time I heard that!" said Mr Chealey to himself. Tears were in his eyes, but they were not tears of misery and exhaustion.

He was coming to bring news so great that it could never have been conveyed in a letter. When it came to the point he found himself unable to convey it even in words. Once more Mr Chealey broke down in the old hall of King's Lodge, but this time it was not because of a terror that unmanned him—it was because of a gratitude that overwhelmed him. On the appearance of the advertisement commissioned by Lord Wopsley of Wick, one of the oldest and best-known of those house and estate agencies in Cheltenham which had manifested their dislike of a new man trying to make a beginning amongst them, had come hurriedly to the conclusion that a new man who appeared to be making so striking a beginning whether they disliked it or not, had better have something else manifested to him. It was their turn to approach Mr Chealey—not perhaps in quite so humble and faint a manner as Mr Chealey had once approached them, but still with considerable urgency and most gratifying politeness. They said it would give them the sincerest pleasure if Mr Chealey, bringing the goodwill of his numerous and distinguished clients with him, would consent to enter their firm in a permanent capacity on the most excellent and advantageous terms to himself.

Tears were streaming down Mr Chealey's face as he incoherently told his news—tears of such thankfulness and gratitude that they could scarcely be distinguished from the smiles with which they were mingled. He was safe. He had been pulled out of the sucking quicksands for good and all, and set upon his feet. He was not to be allowed to suffer for having left his little office stool to suffer to the best of his ability for what had almost appeared to him to be his duty in 1914. He was not to add one more to the millions who, at this most sorrowful moment of the world's existence, sit fast bound in misery and iron, and find no help or hope from man.

"And me that thought that no one cared!" sobbed Mr Chealey.

The King's Lodge car took him back to Lorton Station after tea; and with him, on a slip of paper similar to those which had been reaching Billiken Street from time to time during the recent events, he bore a little statement to be used in case of need or further inquiries: "Mr Chealey is directed to announce that the residence of King's Lodge is remaining in its present owner's hands." Its present owner stood a moment under the King's Lodge portico watching the lights of his car travelling down the drive and turning with a flash out of the gates. The smooth whir of its journeying died farther and farther into the distance till it ceased altogether. The fresh still darkness of the autumn night arched over the quiet Cotswold country, and the beautiful cry of the great white owl who lived in an old elm in the deer-park rose beyond the beeches as he floated past them.

"Well, that's a good thing done!" said the General. He shut the doors and went back to the tea-table in front of the log-fire that blazed on the hearth of the hall. Mrs Bellowes, her charming head resting comfortably against the cushions of her arm-chair, was sitting in reposeful ease watching the flames, and the General dropped into a chair on the opposite side of the hearth and took out his cigarette-case.

"That's a good thing done, Caroline!" he repeated with satisfaction. "And a thing well worth the doing. There's *one* ex-soldier off the roads anyway!"

"And I'm so glad we did it the way we did it, dear," murmured Mrs Bellowes in her serene reflective voice.

"What?" said the General, pausing with his match-box in his hand. "*Glad* we did it the way we did it! Then I must strongly disagree with you, Caroline! The only thing I hesitated over for a moment was the doing of it in the way we had to do it! And Chealey hesitated about it too, and it did him credit. For anything less than the thing we did it for I wouldn't have done it at all. But if the same circumstances arose again, I'd do exactly the same thing again —to-morrow."

Mrs Bellowes said nothing. She watched in indolent silence the flames springing, in gold and rose, like the colour of the beeches, from the piled beech-logs under the great stone canopy of the hearth.

"And I'm especially pleased," resumed the General, proceeding to extract a match from his match-box, "that it's happened to be such a decent little chap as Chealey that we've managed to help. I'd have helped him anyhow, of course, but it's been a real pleasure to play the Good Samaritan to so right-minded a little fellow as Chealey."

"And if we hadn't done it the way we did it," said Mrs Bellowes' idle soft voice, "we could never have made the Levites cross the road and do it too."

The General's match paused in mid-air. He gazed at his wife in blank astonishment.

"Never have made the Levites cross the road and do it too!" he repeated. "Good God, Caroline, what on *earth* are you talking about?"

"Well, not *only* the Levites, of course," said Mrs Bellowes with reflective grace; "they practically *all* came trundling over—even the house-agents who first went by on the other side. I don't think any of them really got past altogether, except perhaps the one that wept in the drive."

The General slowly laid his unstruck match down on the table near him. He sat in silence, gazing at his wife. His mind was absorbedly travelling back over two lines at once—the half-forgotten details of the story of the Good Samaritan and the long procession of Mr Chealey's orders-to-view. Back it went—from Mr Samuel Solomons to the Priests of nature and the stout Surbitites, who, as they were so anxious to assure everybody, had miraculously made an immense fortune in the war without profiteering once.

"I think it's so nice that we've been able to bring a *few* of them over at any rate," went on Mrs Bellowes' leisurely lazy accents. "It amused me so very much to see them trundling across. Not that they quite knew what they were doing, of course," she added, her faintly amused eyes still watching the splendid flames of the beech-logs. "They thought, poor dears, that they were merely travelling here comfortably along their own side of the road to take a charming house for themselves to live in—a house that they wouldn't have been able to take at all if we hadn't won the war. But all they were really doing was to cross the road to help a little ex-soldier on to his feet again out of the ditch."

The General sat a moment longer looking at Mrs Bellowes. Then a grim smile slowly spread over his countenance. He picked up the match again, lit his cigarette and sat smoking and surveying the fire.

THE ORGY.

BY WALTER DE LA MARE.

[Maga, June 1930.]

It was a Wednesday morning, and May Day, and London, its West End too, crisp, brisk, scintillating. Even the horses had come out in their Sunday best. With their nosegays and ribbons and rosettes they might have been on their way to a wedding—the nuptials of Labour and Capital, perhaps. As for people, the wide pavements of the great street were packed with them. Not so many busy idlers of the one sex as of the other, of course, at this early hour—a top-hat here, a pearl-grey Homburg there; but of the feminine a host as eager and variegated as the butterflies in an Alpine valley in midsummer; some stepping daintily down from their landaulettes like 'Painted Ladies' out of the chrysalis, and thousands of others, blues and browns and speckleds and sables and tawnies and high-fliers and maiden's blushes, from all parts of the world and from most of the suburbs, edging and eddying along, this way, that way, their eyes goggling, their tongues clacking, but most of them, their backs to the highway, gazing, as though mesmerised, in and in through the beautiful plate-glass windows at the motley merchandise on the other side. And much of that on the limbs and trunks of beatific images almost as lifelike but a good deal less active than themselves.

The very heavens, so far as they could manage to peep under the blinds, seemed to be smiling at this plenty. Nor had they any need for care concerning the future, for nurse-maids pushing their baby-carriages before them also paraded the pavements, their infant charges laid in dimpled sleep beneath silken awning and coverlet, while here and there a tiny tot chattered up into the air like a starling.

A clock, probably a church clock, and only just audible, struck eleven. The sun from its heights far up above the roof-tops blazed down upon the polished asphalt and walls with such an explosion of splendour that it looked as if everything had been repainted overnight with a thin coat of crystalline varnish and then sprinkled with frozen sea-water. And every human creature within sight seemed to be as heart-free and gay as this beautiful weather promised to be brief. With one exception only—poor Philip Pim.

And why not ? He was young—so young in looks, indeed, that if Adonis had been stepping along at his side they might have been taken for cousins. He was charmingly attired, too, from his little, round, hard felt hat—not unlike Mercury's usual wear, but without the wings—to his neat brogue shoes ; and he was so blonde, with his pink cheeks and flaxen hair, that at first you could scarcely distinguish his silken eyebrows and eyelashes, though they made up for it on a second glance. Care seemed never to have sat on those young temples. Philip looked as harmless as he was unharmed.

Alas ! this without of his had no resemblance whatever to his within. He eyed vacantly a buzzing hive-like abandonment he could not share ; first, because though he had the whole long day to himself he had no notion of what to do with it ; and next, because only the previous afternoon the manager of the bank in which until then he had had a stool specially reserved for him every morning had shaken him by the hand and had wished him well—for ever. He had said how deeply he regretted Philip's services could not be indulged in by the bank any longer. He would miss him. Oh yes, very much indeed—but missed Philip must be.

The fact was, that Philip had never been able to add up pounds, shillings and pence so that he could be certain the total was correct. His 9's, too, often looked like 7's, his 5's like 3's. And as 'simple addition' was all but his sole duty in the bank, he would not have adorned its premises for a week if his uncle, Colonel Crompton Pim, had not been acquainted with one of its most stylish directors, and was not in the habit of keeping a large part of his ample fortune in its charge. He had asked Mr Bumbleton to give Philip a chance. But chances—some as rapidly as Manx cats—come to an end. And Philip's had.

Now, if Colonel Pim had sent his nephew when he was a small boy to a nice public school, he might have been able by this time to do simple sums very well indeed. Philip might have become an accurate adder-up. It is well to look on the bright side of things. Unfortunately, when Philip was an infant, his health had not been very satisfactory—at least to his widowed mother—and he had been sent instead to a private academy. There a Mr Browne was the mathematical master—a Mr Browne so much attached to algebra and to reading the 'Times' in school hours that he had not much patience with the rudiments of arithmetic. "Just add it up," he would say, "and look up the answer. And if it isn't right, do it again."

It was imprudent of him, but in these early years poor Philip had never so much as dreamed that some day he was going to be a clerk on a stool. If he had, he might not perhaps have been so eager to look up the answers. But then, his uncle was fabulously rich and yet apparently unmarriageable, and Philip was his only nephew. Why, then, should he ever have paid any attention to banks, apart from the variety on which the wild thyme grows?

Term succeeded term, and still, though 'a promising boy,' he remained backward—particularly in the last of the three R's. And his holidays, so called, would be peppered with such problems as (*a*) if a herring and a half cost three half-pence, how many would you get for a shilling? (*b*) If a brick weighs a pound and half a brick, how much does it weigh? (*c*) If Moses was the son of Pharaoh's daughter, &c.; and (*d*) Uncles and brothers have I none, and so on. And since, after successive mornings with a sheet of foolscap and a stub of pencil, Philip's answers would almost invariably reappear as (*a*) 18, (*b*) 1½ lb., (*c*) his sister, and (*d*) himself, Colonel Pim grew more and more impatient and Nature had long ago given him a good start.

He had a way, too, when carpeting poor Philip, of flicking his shepherd-plaid trouser-leg with his handkerchief, which seemed useless to everyone concerned. And at last, instead of transferring his nephew from Mr Browne to Christ Church, Oxford, or to Trinity College, Cambridge, or to some less delectable resort at an outlying university, he first (before setting out in pursuit of big game all around the world) consigned him to a tutor, who thanked his lucky stars the expedition would take the Colonel a long time; and, on his return, gave them both a prolonged vacation.

And *then* had fallen the bolt from the blue. On the morning of his twenty-first birthday, which had promised to be so cool, so calm, so bright, Philip received a letter from his uncle. He opened it with joy; he read it with consternation. It was in terms as curt as they looked illegible, and it was merely to tell him that what the Colonel called a post (but which was, in fact, a high stool) had been secured for his nephew, and that unless Philip managed to keep his seat on it for twelve consecutive months he would be cut off with a shilling.

Of these drear months about two and a half had somehow managed to melt away, and now not only was the stool rapidly following them into the limbo of the past, but at this very moment the Colonel was doubtless engaged, and with his usual zest, in keeping his promise. What wonder, then, Philip was not exactly a happy young man as he wandered this sunny populous May morning aimlessly on his way.

There was nothing—apart from Everything around him—to make him so, except only one minute stroke of luck that had befallen him before breakfast.

When he had risen from his tumbled bed in his London lodgings, the sight of his striped bank trousers and his black bank coat and waistcoat had filled him with disgust. Opening the grained cupboard which did duty for a wardrobe—and in the indulgence of his tailor it was pretty full—he took down from a peg the festive suit he was now wearing, but which otherwise he had left unheeded since Easter. He found himself faintly whistling as he buttoned it on ; but his delight can be imagined when, putting his finger and thumb into an upper waistcoat pocket, he discovered—a sovereign. And an excellent specimen of one, with St George in his mantle and the dragon on the one side of it, and King Edward VII.'s head—cut off at the neck as if he had sat to its designer in his bath—on the other. This, with four others very much like it, had been bestowed on Philip many months ago by his Uncle Charles—a maternal uncle, who had since perished in Paris. As the rest of Philip's pockets contained only 7½d. in all, this coin—how forgotten, he simply could not conjecture—was treasure trove indeed.

Now, poor Philip had never really cared for money. Perhaps he had always associated it with herrings and half-bricks. Perhaps he had never needed it quite enough. Since, moreover, immediately opposite his perch at the Bank there hung a framed antique picture of this commodity in process of being shovelled out of receptacles closely resembling coal-scuttles into great vulgar heaps upon a polished counter, and there weighed in brass scales like so much lard or glucose, he had come to like it less and less. On the other hand, he dearly enjoyed spending it. As with Adam and the happy birds in the Garden of Eden—linnet and kestrel and wren—he enjoyed seeing it fly. In this he was the precise antithesis of his uncle.

Colonel Crompton Pim loved money. He exulted in it

(not vocally, of course) *en masse*, as the Pharaohs exulted in pyramids. And he abhorred spending it. For this (and for many another) reason he had little affection for mere objects —apart, that is, from *such* objects as golf clubs, shooting boots, or hippopotamus-hoof ink-stands, and he had not the smallest pleasure in buying anything for mere buying's sake.

His immense dormitory near Cheltenham, it is true, was full of furniture, but it was furniture, acquired in the 'sixties or thereabouts, for use and not for joy. Prodigious chairs with pigskin seats; tables of a solidity that defied time and of a wood that laughed at the worm; bedsteads of the Gog order; wardrobes resembling Assyrian sarcophagi; and ottomans which would seat with comfort and dignity a complete royal family. As for its 'ornaments,' they came chiefly from Benares.

And simply because poor Philip delighted in spending money and hated impedimenta such as these with the contempt a humming-bird feels for the corpse of a rhinoceros, he had never been able to take to his uncle—not even for the sake of what he owned. And it was impossible—as he fondly supposed—for any human being to take to him for any other reason. No, there was nothing in common between them, except a few branches of the family tree. And these the Colonel might already have converted into firewood.

Now, as poor Philip meandered listlessly along the street, fingering his Uncle Charles's golden sovereign in his pocket, he came on one of those gigantic edifices wherein you can purchase anything in the world—from a white elephant to a performing flea, from a cargo of coconuts to a tin-tack. This was the 'store' at which his uncle 'dealt.' And by sheer force of habit, Philip mounted the welcoming flight of steps, crossed a large, flat, rubber mat and went inside.

Having thus got safely in, he at once began to ponder how he was to get safely out—with any fraction, that is, of his golden sovereign still in his pocket. And he had realised in the recent small hours that with so little on earth now left to spend, except an indefinite amount of leisure, he must strive to spend that little with extreme deliberation.

So first, having breakfasted on a mere glance at the charred remnant of a kipper which his landlady had served up with his chicory, he entered a large gilded lift, or elevator, as the directors preferred to call it, *en route* to the restaurant. There he seated himself at a vacant table and asked the waitress to be so kind as to bring him a glass of milk and a bun. He nibbled, he sipped and he watched the people—if people they really were, and not, as seemed more probable, automata intended to advertise the Ecclesiastical, the Sports, the Provincial, the Curio, the Export and the Cast-Iron Departments.

With his first sip of milk he all but made up his mind to buy a little parting present for his uncle. It would be at least a gentle gesture. With his second he decided that the Colonel would be even less pleased to receive a letter *and*, say, a velvet smoking-cap, or a pair of mother-of-pearl cuff-links, than just a letter. By the time he had finished his bun he had decided to buy a little something for himself. But try as he might he could think of nothing (for less than a guinea) that would be worthy of the shade of his beloved Uncle Charles. So having pushed seven-fifteenths of all he else possessed under his plate for his freckled waitress, with the remaining fourpence he settled his bill and went steadily downstairs. Nineteen minutes past ten—he would have a good look about him before he came to a decision.

Hunger, it has been said, sharpens the senses, but it is apt also to have an edgy effect upon the nerves. If, then, Philip's breakfast had been less exacting, or his lunch had made up for it, he might have spent the next few hours of this pleasant May morning as a young man should—in the open air. Or he might have visited the British Museum, or the National Gallery, or Westminster Abbey. He might never, at any rate, in one brief morning of his mortal existence have all but died again and again of terror, abandon, shame, rapture and incredulity. He might never—but all in good time.

He was at a loose end, and it is then that habits are apt to prevail. And of all his habits, Philip's favourite was that of ordering 'goods' on behalf of his uncle. The Colonel in his fantastic handwriting would post him two weekly lists—one consisting of the 'wanted,' the other of complaints about the previous week's 'supplied.' Armed with these, Philip would set out for the building he was now actually in. The first list, though not a thing of beauty, was a joy as long as it lasted. The second, for he had always flatly refused to repeat his uncle's sulphurous comments to any underling, he reserved for his old enemy, the secretary of the establishment, Sir Leopold Bull. And though in these weekly interviews Sir Leopold might boil with rage and chagrin, he never boiled over. For the name of Pim was a name of power in the secretary's office. The name of Pim was that of a heavy shareholder; and what the Colonel wanted he invariably in the long-run got. A chest, say, of Ceylon tea, 'rich, fruity, bright infusion'; a shooting-stick (extra heavy, Brugglesdon tube pattern); a quart size tantalus, for a wedding present, with a double spring sterling silver Brahmin lock; a hundredweight of sago; a stymie, perhaps, or a click—something of that sort.

These 'order days' had been the balm of Philip's late existence. His eyes fixed on his ledger and his fancy on, say, 'Saddlery' or 'Sports,' he looked forward to his Wednesdays like a thirsty Arab in the desert to an oasis of palms and a well of water. Indeed, his chief regret at the bank, apart from little difficulties with his 9's and 3's, had been that his uncle's stores were closed on Saturday afternoons. And on Sundays. His hobby had, therefore, frequently given him indigestion, since he could indulge it only between 1 and 2 P.M. It was a pity, of course, that Colonel Pim was a man of wants so few, and those of so narrow a range. Possibly the suns of

India had burned the rest out of him. But for Philip, any kind of vicarious purchase had been better than none. And now these delights, too, were for ever over. His fountain had run dry; Sir Leopold had triumphed.

At this moment he found himself straying into the Portmanteau and Bag Department. There is nothing like leather, and here there was nothing *but* leather, and all of it made up into articles ranging in size from trunks that would hold the remains of a Daniel Lambert to card-cases that would hold practically nothing at all. And all of a sudden Philip fancied he would like to buy a cigarette-case. He would have preferred one of enamel or gold or morocco or tortoise-shell or lizard or shagreen; or even of silver or suède. But preferences are expensive. And as he sauntered on, his dreamy eye ranging the counters in search merely of a cigarette-case he could *buy*, his glance alighted on a 'gent's dressing-case.'

It was of pigskin, and it lay, unlike the central figure in Rembrandt's "Lesson in Anatomy," so that the whole of its interior was in full view, thus revealing a modest row of silver-topped bottles, similar receptacles for soap, tooth-brushes, hair-oil and Eau de Cologne; a shoe-horn, a boot-hook, an ivory paper-knife and hair brushes, 'all complete.' Philip mused on it for a moment or two, perplexed by a peculiar effervescence that was going on in his vitals. He then approached the counter and asked its price.

"The price, sir?" echoed the assistant, squinnying at the tiny oblong of pasteboard attached by a thread to the ring of the handle; "the price of that article is seventeen, seventeen, six."

He was a tubby little man with boot-button eyes, and his 'pounds,' Philip thought, was a trifle unctuous.

"Ah," he said, putting a bold face on the matter, "it looks a sound workaday bag. A little mediocre perhaps. Have you anything—less ordinary?"

"Something more expensive, sir? Why, yes, indeed. This

is only a stock line—the 'Archdeacon' or 'County Solicitor' model. We have prices to suit all purses. Now if you were thinking of something which you might call resshersy, sir" —and Philip now was—" there's a dressing-case under the window over there was specially made to the order of Haitch Haitch the Maharaja of Jolhopolloluli. Unfortunately, sir, the gentleman deceased suddenly a week or two ago ; climate, I understand. His funeral obliquies were in the newspaper, you may remember. The consequence being, his ladies not, as you might say, concurring, the dressing-case in a manner of speaking is on our hands—and at a considerable reduction. Only six hundred and seventy-five guineas, sir ; or rupees to match."

"May I look at it ?" said Philip. "Colonel Crompton Pim."

"By all means, sir," cried the little man as if until that moment he had failed to notice that Philip was a long-lost son ; "Colonel Crompton Pim ; of course. Here is the article, sir, a very handsome case, and quite unique, one of the finest, in fact, I have ever had the privilege of handling since I was transferred to this Department—from the Sports, sir."

He pressed a tiny knob, the hinges yawned and Philip's mouth began to water. It was in sober sooth a handsome dressing-case, and the shaft of sunlight that slanted in on it from the dusky window seemed pleased to be exploring it. It was a dressing-case of tooled red Levant morocco, with gold locks and clasps and a lining of vermilion watered silk, gilded with a chaste design of lotus flowers, peacocks and houris, the 'fittings' being of gold and tortoise-shell, and studded with so many minute brilliants and seed pearls that its contents, even in that rather dingy sunbeam, appeared to be delicately on fire.

Philip's light blue eyes under their silken lashes continued to dwell on its charms in so spellbound a silence that for a moment the assistant thought the young man was about to swoon.

"Thank you very much," said Philip at last, turning away with infinite reluctance and with a movement as graceful as that of a fawn, or a *première danseuse* about to rest; "I will keep it in mind. You are sure the management can afford the reduction?"

Having made this rather airy comment, it seemed to Philip impolite, if not impossible, to ask the price of a 'job line' of mock goatskin cigarette cases that were piled up in dreary disorder on a tray near at hand. So he passed out into the next department, which happened to be that devoted to goods described as 'fancy,' though, so far as he could see, not very aptly.

Still he glanced around him as he hurried on, his heart bleeding for the unfortunates, old and helpless, or young and defenceless, doomed some day to welcome these exacerbating barbarous jocosities as gifts. But at sight of an obscure, puffy, maroon object demonstratively labelled 'Pochette: Art Nouveau,' his very skin contracted, and he was all but about to inquire of a large, veiled old lady with an ebony walking-stick who was manfully pushing her way through this *mélange*, possibly in search of a *prie-dieu*, how such dreadful phenomena were "begot, how nourishèd," and was himself preparing to join in the chorus, when a little beyond it his glance alighted on a minute writing-case, so frailly finished, so useless, so delicious to look at, handle and smell, that even Titania herself might have paused to admire it. Philip eyed it with unconcealed gusto. His features had melted into the smile that so often used to visit them when as a little boy he had confided in his Uncle Charles that he preferred éclairs to doughnuts. Its price, he thought, was ridiculously moderate: only £67, 10s.

"It's the décor, sir—Parisian, of course—that makes it a trifle costly," the assistant was explaining. "But it's practical as well as sheek and would add distinction to *any* young lady's boudoir, bed-chamber, or lap. The ink, as you see, sir, cannot possibly leak from the bottle, if the case, that is, is held the right way up—so. The pencil, the '*Sans Merci*,' as you observe, is of solid gold; and the pen, though we cannot guarantee the nib, is set with life-size turquoises. The flaps will hold at least six sheets of small size notepaper, and envelopes to—or not to—match. And *here* is a little something, a sort of calendar, sir, by which you can tell the day of the week of any day of the month in any year in any century from one A.D. to nine hundred and ninety-nine thousand, nine hundred and ninety-nine. It could then be renewed."

"M'm, very ingenious," Philip murmured, "and even Leap Year, I see. Is it unique, and so on?"

"No doubt of it, sir. As a matter of fact a lady from Philadelphia—the United States of America, sir—ordered fifty facsillimies, platinum mounts, of this very article—only yesterday afternoon; they get married a good deal over there, sir; wedding presents."

"Quite, thank you, no," said Philip, firmly but pleasantly. "They say there is safety in numbers, but there seems to be precious little else. Have you anything less reproducible?"

"Reproducible, sir? Why, naturally, sir. You see this is only a counter article. While catering for the many, sir, we are bound to keep an eye upon the few. For that very reason, the management prefer to have the costlier specimens under cover."

"Again, thank you," said Philip hurriedly. "What evils are done in thy name, O Philadelphia! I may return later."

He emerged from the Fancy Goods Department, feeling at the same moment crestfallen and curiously elated. His mind, in fact, at this moment resembled a volcano the instant before its gloom is fated to burst into a blazing eruption. Though very hazily, he even recognised the danger he was in. So in hope to compose himself he sat down for a minute or two on a Madeira wicker chair intended perhaps by the management for this very purpose, and found himself gazing at a large black Chinese cat, in the glossiest of glazed earthenware, and as lifelike as Oriental artifice could make it. It was seated in a corner under a high potted palm, and it wore a grin upon its features that may have come from Cheshire, but which showed no symptom whatever of vanishing away. At sight of it—for Philip was not only partial to cats but knew the virtues of the black variety—a secret fibre seemed to have snapped in his head. "Good luck!" the creature smirked at him. And Philip smirked back. A flame of anguished defiance and desire had leapt up in his body. He would show his uncle what was what. He would learn him to cut nephews off with shillings. He would dare and do and die!

He rose, refreshed and renewed. It was as if he had tossed off a bumper of 'Veuve Clicquot' of 1066. He must himself have come over with the Conqueror. A shopwalker lurking near was interrupted in the middle of an enormous gape by the spectacle of this Apollonian young figure now entering his department—Pianofortes and American Organs. There was something in the leopard-like look of him, something so princely and predatory in his tread, that this Mr Jackson would have been almost ready to confess that he was moved. Frenchily dark and Frenchily sleek, he bowed himself almost double.

"Yes, sir?" he remarked out loud.

"I want, I think, a pianoforte," said Philip. "A Grand."

"Thank you, sir; this way, please. Grand pianofortes, Mr Smithers."

"I want a Grand piano," repeated Philip to Mr Smithers, an assistant with a slight cast in his left eye and an ample gingerish moustache. But in spite of these little handicaps Philip liked him much better than Mr Jackson. A far-away glimpse of Mrs Smithers and of all the little Smitherses seated round their Sunday leg of mutton at Hackney or at Brondesbury, maybe, had flashed into his mind.

"Grands, sir," cried Mr Smithers, moving his moustache

up and down with a curious rotary constriction of the lips; "this way, please."

The young man was conducted along serried ranks of Grands. They stood on their three legs, their jaws tight shut, as mute as troops on parade. Philip paced on and on, feeling very much like the late Duke of Cambridge reviewing a regiment of his Guards. He paused at length in front of a "Style 8; 7 ft. 9 in., square-legged, blackwood, mahogany-trimmed Bismarck."

"It *looks* spacious," he smiled amiably. "But the finish! And why overhung?"

"Overstrung, sir?" said Mr Smithers. "That's merely a manner of speaking, sir, relating solely to its inside. But this, of course, is not what we specificate as a *grand* Grand. For tone and timber and resonance and pedal work and solidity and *wear*—there isn't a better on the market. I mean on the rest of the market. And if you were having in mind an everlasting instrument for the nursery or for a practice room—and we supply the new padded partitioning—this would be precisely the instrument, sir, you were having in mind. The young are sometimes a little hard on piano-fortes, sir. They mean well, but they are but children after all; and——"

"Now let—me—think," Philip interposed. "To be quite candid, I wasn't having anything of that sort in mind. My sentiments are England for the English; and Bismarck, you know, though in girth and so on a remarkable man, was in other respects, a little—well, miscellaneous. It is said that he mixed his champagne with stout—or was it cocoa? On the other hand, I have no wish to be insular, and I *may* order one of these constructions later. For a lady, the niece, as a matter of fact, of a governess of my uncle Colonel Crompton Pim's when he was young—as young at least as it was possible for him to be—who is, I believe, thinking of taking—of taking in—pupils. But we will see to that later. Have you anything that I could really look at?"

Mr Smithers's moustaches twirled like a weathercock. "Why, yes, sir. Just now we are up to our eyes in pianos—flooded; and if I may venture to say so, sir, Bismarck was never no friend of *mine.* All this," and he swept his thumb in the direction of the avenue of instruments that stretched behind them, "they may be Grands, but they're most of them foreign, and if you want a little something as nice to listen to as it is natty to look at, and *not* a mere menadjery fit only for an 'awl, there is a little what they call a harpsichord over yonder, sir. It's a bijou model, de Pompadour case, hand-painted throughout—cupids and scallops and what-not, all English gut, wire, metal and jacks, and I defy any dealer in London to approximate it, sir, in what you might call pure form. No noise and all music, sir, and that *mellow* you scarcely know where to look. A lady's instrument—a titled lady's. And only seven hundred and seventy-seven guineas, sir, all told."

"Is it unique?" Philip inquired.

"Unique, sir? There's not another like it in Europe."

Philip smiled at Mr Smithers very kindly out of his blue eyes. "But what about America?" he said.

The assistant curved what seemed an almost unnecessarily large hand round his lips. "Between you and me, sir, if by America," he murmured, "you're meaning the United States, why, Messrs Montferas & de Beauguyou refuse to ship in that direction. It ruins their tone. In fact, sir, they are what's called *difficult.* They make for nobody and nowhere but as a favour; and that instrument over there was built for——"

He whispered the sesame so low that water rustling on a pebbled beach would have conveyed to Philip tidings more intelligible. But by the look in Mr Smithers's eye Philip guessed that the lady in question moved in a lofty, though possibly a narrow, circle.

"Ah!" he said; "then that settles it. A home away from home. Charity begins there. I shall want it to-morrow.

I shall want them both to-morrow. I mean the pianos. And perhaps a more democratic instrument for the servants' hall. But I will leave that to you."

Mr Smithers pretended not to goggle. "Why, yes, sir, that can be easily arranged. In London, I *ho*—conjecture?"

"In London," said Philip, "Grosvenor Square." For at that very instant, as if at the summons of a jinnee, there had wafted itself into his memory the image of a vacant and 'highly desirable residence,' which his casual eye had glanced upon only the afternoon before, and which had proclaimed itself 'to be let.'

"Grosvenor Square, sir; oh yes, sir?" Mr Smithers was ejaculating, order-book in hand. "I will arrange for their removal at once. The three of them—quite a nice little set, sir."

"Pim, Crompton, Colonel," chanted Philip. "R-*O*-M; deferred account; *thank* you. 4-4-4, yes, four hundred and forty-four, Grosvenor Square. I am—that is, *we* are furnishing there."

But his gentle emphasis on the 'we' was so courtly in effect that it sounded more like an afterthought than a piece of information. Nevertheless it misled Mr Smithers. Intense fellow-feeling beamed from under his slightly overhung forehead. "And I am sure, sir, if I may make so bold, I wish you both every happiness. I am myself of a matrimonial turn. And regret it, sir? *never!* I always say if every——"

"That's very kind indeed of you," said Philip, averting his young cheek, which having flushed had now turned a little pale. "And, if *I* may be so bold, I am perfectly certain Mrs Smithers is of the same way of thinking. Which is the best way to the Best Man's Department, if I take in Portmanteaux and the Fancies on my way?"

Mr Smithers eyed him with the sublimest admiration. "Straight through, sir, on the left beyond them Chappels.

On the same floor, but right out on the farther side of the building. As far as you can go."

"That is exactly what I was beginning to wonder—precisely how far I can go. This little venture of mine is a rather novel experience, and at the moment I am uncertain of its issue. But tell me, why is it our enterprising American friends have not yet invented a *lateral* lift ?"

"Now that's passing strange, too, sir; for I've often fancied it myself," said Mr Smithers. "But you see in a department like this there's not much time for quiet thought, sir, with so much what you might call hidden din about. As a matter of fact, when I was younger, sir—and that happens to us all—I did invent a harmonium key-stifler—rubber, and pith and wool—*so*—and a small steel spring, quite neat and entirely unnoticeable. But the manufacturers wouldn't look at it; not they!"

"I don't believe," said Philip, folding up his bill, "they ever look at anything. Not closely, you know. But if ever I do buy a harmonium," he put his head a little on one side and again smiled at Mr Smithers, "I shall insist on the stifler. I suppose," he added reflectively, "you haven't by any chance a nice pedigree Amati or Stradivarius in stock? I have a little weakness for fiddles."

Mr Smithers, leaning heavily on the counter on both his thumbs, smiled, but at the same time almost imperceptibly shook his head.

"I fancied it was unlikely," said Philip. "What's that over there; in the glass case, I mean?"

"That, sir?" said Mr Smithers, twinkling up, "in that glass case there? That's a harp, sir. And a lovely little piece *that* is. Child's size, sir. What they call minnychoore, and well over a century old, but still as sweet as a canary. It was made, so they say, for Mozart, the composer, sir, as you might be aware, in 1781, and up in the top corner is scratched the letters A. W. No doubt of it, sir—A. W. I've seen a picture of the mite myself playing like a nangel in his nightcap, and not a day over seven ; you'd hardly believe it, and his parents coming in at the door. Surprising. Then Schumann, *he* had it, sir—I mean the harp ; and Schumann, though I don't know how he could dissuade himself to part with it, *he* passed it on to Brahms, another composer—and very much thought of even though a bit nearer *our* day. But you'll find it all neatly set out on the brass label at the foot. It's all there, sir. There's many a custo——"

"Indeed!" said Philip; "Brahms, Schumann, Mozart, what scenes we are recalling! And here it rests at last. The knacker's yard. How very, very sad. Why, of course, Mr Smithers, we must have that sent on too—and packed very, very carefully. Is the glass case extra?"

Mr Smithers gulped. "I am exceedingly sorry, sir," he said, "exceedingly sorry, but it's not for sale ; I mean—*except* the case."

"Not for sale," retorted Philip impulsively. "But what is the use, Mr Smithers, of a mercenary institution like this unless everything in it is for sale? You cannot mean for raw advertisement?"

Mr Smithers was covered with confusion. "I am sure, sir," he said, "that the directors would do their utmost to consider your wishes. They would be very happy to do so. But if you will excuse my mentioning it, I should myself very much miss that harp. I have been in this department thirteen years now. . . . My little boy. . . . It is the only thing . . ."

It was Philip's turn to be all in confusion. "Good gracious me, I quite understand," he said ; "not another word, Mr Smithers. I wouldn't *think* of pressing the point. None the less I can assure you that even if it had been for sale I should always have welcomed you whenever you cared to come to Grosvenor Square and take another look at it. And, of course, your little boy too—*all* your little boys."

Mr Smithers appeared to be lost in gratitude. "If only,"

he began, a light that never was on sea or land in his eye —but words failed him.

At the other end of the 'Chappels' Philip again encountered the walker, Mr Jackson, still looking as much like a self-possessed bridegroom as it is possible for a high collar and a barber to achieve.

"I see," said Philip, "you exhibit specimens of the tuberphone (and, by the way, I would suggest *a* instead of 'er'), the tubaphone, the clogbox and the Bombaboo, iniquities at the same time negroid and old-fashioned, but though in a recent visit to Budapest I found even the charming little linden-shaded shops—along the Uffel-gang, you know, not, of course, a fashionable part of the city—crammed with models of the 'Haba-Stein,' a microtonic instrument with five keyboards and Hindu effects, intended, of course, for the polytonal decompositions of the 'Nothing-but-Music' school—*most* interesting; I see *no* trace of it here. I am not a neoteromaniac, but still, we must keep abreast, we must keep abreast!"

He waved a not unfriendly glove over his head, smiled and went on.

Mr Smithers had also watched the slim, grey, young figure until it had turned the corner and was out of sight. He then had a word with his floor chief.

"Pim, eh, Crompton," said Mr Jackson, squinting morosely at his underling's open order-book. "'Setting up house'? Then I suppose the old gent must have sent in his checks. Not that I'm surprised this nephew of his hasn't bought his black yet. Close-fisted, purple-nosed, peppery old ——! There won't be many to cry their eyes out over *his* arums and gardenias."

Mr Smithers, being a family man, felt obliged to seem to enjoy as much as possible his immediate chief's society.

"All I can say *is*," he ventured, "that young feller, and he's a gentleman if ever there was one, is making it fly."

He *was.* At this moment Philip was assuring Assistant No. 6 in the Portmanteau Department that unless the Maharaja of Jolhopolloluli's dressing-case could be despatched next day to reach No. 444 Grosvenor Square by tea-time he need not trouble. "A few other little things," he explained, "are being sent at the same time." No. 6 at once hastened to the house telephone and asked for the secretary's office. The line was engaged.

But he need not have hesitated, for when a young man with a Pim for an uncle and of so much suavity and resource makes his wishes known, this world is amiability itself. Philip was warming up. However bland in outward appearance, he was by this time at a very enlivening temperature. He had tasted blood, as the saying goes; and he was beginning to see the need of setting a good example. Customers, like the coneys, are usually a feeble folk. His little sortie was turning into a crusade.

By this time he had all but finished disporting himself in the Furniture Department. "Three large reception rooms, one of them extensive," had run his rather naked catalogue, "a ballroom, a dining-room, a breakfast-room and a little pretty dumpy all-kinds-of-angles morning-room with a Cherubini ceiling and a Venetian chimney-piece, eighteenth century, in lapis lazuli and glass. Bedrooms, let me see, say, twenty-two—just to go on with (but not in), eleven of them for personal use, and the rest, staff. That, I think, will do for the present. We face east or west as the case may be; and nothing, please, of the 'decorative,' the quaint, or the latest thing out. Nothing shoddy, shapeless, or sham. I dislike the stuffy and the fussy and mere trimmings; and let the beds be ***beds***. Moreover, I confess to being sadly disappointed in the old, the 'antique,' furniture you have shown me. The choice is restricted, naïve and incongruous, and I have looked in vain for anything that could not be easily rivalled in the richer museums. However, let there be as many so-called antique pieces as possible, and those as antique as you can manage. Period, origin, design, harmony—please bear these in mind."

The assistants clustering round him, bowed.

"If I have time I will look through the department again on my way down. Seven hundred guineas for the cheaper of the Chippendale four-posters seems a little exorbitant; and three hundred and fifty for the William and Mary wall-glass—I fear it's been resilvered and patched. Still, I agree you can but do your best—I say you can all of you but do your best—and I must put up with that. What I *must* insist on, however, is that everything I have mentioned—everything—must be in its place to-morrow afternoon—carpets and so on will, of course, precede them—by four o'clock. And let there be no trace left of that indescribable odour of straw and wrappings—from Delhi, I should think—which accompanies removals. 444 Grosvenor Square. Pim—Crompton—Colonel: R-*O*-M. Thank you. To the left? *Thank* you."

This 'floor-chief' hastened on in front of his visitor as if he were a Gehazi in attendance on a Naaman, and the young man presently found himself in a scene overwhelmingly rich with the colours, if not the perfumes, of the Orient. Here a complete quarter of an hour slid blissfully by. Mere wooden furniture, even when adorned with gilt, lacquer, ivory, or alabaster, can be disposed of with moderate ease; and especially if the stock of the tolerable is quickly exhausted. But Persian, Chinese, if not Turkey, carpets are another matter.

Philip sat erect on a gimcrack gilded chair, his cane and hat in his left hand, his gloves in his right, while no less than three sturdy attendants in baize aprons at one and the same moment strewed their matchless offerings at his feet, and an infuriated and rapidly multiplying group of would-be customers in search of floorcloth, lino and cocoanut matting stood fuming beyond. But first come first served is a good old maxim, and even apart from it Philip was unaware of their company. He lifted not so much as an eyebrow in their direction.

In the meantime, however, the cash balance in his uncle's bank, and much else besides, had long since as rapidly vanished as the vapour from a locomotive on a hot summer's day. From the Carpet Department, vexed that time allowed him only one of London's chief treasuries to ransack—such are the glories of Bokhara and Ispahan—he hastened down to the wine counters. Here, childishly confident in the cellarage of No. 444, Philip indulged a pretty palate *not* inherited from his uncle: claret, Burgundy, hock, sherry, cherry brandy, green Chartreuse and similar delicate aids to good talk and reflection. He was ingenuous but enthusiastic. Port he ignored.

From 'Wines' he made his way through the galleries exhibiting curtains and 'hangings' (he shuddered), and china and glass—"most discouraging." His spirits revived a little when yet another defunct and barbaric prince, this time from Abyssinia, supplied him in the Car Department with a vehicle whose only adequate use, to judge from the modesty of its dashboard, the simplicity of its engine and its price, would be a journey from this world into the next. Nevertheless his Highness had left it behind.

Fleeting visits to counters bristling with ironmongery, turnery, kitchen utensils and provisions, and from motives of principle he omitted all mention of mulligatawny paste, chutney, West India pickles and similar fierce and barbarous comestibles, vanished out of memory like the patterns of a kaleidoscope. The rather noisy annexe reserved for live stock Philip left unvisited. After deserts of dead stock it sounded inviting, but Philip's was a dainty nose and he was sorry for orang-outangs.

So too with books. He had clear convictions of what a gentleman's library should be without, but decided that it would take more leisure than he could spare this morning to expound them. Even the sight of a Work of Reference, however, is an excellent sedative; he ordered the choicest of who's-whos, dictionaries, atlases, encyclopædias, bird, flower and cookery books—with a copy of 'Bradshaw'—and retired.

As for pictures and statuary, one anguished glance into the dreadful chambers devoted to the fine arts had sent him scurrying on like a March hare. Nor, as he rather sadly realised, had he any cause to linger at the portals of the Monumental-Masonry Department, and he now suddenly found himself in the midst of a coruscating blaze of the precious metals and the still more precious stones. He had strayed into 'Jewellery'—a feast for Aladdin. Gold in particular—goblets and bowls and tankards, plates, platters and dishes of it; clocks, chronometers, watches—from massive turnips, memorial of the Georges, to midgets like a threepenny piece in crystal and enamel, many of them buzzing like bees, and all of them intent on the kind of time which is *not* wild or always nectarous, but of which Philip had always supposed there was an inexhaustible supply. But not, alas, for all purposes. Indeed, these officious reminders of the actual hour had for the first time a little scared him.

In the peculiar atmosphere that hangs over any abundant array of sago, cooked meats, candles, biscuits, coffee, tea, ginger and similar wares, he had been merely a young bachelor on the brink of an establishment. But at sight of this otiose display of gew-gaws in the lamplit mansion in which he now found himself, his fancy had suddenly provided him with a bride. She was of a fairness incomparably fair. The first faint hint of this eventuality had almost unnerved him. He lost his head and—his heart being unconcerned—his taste also. In tones as languid as the breezes of Arabia he had at once ordered her rings, bracelets, necklaces, pendants, brooches, ear-rings, not to speak of bediamonded plumes and tiaras, that would daunt the dreams even of the complete bevy of musical comedy young ladies on the British stage—not to mention those of Buenos Aires. And then, oddly enough, he had come to himself, and paused.

At the very moment of opening his mouth in repetition of a solo with which he was now entirely familiar—" R-*O*-M," and so on—he sat instead, gaping at the tall, calm, bald, venerable old gentleman on the other side of the counter. He had flushed.

" Have you," he inquired almost timidly at last, his eyes fixed on a chastely printed list of cutlery and silverware that lay on the glass case at his elbow, " have you just one really simple, lovely, rare, precious, and, well, unique little trinket suitable for a lady? Young, you know? An *un*-birthday present?"

The old gentleman looked up, looked at, looked *in*, smiled fondly, reminiscently, and, selecting a minute key on a ring which he had drawn out of his pocket, opened a safe not half a dozen yards away. " We have this," he said.

'This,' at first, was a little fat morocco leather case. He pressed the spring. Its lid flew open. And for an instant Philip went gravel blind. But it was not so much the suppressed lustre of the jewels within that had dazed his imagination as the delicate marvel of their setting. They lay like lambent dewdrops on the petals of a flower. The old gentleman gazed too.

" The meaning of the word 'simple,'" he suggested ruminatively, " is one of many degrees. This, sir, is a Benvenuto Cellini piece." He had almost whispered the last few syllables as if what in workmanship were past all rivalry was also beyond any mortal pocket; as if, in fact, he were telling secrets of the unattainable. The tone piqued Philip a little.

" It is charming," he said. " But have you nothing then of Jacques de la Tocqueville's, or of Rudolph von Himmeldommer's, nothing of—dear me, the name escapes me. The earlier Florentine, you will remember, no doubt referred to in *Sordello*, who designed the chryselephantine bowl for the Botticelli wedding-feast. But never mind. Nothing Greek? Nothing Etruscan—*poudre d'or?* Are you suggesting that the Winter Palace was thrice looted in vain?"

The old gentleman was accustomed to the airs and graces of fastidious clients and merely smiled. He had not been listening very intently. "You will appreciate the difficulty, sir, of keeping anything but our more trifling pieces actually within reach of the nearest burglar with a stick of gun-cotton or an acetylene lamp. This"—he stirred the little leather case with his finger as lightly as a cat the relics of a mouse, and its contents seemed softly to sizzle in subdued flames of rose and amber and blue—"this," he said, "happens not to be our property. It is merely in our keeping. And though to an article of such a nature it is absurd to put a price, we have been asked to dispose of it; and by—well, a client for whom we have the profoundest respect."

"I see"; Philip pondered coldly on the bauble, though his heart was a whirlpool of desire and admiration. He swallowed. The remote tiny piping of a bird that was neither nightingale nor skylark, and yet might be either or both, had called to him as if from the shores of some paradisal isle hidden in the mists of the future. He glanced up at the old gentleman, but his bald, long, grey countenance was as impassive as ever.

"I'll take it," Philip said, and for a while could say no more. When speech was restored to him, he asked that it should be delivered not "with the other things," and not to any butler or major-domo or other crustacean that might appear in answer to a knock at No. 444, but by special messenger into his own personal private hands.

"Precisely at half-past four, if you please." The old gentleman bowed. As there was not enough room in the money column of his order-book for the noughts, he had written in the price in longhand, and was engaged in printing the figures 444 in the place reserved for the customer's address, when a small but clearly actual little voice at Philip's elbow suddenly shrilled up into his ear—

"Mr Philip Pim, sir?" Philip stood stock-still, stiffened, his heart in his ears. "The sekkertary, sir," the piping voice piped on, "asks me to say he'd be much obliged if you would be so kind as to step along into his office on your way *hout*, sir."

The tone of this invitation, though a little Cockney in effect, was innocence and courtesy itself; yet at sound of it every drop of blood in Philip's body—though he was by no means a bloated creature—had instantly congealed. This was the end, then. His orgy was over. His morning of mornings was done. The afflatus that had wafted him on from floor to floor had wisped out of his mind like the smoke of a snuffed-out candle. Yet *still* the bright thought shook him: he had had a Run for his money. No—better than that: he had had a Run *gratis*.

He must collect his wits: they had gone wool-gathering. At last he managed to turn his head and look down at the small, apple-cheeked, maroon-tunicked page-boy at his side—apple-cheeked, alas, only because he had but that week entered the sekkertary's service and his parents were of country stock.

"Tell Sir Leopold Bull"—Philip smiled at the infant—"that I will endeavour to be with him in the course of the afternoon. Thank you. That," he added for the ear of his friend on the other side of the counter, "that will be all."

But Philip was reluctant to leave him. These four syllables, as he had heard himself uttering them, sounded on in his ear with the finality of a knell. He was extremely dubious of what would happen if he let go of the counter. His knees shook under him. A dizzy vacancy enveloped him in. With a faint wan smile at the old gentleman, who was too busily engaged in returning his treasures to the safe to notice it, he managed to edge away at last.

Every mortal thing around him, gilded ceiling to grandfather clock, was at this moment swaying and rotating, as will the ocean in the eyes of a sea-sick traveller gloating down upon it from an upper deck. He felt ill with foreboding.

But breeding tells. And courage is a mistress that has never been known to jilt a faithful heart. Philip was reminded of this as he suddenly caught sight of a sort of enormous purple beefeater, resembling in stature a Prussian dragoon, and in appearance a Javanese Jimjam. This figure stood on duty in the doorway, and appeared to be examining him as closely as if he were the heir to the English throne (or the most nefarious crook from Chicago). As Philip drew near he looked this monster full in his fish-like eye, since he was unable to do anything else. But try as he might he could not pass him in silence.

"Ask Sir Leopold Bull, please," he said, "to send an official to show me the way to his office. He will find me somewhere in the building."

"I can take you there meself," replied the giant hoarsely. He could indeed—bodily.

"Thank you," replied Philip. "I have no doubt of it. But I should be much obliged if you would at once deliver my message."

He then groped his way to yet another wicker chair not many yards along a corridor festooned with knick-knacks from Japan and the Near East, and clearly intended for speedy disposal. He eyed them with immense distaste and sat down.

"Nothing whatever, thank you," he murmured to a waitress who had approached him with a card containing a list of soft drinks. Never in his life had he so signally realised the joys of self-restraint. And though at the same moment he thrust finger and thumb into his waistcoat pocket in search of his Uncle Charles's last sovereign, it was with a view not to material but to moral support. Years before he had often tried the same device when as a small boy deadly afraid of the dark he had managed at last to thrust his fevered head up and out from under his bed-clothes, and to emit a dreadful simulacrum of a croupy cough. He had never known it to fail of effect, and it was always nice to know his mother was *there*.

So, too, with his Uncle Charles's sovereign. It was nice to know it was there, though it was not the dark Philip was now afraid of but the light. Resting the ivory handle of his walking-stick on his lower lip, he began to think. What would his sentence be? A first offender, but not exactly a novice. Not, at any rate, he hoped, in taste and judgment. Months or years? Hard labour or penal servitude? So swift is the imagination that in a few seconds Philip found himself not only—his sentence served, the smiling governor bidden farewell—*out* and a free man again, but fuming with rage that he had not managed to retain a single specimen of his spoils. The Jobbli dressing-bag, for instance, or that tiny, that utterly and inimitably 'unique' little Sheraton Sheridan writing-desk.

He came back a little stronger from this expedition into the future. For reassurance, like hope, springs eternal in the human breast. His one regret was not so much that he had been found out (that might come later), but that he had been found out so soon. How much bolder, less humiliating, nobler, to have actually bearded that old 'curmudgen' of an uncle of his, swapp or bogie in hand, in his den!

That in any event he would have been 'found out' on the morrow, as soon, that is, as the first van arrived at No. 444, he had realised long ago. He certainly would not have been found 'in'! But even one brief night in May seems, in prospect, a long interval between being a Crœsus and a felon in Holloway Jail.

He was recalled from these reflections by a young man whose sleek black hair was parted as neatly in front and in the middle as his morning coat was parted behind. A few paces distant, like a mass of gilded pudding-stone, stood the giant from the Jewellery Department. Were they in collusion? Philip could not decide.

"If you would step this way, sir, to the secretary's office," said the young man, "Sir Leopold Bull would be very much obliged."

Philip mounted to his feet and, though he flatly refused to step *that* way, followed him—to his doom. That, however, was not to be instantaneous, for on his arrival Sir Leopold Bull, rising from his roll-top desk with a brief but thrilling smile, first proffered a plump white hand to his visitor and then a chair. It seemed to be a needlessly polite preamble to the interview that was to follow. Philip ignored the hand but took the chair.

"Thank you," he said. "I do hope you will some day take my advice, Sir Leopold, to *sim*plify the arrangement of this building. It is a perfect labyrinth, and I always miss my way." With a sigh he sank down into the cushions. He was tired.

"My uncle, Colonel Crompton Pim," he continued, "is unable to spare a moment to see you this morning. I regret to say he strongly disapproved of the Bombay ducks, or was it the Clam Chowder, you sent him on Friday. They were beneath contempt."

Sir Leopold smiled once more, but even more placatingly. "I had the privilege of seeing Colonel Crompton Pim only yesterday afternoon," he replied. "He then expressed his satisfaction, for the time being, at the golf balls—the new *Excelsior* brand—with one of which we had the pleasure of supplying him *gratis* a week or two ago. The Bombay ducks shall be withdrawn immediately. I must apologise for not seeking you out in person, Mr Pim, but what I have to say is somewhat of a private nature, and——"

"Yes," said Philip, realising how thin was the edge of the wedge which Sir Leopold was at this moment insinuating into the matter in hand. "Yes, quite." And he opened his innocent blue eyes as wide as he could, to prevent them from blinking. He kept them fixed, too, on the close-shaven face, its octopus-like mouth and prominent eyes, with ill-suppressed repulsion. To be a fly that had fallen a victim to such a spider as this!

"It would please me better," he went on, "if you would arrive as rapidly as possible at the matter you wish to discuss with me. I am free for five minutes, but I must beg you not to waste our time. And please tell your porter over there to go away. Scenes are distasteful to me."

The face of the porter, who seemed to have been created solely for his bulk, turned as crimson as a specimen of *sang-du-bœuf*. He appeared to be hurt at having been described as a 'scene.' But wages are of more importance than feelings, and he withdrew.

"You have had a busy morning, Mr Pim," said the secretary. "No less than seven of my assistants who have had the privilege of waiting upon you have been monopolising me for some time with telephone messages. I hope I am not being too intrusive if I venture to congratulate you, sir, on what I suppose to be Colonel Crompton Pim's approaching——"

"Candidly, Sir Leopold," said Philip firmly, "that *would* be venturing too far. Much too far. Let us say no more about it. What precise charge are you intending to bring against me?"

There was a pause while the world continued to rotate.

"For which article?" breathed Sir Leopold.

Philip gazed steadily at the full, bland, secretive countenance. It was as if once again he had heard that seraphic bird-like voice sounding in the remote blue sky above the storm-clouds that now hung so heavily over his beating heart.

"Oh, I mean for delivery," he said. "Mine was—was a large order."

"But, my dear sir, we shouldn't dream of making *any* such charge. *Any* service to Colonel Pim . . ." The faint sob in his voice would have done credit to Caruso.

Philip stooped to hide the cataract of relief that had swept over his face, then raised his head again. How could he be sure that this was anything more than play-acting—the torture of suspense? "Ah, well," he said, "that is no matter now. I gather there was some other point you had in mind—in *view*, I should say."

"Oh, only," said Sir Leopold, "to ask if Colonel Pim would be so kind as to subscribe as usual to our Fund for the Amelioration of the Conditions of the Offspring of Superannuated Shop Assistants. Mainly orphans, Mr Pim. We must all die, Mr Pim, and some of us have to die earlier in life than others. Still, our average here is little worse than that of any other large London establishment. In Petrograd, or was it Los Angeles, I am given to understand, a shop assistant at two-and-thirty is a shop assistant with at least one foot in the grave. It is the little orphans, the fatherless ones, who, from no apparent fault of their own, have to be left to the tender mercies of a busy world! It would grieve you, sir, which Heaven forbid, if I told you how many of these wee small things there are now on our hands. Chubby, joysome, rosebud little creatures, as happy as the day is long. Nevertheless it is a little thoughtless to marry, Mr Pim, when it is only orphans one can leave behind one. On the other hand, there is a silver lining to *every* cloud. Without these infants we should be deprived of a good cause. An excellent cause. And it's causes that keep us going. Last year I think Colonel Pim very kindly contributed half a guinea."

"In cash?" Philip inquired sharply.

"We debited his account," said Sir Leopold.

"Well, then," said Philip, "please understand that my uncle *regrets* that little laxity. He has hardened. He now entirely disapproves of orphans and of orphanages. The shop assistant, he was saying to me only the other day, is a person who should be grateful to Providence that he has *no* justification for dabbling in matrimony. The more celibate they are, in his opinion, the better. But recollect, Sir Leopold, that until we arrive at the higher and fewer salaried officials in your establishment, I feel myself in no way bound to *share* my uncle's views. Your staff is as courteous and considerate as it appears to be unappreciated. A man's a man for a' that. And *a'* that. Let us talk of brighter things."

Sir Leopold did his utmost to conceal the wound to his vanity. "I am sorry to seem to be persistent," he assured his client, "but Colonel Pim only yesterday was so kind as to say he would *consider* my appeal. I take it, then, that he has changed his mind ?"

"My uncle," retorted Philip tartly, "has a mind that is the better for being changed." For an instant he saw the face before him as it would appear in due course in the witness-box; and his very soul revolted. That pitiless Machine called Society might have its merits, but not *this* cog in its wheel! "I myself implored my uncle," he added bitterly, "to give the orphans the cold shoulder. What in the chronic sirocco of his next world would be the use to him of a mere half-guinea's worth of cooling breezes? Scarcely a sop in the pan. Indeed, only a passion for the conventional prevented him from asking for his previous donations to be returned."

Sir Leopold appeared to be engaged in rapidly bolting something—possibly his pride. It was at any rate not part of his secretarial duties to detect insanity in the family of any solvent shareholder.

"There is only one other little point," he went on rather hollowly. "Colonel Pim asked me to send him a detailed account of his purchases during the last month. We met by happy chance as he was yesterday alighting from a taxicab at the entrance to his bank. After to-day's purchases that will perhaps take an hour or two. But it shall reach him to-morrow morning—without fail."

Philip had risen. It is better to stand when one is at bay. While with a gentle absent smile he stood drawing on his gloves he was faced with the wildest effort of his life—to make sure of what lay in hiding behind these last remarks. Anything *might.*

"Oh, he did—did he," he remarked very softly. "I fancy"—and at last he lifted his gentle eyes to meet his adversary's—"I *believe* there's an empty whisky jar that has not yet been credited to him. Perhaps that was on his mind."

"Well, Mr Pim," said Sir Leopold, 'turning' at last, "if *that's* his only jar it's soon adjusted."

Philip took a deep breath. He playfully wagged a finger.

"Now *that,* Sir Leopold," he said, "was blank verse. I hope you don't intend to put my little purchases of this morning into *rhyme.* The effort, I assure you, would be wasted on my uncle."

He wheeled lightly and turned towards the door. Sir Leopold, his face now at liberty to resume its office of expressing his feelings, accompanied him. Indeed he continued to accompany him to the very entrance of his gigantic abode. And there Philip almost fainted. A deluge, compared with which that of Noah and his family was nothing but an April shower, was descending on the street.

"A taxi," roared Sir Leopold at a group of his satellites in the porch, caparisoned in shiny waterproofs and armed with gigantic *parapluies.*

But though at least nineteen of these vehicles were instantly battling their way towards this goal, Philip with incredible agility had eluded their attention. Before Sir Leopold had had time even to arrange his face to smile a farewell, our young friend had gone leaping up the staircase behind him and had without a moment's pause vanished into the Tropical Department. One fugitive glance at its pith and pucka contents, and at the dusky assistants in attendance, had only accelerated his retreat. In less than half a minute he found himself confronting a young woman seated in the midst of a stockade of umbrellas.

The coincidence was too extreme to be ignored. He would at least carry off *some* little souvenir of his morning's outing. What better value could he get for hard cash than an implement that would be at the same time a refuge from the elements—for other he would soon presently have none—and a really formidable weapon at hand for his next interview with Sir Leopold?

He had but just enough breath left to express himself. He pointed.

"I *want* one, please," he cried at the young woman. "Cash."

"One, two, three, four, *five* guineas?" she murmured, looking as if she were less in need of her stock than of her lunch. "Partridge, malacca, horn, ivory, rhinoceros, natural, *gold?* Union, gloria, glacé, taffeta, cotton, mixture, or *twill?*"

"Not a toy; an umbrella," Philip expostulated. "To keep off rain. A nephew returning to school—ten years' wear. Gingham, alpaca, calico, cast iron—*anything;* so long as it is hefty, solid, endurable, awful and *cheap*."

"We have here what is *called* an umbrella," replied the assistant a trifle coldly. "The 'Miss and Master Brand.' Lignum-vitæ stick, whalebone ribs, blunted ferrule, non-poisonous handle, guaranteed not to break, fray, fade, or scale. Nine and elevenpence complete."

"Bill; in haste; cash; just as it is; thanks," cried Philip, and seized the dreadful object. With a groan he laid his Uncle Charles's sovereign in the narrow brass trough of the pay-desk. The obese young person in the wooden box seemed about to lift it to her lips, glanced at him again, put it aside, smiled and gave him his change.

"The way to the back exit, I think, is over here," Philip murmured, waving his gloves due west.

The young person smiled again, and he withdrew. He withdrew down the back steps and into the deluge: there to face a watery world, the possessor of ten shillings and a penny (in his pocket), a wardrobe of old suits, about a hundred and fifty books, three of them unmerited prizes for good conduct, a juvenile collection of postage stamps, a hypothetical legacy of a shilling, and an uncle who, if he faced his liabilities as an English gentleman should, had to all intents and purposes overdrawn his bank account that afternoon by, say roughly, a couple of hundred thousand pounds.

FATHER TOM AND THE POPE;

OR, A NIGHT AT THE VATICAN.

As related by Mr Michael Heffernan, Master of the National School at Tallymactaggart, in the County of Leitrim, to a friend, during his official visit to Dublin, for the purpose of studying Political Economy, in the Spring of 1838.

BY SIR SAMUEL FERGUSON.

[Maga, May 1838.]

CHAPTER I.—HOW FATHER TOM WENT TO TAKE POT-LUCK AT THE VATICAN.

WHEN his Riv'rence was in Room, ov coorse the Pope axed him to take pot look wid him. More be token, it was on a Friday; but, for all that, there was plenty of mate; for the Pope gev himself an absolution from the fast on account ov the great company that was in it—at laste so I'm tould. Howandiver, there's no fast on the dhrink, anyhow—glory be to God!—and so, as they wor sitting, afther dinner, taking their sup together, says the Pope, says he, "Thomaus" —for the Pope, you know, spakes that away, all as one as one ov uz—"Thomaus *a lanna*," says he, "I'm tould you welt them English heretics out ov the face."

"You may say that," says his Riv'rence to him again. "Be my sowl," says he, "if I put your Holiness undher the table, you won't be the first Pope I floored."

Well, his Holiness laughed like to split; for, you know, Pope was the great Prodesan that Father Tom put down upon Purgathory; and ov coorse they knewn all the ins and outs of the conthravarsy at Room. " Faix, Thomaus," says he, smiling across the table at him mighty agreeable— " it's no lie what they tell me, that yourself is the pleasant man over the dhrop ov good liquor."

" Would you like to thry ? " says his Riv'rence.

" Sure, and amn't I thrying all I can ? " says the Pope. " Sorra betther bottle ov wine's betuxt this and Salamancha, nor's there fornenst you on the table ; it's raal Lachrymal-chrystal, every spudh ov it."

" It's mortial could," says Father Tom.

" Well, man alive," says the Pope, " sure and here's the best ov good claret in the cut decanther."

" Not maning to make little ov the claret, your Holiness," says his Riv'rence, " I would prefir some hot wather and sugar, wid a glass ov spirits through it, if convanient."

" Hand me over the bottle of brandy," says the Pope to his head butler, " and fetch up the materi'ls," says he.

" Ah, then, your Holiness," says his Riv'rence, mighty eager, " maybe you'd have a dhrop ov the native in your cellar ? Sure it's all one throuble," says he, " and, troth, I dunna how it is, but brandy always plays the puck wid my inthrails."

" 'Pon my conscience, then," says the Pope, " it's very sorry I am, Misther Maguire," says he, " that it isn't in my power to plase you ; for I'm sure and certaint that there's not as much whisky in Room this blessed minit as 'ud blind the eye ov a midge."

" Well, in troth, your Holiness," says Father Tom, " I knewn there was no use in axing ; only," says he, " I didn't know how else to exqueeze the liberty I tuck," says he, " of bringing a small taste," says he, " of the real stuff," says he, hauling out an imperi'l quart bottle out ov his coat-pocket ; " that never seen the face of a gauger," says he, setting it down on the table fornenst the Pope : " and if you'll jist thry the full ov a thimble ov it, and it doesn't rise the cockles of your Holiness's heart, why then, my name," says he, "isn't Tom Maguire!" and wid that he outs wid the cork.

Well, the Pope at first was going to get vexed at Father Tom for fetching dhrink thataway in his pocket, as if there wasn't lashins in the house: so says he, "Misther Maguire," says he, "I'd have you to comprehind the differ betuxt an inwitation to dinner from the succissor of Saint Pether, and from a common nagur ov a Prodesan squireen that maybe hasn't liquor enough in his cupboard to wet more nor his own heretical whistle. That may be the way wid them that you wisit in Leithrim," says he, "and in Roscommon; and I'd let you know the differ in the prisint case," says he, "only that you're a champion ov the Church and entitled to laniency. So," says he, "as the liquor's come, let it stay. And in throth I'm curis myself," says he, getting mighty soft when he found the delightful smell ov the *putteen*, "in inwistigating the composition ov distilled liquors; it's a branch ov natural philosophy," says he, taking up the bottle and putting it to his blessed nose. Ah! my dear, the very first snuff he got ov it, he cried out, the dear man, "Blessed Vargin, but it has the divine smell!" and crossed himself and the bottle half a dozen times running.

"Well, sure enough, it's the blessed liquor now," says his Riv'rence, "and so there can be no harm any way in mixing a dandy of punch; and," says he, stirring up the materi'ls wid his goolden muddler—for everything at the Pope's table, to the very shcrew for drawing the corks, was ov vergin goold—"if I might make bould," says he, "to spake on so deep a subjic afore your Holiness, I think it 'ud considerherably whacilitate the inwestigation ov its chemisthry and phwarmaceutics, if you'd jist thry the laste sup in life ov it inwardly."

"Well, then, suppose I do make the same expiriment," says the Pope, in a much more condescinding way nor you'd have expected—and wid that he mixes himself a real stiff facer.

"Now, your Holiness," says Father Tom, "this bein' the first time you ever dispinsed them chymicals," says he, "I'll just make bould to lay down one rule ov orthography," says he, "for conwhounding them, *secundum mortem.*"

"What's that?" says the Pope.

"Put in the sperits first," says his Riv'rence; "and then put in the sugar; and remember, every dhrop ov wather you put in after that spoils the punch."

"Glory be to God!" says the Pope, not minding a word Father Tom was saying. "Glory be to God!" says he, smacking his lips. "I never knewn what dhrink was afore," says he. "It bates the Lachrymalchrystal out ov the face!" says he—"it's Necthar itself, it is, so it is!" says he, wiping his epistolical mouth wid the cuff ov his coat.

"'Pon my secret honour," says his Riv'rence, "I'm raaly glad to see your Holiness set so much to your satiswhaction; especially," says he, "as, for fear ov accidents, I tuck the liberty of fetching the fellow ov that small vesshel," says he, "in my other coat-pocket. So devil a fear ov our running dhry till the but-end of the evening, anyhow," says he.

"Dhraw your stool in to the fire, Misther Maguire," says the Pope, "for faix," says he, "I'm bent on analizing the metaphwysics ov this phinomenon. Come, man alive, clear off," says he, "you're not dhrinking at all."

"Is it dhrink?" says his Riv'rence; "by Gorra, your Holiness," says he, "I'd dhrink wid you till the cows 'ud be coming home in the morning."

So wid that they tackled to, to the second fugee a-piece, and fell into larned discourse. But it's time for me now to be off to the lecthir at the Boord. Oh my sorra light upon you, Docther Whateley, wid your pilitical econimy and your hydherastatics! What the *dioul* use has a poor hedge-master like me wid sich deep larning as is only fit for the likes ov them two that I left over their second tumbler? Howandiver, wishing I was like them, in regard ov the sup ov dhrink, anyhow, I must brake off my norration for the prisint; but when I see you again, I'll tell you how Father Tom made a hare ov the Pope that evening, both in theology and the cube root.

CHAPTER II.—HOW FATHER TOM SACKED HIS HOLINESS IN THEOLOGY AND LOGIC.

WELL, the lecthir's over, and I'm kilt out and out. My bitther curse upon the man that invinted the same Boord! I thought ons't I'd fadomed the say ov throuble; and that was when I got through fractions at ould Mat Kavanagh's school, in Firdramore—God be good to poor Mat's sowl, though he did deny the cause the day he suffered! but it's fluxions itself we're set to bottom now, sink or shwim! May I never die if my head isn't as throughother as anything wid their ordinals and cardinals—and, begob, it's all nothing to the econimy lecthir that I have to go to at two o'clock. Howandiver, I mustn't forget that we left his Riv'rence and his Holiness sitting fornenst one another in the parlor ov the Vatican, jist afther mixing their second tumbler.

When they had got well down into the same, they fell, as I was telling you, into larned discourse. For, you see, the Pope was curious to find out whether Father Tom was the great theologian all out that people said; and says he, "Mister Maguire," says he, "What answer do you make to the heretics when they quote them passidges agin thransubstantiation out ov the Fathers?" says he.

"Why," says his Riv'rence, "as there should be no sich passidges I make myself mighty aisy about them; but if you want to know how I dispose ov them," says he, "just repate one ov them, and I'll show you how to catapomphericate it in two shakes."

"Why, then," says the Pope, "myself disremimbers the particlar passidges they alledge out ov them ould felleys," says he, "though sure enough they're more numerous nor edifying—so we'll jist suppose that a heretic was to find sich a saying as this in Austin, 'Every sensible man knows that thransubstantiation is a lie'—or this out of Tertullian or Plutarch, 'the bishop ov Room is a common imposther'—now tell me, could you answer him?"

"As easy as kiss," says his Riv'rence. "In the first, we're to understand that the exprission, 'Every sinsible man,' signifies simply, 'Every man that judges by his nath'ral sinses;' and we all know that nobody folleying them seven deludhers could ever find out the mysthery that's in it, if somebody didn't come in to his assistance wid an eighth sinse, which is the only sinse to be depended on, being the sinse ov the Church. So that, regarding the first quotation which your Holiness has supposed, it makes clane for us, and tee-totally agin the heretics."

"That's the explanation sure enough," says his Holiness; "and now what div you say to my being a common imposther?"

"Faix, I think," says his Riv'rence, "wid all submission to the betther judgment ov the learned father that your Holiness has quoted, he'd have been a thrifle nearer the thruth, if he had said that the bishop ov Room is the grand imposther and top-sawyer in that line over us all."

"What do you mane?" says the Pope, getting quite red in the face.

"What would I mane," says his Riv'rence, as composed as a docther ov physic, "but that your Holiness is at the head ov all them—troth I had a'most forgot I wasn't a bishop myself," says he (the deludher was going to say, as the head of all *uz*)—"that has the gift ov laying on hands. For sure," says he, "imposther and *imposithir* is all one, so you're only to undherstand *manuum*, and the job is done. Awouich!" says he, "if any heretic 'ud go for to cast up sich a passidge as that agin me, I'd soon give him a lesson in the p'lite art ov cutting a stick to welt his own back wid."

"'Pon my apostolical word," says the Pope, "you've cleared up them two pints in a most satiswhacthery manner."

"You see," says his Riv'rence—by this time they wor mixing their third tumbler—"the writings ov them Fathers is to be thrated wid great veneration; and it 'ud be the height ov presumption in anyone to sit down to interpret them widout providing himself wid a genteel assortment ov the best figures ov rhetoric, sich as mettonymy, hyperbol, cattychraysis, prolipsis, mettylipsis, superbaton, pollysyndreton, hustheronprotheron, prosodypeia and the like, in ordher that he may never be at a loss for shuitable sintiments when he comes to their high-flown passidges. For unless we thrate them Fathers liberally to a handsome allowance ov thropes and figures, they'd set up heresy at ons't, so they would."

"It's thrue for you," says the Pope; "the figures ov spache is the pillars ov the Church."

"Bedad," says his Riv'rence, "I dunna what we'd do widout them at all."

"Which one do you prefir?" says the Pope; "that is," says he, "which figure of spache do you find most usefullest when you're hard set?"

"Metaphour's very good," says his Riv'rence, "and so's mettonymy—and I've known prosodypeia stand to me at a pinch mighty well—but for a constancy, superbaton's the figure for my money. Devil be in me," says he, "but I'd prove black white as fast as a horse 'ud throt wid only a good stock ov superbaton."

"Faix," says the Pope, wid a sly look, "you'd need to have it backed, I judge, wid a small taste of assurance."

"Well, now, jist for that word," says his Riv'rence, "I'll prove it widout aither one or other. Black," says he, "is one thing and white is another thing. You don't conthravene that? But everything is aither one thing or another thing; I defy the apostle Paul to get over that dilemma. Well! If any thing be one thing, well and good; but if it be another thing, then it's plain it isn't both things, and so can't be two things—nobody can deny that. But what can't be two things must be one thing—*Ergo*, whether it's one thing or another thing it's all one. But black is one thing and white is another thing—*Ergo*, black and white is all one. *Quod erat demonsthrandum.*"

"Stop a bit," says the Pope, "I can't althegither give in to your second minor—no—your second major," says he, and he stopped. "Faix, then," says he, getting confused, "I don't rightly remimber where it was exactly that I thought I seen the flaw in your premises. Howsomdiver," says he, "I don't deny that it's a good conclusion, and one that 'ud be ov materi'l service to the Church if it was dhrawn wid a little more distinctiveness."

"I'll make it as plain as the nose on your Holiness's face, by superbaton," says his Riv'rence. "My adversary says, black is not another colour, that is, white? Now that's jist a parallel passidge wid the one out ov Tartullian that me and Hayes smashed the heretics on in Clarendon Sthreet, 'This is my body—that is, the figure ov my body.' That's a superbaton, and we showed that it oughtn't to be read that way at all, but this way, 'This figure of my body *is* my body.' Jist so wid my adversary's proposition, it mustn't be undherstood the way it reads, by no manner of manes; but it's to be taken this way—'Black—that is, white, is not another colour'—green, if you like, or orange, by dad, for anything I care, for my case is proved. 'Black,' that is, 'white,' lave out the 'that,' by sinnalayphy, and you have the orthodox conclusion, 'Black is white,' or by convarsion, 'White is black.'"

"It's as clear as mud," says the Pope.

"Begad," says his Riv'rence, "I'm in great humour for disputin' to-night. I wisht your Holiness was a heretic jist for two minutes," says he, "till you'd see the flaking I'd give you!"

"Well then, for the fun o' the thing, suppose me my

namesake, if you like," says the Pope, laughing, "though, by Jayminy," says he, "he's not one that I take much pride out ov."

"Very good—devil a betther joke ever I had," says his Riv'rence. "Come, then, Misther Pope," says he, "hould up that purty face ov yours, and answer me this question. Which 'ud be the biggest lie, if I said I seen a turkey-cock lying on the broad ov his back, and picking the stars out ov the sky, or if I was to say that I seen a gandher in the same intherestin' posture, raycreating himself wid similar asthronomical experiments? Answer me that, you ould swaddler?" says he.

"How durst you call me a swaddler, sir?" says the Pope, forgetting, the dear man, the part that he was acting.

"Don't think for to bully me!" says his Riv'rence, "I always daar to spake the truth, and it's well known that you're nothing but a swaddling ould sinner ov a saint," says he, never letting on to persave that his Holiness had forgot what they were agreed on.

"By all that's good," says the Pope, "I often hard ov the imperance ov you Irish afore," says he, "but I never expected to be called a saint in my own house either by Irishman or Hottentot. I'll till you what, Misther Maguire," says he, "if you can't keep a civil tongue in your head, you had betther be walking off wid yourself; for I beg lave to give you to undherstand, that it won't be for the good ov your health if you call me by sich an outprobrious epithet again," says he.

"Oh, indeed! then things is come to a purty pass," says his Riv'rence (the dear funny soul that he ever was!) "when the likes of you compares one of the Maguires ov Tempo wid a wild Ingine! Why, man alive, the Maguires was kings ov Fermanagh three thousand years afore your grandfather, that was the first ov your breed that ever wore shoes and stockings" (I'm bound to say, in justice to the poor Prodesan, that this was all spoken by his Riv'rence by way of a figure ov spache), " was sint his Majesty's arrand to cultivate the friendship of Prince Lee Boo in Botteney Bay! Oh Bryan dear," says he, letting on to cry, " if you were alive to hear a *boddagh Sassenagh* like this casting up his counthry to one ov the name ov Maguire!"

" In the name ov God," says the Pope, very solemniously, " what *is* the maning ov all this at all at all ? " says he.

" Sure," says his Riv'rence, whispering to him across the table, " sure you know we're acting a conthrawarsy, and you tuck the part ov the Prodesan champion. You wouldn't be angry wid me, I'm sure, for sarving out the heretic to the best ov my ability."

" Oh begad, I had forgot," says the Pope, the good-natured ould crethur; " sure enough you were only taking your part, as a good Milesian Catholic ought, agin the heretic Sassenagh. Well," says he, " fire away now, and I'll put up wid as many conthroversial compliments as you plase to pay me."

" Well, then, answer me my question, you santimonious ould dandy," says his Riv'rence.

" In troth, then," says the Pope, " I dunna which 'ud be the biggest lie: to my mind," says he, " the one appears to be about as big a bounce as the other."

" Why, then, you poor simpleton," says his Riv'rence, " don't you persave that, forbye the advantage the gandher 'ud have in the length ov his neck, it 'ud be next to on-possible for the turkey-cock lying thataway to see what he was about, by rason ov his djollars and other accouthre-ments hanging back over his eyes? The one about as big a bounce as the other! Oh, you misfortunate crethur! if you had ever larned your A B C in theology, you'd have known that there's a differ betuxt them two lies so great, that, begad, I wouldn't wondher if it 'ud make a balance ov five years in purgathory to the sowl that 'ud be in it. Ay, and if it wasn't that the Church is too liberal entirely, so she is, it 'ud cost his heirs and succissors betther nor ten pounds to have him out as soon as the other. Get along, man, and take half a year at dogmatical theology: go and read your Dens, you poor dunce, you!"

"Raaly," says the Pope, "you're making the heretic's shoes too hot to hould me. I wondher how the Prodesans can stand afore you at all."

"Don't think to delude me," says his Riv'rence, "don't think to back out ov your challenge now," says he, "but come to the scratch like a man, if you are a man, and answer me my question. What's the rason, now, that Julius Cæsar and the Vargin Mary was born upon the one day?—answer me that, if you wouldn't be hissed off the platform?"

Well, my dear, the Pope couldn't answer it, and he had to acknowledge himself sacked. Then he axed his Riv'rence to tell him the rason himself; and Father Tom communicated it to him in Latin. But as that is a very deep question, I never hard what the answer was, except that I'm tould it was so mysterious, it made the Pope's hair stand on end.

But there's two o'clock, and I'll be late for the lecthir.

CHAPTER III.—HOW FATHER TOM MADE A HARE OF HIS HOLINESS IN LATIN.

Oh, Docther Whateley, Docther Whateley, I'm sure I'll never die another death if I don't die aither of consumption or production! I ever and always thought that asthronomy was the hardest science that was till now—and it's no lie I'm telling you, the same asthronomy is a tough enough morsel to brake a man's fast upon—and geolidgy is middling and hard too—and hydherastatics is no joke; but ov all the books of science that ever was opened and shut, that book upon Pilitical Econimy lifts the pins! Well, well, if they wait till they persuade me that taking a man's rints out ov the counthry, and spinding them in forrain parts isn't doing us out ov the same, they'll wait a long time in troth. But you're waiting, I see, to hear how his Riv'rence and his Holiness got on after finishing the disputation I was telling you of. Well, you see, my dear, when the Pope found he couldn't hold a candle to Father Tom in theology and logic, he thought he'd take the shine out ov him in Latin anyhow, so says he, "Misther Maguire," says he, "I quite agree wid you that it's not lucky for us to be spaking on them deep subjects in sich langidges as the evil spirits is acquainted wid; and," says he, "I think it 'ud be no harm for us to spake from this out in Latin," says he, "for fraid the devil 'ud undherstand what we are saying."

"Not a hair I care," says Father Tom, "whether he undherstands what we're saying or not, as long as we keep off that last pint we wor discussing, and one or two others. Listners never heard good ov themselves," says he; "and if Belzhebub takes anything amiss that aither you or me says in regard ov himself or his faction, let him stand forrid like a man, and, never fear, I'll give him his answer. Howandiver, if it's for a taste ov classic conwersation you are, just to put us in mind ov ould Cordarius," says he, "here's at you;" and wid that he lets fly at his Holiness wid his health in Latin.

"Vesthræ Sanctitatis salutem volo!" says he.

"Vesthræ Revirintiæ salubritati bibo!" says the Pope to him again (haith, it's no joke, I tell you, to remimber sich a power ov larning). "Here's to you wid the same," says the Pope, in the raal Ciceronian. "Nunc poculum alterhum imple," says he.

"Cum omni jucunditate in vita," says his Riv'rence. "Cum summâ concupiscintiâ et animositate," says he; as much as to say, "Wid all the veins ov my heart, I'll do that same;" and so wid that, they mixed their fourth gun a-piece.

"Aqua vitæ vesthra sane est liquor admirabilis," says the Pope.

"Verum est pro te,—it's thrue for you," says his Riv'-

rence, forgetting the idyim ov the Latin phwraseology, in a manner.

"Prava est tua Latinitas, domine," says the Pope, finding fault like wid his etymology.

"Parva culpa mihi," "small blame to me, that is," says his Riv'rence; "nam multum laboro in partibus interioribus," says he—the dear man! that never was at a loss for an excuse!

"Quid tibi incommodi?" says the Pope, axing him what ailed him.

"Habesne id quod Anglicè vocamus, a looking-glass," says his Riv'rence.

"Immo, habeo speculum splendidissimum subther operculum pyxidis hujus starnutatoriæ," says the Pope, pulling out a beautiful goold snuff-box, wid a looking-glass in under the lid; "Subther operculum pyxidis hujus starnutatorii—no—starnutatoriæ—quam dono accepi ab Archi-duce Austhriaco siptuagisima prætheritâ," says he; as much as to say that he got the box in a prisint from the Queen ov Spain last Lint, if I rightly remimber.

Well, Father Tom laughed like to burst. At last, says he, "Pather Sancte," says he, "sub errore jaces. 'Looking-glass' apud nos habet significationem quamdam peculiarem ex tempore diei dependentem"—there was a sthring ov accusatives for yez!—"nam mane speculum sonat," says he, "post prandium vero mat—mat—mat"—sorra be in me but I disremimber the classic appellivation ov the same article. Howandiver, his Riv'rence went on explaining himself in such a way as no scholar could mistake. "Vesica mea," says he, "ab illo ultimo eversore distenditur, donec similis est rumpere. Verbis apertis," says he, "Vesthræ Sanctitatis præsentia salvata, aquam facere valde desidhero."

"Ho, ho, ho!" says the Pope, grabbing up his box; "si inquinavisses meam pyxidem, excimnicari debuisses. Hillo, Anthony," says he to his head butler, "fetch Misther Maguire a——"

"You spoke first!" says his Riv'rence, jumping off his sate: "You spoke first in the vernacular. I take Misther Anthony to witness," says he.

"What else would you have me to do?" says the Pope, quite dogged like to see himself bate thataway at his own waypons. "Sure," says he, "Anthony wouldn't undherstand a B from a bull's foot, if I spoke to him any other way."

"Well, then," says his Riv'rence, in considheration ov the needcessity," says he, "I'll let you off for this time; but mind, now, afther I say *præstho*, the first of us that spakes a word of English is the hare—*præstho!*"

Neither ov them spoke for near a minit, considhering wid themselves how they wor to begin sich a great thrial ov shkill. At last, says the Pope—the blessed man! only think how 'cute it was ov him!—"Domine Maguire," says he, "valde desidhero, certiorem fieri de significatione istius verbi *eversor* quo jam jam usus es"—(well, surely I *am* the boy for the Latin!)

"*Eversor*, id est cyathus," says his Riv'rence, "nam apud nos *tumbleri*, seu eversores, dicti sunt ab evertendo ceremoniam inter amicos; non, ut Temperantiæ Societatis frigidis fautoribus placet, ab evertendis ipsis potatoribus." (It's not every masther undher the Boord, I tell you, could carry such a carload ov the dead langidges.) "In agro vero Louthiano et Midensi," says he, "nomine gaudent quodam secundum linguam Anglicanam significante bombardam seu tormentum; quia ex eis tanquam ex telis jaculatoriis liquorem faucibus immittere solent. Etiam inter hæreticos illos melanostomos" (that was a touch of Greek). "Presbyterianos Septentrionales, qui sunt terribiles potatores, Cyathi dicti sunt *faceres*, et dimidium Cyathi *hæf-a-glessus*. Dimidium Cyathi verò apud Metropolitanos Hibernicos dicitur *dandy*."—

"En verbum Anglicanum!" says the Pope, clapping his hands—"leporem te fecisti;" as much as to say that he had made a hare ov himself.

"*Dandæus, dandæus*, verbum erat," says his Riv'rence—oh, the dear man, but it's himself that was handy ever and always at getting out ov a hobble—"*dandæus* verbum erat," says he, "quod dicturus eram, cum me intherpillavisti."

"Ast ego dico," says the Pope, very sharp, "quod verbum erat *dandy*."

"Per tibicinem qui coram Mose modulatus est," says his Riv'rence, "id flagellat mundum! *Dandæus* dixi, et tu dicis *dandy*; ergo tu es lepus, non ego—Ah, ha! Saccavi vesthram Sanctitatem!"

"Mendacium est!" says the Pope, quite forgetting himself, he was so mad at being sacked before the sarvints.

Well, if it hadn't been that his Holiness was in it, Father Tom 'ud have given him the contints of his tumbler betuxt the two eyes, for calling him a liar; and, in troth, it's very well it was in Latin the offince was conweyed, for, if it had been in the vernacular, there's no saying what 'ud ha' been the consequence. His Riv'rence was mighty angry anyhow.—"Tu senex lathro," says he, "quomodo audes me mendacem prædicare?"

"Et tu, sacrilege nebulo," says the Pope, "quomodo audacitatem habeas, me Dei in terris vicarium, lathronem conwiciari?"

"Interroga circumcirca," says his Riv'rence.

"Abi ex ædibus meis," says the Pope.

"Abi tu in malem crucem," says his Riv'rence.

"Excumnicabo te," says the Pope.

"Diabolus curat," says his Riv'rence.

"Anathema sis," says the Pope.

"Oscula meum pod,"—says his Riv'rence—but, my dear, afore he could finish what he was going to say, the Pope broke out into the vernacular, "Get out o' my house, you reprobate!" says he in sich a rage that he could contain himself widin the Latin no longer.

"Ha, ha, ha!—ho, ho, ho!" says his Riv'rence, "Who's

the hare now, your Holiness? Oh, by this and by that, I've sacked you clane! Clane and clever I've done it, and no mistake! You see what a bit ov desate will do wid the wisest, your Holiness—sure it was joking I was, on purpose to aggrawate you—all's fair, you know, in love, law and conthravarsy. In troth if I'd thought you'd have taken it so much to heart, I'd have put my head into the fire afore I'd have said a word to offind you," says he, for he seen that the Pope was very vexed. "Sure, God forbid that I'd say anything agin your Holiness, barring it was in fun: for aren't you the father ov the faithful, and the thrue vicar ov God upon earth? And amn't I ready to go down on my two knees this blessed minit and beg your apostolical pardon for every word that I said to your displasement?"

"Are you in arnest that it is in fun you wor?" says the Pope.

"May I never die if I amn't," says his Riv'rence. "It was all to provoke your Holiness to commit a brache ov the Latin that I tuck the small liberties I did," says he.

"I'd have you to take care," says the Pope, "how you take sich small liberties again, or maybe you'll provoke me to commit a brache ov the pace."

"Well, and if I did," says his Riv'rence, "I know a sartan preparation ov chemicals that's very good for curing a brache either in Latinity or frindship."

"What's that?" says the Pope, quite mollified, and sitting down again at the table that he had ris from in the first pluff of his indignation. "What's that?" says he, "for, 'pon my Epistolical 'davy, I think it 'udn't be asy to bate this miraculous mixthir that we've been thrying to anilize this two hours back," says he, taking a mighty scientifical swig out ov the bottom ov his tumbler.

"It's good for a beginning," says his Riv'rence; "it lays a very nate foundation for more sarious operation: but we're now arrived at a pariod of the evening when it's time to proceed wid our shuperstructhure by compass and square, like free and excipted masons as we both are."

My time's up for the present; but I'll tell you the rest in the evening at home.

CHAPTER IV.—HOW FATHER TOM AND HIS HOLINESS DISPUTED IN METAPHYSICS AND ALGEBRA.

God be wid the time when I went to the classical seminary ov Firdramore! when I'd bring my sod o' turf undher my arm, and sit down on my shnug boss o' straw, wid my back to the masther and my shins to the fire, and score my sum in Dives's denominations or the double rule o' three, or play fox-and-geese wid purty Jane Cruise that sat next me, as plisantly as the day was long, widout anyone so much as saying, "Mikey Heffernan, what's that you're about?"—for ever since I was in the one lodge wid poor ould Mat I had my own way in his school as free as ever I had in my mother's shebeen. God be wid them days, I say again, for it's althered times wid me, I judge, since I got under Carlisle and Whateley. Sich sthrictness! sich ordher! sich dhrilling, and lecthiring, and tuthoring as they do get on wid! I wisht to gracious the one-half of their rules and rigilations was sunk in the say. And they're getting so sthrict, too, about having fair play for the heretic childher! We've to have no more schools in the chapels, nor masses in the schools. Oh, by this and by that it'll never do at all! The ould plan was twenty times betther; and, for my own part, if it wasn't that the clargy supports them in a manner, and the grant's a thing not easily done widout these hard times, I'd see if I couldn't get a sheltered spot nigh-hand the chapel, and set up again on the good ould principle: and faix, I think our Metropolitan 'ud stand to me, for I know that his Grace's motto was ever and always, that "Ignorance is the thrue mother ov piety."

But I'm running away from my narrative entirely, so I am. "You'll plase to ordher up the housekeeper, then," says Father Tom to the Pope, "wid a pint ov sweet milk in a skillet, and the bulk ov her fist ov butther, along wid a dust ov soft sugar in a saucer, and I'll show you the way of producing a decoction that, I'll be bound, will hunt the thirst out ov every nook and corner in your Holiness's blessed carcidge."

The Pope ordhered up the ingredients, and they were brought in by the head butler.

"That'll not do at all," says his Riv'rence, "the ingredients won't combine in due proportion unless ye do as I bid yez. Send up the housekeeper," says he, "for a faymale hand is ondispinsably necessary to produce the adaptation ov the particles and the concurrence ov the corpuscles, widout which you might boil till morning, and never fetch the cruds off ov it."

Well, the Pope whispered to his head butler, and by-and-by up there comes an ould faggot ov a *Caillean*, that was enough to frighten a horse from his oats.

"Don't thry for to desave me," says his Riv'rence, "for it's no use, I tell yez. Send up the housekeeper, I bid yez; I seen her presarving gooseberries in the panthry as I came up: she has eyes as black as a sloe," says he, "and cheeks like the rose in June; and sorra taste of this celestial mixthir shall crass the lips ov man or mortial this blessed night till she stirs the same up wid her own delicate little finger."

"Misther Maguire," says the Pope, "it's very unproper ov you to spake that way ov my housekeeper; I won't allow it, sir."

"Honour bright, your Holiness," says his Riv'rence, laying his hand on his heart.

"Oh, by this and by that, Misther Maguire," says the Pope, "I'll have none of your insiniwations; I don't care who sees my whole household," says he; "I don't care if all the faymales undher my roof was paraded down the High Street of Room," says he.

"Oh, it's plain to be seen how little you care who sees them," says his Riv'rence. "You're afeared, now, if I was to see your housekeeper, that I'd say she was too handsome."

"No, I'm not!" says the Pope; "I don't care who sees her," says he. "Anthony," says he to the head butler, "bid Eliza throw her apron over her head, and come up here." Wasn't that stout in the blessed man? Well, my dear, up she came, stepping like a three-year-old, and blushing like the brake o' day; for though her apron was thrown over her head as she came forrid, till you could barely see the tip ov her chin—more be token there was a lovely dimple in it, as I've been tould—yet she let it shlip a bit to one side, by chance like, just as she got fornenst the fire, and if she wouldn't have given his Riv'rence a shot if he hadn't been a priest, it's no matther."

"Now, my dear," says he, "you must take that skillet, and hould it over the fire till the milk comes to a blood-hate; and the way you'll know that will be by stirring it ons't or twice wid the little finger ov your right hand, afore you put in the butther: not that I misdoubt," says he, "but that the same finger's fairer nor the whitest milk that ever came from the tit."

"None of your deludhering talk to the young woman, sir," says the Pope, mighty stern. "Stir the posset as he bids you, Eliza, and then be off wid yourself," says he.

"I beg your Holiness's pardon ten thousand times," says his Riv'rence; "I'm sure I meant nothing onproper; I hope I'm uncapable ov any sich dirilection of my duty," says he. "But, marciful Saver!" he cried out, jumping up on a suddent, "look behind you, your Holiness—I'm blest but the room's on fire!"

Sure enough the candle fell down that minit, and was near setting fire to the windy-curtains, and there was some bustle, as you may suppose, getting things put to rights. And now

I have to tell you ov a raally onpleasant occurrence. If I was a Prodesan that was in it, I'd say that while the Pope's back was turned, Father Tom made free wid the two lips ov Miss Eliza; but, upon my conscience, I believe it was a mere mistake that his Holiness fell into on account of his being an ould man, and not having aither his eyesight or his hearing very parfect. At any rate it can't be denied but that he had a sthrong imprission that sich was the case; for he wheeled about as quick as thought, jist as his Riv'rence was sitting down, and charged him wid the offince plain and plump. "Is it kissing my housekeeper before my face you are, you villain?" says he. "Go down out o' this," says he to Miss Eliza; "and do you be packing off wid you," he says to Father Tom, "for it's not safe, so it isn't, to have the likes ov you in a house where there's temptation in your way."

"Is it me?" says his Riv'rence; "why, what would your Holiness be at, at all? Sure I wasn't doing no sich thing."

"Would you have me doubt the evidence ov my sinses?" says the Pope; "would you have me doubt the testimony ov my eyes and ears?" says he.

"Indeed I would so," says his Riv'rence, "if they pretend to have informed your Holiness ov any sich foolishness."

"Why," says the Pope, "I seen you afther kissing Eliza as plain as I see the nose on your face; I heard the smack you gave her as plain as ever I heard thundher."

"And how do you know whether you see the nose on my face or not?" says his Riv'rence; "and how do you know whether what you thought was thundher, was thundher at all? Them operations of the sinses," says he, "comprises only particular corporayal emotions, connected wid sartain confused perciptions called sinsations, and isn't to be depended upon at all. If we were to follow them blind guides, we might jist as well turn heretics at ons't. 'Pon my secret word, your Holiness, it's naither charitable nor orthodox ov you to set up the testimony ov your eyes and ears agin the characther of a clergyman. And now, see how aisy it is to explain all them phwenomena that perplexed you. I ris and went over beside the young woman because the skillet was boiling over, to help her to save the dhrop ov liquor that was in it; and as for the noise you heard, my dear man, it was neither more nor less nor myself dhrawing the cork out ov this blissid bottle."

"Don't offer to thrape that upon me!" says the Pope; "here's the cork in the bottle still, as tight as a wedge."

"I beg your pardon," says his Riv'rence, "that's not the cork at all," says he; "I dhrew the cork a good two minits ago, and it's very purtily spitted on the end ov this blessed cork-schrew at this prisint moment; howandiver you can't see it, because it's only its raal prisence that's in it. But that appearance that you call a cork," says he, "is nothing but the outward spacies and external qualities of the cortical nathur. Them's nothing but the accidents of the cork that you're looking at and handling; but, as I tould you afore, the real cork's dhrew, and is here prisint on the end ov this nate little insthrument, and it was the noise I made in dhrawing it, and nothing else, that you mistook for the sound ov the *pogue*."

You know there was no conthravening what he said; and the Pope couldn't openly deny it. Howandiver he thried to pick a hole in it this way. "Granting," says he, "that there is the differ you say betwixt the reality ov the cork and them cortical accidents, and that it's quite possible, as you allidge, that the thrue cork is really prisint on the end ov the schrew, while the accidents keep the mouth ov the bottle stopped—still," says he, "I can't undherstand, though willing to acquit you, how the dhrawing ov the real cork, that's onpalpable and widout accidents, could produce the accident of that sinsible explosion I heard jist now."

"All I can say," says his Riv'rence, "is, that I'm sinsible it was a real accident, anyhow."

"Ay," says the Pope, "the kiss you gev Eliza, you mane."

"No," says his Riv'rence, "but the report I made."

"I don't doubt you," says the Pope.

"No cork could be dhrew with less noise," says his Riv'rence.

"It would be hard for anything to be less nor nothing, barring algebra," says the Pope.

"I can prove to the conthrary," says his Riv'rence. "This glass ov whisky is less nor that tumbler ov punch, and that tumbler of punch is nothing to this jug ov *scaltheen*."

"Do you judge by superficial misure or by the liquid contents?" says the Pope.

"Don't stop me betwixt my premisses and my conclusion," says his Riv'rence; "*Ergo*, this glass ov whisky is less nor nothing; and for that raison I see no harm in life in adding it to the contents ov the same jug, just by way of a frost-nail."

"Adding what's less nor nothing," says the Pope, "is subtraction according to algebra; so here goes to make the rule good," says he, filling his tumbler wid the blessed stuff, and sitting down again at the table, for the anger didn't stay two minits on him, the good-hearted ould sowl.

"Two minuses makes one plus," says his Riv'rence, as ready as you plase, "and that'll account for the increased daycrement I mane to take the liberty of producing in the same mixed quantity," says he, follying his Holiness's epistolical example.

"By all that's good," says the Pope, "that's the best stuff I ever tasted; you call it a mixed quantity, but I say it's prime."

"Since it's ov the first ordher, then," says his Riv'rence, "we'll have the less deffeequilty in reducing it to a simple equation."

"You'll have no fractions at my side, anyhow," says the Pope. "Faix, I'm afeared," says he, "it's only too asy ov solution our sum is like to be."

"Never fear for that," says his Riv'rence, "I've a good

stock of surds here in the bottle; for I tell you it will take us a long time to exthract the root ov it, at the rate we're going on."

"What makes you call the blessed quart an irrational quantity?" says the Pope.

"Becase it's too much for one, and too little for two," says his Riv'rence.

"Clear it ov its coefficient, and we'll thry," says the Pope.

"Hand me over the exponent, then," says his Riv'rence.

"What's that?" says the Pope.

"The schrew, to be sure," says his Riv'rence.

"What for?" says the Pope.

"To dhraw the cork," says his Riv'rence.

"Sure the cork's dhrew," says the Pope.

"But the sperits can't get out on account of the accidents that's stuck in the neck ov the bottle," says his Riv'rence.

"Accident ought to be passablé to sperit," says the Pope, "and that makes me suspect that the reality ov the cork's in it afther all."

"That's a barony-masia," says his Riv'rence, "and I'm not bound to answer it. But the fact is, that it's the accidents ov the sperits too that's in it, and the reality's passed out through the cortical spacies as you say; for, you may have observed, we've both been in real good sperits ever since the cork was dhrawn, and where else would the real sperits come from if they wouldn't come out ov the bottle?"

"Well, then," says the Pope, "since we've got the reality, there's no use troubling ourselves wid the accidents."

"Oh, begad," says his Riv'rence, "the accidents is very essential too; for a man may be in the best ov good sperits, as far as his immaterial part goes, and yet need the accidental qualities ov good liquor to hunt the sinsible thirst out ov him." So he dhraws the cork in earnest, and sets about brewing the other skillet ov *scaltheen;* but, faix, he had to get up the ingredients this time by the hands ov ould Molly; though devil a taste ov her little finger he'd let widin a yard ov the same decoction.

But, my dear, here's the 'Freeman's Journal,' and we'll see what's the news afore we finish the residuary proceedings of their two Holinesses.

CHAPTER V.—THE REASON WHY FATHER TOM WAS NOT MADE A CARDINAL.

Hurroo, my darlings!—didn't I tell you it 'ud never do? Success to bould John Tuam and the ould siminary ov Firdramore! Oh, more power to your Grace every day you rise, 'tis you that has broken their Boord into shivers undher your feet! Sure, and isn't it a proud day for Ireland, this blessed feast ov the chair ov Saint Pether? Isn't Carlisle and Whateley smashed to pieces, and their whole college of swaddling teachers knocked into smidhereens. John Tuam, your sowl, has tuck his pasthoral staff in his hand and beathen them out o' Connaught as fast as ever Pathrick druve the sarpints into Clew Bay. Poor ould Mat Kavanagh, if he was alive this day, 'tis he would be the happy man. "My curse upon their g'ographies and Bibles," he used to say; "where's the use ov perplexing the poor childer wid what we don't undherstand ourselves?" no use at all, in troth, and so I said from the first myself. Well, thank God and his Grace, we'll have no more thrigonomethry nor scripther in Connaught. We'll hould our lodges every Saturday night, as we used to do, wid our chairman behind the masther's desk, and we'll hear our mass every Sunday morning wid the blessed priest standing afore the same. I wisht to goodness I hadn't parted wid my Seven Champions ov Christendom and Freney the Robber; they're books that'll be in great requist in Leithrim as soon as the pasthoral gets wind. Glory be to God! I've done wid their lecthirs—they may all go and be d——d wid their consumption and production. I'm off to Tullymactaggart before daylight in the morning, where I'll thry whether a sod or two o' turf can't consume a cartload ov heresy, and whether a weekly meeting ov the lodge can't produce a new thayory ov rints. But afore I take my lave ov you, I may as well finish my story about poor Father Tom that I hear is coming up to whale the heretics in Adam and Eve during the Lint.

The Pope—and indeed it ill becomes a good Catholic to say anything agin him—no more would I, only that his Riv'rence was in it—but you see the fact ov it is, that the Pope was as envious as ever he could be, at seeing himself sacked right and left by Father Tom, and bate out o' the face, the way he was, on every science and subjec' that was started. So, not to be outdone altogether, he says to his Riv'rence, "You're a man that's fond ov the brute crayation, I hear, Misther Maguire?"

"I don't deny it," says his Riv'rence, "I've dogs that I'm willing to run agin any man's, ay, or to match them agin any other dogs in the world for genteel edication and polite manners," says he.

"I'll hould you a pound," says the Pope, "that I've a quadhruped in my possession that's a wiser baste nor any dog in your kennel."

"Done," says his Riv'rence, and they staked the money.

"What can this larned quadhruped o' yours do?" says his Riv'rence.

"It's my mule," says the Pope, "and, if you were to offer her goolden oats and clover off the meadows o' Paradise, sorra taste ov aither she'd let pass her teeth till the first mass is over every Sunday or holiday in the year."

"Well, and what 'ud you say if I showed you a baste ov mine," says his Riv'rence, "that, instead ov fasting till first mass is over only, fasts out the whole four-and-twenty hours ov every Wednesday and Friday in the week as reg'lar as a Christian?"

"Oh, be asy, Masther Maguire," says the Pope.

"You don't b'lieve me, don't you?" says his Riv'rence; "very well, I'll soon show you whether or no," and he put his knuckles in his mouth, and gev a whistle that made the Pope stop his fingers in his ears. The aycho, my dear, was hardly done playing wid the cobwebs in the cornish, when the door flies open, and in jumps Spring. The Pope happened to be sitting next the door, betuxt him and his Riv'rence, and, may I never die, if he didn't clear him, thriple crown and all, at one spang. "God's presence be about us!" says the Pope, thinking it was an evil spirit come to fly away wid him for the lie that he had tould in regard ov his mule (for it was nothing more nor a thrick that consisted in grazing the brute's teeth): but, seeing it was only one ov the greatest beauties ov a greyhound that he'd ever laid his epistolical eyes on, he soon recovered ov his fright, and began to pat him, while Father Tom ris and went to the sideboord, where he cut a slice ov pork, a slice ov beef, a slice ov mutton, and a slice of salmon, and put them all on a plate thegither. "Here, Spring, my man," says he, setting the plate down afore him on the hearthstone, "here's your supper for you this blessed Friday night." Not a word more he said nor what I tell you; and, you may believe it or not, but it's the blessed truth that the dog, afther jist tasting the salmon, and spitting it out again, lifted his nose out o' the plate, and stood wid his jaws wathering, and his tail wagging, looking up in his Riv'rence's face, as much as to say, "Give me your absolution, till I hide them temptations out o' my sight."

"There's a dog that knows his duty," says his Riv'rence; "there's a baste that knows how to conduct himself aither in the parlour or the field. You think him a good dog, looking at him here; but I wisht you seen him on the side ov Slieve-an-Eirin! Be my soul, you'd say the hill was running away from undher him. Oh I wisht you had been wid me," says he, never letting on to see the dog at all, "one day, last Lent, that I was coming from mass. Spring was near a quarther ov a mile behind me, for the childher was delaying him wid bread and butther at the chapel door ; when a lump ov a hare jumped out ov the plantations ov Grouse Lodge and ran acrass the road ; so I gev the whilloo, and knowing that she'd take the rise ov the hill, I made over the ditch, and up through Mullaghcashel as hard as I could pelt, still keeping her in view, but afore I had gone a perch, Spring seen her, and away the two went like the wind, up Drumrewy, and down Clooneen, and over the river, widout his being able ons't to turn her. Well, I run on till I come to the Diffagher, and through it I went, for the wather was low and I didn't mind being wet shod, and out on the other side, where I got up on a ditch, and seen sich a coorse as I'll be bound to say was never seen afore or since. If Spring turned that hare ons't that day, he turned her fifty times, up and down, back and for'ard throughout and about. At last he run her right into the big quarryhole in Mullaghbawn, and when I went up to look for her fud, there I found him sthretched on his side, not able to stir a foot, and the hare lying about an inch afore his nose as dead as a door-nail, and divil a mark of a tooth upon her. Eh, Spring, isn't that thrue ? " says he. Jist at that minit the clock sthruck twelve, and, before you could say thrap-sticks, Spring had the plateful of mate consaled. " Now," says his Riv'rence, " hand me over my pound, for I've won my bate fairly."

" You'll excuse me," says the Pope, pocketing his money, " for we put the clock half an hour back, out ov compliment to your Riv'rence," says he, " and it was Sathurday morning afore he came up at all."

" Well, it's no matther," says his Riv'rence, putting back his pound-note in his pocket-book, " only," says he, " it's hardly fair to expect a brute baste to be so well skilled in the science ov chronology."

In troth his Riv'rence was badly used in the same bate, for he won it clever ; and, indeed, I'm afeard the shabby way he was thrated had some effect in putting it into his mind to do what he did. " Will your Holiness take a blast ov the pipe ? " says he, dhrawing out his dhudeen.

" I never smoke," says the Pope, " but I haven't the least objection to the smell of the tobaccay."

" Oh, you had betther take a dhraw," says his Riv'rence, " it'll relish the dhrink, that 'ud be too luscious entirely, widout something to flavour it."

" I had thoughts," said the Pope, wid the laste sign ov a hiccup on him, " ov getting up a broiled bone for the same purpose."

" Well," says his Riv'rence, " a broiled bone 'ud do no manner ov harm at this present time ; but a smoke," says he, " 'ud flavour both the devil and the dhrink."

" What sort o' tobaccay is it that's in it ? " says the Pope.

" Raal nagur-head," says his Riv'rence ; " a very mild and salubrious spacies of the philosophic weed."

" Then, I don't care if I do take a dhraw," says the Pope. Then Father Tom held the coal himself till his Holiness had the pipe lit ; and they sat widout saying anything worth mentioning for about five minutes.

At last the Pope says to his Riv'rence, " I dunna what gev me this plaguy hiccup," says he. " Dhrink about," says he—" Begorra," he says, " I think I'm getting merrier nor's good for me. Sing us a song, your Riv'rence," says he.

Father Tom then sung him " Monatagrenoge " and the " Bunch o' Rushes," and he was mighty well pleased wid both, keeping time wid his hands, and joining in in the choruses, when his hiccup 'ud let him. At last, my dear, he opens the lower buttons ov his waistcoat, and the top one of his waistband, and calls to Masther Anthony to lift up one ov the windys. " I dunna what's wrong wid me, at all at all," says he, " I'm mortial sick."

" I thrust," says his Riv'rence, " the pasthry that you ate at dinner hasn't disagreed wid your Holiness's stomach."

" Oh my ! oh ! " says the Pope, " what's this at all ? " gasping for breath, and as pale as a sheet, wid a could swate bursting out over his forehead, and the palms ov his hands spread out to catch the air. "Oh my! oh my!" he says, "fetch me a basin!—Don't spake to me. Oh!—oh!—blood alive!—Oh, my head, my head, hould my head!—oh!—ubh!—I'm poisoned!—ach!"

"It was them plaguy pasthries," says his Riv'rence. "Hould his head hard," says he, "and clap a wet cloth over his timples. If you could only thry another dhraw o' the pipe, your Holiness, it 'ud set you to rights in no time."

"Carry me to bed," says the Pope, "and never let me see that wild Irish priest again. I'm poisoned by his manes—ubplsch!—ach!—ach!—He dined wid Cardinal Wayld yestherday," says he, "and he's bribed him to take me off. Send for a confissor," says he, "for my latther end's approaching. My head's like to split—so it is!—Oh my! oh my!—ubplsch!—ach!"

Well, his Riv'rence never thought it worth his while to make him an answer; but, when he seen how ungratefully he was used, afther all his trouble in making the evening agreeable to the ould man, he called Spring, and put the but-end ov the second bottle into his pocket and left the house widout once wishing "Good-night, an' plaisant dhrames to you"; and, in troth, not one of *them* axed him to lave them a lock ov his hair.

That's the story as I heard it tould; but myself doesn't b'lieve over one-half of it. Howandiver, when all's done, it's a shame, so it is, that he's not a bishop this blessed day and hour; for, next to the goiant of St Jarlath's, he's out and out the cleverest fellow ov the whole jing-bang.

'A LITTLE SAIL.'

BY WESTON MARTYR.

[Maga, May 1925.]

SOME weeks ago I was invited to spend a few days on a farm in Essex, and, being a sailor, I naturally jumped at the chance to discover finally what real degree of truth might lie behind that veiled implication—" Who'd sell a farm and go to sea ? "—which I had listened to many a time growled out by old shell-backs momentarily disgusted with the treatment meted out to them by the element on whose implacable bosom they had chosen to work and to live. My imagination had, of course, created many pictures for me of farms and of the life on farms, but that Essex farmhouse, when I found it, proved to be distinctly unlike anything that I had ever dreamed.

Wicklea Wick, or Wickilywick, as the natives say, was as quaint as its quaint name. It stood, like an island, in the midst of a lone expanse of wistful marshland, painted by the placid evening light in soft and sleepy tints, and full of the plaintive cries of birds. Around the house I found a moat—a veritable moat—with duck swimming in it ; wild ones, too, for they all flew away as I walked up, over what must once have been the drawbridge, under a rounded Saxon arch and into a stone-paved hall. That hall had in it an open fireplace, ten foot square if it was an inch, and on one wall, stuck there like some giant swallow's nest, was a minstrels' gallery !

Now, it occurs to me that all these things may seem quite natural, but to a man whose feet have merely touched his country's pavements, and who has rarely trodden on his native soil, the moat and the minstrels' gallery appeared to be quite out of place—and out of time too; six or seven hundred years out at that. Earlier in the day I had stayed my journey in the ancient British hamlet of St Osyth, and there drunken a tankard of something which I was assured was 'real old oyster-feast,' so now I began to wonder if perhaps the strength of that strange liquor . . .

But my host appearing then, I knew, improbable though it seemed, that I was neither drunk nor dreaming, but merely a pilgrim lost in an England where—I made up my mind to it then and there—I was likely to happen on anything. It was as well for me that I decided to adopt this attitude of mind so early in the proceedings, for presently I found my fellow-guests to be the illustrious members of a far-famed company, resting after their play's successful run, together with a gentleman from the lap of the old Imperial Court in Peking; proud, yellow and aristocratic, Mr Van Ping by name. Of course, if one be fortunate, one may meet such individuals as these without the fact appearing strange at all. But—on an Essex farm! Anyhow, there I found them; and that night a crew of pirates, plus a captive Chinaman, sat down to a most tumultuous feast and barbecued their meat before the great hall fire. Mr Van Ping would *not* make up, but I had a splendid crimson sash and a real cutlass, dredged at some distant time from out the moat, where I think some smuggler in a hurry must have cast it. And here I wish to say that rump-steaks hung on a string and spun gently before a blaze are perfectly delightful; but all the same it astonished me to find this method of cookery still in vogue in England.

The feast completed, our captive women sang and danced before us, and the Lady with the Wonderful Voice intoned, from the dimness of the gallery, words that Masefield has set down concerning ships and the sea and the men who sail upon it, until I found a lump in my throat that badly needed swallowing. It was a night for a sailor unused to pleasant nights to store up in his memory; and so, at last, with the thought of these things stirring in my mind, I limped, tired but very happy, to bed. I limped, because the Lady who Dances had bandaged my piratical leg and painted on it, with a stick of lip-salve, a terrible wound; so, of course, I *had* to limp.

Next morning the light awoke me, and looking forth from my window across the marshes I saw a red-brown sail glide, stately, through the fields. A sail and spar, sustained upon no hull that I could see, sliding across meadows remote from any sea, was a mystery that intrigued me; but I was not surprised, for I remembered in time that this was England, where anything may happen; so I went downstairs (solid oak, without a creak in them) to breakfast.

Then the Lady who Dances, the gentleman from Peking and I set out to solve the riddle of that wandering casual sail. We walked on spongy earth that squirted mud at every footstep, through lush grasses and amongst plovers who mobbed us. I do not know why, but perhaps, being English birds, they disliked our Chinaman. I relate facts merely, and I do not attempt to account for the extraordinary things that happened to me that day. In any case, being English, presumably you will understand, without the help of any theories advanced by a bewildered stranger in this fantastic land.

We fled to escape the infuriated lapwings, until suddenly brought up by something that opened at our feet and yawned at us. It was a thing that, in any reasonable country, I should have called a spruit, nullah, or donga; but this affair, though blood-brother to all three, had sloping banks composed of the muddiest mud I have ever seen anywhere. The colour of the thing was a greasy zinc, and I thought of West Coast fever creeks, and sniffed and looked around for crocodiles—and listened. But there seemed to be no mosquitoes, so we proceeded, cautiously, down-stream —the very twistiest stream in all the world, I think.

I become acclimatised rapidly, I suppose, for I was not much surprised when we came upon the yacht. Rounding the thousandth bend of that incredible ditch, dyke, or drain, a thing I had supposed to be a post upon the bank transformed itself into the masthead of a small black cutter, lying afloat in a scanty trickle of dirty water at the bottom of that absurd fissure of mud. It was as though one had surprised a rakish brig roosting at the bottom of a hole in the sands of the Sahara. But I kept myself in hand, and, after a little while, I hailed her, when a face arose through her cabin hatch and smiled at us. It was a smile of welcome and goodwill, without a trace of wonder or derision in it. Which was really surprising. For we three pilgrims, materialising suddenly from nowhere, must have looked, to say the least, odd. The Lady who Dances wore a blood-red 'kerchief bound about her lovely head, a sweater green as young willow shoots in spring, and a pair of beautiful indigo-blue riding-breeches. The Gent from Peking conveys, at first sight, the impression that he is a kind of toy lion. He has a really splendid mane, and a tail for all the world like a yellow chrysanthemum, and he holds this up in the air when pleased, which he was then. His eyes stick out a great deal, and his tummy, owing to the excessive shortness of his legs, was matted with mud. As for me, in whatever raiment I may clothe myself, I invariably seem to incite strong feelings of scorn and derision in all beholders.

Such were we, but our new friend, instead of calling upon his gods to come down and witness his amazement, merely remarked, "Good-morning. Won't you come aboard?" I looked at the Lady, and I could see, from the lights dancing in her eyes, that her soul thirsted to embark immediately upon this adventure. Then I contemplated the twenty feet or so of sloping bottomless mud that lay between her and her heart's desire, and I tried to think of any way to cross it. I gave it up. And then, not for the only time that day, our friend showed us that he was the sort of fellow who cannot be defeated. " Oh, that's all right," cried he. " I'll heave you the end of the dinghy painter, and you can easily haul her up to you. Then you all get in, you know, and shove with an oar a bit, and she'll toboggan down there like winkin'."

We did these things, and it was even as he said, except that the bit of a shove with an oar was quite unneeded. Indeed, I found it necessary to restrain the boat by force from dashing away with her two passengers before I could fling myself aboard. But I managed it—a flying pier-head jump—and then the toboggan started. Have you ever seen an expert flying down the Cresta Run on his stomach with his legs waving in the breeze? Well, that was me; and I even tried to steer with my feet as that dinghy charged madly down the slimy bank, straight as an arrow for her parent's side. I drove my starboard leg down to the knee in the mud; but it was all useless, for the boat refused to answer her helm, and finished the run by butting the yacht hard, right between wind and water, and fair amidships. There was a 'crack' which told unmistakably of something started somewhere, and the Lady who Dances cried out aloud, surprisingly; while I mentioned the nether regions by another name; and the Pekinese gentleman also threw his tongue. But our imperturbable friend remarked, " Well done! You did it beautifully. The dinghy's bent a bit, but she'll do. If I were you I'd hang my leg in the creek and wash it; and then, if you like, we'll go for a little sail."

I was not at all clear how George (for this he assured us was his name) proposed to sail in that contorted drain, but soon I began to understand that there was a lot more in George than met the eye. " We'll have to drop down stern first," said he, " until there's room to turn; so, if you'll heave up the anchor, I'll shove her along with the pole."

A sailor obeys an order without asking any questions, so I hove up on the chain; and although there was only a fathom of it to come, the mud it brought up with it was impressive, and it covered the fore-deck completely with a species of slimy globigeringous ooze. "Don't worry about that," said George. "She'll wash it off herself when we get out. Will you push with the spinnaker boom, please? If we don't hurry we're likely to stick on the bar. Then, there we'll be, you know."

Twenty-five years at sea is not the best training for punting with spinnaker booms through Essex mud. In theory the thing is simple. You plant your pole on the bottom and push the boat along. In practice, you push and the pole sinks deeply into the mud, and your struggles to get it out again pull the boat the wrong way. When striving desperately to push a boat ahead it is exasperating—nay, maddening—to find that the harder you work the more you are urging her in precisely the wrong direction. And when a confounded son of a celestial and yellow lady-dog persists in getting between your legs with the idea that he is assisting you to repel mythical boarders . . . Well, you kick him, hard; and he is most surprised. But this relieves your outraged feelings, and it makes the Lady who Dances laugh—which is always worth while. Then I did what I should have done before. I watched George, and I found him achieving, with easy grace, feats of the most incredible dexterity. His method was to reach out well ahead, drive his pole into the mud and then pull the boat up to it. It seemed simple enough, and I decided at once to conform to his style. So I, too, reached well ahead with my boom, harpooned the bottom with it and then pulled hard. And the boom withdrew itself from its hole suddenly, with disgusting sounds as of stomach-pumps functioning furiously. I sat down. I sat down hard. I sat down extremely quickly on Mr Van Ping. Which was entirely his own fault, for he should not have determined so continuously to infest me. I retired then.

I refused to play any more, and George said it was just as well.

There was something about that man I liked. I do still—in spite of all he did to us. He was working hard now with his pole, and I gathered that the question of crossing the approaching bar was troubling him. For the bar was approaching, and speedily; for the strongly running ebb now hurried us steadfastly along between the banks of slime, until these presently spread out on either side and fell away from us, revealing, amazingly—the sea! At least George said it was the sea; and the North Sea, too; but we still have our doubts about it. The colour of the water was very queer for one thing—thick and jaundiced—and there was not enough of it there really for a proper sea. We drifted out from the shore a mile or more before I ventured to congratulate George on his successful passage of the bar. But, "We've not got over it yet," said he, thrusting his faithful pole overboard. And, lo, it touched bottom at less than two feet. And this was the sea—the North Sea!

Then, in the midst of that vacant windless stretch of eerie water, our boat, without a stitch of sail upon her, began to list. Gently at first, then direfully, over she heeled, and the still waters slid abruptly into rapid motion and sped, foaming, past our sides. Over we went till the deck was half awash, while against our exposed bilge arose a seething, frothing, yellow wave. George, letting go his anchor, appeared to take these miracles with perfect calm; but to the rest of us it seemed as though some giant hand had seized upon our keel and was dragging us, fiercely, broadside on against the tide. This exciting and impressive performance left us expectant and amazed; but George said we were merely stuck on the bar, and if we did not roll over we would do, which struck me as being a most inadequate way of summing up an apparently miraculous and obviously perilous situation.

I think there must have been a hole in that bar, into which

we mercifully slid, for suddenly our giant let go his hold, and the boat stood once more upright, riding to her anchor, head on to the rushing tide. George, a lucid soul, remarked, "Well, here we are," an accurate observation ; for there we certainly were, and there we remained for six portentous and unforgettable hours, chock-full—all of them—with interest and excitement.

We watched the waters dwindle and recede, to depart at last beyond our horizon, leaving us desolate and encompassed by a very ocean of mud. We leant our elbows on the rail and gazed at those sleek leagues of circumambient mire, until a tinge of sadness begat by the cheerless scene began to steal upon us. And then, upon our nostrils, too, there stole faint whiffs and savours as of fish, long dead ; and from the well arose a sound of snorts and growls and scrapings.

The fight broke out with a crash of upset pails, and we hastened aft in time to see the memorable battle of the Pekinese Dog and the Bucket of Slipper-Limpets. The struggle raged, appropriately enough, on the cockpit floor, and there we found the Gent from China holding his own fairly easily, the short, sharp, fiery dash with which the limpets had opened their campaign having apparently completely exhausted them. Also, it is only fair to add that though they held a decided advantage in numbers, the limpets were sadly handicapped by lack of condition. They were clearly not in training. In fact, it soon became clear to me that the members of that devoted band not already dying or dead were all very far gone indeed with some sort of badly wasting sickness. The Slipper-Limpets had evidently been lying quietly in their bucket, at peace with the world, when the Chinaman unprovokedly attacked them. The heroic band, with a magnificent effort, the bravery of which compels our admiration, had risen as one limpet and hurled themselves upon the head of their enemy, only to fall at last fainting on the battlefield. But mark the heights to which a slipper-limpet rises. Swooning, dying and dead they lay, trampled on, bitten and chewed by their ferocious and barbaric enemy. But in this desperate and hopeless situation do they hoist the white flag, hold up their hands and cry "Kamerad"? No, a thousand times no! For the true slipper-limpet remains unconquerable—even in death. Down their serried ranks they passed the awful word, "Launch the gas attack!" And they did. . . .

We left that place in a hurry, and the dinghy, pushing her through the mud to wind'ard with the oars. Mr Van Ping we also left upon the stricken field. He howled despairingly, but we did not want him. He had been far too intimately associated with his late adversaries to allow us to love him any more.

"George," said the Lady who Dances, "*why* do you carry those horrible things about with you? Are they pets, and are you attached to them? Don't say you eat them!"

"No," said George, "they're bait. They eat oysters, you know, but the dabs like 'em. I'd forgotten about that lot, and they must have been in the bucket a fortnight. Harmless little chaps if you don't rouse them. But, by Jingo, *when* you do! We will now wait here a bit till the whiff's eased off, then I'll go back and clean up, and we'll have some lunch."

When the time was ripe we proceeded hopefully to urge the reluctant dinghy back across the mud. But it was not to be, for she had bedded herself down comfortably in her wallow, and, nestling there cosily, she now refused to budge. George then rashly jumped out to push, and sank to past his middle in the ooze; and when I followed him to help, all of me below my third waistcoat button was immediately swallowed up.

Mr Van Ping, marooned upon the yacht with only the spirits of departed slipper-limpets to keep him company, gave tongue lugubriously. I looked at George, and I think my face was white, and I know I was sweating coldly, for the fear of a very dreadful death had arisen in my heart. George for once had discovered an adversary in whose face he could not smile, and I have reason to believe that icy sweats were afflicting him also. But, "Well, here we are," said he, clinging, it seemed to me, with misplaced affection to an over-worked phrase ; but it showed his heart was in the right place, and this did me good, for by now my last waistcoat button was disappearing.

Then the Lady who Dances began to take an active part in the affair. Without a word she handed out the oars, and whilst with these we tried to impede our lingering burial, she took the dinghy's bottom boards, and planting these unsteady stepping-stones before her as she went, she passed, dainty and sure, across the shuddering surface of the quick-sand. The rapturous nature of Mr Van Ping's welcome was as nothing to the glad fervour with which we greeted the end of the main sheet that presently smacked the mud into our faces. Grabbing it we pulled hard, only to find we were by then so well and truly planted that it was impossible to exhume ourselves.

But George, as ever, rose even to this occasion. "Take your end forward to the windlass and heave on it," cried he. "And you, pass me your oar and make the line fast under your arms. And if I were you I'd throw a bowline or you're likely to regret it." These things being accomplished, the Lady hove away, the rope taughtened and I, strangled and kicking, drew out at last from that reluctant mud. By the time I reached the yacht there was not very much of George above the surface, and what there was of him was sinking visibly by the stern. But we salvaged him in time, and being thin, he uncorked easily enough. We drew him alongside, and his words when he touched the deck once more were, under the circumstances, impressive. "Wash and brush-up. Then grub, I think," said he.

The wash and brush-up was not a success at all, but the grub when it came was entirely amazing. Crouching in that tiny cabin, we watched with awe while George performed miracles upon two Primus stoves. From somewhere, apparently the bilge, he drew forth steaks, which presently, sizzling in olive oil, he anointed with strange and pungent condiments. Onions he produced from dark and mysterious holes, and potatoes also, to be fried cunningly beneath the meat. Coffee boiled in a black and battered pan sounds most unpromising, but, with George presiding at the brew, a fresh and fragrant beverage somehow results. Then I learned, in succession, how toast can be made—to perfection, too—upon a blow-lamp; how beer, in a frying-pan, may be sweetly mulled; and of the divine virtue that may be extracted by an expert from a mere tin of pork and beans. I found out, too, how all these operations, and others besides, may be so synchronised as to achieve in due time that most desirable affair—the perfect meal.

"Dee-licious," said the Lady who Dances, gazing at her empty plates. "I didn't think it could be done. George, you are a wonder, and I feel myself beginning to love you." And I, replete, leant back upon the cushions and agreed with her.

"Being no sea-water within miles," said George, "we can't wash-up; so we'll sit and smoke and wait till she floats."

For the next two hours we sat, in the diminutive but adequately appointed hole which George calls his cabin, well-fed, warm and cosy, while George held forth enlighteningly upon the peculiar difficulties and quaint hazards which beset all navigators adventuring on the besmirched and tide-tormented waters of the Thames estuary. By tea-time a rising wind was whistling through our rigging, with those low mournful pipings which I have found to be a sure prelude to a spell of dirty weather out of the south-west. Across a sky, gloomy and overcast, the scud was even then commencing to hurry, and a line of heaving whiteness across the mud-flats marked the returning of the waters.

"Do you get much sea on these banks of yours with a hard sou'-westerly wind, George?"

"Oh, heavy enough to break us up—if the bottom's hard,"

said George. "But as you know, it isn't. No. That's not troubling me, and I don't care where I go, of course; but this is a dead head wind for you people, and in a jobble the old boat will *not* go to wind'ard."

"That's nice," said I. "Then what's the evolution?"

"Hang on to our anchor, I think, till there's water enough to float us right over the bar, and then run for Harwich."

"Harwich!" exclaimed the Lady.

"I'm afraid so," said George. "It's not far, though. Down the coast, and take the first turning on the left. I haven't a chart, but I can make it all right. But I'm afraid you'll be out all night."

"Can't be done, George," said I. "We've got to get this child home to her little cot to-night. You're a man of resource. How do we do it?"

"Oh, in that case, then Clacton's the only place. I'll take a chance and try and land you on the pier there, and you might get hold of a car to take you home."

"Right, George!" said I. "Clacton let it be."

Our destination thus decided on, there remained only the question whether the Fates would allow us to reach it; and upon this point I had my own grave doubts. It is true the wind was fair, but there seemed to me to be far too much of it, and it was raising a sea by now that promised to jolt us to pieces before we floated clear of the ground. The bottom was soft enough, no doubt, and a sound strong boat would not suffer much from pounding on it. But our boat was neither strong nor sound, and the marks of a very great age were visible upon her.

We waited.

The angry line of breaking waves moved steadily on across the dismal flats, seeming to close on us in menace. Those hurrying waters, reaching us at last, washed high about our sides, and soon each wave that passed us by began to lift us, and let us fall again upon a bottom manifestly changed to stone. The seas grew higher as the water rose, and I waited for our bruised hull to split and fall to pieces under the brutal pounding.

"If she doesn't hit a hard patch or slam the heel of her mast through the bottom, she'll do," said George contentedly. And the boat continuing indomitably to endure her punishment, I ventured to suppose she had been specially constructed for this work. But George assured me cheerfully that such was far from being the case. "Oh, no," said he. "Before I bought her and decked her in she was a Clacton beach boat. You know. Carting a gang of trippers round at a bob a head. Regular old shilling-vomiter she was, in fact."

"Ah, I see," said I. "And she seems to be taking again to her former habits. If I am not mistaken Mr Van Ping already owes you three shillings; and I feel that if this bumping goes on much longer I shall be in your debt too."

"Do it well over the side, then, and we won't insist on our bob," said George, looking at the Lady who Dances, who was palpably scared, but just as palpably determined not to show it. "I believe," said he then, "if we put sail on her now she might drive over the bar. We'll try it anyhow, as things will be quieter if we get her under way."

With that, he set about getting his cockleshell ready for sea in true deep-water style, and as master, mate and crew in turn, he gave and carried out his orders. "Man the windlass," he roared. "And send a hand aft to the wheel. Anchor's away, sir. Then stand by your fore-topmast-staysail halliards. Leave the anchor hanging at the cat-heads and hoist away on that sail. Put up your helm and—damn it, the peak halliards have got away from me." These cheery sounds, floating to us aft out of the darkness, made our Lady laugh again, which all the time had been precisely George's laudable intention. Observing this, and knowing, too, how action tends to banish apprehension, I gave the Lady the tiller together with instructions, and then I crawled forward, to find George wrapped in a Laocöon-like coil of halliards.

I suppose I have set some hundreds of mainsails in my

time, and George must have hoisted that one particular sail hundreds of times too. Yet this time George's mainsail nearly defeated us both. It refused to go up, while all we two able seamen seemed able to do was to fall, heavily and repeatedly, down. The fore-deck was coated with wet and slippery mud, it was listed at an acute angle, and regularly every two seconds the whole boat shook with a shuddering jar that made any sort of foothold impossible. Why say more? The wonder is that we ever set that sail at all. But we did, and while we were doing it, oblivious to everything else in the world except the ultimate setting of that confounded sail, the boat must have somehow bumped and slid and wrenched herself over the bar; for we found, when at last we straightened our aching backs and looked around, that she was afloat again, and sailing.

Then we became aware of cries arising from aft. "Oh, which way shall I push the stick. Which way? Which way?" It was the Lady in trouble with the steering, and, from the note of agony in her voice, she must have been in trouble for some time. "Look out! You'll jibe. Put down your helm," we helpfully cried. "Which way? Which way?" the anguished answer came, and with it the crash and jerk and racket of a most healthy and full-blooded jibe.

"Relieve the wheel," said George, "and keep her before the wind till I get a light in the binnacle and see where we're running to."

I steered the boat, it seemed for hours, while she rushed blindly through a night mysterious, wild and darker than the shades. "Keep your eye skinned," called George, wrestling still with matches in the cabin. "We don't want to knock a hole in any of the banks around here, and there are dozens of 'em, you know." As this perturbing piece of news was being imparted, I felt the Lady who Dances start. "There's something *there*," she cried. "Look! Right in front of us. A low black line. What can it be?"

"Then jibe her, quick!" said George, most suddenly

appearing. " It's lucky our Lady can see in the dark, for that's the beach. I haven't a chart, and, anyhow, there's no oil in the lamp; so we'll keep her running along in sight of the shore, and in time we ought to connect with Clacton pier. I think there's lots of water."

The cheerful and casual methods adopted by George, when navigating in those difficult and tide-ridden waters so afflicted by shoals, impressed me. They were sketchy, perhaps, but most surprisingly adequate, for presently a strange enormous shape loomed in the black above us, and, " Pavilion on the pier," said George. " Bear up or you'll hit it." We had arrived!

Anchoring in the pier's inadequate lee, we drew the dinghy alongside and looked at it. She was small—very small—and very full of water; but George opined that she would take us all " if you bail hard with the bucket." So we embarked, reluctantly, especially the Gent from Peking, who, though strongly reminiscent still of slipper-limpets, simply had to be carried. I know not how we reached the pier; I was far too busy bailing, and the credit is due to George alone for performing this final miracle. Banging and slithering amid encrusted piles we felt, by hand, for a landing-place which even the Lady who sees in the Dark could not make out in that Cimmerian darkness. Mr Van Ping it was who finally showed us the way, for suddenly he sprang wildly out into the night, and we heard him then shaking himself exuberantly upon some platform invisible above us.

" Well, there you are," said George. " Safe ashore again. I'm sorry you feel you have got to go, but some day soon I hope you'll come for another little sail. I'll get back now and shove off for Harwich. Good-bye, you three. I'm awfully glad we met."

And then George disappeared into the night. That was the last we saw of him, and we have never heard of him since. But one thing I am sure of, and that is that he fetched Harwich. I feel that if George made up his mind to it he could fetch Melbourne, say, in a small canoe. And what is more, he would be certain to enjoy his little sail.

In February it seems, to judge from its forlorn and desolate pier, Clacton is out of season; and later, whilst traversing the town in search of suitable wheeled transport, we felt very glad of this fact, for even a native population inured to the sartorial peculiarities of week-end trippers proved able only to regard us with feelings of startled amazement, coupled with a glib derision which was very embarrassing indeed. Even the ancient, and therefore presumably experienced, Jehu of a battered car, as weathered as himself, could scarcely be induced to regard us as possible fares, and it was necessary to make it very clear that the adventure would prove to him most lucrative before he would permit us to embark on his rattling 'randrydan.'

"Wickilywick, you say. Yes, down in the marsh. I know it. I'll risk it—for two quid. But you'll *ruin* my cushions. 'Ere, sit on this nose-bag. And hold the dog on your lap *all* the way, mind, for 'e smells 'orrid. Fish, ain't it?"

And so at length we departed, rattling Wickilywickwards through the night, disturbing as we went, with our outrageous clamour, sleeping suburban Clactonites, blackbirds roosting in hedgey lanes and mournful lapwings hiding in the marsh.

"I'm cold and I'm wet and very, very dirty. I've a bruise on all my corners, and I'm tired out. But somehow," said the Lady who Dances, "I'm happy. We've had a good day to-day, I think, don't you?"

"Perfect," said I. "I didn't know it could be done—in Essex. I've moved about the world a bit, and I've had some good days too; but there's a strange quaint flavour about this one that I've never met before. I'm not thinking of the limpets either."

And Mr Van Ping seemed to agree with us, for just then he sat up and wagged his feathered tail.

Said I, "I only hope they aren't all worried to death about us. It's after one o'clock, and they'll be wondering what's happened. Search parties out all over the marsh, and the police called in, I expect."

Said the Lady, as we at last approached the farm, "They don't *seem* very excited. The house is all dark! I believe the callous beasts have calmly gone to bed."

They had, and our host alone arose to greet us. Awakened doubtless by the tumultuous whirring of our gears, he called from his bedroom window, "I say, did you take Van Ping? Ah! good. He's there. I was afraid he'd lost himself. The side door's open, children, and you'll find a cold duck and a ham and things in the hall. But I'm freezing. Good night, and God bless you."

When I got to bed at last I lay awake a little while, thinking about things. "It's the queerest country in all the world," I thought, "with the very quaintest people. Yes. All these years I've been wasting my time; but I'm home again at last—and I mean to stay here."

And as I fell most peacefully asleep I whispered to myself, "*Dear* England."

GOOD HUNTING.

BY J. F. LIPSCOMB.

[Maga, February 1931.]

I HAD taken a couple of tons of timber down to Longonot Station by motor lorry one afternoon during the rains, and it was on my way back with a half-load of mealie meal and salt that I met them.

The railway runs along the floor of the Rift Valley, and a long seven-mile hill leads from the valley up the escarpment to the plateau from which I had come down, and over which, as I climbed, I could see a mass of grey-black clouds drifting steadily. It had rained hard all day, and in consequence the road was wet and greasy and churned in places into deep mud by passing wagons, so that my engine roared away in low gear, while the lorry, in spite of its six wheels and chains, slipped and slithered over the sticky surface. The ditches at the sides of the road were rushing torrents of brown water, and every leaf on every bush dripped monotonously into the wet grass. For the moment the rain had stopped, and I had thrown the side-curtains on to the roof of the cab and was plugging up the hill at a steady five miles an hour, when I came upon the car.

It had skidded at the edge of a washout, and was now lying half-buried in mud, with its back wheels in the hole and the front ones still on the road, as if clawing desperately at safety. It was a box-body car, and the back was piled high with the usual assortment of valises, blanket bags and suit-cases, while against the front mudguard leant dejectedly a tall broad-shouldered man dressed in khaki, forlornly watching another and younger man, who groped on hands and knees about the buried back wheels.

At the sound of my approach they looked up, and as I drew level I stopped and switched off the engine.

"Can I help?" I asked.

The big man got himself off the mudguard and came towards me.

"You can," he said, "and I'm mighty pleased to see you. I was just considering the choice between a wet night here in the car or a wetter walk somewhere else."

"Shall I try and haul you out?" I asked. "I've got plenty of rope."

"You're very kind," he answered, "but it's no sort of use. We're bust to little bits down in her tail there. That's so?" He turned to the other man, who looked up from cleaning his muddy hands on the grass and grinned pleasantly as he replied, "Sure."

"Then you'd better come with me," I said. "Where are you making for?"

"For Colonel Rayne's farm," he answered. "I understand it's somewhere on top there."

"It is," I said, "about twenty miles farther on, and I pass his door to get to my own place. How about shifting your kit on to the lorry?"

We did so, packing the whole lot on top of my sacks of mealie meal, and covering it all with a tarpaulin.

"Now," I said, when we had shut down the sides of their car and diverted the ditch that was pouring its water into the engine, "are you ready?"

"We are," replied the tall man, "but before journeying farther we will give thanks for our deliverance and drink to the success of our further efforts."

He dived into one of the pockets of his coat—a coat obviously made by a tropical outfitter who had never known the tropics—and produced a flask of gigantic proportions, into the cup of which he poured a generous tot, which he handed to me.

"A mixture of my own," he remarked pleasantly, "and one of which I am proud—yes, really proud—guaranteed innocuous to all but the weakest heads, but at the same time giving a feeling of uplift to the spirit."

"Here's luck!" I said, and drank my tot.

What that drink was concocted of I do not know and have never found out, but it was the perfection of all short drinks, and at any rate, as far as uplift of the spirit went, lived well up to its maker's claims.

We packed into the lorry and set off to face the rest of the climb on to the plateau, and it was while we were grinding up the hill that he told me who he was. His name, it appeared, was Septimus Scudder, being, as he informed me, "the seventh son of my father, Hiram Scudder of Chicago." He was an American citizen, but having lived nearly half his life in England, dividing his time equally between London and Chicago, he declared himself free of any transatlantic prejudices with regard to the British people. Now, with his son Joe, he was touring Kenya in the hope of raising a spice of adventure in a somewhat humdrum life. He intended to go on safari and do a little big game shooting, but, as a start, was paying a few visits "in various localities in your remarkably interesting country." He seemed a cheerful soul with an unceasing flow of conversation, and in that respect differed from his son, whose remarks were monosyllabic in the extreme, a state of affairs probably brought about by lifelong experience of the impossibility of competing with his father. The cab of the lorry being small, Joe sat behind on top of the load. "Say," said his father, "you'll be getting wet if it starts to rain again."

"Sure," replied Joe.

Rather more than a mile from the top of the escarpment the bush thins out and stops, giving way to the open grass that spreads up over the lip of the plateau and on to the plains beyond. It was while we were still in the bush that, on rounding a corner, we came full on to two lions, a dark-maned male and a lioness, walking calmly down the road towards us. When we met them they were not more than fifteen yards away, and instinctively I stood on the brakes and clutch and felt for my rifle, forgetting that, as I had shot a buck for the pot only the day before, on that day of all days I had left my rifle at home. However, the inarticulate Joe, though he might be slow of speech, was quick of action, and almost before I had stopped the lorry he had grabbed a rifle from among his kit and pushed it into his father's hand with the exhortation to "shoot lively." It was needed, too, for as we stopped the lions moved, turning and bolting into the bush at a good pace. Septimus Scudder jumped from the lorry and fired two rounds rapid after them. The first shot was a miss, but the second was a hit rather far back on the lion, causing him to stumble in his stride and bringing a growl out of him.

"I never could shoot straight with this darned gun," said Mr Septimus Scudder.

"That's so," replied his son.

What happened next, when looked at calmly from the present, seems sheer lunacy, and I can only excuse it on the supposition that Septimus' flask was more potent than he claimed, for the fact remains that three supposedly sane men, two of them unarmed, the third with a small-bore rifle with which he never could shoot straight, plunged into the bush on the trail of the wounded lion and the unwounded lioness.

The lion was bleeding freely, and the trail was plain to see, great dots of blood spotting the ground and dappling the wet grass. At first we followed at a run till I collected a few of my senses and insisted on a little care being taken, pointing out that we were following lions and not rabbits.

"I guess there's sense in that," allowed Septimus, and

thereafter we went more soberly, but even so it was a mad enough proceeding.

For half a mile or so the lions kept straight away from the road through fairly thin bush, but then the spoor crossed a small river-bed and turned into the thicker bush which bordered it. As we, too, turned into this bush, there was a growl ahead, and the sound of a body brushing its way through thick grass only a few yards away.

"Gosh, they're there!" said Septimus excitedly, clicking over the safety catch of the rifle.

"And for the love of heaven shoot straight if they come for us," I exhorted him.

"Sure," said Joe with feeling.

But they did not come for us; and pushing cautiously forward we came to where they had waited, and where the lion had left a great pool of blood in the place he had lain down.

This sort of thing continued for another mile or more, the lions waiting till we were nearly up to them, and then slinking on again. Why they never came for us I cannot imagine, and Septimus has since opined that Providence must have been keeping an extra fatherly eye on us that evening.

The spoor had turned uphill, and before long we were getting out of the bush and nearer to the open grass above it; but still we could get no sight of our quarry, and it was as we crossed a small muddy patch of ground that I noticed the lion was now alone ahead of us, and that the lioness must have turned away farther back in the thicker bush and left him to fend for himself.

The sun had set behind the Mau escarpment some little time earlier, and low-flying clouds were dropping misty streamers around us in the falling dusk. I pointed out to Septimus that in a quarter of an hour it would be dark, and that as we were well over two miles from the lorry we had better be turning back.

"Go back!" he said indignantly. "Not on your life I

don't. I'm following that lion till it's so dark he can just open his mouth and wait for me to walk into it," and he went on.

We got out of the bush into the open, but there was no sign of the lion, and the spoor led straight on. We followed, and about five or six hundred yards farther up the hill came on a patch of long tuft grass. As we reached it the lion stood up, hard hit, but with the fight still in him, and not ten yards from us. "Shoot," I said to Septimus, and he shot, and in spite of the fact that the light had almost gone he shot straight this time.

The lion was a fine full-grown beast with a small dark mane, and as we turned him over and felt the muscles rippling under the skin, "He'd sure have made cat's meat of us if he'd got a hold of us," said Septimus.

"I guess so," agreed Joe.

And that was his epitaph.

. . . .

"Well," I said, "if we're going to get back to the lorry before it's too dark to see the way we'd better be moving."

"And the lion?" asked Septimus.

"Leave it here," I said, "and get Rayne to bring you out in the morning with a couple of boys to skin it."

"Ain't there anything that might harm it?" he asked. "I thought this country was just alive with predatory beasts."

"Hyenas would have a meal off it if they found it," I admitted, and regretted the admission immediately afterwards; "but you'll have to risk that," I added.

"Risk nothing!" said Septimus Scudder with considerable heat. "See here! I don't shoot lions every day of my life, and I stay right here till the hide is off this carcase and I can take it away with me."

I looked at him, and he obviously meant what he said.

I looked at Joe, and he was grinning broadly. It seemed that he knew what to expect when his father made up his mind.

"Have either of you got a knife?" I asked.

"No," said Joe.

I pulled out my sheath knife and handed it to him.

"You'll find me asleep in the lorry when you have finished the job," I said, and turned to go.

Septimus looked at me with his faintly mocking smile.

"Young man," he said, "neither of us have ever skinned a carcase in our lives, and, speaking for myself, I am not starting on the king of beasts. Now, are you going back to Colonel Rayne to tell him that you have left his guests sitting out cold and wet in a howling wilderness waiting for some good Samaritan to skin one little lion for them, or——?" He held out the knife to me. "Have a drink before you start," he added hospitably, fumbling for the flask.

From the moment he refused to leave the lion I knew what would happen inevitably. I made no further excuse; I took the drink and started the job.

Have you ever skinned a lion in the dark on a wet night with skurries of rain beating down on your back, out on an open plain across which the wind from the mountains is whipping in long sighing gusts that eat right into your bones? I had never done so before, and never will I do so again. Even though my eyes were by this time accustomed to the darkness, I could see very little, and had to work largely by feel, and within ten minutes my fingers were so numb with the cold and slippery with grease from the carcase that I could barely hold the knife. At the best of times the skinning of a lion is not the pleasantest of jobs, but in the dark, when it is raining, I have never found a more unpleasant.

Except for an occasional request from me for one of them to pull here or hold there, the work was done almost in silence. Even Septimus' tongue was silenced by the wet and the cold. We had all of us left our raincoats in the lorry, and long before I had finished we were wet to the skin.

That skinning stays in my mind as a nightmare—the sort of nightmare in which one is spending eternities of time at something unpleasant that never finishes, and throughout which one's mind is numbed so that one never has any reasonable expectation of ever doing anything else. I kept my back to the wind and the rain as much as I could, but gradually the wet soaked through my clothes till little cold streams of water were running down my back like a slow-motion shower-bath. The others were probably feeling quite as miserable as I was, but they did not show it very much. Suddenly Joe gave a short laugh.

"What the hell d'you find funny about this?" I asked irritably.

"Nothing," he said, "but anyone seeing us would."

After what seemed to me to be hours of wrestling with greasy folds of skin the job was finished, and I pulled the skin clear of the carcase and stood up to stretch my cramped joints.

"And ain't he got any wings?" asked Septimus. "We may as well finish the job properly."

Now a lion has in each shoulder a small floating bone, the shape of a crescent moon and about three inches long, which is quite independent of all other bones, and is said to be a relic of the time when a lion had wings. Obediently I stooped again to the carcase and dug till I had found both of them, when I handed them to Septimus.

"Now," I said, "my part of the job is finished, and your's begins."

"How's that?" asked Septimus.

"Well," I answered, "somebody has got to hump that skin back to the lorry, and I tell you straight that I'm not helping. I reckon I've done my whack in to-night's entertainment."

"I guess that's so," said Septimus.

He turned to Joe. "This is on us," he said.

"Sure," replied Joe, and started to fold up the skin.

I picked up the rifle. "I'll take the gun," I said.

"Now," said Septimus thoughtfully, "d'you know which way we go, because I'm darned if I do?"

"I think so," I answered quite cheerfully. I was feeling better now that my share was over. "There are two ways we can go."

"And they are?"

"We can either go back the way we came, straight downhill into the bush and as direct as we can make for the lorry —it'll be much the shortest way—or——"

"Steady on!" said Septimus. "If we go down the way we came up, ain't it probable that the lady in the case will be hanging around in the same direction?"

"Quite probable," I replied.

"And," he went on, "I reckon she will be feeling kind of hurt and lonesome without her lord and master?"

"She will," I said.

"And she'll be able to smell this hide of his that we'll be taking with us?"

"Can't you?" I asked.

He was silent for a moment. Then he said very thoughtfully—

"And you'll be carrying the gun?"

"I shall," I said firmly.

"Then what is the alternative?" asked Septimus.

"The alternative," I said, "is to keep along in the open here till we strike the road, and then go back down the road to the lorry."

"And how far would we be from the road?"

"Two miles," I replied. "Perhaps three."

"One extra mile is of no significance," said Septimus, "and I reckon that's the way for us."

"Sure," said Joe. "Lead on, Macduff."

In daylight that bit of country looks harmless enough, for the most part plain grass, with here and there clumps of tuft grass, and occasionally a depression that during rain becomes a runnel of water. Perhaps a little rough underfoot, but not difficult to walk over. But at night it was different; it was very difficult to walk over. We slipped and slithered on the earthy patches between the grass, we tripped over the tufts and we put our feet into unexpected holes, and every now and then we floundered through a runnel of water, and when we did so, an icy torrent swished around our legs and filled our already squelching boots. And all the time it continued to rain, steadily and persistently, a heavy drizzle, driven from the mountains by a biting wind. I led the way; Mr Septimus Scudder followed, having found his tongue again and using it freely; and in the rear stumbled Joe, burdened with the lion skin.

Now when a native carries a hide, he folds the outside to the centre, ties the legs and tail in a tight knot on the top, and having made a firm bundle of it, balances it on his head. I suggested to Joe that he should do this; but he said he was not going to balance any dirty hides on his head, and instead tried to carry it on his shoulder, with the consequence that every time he stumbled—which was frequently—some corner of the skin would slide out of the bundle and flap heavily against him at every step he took until he stopped and tied it up again. At short intervals he changed with his father, and from my position in the lead I listened to stertorous breathings and muffled imprecations coming along behind me, and called back warnings of what they were likely to fall into next.

When we had gone about half the distance to the road we crossed a runnel heavily in flood, and after struggling through it, Septimus dropped the skin in a heap and sat himself upon it. He was not a man used to much physical effort.

"Say," he gasped, "wasn't it in the Bible that some fellow disguised a sheep in wolf's clothing?"

"It was," I replied, "or the other way round."

"Other way round what?" asked Septimus.

"Wolf in sheep's clothing," I answered.

"Well," he said, "whichever way it was, that sheep was a better man than I've always thought him before now—if a wolf's skin is any way near so heavy as a lion's."

Somehow we reached the road, æons later in that everlasting night as it seemed, and never were three men more glad to see a road than we were. It had been bad enough for me carrying only a rifle, but what it must have been for the other two I hate to think. But they stuck it, and for all they said during the journey not once did either of them suggest jettisoning the skin until we reached the road.

Then said Septimus, "And now, how far down the hill to the lorry?"

"Not more than a mile," I replied.

"Then," he said with decision, "we will leave this hide right here."

"And stay with it while I get the lorry?" I asked.

"We will not," he replied. "I'm a darn sight nearer dead than alive, and I guess Joe's the same, and there's only one thing that will revive us, and that's a drink. I've got another flask in my suit-case, and I'm not sitting here in the cold waiting for it when I can get it sooner by walking to it. That right, Joe?"

"Sure thing," said Joe.

So we left the skin in a heap by the side of the road, and set off downhill towards the lorry. It had stopped raining by this time, and a few stars were showing between the drifting clouds, and if it had not been for my wet clothes clinging clammily to my body I should have felt almost cheerful, for the bad temper I had felt while skinning the lion had evaporated, and I was beginning to see the night's doings in their true light.

We reached the lorry, and Septimus dived into his suit-case, while Joe climbed on top of the load and started digging into a kit-bag.

"Isn't one flask enough?" I suggested mildly.

Septimus looked up. "Who said anything about two?" Then seeing Joe, "Say, Joe, what's up?"

"Clothes," said Joe.

He stood up and pulled from his kit-bag a large towel, and having done so, proceeded to divest himself of every stitch of clothing he had on, to rub himself thoroughly, and then to put on a complete change of dry clothes.

"That's an idea," said his father, and started to do likewise.

"Well," I said, "if your kit runs to another change of clothes, I'll do the same."

If any car had come up the road just then the occupants would have had the unusual experience of finding in the middle of the night a heavily laden lorry stationary in the road, while on top of it three men stood stark naked and towelled themselves vigorously.

At length, clothed once more, and warmed inwardly and outwardly, we started off. Joe was comfortably ensconced among the sacks, wrapped in voluminous garments and sheltered from any further rain by a tarpaulin. Septimus and I got into the cab and shut down the side-curtains.

Ahead of us the lamps threw a path of light into the darkness, and it was pleasant to think that there need be no more paddling about in the wet for us that night. A comforting warmth rose from the engine, and I began to speculate as to the time we might expect to get to Rayne's, while a faint doubt assailed me as to the safety of the skin during the time we had left it. It must have taken us at least an hour to get to the lorry, change our clothes, start up and get back again, and hyenas—but I did not say anything to Septimus, who was crowing over the night's triumphs and hugging himself for joy.

"Nearly there," I said to him, and he started to fumble for the catches of the side-curtains. At the same time our lights picked up the distant heap that was the skin, and it seemed to me that for an instant a pair of eyes shone in the beams and that a dim shape slunk away into the night. We came close, and a second pair of eyes appeared and gazed fixedly at us till we were within a few yards, when they, too, disappeared; but I still said nothing, and Septimus did not see. By now he had undone the curtains, and as I stopped the lorry he got out, walked to the skin and stooped to pick it up.

"Say," he remarked, "it's a darned wet unpleasant hide," and then his words froze on his lips and his face set like a mask, while even above the hum of the engine I could hear the gasp that came out of him. Joe heard it too, and hauled himself out of his covering and looked down on to his father standing in the road. For a full half-minute there was silence while the whole awful truth sank into them, and then Joe laughed—laughed uproariously. His father turned, and for a moment I thought he would come and hit him, but then he showed what he was made of, for a grin slowly appeared on his face, and then he too laughed, and the three of us laughed at the wreck of our night's work in a way that must have astonished the hyenas if they were listening.

Septimus held up the skin, or what remained of it, a thing of holes and shreds and tatters that such a short time before had been a noble trophy.

"Gosh, but I wanted that skin badly!" said he.

From the wreck we saved the head and mane unharmed, and the claws from two feet; the rest we left for the hyenas to finish.

In the early hours of the morning we arrived at Rayne's farm, and save when we went together to get the lion's skull so that Septimus could have the head set up, I did not see the Scudders again. But some little while later there reached me a parcel containing a real first-class hunting knife, and round the hilt of the knife are the words 'Good Hunting.'

THE PUNDRAPORE RESIDENCY.

BY ALEXANDER ALLARDYCE.

[Maga, August 1872.]

I.

FEW events have caused so great a sensation among Indian officials as did the appearance of a 'Gazette' announcing the appointment of Captain Jones of the 27th Bengal Cavalry —the Junglywallahs—to the political agency of the Pundrapore State. The causes of an Afghan war had been more easily accounted for than the selection of a man who could not command an ounce of interest from head to tail of the service. The post was one of the most coveted appointments in India. Sir Rothie Murkus had, with tears in his eyes, refused the entreaties of a host of Gushingtons, Rattles and Pendlows, whose genealogical trees might have convinced the most sceptical of their special fitness for the Pundrapore Residency. The same venerable statesman affirmed to his disappointed relatives that the wires were pulled by a hand which he could not venture to oppose. What was this mystery of the hidden hand? All Calcutta talked of nothing else; and from Cossipore to Garden Reach the wonderful appointment of Captain Jones to the Pundrapore Residency was in everybody's mouth. No one had more reason to be surprised than the officer who was thus unexpectedly brought before the public. When Captain Jones was solemnly interrogated by his colonel in the presence of the brigadier and other field-officers of the station, he declared, upon his honour as an officer and a gentleman, that he had not a single relative either in the Court of Directors or in the Board of Control—that he had never seen the Governor-General—and that he hardly knew the names of the members of Council or secretaries to Government. And upon cross-examination he was compelled to acknowledge that the only connection between his family and India arose from his uncle having kept a grocer's shop in the East India Docks, where the old man had amassed enough of money to purchase Company's paper and to procure a cavalry cadetship for his nephew. Had the occasion been one of less importance, Jones would have scrupled to be so frank with his brother officers. He had hitherto been somewhat reticent upon the subject of his family, with the exception of a few obscure hints that its origin was Welsh and princely. But Captain Jones felt that romancing would be dangerous at such a juncture; and the brigadier went away more puzzled than before.

Had Jones seen his name in the 'Gazette' as a Knight Commander of the Bath, it would not have occasioned him more surprise than did the notification of his appointment to the Pundrapore Residency. To purchase out his seniors step by step, and to retire from the service in process of time with the title of Colonel, had been the very moderate limit of Jones's ambition. His leisure moments were frequently devoted to the composition of epitaphs, in which he described himself as having been "for *x* years The Gallant and Resolute Leader of the 27th Bengal Cavalry—the Jungly-wallahs," "The Brave and Accomplished Commandant," "Who lived like a Soldier and died like a Christian," with many other similar expressions of self-appreciation. Treasured up in one corner of his desk lay a design for a mural tablet, with an inscription as long as a modern biography. This, as Jones had told Cornet Sniggers in confidence, was a memorial that his sorrowing relatives would probably erect in Cheltenham Church, near which town he meant to set up his staff when his campaigning days were over. Sniggers also informed the mess that Jones had shown him the plan of a cenotaph overshadowed by two palm-trees, erected, as the legend said, "By his grateful and devoted soldiers, Who reverenced him as a Father, And worshipped him as a Leader." In the design for this remarkable piece of sculpture, two native troopers, in the flowing turbans and tight-fitting jackets of the Junglywallahs, were represented as bending over their wounded or dying commander, whose arm was strained in the effort to wave above his head his broken sword. Round the base were skulls, cross-bones and other mortuary emblems, understood to be the remains of Sikhs and Afghans who had fallen by the sabre of the recumbent warrior. The tears had stood in Jones's eyes as he showed these tributes of affection to his subaltern, who gave, in turn, many assurances of sympathy and promises of secrecy. These promises did not, however, prevent Sniggers from acquainting the mess with the little weakness of their brother officer; and for many a day after, Jones had to submit to being dubbed "Old Mortality" at the mess-table of the Junglywallahs.

Probably the whole Bengal army did not contain a more ungainly figure than that of the new Resident. He stood six feet high, with a thin chest and round shoulders. The knees of his long spindle-legs were constantly coming into collision, and the natural pallor of his lean sallow face was set off by a stiff black moustache, gaunt cheeks and a chin generally half-shaven. All the riding-masters in her Majesty's service could not have given him a decent seat in the saddle within the compass of an ordinary lifetime; nor could the smartest drill-sergeant in India have induced him to keep the step for five successive minutes when walking in company. It was a joke in the regiment that Jones turned away his head when fencing, and shut his eyes when shooting.

His unprepossessing appearance might have passed unnoticed but for the *gaucherie* of his manner, which in the society of ladies was especially painful. At balls, where Jones underwent self-torments to make himself agreeable, it was remarked that everybody whom he asked to dance was engaged, and that even the permanent wall-flowers found pretexts for declining his attentions. It was at Bustlepore, where the Commander-in-Chief was holding a levee about the beginning of the first Sikh war, that Jones, in making his bow, jerked his head so close to his Excellency's stomach, that Sir George started back and demanded with an oath "who the clumsy ogre was?" Jones passed along with his white face yet a shade whiter, and something like tears in his grey eyes, but no one ever heard him complain of the Chief's rudeness; and old Colonel Gargoyle of the Jungly-wallahs, whose word was law upon all matters of etiquette, declared that Jones was more of a gentleman than Sir George Blitzen.

The Pundrapore Residency was one of the best pieces of patronage in the hands of the Bengal Government. Successive Governor-Generals had filled the appointment with their favourite aides-de-camp and private secretaries; and when there was nobody in particular to be provided for, a distinguished officer from either branch of the public service had generally been selected. The last Resident, the Hon. Captain Grantley, was the near relative of a former Governor-General, and he consequently enjoyed a full measure of the present ruler's hatred. And his lordship was at no loss for opportunities of evincing his feelings towards Captain Grantley. The Pundrapore territories were at that time in what the Calcutta newspapers call a state of chronic anarchy. Mozuffer Jung, the last ruler, a politic Mussulman, who had kept friends with all parties, had been dead for about two years. His youngest and favourite wife, a Persian beauty who had cost five thousand rupees at Herat, had managed to secure the regency of the State, the custody of her infant son and the control over the other three wives and miscellaneous female appurtenances of the harem. The British Government, knowing the favourite Begum's capacity for intrigue and mischief-making, strongly opposed this arrangement; and the late Nawab had been incessantly urged to commit the administration of the State to his Prime Minister, a Mahratta Brahmin, upon whose fidelity and steadfastness the Government could with confidence rely. But it soon became apparent that Captain Grantley would do little to promote the policy of Government. The fair Persian made the best of the opportunities which her secluded life afforded, to captivate the Resident soon after his arrival at Pundrapore; and Captain Grantley was a man of too much gallantry and too little prudence to decline the flirtation. The result was that he allowed himself to become the instrument of carrying out the Begum's projects, and of thwarting the instructions which Sir Rothie Murkus, the Foreign Secretary, kept continually dinning into his ears. After the Nawab's death, the Begum became less guarded in her intrigues, and Captain Grantley still more infatuated. The Calcutta papers clamoured for his withdrawal, and 'Brutus,' and 'Indignation,' and 'True Briton,' and 'Anglo-Indian' and all the other *noms de plume* of newspaper letter-writers, were constantly employed to express the public disgust at Captain Grantley's proceedings. But Captain Grantley's noble relative was now all-powerful in the Board of Control; and so the Captain snapped his fingers at the Calcutta press, for he knew that the Governor-General would not dare to adopt its extreme suggestions.

There was then an uneasy feeling among the British in Hindostan. The Sikhs had not yet been finally crushed, and their chieftains were swaggering about through the Punjab talking of the speedy approach of the time when Runjeet would drive the British into the sea. Dost Mahomed, too, was looking down from Cabul with a troubled countenance at the progress of the red-coated Kaffirs. And, what was still more serious, there was much discontent among the powerful Rajpoot chieftains, who fretted impatiently at the checks imposed by the British upon the arbitrary exercise of their feudal power. In all intrigues of the day the Begum of Pundrapore took a prominent part. Her agents were in every petty court, fomenting all causes of discontent and encouraging the Rajahs to unite together for the assertion of their independence. Symptoms of open disaffection had been more than once manifested in Pundrapore, until the Government thought it necessary to impress upon the chiefs the uselessness of insubordination by a display of troops. Sir George Blitzen, with a brilliant staff, escorted by a cavalry regiment and by large detachments of infantry and artillery, entered Pundrapore with the ostensible object of paying his respects to the Begum. Sir George was a courtier of the Carlton House and Pavilion school, and his first impulse was to pacify the State by subduing the heart of its ruler. But the Begum would listen to none of his fine speeches. She was at no loss to divine what had procured her the honour of his Excellency's visit, and she determined to express her dislike for the Government by slighting its representative. A grand durbar was held in the palace for his Excellency's reception, and Sir George took his seat upon the right hand of the Begum with so many high-flown compliments and expressions of regard, that Captain Gulstan, his Persian Secretary, could hardly find words to convey to the Begum the due warmth of the Chief's affection. Her Highness in turn complimented Sir George, and expressed her sorrow that his Excellency should be compelled to serve so far from his native country at his advanced age. How sad it was that the young Maharanee of Frangistan should have no younger warriors to command her forces, that she must send the father of grandfathers to lead her soldiers in India. The well-padded breast of Sir George quivered with scarce concealed anger at the taunt, as Gulstan tremblingly translated it, toning down the sneer as much as he dared.

It was Sir George's weakness to look twenty years younger than his age; and barber, dentist and tailor had done their utmost to support the delusion. This was but the beginning of hostilities; and affront after affront, but always within the bounds of diplomatic courtesy, was offered to his Excellency during his stay in Pundrapore, until he began to pray devoutly that the State would really revolt, that he might obtain some satisfaction for the slights he was receiving. If anything could have added to the bitterness of these affronts, it would have been the studied deference with which the Begum treated Captain Grantley's counsels. Sir George did his best to pay back the Begum by bullying her favourite; but Captain Grantley, in his diplomatic capacity, was almost wholly independent of the military authorities, and he did not give himself much trouble about what his Excellency said or did. Sir George at length marched out of Pundrapore in a fury, and reported to the Government that the only salvation for the Pundrapore State was the deposition of the Begum and the immediate recall and degradation of the Resident. The former could only be done with the authority of the Board of Control, and there was little hope that its members would assume so grave a responsibility to gratify Sir George, who was no favourite in Cannon Row. On the other hand, Captain Grantley's noble protector was the referee of the Board upon all political questions, and the Governor-General was too prudent a statesman to draw down upon himself the ire of his predecessor by the recall of the Resident. Fortunately for his Excellency, the residency of Kaifiabad just then fell vacant, and to this post Captain Grantley was at once promoted downstairs. His salary was not diminished, and as his duties were confined to the payment of an annual pension and the forwarding of a weekly budget of complaints on the part of the recipient to the Foreign Office, he had little ground for grumbling; and it was at this juncture that Captain Jones took charge of the Pundrapore Residency.

II.

The Junglywallahs gave a dinner to their departing comrade, and said so many kind things about him that Jones really began to believe in himself, and to think that the Governor-General had shown great discrimination in filling up the Pundrapore agency.

"I should not wonder, my boy," said old Gargoyle, after many bumpers of 'Simpkin' had been quaffed to the success of the new diplomatist, "but that, after all, you owe your success to the Begum herself. Her ladyship may have seen and fancied you when we marched through Pundrapore last relief time, and have hocussed the G.-G. into sending you to console her for the loss of that puppy Grantley."

Jones blushed, and the mess set up a roar of laughter, as they were in duty bound to do, at this witticism of the colonel's, while M'Gonigil, the senior captain and chief Adonis of the regiment, who would himself have gladly accepted the responsibilities of the Pundrapore Residency, not excluding the Begum, threw a contemptuous glance across the table and muttered, "The divil resave her oisight if she did."

Captain Jones arrived in Calcutta, and put up at Spence's, where he soon found that the Resident of Pundrapore was a very different personage from the young cadet who had lived there upon a hundred rupees a month twelve years before. *Khidmutghars* flew to anticipate his orders, *punkah-wallahs* pulled as if for life or death whenever he came into their vicinity, and even the manager of the hotel—great man as he was—bowed with an appearance of politeness when Captain Jones appeared in the breakfast-room of a morning. At the club in Chowringhee, everyone who had the slightest acquaintance with him asked him to dinner, and people whose names were scarcely known to him offered him their carriages for a drive on the course. So much for being a political officer on fifteen hundred a month, thought Jones, as he blessed the hour when he had been gazetted to the Political Department. There was still one ordeal to be gone through: he must report himself at the Foreign Office and receive his instructions; and he much feared the result, if Sir Rothie Murkus were to subject him to a cross-examination upon the duties of a Political Agent. He had read all the article "Pundrapore" in 'Thornton's Gazetteer,' and had attempted to commit to memory the six treaties which the British Government had made with the rulers of that State, none of which had ever been worth the parchment that bore the originals. And when he had mastered the Foreign Secretary's "Thoughts on the Duty of British Intervention in Native States," and the Under-Secretary's "Notes on Annexation," and the Deputy Under-Secretary's "Quousque Tandem: A Plea for the Deposition of Indian Despots," he thought he might venture into the lion's mouth, and he accordingly sought the sanctum of Sir Rothie Murkus.

As he passed through the Deputy Under-Secretary's room, that gentleman, who was engaged with the editor of the 'Bengal Peon,' abruptly broke off the conversation and stared at Captain Jones as if his eyeballs would start from their sockets. In the next apartment, where the Under-Secretary, a small young gentleman of weak eyesight and bilious temperament, was similarly occupied with the editor of the 'John Bull,' he was honoured with an equal share of attention. Mr Waspbite wiped his spectacles, put them on and said, "God bless me! are you Captain Jones, the Pundrapore man?" and having received an affirmative bow, he again said, "God bless me!" and appeared quite struck by the circumstance. At the next door stood Sir Rothie himself, shaking hands with the editor of the 'Padrepore Monitor and Weekly Evangelist,' for the Foreign Office knew well the value of cultivating the Exeter Hall interest. Though Sir Rothie had more politeness than his subordinates, he too seemed to share in the general curiosity, and he subjected

Captain Jones to a critical examination as he conducted him into his office.

"And so you're the new Resident of Pundrapore, are you, hey?" said Sir Rothie, as he seated himself at his desk; "I suppose you did not expect such promotion, eh?"

"I did not, sir; but I assure you I am very grateful for it," said Jones modestly; "and I hope I shall prove to Government that its confidence has not been misplaced. May I ask to whom I am indebted for my good fortune?"

"Oh, to nobody in particular. The Government of Bengal always knows where to lay its finger upon the right man. And now for your instructions—here they are. And Captain Jones, if I were you, I would follow Mr Harcourt's advice as much as possible. He has been long in the Residency, and knows its ways. I shan't detain you longer; but stay, I think the Commander-in-Chief had something to say to you. You know he has just returned from Pundrapore? Well, I'm going now to Government House, where we shall meet Sir George. You may as well come along with me."

Jones trembled as the recollection of the fatal day at Bustlepore, when his awkwardness had imperilled the portly paunch of the Commander-in-Chief, flashed across his mind; but duty compels the soldier up to the cannon's mouth, and Jones resigned himself with a sigh to the prospect of meeting Sir George Blitzen.

He was, however, spared the pain of an interview. The Commander-in-Chief had already entered his carriage, and was driving off as Sir Rothie and Captain Jones came into the compound. "Hey, Sir George, Sir George! this is Captain Jones, the new Resident of Pundrapore, whom you wished to see!" cried the Foreign Secretary; but the Chief's impatient horses would not be stayed. Sir George put his head out of the carriage and threw a penetrating glance in the direction of our hero. "All right," he cried; "I am off to Barrakpore to inspect the station. Ugly as ever, Springer," he muttered to his aide-de-camp; "he is just the man I wanted"; and his Excellency was whirled away, leaving Jones and Sir Rothie standing on the steps of Government House.

"It's all right, I suppose," said Sir Rothie; "if he had had anything particular to say to you I daresay he would have said it. I suppose he just wanted to congratulate you. Good-bye, Captain Jones. I hope you'll have a pleasant time of it. Take care and don't be fascinated by the Begum"; and Sir Rothie disappeared within the *penetralia* of Government House.

The Calcutta journals next morning had each a leader upon the Pundrapore Residency. The 'John Bull' said that the time had come when the British public must demand, by its representatives, an impartial review of the exercise of the Governor-General's patronage. "When we see the public interest sacrificed to private considerations, and nameless and unknown men promoted to positions which they are perfectly unqualified to fill, it is the duty of a free and conscientious press to demand that the axe should be laid to the root of the tree, and that such abuses as we have recently seen in the case of the Pundrapore Residency should be rendered impossible in the future. The claims of Lieutenant-Colonel Thomas Robinson, Political Agent at the Court of Chotasahebpore, are too conspicuous to require that public attention should be directed to the gross injustice which has been sustained by that gallant officer; but in another quarter the Government that has offered so flagrant an insult to a meritorious servant, and that has thus hurled defiance at public opinion, will infallibly be called to account." The 'Peon' was more mild, and expressed a doubtful hope that Captain Jones might prove equal to his responsible position; but feared that Mr Rattle, the Commissioner of Saugor Island and the Lower Sunderbunds, was the only official who could have saved the Pundrapore State. "We have it upon excellent authority that Captain Jones's appointment has been made under pressure from the Home authorities, and that it has formed the subject of a dignified protest on the part of the Government of Bengal. How long, we ask, are the hands of our administrators to be paralysed by the ignorant and interested action of their English masters, the Plutocracy of Leadenhall Street, the Octogenarians of Cannon Row?" The 'Padrepore Monitor' said the others were all wrong, and that there were special reasons for Captain Jones's appointment—reasons which could not at the present moment be laid with propriety before the public; and so people began to think that Jones must be somebody after all, for the 'Padrepore Monitor' was supposed to have good information about what went on in the back staircases of Government House.

Captain Jones went away from Calcutta with his good opinion of his own capacity very much strengthened. He had come to look upon himself as an embryo Malcolm, and he dreamed already of missions to Persia and to Cabul, of the Foreign Secretaryship, and of a seat in Council, with perhaps the government of one of the minor Presidencies. Who knew? Such things had been, and his foot was now upon the first step of the ladder. At the *dak* bungalows on the road to Pundrapore he utilised the stoppages for the composition of a new series of epitaphs, in which he provided for all the possible contingencies of his future career, from the Pundrapore Residency to the government of Bombay. A statue in the cathedral of Calcutta, with an inscription, "To the Memory of Major-General Sir John Jones, Knight Commander of the Bath, of the Order of the Douranee Empire, of the Burmese Tsalway, &c. &c., Whose brilliant diplomatic talents, For so many years, Shed a lustre upon the Indian Service, And secured to the British Possessions Peace and Uninterrupted Security," occupied his mind during the most of the long and wearisome journey.

When he arrived at Pundrapore he found his predecessor already gone. So disgusted was Captain Grantley at Jones's appointment, that he did not take the trouble to make over the office to him in person, but hurried off to Agra to have, as he said, "a fling" before settling down in the solitude of Kaifiabad. "Tell the fellow," he had said to Mr Harcourt, "that he will find it not quite so easy to keep the peace in Pundrapore as to smoke cheroots at the mess-table of the Junglywallahs. The Government has taken away the only man who could have held down disturbances, and the consequences be at its own door. Good-bye, Harcourt, and God send you a good deliverance from Pundrapore; for if I know anything about the place, there will soon be mischief with this new booby." Mr Harcourt thought so too, and he had put in for a transfer from the Political to the Administrative Department as soon as he had heard of Captain Jones's appointment. But he received his new superior with formal civility, and did his best to instruct him in the duties of the office, although his surprise at the Government's selection continued to increase as he found opportunities for gauging Captain Jones's mental abilities.

The curiosity regarding the new Resident had extended even to Pundrapore. Rumour, which is always distorted in native gossip, had described the new Resident as little better than a *pagul* or fool. Fools, they said, were always fortunate, and the Big Lord Sahib had read in the stars that Pundrapore would be given over to the British by the greatest fool in the army; and so Captain Jones had been selected. If the Begum did not share in the general belief, she at least shared in the general curiosity, and waited with much anxiety for the arrival of the new Political, whose mysterious appointment she could not but think boded no good to the continuance of her authority. At this time her Highness was more than ever immersed in political intrigue. There were daily reports of a rising in Lahore, and the Begum was only waiting for the Sikhs to take the field to proclaim the independence of Pundrapore, to massacre the English in the Residency and to declare herself sole ruler of the State during the rest of her life. The great obstacle to the Begum's scheme was Taptee Rao, the minister of her late husband, who still nominally held the office of Vizier, although he did not share in the councils of his mistress. Taptee was a shrewd old Brahmin, who had sense enough to be faithful to the British and to the cause of the youthful Nawab. The many slights which the Begum had heaped upon him, and the contempt with which his advice was always treated, had sunk deep in Taptee's heart, and he was eager to thwart her ambitious designs and to reveal her plots to the Foreign Office. But the Begum conducted all her intrigues through her favourite, Faizul Khan, a wily and truculent Pathan who commanded the Pundrapore troops, and whose detestation of the pork-eating English and dogs of Hindoos had raised him high in the good graces of the Regent. Faizul, it was said, even aspired to share the Pundrapore *musnud*, if the Begum were once at liberty; and it is certain that he looked with no favourable eyes upon her intimacy with Captain Grantley. The Begum had a difficult task to conciliate her two admirers, but she managed to make tools of them both, and sneered at both alike when their backs were turned.

A grand durbar was held for the reception of the new Resident shortly after Captain Jones's arrival. It was with no little trepidation that Jones prepared himself for the ceremony. He had never been a Mæcenas to military tailors, but his position now demanded that some attention should be paid to costume, and a number of boxes from Harman's had accompanied him to Pundrapore. When he had equipped himself in full diplomatic uniform, he stood waiting for Mr Harcourt, nervously handling his cocked-hat and wishing that the durbar was well over. Harcourt came in smoking a cigar and looking provokingly cool. "Hilloa!" he cried; "going to tame the Pundrapore tigress by love and the language of flowers, instead of Sir Rothie's despatches. I declare it's quite refreshing to see a new Calcutta coat, if it didn't awaken painful reminiscences of unpaid bills. Well, shall we go and make our salaams to the Begum? It's a deuced nuisance in such a hot morning; and I hope we shall get away as soon as possible."

"Well, really, I suppose we must get it over," doubtfully replied the martyr to the mysterious policy of Government; "but you see, the fact is, that I'm somehow new to this kind of work. I never was but at one levee in my life"—and here the ill-omened recollection of his rencontre with Sir George Blitzen darted across his memory—"I'm rather afraid—that is, I'm anxious that—that—well, yes, that the dignity of the British Government should be properly represented upon this important occasion."

Jones looked towards his subordinate with much solemnity, as if he would have Mr Harcourt believe that his mind was troubled with official responsibility and not with a nervous dread of appearing in public. But Harcourt was too astute a diplomatist to be thus imposed upon.

"Ah, yes, I see," he said, casting a keen glance at the Resident. "Well, all you have got to do is to look wise and ill-natured, and follow my directions: to be coldly complaisant to the Begum, to be particularly civil and gracious to old Taptee Rao, and to put on as sulky a frown as you can whenever you look in the direction of that confounded *soor* Faizul Khan."

"I suppose I had better do something, too, about seeing the boy Nawab. Sir Rothie, in his instructions, lays special emphasis upon 'guarding against the injurious results of maternal fondness and female indulgence.' The child, of course, will be thoroughly spoiled by his doting mother."

"Ah, well, perhaps," rejoined Mr Harcourt doubtfully. "Has it never occurred to you, Captain Jones, that by 'the injurious results of maternal fondness' Sir Rothie may have meant such mistakes as giving the child poison for sweetmeats, or wringing his neck round when playing with him in her arms? Of course you understand your own instructions better than I do, but I have known such *double entendres* often conveyed under cover of a diplomatic phrase."

"Good heavens! you are surely not in earnest, Harcourt?" cried the astonished Resident. "The Begum surely cannot be such a fiend as harm her own flesh and blood."

"You see there is flesh and blood and flesh and blood, and the Begum cares so much for the flesh and blood that is contained within her own pretty epidermis, that she has but little affection to bestow upon external animal matter," said Mr Harcourt deliberately, as he lazily puffed forth smoke. "The child is in her way, and if it were not for the Government she would throttle the poor *chhokra* with as little reluctance as she would order that big brute, Faizul Khan, to knock you and me both upon the head. However, let her do her worst, and I am very much mistaken if she do not find that F.O. trumps her tricks for her."

The two set out together for the durbar, Captain Jones's equanimity being by no means restored by Mr Harcourt's communications. The Resident looked admiringly at his companion, envying him his coolness; and indeed Mr Harcourt would not have been put about if he had entered the presence of the Great Mogul in the palmiest days of the Delhi empire. He sucked at his cigar until he was at the very door of the palace, where they were received with great ceremony by Taptee Rao and Faizul Khan, who marshalled them to the durbar room. Here the Begum, a shapeless mass of silks and embroidery, showing neither features nor figure, was crouching upon a mass of velvet cushions. The officers made their salaams and took their seats, while the Residency *Munshi* read over Captain Jones's credentials in Persian for the edification of the Princess. Harcourt, who was used to Oriental fashions, squatted cosily among his cushions and began to stare nonchalantly about him. Poor Jones, who had never sat upon anything but a chair or a regimental saddle, had much ado to arrange his long legs in a position at once easy and dignified; and he shifted about painfully all the time the Munshi was drawling over the despatch. Faizul Khan marked his awkwardness, and a sneer which he scarcely took pains to conceal crossed his haughty face. But it did not escape the Resident, whose eyes were wandering uneasily about the room; and remembering Harcourt's advice, he looked at Faizul Khan with a steady scowl which evidently discomposed the Pundrapore commandant. Taptee Rao saw his byplay, and enjoyed the discomfiture of his rival, making a mental resolution to turn the incident into account.

At the conclusion of the Munshi's prelection, Captain Jones, by Mr Harcourt's direction, placed a *nuzzar*, or present of a few gold coins, in the Begum's hand, who muttered something in Persian of her respect for the British Government and her happiness to receive the distinguished Sahib who had been sent to shed light upon her court by his presence. The Resident read a few sentences in Persian from a paper which Mr Harcourt's forethought had caused to be pinned to the inside of his cocked-hat, assuring the Princess of the friendship of Government and guaranteeing the liberties and independence of Pundrapore. The ceremony was then virtually at an end, as the attendants served the company with *attar* and *pan*; and then ensued that awkward pause which always precedes the end of an Indian visit. Captain Jones waited for the Begum's permission to go, and the Begum was on thorns until Captain Jones would take his departure. At last Harcourt's winks and nods admonished his chief to break up the meeting, and he asked her Highness's permission to depart, which was graciously granted. The mass of silks then moved from the room, and the two officers took their departure, attended by old Taptee Rao, who was all bows and smiles for the new Resident, whose arrival, he declared, "was welcome as a rain-cloud in the thirsty month of Jeth."

"*Anglicè*, welcome as a wet blanket," muttered Harcourt, *sotto voce*; adding aloud, "Here comes that amiable individual, Faizul Khan, doing his visage the gross injustice of trying to make it look agreeable and benevolent; what can be in the wind now? 'O grandmamma, what great eyes you have got!' 'The better to see you, my sweet little pet.' Upon which of us little Red Riding Hoods would the wolf like to sup?"

Faizul Khan heard the conclusion of Mr Harcourt's remarks without understanding them in the least, although he was well acquainted with English. "Captain Sahib," he said, "her Highness has sent me to beg that you will allow her to present to your Honour her child, the young Nawab. Her Highness awaits you in the *Dewan-i-khas* of the palace."

The *Dewan-i-khas*, or public drawing-room, was a large bare-looking apartment. Its furniture presented a curious mixture of European civilisation with Oriental barbarism. Veneered cane-bottomed chairs stood side by side with rich velvet couches. The walls were hung with tawdry Parisian prints of questionable delicacy, interspersed with the weapons which the late Nawab had borne when he rode with Holkar and Ameer Khan; and the floor was bare, with the exception of a patch in the middle covered by a rich Persian carpet of gaudy colours. Captain Jones had never set his foot in a Begum's drawing-room before, and he stood wondering at the curious pictures and the strange furniture, until he heard a rustle behind him, and the Begum entered carrying her son in her arms. Her figure, no longer concealed beneath a mass of drapery, was shown to its full advantage by the simple white robe wound gracefully round her body; and a *chudder*, or mantle of airy muslin—called 'running water' from the fineness of its texture—was thrown carelessly over her head and shoulders, its spotless whiteness setting off the raven lustre of her luxuriant hair. Her face was fair—singularly fair for an Oriental; her features were small and delicately chiselled; and her eyes, the chief criterion of a native beauty, were large, lustrous, fawn-like and shaded by exquisitely pencilled lashes. The little head was proudly carried upon a lithe and shapely neck, and her hands were tiny and of delicate whiteness. The little Nawab had taken after his father rather than his beautiful mother, for his face was black and swarthy and his neck thick as that of a bull-calf. Captain Jones stood rapt in admiration of the Princess, and wondering how it was possible that so fair a creature could be as ruthless as Harcourt had represented her. Before he could acknowledge her presence, even by a bow, the Begum had thrown herself at the feet of the astonished officer and held up her hands in an attitude of pathetic supplication.

"O Sahib!" she cried, "Allah has indeed been good to Pundrapore in sending you here to protect me and my helpless child. I have heard so much of your honour and valour that we can sleep sound under your protection. Graciously accept me and my son as the humblest of your slaves."

The Princess spoke English well; probably her intercourse with Captain Grantley had aided her to acquire this somewhat unusual branch of an Eastern lady's education.

"Madam, I mean your Highness, I cannot bear to see you in this posture," stammered Jones, who devoutly wished that he had brought Harcourt with him; "I entreat you to rise and be seated. You may ever command my services in anything that relates to yourself or your territories, so far as consists with my duty to Government."

He took the Begum's hand and led her to a seat. "How fortunate I am, Captain Sahib, in having you sent here to aid me, a poor weak woman, in ruling this troublesome country!" said the Begum, turning her eyes full upon Jones with a look of soft blandishment. "Lord Blitzen Sahib, when at Pundrapore, said that your bravery was like that of Jamshid and your justice renowned as King Naushirvan's."

"The devil he did," thought Jones. "It was very good of Sir George to say so, but how on earth could he have known it! He must have watched my career very closely to have such an intimate knowledge of me."

"I have many enemies, Sahib," continued the Begum. "They wish to take away the *musnud* from me and my son, and they tell lies of us to the Lord Sahib at Calcutta. How can I, a helpless widow, stand up against the words of the *Sahib log* (Englishmen)? But you will assist me; say that you will assist me! Oh protector of the poor, lay your hand upon the child's head and be a father to him!"

Captain Jones, though much disconcerted by the idea of so close a relationship, did as he was requested, and promised that he would do his best to remove any misunderstanding between her Highness and the Government. The beauty and apparent helplessness of the Begum were making a considerable impression upon Jones's heart, and he mentally vowed that he would be her devoted knight and champion.

"You will not heed what Harcourt Sahib may say to you. He is deceived by Taptee Rao, my late lord's wicked minister, who hates me, and has sworn to take my life. He wishes to be regent himself. But now I may rely upon your honour and defy him."

Jones again assured her Highness of his disposition to assist her; and begging permission to take his leave, he bowed himself out of the room, the Princess saluting him with profound salaams and casting tender glances after him so long as he was in sight. Scarcely had the doors closed after the Resident, when the Begum sprang to her feet, set down the child upon the floor with a bump that made him squall lustily, and ran to the window overlooking the courtyard, where Captain Jones was already getting on horseback.

"Why have they sent that father of asses here?" she muttered in her native language, her little hands passionately clenched and her eyes sparkling with rage. "Can the English Sircar have meant to throw dirt upon me by sending an unknown fool to reside at my court? Well, well, upon their own heads be the issue. I shall turn their insult to my own advantage, and *when the time comes* they will miss Jones Sahib less than a better officer." A smile of diabolical significance passed over the Begum's face as she said this, which boded no good to the officer who had just ridden out of the palace courtyard.

"It is utterly impossible that so lovely a woman can be so bad as they call her," soliloquised Jones, as he rode through the bazaar towards the Residency. "Harcourt must be mistaken, and I should not be surprised if that old villain Taptee Rao was at the bottom of all the slanders that have been raised upon her Highness; however, he won't deceive *me*. Who on earth could have believed that old Blitzen would have given me such a good character to the Begum? Though rough and *brusque* in his manners, Sir George is an officer of great penetration—of remarkable penetration, in fact—and he knows the service from head to tail, else he could not have known that *I* was the right man for Pundrapore. I think I ought to write and thank him for his good opinion."

And Captain Jones did write a most grateful letter to Sir George Blitzen, in which he returned his humble thanks for the favourable opinion his Excellency had expressed of him to the Begum, and concluded by saying that he should ever strive to perform his duty so as to merit the continuance of his Excellency's approbation.

Sir George read this epistle with a puzzled look, and then after a minute's reflection burst forth into a prolonged whistle. "See here, Springer!" he cried, tossing over the letter to his secretary. "The infernal jade has got that damned booby in her toils already. I never said a word about him. However, it's all right. Just give a hint to the Quartermaster-General to see that the Pundrapore routes are correctly laid down in the road-book, for if troops aren't wanted there before the *chota bursat* (early rains), my name isn't George Blitzen." And the gallant warrior expressed his satisfaction at the posture of affairs by a volley of oaths which need not be reproduced here.

III.

Sir George Blitzen proved, however, a false prophet, for time passed on and no disturbance occurred in the Pundrapore territories. No event had yet transpired to put the Resident upon his mettle, and, fortunately for himself, his intercourse with the Begum had not passed the bounds of diplomatic routine. Her Highness professed the utmost respect for Captain Jones's opinion, and consulted him upon everything in which she was *not* seriously interested. Jones soon began to take great credit to himself for the change he had produced in the Begum, and to boast that by a little judicious diplomacy he had transformed Pundrapore from a hotbed of sedition into one of the most loyal States in India.

"Wait a bit," said Harcourt; "don't halloo until you're out of the jungle. I like this quietness worse than her old tantrums. Although I don't see her cards, I'll give you twenty to one in gold mohurs that she is up to some preciously deep mischief all this time. It's a pity that you aren't friends with Taptee Rao nowadays, for he is the man that would be most likely to give us a tip upon the event."

But even Mr Harcourt's scepticism was somewhat staggered when the Begum one day placed in the hands of the Resident a proposal which had been made to her by the Rajah of Thagabad, a petty princeling whose lands abutted on the Pundrapore territory. The Rajah had offered his services to the Pundrapore State in case of a rising against the British, and pledged himself to bring five hundred men to the Begum's banner, provided a grant of lands which his family had formerly enjoyed in her Highness's territory were again confirmed to him. It was, after all, a cheap demonstration of loyalty upon the Begum's part, for she knew well that the Rajah could not put fifty men in the field. She had not forgotten, either, that in a recent dispute about the marches, the Rajah had designated her by a name unpleasant to the ears of woman; and lastly, she held at that very moment, under the signature and seal of the Lion of the Punjab, a grant of the Rajah's own lands and principality. So the Rajah was relieved of the care of his property, and requested to reside in the holy city of Benares, while the Begum received a letter of thanks for her loyalty written by the Governor-General's own hand. Her Highness gave a malicious little laugh as she crumpled up his lordship's letter, and read the punishment which had befallen her enemy of Thagabad; but she professed herself to Captain Jones to be overjoyed beyond measure at the honour which his Excellency had done her.

Captain Jones sat upon his verandah on a hot September evening, smoking a cheroot and reading a Calcutta newspaper. Harcourt was away upon privilege leave, playing havoc among tigers in Dehra Dhoon, or flirting with the languid belles of Landour and Mussoorie. There was not much news in the Calcutta journal. He read of a horrid murder in Lall Bazaar, and how the police had failed to find the perpetrator. There was a column and a half of a lecture upon "Female Education" by Baboo Bunkum Chunder Chintamony, whose own wives and daughters could not have read their *ka kha, ga gha* (the Bengalee alphabet), to have saved them from the burning ghat. And there was another address upon "Pure Theism, the only True Religion," delivered before the Cossitollah Literary Association by Baboo Jotendro Churn Chatterjee, who, a few days before, had given a thousand rupees to buy new ornaments for the family idol at Guddhapore. There was, of course, an account of another squabble among the justices, in which Commissioner Bacon, the chairman, had received the lie direct from Mr Benediction Williams, and had retorted by calling his opponent "a beggar on horseback"; but it had with some difficulty been adjusted without the intervention of fisticuffs. This was no novelty, and Jones turned languidly away to the editorial columns, where a leader announced that the Punjab was in a state bordering upon insurrection, and called upon the Government to take immediate steps for insuring the safety of the country.

It was too true. The old Lion of Lahore had been gathered to his fathers, and his sons and grandson, who inherited neither his valour nor his prudence, rapidly followed him; until the sceptre of the Khalsa came at last into the boyish hands of Dhuleep Singh, the last prince of the Punjab. His mother, who now became the animating spirit of the Lahore Court, entertained a bitter hatred towards the British; and she was at this time the centre of a widely spread conspiracy, which had for its object the expulsion of the English forces from at least the upper provinces of Hindostan. Of this conspiracy the Pundrapore Begum was a most active member, and constant communication was kept up between the two durbars. And upon this very evening, while Captain Jones was quietly smoking his cheroot, her Highness was reading the following missive which a Sikh soldier, disguised as a mendicant, had just brought her:—

"To the beautiful among women, excelling in wisdom and of manlike courage, Murwarid, Begum of Pundrapore—Receive our wishes for your prosperity, and know that all our preparations are made for crossing the river, and the thirst of the Khalsa can only be sloked by a deep draught of English blood. You are entreated, when this reaches you, to take the field. What need of more? Prayers for the prosperity of the reign. The communication of the lowly slave, Gulloo, Maharanee of Lahore."

The Begum well knew the meaning of this missive, which was written in a cipher intelligible only to the conspirators. All their plans had been arranged beforehand, and now the signal of insurrection was given. Impatient as the Begum had been for revolt, she felt a hesitation to engage with the paramount power now that the time had arrived, and an ominous distrust of the issue. But it was too late to draw back. Lall Singh was by this time advancing upon the Sutledge, and the success of his forces must depend in a great measure upon her co-operation.

The Begum was for many hours closeted with Faizul Khan and a few of the most trusted officers of the Court. In a short time messengers were getting to horse and galloping over the territory, commanding the attendance of all the Mohammedan chieftains, with their vassals. There was a considerable force always kept under arms within the State, upon pretence that troops were necessary to repress the haughty Rajpoot landholders, who could but ill brook Mussulman rule. Of this force both the Resident and Government were perfectly aware; but beyond keeping a keen eye upon its movements they did not interfere further. A small British force was stationed at Malariabad, near the Pundrapore frontier, where such of the officers as were not suffering from the climate of that salubrious station dispensed a lavish hospitality and organised monster sporting excursions into the thick Pundrapore jungles; and over the movements of the Malariabad garrison the Resident had a discretionary power, should circumstances render their services necessary to him.

Captain Jones had despatched his dinner, and was sitting with open jacket and unbuckled waist-belt over a cheroot and a glass of iced brandy-and-soda, when a message was brought from the Begum, begging his instant attendance, upon a matter of importance. "What on earth does she want, I wonder?" growled Jones, reluctantly fastening his belt and taking up his helmet and sword; "nothing that wouldn't have kept until to-morrow, I fancy. Perhaps the little Nawab has got a colic from eating too many mangoes; or some zemindar has refused to pay his rent, and the Begum wants my sanction to send a lot of troopers to recover the arrears. Wonderfully simple and beautiful is the law of distraint here in Pundrapore."

And so Jones, attended only by a single orderly, walked briskly to the palace, and was shown up into a room that had been the *duftur khana*, or business-room, of the late Nawab. The Begum had not yet made her appearance, but the little Prince, who had taken a great fancy for Jones, came running into the room and clasped him by the knees.

"*Tulwar do hum ko, Capitan Sahib*" (Give me your sword, Captain), cried the child; and the boy was soon astride of the Captain's long cavalry sword and galloping wildly about the room.

While Jones stood watching the child's gambols, Faizul Khan, with half a dozen Pathan troopers, came suddenly behind and threw themselves upon him. An unequal struggle took place, and in a few minutes the Resident was lying on the ground, bound hand and foot, while Faizul Khan stood over him, with a drawn sabre pointed at his breast, threatening to slay him if he uttered a single word.

"*Mat maro Capitan Sahib, mat maro!*" (Don't beat the Captain, don't beat him), cried the little Nawab, as, with tears in his eyes, he dragged the Resident's sword towards Faizul Khan and endeavoured to strike down the Pathan's sabre.

"Take away the boy," cried Faizul Khan hoarsely, "and secure the doors and windows. Place a sentry at each door, and let them stab the prisoner if he speaks above his breath. Make ready my horse there," he cried, as he clanked out of the room.

Jones was now left alone, lying upon the floor, and the doors were locked upon the outside. He was stupefied by the turn affairs had taken, and his mind was perfectly unable to suggest any cause for the attack which had just been made upon him. Two things were, however, apparent: that his life was in serious danger, and that there was a political disturbance about to take place. But the Begum! what of her? Had he been seized by her consent, or was Faizul Khan the leader of the insurrection, and the Princess herself also a prisoner? So sudden had been the outbreak that he could scarcely convince himself of its reality. It must be the aged and indigestible fowl that he had eaten at dinner three-quarters of an hour before, or the brandy-pawnee ; and it would all pass away in a headache to-morrow morning. But no ; the cords on his wrists and ankles were no nightmare phantasm, and the hard floor beneath him was a sensible reality. Brief time had, however, been given him to meditate upon his situation when the Begum hastily entered the room, attended by two armed Sirdars. Her Highness seemed to have undergone a complete transformation since Jones had last seen her. She was no longer the meek and humble widow, who had boasted of her helplessness, and had been too timorous to do anything upon her own responsibility without consulting the Resident. Her delicate features, distorted by passion, and her flashing eyes, now showed how well she merited the title of Tigress of Pundrapore. She carried a naked dagger in one hand and a sheet of paper in the other.

"You are in my power, Captain Sahib," she said coldly; "listen now to what I have to say. In a few weeks the chiefs and princes of Hindostan will have beaten the British beyond the Carumnassa, and not an Englishman will be left in the upper provinces except as a prisoner. I might kill you just now, but I prefer to spare you ; that is, provided you will purchase your life by obeying my commands."

"My life is in your hands, and you may do with it as you please," said Jones, raising himself on his elbow and looking the Begum boldly in the face ; "but never will I consent to purchase it at the expense of either duty or honour. I warn your Highness of the dangerous game you are playing—a game that can only end in the destruction of yourself and your principality ; for the British power is like the ten heads of your demon Ravuna, which grow on again as fast as they are cut off."

"I came not here to ask your advice," said the Begum haughtily, "but to give you my orders. Here is paper ; on that table are pens and ink. Write to the commandant Sahib at Malariabad to draw off his troops to Agra, to join the division there which is about to march to the Punjab to repel the Sikhs. Do this, and I swear by the Koran that your life shall be safe. Refuse, and you die before midnight."

"Never," said poor Jones, with a groan: "do your worst, but I'll never disgrace my commission by such an act."

"Slave!" cried the Begum in a fury as she flashed the dagger above her head, "shall I have to torture you into obedience? I know not what prevents me from plunging this into your heart. Hearken, Jones Sahib; it is your last chance. I give you half an hour to consider; and if you refuse on my return, I shall put you to death with such tortures as never Englishman yet suffered. Think well what awaits you before you make up your mind."

So the Begum and her attendants left the room, leaving Jones again to his solitary thoughts. They were far from pleasant. Death stared him in the face, for he would never save himself by complying with the Begum's commands. Though by no means possessed of a vigorous intellect, Jones had plenty of courage, and would have scorned to disgrace the British service. He tried to think seriously of his latter end, but his thoughts strayed to the Begum, to the rebellion in the Punjab, to what they would say at Government House when they heard of his murder, and to a hundred other subjects wholly irrelevant to the dread change that was approaching. He began a prayer, but long before he had got to the end of it he found himself at his old occupation of epitaph-making, composing an inscription for a memorial which Government would erect over his slaughtered remains. He felt he could almost die in peace if he might leave behind him a suitable design for a monument; but, alas! his wrists were tied, and the hour of his death was at hand. He rolled over upon his other side, and again attempted to compose himself for prayer. "Hist, Sahib," was whispered close beside him ; and rolling round again, Jones saw by the light of the lamp that swung from the ceiling, the round bald head and smooth puffy cheeks of old Taptee Rao protruding from the floor; "write, Sahib, write, and trust to Taptee. I faithful slave of Company Bahadoor. I shall save the Resident Sahib and turn the plots of the Begum *ulta pulta* (upside down). She very clever woman the Begum, but Taptee Rao very more clever. Write, Sahib, and give me your seal-ring."

"Can I trust him?" thought Jones; "or is this a new artifice of the Begum's? She hates him, and he has as much to fear as I have. It is a forlorn hope to grasp at it."

"Quick, Sahib, quick! Begum come back directly. Give me ring, and I send for sepoys to Malariabad. I offer reward to all who desert the Begum, and I surround the palace before daybreak and take the Begum prisoner. May dogs devour her!" added Taptee, revenge lighting up his generally stolid countenance. Jones could only reply by rolling round and turning his back, behind which his hands were bound, towards Taptee. The Minister slipped off the ring and said, "Do as Begum bids you, Sahib; make believe to write. I tell the commandant Sahib all beforehand. I come back directly; they not hurt a hair of your head, Sahib." And Taptee disappeared with a reassuring wink towards the Resident. Five minutes after, two horsemen had started for Malariabad, a distance of five-and-twenty miles, carrying intelligence of the rebellion and commanding the instant despatch of a force to Pundrapore.

When the Begum returned, she found Jones sulkily resigned to her wishes. "Will you write, Jones Sahib?" she cried, with a menacing flourish of her dagger; "or will you try the fare which the Begum of Pundrapore has prepared for her English guest?"

"I take these men to witness," said Jones in Hindustanee, avoiding a direct answer, "that I act under compulsion and against my own free will."

A contemptuous smile curled the Begum's lips. "It is well," she said; "life is sweet. Loose his hands and give him the pen and ink; and if he dares to make the slightest struggle, stab him to the heart."

Jones, with a sheet of paper upon his knee, wrote a formal order to the colonel commanding at Malariabad, directing him to join his division at Agra with all the garrison, in consequence of an outbreak in the Punjab, of which he, the Resident, had just received information from Government. When he had finished, the Begum took the letter and narrowly examined it, as if she would convince herself that no private communication had been conveyed under cover of the official message.

"Good, Sahib," she said; "for the present your life is spared, but if within two hours after he receives this the commandant Sahib does not march for Agra, I shall have you blown from the biggest gun in Pundrapore."

The attendants again bound Jones's hands and left him, securing the doors and placing sentries on the outside as before. "After all, then, it is only a brief reprieve," thought Jones, "for she will of course come down on me as soon as she hears that the troops are marching to attack her. Heavens! what a booby I have been to allow myself to be deceived by that woman."

Jones lay keeping his eyes anxiously fixed upon the spot where Taptee Rao had formerly appeared. A vision of angels or cherubim would have been less welcome at that moment than Taptee's bullet-head. He had not long to wait. A piece of matting began to heave, a portion of the floor was cautiously raised, and Taptee peered warily into the room.

"All right, Sahib," he whispered; "soldiers come directly, and I send for Doorga Singh with three hundred horsemen, all Hindoos who faithful to Company's salt. Malariabad sepoys be here before morning, and then the Begum's *raj* is done, gone, finished."

Nothing but the close proximity of the sentries, and their critical position, could have prevented Taptee from relieving his exuberant feelings by a triumphant dance over the approaching downfall of his enemy. He drew himself up through the aperture, and, taking a knife from his girdle, severed the cords that confined the Resident. "You must go from palace, Sahib," he said; "go along Malariabad road, and stay in old pagoda till I come." Jones went first through the trap-door into the room beneath, and Taptee followed, carefully arranging the flooring and mats so that the secret of the Resident's escape might remain a mystery. They found themselves in Taptee's private room, and the trap-door may perhaps serve to explain the extraordinary acquaintance which the Minister possessed with all his late master's secrets.

Taptee gave Jones a sabre and pistols, and, letting him out by a private gate, directed him to the pagoda, where the Resident was to wait for his arrival.

A grand council had been summoned for one o'clock in the palace hall, in which the Begum was to declare her intention of joining the Sikhs, and the nobles were to proclaim her sole ruler of Pundrapore during her lifetime. Her Highness had been closeted with Faizul Khan and other Sirdars, devising ways and means for equipping a large force which was to be instantly despatched to the Lahore army. The point of greatest importance that still remained to be settled was the fidelity of Taptee Rao. Faizul Khan, who wanted his place, volunteered to murder him without further delay; but the Begum knew the influence which the Minister possessed among the Hindoo chiefs and Brahmins of Pundrapore, and resolved if possible to obtain his assistance. Taptee entered the hall where several chiefs were already assembled, with a face of smiling innocence, making careless inquiries why the council had been summoned. His jocular manner formed a singular contrast to the anxious and restless demeanour of the other councillors, who stared aghast at

Taptee's reckless appearance and turned away impatiently from his broad jokes. At last the Begum entered the hall, attended by Faizul Khan and half a score of Sirdars. Without preface, her Highness explained the state of affairs, and eloquently urged the nobles to take up arms for their country and for religion. She had, she said, at the earnest request of her subjects, consented to rule over them so long as she lived; and she now begged the council to show its confidence by committing to her the sole direction of the expedition which was to be sent to the Punjab. Loud cries of "*Din! din!*" (for the Faith, for the Faith) showed that the enthusiasm of the Mohammedan chiefs had been aroused; and the Begum, smiling graciously, continued, "But first we must know who are our friends and who our foes. Taptee Rao, you have heard our proposals; will you, who have eaten our bread and our salt, turn against your rightful ruler and take part with the infidel English against your country?"

"Gracious Queen!" said Taptee, sidling forward with a bland visage, "Asylum of the Universe and Protector of the Poor, if my humble services can in any wise be acceptable, deign to cast thine august eyes with favour upon the humblest of thy slaves."

"I commend your fidelity," said the Begum. "Retain your present post in our court, and when the British are driven from the country we shall find some means of rewarding you!"

Taptee clasped his hands in an ecstasy of gratitude. "Most mighty sovereign," he said, "if your slave might be permitted to speak, he would say that in three hours he will bring his kinsman, Doorga Singh, with three hundred troopers, to your Highness's standard."

The Begum uttered an exclamation of joy. Doorga Singh was a haughty Hindoo noble with whom she had been long at feud, and she had never dared to expect assistance from him.

"Taptee Rao," she cried, "the *raj* of Thagabad is yours from this day, for the Lahore durbar has gifted it to me. Continue as you have begun, and your reward shall be great beyond your conception."

Faizul Khan ground his teeth and muttered an oath, while Taptee again prostrated himself before the Begum, overpowered by his grateful feelings. The wily Princess had not abated any of her hatred to the Minister, but she knew how important it was at so critical a period to appear generous and conciliatory to her Hindoo subjects. Taptee begged her Highness to allow him to depart for a space that he might send the necessary instructions to his kinsman, Doorga Singh; and he waddled out of the room, pausing every second to invoke a blessing upon the head of his benefactress and a prayer for the prosperity of her reign.

As soon as he quitted the hall, Taptee hurried off to his room, and hastily concealing a small bag of precious stones beneath his clothes, and catching up a sword, he hurried off to the old pagoda to join the Resident. He found Captain Jones pacing up and down the ruins in a fever of anxiety. Every few minutes the stillness was broken by the clatter of hoofs, as messengers dashed off with intelligence of the revolt. What delayed the troops from Malariabad? surely they ought to have been here before this time. But Malariabad was a good five-and-twenty miles off, and Taptee Rao's messenger would have little more than reached the cantonments. He felt relieved when Taptee joined him, and the two waited in the ruins, looking out anxiously towards the palace, where lights flitting about from window to window told of the bustle that was going on inside.

The council was not yet broken up. The Begum, assisted by Faizul Khan, received from the various chiefs the strength of the forces they could bring to the Pundrapore standard, and by bribes and lavish promises settled rival claims to command. Still no troops had arrived, and her Highness ever cast an anxious look towards the door for the return of Taptee Rao and his promised auxiliaries. The Begum started as she noticed a Sikh sowar, his dust-coloured uniform bespattered with mud and his blue turban torn by riding through the jungles, make his way into the hall, and with little ceremony elbow a road through the excited crowd of Mohammedan chiefs, who were boasting loudly of the feats which they were to perform in the coming campaign. With a rough salaam he handed a note to the Begum and fell back among the throng.

The note ran thus, after the usual compliments :—

"The Sirdar Juwaher Singh, our trusted vizier, has been slain by traitors before our eyes. The 'drum of religion' is for the present silenced. You are entreated to take no steps until you hear further from us. May the hour of our deliverance be at hand.—GULLOO."

The Begum, as she read the letter, drew a long breath and looked down upon the scene before her. There they were, everyone clamouring for battle; the nobles with drawn swords vaunting their bravery or disputing for precedence; Moulvies bustling about and stimulating the doubtful to war against the English *Kaffirs;* and there in a corner stood Faizul Khan, surrounded by a group of chiefs, with whose assistance he was laying down a plan of the morrow's march. And now the game was all up. She had cast the die, only to be beaten at the first throw. What was to be done? Should she at once tell the chiefs whom she had duped and yield herself a victim to their fury, or wait rather until General Linstock came to carry her off as a prisoner to Benares or Chunar? Then there was the Resident—what was to be done with him? Should she give him his liberty, and make him an intercessor for her with the Governor-General, or slay him on the spot as an atonement to her baffled ambition? A thought struck her; why should not she escape to the Punjab with a few trusty followers, and take with her the Resident as an offering to the Sikh chiefs? He would at all events be useful as a hostage.

"Faizul Khan," she cried, "bring down the prisoner. I would learn from him the strength of the garrisons between this and Lahore."

Faizal Khan readily departed, delighted at the opportunity afforded him of annoying his enemy Captain Jones. Scarcely had he left the hall when the tramp of a body of horse was heard, and attendants came running to announce the arrival of Doorga Singh and his troopers. The Begum's face became yet more ashy pale. "Fresh victims," she muttered; "but why should I regret them? they are only Hindoo dogs. Would that no blood of the Faithful may rest upon my head. Greet the leaders from us," she said aloud, "and invite them into our presence."

Doorga Singh came in, surrounded by a throng of Hindoo chieftains. He was a tall thin Mahratta, whose broad shoulders and long arms indicated great personal strength. He was armed with sword and shield, and bore the long Mahratta spear in his right hand. The Mohammedan chiefs twirled their moustaches, and looked with scarcely dissembled disgust upon the group of infidels as they pushed through the throng to the Begum's presence.

No reverence did Doorga Singh make to her Highness, and the Begum sat pale and almost shivering, waiting for an explanation of his strange demeanour; but before she could summon courage to speak, the Hindoos parted, and forward stepped the Resident with Taptee Rao hard at his heels.

"*Khiyānat, Khiyānat!*" ("Treachery, treachery!") shrieked the Begum, springing from her seat as the truth flashed upon her mind. "Faizul Khan, Abdul Ruhman, down with these Hindoo dogs! slay them for sons of burned fathers!"

"Hold!" cried Captain Jones before a man could stir, "your Highness is entirely in our hands, and resistance is useless. The palace is filled with Mahratta troopers, and a large British force is close to the city. Resistance is worse than madness. Surrender, your Highness, and you, chiefs and sirdars, lay down your arms and be assured that all possible leniency will be shown to your fault by Government."

Faizul Khan here came rushing in in alarm. "Asylum of the Universe," he cried, "the prisoner——" but seeing the aspect of affairs, he drew his sword and sprang upon the Resident. Doorga Singh received the Pathan upon the point of his spear, and in an instant the wretched man lay writhing in the death-struggle at the foot of the *musnud*. A *mêlée* immediately ensued. Doorga Singh, shouting the Mahratta war-cry, "*Hur, hur Mahadeo!*" threw away his spear and rushed sword in hand upon the Mohammedans. Mahrattas came crowding into the hall, and, wielding their long spears over the heads of the combatants, galled the Mussulmans, and made them an easy prey to those with whom they were engaged. The Resident stood by the Begum shouting to the Mahrattas to spare all who laid down their arms, but his words were unheeded in the heat of the conflict. In a few minutes the rebels were all overpowered or slain, and the Pundrapore rebellion was at an end. As for the Begum, she had tried to stab herself with her dagger, but Jones and Taptee had snatched it from her hand. She now sat looking upon the scene, like a tigress that has been disappointed in her prey. "Take me away, Captain Sahib; take me away," was all that she could utter, in a voice so husky as to be almost inaudible; and away she was led, Taptee taking care that her prison should be more secure than the one she had provided for the Resident.

Morning was beginning to glint through the hall windows, revealing Jones upon the Pundrapore *musnud* refreshing himself with pale ale and cold pie which a servant had fetched from the Residency. By him squatted Taptee, who, regardless that the sacrilegious Sahib was eating the sacred flesh of kine, was holding an animated discussion with him on the future management of Pundrapore. At a respectful distance lay or squatted Doorga Singh and his officers, sleeping or smoking their *hookhas ;* and close by them were the prisoners bound hand and foot, while the corpses of the slain were being carried from the hall. The noise of cavalry interrupted Taptee's confidences, and Colonel Beaton, of Beaton's Horse, the commandant of Malariabad, came rattling into the room.

"Why, damn it, Jones, you don't mean to say that it is all over ?" cried he pettishly, as he looked round at the prisoners. "Couldn't you have kept them going until we came up ? It's what I call doing the shabby thing to take fellows off their *charpoys* (beds) at one o'clock in the morning for nothing, and we have nearly blown every horse in the regiment with the gallop."

Jones rapidly explained the events that had occurred during the night, and told Colonel Beaton that it might still be necessary to scour the state to suppress any chief that had taken arms by the Begum's orders.

"All right !" cried Beaton eagerly, "we may have some sport yet. Let the men breathe their horses, Morris, and let them sound to saddle in an hour and a half *tik* (exactly). I wonder if there is anything edible to be had here for *chota hazree* (early breakfast) ? And I say, Jones, I'll tell you what I shall do for you. I'll leave you Penninck, who writes for the 'Peon.' He is a dab at doing reports, and will make up a beautiful story to tell the Government. Besides, the little beast has no more seat than a wool-pack, and would be always tumbling off if we came to any stiff riding."

And so when Colonel Beaton and his officers had done justice to a nondescript though plenteous meal, they galloped off to hunt for rebels, leaving Cornet Penninck on special duty at the Residency.

IV.

The Pundrapore insurrection caused a great sensation in Calcutta. Would Government annex the territory? Some said that Sir George Blitzen was already marching to Pundrapore at the head of two divisions of all arms of the service to depose the Begum and annex the state. Others were certain that the Governor-General would do nothing of the kind; that the present crisis demanded conciliatory measures; and that the Begum would be well 'wigged' and reinstated in the Regency. Mr Waspbite, the Under-Secretary at the Foreign Office, was besieged with inquiries at his club in Chowringhee, until even *his* amiable temper was exhausted, and he said, "Damn the Pundwapoah Wesidency. If you want to know you should ask the Govenah-Genewal."

The press likewise had its say upon the subject. 'The Padrepore Monitor and Weekly Evangelist' reminded its readers how often in the course of the previous ten years it had constantly predicted that affairs at Pundrapore would turn out exactly as they had happened. The editor conjured the Governor-General to do his duty and annex the principality, undeterred by the howls of native opinion and regardless of the ignorant and interested views of English statesmen. "With an able British officer, such as Mr Caird, the energetic Magistrate of Cholerapore, at the head of the administration, and an efficient educational staff under the Rev. Fungus M'Bain, the eminent Free Church Missionary, as Director of Public Instruction, upon a salary of not less than Rs. 700 per mensem, with a free bungalow, a new and happier era would soon dawn upon the benighted regions of Pundrapore. The importance of the last-named appointment cannot be too strongly impressed upon his Excellency's consideration," &c., &c.

The 'Peon' scarcely expressed an opinion, but, as might

have been expected, dwelt at length upon the valuable services which Cornet P. R. Penninck, of Beaton's Horse, had rendered in restoring order at the Residency and the Palace, an account of which occupied one and a half columns of leaded type. The 'John Bull' bluntly said that the Government ought to do justice. "Visiting with a fitting punishment the Begum and her fellow-conspirators, but why should an innocent child suffer for the misconduct of his guardian? Let us train the young Nawab to be a wise and judicious ruler, and place an experienced officer in charge of the state during his Highness's minority. In this manner we shall best refute the slanderous writers who would attribute to the Company's government an insatiable lust for territory. The name of Lieutenant-Colonel Thomas Robinson, Political Agent of Chotasahebpore, must of course occur to everyone who has bestowed a serious thought upon the guardianship of the young Nawab and the future management of the Pundrapore state," &c., &c.

When the news of the Pundrapore insurrection reached Government House, a special meeting of the Executive Council was forthwith summoned. The members met in the evening in the old Council Chamber to determine the destiny of Pundrapore. If the *genius loci* could have prevailed, the independence of Pundrapore would have stood but a sober chance, for around them upon the walls hung the portraits of the statesmen and warriors who had done most to extend the British power in India. There was Clive, who gave Bengal, Behar and Orissa to the Company's territories; Wellesley, the conqueror of Mysore, the Carnatic and Maharashtra; with Hastings, Cornwallis, Eyre Coote and Minto. But the golden age of annexation was past, and the pagoda-tree was fast falling into the sere and yellow leaf. There was a strong party in Parliament hostile to the Company, who never ceased to denounce each fresh extension of territory as another instance of arbitrary rapacity, seizing eagerly upon every new aggression as a ground for renewing the attack; and so the Calcutta statesmen were compelled to go cautiously to work in the case of Pundrapore.

"It appears to me, gentlemen," said the Governor-General during that little standing confabulation which always preceded the formal sitting, and in which the real business of the meeting was generally settled—"it appears to me that we have no real ground for proceeding to extremities against the state. The Nawab is but a child, and it would be hardly fair to make a minor answerable for the misdeeds of his guardian."

"All owing to that fellow Jones," growled the Honourable Mr Elchey, who, having been Resident at the Court of Cooch Behar, claimed a leading voice in all diplomatic business. "If he had but kept out of the way and given them rope enough, the whole state would have been up, and then there would have been a good excuse for annexation. But the political department is going to the devil. When I was resident at Cooch Behar, your Excellency, there was an old Thakoor who had got a *ta' allukae zabardasti*, and the Government wanted——"

"But in this case, Mr Elchey, I don't think any blame can attach to the Political officer," said the Governor-General, unceremoniously interrupting the ex-diplomatist, whose reminiscences of Cooch Behar were notoriously prosy and so full of Hindustani phrases as to be intelligible only to a member of the Revenue Board. "Captain Jones appears to have acted as judiciously as the circumstances admitted, and his report is really an admirably written document, quite different from anything that we have had before from Pundrapore. Besides we shall have the Punjab soon upon our hands, and can easily forgo the pleasure, for the present, of gathering Pundrapore under the Company's wing."

"What was that mystery about Captain Jones's appointment, my Lord?" asked Mr Elchey; "everybody said there was some special reason for his selection that has never come before the Council? None of the members, to my certain knowledge, ever heard the man's name before."

"Really, Mr Elchey, you have no more reason to complain than I have. Sir George Blitzen had been down in Pundrapore inquiring into Grantley's management, or rather mismanagement, and his Excellency reported so strongly in favour of Grantley's withdrawal that I had him at once transferred to Kaifiabad; and I wrote to Sir George begging him to recommend one of his best officers for the vacancy, for it was necessary in the unsettled condition of Pundrapore that the Resident should be a military man. He recommended Jones, and I appointed him on Sir George's recommendation, and there the story ends; and I must say that Captain Jones has not disgraced the Commander-in-Chief's patronage."

"Well, he must have been a very modest man to hide his light so completely under a bushel," said, with a satiric laugh, General Brymston, the military member, whose nephew, Colonel Congreve, had been among the disappointed candidates.

"Just what I said to Sir George, General," said his Excellency; "and all the answer I got was, '*he's the man for Pundrapore*'; and really I don't think we have any reason to complain."

And so the Council sat down, and resolved that the Begum of Pundrapore should await the pleasure of Government, under surveillance, at the fortress of Chunar; that Taptee Rao should be advanced to the dignity of Rae Bahadoor, and should take charge of the fiscal and judicial management of the Pundrapore state, in conjunction with the British Resident; and that the latter officer should act as guardian of the young Nawab's person, and make such provision as was necessary for the maintenance and education of a prince of his rank.

But the public had not yet heard the last of Pundrapore. Mr Deek, M.P., who wanted to get into the Board of Control and was taking a course of the Calcutta papers, had stumbled upon Captain Jones's appointment. To find Pundrapore in the map of India, and to turn up the history of the principality in 'Thornton's Gazetteer,' was the work of an instant; and that very night Mr Deek gave notice that he would call the attention of the Right Honourable the President of the Board of Control to a recent instance of the exercise of the Governor-General's patronage, and call for the production of the papers connected with the appointment of Captain Jones to the Pundrapore Residency. And Mr Deek did call attention to the Pundrapore Residency in a speech which lasted two hours and a half, in the course of which he detailed the history of Pundrapore from the invasion of Mohammed of Ghizni down to Captain Jones's appointment, quoting largely from 'Mill's History,' 'The Collection of Treaties, Engagements and Sunnuds' and the 'Charter Blue-Books.' There were scarcely forty members present when the President was roused from his slumbers to defend the Government of Bengal. "There would nothing," said the right honourable gentleman, "have given the Board of Control so much pleasure as to produce the papers which the honourable gentleman had so eloquently called for, *if they only had existed*. As for the appointment of Captain Jones, it was easily explained; he was the fittest man for the post. I may mention," continued the President, "that a despatch has this day been received by the Board, stating that the officer whose appointment has been called in question has saved the Pundrapore state from a very serious insurrection, and has probably spared the Government the unpleasant task of annexing the territory. I shall be very happy, in the course of a few days, to lay the paper upon the table for the information of the honourable member who takes such an interest in the affairs of Pundrapore." The President sat down, and Mr Deek collapsed into the smallest possible bulk, cursing his unlucky curiosity, as he read next morning in the 'Times' that, "in reply to a question from Mr Deek, the President of the Board of Control said so and so." His great speech was thus denied to posterity.

The President was right; there were no official papers connected with Captain Jones's appointment. Sir George Blitzen is dead and gone, and we shall offer no indignity to the memory of that distinguished soldier if we print the following private epistle which has come into our hands:—

"From Major-General Sir GEORGE BLITZEN, K.C.B., K.H., to Major SPRINGER, Military Secretary on leave at the Presidency.

"MUSSOORIE, 16*th March* 18 .

"MY DEAR SPRINGER,—I have just got back here again, and deuced glad I am to escape the infernal heat of the plains. The march from Pundrapore was as hot as if there had been only a sheet of pasteboard between us and the devil's own dominions. Talking of Pundrapore, there will be a nice mess there one of these days. The Begum is a tigress—a perfect hyena for untamableness. In fact, I may say she is the only woman that ever braved George Blitzen, and I saw *something* of the sex when I was a *chhokra* with Sir Arthur in the Peninsula. A nice game she and that drawing-room soldier Grantley are playing, but I will put a spoke in her wheel. The Governor-General has given me the nomination of the next Resident, and by G–d I'll send her the ugliest fellow in the Service. Now, Springer, you must find out who that clumsy clown was that poked his head into my stomach at Bustlepore, for as sure as my name is George Blitzen he shall have the post. My lady Begum will then find that, if her plots can only be carried out by making love to the Resident, she must at least make love to a less pleasant object than Grantley. As for his qualifications, they be d–mned. Pundrapore must be annexed within the year, and it does not matter a straw what sort of a Resident is sent there. If the Begum knock the new man upon the head, the service will more easily spare him than a better officer. Bring up a lot of pickles and tinned meat with you, for the *ménage* here is beastly; and try and persuade Mrs Cockett—Cockett of the Toshakhana Office's wife, you know —that the air of Mussoorie would be salubrious for her constitution during the next two months. There are three or four Rattle girls here, who are very jolly, and have been flirting heavily with some of the 14th. Order every 14th man to join his regiment without delay. Send a packet of 'Calcutta Christian Intelligencers' by overland mail to Lady Blitzen, who is fond of that sort of literature.—Ever yours,

"GEORGE BLITZEN."

This letter bears the following indorsement in the hand of the late Colonel Springer, C.B.: "Poor Sir George! will ever the man grow old? Captain Jones, of the Junglywallahs, may thank his Excellency's *spretæ injuriam formæ* for a snug berth."

And this was the mystery of Captain Jones's appointment. Captain Jones discharged the duties of his post with some credit until Captain Grantley's retirement from the Kaifiabad Residency, when, upon the recommendation of his patron, Sir George Blitzen, he was transferred to that innocent office, and Mr Harcourt succeeded to the Pundrapore Residency. During the remainder of his service in the East, Jones continued to be held in great respect among diplomatists, and when he retired, the 'Peon' devoted half a column to his merits and services—it was in the 'silly season,' when news was scarce. The Captain—he is now Colonel, however—still lives upon his laurels, and devotes his leisure to his favourite task of composing epitaphs, in none of which does he omit his valuable services rendered to Government when he filled the Residency of Pundrapore.

MY ONE ACCOMPLISHMENT.

BY R. W. K. EDWARDS.

[Maga, April 1902.]

I.

"AND so," said the man with the silky frock-coat, who sat in the centre chair, "you would be willing to go out to the Bangowango Protectorate in the interests of the Company? Very good. I think we can promise you the appointment—on one condition: it is essential that our agent should be master of the Opeku language. It is impossible to explain the principles of European commerce to the Bangowango native in English, and all interpreters are unreliable. At the same time, we are not aware of any means by which you can obtain instruction in Opeku. Being, however, as you say, an ex-student of University College, you will doubtless be able to find some source of information. You shall have three months in which to prepare yourself; by that time we expect a Bangowango headsman to have arrived in London in one of our sailing-vessels. We will confront him with you; and we shall no doubt be able to offer you the opening."

I was quite pleased with the prospect, and was turning to go, as, from a wave of the hand, I felt was expected of me, when a second person at the board, an older man, who somehow suggested having torn his conscience to shreds but still having it about him, asked leave to address me. The chairman, with a shrug, as of patient forbearance shown to a fool, assented.

"I forget your age," said my new questioner.

"Twenty," I replied, feeling very young beneath his gaze.

"Ah!"

"You know, of course," he continued, "the kind of country you are going out to?"

"Why, I suppose it will be all very interesting," I said.

"Exceedingly. Almost entirely unexplored. The Opeku tribes of the Protectorate are specially remote from all civilising influences."

"Then I shall be a sort of explorer?" I replied, swelling with the proud thought.

"Exactly. If ever—that is, I mean to say, *when* you return, you should be able to interest all England with a book giving faithful impressions of many barbarous habits. Cannibalism, for instance, you will be in a position to describe minutely."

The chairman looked as if he thought his colleague might have spared us these unsavoury details; but finding it produced no effect on me, he did not demur. I merely said that the natives would be welcome to dine off me if they cared for anything so tough, and the speaker went on—

"Perhaps you may be interested in the study of tropical disease. Here again you will have a wide field for observation. The Opeku district of the Bangowango territory lies, as you know, on the equator. Every conceivable form of malarial microbe abounds. You will be able from first hand to study their effects, and possibly experiment with specifics."

I replied to the effect that the prevalence of an ague which could attack a quinine-bottle would be no deterrent.

"You will have opportunities for studying poisonous plants, reptiles and insects; in short, you will find to what possible limits of insecure and insanitary surroundings European life may be with immunity exposed."

"I don't care," I said, as I saw his drift. "It suits my

book; and if it will help up the dividends of the British Bangowango Trading Company, I daresay it will suit yours. You may depend upon me; and I shall set about finding an instructor in the Opeku language without delay."

And I walked out of the board-room with a jaunty air. On the morning of the day before, I had made the discovery that Norah was engaged to Captain Chalmers.

II.

Yes, I would go out to the Bangowango Protectorate. Norah should marry her precious Chalmers, and in the meantime my bones should lie rotting in a tropical swamp, or I would come back to be the lion of a London season, completely eclipsing all such nonentities as mere captains.

I would not let Norah know of my plans till I had gone. She should see no sign in me of being crushed. I would not cut the house even. No, I would go there a good deal as usual, be grandly civil to the Captain and coldly chivalrous to the faithless one; and I would make great friends with Norah's younger sister, Kate, who, after all, was quite worth cultivating, with plenty of go in her, and, I believed, a kind of sympathy with the victim of the fickle siren's fascinations.

I had an object in life now, more definite than engineering had ever held out to me through the exceedingly unattractive vista of dry mathematics. Not but what I must work; and I braced myself up to tackle the Opeku language and polish it off in a couple of months.

Here, however, was a difficulty which at first seemed insuperable. Professor Mąhlströñ (I hope I have got all the correct orthographical tags to his name) could say little about it. If, however, I referred to Vummerhausen on 'The First Efforts of Primeval Man at Articulation,' I might find some allusions that would help.

I went to the British Museum reading-room, took down

Vummerhausen and wrestled with him. Vummerhausen consists entirely of footnotes, and these are not indexed; so that it took many hours to cull the few references to Opeku which that learned old ichthyosaurus had permitted himself. At the end of several mornings' work (and the desk at place H 97 in the reading-room must surely bear the dints of my elbows) all I could say of Opeku was that it was dimly and remotely allied to Arabic, and that it was chiefly a string of grunts and groans, varied by an occasional snake-like hiss.

I tried not to be discouraged, and seriously set about learning Arabic—no easy business—hoping that something would turn up, as it shortly afterwards did, to help me in my search for knowledge.

I was leaning back in my chair at seat H 97, mentally wearied and needing some change of thought. The British Museum reading-room is not a place where men usually study each other, but my attention was attracted at that moment to the elderly man who was advancing to take place H 98. I like to speculate on the life-stories of people who sit opposite me in omnibuses and trains; and my own little disappointment happily had not robbed me of this resource.

In this particular case it was not hard to sketch the general outline of the man's story from his appearance. He was of good height, erect and well built, with a noble head and a leonine shock of white hair. But his boots were terrible, and his trousers frayed at the ankles. His frock-coat was green with age and filthy with stains; its collar was turned up, and it was buttoned so closely that you could not help wondering if there was any clothing beneath it. There was a sort of forlorn dignity in the way he shuffled along, looking down and around, as one whose path is beset with phantoms. He looked like a seer; he was, alas! a seer of snakes.

He sat down and waited for his books. He smelt of drink; but it was plain that drink had long ceased, in his case, to promote hilarity; he sat for the most part perfectly still; when he did stir, it was with extreme deliberation, as if any undue movement might rouse a spectacle in his brain and an apparition of some horror that his shaken body would insist on though his mind might rebel against belief in it.

I say all this because I can never hold as lightly as some can the ruin that drink brings a man to. I suppose the tragedy has comic interludes. But I never saw this old man without feeling that he was a standing warning of the dangers of conviviality.

When his books came they were not many or large; but he received them with a sort of dejected appetite, felt inside his coat for a pair of eyeglasses and was soon engrossed. I daresay I should have forgotten about him had not my eye fallen on the title-page of the book he was reading. It was a work on the influence of climate on dialect. I immediately wished to know the name of the author: Opeku would undoubtedly be mentioned in the tropical section; and this would be the sort of clue to be followed up. I dared not for some time, however, interrupt the reader; but at last as he laid aside one volume to take up another I touched his arm and said—

"Can you kindly tell me anything about the Opeku language? I am anxious to learn it, and don't know where to find anything about it."

He turned a lack-lustre eye upon me, and pushed towards me the volume he had just been reading, merely saying, "Folio three-thirty-six."

"This is no use to me," I said, after referring to page 336. "I've read all this in Vummerhausen."

The old fellow grunted. He seemed ill-disposed to talk, and clinched matters by simply saying, with a distinct Scottish accent, "Vummerhausen's a fool!"

Now the man who could confidently call Vummerhausen a fool must have some pretensions to being a scholar in the direction I was seeking. I therefore returned to the attack.

"How am I to learn Opeku?"

"Get away to Bangowango," says he, without looking up.

"That's just it," I said; "I want to go to Bangowango, but it's no use till I know Opeku. Do you know Opeku?"

"Does Jebb know Greek?" said he, with a kind of seedy conceit. "He knows mair, he knows all round it. I'm no' such a dunce as I look."

"Could you teach me?"

He turned impatiently to me. "There's a rule of silence here for havering tongues. I'm no teacher: do I look it?"

"No," I thought, "you don't"; but I only said—

"Well, there's my card, sir. If you know of anyone who will undertake to give me lessons in Opeku, I will give him liberal terms."

And I left him.

It was about a week after this, and I was still groping about, almost in despair, for a solution of my difficulty, when I heard a slow shuffling step ascending the staircase of my quarters at the Inn. He walked in with a certain stiff solemnity, holding my card, which was by this time exceedingly dirty, and, without the semblance of a bow, said—

"My name is Sutherland. Are you the gentleman who was yon day wishing instruction?"

"In Opeku? yes," I said; "sit down."

"You said liberal terms, I believe," he continued, with a kind of toneless sigh, looking down his shabby frock-coat, now dirtier than ever.

"I am ready to give liberal terms," I said.

He looked irresolutely at me, then seemed to gulp down some remnant of pride, sat down and began at once.

"With regard to the structure and formeetion of this language, we shall notice that absolute simplicity characterises every detail. While it may be regarded as essentially a language of inflection, irregularities are of course conspeecuous by their absence; and it is to be noted that the so-called irregularities in any language are merely an aspect of our defective grasp and arrangement of its principles. It must be remembered that the birthplace of every language is the glottis, and that orthography is the servant, and should never be the master, of any tongue. We shall therefore in this present instance prepose an alphabet of twenty-five consonants and ten vowels, as follows. . . ."

And so, volubly and clearly, he gave me a masterly sketch of the language in which he was about to instruct me.

I was amazed at the learning which had acquired all these details of a language which my teacher had probably never spoken in its native surroundings, and the skill that had so clearly arranged them for my benefit. Of course writing was unknown among the Bangowango natives; but he had apparently invented symbols to convey precisely the sounds used, and from the first I felt absolute confidence in his knowledge. I took copious notes—he was by no means easy to keep up with—and invented a sort of shorthand in Opeku. I found it best not to ask my instructor questions, but to let the flood of his knowledge gush out spontaneously, and to collect as much as I possibly could in the time. At the end of an hour I had enough taken down to occupy my time in learning; and he then dictated to me a vocabulary and some exercises, Opeku into English and *vice versa*.

I now felt a difficulty about the fee.

"When will you come again?" I asked.

"That depends."

"Shall I pay you at the end of the time? I suppose that will be better," I said, thinking to myself that this would be the safer arrangement.

He hesitated, and I saw a blank look of dismay steal over his face. There was not much variety of expression there, but at that moment it spoke of hopeless disappointment.

"How do I ken you?" he at length burst out with a sort of dull vehemence. "Next time I come ye may have flitted. Or ye may be deid—or me."

"There, there," I said; "will that satisfy you?" I pressed a sovereign and a shilling into his hand. (Your guinea is your only professional unit.) I am convinced, however, that he believed himself at the moment to be the recipient of two shillings merely. He stole out of the room hurriedly.

It was some days before he came again. This time he sported a linen collar and had had his boots cleaned. The stains on his coat had been inked carefully over, and he gave me the impression of having been at some pains to pull himself together. He still reeked of spirits—but of spirits, I imagined, of a better quality. His white moustache was browned at the centre, I thought, by the passage of good French brandy. He took up the thread of the language exactly where he had left off. He seemed to warm to his work much more quickly, and spoke sonorously and well for fully the hour, I writing like a demon the while.

After this his visits were fairly regular. Sometimes he would be absent for several days at a time, and then turn up rather dilapidated. But on the whole I came to the conclusion that my work kept him in a state of affluence to which he had long been a stranger. His tone towards me was not pleasant; but I humoured him, as I wished to get the best possible value from him. He was an extraordinarily enthusiastic exponent of the language he taught me, and his enthusiasm infected me. I felt disposed to do him credit in spite of his rudeness. Once when I demurred that I was learning more than was commercially necessary, he jumped down my throat with some violence. Was I master, or was he? There was a literary value in what I was learning, or there would be in the future: had I no mind for it, or was I a mere groveller? I took the hint and was silent. In the future I saw myself as the exponent of Opeku to the educated of England. Perhaps some day I might even fill a newly endowed chair in Opeku at one of our universities. At any rate I had now got an opportunity I might never meet with again. So I worked like a Trojan. I found it more than interesting. The language had more capabilities in it than I had ever dreamed of, and it was (possibly because of the excellence of my teaching) so beautifully simple. I grew to be able to translate almost any English; I even learned how to write the rude pentameters in which—so my ancient tutor informed me—the Opeku priests conveyed their religious precepts. He was much pleased with my efforts at times, and his memory seemed inexhaustible; it was practically a dictionary as well as a grammar. Once when I recited a poem by himself in Opeku the tears stood in his eyes, and a minute afterwards he was calling me a "doited fool."

"I'm not a fool," I said.

"Are you not?" said he.

"I don't know that I am," was my lame reply.

"That's it—ye don't ken it yet," he said with a rude laugh. "But ye will some day," and he pocketed my tenth guinea and went off.

III.

All this time I was taking care not to forget that I was a blighted being. I called up the image of Norah as often as I could remember to do so, beat my breast and soliloquised, and tried not to feel better. I used to go to her people's house pretty often, and I delighted in affecting indifference to her charms—or at any rate thinking that I affected it.

I did not tell her of my designs for the future; indeed she never asked me; nor did I impart them to Kate, to whom I paid the very particular attention I thought she deserved as being a good and steady girl.

"You're a jolly good sort, Kate," I said one day. "I should like to talk to you about my work, or rather about my hobby."

"I shall be awfully glad if you will," she said.

"I'm getting a new accomplishment," I said, "and am working tremendously hard at it."

"I thought you were rather *distrait*," said Kate.

"Quite natural that I should be *distrait*," I remarked,

looking woundedly at the fair Norah, who did not care a rap. "However, working at it has proved a great resource," I said, "and I really feel as if I were beginning to get on. There's nothing so bad for a man inclined to brood as idleness."

"Is it the 'cello ? " said Kate.

"No, it's a language," I said ; and I told her of Opeku and its resources.

"I wish it were the 'cello," said Kate, "and I could play your accompaniments."

"Thanks ; that's very nice of you," I said. "But I never could excel in music as I can in Opeku. Many people can play the 'cello ; but there can be hardly half a dozen people in the kingdom who can speak Opeku. When I've studied it for a few years I shall probably be, without boasting, one of the leading authorities on the subject—so my teacher tells me."

"That's a very nice ambition," said Kate.

"Oh, I daresay it's not so fine an ambition as dying for one's country," I said pointedly. I always believed that Captain Chalmers was not exactly the kind of soldier who is attracted by war's alarms. "But still it's something to go on with. I'm sure, a fortnight ago, I'd no idea such an ambition would ever occur to me."

"I respect you very much for it," said Kate earnestly. "It seems to be a modest ambition—one bound not to lead to disappointment. You aren't going to pit yourself against men of greater opportunities and possibly higher intellectual abilities" (if Kate has a fault it is, perhaps, that she is a trifle blunt), "but you are going to do something unique and at the same time exceedingly useful."

"And not unornamental," I responded. "If I could interest you in Opeku, you'd be surprised what a lot there is in it."

"Perhaps you can interest me in Opeku," said Kate, smiling.

I tried, and it was no failure. It is no exaggeration to say that I learnt as much Opeku at the feet of Kate, telling her about it, as I did at the hands of that bibulous old bully, Dr Sutherland. I have since realised what it means when a person says that to learn a thing properly you must teach it. Perhaps the Doctor learned much in his bellowings at me; but he could not have a finer whetstone for his knowledge than I had in the gentler intellect of Kate. She was so full of interest in a subject which I had thought would be a bore to her, that my own enthusiasm was redoubled. She came to possess some knowledge of what I was learning as well, by hearing it, though I am inclined to believe she has by now forgotten it. Norah pretended not to care to hear about it. She was always writing letters or going upstairs to look at her dresses when I was there. At any rate those evenings were to me, somehow or other, exceedingly pleasant.

However, the pleasantest periods must have an end; and ere I was aware of it the time was approaching when I must finally enter into my contract with the British Bangowango Trading Company. I will not say that I anticipated it with wild joy. But I had quite made up my mind long ago; I felt certain of my fitness for the work, and did not at all mean to relinquish the scheme.

"Now, Dr Sutherland," I said one day, "next lesson must be my last. The week after that I am to have my interview with an Opeku chief at the office in the City of which I told you, and I shall be able to put your instructions to the test. I am confident you have done the best that could be done with me, and I feel that I owe you a good deal that can't be repaid. Of course, however, I shall be unable to afford to go on working with you when once arrangements are made."

The old fellow was not best pleased. The last few weeks had been to him a time of comparative prosperity. Drinking on a full stomach, however sorry a pursuit, however dull a slavery, however joyless a necessity to the inebriate, is some thousand times better than the horrible extremity of drinking on an empty one. I felt certain he would get back to the lowest ebb again, as I had found him. No one would employ him—few would stand his temper or his irregularity. I offered to mention him to my future employers; but he refused to give me any address, and I could do nothing more for him.

As I paid him for the last time, I felt really sorry for him. The depth of the shadow he was about to re-enter after the less sombre gloom of the last period seemed so dreadful.

"Dr Sutherland," I said, "I'm a young man and you are an old one. I can't do anything for you. But can't you —I hate to say it—can't you keep off the drink?"

"Ye're owre late, ye fule," he said; "ye're owre late. D'ye think I wouldn't if I could? Look to yourself. The drink's played the deil with my maurals, or I should never be taking your dirty money as I have done. Ye'll greatly oblige by leaving me to my lane the now," and he disappeared, never to cross my path again.

That evening I for the first time broached my plans to the two sisters. It came about in this way. Norah came in whilst Kate and I had our heads together over my work.

"Opeku again!" she said pettishly. (I have reason to believe that the Captain had that afternoon sent her a necklace with only three turquoises in it, when she had expected five.) "Opeku again! Aren't you sick of it?"

"*I'm* not," I said; "I don't know about Kate."

"Oh, Kate's got Opeku on the brain. It's about time she stopped it, I think. It's all you and Opeku. She jabbers Opeku in her sleep now."

Kate coloured, and I could see that Norah was in a temper. So I promptly developed one of my own.

"Very well," I said. "I can promise you you shan't be bothered by *my* Opeku much longer."

"I'm glad to hear it," retaliated Norah.

"Quite so. You may be interested to learn," I went on hotly, looking straight at her, "that I am very shortly going to put my knowledge of Opeku to the test. I am going out where it is spoken—yes, where it is spoken; and that is, Norah, in Bangowango, away just the other side of the equator. Yes, that has been my plan ever since *October*, Norah. That's where I'm going—Bangowango. It isn't much of a place for a white man to go to, but it's quite good enough for the likes of me, and that's where I'm going. It's the most horrible place in the world. It's all swamp, and snakes, and leeches. There's miasma there that you can cut with a knife—that is, if you've the strength left to hack at it at all. Very few white men ever come back alive from it. The inhabitants are all cannibals and delight in blood. The man whose place I am filling died a horrible death. But it doesn't much matter to me where I go——"

I thought I had petrified Norah into a pallid silence with my eloquence; but now she was pointing in alarm beyond me.

"Kate—look to her!" she said.

I turned round and saw that Kate was fainting. I ran and raised her in my arms to the sofa, whilst Norah rushed out for restoratives.

"Oh! oh!" said Kate, as she came to. "It's very stupid of me. I—I can't bear to hear of—of people going out to such dreadful places."

IV.

The day appointed for the interview arrived. During the interval I should, of course, have been busily engaged in revising Dr Sutherland's notes and finally rubbing up my knowledge of the Opeku language. I did nothing of the kind. I simply wandered aimlessly about, trying not to analyse my feelings with regard to the whole business. For one thing, however, I did not go near either Norah or Kate. I was man enough to feel that it was unsettling, and one-half of me was determined not to be unsettled. But I blamed myself considerably for having allowed myself such pleasure as I now discovered the series of evenings spent with Kate to have been. I only realised what it had been when I saw how she took the announcement of my travels.

But that was all over, and I must go through the next epoch of life as best I could. Perhaps I should come back safe and sound from Bangowango, and then be able to take up the thread of friendship again. It was not easy to reason in this way, and the word 'perhaps' cost me an effort; but I had the courage to trample on sentiment, or at any rate the kind of sentiment which leads a man on to getting engaged to a girl on the eve of leaving her behind him.

I went to be examined by the doctor who acted as medical adviser to the Company. I had a lurking hope that he might find a varicose vein; but I could not claim even this mild disqualification for facing the tropics. He reported upon me as perfectly sound in body, although he privately informed me with some asperity that he would not vouch for the mental condition of a man who with so good a physique elected to go where I was going.

I ultimately wrote to Kate and Norah, and told them that I should not see them again before my departure. There was much business to attend to, I said, and I meant to avail myself of what little leisure I had in making farewell visits to my relations in the country. I wrote as coldly as possible; and this done, I felt something more like a man than I had done for some days past.

The day for the interview arrived, and I once more found myself in the board-room of the Company. The same fat pale man was in the chair. His proportions, however, were quite dwarfed, and he looked even flabby beside the native chief who was present.

This was no other than the notorious Hwatowayo, of whom the newspapers had not long before been full. He was supposed to have been converted from cannibalism; but I thought I read a discerning appetite in the glance with which his yellow eyes feasted themselves on me.

He was the most magnificent specimen of a glutton I have ever seen. Diametrically he was stupendous. And all his points were emphasised by his costume, which was what I should call ultra-London. He had the shiniest possible broad-brimmed silk hat, set at a knowing angle on his curly head. He wore a frock-coat and a double-breasted waistcoat of enormous frontage, in itself a complete jeweller's shop window; and he carried a noble gold-headed cane. I immediately inferred that with the Bangowango aristocracy gluttony is a fine art, and Hwatowayo its chief exponent. Every feature was in keeping with this idea. His mouth was large, mobile and prominent; his nose flat and dwarfed. Magnificent was his fat neck; and the lobes of his ears were like Rugby footballs, and laden with golden adornments.

"You will now be able," said the chairman to me, "to carry on a conversation with Hwatowayo. He knows no English, and the interpreter had been dismissed; and from the facility with which you can make yourselves understand each other, we shall know if we can avail ourselves of your services. Will you kindly address some remarks to Hwatowayo?"

I felt very foolish in the silence that followed, and under fire of a scorching grin from Hwatowayo.

"I don't know what to say," I said.

"Ask him how he likes missionary cooked," said the older man who had on the last occasion informed me about the little drawbacks of Bangowango life.

"Silence, gentlemen," said the chairman, as the rest of the directors laughed. "This is no time for levity."

"I'll ask him how he likes our restaurants," I said. Whereupon I rapidly evolved a flowing sentence, expressing hope that his august digestion was in good order and that he found himself well fed in London.

Hwatowayo said nothing, and looked as if he were still waiting for me to begin; so I repeated my remark, this time with a few nods and smiles and encouraging waves of the hand.

He still left it unanswered, and I began to fear that something must be wrong with my accent. I tried again, this time speaking with slow and impressive earnestness. Again I failed to elicit any response. I now began to get hot and anxious, and made another desperate attempt to 'make him sensible,' as the Irish say.

"It appears to be no go," said a director. "Let the nigger have a shy this time. Go it, Hwato, old boy. Speaky Opeku white man, you useless great swine, go on. Speaky Opeku, *encore, vite, allez, marchons.*"

Thus adjured, Hwatowayo seemed to understand, and rose to the occasion. He fired at me a volley of consonants, dentals and sibilants. But there was no word in it that bore the smallest resemblance to the language I had learned from Dr Sutherland. "Tampe, tampe," I said, meaning "slowly, slowly"; but he paid no attention to me, raised his voice gradually to a vociferous boom, struck the upper part of his body a reverberating blow with his swarthy fist, rolled his yellow eyes, gobbled like a turkey-cock, and paused, evidently expecting a reply.

"There seems to be a considerable amount of sense in his remarks," observed a Yankee director and shareholder. "Can you put it into English for us, young fellow?"

"I'm bound to say I can't," I replied. "He speaks very rapidly; but I cannot even distinguish a syllable. His Opeku, if indeed it is Opeku, differs very considerably from mine."

"Well, tell him so; make that amount clear to him anyway. The interpreter worked the oracle somehow, and he's about half your size."

"Well, I'll try again," I said, and I strung together a masterly phrase (my Opeku is an extremely comprehensive language) indicating my respect for him, my wish to understand him, and my inability to do so, arising no doubt from the careless rapidity of his utterance and my own want of practice. In a word, I remarked—

"Titta pŭtche lalla foofoo."

Hwatowayo grunted. He held his hand to his ear to catch my words again, and I repeated—

"Titta pŭtche lalla foofoo."

No answer.

"Titta pŭtche bully jujah," remarked a wag at the table. "Lalla foofoo," I corrected him gravely; and in a few moments all the members of the board were inanely pointing at Hwatowayo and calling out—

"Titta pŭtche lalla foofoo."

Hwatowayo looked fogged. He smiled, and leaning forward said plaintively—

"Me no Dutch, no Dutch: spik plenty Opeku."

The air was now rent with laughter, in which everyone joined excepting myself and the chairman. The latter looked exceedingly worried, and his skin began to act freely—a contingency which stout men who wear silky frock-coats are ever anxious to avoid. I confess I felt humiliated: it dawned upon me, of course, that I had been considerably bamboozled by that old reprobate, Dr Sutherland; this was evidently what so amused everybody around me.

The interpreter was recalled, and it was soon definitely established that I knew no more Opeku than I do Dutch, and I tailed out of the room, very glad to make my escape.

. . . .

What the language is that I so thoroughly mastered I cannot even now say; but it remains with me, a sort of phantom accomplishment of which I can make no possible use. It is curious that I cannot forget it, whereas the solution of a quadratic taxes my memory most severely. I spend hours when I am travelling alone in converting passages of English into that remarkable tongue, and in composing long pieces of verse and prose. I never see an alien on these shores but I try it on him, always without result. Kate and I (for I may mention that we are married now) used often to dwell upon a project, to be carried out when the ship of fortune should have sailed into our little harbour, of travelling round the world, visiting every accessible corner where articulation exists, until we should discover the tribe of natives to whom my language would convey a meaning. But it does not seem likely to come off: the family demands so much more attention every year, and there would perhaps be no one to take my place at the works. (I went back to the engineering after my failure as a scholar of Opeku, and am now a partner in a firm in Whitefriars, where we make the metallic fittings necessary for certain parts of refrigerating machines, and turn out some millions of these fittings every year.) I am said, I believe, to have a peculiar influence over the class of British workmen we employ: perhaps it is that, when anything goes wrong, I am able to fire off a series of interjections of appalling sonority, of which no one knows the meaning but myself.

No; I do not think our project will carry us farther than the south coast, where we go every summer. Besides, the other day, when hastily looking at the books in a second-hand shop window, my eye caught the following title: 'Some Suggestions for the Formation of a Universal Language. By Donald Sutherland, M.A., Ph.D., &c., &c. Aberdeen, 1846.'

I fancy that an investigation in this direction might throw some light upon the matter.

THE MISOGYNIST.

BY HENRY PROTHERO.

[Maga, June 1882.]

LAST year I was taking a solitary walking tour in out-of-the-way parts of Normandy, and towards the end of the summer I found myself at a little unfrequented village-town, composed of one dull 'Place' surrounded by white-shuttered houses, a few little smelly streets, a fine Flamboyant church, a 'mairie' and a convent or two. It was an old-world place, but not specially picturesque; and as the guide-book contemptuously dismissed it in a couple of lines, I expected to be alone, so far as the society of my countrymen went.

A morning walk with my knapsack from another little town (also composed of a dull 'Place,' a Flamboyant church, &c., &c.) had brought me to this place a little before noon on a blazing September day. "And now," thought I, "for *déjeuner;* then a quiet afternoon's sketching at the church or by the stream, and some letter-writing at night"—that was my programme.

There was an unpretentious hotel—the "Singe d'Or"—on one side of the square, with an awning and little tables, and a landlady with a surpassing white cap. "Could madame give me a room?" But certainly she could. "And *déjeuner?*" Immediately—would monsieur enter? So monsieur entered, and after due ablutions descended to the *salle-à-manger.*

In a moment my expectations and hopes of isolation from

my countrymen vanished; for there, waiting for his breakfast, sat a large, heavy-looking, respectable, middle-aged English gentleman, on whose countenance solemnity, pomposity, dulness and self-satisfaction sat enthroned. There was no escape. He recognised a compatriot, and for the rest of the day I was a prey to him.

First he regaled me during our meal with slow and measured complaints about his food, and he would fain have made me the medium through whom our good-humoured hostess was to have her soul vexed and harassed; but as I contrived to frustrate him in this matter, he essayed to explain himself, happily without one word being intelligible to madame.

After breakfast he lay in wait for me, and caught me going out; and throughout that unhappy afternoon his dissertations on the Church of Rome, while I was looking at the church (*I*, not *we*; for he looked at nothing), and on the position of women when we passed a convent, together with his glorification of his own domestic arrangements, and of the high moral and mental state to which he had brought his wife and daughters (whom he was to rejoin next day, poor things!)—all this, combined with the thought that I should have more of it at dinner, drove me nearly frantic.

So great was my dread of further infliction, that the thin *potage*, with paving-stones of bread, was already on the table, and madame had been up to say that "*Monsieur est servi,*" before I ventured to face my dinner and my enemy. But hunger drove me down at last, and in deep dejection I opened the door of the *salle-à-manger*.

Pomposity was there; but, oh joy! he was not alone. The slow pounding tones of his voice were being addressed to other ears than mine. He had a new victim!

Sitting opposite to him was a little, plump, rosy-faced, elderly man in an auburn wig. He had no whiskers, moustache, beard, eyelashes, or eyebrows, but above his little twinkling eyes were two reddish marks where eyebrows ought to have been; and never did I see so much expression and humour in any human countenance as I now saw flitting about in those little twinkling eyes and red marks, and the odd little wrinkles and dimples on the plump red cheeks.

The old story was being dinned into his ears: all through dinner, from the soup to the *Gruyère*, we heard about the low state of morals in France, the high position of the English matron—especially, we were to infer, of Mrs Pomposity, and her family, the Miss Pomposities—the horrors of conventual life, and so on, until our *convive*, hitherto silent but making wonderful little faces, now lit his first cigarette.

Then he said quite suddenly, "There is one thing to be said for convents—they keep a lot of women out of the way."

At this sally, uttered in a cool crisp voice, I was fairly electrified; but joy was the prevailing feeling. There could be no remark so shocking, so contrary to all received morality, but I should have welcomed it at that moment with ecstasy.

As for Solemnity; he sat aghast. The Wig had hitherto been a good listener: he had apparently drunk in words of wisdom; he had accepted interminable platitudes on the true position of women, as lying between political forwardness on the one side, and conventual seclusion on the other. But now, what was this ribaldry? Pomposity determined to put his foot on it.

"No Englishman," said he, "or at least no Protestant, can approve of the immuring of females."

"Cranmer did," retorted the Wig, with an impassive countenance. "He shut up his wife in a box."

In a voice of indignant but ponderous contempt, Pomposity demanded, "A member of the Church of Rome, I presume, sir?"

"Not at all," said the Wig, with a chuckle of suppressed merriment; "I am no more a Papist than Cranmer was." Then, after a moment's pause, he added, "I don't believe the story about Mrs Cranmer." At this statement Solemnity was slightly relieved, and was beginning, "I should presume not indeed,' when the other cut in—

"For this reason—that if the Archbishop had once got her safe in the box, it is incredible that he should ever have let her out again."

By this time I was enjoying myself; the discomfiture of my tyrant was delightful to me, and my only fear was that he would not provoke further argument. As for him, he dimly saw that he was being jested with, and his slow soul was roused; he must bear testimony against this levity. So, after a truly awful allusion to the Wig's 'facetiousness,' he gave us several minutes on the blessings of a married clergy. My spirit sank again, but an unwary pause gave the foe a chance of interposing.

"Some great authorities, speaking from actual experience, have thought otherwise," said he. "Look at Archbishop Usher, whose wife burnt all his pet MSS. against Bellarmine. Bishop Hooper's wife, I have heard, was a sad scourge; and you will doubtless remember, sir" (this with an air of assumed deference to Pomposity, who did not remember, for he had never heard these items of ecclesiastical history), "how a bishop of Down in the seventeenth century said of his wife that he was *pertæsus*, utterly weary of her? So also the Reverend Laurence Sterne declared that he was *ægrotus ac fatigatus*, sick and tired—*uxoris meæ*—of Mrs Sterne. Then again——"

But Pomposity would hear no more. He took up a French paper (which he could not read, and would certainly not have studied so intently, respectable man, if he had had any notion of the contents) and retreated from the distasteful conversation.

The misogynist blinked peacefully over his cigarette at the now averted figure of his antagonist; then turning to me, he remarked that some of the leading Reformers had a very just estimate of women; and he proceeded to quote some very rude remarks made by John Knox in his 'First Blast of the Trumpet against the Monstriferouse Regiment of Women.' This led him to a few anecdotes reflecting on queens generally, and his face was a study when he alluded to the Empress Bianca's unfortunate decease from a surfeit of snails.

This discourse on queens once more brought Pomposity into the field, who, being unable to read his paper, had reluctantly listened. "You speak, sir," said he, "thus disrespectfully of crowned ladies, as though they were all Jezebels——"

("Jezebel was a woman of some spirit," put in the misogynist meditatively.)

"Or Messalinas." And now we had to endure a solemn eulogy of good queens as a set-off against what we had heard about bad ones. Fortunately, a rash challenge as to what he thought of Queen Elizabeth brought the Wig to the front again.

"Aylmer, in his 'Harborough,' does certainly make an exception of Queen Bess," said he, "but I don't know why. He contrasts her with all other women, whom he calls 'triflers,' 'folyshnes,' 'flibbergibbes' and so forth."

This, it will be observed, was a new move in the campaign. We had passed from clerical wives to queens, and now we were passing from queens to an attack on the sex generally. There is no need to give Pomposity's homily which followed. The British matron had a stout but wearisome defender. Her deportment, we were told, unlike that of the French matron, gave respectability to our very streets.

"Ah, that's just it!" cried the Wig. "How true is Washington Irving's description of such matrons! 'Thus have I seen,' he says, 'some pestilent shrew of a housewife, after filling her home with uproar and ill-humour, come dimpling out of doors, swimming and curtseying and smiling upon all the world.'" After this, with his queer little face puckered up in enjoyment of his theme, he launched out into a diatribe on the disadvantages of matrimony. First he quoted a rude comparison—I think by Seneca—between telling one's wife a secret and unnecessarily taking a sea voyage. Then he bethought him of Montaigne's saying, "Cato, like ourselves, was disgusted with his wife." From that he proceeded to another saying of Montaigne's, that marriage was like a cage; those who were out of it were always wanting to get in, and those who were within were all for coming out—a saying which, he said, was no doubt borrowed from Chaucer's lines:—

> "Marriage is such a rabble rout,
> That those who were out would fain get in,
> And those who are in would fain get out."

The last line, he thought, was certainly true, the second one less universally so. Then he had a fling at people who married twice, and wondered if anyone had ever been so fortunate as Mabœuf in 'Les Misérables,' who, being asked whether he had ever been married, replied, "*J'ai oublié!*"

Thus he chatted on, encouraged by my attention and Pomposity's dismay, till it was time for me to retire and write my letters.

"You deserve," said I, as I rose, "as a punishment for your misogynism, to spend a long purgatory with a mother-in-law!"

"A mother-in-law!" cried he. "Ah! see there again!—the monster of modern comedy, the byword of all ages! Yet she, like the *Injusta Noverca* of ancient times, is only the matron moved one step on! Did you ever"—this to Pomposity, who only answered by a solemn stare—"did you ever read 'Holy Living'? You will find there what a saintly man thought of mothers-in-law. He tells how a man threw a stone at a dog; the stone missed the dog, but hit his mother-in-law. 'Thus,' says the pious author, 'the stone was not wholly in vain.'"

The party was now breaking up. Pomposity was for bed, after spending, I fear, a most disagreeable evening. The auburn Wig was lighting a fresh cigarette. "Good night, sir," said I. "I wish I could keep you company a little longer, but I shall have to spend half the night over my letters, and must keep myself awake with endless cigars."

Pomposity thought that I was speaking to him, and answered with friendly gravity, "It is a pity to do that, young man. One of the advantages of that holy state which we have heard so strangely aspersed, is the influence of the matron in discouraging irregular hours. I wish you a good night, sir."

"Good night, sir—good night," chirped the voice of the misogynist after us. "You know what Jeremy Taylor says? 'Better sit up all night than go to bed with a dragon!'"

The next morning, waking rather late, I looked out upon the 'Place.' Pomposity was just departing in a *voiture*, with an air of perplexity and displeasure on his countenance, caused by madame's *bon voyages* and *à plaisirs*, which he did not comprehend, and dimly conceived to be connected with the bill which he still held in his hand; and so, without a smile or a wave of the hand, he departed.

Then I turned my eyes to a little marble-topped table below my window, over which the awning was stretched later in the day. There I beheld our friend the misogynist taking his *café au lait*. His wig was surmounted by a grey wide-awake, so that I could not see his face, but his voice mounted up from under it in cheery strains; and what was he doing? He was actually engaged in presenting chocolates to two little girls in very tight white caps—one our hostess's Cecile, the other from the *boulangerie* opposite—who were capering and dancing round him, like the "daughters of the Horse-leech, crying, Give, Give"; and at the same time justifying his conduct with sundry bows and compliments and wavings of the wideawake, to the two *mamans*, who were laughingly scolding him for spoiling *les petites*.

As I surveyed this prodigy, there arose in my mind some very profound, original and philosophic considerations, which I here set down in order :—

First, That things are not always what they seem.

Secondly, That when any person endowed with dulness and authoritativeness says one thing, then it is pleasing to unregenerate human nature to say the opposite.

Thirdly, That this faculty for opposition is a very useful one ; for see what a miserable afternoon I had spent for want of it.

Hear, then, in one word, the moral of my tale :—

When anyone bores you, start a paradox.

THE TENDER RECOLLECTIONS OF IRENE MACGILLICUDDY.

BY LAURENCE OLIPHANT.

[Maga, December 1877 and January 1878.]

I.

THERE is something very appalling to one so young and inexperienced as myself in the effort of sitting down for the first time in my life to address the public. Apart from the horrid doubt which haunts me, and which seems to paralyse my pen, that perhaps after all my trouble I shall not be able to find any publisher with a sufficient appreciation of my talent to accept my manuscript, there is the conviction that the little story I am about to tell will produce a very considerable sensation upon one, if not upon both sides of the Atlantic; possibly it may not be altogether favourable to myself. I shall be called unpatriotic, unladylike, calumnious, perhaps even indelicate, for describing a few episodes of my somewhat rapid career, not with any view of forcing my own insignificant personality upon the public, but because it is impossible for me otherwise to illustrate the manners and customs of the society in which I was brought up. Ever since I was transplanted from the splendid brown stone mansion on Fifth Avenue in New York, where I passed the giddy seasons of my girlhood, to the modest luxury of the villa in Richmond from which I am now writing, I have felt possessed by an absorbing desire to 'show up,' so to speak, the life led by the world of fashion in the American metropolis, from a purely philanthropic point of view. It has seemed to me that the only chance of doing it any good was to expose it, not unkindly, but with the faithfulness and affection of a friend who tells another his faults. I think it will be new to my English readers, who may rely upon its accuracy; but they need not on that account flatter themselves that the present condition of London society is in any respect superior to that of New York. I tell you, mothers of London, that in your powers of setting matrimonial snares, and of successfully disposing of your marriageable wares, you are more than a match for the 'smartest' of your American sisters, who leave their daughters to take care of themselves; and you young married women of high degree, do not imagine that the frisky matrons of New York can teach you anything you did not know before. Indeed I think it is fortunate for you that the social *convenances* of London deny you the freedom which they enjoy. It is not to either of these two classes that I have anything very new to reveal, though they may pick up a few hints, or draw comparisons invidious or otherwise. It is you, my dear girls, who are heedlessly flirting and fluttering on the brink of the matrimonial abyss, whose good I have at heart.

I have tried both Worlds, Old and New; and so far as faults and follies go, I do not think there is much to choose between them. My present business is with the faults and follies of my own country, with which I feel more especially competent to deal, and which I am most desirous to see corrected and reformed. Having violently reacted from them myself, it is only natural that I should be consumed by the fervour of proselytism, and should, regardless of consequences, exhibit myself as a warning, if need be, to those I wish to serve. When I first appeared upon the social horizon, I may say without vanity that I was the kind of girl who in London would have been called a 'stunner,' a 'screamer,' and who in New York is sometimes described as a 'bouncer.'

My father was the son of a Scotch gardener of the name of

Macgillicuddy, who had emigrated to New York, engaged in the grocery business, and by superior shrewdness and Scotch caution had amassed a considerable fortune, which enabled him to give his son a good education—in other words, to make a gentleman of him. Unusually successful in early life in railway and stock speculations, my father soon became the possessor of a handsome mansion on Fifth Avenue and a financial man of some prominence. Far too respectable himself to become a politician, he nevertheless enjoyed great influence with his party; and there was an air of substantial dignity about him, which, taken in connection with the invariable success that attended his business operations, secured him a commanding position in society. Originally a Presbyterian, he had become attached to an Episcopalian church with ritualistic tendencies, a theological step almost rendered necessary by his fashionable standing; and his box at the opera, which cost him £3000, and expensive pew in St Grace's, for which he paid £2000, though apparently useless luxuries—for he never practised what he professed in the one, and rarely went himself to the other, as he did not know the difference between the wedding march in "Lohengrin" and "Tommy make room for your Uncle"—were, nevertheless, a recognition of the claims of God and of society with which he could not afford to dispense. He had one brother who had never risen above the level of a stonemason; and to him, therefore, it is not necessary here further to allude. My mother had been quite a 'belle' and an heiress in her time. Her father had made his fortune in 'dry goods,' and my maternal uncles were both men enjoying great social consideration on account of their wealth. One was in the hardware business, and the other had struck oil. My mother was a remarkably clever and well-educated woman. She had spent several of the early years of her life in Europe, where she had acquired a taste for art, which my father also affected, without, however, knowing anything about it; and the result was, as their combined taste was somewhat florid, that our house looked like a badly arranged museum. She was, moreover, an accomplished musician, with a magnificent contralto voice; indeed, she was as much superior to the average amateur performer as her cook was to ordinary culinary artists: hence it happened that our dinners and our music were both celebrated. In addition to all this, she had an unrivalled knack of capturing distinguished foreigners, and especially British aristocrats, immediately on their arrival in New York. It is needless to say that we had a cottage at Newport, where we spent three summer months in a perpetual whirl of gaiety; from all which it must be manifest that nothing was left undone to secure that social position which became at last an object of envy and admiration to every well-constituted New York mind. It would be a mistake to suppose that this eminence was attained without infinite trouble and contrivance. I was too young to take an active share in my mother's early social struggles; but even to the end, she never succeeded in thoroughly breaking down an indefinable sort of barrier, behind which a certain ultra-exclusive set chose to intrench themselves. I used to think the presumption and conceit of these people quite intolerable. The idea, in a democratic country like ours, of a select few priding themselves on their ancestry and gentility and hereditary refinement, and all the rest of it, and thinking us not good enough to be admitted into their circle, was quite preposterous. There were the Persimmons, for instance, who assumed the arms of the noble family of Persimmons in England, and claimed relationship with them, and had actually family portraits of knights in wigs and ladies in stomachers, and all that sort of thing (young Dick Persimmon was a clerk in a wholesale tobacco store); and there were the Poppinjays, and the Barebones family, that had a fancy portrait of their great historical ancestor, Praise God Barebones, who came over in the *Mayflower*, and whose descendant, as is well known, signed the Declaration of Independence. They turned up their noses at us because grandpapa had originally been a gardener —as if anybody could have told what the original old Barebones had been. Then in close alliance with these there was the old Knickerbocker set, the Van Twillers, descended from the original Wouter van Twiller, and the Van Didntoffers, of whom more anon, and several others, who, for some mysterious reason, thought themselves better than we were. Mamma's principle was to feel thoroughly democratic towards everybody in a democratic country who thought that they were above her, and to feel thoroughly aristocratic towards all those whom she thought beneath her, or whom it was inconvenient to treat as equals; and I suppose that was the principle which the others applied to her. Every now and then our efforts would be crowned with a new triumph, especially after I became a recognised belle and we had formed closer intimacies with this set, and then the airs mamma used to give herself for some time afterwards were quite alarming. Of course, as we progressed we dropped a good many of our earlier acquaintances.

As for myself, I never regularly 'came out'; in fact, I may be said to have been more or less 'out' all the time. From the days when, in short frocks, I used to help my mother to receive her guests, I was recognised as the principal personage of the family. My father yielded to me in everything, and my mother soon perceived that I was destined to become a most valuable element of social success. First I had a French *bonne*, then the best masters that money could procure; and when I was sixteen I was taken to France and Italy for a year, to acquire a knowledge of art and to pick up the habits of polite society in Europe. I was very quick and industrious; and when I compare my proficiency at this age, in music, languages and painting, with the accomplishments of English girls, I think I may say, without undue conceit, that I far surpassed them. It was with a fluttering heart that I viewed my native shores from the deck of a

Cunard steamer, as, thus armed and equipped for the social fray, I returned to New York. It was no feeling of timidity, but a daring and confident longing, that caused this sensitive organ to palpitate so wildly; perhaps also there was a suspicion that before very long it might be beating for other reasons. Come what might, I was prepared to meet it. I knew I was beautiful, thanks to my mother, whose good looks I had inherited. I was an only child, and therefore a large heiress, accomplished, clever and self-reliant. Nothing was more incomprehensible to me than the shy silence of the bread-and-butter misses whose acquaintance I made during my short stay in London. Even their brothers I was often obliged to help on in conversation—they never seemed to know what to say, or how to say it; while I never knew what it was to be at a loss.

My mother was a woman exceptionally well qualified to launch a girl in the society of New York; she had made it a study, and I felt I was in good hands. Before I went to my first ball she gave a series of dinner parties. To these she especially asked all the young married men who have it in their power to make or mar the *débutante* in her first season. It is they, not their wives, who are the leaders of fashion; and it is to them that the would-be belle must pay her court if she wishes to succeed. Of course the unmarried men are important; but they take their *queue* from the older hands, who, in spite of having wives, are still the most indefatigable ball-goers, the recognised leaders of the 'German,' and the established authorities on matters of fashionable etiquette. Where society has no regular hierarchy, as it has in England, its leaders are self-constituted or tacitly acknowledged. The men, as a rule, marry so young that they have not had time to become *blasés;* and the consequence is, that they flirt as actively with unmarried girls, and flutter about as flippantly, as if they were still single. In some cases they keep this up until their own daughters come out, overwhelming the girls of their choice with bouquets, *bonbonnières* and trifling presents, taking them solitary drives, giving them dinners, boxes at the opera, and distinguishing them by such marks of delicate attention as are always grateful to the female mind. Occasionally these are pushed to such a point that they give rise to unpleasant gossip, but I have never known any real harm come of them. The girls are always thoroughly well able to take care of themselves; and upon the occasions, which sometimes happen, of a man becoming so desperately in love as to forget his conjugal duties and propose an elopement, he invariably meets with a positive and decided refusal. In this respect they show a sagacity and sense of propriety which the aristocratic mothers of young families in London, who think nothing of running away with the husbands of their lady friends, would do well to imitate. Of course an exclusive devotion of this sort has a tendency to injure a girl, because it keeps off the young men while it lasts; but perhaps on the whole she gains a sort of *prestige* by it, which only renders her more attractive to them when it is over.

When the great occasion of my first ball arrived, the carriage could hardly hold all the bouquets that were sent. Unfortunately mamma was taken suddenly unwell the very day of the ball; but she did not wish me to be disappointed, as I had been taking so much trouble with my dress and looking forward to it so eagerly: so I arranged with Harry Hardpan, who had stamped me with his approval, and indeed shown me a good deal of attention on the strength of having been fond of me in a fatherly way when I was a little girl, to send his wife for me—she was only two years older than I was; and he met us at the door with several of my friends to help to carry my bouquets. There were thirteen altogether, of which eight had been sent by married men and five by bachelors. I calculated that their united value was upwards of a hundred and twenty dollars, or about £25. All my bouquets had come with cards on them; and as I read the senders' names, I felt that my success was assured. This inspired me with still greater confidence as I entered the ballroom. That night was a triumph—I was literally besieged; but I was determined to act with caution, for fear of making the other girls jealous. I felt at once the importance of establishing myself in a feminine coterie—so much can be done by combination. I am convinced that there is no greater mistake for a girl than to be misled, by the admiration of the opposite sex, into losing her popularity with her own. Young men are intimidated and kept in their proper place by a strong phalanx of girls, if these hold together properly. It requires a youth of uncommon nerve boldly to face half a dozen girls all tittering together in a corner, who, he knows, will pick him to pieces the moment he leaves them. We New York girls used to keep our little heels on the necks of our beaux and trample over them ruthlessly. In London the case is exactly reversed, and the poor girls are crushed by the aw-quite-too-awfully-aw kind of youth, to a degree which makes my blood boil. It is partly because London girls do not understand how to combine and organise, so to speak, against the men, and partly because they have to compete against the young married women, that they are treated with such indifference. Now in my day, in New York, the young married women were nowhere, or, in the vernacular of that city, they 'had no show'; but I hear that they are making a good deal of running of late years, and that the girls are beginning to complain seriously. Another reason why American girls have such a much better time than English girls is, that as they have so much liberty, they can offer more inducements to the young men to pay them attention. A young man will submit to be crushed and bullied and sat upon, if you make it all right at the end of the evening by asking him to take you a sleigh-ride next day, or to give you a dinner at Delmonico's, with only a young lady friend of your own age, and her husband, who admires you, to do proper. What fun we girls used to have, and what plans we used to concoct for robbing our beaux of their affections, of exchanging them when we got tired of them, or of drawing them on to the proposing point! In my first season I had seven proposals. I had several far better seasons than this later on; but mamma said I could not have expected to have done more the first winter, considering the girls I had to compete with, some of whom possessed all my advantages, combined with far greater experience.

Here again I am struck with the difference between England and America. I do not suppose English girls get one proposal for ten that we get. I know one girl, now twenty-four, who has had 157. This I can vouch for, as she showed me the list; but some of the men must have been very slightly wounded, for one asked to be introduced to her not long since. He had been in California for four years, and had forgotten that when he last saw her he had proposed to her, and she had forgotten that she had refused him. He had, in the meantime, made a large fortune in Bonanzas, the absence of which was her objection to him at the time; and they are now engaged to be married. She says she does not see why she should put off getting married any longer, especially as the young married women are beginning to have such a good time.

On the whole, however, I used to think there was far more fun to be had at Newport than in New York. That is the place to contract intimacies both with the girls and the young men. The picnics and games, the perpetual drives with the temporary beau of your choice, the garden parties and constant contact with the same set, tend to establish your position. At the end of one season in New York, and another at Newport, you may be said to have learnt the whole game thoroughly, and can judge for yourself whether you are *de la première force* or not. You now feel perfectly able to take care of yourself, and can allow yourself all sorts of liberties that you could not have ventured upon at first. You have even got so far as to call one or two young men by their Christian names; in talking of them among ourselves we never think of alluding to them except as Dick, or Tom, or Harry, and so forth.

My intimate friend, *confidante* and rival was my cousin, Flora Temple. In spite of her grand name, she was not so well born as I was, or as her namesake on the turf—for her father was originally a tailor, who had made his fortune during the war by taking army contracts; and when he had risen to the social surface, he married my mother's sister, and then, rather fortunately for my cousin, died, for he was a very shoddy sort of person, and left her two millions of dollars. This, together with her own beauty and talent, and my mother's social influence, soon pushed her into the front rank. She was more than two years my senior, and had commenced her career by a tremendous affair with the celebrated Iky Bullstock, who for the last fifteen years has been devoting himself to ensnaring the affections of girls as soon as they come out. Since his marriage, his name has been connected with no fewer than ten. I was counting them up with Flora not long ago; but then, I think, in the cases of several, it was mere idle gossip. Anyhow, it did not do Flora any harm, for Charlie van Didntoffer was simply wild about her. Charlie belonged to one of the oldest Knickerbocker families; he was very handsome, a banker of the highest standing and had charming manners. I am sure many of my English readers must remember him in Paris and Rome. He was almost omnipotent at the fashionable Spuyten Duyvel Club, was prominent in all matters of sport and was universally popular. To begin with a flirtation with Iky Bullstock, and go on to an engagement with Charlie van Didntoffer, was enough to turn any girl's head. In my own secret soul, though, we girls were much more reticent in these matters than English girls are; and, I cannot say for certain, I do not believe Flora cared so much for Charlie as she pretended, and mentally reserved the right to throw him over if sufficient inducement should offer, but she enjoyed what you in England call the 'swagger' of the thing. Whether Charlie suspected this or not, I do not know; but certain it is that at Newport, where we were all three thrown a good deal together, I began to perceive indications of a wavering in his affections in my direction. Now I am no base, ungenerous, or treacherous girl; but I do not think that it was in flesh and blood to help reciprocating just the least bit, more especially as Iky was still fluttering around: and on several occasions I did not think Flora's conduct quite fair towards Charlie, and felt quite sorry for him, poor fellow; and so by degrees it came about—I know I was to blame, but I really could not help it—before I knew where I was, Charlie had proposed to me. He said he felt sure Flora was only trifling with him, and if I would only accept him he would throw her over. I never consulted mamma much on these subjects, as I always felt she took such a mercenary view of them—she seemed to make no allowance for sentiment; so I had to work it out for myself, and as I was barely eighteen, I was determined to do nothing rash. So I told Charlie that I could not disguise the fact that I cared for him more than for anybody else; but at the same time as he was engaged to Flora, I could not countenance his jilting her on my account, but I thought we had better all wait as we were for a year. If at the end of that time Flora still cared for him, and he still cared for me, and I did not care for somebody else, then we could discuss the whole matter over again; and in the meantime we could remain upon the nice intimate terms which this little confidence would produce. You see, I thought a year would surely bring about a change in the situation somehow, which would make it all easier. What does the stupid boy do but go straight to Flora and tell her he finds he does not care for her any longer! Of course Flora was furious, and said I had behaved shamefully; and for some weeks we did not speak. The affair made quite a stir at the time; all Newport was talking about it, and it was one of the standard pieces of gossip in New York when everybody returned from their various watering-places and exchanged the several scandals which had occurred at them respectively. Although

Charlie was very devoted to me, I felt rather uncomfortable, and refused to be definitely engaged to him. In spite of being so fond of gaiety, I was also a devourer of all kinds of literature and general information, and really studied as hard as my other avocations would permit. Now, although Charlie was most refined and gentlemanlike in his manners, he lacked what in Boston (pronounced not inappropriately Boreston) is called culture (pronounced culchaw). What between banking, driving his four-in-hand and attending to Flora or me, he seemed to have no time to inform his mind. In this respect he was not inferior to Iky Bullstock, Harry Hardpan, or any of the others; but I wanted to marry a mind as well as a man, and I told him so. After that he used to come and read Dickens to me for an hour a-day. I told him when he had finished all Dickens's novels, I would put him through a course of "New England thought," and by that time I should be in a position to give a definite answer in regard to our marriage.

For the reason I am about to narrate, that time never arrived. We were in the middle of 'Bleak House,' and I was thinking how in the world to make it up again with Flora, when Charlie came in panting one day with a most important piece of intelligence. Letters had just been received by his firm announcing that the Earl of Chowder, eldest son of the Duke of Gumbo, and Viscount Huckleberry were to arrive by the next steamer, enclosing letters of credit and requesting the Van Didntoffer Brothers to do all in their power to make their stay in New York agreeable to them. The agitation into which this intelligence threw mamma at once revealed to me the vast ambitions of which that excellent woman was capable. Magnetically her noble aspirations seemed instantly conveyed to my own bosom; and though Charlie was reading about Lady Dedlock, a theme which at any other time would have absorbed my attention, "the beating of my own heart was the only sound I heard." Here was a splendid opportunity for setting matters right with Flora; besides, I needed her co-operation and advice. There was one for each of us; and provided we did not interfere with each other and go for the same one, as we had in the case of Charlie, there was no reason why, with the advantage of an early start, we should not have it all our own way. The fact is, we were both considerably put upon our mettle by the triumphant success which had just crowned the efforts of our two most intimate friends—Ida Straddle, daughter of Billy Straddle, of the well-known firm of Puff and Straddle, brokers—and Laura Berstup, whose father is a railway magnate, and well known amongst English shareholders for the talent with which he has made his fortune out of the dividends they fondly hoped to pocket. Ida, after a rapid campaign extending a little over a fortnight, had captured an impecunious Spanish grandee who valued his dukedom at half a million of dollars. Billy, who has always shown himself a most fond and indulgent father, had the cash down on the nail, and Ida became the Duchess of Virdemonio, to the great envy of us all, and has already sent those of us who wish to contract alliances with the Spanish aristocracy, invitations to visit her in her "Château en Espagne"; and here I may remark, that whenever one of us makes a successful hit of this sort, she always does her utmost to help on her friends. Then Laura was engaged to be married to the Russian Prince Schamovitch: he was next door to being a *crétin*; but as he was distantly connected with the Romanoffs, the splendour of the alliance reduced every other consideration to insignificance. Besides, as Laura said, they were going to live principally in Paris, where it was rather convenient than otherwise for a very pretty woman to have a fool for a husband. As the Prince is enormously rich, and Laura is not badly off, I have no doubt they will have a good time; but you may imagine how all this was calculated to stimulate our energies. Any girl with a well-balanced mind would rather be an English countess, or even viscountess, than a Spanish duchess or a Russian princess. We classify them somewhat as follows:

First, the British aristocracy down to baron—we do not think much of baronets and knights; next, we like French and Russians, because that involves living a good deal in Paris; but titles below dukes and princes are too common to be really much prized, unless attached to a very old historic name or great wealth. Italians and Spanish come next, the former preferred on account of the climate and social advantages of Rome and Naples. Germans we do not so much care about; I think, perhaps, because there are too many Germans in the country already.

But all this is a digression; only I was obliged to enter a little into it in order to explain why the arrival of the Earl of Chowder and Lord Huckleberry was likely to produce so much sensation amongst us. So I posted off to Flora with the news. The fact is, that Flora was as tired of our estrangement as I was. So when I rushed into her room, and said, "My dear, I have come to tell you such a piece of news!" she said, quite cordially—

"You can't think, Irene, how I have been longing to see you lately. Why have you been keeping away so?"

As if she did not know that it was no pleasure to me to come and be snubbed, and that my absence had been due to her own crossness. However, I was not vindictive; so I said impetuously—

"Oh, Flozie!" (this was my pet name when we were in our most loving moods), "who do you think are coming to New York? and Charlie is to bring them to us the first day. Why, the Earl of Chowder and Viscount Huckleberry! Isn't it puffectly splendid?" Candour compels me to state that, in my excited moments, I am in the habit of describing most things as "puffectly splendid." We all do; and, on the whole, I think it is better than the expression used by English girls under the same circumstances, of "quite too awfully nice."

"Oh, lovely!" said Flora. "But poor Charlie; what are you going to do with him?" she asked maliciously.

"Oh, Charlie can stand it," I replied. "Don't you remember, before he was engaged to you, he was engaged a whole year to Lizzie Puff, and something always happened to put off the marriage, till at last he told her that he was sorry to find that he did not care for her; but that if, knowing this, she still wanted to marry him, he would make the necessary sacrifice? I don't think we need have any compassion for him."

"Darling," said Flora, "you are quite right. How stupid we were ever to quarrel about him! but, my dear, we must take care not to make the same mistake again. How shall we manage? After what you did about Charlie, I don't see how. Can I trust you, dear?"

This led to a long discussion about Charlie, in which I explained to her that I had previously refused to be engaged to him until they had both got tired of each other, but that he had been unwarrantably premature; and Flora became satisfied at last, and we swore eternal friendship and mutual co-operation, and perfectly square and honest conduct in all future complications; then we kissed each other a good deal and sat down to discuss the plan of the campaign in earnest. After mature deliberation, we decided that the first step should be a reconciliation between Flora and Charlie, and that, in celebration thereof, he should be made to give us a little dinner at Delmonico's, to which should be invited Fanny and Harry Hardpan, Prince Schamovitch and Laura, Lord Chowder and Lord Huckleberry, Iky Bullstock and both of us girls. Under these circumstances, it is not at all a bad plan to have one or two old admirers. The dinner was to be arranged for the night after the arrival of the Cunard steamer, and we were all to hold ourselves disengaged accordingly. Dear Charlie was so anxious to make the *amende* to Flora, that he entered into the scheme cordially and without the slightest suspicion. Indeed he was a great deal too much pleased to be the entertainer of the two British noblemen to think of anything else. Moreover, there was no man in New York who understood the art of giving a little dinner of this sort more perfectly than Charlie, and he was not sorry for the opportunity it afforded him of distinguishing himself; so we were happy and satisfied all round. I think my Lords Chowder and Huckleberry may travel far before again finding themselves at dinner with four such pretty and agreeable women as Laura, Fanny, Flora and myself. Though not given to manifesting more astonishment than they could help, I was amused to see how completely they were taken by surprise. Chowder was a somewhat heavy blue-eyed blonde, with a large light beard and rather vacuous smile; but he had a sort of smart way of sharply dropping his eyeglass with a little twitch out of his eye, which, every time he did it, seemed to impart a flash of intelligence to his countenance. As I came to know him better, I accounted for it by the fact of his having suddenly to change the focus of his eye. He seemed intensely amiable and good-natured. He evidently had a sluggish protoplasm, and was very easily amused, but took his jokes in a heavy sort of way, just as some hunters do their fences—they always manage to get over, but bungle so much that they lose their place in the field. Now Huckleberry, on the other hand, was all 'snap.' Tall, dark, thin, with a pure classical profile and a bright sparkling eye, he took in the whole situation before we had finished the preliminary oysters, and by the time we had done our soup, had proved himself a match for Flora, who is recognised amongst us all as having the quickest wit and the sharpest tongue for repartee of any girl in our set. She seemed to be an entirely new specimen to Huckleberry, and evidently piqued him by a certain brilliant *nonchalance*, which I fancy made him feel rather smaller than he had ever done in the society of any girl of the same age in his life before. Flora was not the kind of girl to stand the patronising air with which the young British Peer of immense landed estates and acknowledged talent is accustomed to address the young ladies of his own class in London. She was wise enough to see that if she wanted to hook her aristocrat, the best plan was to treat him upon thoroughly democratic principles. She rightly judged that the novelty of finding himself patronised, instead of patronising, of being condescended to, instead of condescending, would produce a strange and rather fascinating sensation. In the struggle to assert himself, to conquer and subdue this rebellious and independent belle, the chances were that he would fall in love. By the time the cigarettes were put upon the table, there was a glitter in his eye that convinced me he would fight Flora with her own weapons till he had subdued her; and I knew that if ever Flora met her match, she would fall hopelessly and desperately in love with him. It would not be a skin-deep affair this time, as it was in the case of Charlie, but a real serious business. I should rather have preferred Huckleberry to Chowder myself: but, in the first place, I could not again interfere with Flora's affairs; in the second place, I do not think I should have had a chance with Huckleberry. It was Flora's 'cussedness,' to use an unladylike expression, which proved so irresistible to him, and my temper is calm and equable. And, lastly, the Earl of Chowder would be Duke of Gumbo on the death of his father; and Lord Huckleberry's father was already dead, so he would never be anything more than a Viscount. When Flora was Viscountess Huckleberry, I should be Duchess of Gumbo, and go in to dinner in London miles before her; so I devoted myself to Chowder. He was so soft and gentle and unassuming, I got quite to like him. He was not a bit like my idea of a lord.

The day following the dinner was race-day, and Charlie invited the whole party to drive out with him on his drag. I insisted on Fanny taking the box-seat—poor Fanny! Charlie had been a *passion malheureuse* at one time in that quarter, and she had married Harry out of pique. Then after he had lost her, Charlie seemed rather to regret it, until he fell in love with Flora. Now that we were both likely to be otherwise provided for, I thought it would only be kind to both of them to bring them together a little, and I knew Harry would not mind, as he was otherwise engaged. Now I know all this is very wrong. I do not defend it—on the contrary I regret it. I am deeply penitent for my past follies; but believe me, it was all not half so bad as it looks to the less innocent mind of Europe. This trifling with each other's affections, even if it does not lead to anything worse, is not a custom to be applauded; but the social *convenances* of America lend themselves to such flirtations far more than do those of countries where the external restraints are so great that the very necessity which exists for them suggests the frequency of far graver consequences than we in New York know anything about. Besides, I wanted to sit next Chowder; and how could I do that if I sat next Charlie? And so it was arranged, and Schamovitch and Laura sat behind; and I think it rather encouraged Huckleberry to find that Schamovitch, whom he had known in Petersburg, where he occupied a high social position, was so irretrievably captured, and so desperately in love with Laura Berstup.

Chowder and Huckleberry had both left cards on mamma; and the next day being Sunday, mamma gave one of her Sunday dinners, with music, and a general society afterwards, as was her wont, and she and I sang duets together, and I felt all the time Chowder's blue eyes fixed upon me, sometimes through his glass and sometimes without it. I had to devote myself to the world in general, but I rather appeared to advantage in entertaining mamma's guests, and was not sorry that he should see how competent I was for the task; besides, every now and then I fluttered up to him, and I could see by the brightening of his eye that he liked it. He was too unenterprising to make new acquaintances, and already began to look upon me as an old friend, so I felt pretty safe, and was amused to see how little success one or two other girls had with him to whom I introduced him. They pronounced him utterly stupid, and declared they could get nothing out of him—dear old Chowder! That was because they did not know how. English mothers and their daughters may wonder how it is that, though they have tried to catch Chowder and Huckleberry with untiring energy for the last seven or eight seasons, we American girls found so little difficulty. I can explain it quite easily. It is because in England the mothers do not allow their daughters to manage their own affairs; and, even if they did, the latter are hampered with all sorts of restrictions of so-called propriety, which seems to us unnecessary. There appears to be a tendency of late to introduce European notions in these matters, but it will utterly spoil the market. The more American girls give up their own manners and customs for those of the foreign aristocrats they covet, the less likely are they to succeed in attracting them. In the cases of Chowder and Huckleberry, for instance, those young noblemen were overcome with the novelty of the thing. Neither Flora nor I let a day pass without having a quiet hour or so with them. What with nice solitary drives, pleasant little dinners, theatres and balls, we managed this easily enough. The 'German,' as danced with us, is most useful as a means of securing your prey for a whole evening; he has no means of escape. Thus young women with us are not afraid of being talked about in connections with young men, or *vice versa*, as in England; while the young men, on the other hand, are not haunted by the dread that a stern parent will ask them their intentions, or a big brother inflict condign punishment on them for not behaving honourably. Such accidents have, it is true, been known, but only in very extreme cases; but they are not frequent enough to operate as checks upon "the course of true love." In London the young men devote themselves to the young married women, with whom the poor girls get no chance to compete, because they have so much less liberty, and are so closely guarded by chaperons; the consequence is, that they lack the necessary experience and practice. We are as much superior to them in flirtation, considered as a fine art, as an expert fly-fisher is to one who has never used anything but a worm and a pin.

As for Flora and Huckleberry, if she had had a twenty-pound salmon on a single gut she could not have had harder work to play him. The way he dashed down the rapids and she after him was something frightful to behold. Just as she had reeled him up to the bank, so to speak, and she began to breathe, he would make a dash, or jump madly in the air, and nothing but the most consummate coolness, intrepidity and skill prevented his breaking away altogether. At such a moment interference would have been fatal, and those most interested in her success wisely refrained from offering her either reproval, assistance, or advice. With Chowder it was a very different matter: he was like a sluggish old cat-fish; occasionally he made feeble attempts to break loose, but I never slackened my line for an instant, and soon found I had only to be watchful and patient to make sure of him. Matters came to a crisis during a trip which we made to Niagara under the following circumstances: Our party consisted of the Hardpans, Huckleberry and Flora, Prince Schamovitch and Laura Berstup, Edith Persimmon and Charlie, Chowder and myself. And by this time Charlie was becoming devoted to Fanny Hardpan, and Harry had long been rather a favourite of Edith's. Of course we followed our devices in visiting in pairs the spots which we considered to possess the greatest amount of natural interest and beauty; and Chowder and I, who were of an enterprising and exploratory turn of mind, determined to try to push our way under the Falls to the point reached by Professor Tyndall. Encased in voluminous suits of tarpaulin waterproof, and led by a guide, we descended the stairs and crept along the slippery path that leads into the blinding spray. Chowder would not let the guide hold me, but took my hand and told him to lead the way; and at last we came to a point where we had to wade, and where the spray was so dense that though the guide was only a few paces ahead he was invisible. At this point I slipped, and the noise of the rushing waters was so bewildering, the difficulty of breathing was so great, that I lost my presence of mind and clutched my companion wildly. I do not know whether he mistook my alarm for a more tender sentiment, but he responded by immediately clasping me in his arms—I should certainly have fallen if he had not—and then in a voice of thunder he suddenly bellowed—

"Dearest Irene, I love you!"

He was obliged to roar, otherwise I should not have heard him on account of the noise of the water, and he could not say more at one time, for it was so extremely difficult to breathe. It was so unexpected, and I was so utterly unprepared, that I could only respond by a sort of inane scream—

"You don't tell me!"

Apart from being an Americanism, I have often thought since what a perfectly absurd reply this was; but he seemed quite satisfied with it, and apparently regarded it in the light of a consent, and I was too confused to know whether it was or not. Luckily I slipped again, and escaped the dripping caresses which, like some huge Newfoundland dog, he seemed determined to lavish upon me. I could just pant breathlessly, "Back! back!" when fortunately the guide came, and finding I was completely exhausted, extricated me from Chowder's embrace—just a moment before that nobleman, unable to keep his own footing, fell flat on his back on the rocks—and carried me out of the rushing waters. I was quite afraid that Chowder had been swept into the river, and sent the guide back for him: poor fellow! he was so much bruised that he required all my sympathy for some days afterwards; but as I had become his *fiancée* in this accidental way, this was a duty as well as a pleasure.

The first thing Chowder did after straightening himself up and putting on dry clothes, was to make me promise not to tell. He said that the Duke and Duchess of Gumbo would be violently opposed to his marrying me. Considering that papa had promised to settle a million of dollars upon me as soon as I was engaged to him, I felt myself to be quite as good as they were, and could not conceive why they should object. He muttered something about my having such an unfortunate name; but I told him that my father had been at some trouble to trace his pedigree to the celebrated "Macgillicuddy of the Breeks," a Highland chieftain of a clan which has now become extinct, but that we in America attach no importance either to rank or family, and that I loved him for his own sake. Then he wanted to kiss me again, and said, that for reasons which were inexpressible, if my ancestor had been a Highland chieftain, he could not have been Macgillicuddy of the Breeks, and that there must be some mistake, and I was probably originally descended from the Irish Macgillicuddies of the Reeks. This doubt thrown over my pedigree made me feel very uncomfortable; for although we pretended not to care about such things, papa is very proud of his Highland ancestor, and, as I told Chowder, had even got his coat of arms. Chowder laughed in a ridiculous way, and said something about his trousers of arms, which I did not understand; but he often, like so many of his countrymen, made silly remarks. From the way Chowder spoke, I saw that the whole affair would have to be managed with the greatest care on account of his parents, and I did not even confide it to Flora, who had by no means succeeded with Huckleberry. In spite of the extremely intimate relations which subsisted between them, she could not get him to commit himself—so, privately, I enjoyed my little triumph over her.

Alas that my own mother should have been the one to ruin everything! No sooner did I tell her of our engagement than her exultation knew no bounds. Nothing would satisfy her, on our return to New York, but to make it known. In vain I explained to her the peril of such a course. In vain did Chowder himself remonstrate with her; it was all to no purpose. In a week all New York was ringing with our engagement, and it had been announced in all the papers. Huckleberry dived off to Utah and San Francisco, without having declared himself, in a sort of panic, just at the moment when Flora thought she had brought him to the point; and I came in for some strong language from my cousin for having secured my own prize and frightened away hers.

Meantime Chowder had not sufficient decision of character to propose a wedding right off. The parental terrors were heavy upon him; he talked vaguely about being 'cut off,' whatever that may mean; and, in fact, doggedly resisted anything like prompt action, while he seemed more hopelessly in love than ever. To be honest, I cannot say that I reciprocated to the same extent; I had a *tendresse* for him, but certainly should never have thought of accepting him had he been Mr Smith of London. Meantime Chowder had been obliged, by the publicity of our engagement, to write to the Duke. We concocted the letter between us, and he enclosed a note and my photograph to the Duchess, who usually spoiled him and was more susceptible to attack. After that we had nothing for it but to await the answer in an agony of suspense. Meantime, to clinch the matter, my father settled a million upon me—a fact which Chowder telegraphed to the Duke. How long the month seemed before the dreaded reply arrived, and what a terrible blow it was when at last it reached us! Chowder was literally crushed. His face became so limp under the emotion and agitation of his mind, that his eyeglass would no longer stick in his eye. It was useless to urge him to open rebellion; he was ordered peremptorily to return to his ducal parents, and to his duties in the House of Commons, and seemed incapable of resistance. Such is the tyranny of an effete and bloated aristocracy. How I raged against it! What chiefly aggravated me was the idea that they evidently considered themselves superior to me. The Duke had the impertinence to talk about Chowder "marrying beneath him," as if the aristocracy of New York was not equal to any other aristocracy in the world.

When I told Chowder this, he said that there could not be any aristocracy in a democracy; that he himself was rather democratic in his principles (he is a follower of Gladstone's, and there is no saying where he will end); but that, while he fully admitted my equality with him, he also accorded the same equality to my maid Biddy. I was going to retort upon him as he deserved, when I remembered that my cousin, Maggie Macgillicuddy, was actually a factory girl at fifty cents a-day at Lowell—her father, who was a stone-mason, having taken to drink. This confused me for the moment so much that I scarcely knew what to say, so I asked him whether he thought it would have made any difference supposing I had been a Van Twiller or a Persimmon? He said that it would not have made the slightest difference, and the objection would have been quite the same. As in England it was not supposed that distinctions based upon the idea of birth or caste could possibly exist in a democracy which expressly repudiated them. Hence, all Americans who came to England were considered equal; no one ever thought of inquiring about their families; and, so far as marrying went, he considered all American girls equally charming, and me the most charming of all. This was not very logically expressed, but I understood what he meant, and it consoled me very much. He further tried to comfort me by assuring me that he had only to see his parents to make it all right. He attributed all the blame to its having been prematurely announced before he had time to prepare the ducal mind; and explained that to marry without arranging things first, would put us in a very awkward position if his family refused to receive us. He said I did not understand London society, and that I should never be able to bear the position in which we should be placed; but he had no doubt about smoothing over matters in a few weeks, when he would at once come back and make me 'his own.' This was highly unsatisfactory, but it was the best that could be done. What annoyed me most was Flora's sympathy, through which I could see a thinly veiled satisfaction. She was in constant correspondence with Huckleberry, who wrote her most interesting letters from Utah, where he was being hospitably entertained by the late Brigham Young.

We had a very tearful parting ; and in spite of Chowder's protestations, I felt my heart sink within me when he turned away from me for the last time—looking, poor fellow, quite crushed and heart-broken. I think he suspected himself how small his chances were of success. It was very disagreeable to feel that all the other girls were canvassing my chances. Of course, as they had all envied me, they all secretly hoped he would be obliged to throw me over ; and this, I may just as well say, without further circumlocution, he did, in exactly six weeks from the day we parted. I will not recapitulate the reasons which made it impossible, the objections urged by his parents, which he was obliged to admit were insuperable, the agony which he described was racking his brain and lacerating his heart. It was far too well written and pathetic to be his own composition, and bore the trace of the delicate hand of his mother all through it. The revulsion of feeling to which this disappointment gave rise is too painful for me to attempt any analysis of here. I now know that I have every reason to be deeply grateful to it, for it changed the whole current of my views and aspirations in life ; and to it I owe the happiness I now enjoy ; but it was inexpressibly distressing at the time—wounded self-love, mortified vanity, blighted hope and affection—for I really found, now that I had lost him, that I had more affection for him than I had imagined—all combined to make me utterly miserable. I railed against mamma as the cause of it all, though I really do not suppose she did so much harm on the whole. I shut myself up and refused to be comforted. The consolation of my own sex only enraged me less than the amiable attentions of the other. Charlie van Didntoffer, who was carrying on quite scandalously with Fanny Hardpan, had the impertinence to offer me 'brotherly' sympathy, forsooth, as if I wanted his sympathy, or Fanny's either. It was quite shameful the way that pair drove round Central Park every day with ostentatious effrontery in one buggy, while Harry was carrying on in another with Edith Persimmon. Then to make matters worse came the marriage of Prince Schamovitch with Laura, and I was one of the bridesmaids, and had to endure the condolences of the other bridesmaids, some of whom were to have acted in the same capacity for me, and make myself agreeable to the 'ushers'—an institution you do not have at your English weddings, and a very good thing too. However, I will not let my ill-temper run away with me—though even, after this distance of time, the recollection of what I suffered then seems to envenom my pen.

I was fortunate in being able to turn to my books and studies; and I even tried going to a Bible-reading, which took place once a week, and which was largely attended by the ladies of the fashionable world. It was considered quite consistent to go to this and to all the gaieties that were going on besides; and yet I observed they seemed to make distinctions among themselves. For instance, Fanny Hardpan was a regular attendant; and when Edith Persimmon came once, there was quite an objection made to her on the score of her being too fast. Now I would have thought that these were just the kind of people who should have been the most welcome, because of the benefit they might derive from meetings of this sort; but after a little time I began to doubt whether they exercised any appreciable influence on the daily lives of those who attended them, and as I did not see that they did I gave them up. From all which you see that my mind was undergoing a change; and when Huckleberry returned from the west four months later, I was able to watch the fortunes of Flora with far more charitable feelings than I supposed possible. Indeed I felt sorry for her, for she was evidently really and honestly in love, and beginning to get uncommonly nervous about the result—which was not to be wondered at, considering the frightful warning she had before her eyes in my own case. So I determined to speak seriously to Huckleberry, and show him the harm he was doing to my cousin, and insist upon his either going back to England at once or proposing to her definitely. Huckleberry was very nice about it. He said he had no idea that Flora was really so 'far gone'; that he was very 'far gone' himself; that he thought Flora a girl calculated to make any man happy, and clever enough to fill any social position in any country, and one that any man might be proud of; and that he had never been in love with a girl in his life before, and had only delayed on account of the novelty of the situation; and he hinted that it would be a severe blow to Lord Somebody's wife in England—he did not tell me her name—but that perhaps it would be the best way of ending 'it'—he did not say what; but I thought it best to agree with him, so I said at random that 'it' ought never to have been begun, at which he looked rather red and surprised, and took my hand and kissed it. And two hours afterwards Flora came bursting into the room, radiant with delight. Huckleberry "had placed his hand and heart at her disposal, and he had no tiresome family to consult, and he was in a great hurry to get home, so the marriage would have to be in a fortnight, and would I be bridesmaid? and Huckleberry was the most rising young peer of his day, and sure to be Prime Minister some time; and when she was married I was to come and stay with her at Huckleberry Castle in England, and might marry Chowder after all"—with a great deal more, all in a breathless torrent of bliss and expansiveness, which made me feel thankful that I had forgotten all my envious feelings and been the means of securing her happiness; for I really think my conversation with Huckleberry turned the scale at the critical moment.

Flora's wedding was a very grand affair. The entire New York aristocracy honoured it with their presence, including the Van Twillers, Persimmons, Van Didntoffers, the Poppinjays and the *crême de la crême* generally. Our old beau Charlie, Dick Persimmon, Tommy Straddle, Billy's son, and three or four more of the most distinguished members of the Spuyten Duyvel Club, were all ushers, and I was surrounded by a galaxy of lovely bridesmaids, whose names, together with an exact description of our dresses, are contained in the columns of the papers which appeared next day. In the same veracious chronicles will be found a list of the unusually costly and magnificent presents which came pouring in upon the happy pair, with their probable values attached; while the reporters vied with each other in extolling the good looks of both bride and bridegroom, and in conveying to their interested readers a most minute and detailed account of their personal appearance and conduct upon the trying occasion.

A few days afterwards they started for England in the same steamer with the Schamovitchs, who had been making a tour in Canada, and I relapsed into a resigned condition, conducive to much moralising on the vanity of sublunary affairs, and felt very much as if the world was stuffed with sawdust. Little did I then dream of the thrilling nature of the episode still in store for me.

II.

For the next two years after my misfortune with Chowder, I oscillated a good deal. Sometimes I sought distraction in gaiety, and then swung back into study. One of my principal excitements was fighting papa in the matter of my settlement, which, now that there was to be no Chowder, he wanted me to consent to cancel. This I stubbornly refused to do, and, as will appear later, to good purpose. By degrees, I found myself becoming rather an awe-inspiring creature to the young man of the period, which was all the more aggravating to him, because, pecuniarily, I was so desirable. Now and then one in a shy timid sort of way would muster up courage enough to propose to me on quite inadequate encouragement; and one pertinacious man would not be content with four refusals. This made me rather cynical; and when I was not cynical, I was learned, with a materialistic tendency and a theory of evolution of my own. Decidedly I was rapidly becoming disagreeable, and so, finally, I found myself drifting away from my old associates into a sort of literary *coterie*, where my talents were more appreciated, and where I could meet men whose conversation was more congenial to me than that usually indulged in by the Spuyten Duyvellers. And here I would wish, *par parenthèse*, to say a few words to those young gentlemen, for whom I have a cordial and tender feeling. In the words of the old song, "We have lived and loved together"; so I am sure, if I venture to give them a little wholesome advice, they will take it in the spirit in which it is offered. I am speaking not only for their good, but in behalf of my own sex. I remember one evening half a dozen of us girls counting up the young men who could converse intelligently on any of the literary, scientific, or even political questions of the day. When we had got up to two, we were obliged to stop. Now this is very hard upon us. We don't want to be driven to resort to old married men or foreigners for intellectual recreation: but what are we to do? When you are not down in your eternal Wall Streets, you are out at Jerome Park, or looking out of the club windows; but as for informing your minds and giving your naturally bright intellects some wholesome food to digest, which should make you instructive as well as agreeable members of society, you won't do it. No wonder we have to fall back on English dukes, or any distinguished stranger we can find, when our own countrymen will not qualify themselves properly to be the husbands of intelligent and well-educated girls. I am sorry to have to speak so sharply, but nobody seems likely to do it if I do not, and I feel that I owe you some explanation for having taken an Englishman when I had the whole Spuyten Duyvel Club to choose from. I have made it, and I hope you will ponder over it, and profit by it.

Thus it happened that, dining one evening with the celebrated Professor Bivalve, whose researches have done so much to throw light upon the early history of the human race in connection with the remains of jackasses recently discovered in a transition state in the western part of this continent, I found myself sitting next to a remarkably handsome man of about thirty; evidently, from his accent, English, and from his haughty look and polished manners, aristocratic. There was a breadth and power in his massive forehead, a light in his grey eye and a decision in his strong firm mouth and jaw which captivated me at once; in a word, he was a magnificent illustration of the survival of the fittest. I was evidently still susceptible, whatever I might have thought to the contrary. The brilliancy of his conversation was quite in keeping with his intellectual appearance, though it had not as yet been addressed to me, as we had not been introduced. My kind host, however, soon relieved us from all embarrassment on this score, by presenting him to me as Mr Tompkins. It took me a minute or two to recover from the blow which this very plebeian name inflicted upon my feelings, and in my confusion I quite lost some very curious facts which the Professor was narrating to us regarding his own special origin as bearing upon natural selection in general. However, I soon recovered, and, as an agreeable preliminary remark, I opened the conversation by asking my companion whether he did or did not consider the existence of Battrybius put in doubt by the voyage of the *Challenger*. It is needless for me to attempt to give here, in my imperfect language, the entirely new and startling theory in regard to the past history, the present condition and the future prospects of the human race, which absorbed me by its entrancing interest throughout the whole of dinner.

Mr Tompkins found me such an intelligent disciple and listener, that he readily agreed to take me with him on the following day to investigate some curious geological phenomena which have heretofore been overlooked on the banks of the Hudson, in connection with the Palisades. Indeed, all round New York, if people only knew it, there is an immense field of inquiry for the scientific mind. Mr Tompkins and I, regardless of the risk of chills and fever, examined it thoroughly. There was nobody to interfere with us; he never went near the gay and fashionable world. I was too happy to abandon it utterly in such delightful company, and thus keep him away from the snares of the other girls, who, although they could not have appreciated his lofty intellect, would certainly have been fully alive to his manly beauty. Mamma had apparently given me up as hopeless; I was quite out of her depth; and I did not think it worth while to introduce Mr Tompkins to her during the early stages of our acquaintance as I felt sure they would not suit each other. The only aggravating thing about him was, that he never would for a moment leave the ground of science for that of sentiment. We chipped rocks and dissected molluscs together, but he appeared to be profoundly unconscious of the fact that he was chipping my heart and dissecting my feelings all the time in the most ruthless manner, and it seemed quite impossible to make him take a hint. He was apparently absorbed in working out his theory to the exclusion of every other consideration, till I got quite to hate it; for, after all, whatever our origin may have been, or whatever may be in reserve for us in the future, it is evident that if the 'species' is to be kept going at all, it must occupy itself with the present. I often tried in the most delicate way in the world to suggest this view of the question to him. Theory is valueless if we neglect the most favourable opportunities of practical experiment and test. Imagine my horror when, one day, in answer to these hints, he gave me to understand that he had completed his labours in the neighbourhood of New York; but that there was still a missing link of which he was in search, and that he could only hope to discover it by going out West and living among the Indians, where he could make the acquaintance of a squaw.

That afternoon I brought Obadiah—I forgot to say that was his dreadful name—to our house, introduced him to papa and mamma and made him stay to dinner; it was getting too serious. The idea of his continuing his ridiculous investigations at the price of the most treasured feelings of my nature was insupportable. Moreover, I felt sure that he was under some extraordinary delusion. It was nonsense to tell me he did not care for me. It was impossible for two such congenial souls to be thrown together as we were, having every thought and interest in life in common, and not to care for each other. As for myself, I have been so frank hitherto, that I may continue my confessions recklessly. I never knew what love meant till I met Obadiah. When I compared my weakness for Charlie, my inclination towards Chowder, with my devouring passion for Mr Tompkins, I felt indeed how little there was in name, in family, in wealth, or in rank. By the way, it had never occurred to me to ask him about either his family or his means; and when mamma cross-examined me about them, I was obliged to plead total ignorance. This alone shows pretty plainly how genuine my affection was for him. Next day we went by the ferry across to Staten Island, in order to examine a rock undergoing the process of spontaneous concentric exfoliation. He told me it would probably be our last excursion together. This announcement brought matters to a crisis. We were going up a steep hill, and he had given me his arm, when he told me this. I suppose he felt some kind of pressure on it. I know I did on my heart. I thought I should have dropped. Then he stopped and looked kindly and gravely into my face. My eyes filled with tears, and I made a desperate but unavailing effort to look as if I was absorbed by the magnificent view; but I could see nothing except through a watery mist; and all the time I felt so angry with myself that I could have boxed his ears. Well, it could not be helped.

He felt he had to say something, and, as he was a very cool, composed sort of person, he suggested that we should look for a nice comfortable place to sit down. So we found a tree big enough for both our backs to lean against; and then he said, as he was going away so soon and might never see me again, and as we had become such great friends, he would tell me all about himself and his plans. Then the real cause of his indifference flashed upon me suddenly, and I felt sure that he was married, so I said impulsively, "Oh, don't!"

"Don't what?" he asked.

"Don't tell me about her; where is she?" I almost sobbed.

"Either in Utah or New Mexico," he said; "I don't know exactly which, but it does not much matter. I can easily find the ones I want out West."

It was too awful. My wildest imagination had never pictured such a fearful catastrophe. It was all explained now; Mr Tompkins was a Mormon. He had been afraid to break it to me before, because he had not been sure of the extent of my passion; but now that I had been unable to conceal it, he was evidently going to propose to take me to Salt Lake City, and from there we should go on and join his other wives, about whom he apparently cared so little that he did not know whether the particular ones he wanted were in Utah or New Mexico. The wily and artful way in which he had lured me into his toils, his wonderful devotion to science, had all been a snare by which to entrap my young affections. All this passed through my mind like a flash of lightning. All the hearts I had tried to break, all the affections I had deliberately blighted of youths whom I had wantonly encouraged to propose, rose up in judgment against me. How fearful was this retribution! In what a cruel form had my Nemesis overtaken me! sitting on the grassy hillside, just above that well-known village called, with a ghastly sort of appositeness, Tompkinsville. Mr Tompkins paused as if he had nothing more for the moment to say, and I felt that he was purposely giving me time to make up my mind. I was too fond of him to decide hastily in the negative. I know this may seem very horrible to some of my readers, but they must really make allowance for the vehemence of my feelings. I knew that if I did not marry him I should never wed. It was impossible for me ever to feel for another what I felt for him, and it became a serious question with me whether I should blight my whole existence in consequence of a mere prejudice against a custom practised by all the patriarchs most eminent for piety, and by the inspired prophets of the Bible. I thought it would all depend upon the share I should be likely to have to myself of Obadiah; but then how could I ask him how many he had got? He evidently did not care about them all, for he had spoken only of the "ones he wanted." Now they might possibly be only two, in which case I should have a third of him, and besides, I could trust to my own wit for establishing myself in the first place, and I had little doubt of forcing them both into the position of "ones he did not want," in time. Still, if instead of being two, there were six or eight whom he wanted, the case would be entirely altered. It was evidently of the first importance, before making up my mind, to find this out accurately. I internally decided that I would go if he could offer me one-fourth share of himself, or more; but that for anything less than that I should refuse positively. As he maintained a persistent silence, when I had fully made up my mind to this I had nothing for it but to try and obtain the desired information.

"Are you very fond of those you want?" I asked timidly.

"I am fond of every object in nature which helps to produce the desired results," he said with a smile.

I was not surprised that he alluded to his wives in this Platonic sort of way, as he was so absorbed in science that I had ceased to expect anything in the shape of sentiment from him; but I did not like his allusion to the desired results.

"Have you many?" I asked, with some hesitation.

"Many what?" he inquired.

"Many results."

Obadiah looked for the first time during our acquaintance thoroughly puzzled, and, I thought, a little confused.

"Very few," he replied, "and those are, so far, very imperfect. Ah," he went on, with his eye kindling with enthusiasm, and yet with a certain sadness, "how delightful it would be if you could come with me, to help me to discover the reason of the abnormal formation of their skulls!"

I was inexpressibly shocked. So this was all he wanted me to go West with him for! and this was his way of proposing to me!

"Never!" I exclaimed, with a passionate cry, "the very idea of such a thing fills me with disgust and indignation."

He seemed surprised and pained at my vehemence.

"You compel me to explain myself in my own justification," he said, in a more agitated tone than he had yet used. "I am aware I was to blame for inadvertently allowing an expression of a desire for your company to escape me, which may have betrayed a sentiment I have hitherto striven resolutely to conceal. Irene," he went on, "you do not know how much I have suffered during the past month, and how difficult it has been for me to disguise my feelings. If I have refrained from telling you how dear you are to me, it is because I felt I had nothing to offer you."

Nothing to offer me, indeed! I thought savagely. Does he call his wives and his results nothing? But it was pleasant even to hear him confess his love, so I was silent.

"You force me to tell you what I had determined to conceal," he continued, "for I cannot bear to leave you under the impression that I am cold or insensible to your attractions; but, situated as I am, I felt that it would be dishonourable to take advantage of our intimacy and allow it to ripen into any warmer feeling."

Well, I thought, he seems to have some feelings of decency left in him after all, and yet I confess to a tinge of anxiety at the notion that he might prove too honourable to take me with him, though I had not quite made up my mind to go.

"At one time, I confess," he added, "I had almost determined to make a clean breast of it to Mr Macgillicuddy and throw myself upon his mercy."

"Mercy!" exclaimed I, by way rather of an oath than an echo. "What madness! Why, how could you expect that either he or mamma would even listen to such a proposal? Under no circumstances must you ever breathe to them what you have told me."

"Ah," he said mournfully, "then I was right, and I should only have put myself in a false position; so there is no hope."

"It seems to me," said I sharply, "that you are in rather a false position already."

"Irene," he replied pleadingly, "how cruel of you to taunt me with it, when you yourself have forced from me an avowal that I had resolved should be for ever buried in the most secret recesses of my heart!"

A bright thought struck me; perhaps he loved me so much that he would abandon all his other wives and their wretched little results, and his peculiar views, conceal the whole story, and agree that we should be married like reasonable people and go and live decently in Europe instead of in Utah.

I looked tenderly and tearfully into his face. His large expressive eyes seemed melting with the glow of his ardent love as he returned my gaze.

"Darling," he murmured.

It gave me courage; I would frankly tell him my thought. This was not a moment to stand upon ceremony; so I said, and I found myself blushing and stammering painfully—

"Don't you think you could give up your pe—pe—culiar views?"

"My peculiar views!" he replied; "why, what can they have to do with it? I know I have a somewhat different theory from Darwin and Huxley, and perhaps it is not altogether orthodox theologically, but surely that need not be a barrier."

"Oh, I don't mean those," I said pettishly, and perhaps a little incoherently, but I thought he was trifling or trying to deceive me. "I mean *them*," and I placed a stinging emphasis on 'them.'

"Them!" he replied; "who are 'them'?"

His obtuseness was more than exasperating—it was brutal. Why should he force me to name the creatures I loathed? But he had goaded me beyond the bounds of delicacy.

"Your wives," I almost screamed.

If he had been struck with a bullet through the heart he could not have given a more spasmodic start, and then his eyes expanded and his lips trembled and his whole face expressed such terrified amazement that I thought he had gone mad. He afterwards explained that he thought I had.

"I don't understand you," he gasped at last.

A ray of hope shot into my heart.

"Oh, tell me, you're not a Mormon!"

I was literally panting by this time in an agony of suspense, for upon his reply my future happiness depended.

It came at last in the form of an uncontrollable burst of laughter. I have seen many large men laugh, but I never saw anyone laugh as Obadiah did when I made this announcement. Certainly my experiences with Englishmen on the two occasions when they have offered me their hearts have been very peculiar. One chooses the moment when we are so drenched and blinded with the spray of Niagara that we can scarcely speak, precipitately to propose, and try to embrace me, and the other, at the very crisis when his happiness is secured, and I am dying to be pressed to his heart, is rolling on his back on the grass in convulsions of stentorian laughter. As soon as he could control himself, Obadiah put my hand to his lips, and then clasping it firmly, and with the tears resulting from the violence of his risible emotions still streaming from his eyes, began to apologise. He explained to me that the women he wanted to go to the southern part of Utah to find, were the squaws of the Piute Indians; that it was rumoured that their skulls were differently formed from the skulls of any other family of the human race, and presented very marked peculiarities when compared with the male skulls of their own tribe—a type quite unknown not merely among American Indians, but among people anywhere else. At least I think he said all this, but I may be mistaken, for I was a prey to such mixed emotions that I could not attend to him very closely. Mortification at the extraordinary and ludicrous mistake into which I had been led almost overpowered my delight at discovering it to be one, while my anger with Obadiah for laughing at me so immoderately was more than counterbalanced by the certainty that he loved me quite as immoderately. I never imagined it possible I could have been so humiliated, and at the same time so happy. Still, I felt rather indignant with him for having misled me into such an absurd position and made me appear so ridiculous. What could this insuperable difficulty have been which had made it impossible for him to tell me that he loved me, and even made him try to prevent me from caring about him, if it was not that he was already married? What was this awful mystery which raised so terrible a barrier between us? Indeed, before he had done telling me about the Piute squaws' skulls, he had gently dropped my hand, a shade of melancholy stole over the countenance so lately convulsed with merriment, and he heaved a deep sigh.

There was no need of reserve between us now: we knew we loved each other—for he could not be mistaken in regard to my sentiments—so I boldly said—

"Dear Obadiah, what is this fearful secret that you could not venture even to tell my father, that has made you suffer so much while we have been together, that has been the cause of the terrible misunderstanding to which I have been a victim?" At this I saw the corners of his mouth twitch, but I suppressed my irritation and went on: "Tell me, dear, what it is that you feel must keep us apart? I can bear anything, only do not leave me in this dreadful doubt and suspense."

"Dear one," he answered, "it is very simple, and there is very little mystery about it: the fact is, I have not got any money excepting what I can earn by my pen, while you are very rich, and among gentlemen it is not considered honourable for a poor man to engage the affections of a girl who has a fortune without first discovering whether it would be agreeable to the parents. Now, from what I had heard of Mr and Mrs Macgillicuddy, I felt quite certain that they destined you either for an American millionaire or a foreign nobleman; and as I supposed you would not marry without your parents' consent, and as I knew that it would be impossible to obtain this—and as, moreover, if it could be obtained, I should shrink from the suspicion, either on their part or yours, that your fortune had influenced me in the matter—I determined, as soon as I felt that our intercourse, which has been so delightful to me, was leading to danger, to start off at once on my search for the missing skull, upon which, I may say, one whole theory in regard to our origin is built."

I am afraid I very nearly said, "Oh, hang our origin!" I know I felt it, for I was so completely puzzled by his novel and ridiculous theory about my being rich and his being poor that I could not bother with his other theory. I had never heard of such a thing as a man, because he was poor, thinking he ought to keep away from a girl who was rich, or first ask her parents' consent, and absurd rubbish of that sort. Why, with us the rich girls are besieged by the poor men, who do all they can to engage their affections, and the girls, as a rule, take tolerably good care not to marry them, though they do not mind getting engaged, just for the excitement of the thing. Edith Persimmon, for instance, has been engaged five times and has never been jilted herself once; in every case she threw over the man. The notion struck me as so truly ludicrous that I thought I would pay off Obadiah in his own coin, and when he had finished his explanation, in tones of great solemnity and propriety, I went off into quite as violent convulsions of laughter as he had. The fact was, the objection was in reality so utterly absurd, that I saw that our union was secured, and I felt so happy that I really had something to laugh about.

"Oh, you goosey!" I cried; "all my money is my own, and nobody can prevent my giving it all to you; and I don't care about anybody's consent"; and I felt inclined to scream with delight and enjoyment. What a relief it all was! What fools we had both of us been!—he, through not knowing the manners and customs of the country, and I through impetuously rushing to conclusions, and acting upon them, which is also one of its manners and customs. However, all is well that ends well, and when he found I had actually been prepared to sacrifice everything to my love for him—even to being content with only a share of him—he consented to waive his scruples and take my money and use it as if it was his own. Why, as I knew I had plenty for both, it had never entered into my head to inquire whether he had money or not till mamma had asked me about it, and this reminded me that I had not said anything to him about his family, so I remarked—

"Well, now, we may consider all that foolish pecuniary matter settled, because, although papa and mamma may raise objections, I am master of the situation, thanks to the almighty dollar. I suppose, however, you will have to write home to your family about it?"

My experience with Chowder led me to suppose that this was an inevitable part of the performance.

"Oh dear, no," he said, "that will not be at all necessary. The fact is, I have, so to speak, no family to write to: my parents are both dead. My father was a civil engineer, and had just money enough to send me to Eton and Oxford; but I have had to make my own way since then, as he died a poor man. I have a brother, who is on some Indian railway, and some more distant relations, who do not trouble themselves about my fortunes."

This was a great comfort. The only thing remaining to be done was to announce it to my respected parents; but they were both out when I reached home.

"Mamma," I said, as soon as she came in from her drive, "I am engaged to be married to Mr Tompkins."

As I fully expected, she was furious.

"Irene!" she broke out, "I thought you were a girl to be trusted. You know I never interfere with your flirtations, but, in return, I don't expect you to engage yourself in this way to the first obscure Englishman that comes along. You have refused at least six men since Chowder's affair was broken off, the poorest of whom was worth half a million, and some of them worth a great deal more, and now, with all your experience, you go and throw yourself away on this Tompkins—what Tompkins is he, anyhow? and what fortune has he got? Why, even if he was a Sir, or an Honourable, unless he had a large fortune, or was a distinguished statesman, or something of that sort, I never imagined you could have thought of him."

Just then the bell rung; it was Obadiah himself, who, in his blunt straightforward way, would not wait until I had prepared matters, but must needs come and beard the lioness in her den.

"Here he is, mamma, to speak for himself," I said as he entered the room.

"So, Mr Tompkins," she abruptly commenced, "it seems you and my daughter are engaged to be married?"

"Not without your consent," he replied calmly.

This rather took mamma by surprise; she did not expect so meek a response, and continued in a milder tone—

"You know, we American mothers have a strong prejudice against our daughters marrying foreigners."

"I was not aware of it," he said.

"I mean, of course, foreigners who are not persons of distinction in their own country."

"I am sorry I can lay no claim to any such distinction," he observed.

Mamma got rather exasperated by these calm brief answers.

"You are aware my daughter has a large fortune of her own?" she went on, with something approaching a sneer in her voice.

"It has been a matter of regret to me for the last month that it is so," he replied, "as I am absolutely penniless."

This remark struck me not only as illogical, but entirely wanting in common-sense, so I indignantly interposed. "This is a matter between Mr Tompkins and myself, mamma, with which neither you nor papa has any concern whatever."

"Well, my dear, I will leave you to discuss that question with your father. And now, Mr Tompkins," continued mamma, "as you have told us so frankly that you have nothing in the way of money, would you kindly inform us what you have in the way of family?"

I again rushed to the rescue before he had time to say anything.

"All the Tompkinses belong to the same family, mamma. You know the Virginia Tompkinses spell their name with a 'y,' and claim to be descended from the original Tompkyns who came over to Virginia with Captain Smith. It is now historically proved that he was best man on the occasion of the Captain's marriage with Pocahontas: don't you remember, dear mamma?"

I knew the history of her own country was not her strong point and that she could not contradict me. "Obadiah is a younger branch of the same family," I continued; "are you not?" And I turned to him with an expression as nearly conveying a wink as I thought safe.

"Very much younger indeed," he replied. "I am afraid my branch only goes back one generation."

"Only one generation!" exclaimed mamma. "What do you mean? you must have had a grandfather!"

"Two, madam," said Obadiah very stiffly; "but I only know the name of one, and it was not Tompkins, it was Jones, which was my mother's name."

"Then you don't know who your father's father was?"

"I do not," said Obadiah, and he drew himself up with an air of haughty dignity which made him look superb, as if in his absence of pedigree he defied the world. It proved to me that the pride of no birth could be more commanding even than the pride of birth. It seemed to cow mamma for an instant, and I took advantage of the pause to exclaim enthusiastically, 'Why, I know my grandfather was only a gardener, and though you don't know it, perhaps yours was a lord." Then I got very red, and felt somehow I ought not to have said it.

"Irene, I am ashamed of you," said mamma sternly. "You see, Mr Tompkins," she went on, "while in our own democratic country we are not usually very particular in making inquiries into the origin of the families with which we contract alliances, provided the money is forthcoming, it is not the same where foreigners are concerned. We wish our daughters to move in the very highest circles in the country of their adoption by marriage. With our democratic views it is very disagreeable for a girl to encounter the possibility of having to walk in after anybody because of the accident of her husband's birth. This is why really no American girl should by rights ever marry anyone less than a duke; and then," she added thoughtfully, "supposing he was not the premier duke, she might still be placed in an inferior position to the premier duchess. Now here is Irene's own cousin Flora married to Lord Huckleberry; just think if she were to meet Irene in society as Mrs Tompkins, what a difference there would be in the position of the two girls! I am quite sure, Irene, you could not bear it," and she turned to me.

"Your daughter would never be called upon to bear it," said Obadiah; "she would never, as my wife, be likely to move in any society where she would meet Lady Huckleberry."

"Worse and worse," said mamma—and I confess I did not much relish the prospect; but it was far better than that other fate I had nerved myself to encounter for Obadiah's sake, so I determined to put a bold face on the matter.

"If ex-President Grant could stand going in after people, I suppose I could," I said with a pout; "at any rate, I am not going to give up Obadiah for all the Lady Huckleberrys in the world." You see I was becoming desperate. I was rewarded by the grateful look my lover turned upon me.

"Well, my dear," said mamma with a bitter sneer, "I have said everything that as a mother it was my duty to say; you may please yourself—only don't reproach me if you are unhappy in your degradation, and don't expect me to come and pay you a visit, to be looked down upon as the mother of Mrs Obadiah Tompkins. I shall go and stay with Flora at Huckleberry Castle, and we can meet at railway stations or in picture-galleries."

With this my mother marched solemnly from the room and left me to console myself with my darling. Obadiah was a good deal surprised at the suddenness with which she collapsed, and said English mothers did not give in so easily; but I explained that as the daughters here never give in at all, and as, after all, it was I, and not she, who was going to be married, she knew very well that sooner or later she would have to beat a retreat, and, like a wise woman, she saved her dignity by not allowing herself to be drawn any further into a struggle which could only end in defeat. He was very much relieved at the unexpected turn affairs had taken, and we sat together on the couch and had a lovely time.

In spite of my mother's threat, my father directly avoided any encounter with me on the subject of finance. Where she had been vanquished, he felt that he had no chance, and he contented himself with behaving as rudely as possible to my intended upon all occasions.

Obadiah at once agreed to postpone indefinitely his journey to the country of the Piutes and content himself with the skull which I offered him as a substitute, and in order to avoid any protracted gossip in regard to our affairs, we determined that our marriage should take place with the least possible delay and in the most private manner. Mamma, of course, would have nothing to do with the preparations, though my parents were both to be present at the ceremony, and I contented myself with Rose Poppinjay and Edith Persimmon as bridesmaids; while Charlie, who, I must say, is always willing to make himself useful, did duty for Obadiah, to whom I had introduced him some time before, in the hope that he might take advantage of the opportunity to improve his mind.

We were married in the little church round the corner, and started immediately afterwards to spend a quiet fortnight at Levox. As my fortune produced an income of about £12,000 sterling a year, Obadiah agreed with me that there was no spot better adapted than London for spending it. So in due time we took our passage in a Cunarder, and I once more turned my back upon my native city to begin life under entirely new conditions. Almost the first person I met upon the deck was, to my amazement, Edith Persimmon.

"Why, Edith!"

"Why, Irene!"

These two words, ejaculated with immense emphasis, is our invariable mode of expressing surprise and delight at an unexpected meeting of this sort. Then I saw a number of young men hovering around her, and her hands full of bouquets, and I knew that she was bound for Europe, and that all her beaux, married and single, had come to see her off. Under ordinary circumstances, we should have been similarly attended. I should think, for instance, when we went to see the Huckleberrys off, we must have been a party of fifty or sixty. But Obadiah was of a very retiring disposition and hated what he called 'functions' of this kind. Since our marriage, all our thoughts had been in common, so I, of course, quite agreed with him, and we had slipped on board quite quietly. However, as all Edith's friends were mine, there was no escape now; so we had a grand kissing, and hand-shaking, and leave-taking. The young men rather like these occasions, as they can take advantage of the pretext of sudden and overwhelming emotion to steal the chaste salute from the departing fair one for which they have so long been pining in vain. The poor thing being in a kissing, tearful mood, grows confused with so much embracing, and thus gets taken advantage of. I saw it happen to Edith in three different cases, and she seemed scarcely to have known what she was doing. Obadiah, who was looking on with a view to discovering "the hidden principle of nature which was at work," said she was perfectly well aware all the time what she was about; but I think science makes people a little cynical. However, as he said it, of course it must have been true. "Why, my dear," said Edith, as soon as all her admirers had hurried down the gangway, at the imminent risk of jostling one another into the water—for they had clung to the ship to the last—"why, my dear, only to think of our going over together in the same steamer! why, it's perfectly splendid!"

"But are you going over alone?" I asked. "I don't see Mr and Mrs Persimmon."

"Didn't you hear, dear, that Flora sent to invite me to pay her a visit at Huckleberry Castle. She said there was no room for papa and mamma, but that she would be glad to see me alone, and they were expecting a visit from Lord Chowder. So, as dear Captain Codd is such a friend of ours —you know, we made our last passage with him—he agreed to take me under his charge. Besides, Iky Bullstock, and old Mr and Mrs Barebones, and Mary, are crossing with us ; so I shall not feel a bit alone ; and now I shall have you as well— and I am never sick, so I expect to have a beautiful time."

And here I should observe that I had received a letter from Flora, couched in rather cool terms, congratulating me on my marriage, but regretting that it should have happened just at the moment when she was going to invite me to pay her a visit. Now that I was married, she supposed I was too much absorbed in my husband to care about paying visits— which was a delicate way of insinuating, that though she would have been glad to see me alone, she did not want Obadiah. Thus it came to pass that Edith Persimmon was asked in my stead, and that I now found her on board the same steamer with myself, starting in pursuit of Chowder. I was standing with my arm through Obadiah's as I made this reflection, and thought how nearly Chowder had been my fate, and when I compared what it really was with what it might have been, I felt inclined, then and there, to fall on my knees with gratitude ; for I would not have exchanged my Obadiah for a million of Chowders, or have descended from my lofty position as Mrs Tompkins to be her Grace the Duchess of Gumbo for anything the world could offer. Obadiah said that this sentiment arose from a hidden law which had been prevented by the intellectual forces of nature from development in the most civilised portion of the human race, but that in my case it was struggling to find expression, and he hoped in time I should be morally as much superior to the rest of my sex as the recently discovered male aborigines of the eastern part of New Guinea are to the most advanced men of science in Paris, or London, or New York. This may give the reader a hint as to my husband's evolution theory. I may be able to refer to it more fully on another occasion; for the present I must return to Edith. She was extremely anxious to know all about Chowder. In other words, she wanted what in America are called 'points,' and in England 'tips,' from the one person who, of all others, could give them from personal experience. She evidently considered it in a manner providential that she, bent upon the capture of that special coronet, should find herself making a passage in the same steamer with one who had already captured the heart to which it was supposed to belong.

"Edith," I said, "you don't need any instruction of this kind. You have had enough experience, goodness knows, without asking me. You can't catch him under a waterfall, as I did, because there are no waterfalls worth talking about in England; but if you can't get into difficulties in the hunting-field, for instance, and sprain your ankle, and both lose your way, and then—oh, Edith," I broke off, "how silly you are—or rather, I am! I will not go on talking such nonsense. There is only one thing I will tell you: it is not Chowder that you will find any difficulty with, but the Duchess. She will be your Plevna. Take the Duchess, my dear—assault her, sap her, mine her, starve her—anything you like—only capture her. She and you together must then lay siege to the Duke, and the walls of Chowder, like those of Jericho, will fall down the moment you blow your trumpet, if your flag is floating triumphantly from the parental battlements."

Obadiah came up just as I had exploded in this magnificent burst of allegory, and I felt so dreadfully ashamed of myself when I remembered how differently a Papuan woman would have advised any young aboriginal female in regard to matrimony, that I found my eyes filling with tears at this descent from my high ideal.

Two years previously, as the Countess of Chowder, I should have looked forward to a London season with a delight bordering upon frenzy. Now, as Mrs Obadiah Tompkins, deeply interested in the problem of humanity, I anticipated, with a far keener and more real enjoyment, a quiet life with my husband in a suburban villa, surrounded by a congenial society of his literary and scientific friends. I will not describe the intensity of my devotion to him, nor the absolute unity of our feelings and aspirations, for there are none of my married acquaintances who could sympathise with or understand it. He always insisted upon my sitting near him when he wrote, because, he said, I inspired him; but I dare not flatter myself that it is due to this that the remarkable series of articles which have appeared in the 'Nineteenth Century,' signed "Obadiah Tompkins," on "The Moral Attributes of Physical Forces," should have produced so profound a sensation. Their importance may be gathered from the fact that we are credibly informed that Mr Gladstone is at this moment writing a reply to them in a series of articles entitled "The Physical Attributes of Moral Forces," and that the entire subject is to be discussed at a later period in a "Symposium." The more I think of it, however, the more I feel that the true arena for debating topics of this kind is the House of Commons. It is only natural that, being an American, I should be strongly Conservative, and I need scarcely add that Obadiah entirely shares my views. He feels with me that it is not to be tolerated that all the scientific talent should be on the Liberal side of the House, and that Dr Lyon Playfair and Sir John Lubbock are to be allowed to have it all their own way on a certain class of questions. We have therefore made up our minds that he is to stand at the next general election. I confess that it is not without a certain feeling of triumph that I am looking forward to the day when Obadiah will be called upon to join a cabinet, of which Huckleberry will probably be a member.

Meantime, Flora has fully justified my expectations. Her beauty, her brilliant talent, her great adaptability and powers of imitation, enabled her to assume her new *rôle* with eminent success, and she soon secured the admiration, I had almost said devotion, of the leading personages of London society. Thus she gallantly fought her way into the front rank of that set in which Lady Twickenham and the Hon. Mrs Hurlingham are such distinguished ornaments. Before the first season was over, she had got herself enormously talked about, and there was a certain reckless dash about her which captivated all who found themselves drawn within the influence of her magic circle. Chowder was one of her most assiduous worshippers, and Edith had some difficulty in luring him off. Flora, however, far from being jealous, made use of her friend as a sort of decoy, and the two were inseparable. By these means Edith made a round of country-house visits under most favourable circumstances, for no one thought of inviting the Huckleberrys without Miss Persimmon, and thus it happened that she found herself a guest at "Clam Towers," the seat of the Duke of Gumbo, and in the most advantageous position for laying siege to the Duchess. Curiously enough, I had, in advising Edith, underestimated the lasting nature of the impression which I had produced upon the susceptibilities of his lordship. When that enterprising young woman, after infinite exertion, had vanquished the Duchess, she found her blandishments altogether powerless to captivate Chowder, who has given out that he never intends to marry, and who entertains a sincere and respectful friendship for Obadiah and myself. Edith, therefore, has abandoned the pursuit, and, as she has made a sufficient number of aristocratic friends of her own, has parted company with Flora, and has obtained quite an independent position both in London and Paris, at which gay capital she is at present disporting herself with some newly arrived Americans, to whom she is temporarily attached. It remains, therefore, still a matter for conjecture to what nationality her noble husband, when she finally captures him, will belong. Mamma has written to Flora, proposing a visit; but Flora wrote back that she had not a single room in the house to spare. When the latter heard that all London was talking about the remarkable lecture which Obadiah delivered the other night at the Royal Institution, she was foolish enough to give us an opportunity of refusing an invitation to Huckleberry, with which she thought fit to honour us. We finally met at the South Kensington School of Arts. Perhaps I ought to have said, what my modesty shrinks from, that I was as much talked about by this time as Obadiah. In fact, without meaning it, we had suddenly appeared upon the social horizon of a certain class of London society which prides itself upon its intellectual attainments, and had taken it by storm. This led to our being forced upwards, whether we liked it or not, and upon the evening in question I was conscious of a sort of buzz of admiration going on in my immediate vicinity, when Flora rushed into my arms, and I was further conscious that it was I, and not she, who caused it. I went and saw her next day, and made the discovery which suggested this record of my tender recollections, for I thus became aware that I had developed a great deal more heart than I ever imagined I possessed, while she seemed entirely to have lost any she ever had; so I went home to Obadiah, a sadder and a wiser woman.

I thought my little history would convey a moral if it were written, which my readers could find out for themselves, the more especially as Obadiah said he did not mind the publicity of so much that is usually considered confidential, if I thought it would do any good. So I have written because I hope it may; not to the society of London—I almost fear that is past redemption, but my own old society, to which these tender recollections more especially refer, is still young and fresh enough to improve. I have not meant to expose its faults ungenerously, or to dwell too severely upon its weaknesses. At all events, I will comfort myself with the reflection that those who honestly feel that I have maligned them will be far more likely to forgive me than those whose consciences convict them, and to whose forgiveness, therefore, I am indifferent.

MY FIRST HUNT. BY A SAILOR.

[Maga, March 1910.]

LIKE all great events, my first hunt was the result of small unthought-of beginnings. I was asked to spend a couple of weeks with some relations in the country who, from advancing age, had given up their horses. The stable, although large, had a neglected appearance. The old coachman found more occupation in keeping the garden up to date than in grooming horses, a pursuit in which he was encouraged by two unmarried daughters, who were now well beyond the age of love at first sight. They found that the memory of past years was refreshed by the fragrant perfume of deep-scented roses in the summer and Neapolitan violets in the winter. The outhouses and garden were certainly a dream, but after two days I awoke from it and looked round for a possible antidote to utter inactivity.

A well-known pack of hounds, and a suitable stall for a horse untenanted, appealed to me as factors not to be overlooked. I asked old Tom, the coachman, in confidence, whether it would be possible to borrow or hire a horse on which to ride about the country. He told me that horses were brought into the county town at this time of year specially for letting out, and I could get a very nice mount without doubt. As he seemed quite keen about it, I approached my host for permission, making a contract that I, not he, was to pay. He was extremely kind and generous, and wanted to make me enjoy my visit, so I had the biggest difficulty in getting over this obstacle. The preliminaries being completed, I came out and consulted again with old Tom. I asked if the food locker wanted replenishing in the stables, but found there was always plenty kept for visitors' horses.

After this there seemed nothing else for me to do but to go straight in and see the hostler people about the hire of the horse, and for this purpose I went back to the house and up to my bedroom to rig myself out for the possible ride back. Fortunately, I had brought what I thought was practically an unworn pair of riding-breeches with me, but on examination I found them nearly worn out, especially at the knees. Then I remembered that I had some time ago lent them to a friend of mine who was going through his military riding-lessons at Woolwich—I had never expected they would have been so much appreciated by him. At least, however, they gave me the appearance of being an old hand with horses, and therefore came in very usefully in support of my contention before my host and his daughters, that there was really no fear of my having an accident, as I was quite used to riding. They knew I had been used to a pony as a boy, and from the dilapidated appearance of my breeches considered that I must have kept it up. I felt very guilty all the time, but wished particularly to avoid making them nervous. It came as a great relief that I could tell old Tom how the land lay, and I gathered a considerable amount of confidence in talking over the matter with him.

On getting into the country town I found that what he said was right, namely, that it was the custom to take in horses for hiring out to the gentry, and I had no difficulty in finding the stable to which I was told to go. Here there were several nice-looking horses assembled, mostly for hacking purposes, however.

I had in my mind, when talking to the hostler, the possibility of being able to follow the hounds if everything went well, but did not wish to say anything about it ; so I only approached him with the statement that I wanted a horse for a couple of weeks, on which I could ride about the country and perhaps go to a meet or two. The horse I chose turned out, upon the diagnosis of experienced horsemen (confirmed afterwards by the hostler), to be an Irish mare possessing good quality. This I could understand, as she carried her tail and head so high. Her tail was anything but good-looking, being practically destitute of hair; but in spite of this defect she used to swing it backwards and forwards as she walked, as much as to say how well it looked. Altogether, however, as facts subsequently proved, my choice turned out remarkably well, and after a time the mare and I got on capitally.

It was late in the afternoon when the saddle was put on her. I boldly mounted, in order to ride her out to my host's stables, where the old coachman was quite excited about getting ready for a live horse once more. He told me before I started that he felt quite young again at the prospect, but personally I was feeling quite old with the excitement and the strain of doing business with a horse-dealer. I always gathered from 'Punch's' descriptions and drawings that such folk invariably had a parcel of jokes ready for you, and generally succeeded in doing you right and left. I got to the vicinity of the house all right, but before going into the stables I wanted to show my horse to the household and see what they had to say. Everybody turned out on hearing the horse's steps in front of the house; but instead of posing as an accomplished equestrian, I was obliged to stand on my own feet, hanging on to the mare's nose, while they inspected her.

It was this way. I found that opening the drive-gates from a horse's back was quite beyond me in my present condition, and in fact I found all along that gates were very trying obstacles. Once inside the gates, I tried to mount; but the dark, and the fear of walking over the borders as the mare quietly but firmly waltzed round and round, were too much for me. I decided I had better lead her straight up to the house and have done with it.

As far as the assembled household could see in the dark, the general consensus of opinion was that I had got a weight-carrier of no mean order. Seeing that my weight was only slightly over ten stone, this feature did not appeal to me as important. The old coachman, like the rest of the household, had heard my animal's footsteps, and came through a side gate from the stables. The mare at once seemed to feel at home : up till then I am certain, from her restlessness, that she was looking out for someone who could understand her language. I expect she thought it was getting somewhere near bedtime, and from her position in front of the house could see no signs of a stable.

What with a detestable feather-bed, and the mental rehearsal of all I was to go through next day in the way of falling on and off the mare's back, I felt so hot all night that I could hardly sleep, and awoke, or rather got up, next morning eager to jump into a cold bath. I was down slightly before breakfast was ready, and such was the state of my nerves that I decided to go into the stable to see if the mare had by any luck died during the night, or possibly hung herself by her halter. I opened the stable-door, at which she neighed and seemed pleased to see me or the daylight : anyhow, she was alive. I found the cat, an old inhabitant of the stable in bygone days, had forgone his usual rug in the Hall and night wanderings in the house, and apparently had spent the night coiled up on the mare's back, as he was just jumping off on to one of the partitions of the stall when I came in. I could see at a glance we were all going to be a happy family for the next two weeks, if none of us got injured.

After two or three days of hacking along roads, and one or two bursts of speed on grassland, I felt qualified at least to go and look at the hounds at the next meet, which was taking place about six miles away. I made up my mind not to do anything rash, but simply to follow them to the cover-side.

The fateful morning came. I made a poorish breakfast, and was delighted to get started along the road: the morning was crisp and hazy, giving promise of a lovely day. Old Tom had fed the mare well, or else the fresh air had taken charge of her, as she seemed to prefer hopping to walking, and was full of life. During the two or three rides I had had on her before, we appeared to have come to a complete understanding, and I felt serenely sure that I was able to look after myself and that she would look after herself. She was not a frisky, insane, empty-headed creature, this mare, but rather was full of valour, and tried to bite any alarming object, such as a motor-car approaching at full speed or a grunting pig. Letting her do exactly as she liked, old Tom told me, was a great mistake; after which advice, when occasions arose, we sometimes had to split the difference: but it was not so at times when real judgment was required; then I usually found her correct, especially when negotiating difficult obstacles. I did object, however, to being carried across a ploughed field at lightning speed, with her nose just missing the furrows, straight into a bunch of horsemen assembling together to go through a gate or gap in turn. I felt like a ball in a skittle-alley knocking the nine-pins over, with the pins objecting in the profanest language. But I am anticipating.

As I approached the scene of the meet all the cross-roads and bylanes seemed to add to the general throng of horsemen, and carts and carriages gradually collected as we went along. Motor-cars with hunting people in them seemed to be in the predominance, and I found that they had apparently sent their horses on, some by train and others by road. My 'get up' consisted of a bowler hat, Norfolk jacket, and the above-mentioned riding-breeches and gaiters. In this uniform I was glad to find I attracted no undue attention, as there were several mounted men got up in similar attire, mostly looking like farmers' sons out for a day's sport. The cavalcade, when in line of march for the attack upon any particular ground, took up a definite formation. First went the officers of the hunt, then the county squires and their ladies, the men being mostly tall, thin and immaculately dressed, and, it was easy to see, splendid riders; next came the weight-carriers, with talkative old gentlemen on their backs, chatting together, and usually paying compliments and great attention to the younger ladies when any of them happened to be at hand.

I found myself in the rear rank amongst the grooms and the aforesaid farmers' sons, and saw to my surprise the hostler from whom I had hired my mare. He seemed quite proud of his mare, as old Tom had put in some good work grooming her and had made her look smart. I told him I only intended going to the meet, but this, as I found out, was an old way of saying you were going to follow the hounds. He was quite convinced I was going to do so in spite of my remonstrances: I did not think he would like it, and for my part did not dream of going any farther. Instead of being annoyed, however, he seemed to want me to follow, and told me then that she was an Irish mare, well used to bank jumping in her native wilderness, and although very sensible, she wanted to be taught nice manners. I told him I did not think that I could teach her any manners, as I did not know any myself. However, I tried to do what I could, as being of a sensitive nature I rapidly grasped the meaning of the severe glares I received from the hunting people when we did anything wrong.

The contingent from our part of the country, by the time we reached the park gates of the house at which the meet was to be held, had assumed quite large proportions, and in course of conversation I gathered that there was a breakfast waiting for us all. Not having eaten much, I thought I could do justice to the meal, but up to then had never partaken of a hunt breakfast, so did not know of what it consisted. Things all seemed strange to me: instead of coffee I drank champagne, and instead of bacon and eggs I ate lobster salad. The consequence was that when I came out, with a big cigar in my mouth, and took my horse from a groom who was holding it, I felt distinctly as if I had eaten a lump of lead, though my courage had risen.

The sun by this time was shining brightly, but the air was still crisp. The scene outside the house was enchanting to the last degree—quite beyond my descriptive powers—and I could see that it was a case now of do or die. All intention of turning back directly the field started had left me. The Master of Hounds arrived and took charge of his pack, being received with salaams from the assembled audience. We swung into our column of route (myself astern), and the move began. My next-door neighbour knew where we were going, mentioning some place sounding rather like Timbuctoo. Everybody, whether it was the effect of the breakfast or the anticipation of sport, was showing distinct signs of life and a mood different from that of the early morning contingent which I had brought along with me.

Horsemen and horsewomen, with obvious skill, passed up and down the lines on either side of us—sometimes in the ditch or just on the edge of the road. A halt came at last on the highway, and, looking along the hedge where I was standing, I could see the hounds and huntsmen, together with some of the field, slowly trickling through a gap into a dense wood which appeared to embrace the whole of the countryside. This obviously meant the start of the business. My turn came to enter the wood, and I found that the gap through which we were passing was the beginning of a long bridle-path. Now and then, when the path straightened itself out, I could see the whole field, looking very much like an extended and beautifully coloured caterpillar creeping through the wood. Next, I saw ahead of me what seemed to be an undulation taking place in the caterpillar's body. I found, as the wave got nearer to me, that the cause consisted of a large tree-trunk lying across the path. This was my first experience of a jump on horseback. I never hesitated for a moment—in fact I could not, as I was pressed from behind by hordes of other horsemen. I only hoped to goodness I would not make a complete fool of myself in front of everybody by falling off. The mare took the tree with a little hop, and I hardly knew that I had passed over it. In course of passing through the wood more trees were encountered, which sometimes required a little manœuvring, to judge by the fuss some of the horses made.

The pace of the rear-guard livened up a bit presently, as apparently the leading files had come out clear of the wood and were making quicker progress along the field beyond. This made it more difficult to pick one's way, but I simply let the mare do everything herself. There was some confusion at the gate, which was at the end of this bridle-path, as unfortunately I had not brought a crop with me and could not therefore take my turn at keeping it open. It had a pronounced tendency to shut. We got all bunched up, and the horses inside the wood were beginning to get restless, wanting to join their comrades whom they could see cantering along the field in the open. Matters were getting uncomfortable, and so many people looked annoyed at me for blocking the gangway that I thought I had better dismount, if I could do so without being trampled on, and cut a piece of wood to help me in this sort of business. However, I was helped through by someone who kindly kept the gate open for me, and I decided in future to keep well behind, so that I should not get in the way of other people again. But I found this did not suit the mare at all, and was in fact impossible: I supposed that her desire to forge ahead was one of the bad manners which I had to get her out of.

The outskirts of the wood turned at right angles and ran up the side of a valley. At the bottom end where we now were, a lot of people stood in a cluster. I went on with others, and proceeded higher up till I reached the other end of the wood, situated at the ridge overlooking the valley and the most lovely country, covered with heather, silver-birch and pines.

Whilst admiring the beauty of the scene, I heard a roar of, as it were, thunder, and looking round saw the group of horsemen that I had passed, about fifty perhaps in number, galloping up to where we were standing. The noise of the approaching cavalcade absolutely drove terror into me, whilst everyone's animal looked and snorted in the direction of the unearthly rumbling noise coming up from the valley. The mare became exceedingly restless, and I hardly knew which way to look, what to do, or how to keep seated. Suddenly the huntsman broke cover near where we were standing, trotted to a piece of rising ground, and, turning round in his saddle as if to speak to me, gave a war-whoop that no Indian or cowboy could ever emulate. The piercing minor key, the countryside stretching away before me, and a horse obviously asking to be let loose, deadened my sense of fear. Before the echo had died away the countryside seemed to thunder with horses' hoofs, and I was swept away with the avalanche.

I could see no hounds, and had no idea at all of the direction we were taking: all I knew was that we were galloping hard on a broad front. I stuck to a little group of horsemen —five or six in number—who seemed to know their business. My first jump—a bank with a hedge on it—although well cleared by the others who had gone first, brought me on top of my horse's neck, but I sat tighter at the second one. I leaned back as far as I possibly could before landing, and came up with a firm seat. We then covered what seemed to be a mangel-wurzel field full of sheep-wattles or hurdles, over which we jumped in and out just like grasshoppers. I remember noticing with interest that I seemed to be in the best position for landing when my feet were about in line with my horse's ears. I do not say that this was actually the case, but it was certainly my impression.

Two stiffish banks and about six sheep-wattles taken at full speed gave me confidence, and instead of paying exclusive attention to remaining seated I began to try to find out how the people ahead of me knew where to go when there seemed nothing to guide them, and in what direction the hounds were running. Complete knowledge of the country must, I came to the conclusion, be a *sine qua non.* Before I could do much more towards thinking out this problem we were scrambling into a highroad, across which we passed and manœuvred through a gate leading into a sort of a pine-wood. I let everybody go through first, and got through in time to hear the last horseman in front of me galloping away through the wood. Once through, my horse seemed to want to catch him up, and went in the direction of the sound, at what seemed to me lightning speed. The ground underneath consisted of sandpits fringed with heather, then thick clusters of pine-trees. Presently I could hear him no longer, and the track of my leaders got lost in the zigzag, so I simply had to take pot-luck with my horse and trust that she would know the best path to follow. It was quite impossible to steer her at the speed we were going, and equally impossible to stop her.

On breaking cover from these terrible pine-trees (the branches of which I thought every minute would sweep my head off my shoulders), an extensive valley of ferns and rocks and rabbit-holes opened out, into which the mare plunged much against my will, partly I think because she saw another horse in the distance climbing down like a cat towards the bottom. How I got down to the other man in safety I cannot say, but just as I did so he fell into a pit, which my horse managed to avoid. A glimpse ahead, through water-streaming eyes, showed me the hounds clustered together, with nobody in attendance, at the bottom of the valley. The mare was quite beyond my control still, and I hoped sincerely I was not going to play skittles with the hounds by hustling into the middle of them. Also the ground I was covering seemed exceedingly precipitous and unsafe. After two or three last spurts at the bottom of the valley, I managed to pull up, more or less, and headed my horse in the direction of the hounds at a trot. The place where they had assembled was obviously a fox-earth, but it had been stopped. I looked round to see if anybody was about to take charge of them, but could only hear a distant note on the horn. Presently the other horseman joined me, after extracting himself from the pit, and together we wondered how we had got there and what was the next thing to do. We waited quite ten minutes before I saw a hound disappearing at full speed round a turn of the valley, and thinking he must be bent on some hot scent, I suggested that we had better try and get the other hounds along after him. Putting the words into action, I trotted away after the hound and tried to call the rest to follow. They did not understand my lingo, so I waved my hat, as much as to say, 'come along,' which they all did. I had not gone far before they began to leave me, stringing themselves out along the same path which their comrade had taken. I had to break into a gallop to keep up. The bottom part of the valley where they were running was very good going, except for a most awkward-looking rutty cart-road we had to cross, which had a broken-down bank and a ditch at each side of it. My companion was alongside of me, so I asked him to go first if he would, as I did not know much about jumping. He went ahead, and fell broadside on with his horse right in the middle of the road, but fortunately was quickly up, as my horse, in spite of all my efforts, took off exactly at the same place and nearly jumped down on top of him. How I got over I cannot explain, for the bank seemed to give way with the first horse; but in my case it held, possibly because it was strengthened by being knocked down, if that is not an Irish way of describing it.

We were not to be left long by ourselves in this blissful state, with a well-known pack of hounds at our beck and call. Looking up on both sides of the valley, I could distinguish scarlet coats keeping well abreast of us, ready to meet us when we ascended to the top. The ascent soon came, with a distressing climb up a steep slope, which I was glad to find did not tax my mare unduly. I found myself swallowed up again amongst the field, who by this time were swarming up from every direction.

A few minutes afterwards I again seemed to find myself becoming one of a small and isolated group of horsemen. This group consisted of a very red-faced gentleman, a nice-looking girl on a grey horse and two other men who appeared to be friends of hers. They seemed to know the country well, and chose very good ground for riding on. The red-faced gentleman had a most wonderful horse under him, which, whenever there was a chance, always climbed. The rest of us invariably had to jump the lot. A climbing horse seemed to me to be the ideal way of getting along, especially as, when occasion arose, this one could jump like a deer: some of the obstacles could not be surmounted by climbing only. With a group such as this to lead one, the jumping seemed quite easy, as they invariably chose good ground, and the pace seemed to be my only trouble now. However, I think my mare, dear old thing, felt that she was not going to be outclassed by any dashed three-hundred-guinea hunters, and kept going full bore. I was beginning to feel like a sack of potatoes. Tired and weak, I longed for a halt. Presently I got a nasty hit on the nose from the horse's forehead when landing after a jump—not a particularly stiff one. What I thought at first was moisture running down my ears, I found quite by accident to be blood streaming from both sides of my nose. I could not understand how it had got into my ears, and tried to wipe it off with my handkerchief, but owing to the motion of the horse simply smeared it all over my face.

I must have looked very terrifying, as at the next slight pause we had, the girl with the grey horse, who was nearest to me, asked if I would like her to hold my horse while I jumped down in order to wash my face in a little runlet of water by the side of a hedge. I had not got a looking-glass, so could not see what result I had achieved. In any case it was not worth doing, and if I had known the bother I was to have remounting I would never have attempted it. I had hardly wetted my handkerchief before they were on the move again: the girl was having trouble in holding her horse and mine, and I had to run after her and catch my bridle so that she might get on. Directly she went off, I was pulled along by the mare, holding desperately on to the bridle and trying to get her to stand for a moment whilst I mounted. The ground, a ploughed field, was very soft and the mare was very high, and what with the feeling of stiffness and weakness in my legs I hardly knew what to do. At last I got her to stand for one second, and was on her—at least I left the ground, but had to do some climbing before I got properly fixed in the saddle. I was fearfully bumped once or twice during the process, which made me very angry and more determined than ever to see the finish. I looked ahead to find out if I could see the group of people and the girl, but had lost them, and was quite upset at the idea of having to choose the place where I must jump out of the field. I just caught sight of someone jumping at the far end, and made straight for it, as the hedge all along the side of the field was a most treacherous-looking unknown quantity. It had the appearance of being a long extended wood rather than a hedge, but I felt its real function was to hide a ditch. However, possibly it was better where the other horse had gone. I approached the place at full gallop. I spoke to the mare to steady her, and tried to check her. She obviously took this for a warning signal, as I felt her swell her ribs out, and with a leap that made plenty of allowance for unforeseen dangers, we landed safely on the other side, in spite of it being a good deal higher than the take-off side. We had something of a scramble in pulling ourselves together, as the mare's nose almost touched the ground before she recovered herself. As for me, I had leaned back too much, expecting a drop on the other side. My right leg must somehow have crossed over the mare's neck, carrying with it my offside rein, as I found myself riding side-saddle like a girl, with both reins on the same side. I hung on as well as I could, and as quickly as possible got home into the saddle.

I patted the mare on her neck, and would have liked to have called her by her name, but regretted very much that I had forgotten to ask the hostler what it was. I had not lost sight of the horseman who had led me over this jump, and noticed he was going very hard. I soon settled down to our general speed, and finally caught him up. He seemed to know the country very well, and during ten minutes in company with him I admired the way in which he always chose the best place in every hedge, without wasting time by looking about him. Suddenly he turned round and shouted something to me, which sounded like, "They were swinging, and running in full view." I had no idea what this meant, and did not seem to have the strength to work out mentally what I was to do, but could only follow as before. Instead of jumping out of the field in the direction in which we had been heading, we turned at right angles and continued right down the field, which was of considerable size. As we proceeded, horses seemed to be jumping into our field from all directions, and incidentally I saw the red-faced gentleman and the girl with the grey mare closing in upon us. I felt it was very fortunate that I had not lost all scent by the face-washing incident, and that I was apparently directly in the running. All the horses I now saw were showing signs of distress, and I wondered if my old mare was looking like them. Anyhow I felt quite sure that she could not feel any worse than I did. Surrounded by such high-class animals (I found out about some of them afterwards), she seemed to feel she was not going to be outclassed, and I tried to respond to her efforts by endeavouring to shake off the potato-sack feeling that was coming over me. The leading horseman had slackened his pace a bit: the reason he did so was clear when I got a little closer to him and saw the hounds racing across the next field, with two pink coats closely following. In an instant the hounds and horsemen seemed to close up like a concertina right in the middle of the field. Someone called out, "They've got him," but I seemed to have lost all strength for pulling up, until I heard someone else shout to me to keep away from the hounds. With that I leaned over for a swing to the right, and swerved in the direction of a man standing with a sheep-dog by his side. I felt I was going to run him down, and seemed unable to do anything to prevent a collision in spite of the whole countryside being at my disposal. If he had remained still, I think we should have passed him safely, but he literally dived into the mare's legs, whilst I paid the sheep-dog my respects, flying off in the other direction right on top of it. The man, and I daresay the dog, were very much annoyed, and could not understand any more than I could why I had run them down. Nobody was injured, however, so leaving the mare catching her wind in the middle of the field, and the man also catching his and threatening all sorts of violence, I tried to walk over to where the hounds were now lying flat on their stomachs and sides, stretched out panting. Walking seemed like a nightmare, my legs sank under me in a bow, and although I stepped out and apparently walked as one usually does, the progress seemed so absurdly slow that I looked down on the ground to make sure I was actually covering it. All the horses were breathing hard, their tails beating time, whilst a pink-coated man was busily engaged in dissecting the fox. I was glad that blood had been shed—

it seemed a satisfactory ending. I was asked if I would like the paw of the fox, termed the pad, whereby to remember the run, timed to have lasted one hour ten minutes. The girl on the grey horse took the brush, and when the fox had been thrown to the hounds people began to talk the run over, and quite incidentally to consider how they were to get home. Some knew the country well and the road home, whilst others, like myself, did not.

The red-faced gentleman heard me inquiring, and immediately asked me where I lived: I told him, and he said that I was to come along with him, in fact to follow the hounds, as they lived, together with the Master, on our road, and he himself lived only four miles from my place. I ascertained from him that I was about nineteen miles from my home. The little group from our part of the country began to make tracks, following behind the hounds, whilst the red-faced gentleman and the Master rode on in front. We were a little time in reaching a highroad, but once having done so set off at a trot. As we put the miles behind us the group slowly dwindled in numbers, as short-cuts to their respective homes were reached. Finally I found myself alone, riding with the servants of the hunt behind the pack, whilst my guide rode on ahead with the Master.

Being now left alone, I began to think of being terribly hungry. I knew I had brought a little flask of wine with me in my breast coat-pocket, as my ribs had felt quite sore where it had been rubbing up and down all day. As for the sandwiches, they seemed to have disappeared, but on further sounding in my pocket I found them, very much reduced in size, forming a compact mixture of paper, butter, bread and ham. I was not long in dissecting the eatable portion, however, and inside everything I found a bar of chocolate. I ate, drank and lit a cigarette to complete the feeling of satisfaction. A little later on my guide waved for me to come up alongside, as the Master was just about to say good-bye and turn off the highway. We were finally left alone, and set off at a faster trot—fifteen miles for me and twelve for him. It was no joke, but it passed quickly.

Luckily I had not the feeling of riding a tired horse, as my mare responded to the slightest indication that I wished her to step out. I realised vividly how distressing it must be riding a tired horse a long way home, and can imagine it would make the distance seem much longer. My guide also cheered me up, remarking what a good horse I had, and particularly admiring her walking powers. All horses, he said, that could walk well galloped well: he obviously took a great fancy to her—for all I know has since bought her.

The time came at last when I had to leave him. He asked me if I would like a nip of cherry brandy at his lodge gate: I did not want anything myself, but thought perhaps my mare would like something, and asked if he thought it would be advisable to give her anything, but he said that beyond a short drink of warm water (which he ordered to be brought), he always let well alone until he got home, and assured me that the mare would gallop me all the way in her present condition, if necessary. I was anxious to push off and get home, so saying good-bye, trotted away into what seemed pitch-black darkness. I knew my way, but riding through heavily wooded country I really could not see where I was going, and judged where I was by the sound of the horse's hoofs. When it sounded soft, I knew we were near the hedge; when crisp and resounding, well in the middle of the road. I met one or two market-carts, everybody on them asleep, with no light showing. The mare was nearly squeezed in between the wheels and the hedge by one of them.

I got home at last safely, and found old Tom up and about waiting for me, with a hot supper ready for the mare. I was in time for dinner, and everybody was glad to see me, as they were beginning to get nervous. I proudly showed them my fox's pad, and waited until dinner before giving them a full account, as there was just time to get a warm bath before it was ready. I cannot see that being eaten by a lion could give one more varied sensations or greater excitement than following hounds. People who have never hunted cannot possibly understand where the sport comes in, and this is why they waste their eloquence over the death of the poor fox.

The sea calls for my time, and is my pastime too, but for all that I am glad to have had a run with a famous pack of hounds, and consider that hunting is the finest sport in England, and probably in the whole world.

THE PIPE PUSHERS.

BY WESTON MARTYR.

[Maga, August 1929.]

I.

THIS is the story of an obscure but potent branch of the British Army. It is, in fact, the saga of that immortal band known to some irreverent souls as the Pipe Pushers. I propose to sing this saga myself, because it seems no one else will do so, and from what I know of Cornelius I am absolutely certain *he* won't. So the job is obviously up to the other Push Pipe officer, which is me. I wish to make it clear, though, from the very beginning, that my connection with the Pipe Pushers was due solely and entirely to the fact that it was my luck, or rather my fate, to be sharing a billet with Cornelius whilst the great pipe-pushing idea germinated, budded and finally burst into flower in that distinguished officer's brain. I am anxious that all the credit and glory, and so on, should be heaped exclusively upon the head of Cornelius, where they unquestionably belong.

The Great Pipe Pushing Scheme originated at some time towards the end of 1916. I am sorry I cannot be more definite concerning this important date. My memory for dates is poor; but I do remember that the First Somme Battle was hardly over before I decided that life in the infantry was unsuitable for a person of my retiring temperament, and that shortly afterwards I managed to wangle a transfer to a Tunnelling Company, R.E. It was within a month of this jump of mine out of the frying-pan into the heart of the fire that I underwent a course of instruction at the Army Mining School; and as Cornelius was undergoing that same course of instruction when the divine afflatus affected him, the fact serves to establish the vital date as closely as I am able to fix it.

In fairness to that Army Mining School, I must give to it, as well as to Cornelius, a place in the roll of Fame, because it seems to me Cornelius' brain might not have blossomed as it did had its owner not undergone that unique and stimulating course of instruction. The School functioned near a peaceful village situated some twenty miles behind the line. The scholars slept in billets, messed and conducted the theoretical portion of their studies, in two large, ugly, corrugated iron huts, and perpetrated the practical part of the School curriculum in the bowels of an adjacent field, where a maze of dark and narrow tunnels were driven thirty feet below the roots of an unsuspecting crop of sugar-beet. The scholars deserve mention, too. There were about an hundred of them, and they were a queer lot. They were mature men, all of them—quite mature, I should say. The majority had been mining engineers or something or other to do with mines in civil life, and they had gathered at that Army School from all the ends of the earth. They were undoubtedly the toughest lot of men I have ever seen collected together in one place. There were gold men from the Rand, silver men from Australia, copper men from Nevada, tin men from Cornwall and the Straits, iron men from the States and Spain, soft coal men from the Midlands and North and hard coal men from Wales. And between them they knew all there was to know about sin, wickedness and mining for the metals, either precious or base.

The Officer Commanding the School was a little Sapper Major who knew nothing about commercial mining, and cared less; but he was a past master at his own job, which was fortunate, because I think if his pupils had become bored, they would, in the face of all the Army Council, have torn that School up by the roots. Instead, they were well content to sit at the little Major's feet and listen most attentively to his discourses on the best and quickest methods of undermining an alert and probably counter-mining foe and blowing him off the face of the earth. I wish to pay my tribute to the Major. He was a great man.

Cornelius was also a great man. He weighed two hundred and twenty pounds, at any rate, and he hailed from a portion of our far-flung Empire called, as nearly as I can remember it, Zwartruggensdamfontein. He was further remarkable in that he smoked perpetually a brand of tobacco which smelt like a fire in a fish manure factory, and exuded gouts of molten saltpetre that burnt little holes all down the front of Cornelius' uniform. Which was a pity, because Cornelius' uniform had apparently been fashioned by a Zwartruggensdamfontein craftsman, and no open-work embellishments were needed to heighten an effect already sufficiently striking. Cornelius' face well matched the rest of himself. It was big. It was, in fact, the largest front elevation I have ever observed on any human head, and all parts of it, except for those areas specifically exempted by Army Regulations, were covered with a matted growth of extremely ginger hair. In mentioning these matters I am not endeavouring to be funny at Cornelius' expense. Far from it. I am merely trying to show you what Cornelius looked like, so that you may understand how it was that I could sleep in the same room and work in company with Cornelius for nearly a month without suspecting that he was, actually, a genius. It is easy to say, after the event, that I ought to have recognised, in that weird appearance and those strange clothes, two of the hall-marks of genius; but—well, I wish you had seen Cornelius yourself. You would then, like all the rest of us, most certainly have regarded him not as a genius but merely as a joke.

Cornelius has proved that he possessed a unique set of brains; but I am personally inclined to the opinion that his processes of cerebration were normally inclined to be a trifle sluggish. His was the type of mind which needs some external and abnormal stimulus before it proceeds to function, and it is my belief that the stimulus which in his case did the trick was the enforced state of intoxication into which he fell twice daily, in common with the rest of us, on each and every day that Army Mining Course lasted. I am aware that this is a grave charge to make against the authorities, but I repeat it. Twice each day during a period of six weeks, British officers, in numbers approximately one hundred, were forced to reduce themselves to a state of intoxication under orders imposed upon them by the Officer Commanding that Army School, such orders being, I imagine, well known to and approved by the high Army authorities. The state of affairs on which I now throw the light of publicity was doubtless very terrible; but, as one of the victims, I must in fairness add that it was a most pleasant state while it lasted.

The root cause of the whole business was the Major's determination that every officer passing through his School should acquire a thorough and practical knowledge of mine rescue work. Which, I am afraid, involves me in a boring explanation of what mine rescue work is. However, it must be done, so let me gild the pill with silver from the little Major's tongue. I should mention that the Major invariably commenced his lectures in true pedagogic style, but soon forgot himself and lapsed into his normal manner. His opening lecture, I remember, ran something like this: "Gentlemen (I include, erroneously, I fear, the large and red-haired officer in the rear row with the open mouth and the shut eyes. Oblige me, sir, with the appearance at least of your attention. In fact, dammit, WAKE UP). Er. Hum. When you return to the line, gentlemen, the duty will certainly devolve upon you sooner or later of—er—pooping off a mine under Fritz. That is, the Enemy. The product of an explosion is gas,

Expansion. Pressure. You know all about that. One result—a hole in the ground and some Bosches squandered or given a rise in life. Another result—you fill your own galleries with gas and do yourself and your own men in. That is, you *will* if you do not listen attentively to what I am going to say. I propose to tell you how you may preserve your lives—but I have no objection if the large and red-haired officer in the rear row goes to sleep again while I am doing so. This product of explosion—this gas, gentlemen—is odourless, invisible and deadly. You may breathe it without being aware of the fact, after which you become quickly oblivious to all facts and presently die. That is, unless you are quickly removed into the fresh air. The man who does the removing will also be gassed unless he is carrying his own supply of fresh air with him. He can do this, thanks to the mine rescue apparatus which I will now proceed to describe. And I suggest that you give me your close attention while I am doing it, because when you return to the line you are the men who will have to do the rescuing, in view of the fact that you have been through this course. Now this is the apparatus. This cylinder contains oxygen under high pressure. You strap it on your back. This leather bag is connected to the cylinder by a pipe, with a valve in it which controls the flow of oxygen from the cylinder to the bag. You strap the bag on your chest. This tube and mouthpiece leading from the bag you fasten over your mouth. You screw up your nose in this clip, and breathe from the pipe through your mouth. You breathe in oxygen. You breathe out again into the bag. You then breathe in a mixture of oxygen and your own breath. You breathe it out again. You go on doing that. The bag swells up; but the pressure may be relieved by this adjustable exhaust valve. You have thus two valves to play with—the oxygen supply valve and the exhaust valve on the bag. If you open the oxygen valve too much, you blow up your bag and choke yourself. If you open your exhaust valve too much, you loose your air supply and smother yourself. To play on your valves properly and so attain the happy mean requires practice—lots of practice. Each officer present will therefore be provided with an opportunity of practising with a rescue set for one hour twice daily for the duration of the course. Those of you who may suffer from weak hearts will do well to report to the M.O. at the conclusion of this lecture."

Practical instruction in the use of the rescue apparatus was given us, in squads of twenty, by a Sergeant Harris, who must certainly be given a place in the pages of this history. The Sergeant, like the Major, knew his job. "Fall in, gentlemen," said he, "In two ranks, if *you* please. Not that this 'ere's a parade. It arn't. It's a lesson on 'ow to use rescue sets without doing yourselves in. And I may as well tell you gentlemen, right 'orf, I got *my* rank and job because my trade before the war was *making* these rescue sets. I don't know overmuch about Army ways, and I'm telling you this because I 'ad a little trouble with my last lot of gentlemen, before they tumbled to it. I knew what I was talking about, even if I couldn't talk Army talk! *So*—you fall in two deep, because I wants you to work in pairs. Front an' rear rank men is mates, an' you'll work together and go through your tests together according."

Now, as the Fates would have it, Cornelius was my front rank man. Thus did Destiny mate us.

Sergeant Harris, thank heaven, believed in breaking in his pupils gently. He matured us slowly, allowing us to accustom ourselves to the multifarious horrors of those rescue sets step by step and one horror at a time. We passed our first hour with him breathing through our mouths with our noses screwed up in little vices. This is worse than it sounds. At the second lesson, in addition to wearing our nose-clips, we were gagged with a large and evil-tasting mouthpiece strapped firmly on to our heads. This is much worse than it sounds, and thus gagged one dribbles—surprisingly. The next step was to wear the complete outfit minus the nose-clip, which is not so bad—unless a desire to laugh suddenly overpowers one. This happened to me when I caught sight of Cornelius arrayed in his obscene panoply. The effect of a hearty burst of laughter produced exclusively through the nose is devastating. Also it hurts. The first hour spent gulping down oxygen heavily impregnated with the stench of warm damp leather was a period of pure and unadulterated horror, during which I, Cornelius and the rest of the squad sweated cold sweats, felt death in dreadful form bearing down upon us, fell into a panic and tore those stifling clips off our noses. Nor did it cheer us at all when the Sergeant improved the occasion by remarking: "Come, come, gentlemen. This won't do. Nose-clips on again, *if* you please. Supposin' you was down a gas-filled mine *now*. You'd *'av* to keep them clips on. So, if you take my tip, you'll get used to 'em—while you've got the chance."

It appears one can get used to anything if one has to. Within ten days of our first painful session with the Sergeant the twenty members of our squad could have been seen squatting in a row in a low, hot, narrow tunnel thirty feet underground. We wore our rescue sets, and the tunnel was dark and filled with a particularly virulent brand of smoke, generated by the thoughtful Harris as a deterrent to the surreptitious slipping off of nose-clips. And the point to note is that we were filled, not with fear this time, but merely with boredom.

It was about this period that I began to notice the effect produced on us by our daily doses of raw oxygen. High spirits became the rule and appetites grew enormous. We were all, in fact, abnormally stimulated in mind and body by that oxygen to an extraordinary degree. Take my own case, for example. When I entered that Mining School, the fifth proposition in Euclid was a mystery I had never been able to master, and I had a vague idea that a theodolite was either an irregular Greek verb or a geological specimen. I believe I inclined to the latter hypothesis. When I passed out of the School, however, I was the proud possessor of a certificate in which the Major vouched for me as a " Mining Surveyor, First Class." There is thus no doubt of the power of oxygen to work miracles.

It took a long time before the effects of the gas appeared upon Cornelius, though. Cornelius was, shall I say, an exceedingly solid sort of person. It took a good deal to move him at the best of times, and the doses of oxygen imbibed twice daily by Cornelius had about as much effect on him as upon a lump of cold suet pudding. At the end of one hour spent in swallowing neat oxygen I have seen our squad of twenty grown men gambolling together like so many playful lambs. No one ever observed Cornelius gambolling, though. When he had to move, he walked—slowly, and each foot came down flat. His mind, I think, moved at a similar gait, and I suppose I know as much about Cornelius' mind as any-one. Were we not mates, who worked together and slept in the same room ? But even so, I do not pretend to know much about Cornelius. He seldom talked, and during the first month we were together he only really opened his mind to me once. I asked him one night, as we lay in our beds, what he thought of the Major's lecture that day on Mining Strategy and Tactics. Said he : " I do not listen to the man. When I was sixteen I learned to fight in Pieter de Wet's Commando ; and my uncle, Jan Niekerk, who is shift boss at the Simmer and Jack Deep, *he* taught me about mining. So what is there that I can learn from the Major ? "

It was the day after Cornelius had given me this little glimpse of himself that he received the overdose of oxygen which produced such extraordinary results. The programme provided for us that day was in the nature of a ' test,' devised by Sergeant Harris and the Major with diabolical ingenuity. Working in pairs and encased in our full mine rescue apparatus, we were to descend a 30-ft. shaft and proceed along a tunnel, where we would find a sack containing 120 lb. of sand and gravel. This sack represented a gassed man, and our task was to carry it out and bring it to the surface. To make the conditions more realistic, the tunnel was filled with smoke and partially blocked with some timber and sand-bags to represent a 'cave-in.' When our turn came to go down, Cornelius went first and I followed closely. By means of my electric torch I could see Cornelius floundering along the tunnel ahead of me through the darkness and the smoke. I should mention that the dimensions of the tunnel and Cornelius were almost identical, both being about 6 feet high and 3 feet wide. Cornelius had evidently made up his mind to get an unpleasant job over and done with quickly. He went ahead fast, and presently came to the cave-in, a barricade of sand-bags 4 feet high. He thrust both arms, his head and his air-bag through the 2-feet hole and wriggled ahead a little. Then he stuck, because he is decidedly 'Dutch built,' and he had also his cylinder of oxygen strapped on behind him. I am not quite sure what happened next, and Cornelius refused to tell me; but, judging from the effects, I think I can reconstruct the business. Cornelius, unable to go on, decided to withdraw, but found he could not do so, because, while struggling in the hole, he had neglected to manipulate his exhaust valve, and his air-bag consequently filled itself with gas and swelled up like a balloon. Here, I regret to state, Cornelius got rattled. He should have opened the exhaust valve and released the pressure, but he opened the oxygen supply valve full on instead. This allowed oxygen at a pressure of something like 100 lb. per square inch to flow into his already over-inflated air-bag. There was one channel only by which the gas could escape, and that was through the mouthpiece and down Cornelius' gullet. Cornelius accordingly swelled up too. At the time I was unaware that Cornelius was being blown up like a motor tyre before my very eyes. It is true his legs thrashed wildly like a couple of mad flails; but I took all this activity merely as an indication of the strenuous efforts Cornelius was making to get ahead through the hole. The next thing I remember was a loud explosion. (Blanch not, gentle reader. It was not Cornelius, but only his air-bag.) Then I was knocked down and trampled upon as Cornelius rushed madly past me back to the open air.

Had Cornelius been an ordinary man this overdose of oxygen ought to have killed him. Its first effect, however, was merely to make him very drunk indeed. He climbed up out of the shaft, tore off his rescue set and kicked it savagely three times around the beetroot field, after which he fortunately collapsed, and we carried him off to bed.

When I went to bed myself that night Cornelius was fast asleep and snoring. In the middle of the night he woke me up by throwing his boots at me. " Wake up ! " said he. " I've thought of a thing, man, and I must tell you."

" Go to sleep," I said. " You're drunk, Cornelius, if you only knew it. The M.O. says you're suffering from oxygen intoxication, and you've got to keep quiet. If you do, he says you'll be all right in the morning How do you feel ? "

" I am well and I am not drunk," replied Cornelius. " How should I be drunk when I have drunk nothing at all ? The M.O. is a fool. All you English are fools. Listen ! When you attack a trench, what do you do ? First you tell the enemy you are coming with much firing of guns, and then you attack in front. It was so you fought us in my first fight. I was on Talena Hill, and much afraid because I thought you would attack from the flanks and also from behind us. But no. You came on from the front like sheep. And like sheep we shot you. It was always so when I fought against you. And it is still so now I fight for you. Always the attack in front. You cannot learn. You are fools. I told this to my Colonel before we attacked at La Boiselle. At first he was astonished. Then he told me I was a fool."

" I bet he did," said I. " Who was he ? "

" A stiff-necked man and brave, but foolish," went on Cornelius. " He laughed always when he looked at me.

and he called me his old Oom Paul. And now he asked me how it was possible to turn the enemy's flanks when there were no flanks to turn. And I said that we also had no flanks, so that we should sit down and wait until the enemy became foolish and attacked *us* in front. This was truth, and he said it was so, but he said also he could not wait in France until he was old. And he said, 'We may be fools, Oom Paul, but remember, we did take Talena Hill and we did beat you in 1901.' And these being childish words, I did not talk with him any more then. On the next day we fought against the barbed wire and the machine-guns. We fought in the open, there being no cover in that place at all. On the next day we trekked back to rest, licking our wounds. And the Colonel came to me laughing, being pleased because the regiment had taken La Boiselle. 'You see, old Boer,' said he, 'it can be done, in spite of all.' And I replied, 'In truth, it is so. But—have you counted the cost?' Then we stood at the roadside and watched the battalion march past. And when the strength of one company passed us, no more men came. There were no more. *That* was the cost. And I said, 'La Boiselle was not worth it.'

"When the battalion was to go to the line again the Colonel called me before him. He held a paper in his hand. It was a call for officers for the tunnelling companies, and the Colonel said that I, being a miner, should transfer myself to them. He said, 'You are too clever for the infantry, Oom Paul. You know too much.' And then he made a joke. 'You do not like frontal attacks,' he said, 'and you cannot go round any flanks in *this* war. But if you become a tunneller you can try going *underneath*.' Then he laughed, and I went away. But I have thought about his words. For it seemed to me that here *was* a way, and that the Colonel unknowingly spoke truth. To attack from beneath! A new way, and therefore good—if it could be done. I have thought about this for a long time, but never could I find an answer. But to-night, lying here in my bed, I found the answer.

So I woke you to tell. Listen! It can be done with pipes!"

I remember getting up at this point and going over to Cornelius and putting my hand upon his forehead. I judged that Cornelius was delirious; but his head was cool and he seemed quite calm. And he refused to stop talking. "You think I am mad," he said. "But I am not mad at all. Go back to bed, man, and listen. Then you also shall see. And listen well! For with my plan which I tell you now we shall win this war! We shall need pipes—6-inch steel pipes, I think—screwing together in short lengths. We must dig pits, 10 feet or 12 feet deep perhaps, in our front trenches, and from these pits we can push the pipes with jacks—screw-jacks or hydraulic jacks—beneath the earth, under No Man's Land, until they lie beneath the Germans' trenches. Then we must clear the earth core from inside the pipes and charge them with explosives. Then, when all is prepared, we will explode the pipes—and the rest will be quite simple. To-morrow I will explain my plan to the Major, and here in the root field we will make an experiment. But already I know it is good. It cannot fail. *Do you not see?*"

I do not think Cornelius talked any more that night. I seem to remember that, having delivered himself of his great idea, he then fell fast asleep. But I did not sleep. I lay there thinking of Cornelius and his fantastic scheme. His words, of course, were the babblings of an idiot, and I wondered how long the effects of oxygen intoxication lasted, and felt glad that Cornelius had at any rate not been violent. I thought how queer it was to hear Cornelius, who so seldom said anything, go rambling on like that. He had been so ridiculously serious, too, with it all. "And the rest will be quite simple," he had said. "Do you not *see?*" I remember saying to myself, "I wonder what Cornelius does see? There's no doubt if only one *could* push a pipe filled with high explosive beneath No Man's Land, it would give Fritz a nasty surprise. Let's see. The thing to do would be to push out our pipe from a spot that enfiladed his trench. You might get your pipe planted under a good length of his line that way. And when you exploded it you certainly ought to kill everyone there, and smash up all dug-outs and machine-gun emplacements. What a scheme for a raid! By Jove! If only you could do it, Cornelius would be right. The rest *would* be simple. You would merely have to walk across and collect the wrecked trench. The enemy on either flank might make it nasty for you while you were going over, of course, and there'd be the wire to get through. But—wait a bit! Why blow up the enemy's bit of trench only? Supposing that part of the pipe which passed under the wire and No Man's Land were filled with explosive, too. Then when you blew up Fritz, you'd blow a passage through his wire as well—*and*, by gum! you'd blow open a sort of communication trench at the same time, right from your own front trench to his. An attack under such conditions would be absolutely foolproof."

I think the above is roughly the manner in which the possibilities of Cornelius' scheme unfolded themselves in my mind. I remember I got quite excited at last, lying there in my bed, as the beauty of the thing dawned gradually upon me. And the more I thought about it, the better it got. I began to realise the many gorgeous ways in which Cornelius' push-pipes could be used. For instance, if no enfilading position was available, then converging lines of pipe could be pushed out from two separate positions in our trenches. The pipes would meet, and when exploded form a V-shaped salient with its point in the heart of the enemy's defences. And if two pipes were not enough to prepare the ground properly, then use more. Use a hundred! A thousand! Why not? And then I began to dream dreams and see wonderful visions. In fact, before the morning came I envisaged the whole of the British front, with its explosive pipes pushed out before it in a cunningly laid network. I saw, at the stroke of zero hour, the whole German front trench system blown wide open

—all of it, from the Channel to Switzerland—a fitting prelude to the victorious conclusion of the war! This was such a splendid vision that I sprang out of bed and woke Cornelius.

"Do you remember what you were talking about last night," I said.

"Of course," replied Cornelius. "My pipes. And to-day I will tell the Major about them."

"Well, I've been thinking about your pipes all night," I said. "They'd be better than the tanks—if they'd work. But the trouble is, they won't. What makes you think you can push pipes underground like that with a jack, you old jackass?"

And then Cornelius really did surprise me. "Because," said he, "I already have done it." And he then proceeded to relate how, once upon a time, he had taken a contract to cut a drive to connect the bottoms of two prospecting shafts. He had only a rough survey to go by, and was therefore not sure of the precise level and direction in which to make his drive. But it occurred to him that if he could force a small pipe through the intervening ground from one shaft to the other, and that if the end of the pipe eventually penetrated the second shaft, he would then be certain he was on the right line.

"I used," said Cornelius, "some 2-inch pipes. I drove them, one length at a time, through the solid schist with a 5-ton screw-jack. It went in as fast as we could work the jack. There was no trouble. In nine hours the pipe came through to the second shaft. Through 45 feet of schist we drove in, and I tell you, man, it was no trouble at all."

We told the Major all about it after breakfast, and the Major being, as I have said, a great man, grasped all the possibilities of the thing at once. "It sounds," said he, "like a good thing. But it's sure to be full of snags. In practice it probably won't work, but we'll certainly try it. If you pushed a pipe through solid schist, Potgieter, as you say you did, then we ought to be able to deal with the ground underlying the trenches. The fact that the stuff's mostly clay and chalk is clearly providential. I'm beginning to like this idea. In fact, I'll drive over myself to-day to see the C.R.E., and wheedle a jack and some pipe out of him. Then we'll try out the thing here."

When the Major returned that afternoon he had acquired a hydraulic jack, twelve pit-props and twenty 10-feet lengths of 6-inch steel pipe. And these things presently arriving in a lorry, the Pipe Pushers paraded for the first time in history and dumped their material in the middle of the beetroot field. The personnel of the Pipe Pushers, be it noted, consisted of two officers, one N.C.O. and eight other ranks; in other words, of Cornelius, me, Sergeant Harris and eight lusty ex-coal miners disguised as privates, R.E. From such small beginnings do great events spring.

We commenced operations forthwith. Sergeant Harris led off by winning three picks and two shovels from somewhere, and with these invaluable tools we dug a trench. Our trench was 15 feet long, 3 feet broad and 12 feet deep, and we sunk it through 2 feet of top-soil into 10 feet of solid clay. We assumed that the eastern end of our trench was pointing at the enemy, and placed our jack 10 feet from the east face. We bedded it down firmly on the bottom, and chocked it off with pit-props wedged between the jack and some planks (won by Sergeant Harris) placed against the western face. We laid a plank on a clay foundation between the jack and the working face, and levelled the plank by means of a spirit level which Sergeant Harris found somewhere. This plank formed a bed and guide, and we placed upon it a 10-feet length of pipe, screwed up the jack and forced the pipe forward, finding that it cut into the clay as if the stuff were so much cheese. The stroke or reach of the jack was 1 foot. It pushed the pipe forward 1 foot, when it reached its limit. We then screwed back the jack, placed a 1-foot length of pit-prop between it and the pipe and screwed the jack up again, thus forcing the pipe another foot forward.

We repeated this process, using a longer section of pit-prop each time, until the 10 feet of pipe were pushed into the clay. A second pipe was then screwed into the rear end of the first one, and the operation proceeded as before. While the pipes were being pushed forward we removed the core, or filling of clay which they contained, and in the course of our experiment we devised a variety of strange implements to enable us to do this. In this connection Sergeant Harris must again be mentioned in despatches. He, good man, lured into our trench the village blacksmith, who speedily became engrossed in the proceedings. Thanks to this worthy, the working equipment of the Pipe Pushers was supplemented by one giant chisel, one large auger-like affair and a spiral wire-bristled brush which resembled a chimney-sweep's chief implement. We attacked the core with these weapons, screwing them on to lengths of 2-inch pipe and using the pipe as a handle. We battered at the core with the chisel, screwed and scraped out the fragments with the auger and cleaned up with the brush. Sometimes, if we were lucky, the auger got a grip on a length of clay core and drew the whole thing out intact, exactly like pulling a long cork out of a bottle. As the push pipe lengthened, so did we extend the handle of our core-extracting tools, screwing on additional lengths of 2-inch pipes, precisely as a sweep does when cleaning a chimney.

Working like this we found we could push our pipe forward at an average rate of 5 feet per hour. In that first experiment we pushed 100 feet of pipe and cleared it of its core in twenty-six working hours, and the thing showed so much promise that even the Major began to get excited. Said he, "We'll need a lot of explosive to fill that pipe, and I don't quite see how I'm going to get hold of it. So I think I'll try and get the General to come and have a look at this. If we can impress him, the problem of supplies should be solved."

In due course the General turned up. I do not know if he was impressed. He watched us push 2 feet of pipe, and then he said "Humph" and went away. But if not impressed, he must, I think, have been at least intrigued, otherwise I am unable to account for the 500 lb. of ammonal which presently appeared. Ammonal, thank goodness, is not by nature one of those touchy and irritable explosives. You can drop the stuff and knock it about and treat it generally in a careless and offhand manner without causing it to react violently, as will, for instance, gun-cotton, which possesses a tricky and most artistic temperament. Our ammonal was packed in little canvas bags, and we found that by rolling the bags between two boards we could make them assume a sausage-like form ideal for stuffing into the push pipe. We fitted a wooden head to our 2-inch pipe, and using this as a ram-rod we forced our ammonal sausages one by one up the pipe as far as they would go. We filled about 50 feet of the pipe with the 500 lb. of ammonal, and in the last bag we placed a stick of blasting gelatine and a detonator attached to a length of insulated electric fuse. This fuse led back through the pipe into our trench, where it could be attached to an electric exploder when the time came to blow up the charge. Then we filled up the rest of the pipe with clay, tamped it in firmly and rested from our labours. The first push pipe mine was laid and ready!

I regret to state that Cornelius, if left to himself, would probably have then ruined the whole business. "We will now blow," said he, "and show that it is good." Fortunately Sergeant Harris intervened. Said he, "Excuse *me*, sir, but Gor bless your 'eart, don't you go and *waste* it! If you blow it now, all we'll 'av to show is a hole in the ground—an' no one ain't going to get excited about that. You take my tip, sir, and wait an' get the General and all here. An' *then* fetch 'em with the fireworks." And the Major approving these words of wisdom, the Pipe Pushers perforce waited itching with a great impatience, while the Major pulled the strings.

We waited for three days, but the audience which ther

assembled to witness our demonstration was, it seems to me, well worth waiting for. It consisted of one General Officer Commanding an Army Corps and his Staff, two Staff Colonels, one Staff Major and two Staff Captains, all from G.H.Q. itself. "Gawd!" said Sergeant Harris as he observed the Major conducting these mighty personages towards us across the beet field. He dropped into the trench and I followed him, because I believe in taking cover when danger threatens, and that was my first experience of a mass attack by officers of the General Staff. Cornelius, however, was made of sterner stuff. While I cowered at the bottom of the trench, Cornelius stood his ground, and gazed unwinkingly at that glittering array of scarlet and gold advancing upon him. He listened to the Major explaining the details of his Pipe Pushing Scheme; and when he was indicated as its author, he scratched his fiery head and favoured the assembly with a grin. "With my pipes we win the war," said he. The assembly then also grinned. To tell the truth, the assembly burst out laughing. Said Cornelius, "Now, General, if you permit, I will blow my pipe. Then you will see it is good, and I do not think you will laugh any more." He then jumped into the trench and pressed down on the handle of the exploder.

I remember a mighty "THUMP," as if some angry giant had belaboured the quaking earth. I remember most of the trench falling in upon me, and I remember a glimpse of an atmosphere thick with flying beetroots, Staff officers and lumps of clay. And I shall not forget in a hurry a red and horrid fragment, raw and bleeding, that fell with a thud at my feet. I prepared to be sick, but recognised in time that the thing was merely a lump of lacerated beetroot, and scrambled out of the trench. I viewed the stricken field. In the middle of it gaped a crater 50 feet long and 10 feet deep. On its brink stood Cornelius, the Major, the Corps Commander and Sergeant Harris. They looked pleased. Scattered about amongst the beetroots crouched the disconcerted members of the General's Staff. They bore all the hall-marks of having recently undergone a very harrowing experience, and they did not look pleased. At the far end of the field stood the School's one hundred mature and hard-bitten pupils. They seemed to me to rock strangely on their feet. They bent double, and their bodies heaved as if in pain, and they seemed to cling desperately to each other. It was some little while before I understood that they were laughing.

I approached the group at the crater's edge, and I am glad I got there in time to hear the General. Said he, "A fine show. I congratulate you. Devastating! Absolutely devastating. Pop off a thing like that under a trench full of Huns, and they'd vanish. Simply vanish. Just like those boys of mine did. *Did* you see 'em go? Blown clean out of the field! But I think I showed 'em the old man can still stand being shot over, what? Splendid! I'll devastate 'em. It's been a real good show. By Tophet! and I'm pleased with you. And I'll give you a chance to show what you can do in the line. I'll arrange it at once. And now let me go and tell my boys what I think of 'em. Rattled, they were! Properly rattled, by Gad! And by a barrage of bally beetroots!" Saying which, the General patted Cornelius on the back and trotted off chuckling.

Said Cornelius, "Almachty! *There* is a fine man. I did not know. If we have more Generals like him we win this war after all. When they laughed at me I became angry—but I am glad I did not hurt *him*."

Four days after the successful demonstration of their powers the Pipe Pushers received orders to carry out their first offensive operation against the enemy. "The scheme seems to be," said the Major, "for you to prepare the ground for a raid the Nth Brigade are making. Zero hour is 2 A.M. next Monday, which gives you four days to get ready. They're sending one company over without any artillery preparation whatsoever. The General says he is relying on you to do all the preparation. He wants you to blow up 200 feet of the

Bosche trench, and then the infantry go over and pick up the pieces. The General says he needs some prisoners for identification purposes; but I think his main idea is to give you a chance to show what you can do. I may tell you the General seems to be the only person at Headquarters with any faith at all in your pipes. Everyone else laughed at the idea or condemned it outright. And I hear the infantry people are dead set against the Push Pipes, and have definitely asked to be allowed to make the raid on their own. So, you see, you've got to make good this time, or I doubt if you'll get another chance. I've been up the line myself and examined the position, and I think you might, with luck, bring the thing off. The trenches there are no more than 100 feet apart, and you'll find there is one place from which you can enfilade about 200 feet of the enemy's firing trench. That gives 300 feet of pipe to push. The ground is soft clay over chalk. Practically made for the job, in fact, except that I noticed some flint boulders in it which may give you a little trouble perhaps. You will go up the line to-night, taking Sergeant Harris and your eight men, and I've arranged for a lorry to take you, together with 300 feet of pipe, the necessary timber and a jack. You will report at Brigade Headquarters, and they will provide a guide and a carrying party. You'll be ready to start pushing by daylight to-morrow, I should think. To-morrow's Friday, and that gives you three clear days. The Tunnelling Company in the sector have been ordered to ration your men and provide all the ammonal you may need, and Battalion Headquarters will give you all details concerning the raid. You will, of course, co-operate closely with them throughout. Here are your orders and a plan of the front lines—and that seems to be about all I can do for you. So—good luck!"

Behold now the Pipe Pushers, marching on to war—or, rather, struggling up a narrow, slippery communication trench in the black dark. Cornelius follows the guide and I follow Cornelius. And behind us trails a staggering line of men bearing heavy burdens and cursing. Sergeant Harris brings up the rear, because it is much simpler to drop in the mud such awkward impedimenta as pit-props, planks and pipes than to insinuate them along a twisty overcrowded trench in the dark.

It seems to have been the fate of the Pipe Pushers to be unpopular from the first. At Brigade Headquarters we were treated with hauteur, derision and scorn; our carrying party quite obviously hated us; the people who encountered our jack, pipes, &c., in the trench most violently disapproved of us; and when at last we arrived at the scene of our operations in the firing line we found we were far from being welcome. Said the Company Commander, "My God! What's all this? You can't dump that junk in my trench. I won't have it. Go away. Who *are* you, anyway?"

"The Push Pipe Party," replied Cornelius.

"Oh, you are, are you?" said the Company Commander. "Then you push off, my son. And take your damn pipes with you." He then flashed an electric torch on Cornelius' face, cried out in a loud voice, "Perishing Muckings! If it isn't old Uncle Oom Paul!" and collapsed upon the firestep. "Oh, don't—*please* don't tell me," he went on, "that *you're* the maniac they've sent to mess up our raid with a drain pipe!"

And then I heard Cornelius groaning in the dark. "Almachty!" he cried, "*it is my old regiment!*"

II.

Cornelius' old regiment boasts a list of battle honours as long as my leg. Its unofficial name is 'The Bull Heads,' because of the regimental tradition that the best way to defeat an enemy is to go for him bull-headed and toss him away. The Bull Head's pet weapon is the bayonet; they regard barbed wire and bombs as unsporting, and look with scorn upon such accessories to infantry action as tanks and machine-guns. As this is a respectable family magazine, I cannot give you the Bull Heads' views on push pipes and Pipe Pushers, which is a pity, because the Bull Heads' views, though devastating, were diverting. And I know what I am talking about, because I had to sit and listen to the Bull Heads expressing themselves for twenty-three consecutive hours. During that time each single man in the battalion took trouble and pains to get himself to the fire-bay in which we were working in order to express himself on us. 'C' Company's Sergeant-Major, I remember, was good; while No. 9 Platoon Commander was even better; and the R.S.M.'s discourse was, I think, a most masterly effort. But how—oh! *how* I wish I could give you the imperishable words let drop into the Pipe Pushers' trench by 'C' Company's Sanitary Orderly.

The unusual amount of traffic flowing into our trench inevitably attracted the enemy's attention, with the result that all that day we worked under a barrage of light shells and heavy trench-mortar bombs, which made life almost as uncomfortable as the hail of scorn and jeers directed upon us by the Bull Heads. But in spite of all this sound and fury the Pipe Pushers worked on. We arched our backs and pushed —furiously. For we were angry. We meant to show the Army (especially the Bull Heads) how to win the war. Our answer to the scoffers was, "You wait—and watch US." We meant to blow sky-high as many Germans as we could get at, not because we hated Germans particularly, but because by this time we hated those confounded Bull Heads, and we proposed to show them what the Pipe Pushers really could do. By 6 P.M. that night we had pushed 70 feet of pipe clear under No Man's Land, and we knew then that, unless some accident befell us, our 300 feet of loaded pipe would be ready and waiting well before zero hour.

Said Cornelius, "All goes well. Go you now to Battalion

Headquarters and tell the Commanding Officer that our mine will be ready—on time."

"Hang it all, Cornelius," I said, "*you* go. You're the officer in charge, and you ought to go. I've heard what the battalion think of us, and I've had enough. I don't want to hear the Colonel."

"Yes," replied Cornelius, "I am in charge, and so I tell you to go. The Colonel he laughed at me always. Now he will laugh more, and I shall become angry. Go you, then. Give him greetings from his old Boer. Tell him I have not forgotten. There are no flanks in this war. No. In front, waiting for the Bull Heads, is the wire, thick as a forest of wachtenbitche thorn. But tell him I, Cornelius Potgieter, will clear the way for the Bull Heads. Tell him that. Go!"

I went; but I toned down Cornelius' message considerably, because I am frightened of all Colonels; and the Bull Heads' Colonel, when I crawled into his dug-out, regarded me as a M.F.H. might regard a vulpicide.

"I have to report, sir," I said, "that our work is going ahead more quickly than we estimated, so that the pipe-mine will be ready for firing before zero hour. That is, unless they dump something on top of our jack first, sir. They've been feeling for us with heavy Minnies all day."

"They have?" said the Commanding Officer. "Ah! then perhaps there's a chance yet. Not that I wish you people any harm, of course; but the Corps have forced these confounded pipes of yours on to us, and, I feel it in my bones, they'll be the undoing of our raid yet. So you'll understand I'll be glad to see 'em put out of action. May heaven forbid that I should interfere with the G.O.C.'s orders; but what I say to you, young man, is this: We go over at 2 A.M. on Monday whether you explode your filthy pipes or whether you do not, and all you have to see to is that you don't blow any of my men up. It really is too bad of the General to saddle this—er—sewage scheme on to the Bull Heads."

"Very good, sir," said I. "But I hope you will think a little better of us when the raid's over. Captain Potgieter told me to report that he's going to blow open a communication trench right across No Man's Land, destroy the wire in front and put out of action every man in the trench you are going to attack. Surely that ought to help a bit, sir?"

"Ah! Potgieter. Yes," said the Colonel, smiling grimly. "So they told me. I think I'll come up later and make sure that old Boer doesn't dish the lot of us with his slim tricks."

"Did you tell him?" asked Cornelius when I returned.

"I did," I said. "And he's coming up later to bite you. He regards us as a joke. They all do. And I gather from some pregnant remarks the Adjutant let fall that the Bull Heads intend to savage us if we dare to kill any of their Bosches. They say they're making this raid to get identifications—and they want live ones. As far as I can make out, their plan was to go over in the dark, wire-cutters in one hand and pick-handles in the other, collect all the Fritzes they could find, and then get back without making any noise, fuss, or bother. So they naturally think that our mine popping off at the start of the proceedings is bound to jigger the whole show."

Cornelius gave vent to something that sounded like "Verflootundhochnamalia," which seemed to do him good. "The frontal attack as always," he then growled. "He will *not* learn, that man. But, this time, I will teach him."

The Pipe Pushers worked on. A little after dark we had some trouble. The Pipe jammed, and it felt as if the end had run against some hard substance, probably one of those flint boulders the Major had warned us about. There being nothing to do except try and push past it, we fitted a lever to the handle of the jack, and all hands hove mightily upon it. The pipe buckled under the strain, twanged once like a banjo string and suddenly moved forward. The Pipe Pushers breathed again. We had evidently forced our pipe past the obstruction, and from then on for the rest of the night we had no more trouble, the pipe, in fact, after this incident, appearing to go forward more easily than ever.

By 4 A.M. we had pushed out 120 feet of pipe, and Sergeant Harris was hard at work removing the core. "Go easy," I warned him. "Remember you're working now right under the enemy's trench. You're only two or three feet beneath his trench boards. It won't do if he hears us."

"It won't!" said the voice of the Bull Heads' Commanding Officer from out of the darkness above us. "Although I think, from the way they're behaving, they know all about you already. I don't quite like all these lights they're sending up, and I mistrust this unusual trench-mortar activity. When I had the honour of being your Commanding Officer, Potgieter, I remember you used to lecture me on the superiority of Boer over British tactics. Well, if it's your idea to knock at the enemy's door before you attack him and tell him you're coming, you seem to have succeeded perfectly."

"Ah! You laugh at me still, Colonel," replied Cornelius. "But, wachtenbitche! Our people have a saying that he laughs the loudest who laughs last. So—we shall see!"

At this speech from Cornelius, visions of court-martials and shootings before dawn rose up before my horrified eyes; but the Bull Heads' Colonel must, I think, have had a soft place somewhere in his heart for old Cornelius, because all he said was this—

"*Our* people, too, have that same saying, old Boer. I think it is a very true one."

And with that the Bull Heads' Colonel climbed to the fire-step above us and looked out across the wire. For the dawn was breaking, and the Bull Heads, as their custom is, were standing-to. I climbed up also, to join that line of silent men who watched and waited so intently for what the new day might bring to them. The first faint gleamings of the light sifted across the eerie ground between the trenches, revealing nothing. Then suddenly the light grew—and we saw. We saw, reared in the middle of No Man's Land, an incredible pillar! A mystic column. A long, thin stalk that sprouted from the ground and rose up astoundingly 60 feet into the air. It drooped, as if weary, and it wavered drunkenly in the little dawn wind. And from its top appeared, twirling, the head of a chimney-sweep's broom.

I stumbled backwards at the sight, and fell. And in my ears arose, above the thunder of the guns, a crash and a rumble and an exceedingly great roaring.

It was the Bull Heads—laughing!

'STUMPY.'

BY LUNAR BOW.

[Maga, April 1933.]

It was a rough and bitter winter's morning. A smear of daylight showed a suggestion of Esquimalt Harbour, a small collier weighing her anchor and H.M.S. *Alleluja*, flagship, with her port side prepared to receive the collier. On the whole a most revolting scene, at that time, on such a morning. The flagship's port after-gangway was lowered, for the collier was a mere stickleback of but 2000 tons or so, and would lay well before it when alongside. A whaler with her crew in oil-skins and sou'westers lay ahead of the gangway.

'Stumpy' Jones, the senior midshipman, was on watch at the time and viewed the proceedings of the collier with a melancholy air worthy of a Soviet farmer. In a few days Stumpy was to appear before an awesome board of brass hats, to be examined in seamanship and naval construction. If he survived, the ship's tailor would remove his white patches from the lapels of his monkey jacket and sew a gold orris wire lace stripe on each sleeve. He had them ready in his sea-chest.

The collier had the flagship's wire on board and brought-to her windlass drum; but windlasses, like shore lasses, are temperamental: they will or they won't. In this case she would not. So the collier's men merely hung on to the wire abaft the drum. The slack, which should have been hove in by the windlass, straightened out, and the collier sagged astern until it was taut, then she began to close in to the side of the *Alleluja*, which was festooned with fenders. The collier, owing to this slack wire, was much farther astern than she would have been had all gone well, and the people forward did not know there was a whaler alongside. The master of the collier caught sight of her too late to go ahead for fear of chopping her up with his screw. The whaler could not now drop astern out of the way because of the gangway ladder. She was, in fact, trapped.

The fenders groaned as the collier closed in on them. The whaler was saved from being crushed at once, by their resistance. Then she began to rise up and tilt over between the two ships, and as she did so the crew climbed out and up the flagship's side. All except one, whose legs were foul of something in the boat. The whaler turned bottom up, imprisoning the man beneath, and still the collier crunched in on the fenders; and fenders can be squashed. Overhanging the whaler on a small davit was the copper punt; officially known as a Balsom raft, but still retaining the old service name when it was used for cleaning the copper sheathing of the ships of the old Navy. She was a strongly built craft.

Stumpy, standing on the gangway, saw three men come up to safety, but not the fourth.

"Let go the copper punt!" he ordered.

The punt crashed down between the two ships and jammed there. Then he kicked off his sea-boots and went down into the black and icy water under the mess of the copper punt and whaler. The punt checked the last of the crushing in of the collier's stern. Half a minute later Stumpy rose to the surface dragging with him the seaman. Both were hauled on board and the doctor took charge of them. A doughty deed whose immediate reward was pneumonia for both Stumpy and the seaman. As the *Alleluja* was proceeding to sea the next day, and a ship at sea is no place for pneumonic patients if it can be avoided, the two were sent ashore to the little naval hospital. A gem of a hospital set in grounds surrounded by pine and spruce trees, the charge of which was a much sought after job. The M.O. was a staff surgeon.

Stumpy's little effort had not escaped the notice of the press, though how they nosed it out is beyond comprehension. But there it was, on all the breakfast tables and side-walks, the next morning. Horrible headings such as "Valiant Sea Pup," "Put it there, Middy" appeared. Had Stumpy seen them his temperature would have risen still higher; but the M.O. took care that he should not. Reporters besieged the hospital, but were firmly met by the matron, one of the old sort who had tamed post captains to feed out of her hand and whose corsets creaked like a new manilla hawser stretching. She shoo'd them off, so they went away and worried the cook. The wives of "prominent citizens" of Victoria brightened the "dear little Middy's" bedside with a flood-tide of flowers, which made the porter's office—for they never got any farther—look like the beginning of a funeral.

Time came when Stumpy was convalescent and sat about the grounds breathing in the sweet scent of the pine trees or was told off to roll bandages by the matron, who had a heart of gold but could not think of jobs that appealed to Stumpy. The staff surgeon's wife was a mother to him. But when he was fit, he got restless. He had no ship to go to, for the harbour was deserted; so he had nothing to do. The old hospital game of rolling bandages was insufficient for his active mind. Nor was any ship expected to return for many weeks. Once, he went to Victoria and lunched at the 'Poodle Dog,' but the tram conductor, who knew him, gave him away to a reporter; so he fled like a frightened rabbit back to the hospital.

The next day he went to the staff surgeon and asked for something to do.

"You can take me gun whenever you like and go off into the woods after the pheasants. Ask the wife to make you up some sandwiches and fill me flask for you. I'll come with you myself, when I can."

And so for a couple of weeks he roamed the woods. He learnt that the moss grew thickly on the south and west sides of the giant pine and spruce, and that if he got lost he should sit down, light his pipe and wait till he heard a cow-bell and then follow the bell cow home to her ranch. He also learnt that rancher's wives considered he wanted feeding up. So he put on weight rapidly and felt good.

Nevertheless, always in the background of his thoughts was the fact that he was overdue for promotion and that no ship was due for some time which would provide the necessary board of officers who could examine him. He had been well over three years on the station, and felt that he ought to be getting on with it. He longed to get home; he had grown out of his clothes twice already and it was not worth while getting more, though he looked a fool in his present ones. He was, in fact, generally disgruntled; moreover, he had had no pay for some time. He went to the M.O. about these things.

"Of course you can get your pay, me boy. I'll give you a chit to the cashier of the dockyard and he'll square up with your paymaster. As to being examined for sub-lieutenant, me son, I'll cure you or kill you and post-mortem you afterwards, but I'll be damned if I examine you in seamanship. And why the hurry? You young fellows seem to think the Navy'll go to the dogs unless you get enough stripes on your sleeves to stop it. Run away and play, me boy."

There! That was it, "Run away and play," like a ten-year-old kid; and he was nineteen. It would not do. He went over to the dockyard cashier to draw his pay and found him a very friendly fellow.

"Glad to see you looking so fine, Mr Jones. Pay, certainly. I suppose you don't find much to do with yourself nowadays?"

Stumpy admitted that it was so.

"Well, how about coming along with me and calling on

the chief engineer of the dockyard? He's a good old soul, and his wife is charming."

"Thanks awfully. I will," replied Stumpy.

Why on earth had not he thought of that before? Here was a perfectly good senior naval engineer who could examine him in naval construction, and that would be one thing off his chest.

Mrs Engineer was rather inclined to fuss over Stumpy. Some of the things she said about the whaler business made him feel hot under the collar, more especially as there were two rather pretty flappers there, who grinned at him for no reason at all so far as he could see, except that he had grown out of his clothes. But eventually he got a chance to broach the subject to the chief engineer of being examined in naval construction. The chief, who never talked shop at home, told him to come and see him at his office the next forenoon.

"Well, I've been looking up the regulations," said the chief on the following forenoon, "and I'll examine you on Monday. If you satisfy me I'll give you a provisional certificate, as I haven't been told off to do the job officially."

"Thank you, sir. Provisional means, I suppose, that I've qualified unless someone says it is irregular?"

"That's it, Jones, the 'somebody' being some sleuth-hound in the C.-in-C.'s office."

At this moment Mr Bursey, the chief boatswain of the dockyard, accompanied by the gunner of the dockyard, entered, bringing with them a newly arrived chief boatswain, who was to relieve the one in the *Alleluja* as soon as she returned.

"Let me introduce Mr Jones to you," said the chief engineer.

"Glad to see you about, Mr Jones."

A chief boatswain is senior to a midshipman; he calls him Mister, but not Sir. The point is important. Most important, as the boatswain was, at that time, the senior naval officer of Esquimalt.

Stumpy duly sat for his naval construction exam. and got a certificate (provisional).

It had not escaped Stumpy's notice that there were now three officers of the executive branch in the harbour: the dockyard chief boatswain, the new chief boatswain and the gunner. This was brought to the notice of Mr Bursey, chief boatswain and S.N.O., by the following letter:—

"SIR,—I have the honour to submit that I may be examined for the rank of sub-lieutenant.

I enclose my certificates (1) for engineroom watch keeping, (2) my naval instructor's certificate confirming that I have taken and worked out all the navigational observations required by the King's Regulations and Admiralty Instructions before sitting for examination.

I have the honour to be,

Sir,

Your obedient servant,

—— JONES, Midshipman."

To the S.N.O.,
Esquimalt.

This flattened the old boatswain out. He took it over to the chief.

"Look at this, sir!" he said, handing him the letter.

"Well!" said the chief; "you are the S.N.O., aren't you?"

"Yes, sir, in a ways, so to speak."

"My dear Mr Bursey, there are no 'ways' about it. You are either the S.N.O. or not. If you are senior to the other chief boatswain, then you are the S.N.O., until somebody else turns up. And I may tell you that I have just examined the young gentleman in naval construction myself and passed him provisionally."

"Ah! yes, sir, but you are a senior commissioned officer and an expert in engineering."

"Well, aren't you an expert in seamanship? Don't you know enough to examine a young snotty?"

The chief boatswain gasped.

"Me! After thirty-five years—man and boy—not know enough?"

"Well, there you are. Order the new chief boatswain and the gunner to form a board and make the young man wish he had come up against a post captain and a couple of commanders, instead of your little lot; and make it provisional, as I did."

"I will, sir, and he'll have the exam. of his life."

"Don't be too hard on him; he's young."

"I hadn't the gall he's got when I was his age, I give you my word. There's another thing, sir. I've been looking up the subjects for the examination, and one of them is 'fleet ta'tics'; I'm a little bit shaky there, sir."

"Considering," said the chief engineer, "that the ships of this fleet might well be compared in homogeneity to a buffalo, a cheetah, two Maltese bulldogs and two cock pheasants, I shouldn't worry much about that. But, anyhow, you can get hold of a signal book and read it up."

The chief boatswain departed, muttering the same old things about the new Navy as the Thranite did about the Navy of his day.

In a few days Stumpy was ordered to appear for examination before the board of the two chief boatswains and the gunner. Mr Bursey was the president.

It was not an examination, it was more of an inquisition. They hunted him from stun' sails to dunnage, from canteen management to rats in the boatswain's store. They tacked and box-hauled him; they sprung every spar in his imaginary ship; they fouled his cables, burst his rudder and finally left him a total wreck on a lee shore, with his fore compartment full of water and nothing but hammocks and oilskins to make sail with, and nowhere to put them. 'Hardy' of the *Victory* would have failed, and so would the board itself. Then came the tactics part; the wily old boatswain had only one question on this subject, which he had worked out beforehand; and, bless his old soul, he had got it wrong. He placed eight matches on the table in a fleet formation and handed Stumpy a written signal.

"Mr Jones, the fleet is like this and you get that signal. What do them matches do?"

Stumpy moved the matches quite correctly.

"Wrong! Mr Jones, you're wrong; they should do this," and he twiddled the matches about.

"Of course! Sir. I meant that"—lying hard.

"Oh! no, that won't do, my son—er, I mean Mr Jones. One mistake like that and a 'ole fleet is sunk."

"Sorry, sir."

"Experience in 'ta'tics' is what you want. 'Ta'tics' is like seamanship, easy when you knows how. You can go now, and the board will let you know the result of your examination shortly."

An hour later the board sent for Stumpy, and the president presented him with a third-class certificate. It would have been a 'fail' had not the gunner, who had served in a torpedo boat flotilla, pointed out that the president had been wrong in his 'ta'tics.'

"Here is your certificate, and I congratulate you, though you might have done better, Mr Jones."

"Sir, you mean, Mr Bursey."

"Eh!"

"Sir, when you address me, is the service custom, I believe."

"Eh!" repeated the old boatswain with a hand to his ear.

"You have just made me your senior officer," said Stumpy with dignity as he left the room.

The longing for home still abode with Stumpy. Moreover, the old chief boatswain had pulled himself together and was now bombarding him, as the new S.N.O., with all the correspondence and cables, and Stumpy had to admit that the old boy was getting his own back. In addition the staff surgeon fell upon him.

"Look here, Jones, I don't know what you are playing at, but this is a hospital, not a general post office. I can't have my staff bothered with these fellows hanging round all day with letters and telegrams for you."

Stumpy seemed to be stumped.

After a day of intensive thought he visited the cashier's office and came away with several forms. These he filled in and signed as Senior Naval Officer, Esquimalt. They consisted of a warrant for a pass on the Canadian Pacific Railway, first class; a passage to England in one of the Allan Line Steamers, also first class; and an advance of three months' sub-lieutenant's pay.

The cashier seemed a bit dazed when they were presented; but still the magic words, Senior Naval Officer, were not without effect. So long as he got his receipt forms signed, it was none of his business.

On the last night Stumpy gave a dinner-party at the 'Poodle Dog,' Victoria, to the officers of the board who had examined him. It was a great night. 'Ta'tics' were performed with knives, forks and tooth-picks, and the bill for glasses broken in collision was large. They ended up with a music hall, and finally the board saw him off in the steamer to Vancouver, the first stage of his journey.

Some three weeks later H.M.S. *Alleluja* arrived and secured to her buoy. Amongst other signals was one arranging for Midshipman Jones to sit for examination in seamanship on Tuesday next.

The old chief boatswain, late president of the Seamanship Board, began getting into his frock-coat and sword in order to go on board and explain matters. And as with difficulty he forced each button home, he said—

"The young devil—blast 'im."

DOLLIE, AND THE TWO SMITHS.

BY LAURENCE OLIPHANT.

[Maga, July 1870.]

My father was an Irishman and a writer of articles for magazines. I have never written in a magazine or anything else myself. My mother I do not remember. She died shortly after my birth. One of my earliest arithmetical efforts consisted in the discovery that I had nine brothers and sisters, concerning whom, as they are all alive and are some of them Fenians, I desire to speak only in complimentary terms.

I believe publishers did not pay so liberally in those days as I have reason to hope they do now, or possibly my father may have acquired dissolute habits through his contact with literary men; but from some cause or other I was so slenderly provided with food, clothing and education, and my home was so inconveniently crowded and uncomfortable, that I left it at the age of fifteen with an outfit consisting of one extra shirt, one ditto pair of socks, a comb, and thirteen-and-sixpence that I borrowed, without alluding to it at the time, from my eldest sister, who was keeping house and acted as treasurer generally, and whose balance in hand consisted of that amount. I have since paid it her back, with interest at 7 per cent. As, however, my present purpose in writing is not to dwell upon the varied and striking incidents in my own fortunes through life, so much as to portray certain scenes into which its destiny has led me, I will skip over the first twenty years after leaving home and land myself in a neat white clapboarded house, with green venetians, and a verandah half round it, situated on a wooded hillside, and commanding a lovely view of a secluded lake about ten miles long and three wide, on the shores of which a few scattered clearings indicate that we are across the Atlantic and in a part of the country not yet very thickly settled. Nevertheless we are in one of the eastern States of America, at no very great distance from a city of fifty thousand inhabitants, and can hear the shriek of the engine as the cars stop at the little village at the head of the lake. As to whether that lovely creature with fair hair and blue eyes, and hands so small and white that it is a marvel how she can do so much house-work and preserve them as she does, and a pleasure to look forward to eating the bread they are now kneading—I say, as to whether this young lady is my wife, or the 'chattel,' to take the legal English view of her, of that handsome broad-shouldered man unyoking a team at the door of the barn, is a matter in which we three alone are concerned. It does not signify, either, who the farm or the two little chubby children belong to: the point to which I wish to call my readers' attention is this. Here I am, an Irishman by descent, an Englishman by birth, a citizen of the United States by naturalisation and of the world by an extended knowledge of it. I confess to only one inveterate prejudice, acquired doubtless from a long residence among pure and simple Asiatics, and this is an intense abomination of, and contempt for, all society calling itself civilised, and especially for that mongrel race of money-grubbers, whether they are located on one side of the Atlantic or the other, which calls itself Anglo-Saxon, and which, to an inordinate conceit, adds an almost inspired faculty for 'peddling.' If, therefore, the extremely sensitive feelings of my American readers are hurt by this record of my experiences of village life in their country, I only request them to wait until I publish a few observations upon which I am engaged in regard to the commercial morality of London as compared with that of New York, when they will have an opportunity of judging for themselves of my extreme impartiality, and of venting their spleen against England, by republishing my very original and uncomplimentary criticisms on that country and pocketing the entire proceeds of the labour of my brains. I give them fair notice that for every dollar of which I am thus robbed I shall stick a pin into them somewhere; and people with such very thin skins had better make friends with me in time. I am to be bought. I have not purchased and paid for so many of my fellow-citizens without knowing to a cent what my own price is. My stock-in-trade consists of a certain faculty I have for washing the dirty ('soiled' we call it on this side—'dirty' is considered coarse) linen of the Anglo-Saxon race in public. So much as regards myself.

The name of my broad-shouldered companion and fellow-labourer is Orange Z. Smith. As there are two other Orange Smiths in the neighbourhood, we have to be very particular about the Z, pronounced zee, and not zed, in America, and so taught throughout the schools and colleges of the country. In the case of Orange, it does not stand for the first letter of any name, but is simply a distinctive middle initial; hence it follows that he is popularly known as Orange Zee. When our first little cherub was born, we called him Zuyder Zee, out of compliment to a Dutch ancestor on his mother's side. I may here remark that my name is also Smith. I dropped my Celtic patronymic and appropriated the English one upon the occasion of my taking the thirteen-and-sixpence from my sister above mentioned. The name of Zuyder Zee's mother is Mary, but she is called 'Dollie.' All the pet diminutives of female names in the States end in *ie*, and not in *y* as in England, perhaps because there is a more refined flavour about *ie* than about *y*; and all Dollie's correspondents address their letters to her, not by the Christian name of her husband, or even by her own Christian name, but tenderly and affectionately as 'Mrs Dollie Van

Snook Smith,' thus as it were inviting the affectionate sympathy and interest of the clerks in the post-office. So when I was so unfortunate the other day as to upset her out of the buggy, and she broke her leg, the editor of the 'Van Snookville Democrat' touchingly alluded to "the limb of Mrs Dollie Smith, one of the most beautiful and highly respected residents of this township." Dollie's grandfather, Van Snook, had been the first settler here, and the town was called after him. When Zuyder Zee was born I asked Orange Zee whether the event ought not to be announced in the 'Van Snookville Democrat,' but he said it would not be considered proper to make any public allusion to the incident; and I remembered afterwards that I never saw a column for births in any American newspaper. Long may it be before our Dollie figures in any other column! but whenever she does, her affectionate relations will stick to the pet diminutive, and will announce the departure, not 'of Mary, wife of —— Smith,' but of 'Mrs Dollie Van Snook Smith.'

It is not necessary to say how Orange Zee and I first became acquaintances and then friends, and then decided 'to go farming' together, and were attracted to this pretty hillside and to the immediate neighbourhood of the farm where Dollie was living with her parents. I had to trust to Orange Zee's farming experience in everything. My ignorance was so great that he never ceased wondering where I had been 'raised.' I should like to know how many of my readers know how to drive a nail so as not to split the wood. I think the profound contempt with which Orange Zee regards all Englishmen, to whom he owes his origin, is principally based upon the information which I gave him that there were actually many people in England who did not know how to drive a nail. Nor does he yet understand—as of course everybody must be constantly wanting to drive nails in England as in America—"what on earth they do, if they don't know how."

After Orange Zee and I had seen Dollie, and found that

the adjoining farm was for sale, we determined to buy it; and we accordingly went to Dollie's uncle, to whom it belonged, and told him that the fences were all out of repair and the house was falling to pieces, and the meadows were all 'run out,' and that it was a miserable old place 'anyway' and not worth taking at a gift. Dollie's uncle saw at once from this that we were dying to get hold of the place, and, as he was equally anxious to sell, he said that he had now given up all idea of selling and intended to 'hang on' to it. Orange Zee told me afterwards that the great art of buying and selling was to appear as if you did not want to buy or sell, and always to seem to hang back. So we hung back. As we were boarding with Dollie's parents, I found 'hanging back' quite a pleasant occupation. At last one day Dollie's uncle came and said that he had been offered 75 dollars an acre for his farm, and that if we wanted it we had better speak, as he was going to let it go at that. To my surprise, Orange Zee said he had just offered 50 dollars an acre for a better farm on the other side of the lake, and expected to get a decided answer from the proprietor to-morrow. I felt quite angry with Orange Zee when I heard this, as I hated the looks of the other side of the lake; and when Dollie's uncle went away, I told him he might go there if he liked by himself, but that I should continue to 'hang back.' He laughed at my innocence, and assured me that what he had told Dollie's uncle was only as big a lie as what Dollie's uncle had told him, and "how else could we expect ever to get hold of the farm?" So then, of course, I said that it was all right, and we went on 'hanging back.' Finally, we had a talk with Dollie's father on the subject; and he said that if we would give him a hundred dollars down, and a note of hand at six months for a hundred more in case he succeeded, he would get the farm from his brother at 50 dollars the acre; but in that case we must leave the place for the present and seem to have given up all idea of settling here. Orange Zee told me afterwards that the old man (we always called Dollie's father 'the old man') had held a mortgage over his brother, and by threats of foreclosure forced him to sell. The old man was highly respected and looked up to for many miles round as being the best horse-doctor and the 'smartest' man at a trade generally to be found in that part of the country. He was also an elder of the Baptist Church, and exercised a most powerful gift on the occasion of 'revivals' and 'protracted meetings.' When he found out how matters stood between Dollie, Orange Zee and myself, he got nearly all our money out of us by secret promises of Dollie—first to one and then to the other; and nothing but the accident of Dollie herself taking a decided stand of her own prevented our being turned out of the house Dollieless and penniless. The whole details of this financially romantic transaction were afterwards reported in the 'Van Snookville Democrat'; and the old man received a sort of ovation for some time afterwards whenever he entered a store in the village, in compliment to his skill in having thus turned the charms of his Dollie to such good pecuniary account.

This did not prevent our having a wedding, which was the occasion of great rejoicing amongst all the members of the church to which Dollie belonged, and which bore grateful testimony to her popularity among the farmers' daughters in the neighbourhood, who flocked to her marriage, in very elaborate Parisian toilets, in buggies and spring-waggons, and accompanied by 'beaux' the honesty of whose intentions it was refreshing, to one accustomed to less primitive conditions, to contemplate. If I decline, for reasons which may hereafter appear, to say whether Dollie was married to Orange Zee or myself on this auspicious occasion, it is not because either Dollie or her husband have ever since done anything to be ashamed of. Of the purity and simple innocence of our menage there has never been a question. Nor did the fact that one of us had failed to realise his aspirations in respect of this estimable young lady, embitter our home relations. The sceptics in virtue on the other side of the Atlantic may sneer, but I am proud to say that no cloud of jealousy ever disturbed the serenity of our domestic horizon. Nor was the disappointed Smith ever for one instant false to the pure and innocent sentiment of fraternal affection which bound him to the other two. Indeed I may say that we were (and I trust still are) all three very justly considered models of propriety by the highly moral community of the village.

The said village consists of a single street, with three churches and a schoolhouse, all facing each other, in a little square in the middle, with pugnacious-looking steeples and a hostile cock to the gables, as though they were all longing to fly at each other. There are three dry-goods stores, and a hardware store, and a drug store, and a blacksmith's shop, and a billiard saloon, and two taverns, besides grist-mills, saw-mills, carpenters' shops, &c. The population is a genial, good-natured race enough. Everybody is familiarly known by his or her abbreviated Christian name; and the most minute details of the daily life of every family, and every obscure member of it, are accurately known and carefully discussed at post-time in the store that keeps the post-office, and which serves as a club and resort for idlers generally throughout the day. For although the inhabitants of Van Snookville are a tolerably industrious and prosperous community, they manage to spend a large share of their time in gossip, and find in the ever-varying excitements of politics and religion abundant occasion for quarrel and intrigue. To one not familiar with their habits, their severe language and the harsh judgment they entertain of each other might be supposed to lead to irreconcilable feuds. But this is rarely the case, for the simple reason that an irreconcilable feud is a very unprofitable investment of time and temper; and men seldom hate each other so much as to interfere with their prospects of being able to cheat one another. Of course the more rich and influential a man is, the more he can afford himself the luxury of a temper. In America, as in England, civility is a marketable commodity; and I had frequent occasion to remark with admiration that my Van Snookville friends rarely permitted their warmth or indignation of feeling to interfere with their prospective pecuniary interests.

Orange Zee said that, until we could increase our capital, our best chance of becoming respected in the village would be to join the Methodist Church and get the better of the old man 'on a trade.' He has therefore already become a 'class leader'; and in consequence of certain secret information regarding her father, conveyed to us by Dollie, we see a way by which we shall be enabled to obtain possession of a good deal of the old man's property without rendering ourselves liable to imprisonment. We are indebted for the idea to Swomp, the pettifogging lawyer, who is the old man's rival in politics and in piety, and who is to obtain a percentage on the whole amount resulting from the transaction. After we had obtained possession of the farm and of Dollie, we found that it would be necessary to improve our living accommodation; and instead of building, we determined to buy a ready-made house which was for sale half a mile distant, and move it to our own land—a proceeding which involved a great deal of the process known as 'dickering.' To 'dicker' successfully, one must have a great aptitude for chewing straws and whittling. The great art is to force your opponent to be the first to put a value on the article to be bought or sold. You choose a morning when you are not busy, for it is ruinous to let any indication of anxiety or haste appear. You walk slowly with your opponent to a fence-rail, and both sit leisurely across it and chew straws thoughtfully. I say opponent, because in one sense every man is your natural enemy—all the members of the community, whether they are engaged in agriculture, commerce or politics, being trained from their earliest infancy to prey upon each other's pockets. You find yourself engaged in a gigantic game of grab (which means getting all you can, and giving as little as possible in return), and the weakest goes to the wall. Some win the game as bullies, others as sneaks; but you have very little chance unless you are either the one or the other. Moreover, it is important to remember that if you do not treat every man with whom you have any dealings upon the assumption that he is both a liar and a rogue, he considers you a fool; nor is there the least danger of his feelings being wounded by your openly doubting and requiring proof of his most solemn asseverations. This entire absence on your part of any gentlemanlike feeling excites his respect for your 'smartness,' and leads him to doubt equally every statement made by you in return as the highest compliment he can pay you. I remember my first attempt at a trade was made in Dollie's presence, and what I imagined were feelings of delicacy, she called weakness, and my sense of honour she said was *non* sense—a fossil sentiment which had its origin in ages fitly called 'dark,' when idiots in armour devoted themselves to the protection of weak-minded women when they might have been making money, and sacrificed their material progress to an abstraction called Chivalry. I explained to Dollie that among the Anglo-Saxons on the other side of the Atlantic it was only considered honourable to tell lies when they were necessary to screen the woman you had betrayed; and that, according to modern ideas of chivalry, it was not considered important that you should respect the virtue of your friend's wife, if you religiously paid him your gambling debts. Nor could I get this obtuse Dollie to admit that the unscrupulous pursuit of dollars by men of business in the New World was a more degrading occupation than the unlicensed pursuit of women by men of pleasure in the Old.

Orange Zee, who has an immense physique, trusts a good deal to his overbearing voice and manner in a trade; and it was amusing to hear him endeavour, by sheer force of will, to extort from little Deacon Brown a price for his house, and to see the little Deacon wriggle and writhe and protest that he had not the faintest idea of how much it might be worth, that he had never sold a house in his life before, and that unless Orange Zee would make him an offer, he felt quite powerless and paralysed. At least two hours elapsed before either of them would name a figure. I think it was Orange Zee who, in spite of his browbeating, was forced to name a sum, which so wounded the Deacon's feelings that he quietly rose and walked off without vouchsafing a word in reply, leaving our big Orange Zee ignominiously chewing his straw. In this game the little Deacon made the first score. It was protracted over many days with varying fortunes, and might finally be considered drawn, as I do not think we paid either too much or too little for the house.

The next thing was to dicker with the 'house-mover' to transfer our new residence bodily on to our farm, which he did for a hundred dollars, with the assistance of an old broken-winded horse, a man and a boy. The *modus operandi* is simple enough. You go into the woods and cut down two trees long enough to pass under the whole length of the building, which is of course of wood. By means of screws the house is raised from its under-pinning and placed upon these timbers, which are in their turn placed upon wheels; the old horse walks round and works a sort of capstan fixed in the middle of the road, and attached by a rope to the house, which moves upon the wheels along planks placed under them as it slowly progresses. Most farmers in America are carpenters as well, and build their own houses without any assistance; but we were in a hurry, and Orange Zee had too great a contempt for my powers as an assistant for us to undertake it.

The most expensive operation was the purchase of stock. Twenty-five cows at from 60 to 80 dollars apiece made a considerable inroad into what the old man had left of our capital.

Orange Zee and I work our whole farm of 100 acres without any help. We have a team for which we paid 300 dollars, and a lumber-waggon and a mowing-machine, with ploughs, harrows and other farm implements. Dollie has a German 'help' called 'Lizer,' who is not considered worth more than her board until she can speak English. We are consoled for her stupidity by her cheapness. She and Dollie milk all the cows, make all the butter, wash all the clothes, bake all the bread, cook all the food and mend and make a great part of our clothing, to say nothing of looking after the children and the house generally.

We have a parlour with some ornaments made with dried 'fall' leaves, and some cheap china shepherds and shepherdesses, and a picture worked by Dollie's mamma in worsted-work. This room is kept carefully closed, and its finery covered up, excepting on the monthly occasions when Orange Zee, in his capacity of class leader, has a prayer-meeting in it. We live in the kitchen, out of which open two bedrooms, a buttery, a wood-shed, an attic staircase and a cellar staircase, so that the walls may be said to be almost composed of doors. Lizer shares the attic with dried apples and empty trunks.

The cooking is all done at a stove, not at an open fireplace, a thing never to be seen in an American farmhouse. The staple articles of diet are pork and beans and apple-sauce; besides which, Dollie is an excellent hand at corn-bread and griddle-cakes. We get up at five, and Orange Zee and I go out and do 'the chores'—in other words, attend to the stock, draw water and make Dollie's fire, chop wood, &c. At six we breakfast, and at mid-day we dine, and at six we have supper and do our 'chores' again. The quantity of things Dollie does by machinery is surprising. She washes with a machine, and she dries with a machine, and she sews with a machine, and can knit a pair of stockings in half an hour with a machine, and makes butter with a machine, and pares apples with a machine; and she 'cans' tomatoes and sweet corn, and preserves blackberries, and saves wood-ashes and makes soap with 'lye' (which is water that has soaked through them), and is a perfect repository of domestic receipts; and turns out on Sunday to go to meeting with a big 'chignon,' which she calls a 'waterfall,' and a long train, as neatly *chaussée* and *gantée* as if she lived on the Boulevards instead of on Beaver Lake. How she manages to effect these sudden and entire transformations is only one of the mysteries which attach to Dollie and are a source of perpetual wonder and admiration to Orange Zee and myself. Then she takes in 'The Revolution,' and seems to me to have more advanced opinions on 'Woman's Rights' than Susan B. Anthony herself; and she reads 'The Radical' regularly, and watches the new development of the religious idea of Boston with such keen relish that I sometimes suspect she is a secret contributor. I verily believe she is corresponding with those two strong-minded opponents of stringent ceremonial observances, Olive Logan and Eleanor Kirke, on the marriage question; but she does not at present admit either Orange Zee or myself into her reasons for always going to the post-office herself for her letters. We have perfect confidence in her, and are waiting without alarm for the results. So long as she is the most efficient housewife in the county we have no right to complain; and I believe that it is when she is on her knees scrubbing the floor that her most brilliant inspirations come to her, and suggest those abstruse problems of theology with which she occasionally plies Elder Fisher, much to that poor orthodox minister's embarrassment. Notwithstanding all which, there is not a Sunday-school teacher in the district (pronounced *dee*strict) more univers ly respected and beloved; and no 'sewing bees' are so popular as those which our pretty little Mrs Dollie gives alternately with Orange Zee's prayer-meetings in the front parlour. Upon these occasions the neighbouring farmers' wives flock to the manufacture of our 'pants' and petticoats, and discuss the latest inventions in sewing-machines and theology over an abundant supply of tea. Dollie is a specimen of a new type developed since the race was transplanted to America, and is as peculiar to the soil as are the beavers which used formerly to inhabit our lake ; and I believe, notwithstanding her regular attendance at Elder Fisher's, she is surely but silently sapping the foundations of his theology in the minds of a large section of his congregation. Like the beavers aforesaid, I sometimes think that Dollie acts entirely by instinct and without any exercise of the reasoning faculty. She always speaks under some strong, quick impulse, which is irresistible to the listener. A beaver is taught by intuition how to make use of his tail: why should not the same intuition teach a woman how to use her tongue? The fact that it has never done so yet does not cause me to despair. Since I have known Dollie I have become sanguine. Orange Zee and I both feel that she is rapidly developing us into something, but we do not yet know into what. Time will show.

Meantime, like Dollie, we do as much farm-work as we can by machinery too. We have a sowing-machine and a mowing-machine and a reaping-machine. In the hot haying-time we mow before breakfast, and rake and cure our hay with horse-rakes and tedders, and load it by a patent process on to our waggon, and get our bright 'Timothy' into our barn with another patent thing like a harpoon, the same afternoon. Think of that, you poor befogged farmers of the old country! The amount of hay that we two can cut, cure and stow away in one day, is so great that I shall not mention it, lest you should imagine that I had been born as well as naturalised in America. We never stack it outside, and have a hay-press of our own, which we work as we do most things, by horse-power, and press for our neighbours as well. We have a horse-power threshing-machine also, with which we thresh our neighbours' grain at from four to eight cents a bushel, and make a good thing of it ; and by killing all our calves two days after they are born, and sending all our milk to the cheese factory, we are able to contribute to the large cargoes of cheeses which annually cross the

Atlantic for consumption in the British Isles. What old fogies you British farmers are not to kill your calves and so save the milk!

Then Orange Zee can do almost anything he wants with a plough and team; he has surface-drained all our farm with open ditches three feet deep with the plough alone. As for me, all my most brilliant inspirations in regard to agriculture have been suggested by the remarkable farming experiences published by Mr Horace Greeley in the columns of the 'Tribune.' I believe, in spite of Orange Zee's knowledge, we should have been repeatedly ruined had it not been for the original ideas we derived from the lucubrations of that truly great man. Indeed, as I cannot be of much assistance to Orange Zee by my practical knowledge, I endeavour to make up for it theoretically by studying the rural 'New-Yorker,' 'The Country Gentleman' and other agricultural journals. Had I been allowed to have my own way, I should have invested in a variety of advantageous patents and entered upon a large scale upon experiments with all the numerous varieties of oats, potatoes, tomatoes and other produce which are warranted to make the fortunes of farmers courageous enough thus judiciously to risk their capital. Among the varied occupations of Orange Zee, however, he had passed a year of his life peddling patent rights, and the information he had thus acquired in regard to their value induced him invariably to prohibit my ever buying one. This was a great trial to me, for scarcely a week passed without some eloquent traveller calling, and offering for a few dollars the exclusive right to make and sell in the county stoves warranted to season as well as cook meat; or fences which were cheaper and more durable than either wood or iron; or clothes-pegs which possessed the remarkable property of drying the clothes as well as of attaching them to the lines; or lightning-rods which not only protected the house from lightning but bottled up the electricity for private consumption—besides many other ingenious contrivances which marked the fertility of the American brain. In fact I feel sure that, had it not been for Orange Zee, we might have become proprietors of many exclusive privileges which would have secured us a comfortable independence for our lives. I was confirmed in my opinion of my own good judgment and ability in these matters by overhearing myself spoken of one day as a "good, clever sort of fellow." As Dollie made the same remark in regard to the stupidest man in the neighbourhood, I afterwards discovered that a 'clever fellow' signified here a 'good-natured fool.' After this personal application it was natural that the violent transformation which English words undergo after crossing the Atlantic should rouse my indignation. I once seemed to plunge a whole supper-table into a douche-bath because I remarked that a species of porridge called Graham Mush was 'nasty.' I do not yet know the exact meaning of this awful word, but it is evidently something more than the opposite of nice; and certain it is, that this cock-and-bull account of farm-life in America will be called there a 'Rooster-and-Ox' story.

Besides our agricultural operations, we are called upon as good citizens to devote some of our attention to politics. The election of the town officers every year is an occasion of great excitement and intrigue. It is here that the youthful American mind acquires the rudiments of that exalted statesmanship which finds its full fruition in the adroit achievement of great state or national financial frauds. A 'State' in America is divided into counties and towns; the towns are in fact rural districts, each one large enough for half a dozen ordinary English country parishes; in each town there may be one or more villages or hamlets, though the villages properly so called require charters of incorporation giving them municipal officers and independent local government. Where there is no such village incorporation, the town chooses annually its own officers: these consist of town supervisor, road commissioner, sheriff, constables, &c.

Politics may thus be said to be brought into the minutest details of every man's daily life.

For instance, Orange Zee, vowing vengeance against the old man, Dollie's father, and being also animated by the desire to attain the first round of the ladder by which he might possibly ultimately climb to the presidential chair at Washington, determined to put himself forward as the Republican candidate for the exalted office of town constable. In pursuance of which design Orange Zee donned his go-to-meeting coat, and after consulting Swomp, who was going himself to run for supervisor on the Republican ticket, drove to several of the leading Republican farmers and announced to them that he had been so urgently pressed by his friends to have his name put upon the ticket as constable, that he had reluctantly consented, and that he would consider it a favour if they would support him. Meantime Swomp having held a private caucus of his friends at one of the 'stores' in the village, decided upon the list of officers which they would offer to the Republican party in opposition to the list headed by the old man, who comes forward as Republican candidate in opposition to Swomp. A few days after, all the Republicans in the town rally to the Republican tavern, where Swomp's supporters hand each arrival a ticket containing his own name at the top and Orange Zee's name at the bottom; and the old man's supporters hand each arrival a list with his name at the top: on receiving which the voters plunge into an inner room reeking with humanity, smoke and profanity, where all the respective candidates and their supporters are struggling round a table, at which are seated the scrutineers; and after a day of confusion and excitement, Swomp's supporters announce triumphantly that they have carried their ticket, and Orange Zee returns to our longing arms, covered with dust and glory and smelling of whisky. But this is only a preliminary stage. The Democrats go through the same form a few days afterwards, and then both political parties having thus decided on their tickets, try issues with each other. It is only to be expected that a number of the old man's supporters, disgusted with their defeat, vote Democratic ; but then a number of Democrats on the same ground vote Republican—so the one set of malcontents about balances the other. Still the issue is as uncertain as it is in England, because a vote in America is worth as much money as it is in England, though it is only for the State or United States Legislatures that they are worth paying for in money : in their local elections the consideration is various, and may be illustrated by Orange Zee's own proceedings. He having a marvellous faculty for diving into the private affairs of his fellow-townsmen, went to some who had large amounts owing to them, and promised, if they would vote for him, to collect their debts in his capacity of constable and charge them nothing for it ; and he went to others who he knew were overwhelmed with debts, and promised that if they would vote for him he would always give them warning before he came to distrain, so as to enable them to convey their goods away in time : in fact Orange Zee managed so to impress people with the extent of the powers which he could wield to benefit those who voted for him, and to injure his opponents, that many who voted Democratic scored out the constables nominated on their own ticket and substituted Orange Zee's name. Thus it happened that although the Democratic ticket was finally elected, and Swomp and the old man both defeated, Orange Zee came in triumphantly at the tail of the Democrats ; thus in these early days proving political capacity of a very high order, and inspiring both Dollie and me with great expectations for the future. I did not then know that Orange Zee had began life as a boot-black in the lobby at Albany, and thus at a tender age had imbibed, as it were, through the soles of eminent politicians, those first principles which he was turning to such excellent account. Where life is one gigantic system of barter, one of the earliest lessons to be learnt is, how much one's social position, political influence, professional knowledge and religious standing, are severally worth 'on a trade.' Take the case of Gouge who was elected Democratic town supervisor against Swomp and the old man. Gouge was a director of the Van Snookville and Boghole Branch Railway. The V.S. and B.B.R. is Democratic; no Republican conductors, porters and brakesmen need apply. At the State elections the V.S. and B.B.R. vote Democratic to a man; and the nomination of the Democratic candidate for our Congressional district may practically be said to rest with the President and Board of the V.S. and B.B.R. Gouge had been first a porter, then a conductor, and finally had run a wild-cat on said railway with such success that he was promoted to station-master. To run a wild-cat for any length of time on a single line without an accident requires both skill and daring. A wild-cat is a sort of extra goods train that has no stated times for running, but dodges from one station to another between the regular trains whenever the line happens to be vacant and the engineer thinks he can reach the next station before any train leaves it, and go fast enough not to be overtaken by the lightning express behind him. Metaphorically, Gouge had run a wild-cat all his life; he had a wonderful faculty of dodging past people on his upward career. He knew so well the value of his position as station-master, that though his salary was only a thousand dollars a year, he managed by dexterous trading to exchange the information, opportunities and power which his position gave him, for over twenty thousand dollars in two years. Gouge it was who saw how much money was to be made by a hotel at the depot; and he sent for his brother, who was a hotel-keeper, and promised to secure the privilege of the hotel to him, on condition that he should receive a share of the profits; and so he introduced Gouge junior to the President, who saw no objection to the scheme, provided he had another share in the profits. So the President and the two Gouges share the profits of the hotel between them. In the same way he secured a valuable railway contract for the leading Democrat in Van Snookville, upon the understanding that he should command the whole vote whenever he required it, a few refractory Democrats being 'squared' with small shares in the contract, and the whole helping to swell the political influence of the President of the V.S. and B.B.R., who received besides a large pecuniary share in the profits of the contract. And so Gouge quietly slipped with his twenty thousand dollars from being station-master into the proprietorship of the 'Van Snookville Democrat,' which paper he worked so successfully for the interest of the railway and the Democratic party in general, and himself in particular, that when the Van Snookville National Bank was started, the voice of public opinion unanimously pointed to Gouge as president; and Gouge finding himself, to use his own words, "reluctantly forced into this position of responsibility and prominence by his appreciative fellow-townsmen" (who are by this time so completely cowed by him that they are afraid to call their souls their own), runs that flourishing institution, the First National Bank of Van Snookville, as he did the wild-cat, entirely for his own benefit. Is there any wonder therefore that, though the majority of the population of Van Snookville is Republican, by some mysterious dispensation the vote of the town is always largely Democratic? for could not Gouge, who is President of the First National Bank, Director of the V.S. and B.B.R., town supervisor, proprietor of the 'Van Snookville Democrat,' part proprietor of the Van Snookville Railway Hotel, and joint-owner with his son, who 'runs it,' of the principal store in the village, with one-half of the population in debt to his bank, and the other half dependent in some form or other on the V.S. and B.B.R.—could not Gouge, I say, bring such terrific pressure to bear upon any luckless individual who ventured to thwart his sovereign will, that life in Van Snookville would be a burden to him? If Gouge wants to force a public road across a man's field, all he has to do is to tell the judge, who owes his election to Gouge's influence, that he had better appoint assessors prepared to 'lay' the road thus and do his (Gouge's) will, or he need never more hope to dispense justice in that neighbourhood. Gouge's life seems bent on the invention of political and social screws and instruments of moral torture; and as all the functionaries are elected, and he practically controls the elections, he manages to work the electors and the elected against each other with such adroitness that the power he wields may be said to be absolute. Providentially Gouge drinks! Van Snookville, as ungrateful as her rival Paris, to the man to whom she owes, if not her beauty, at least her prosperity—Van Snookville, less bold than her 'irreconcilable' sister, is afraid to vote 'no' against her oppressor, but finds a grateful solace in the consolatory reflection that he drinks. For a week at a time whisky renders Gouge unable to rule over us. Then Swomp, who is perpetual arch-grand knight of the Good Templars, rallies his sons of temperance, and the leading church members enter into deep mysterious conclave as to the best means of ridding themselves from the hated yoke of Gouge.

The old man and Swomp sink their religious and trading animosities to combine against the common enemy; and a holy alliance is formed between the Methodists and Baptists, which results in the announcement that Splurge, the great revivalist preacher, will shortly arrive, to quicken the slumbering consciences of the Van Snookvilleites; and the junior members of the community, of both sects and sexes, look forward with some little flutter of excitement to the prospect of 'a protracted meeting' and unlimited opportunities of flirtation. It is hoped that by a tremendous effort of religion and morality Gouge may be crushed. I did not take any part in the revival myself, because Dollie did not approve of it, and she only allowed Orange Zee to go because he said he ought to be there in his capacity of town constable; but his real object was to act as spy upon Swomp and the old man and report their machinations against Gouge to that accomplished operator and boon-companion. Orange Zee, you see, did not believe that the great Gouge could be crushed, even by a Splurge, although that distinguished divine likened him to a roaring lion seeking whom he could devour, and called upon his hearers to "flee from him and his contracts, and his newspaper, and his hotel, and his store, and all his works."

During the fortnight that the protracted meeting lasted, all farming operations were suspended. It took place at a season of the year when work was not pressing, and day after day waggon-loads of old and young of both sexes, in their best costume, drove up alternately to the Methodist and Baptist churches; and the voice of Splurge might be heard for some distance down the village street exhorting his hearers to come forward to "the mourners' bench." Here those who had been most powerfully acted upon made their confession and their profession, and from that time forward they were said to have 'got' or 'experienced' religion. The exact number of persons who 'got religion' during this visit of Splurge's was afterwards published among those interesting heart-statistics, if I may be allowed the phrase, which are to be found in those spare columns which the religious journals do not devote to abusing each other. It is quite an interesting study to turn over a file of these, and add up the total of broken and contrite hearts that have resulted during the year from the labours of the various Splurges all over the country, and to read how bitter these rival Splurges sometimes get with one another, and how jealous of each other's special gifts, and how furious are the feuds which arise from the difficulty of sharing the spoil. Even now the war which resulted from the Van Snookville revival is still raging, for Swomp declared that the old man had persuaded a number of those who intended to 'experience' Methodist religion, to join the Baptist Church; whereas it had been clearly understood, before Splurge's arrival, that all the broken hearts he made were to be divided equally between the two denominations; but the fact is, on a trade, whether it be in human consciences or anything else, the old man is always more than a match for Swomp.

The practical inconvenience of this revival was, that its influence was not confined to quickening the consciences only of those who benefited by it; they seemed to get quicker all over. One young man, before he got religion, with whom I was dickering for a horse, positively assured me he had paid 200 dollars for it, and could not sell it to me for less. Our trade was interrupted by Splurge for a fortnight, and at the end of it he had undergone the quickening process, and swore as positively he had paid 245 dollars for the animal.

This is only one illustration. I did not know of a single instance of greater honesty in trade after the revival than before it. It never once seemed to occur to two men of contrite spirit to say to each other, "Come now, we have persistently thought everything worth whatever we could get for it, irrespective of its intrinsic value, and have considered false representation in regard to articles we had for sale a merely venial offence; let us, now that we have got religion, never try to get more for anything than it is honestly worth." If even Splurge cannot venture to recommend people when they are asked for their coats to give their cloaks also, without extinguishing himself and his popularity as an imparter of the Christian religion for ever, let him, at least, suggest that when a man asks for your coat, you should not turn upon him and strip him naked as an evidence of Christian 'smartness.' O my dear Splurge, I am sorry to have to tell you that my experience has been that the sooner men get over the effects of your labours on their consciences, the more I like to deal with them; and I would also venture to suggest that it is very difficult to give to others what you have not got yourself.

Orange Zee did not get religion, but he got a good deal of

useful information, by the dexterous management of which he hopes to increase his social and political influence and thus rise to higher spheres of usefulness.

I do not mean to divulge what these are—in fact I am at this moment interrupted by a piece of intelligence which for a time will disturb our domestic arrangements, and which involves to no small degree the future happiness both of Orange Zee and myself. I have before alluded to the remarkably philosophical and speculative character of Dollie's mind, and that we have both been conscious that her advanced habits of thought were not unlikely to produce a strong influence upon us. She has just imparted to us the important discovery that she has married the wrong Smith. I need not say that we saw it both in the same light instantly. Why it never flashed upon us before during the last five years it is useless to attempt to inquire. It was the real solution of a great domestic problem, which, like Columbus's egg, we had missed from its extreme simplicity.

As the laws of divorce in the State in which we are now residing interfere in the most absurd and arbitrary manner with the private matrimonial arrangements of its citizens, we have determined at once to proceed to the more enlightened State of Indiana, and have telegraphed to have the preliminary measures taken ; this will enable us to start to-morrow. Dollie, who has made herself acquainted with the whole course of proceedings, assures us that in that State the ceremony of divorce by mutual consent will not occupy above half an hour, and she then wishes to proceed to New York to have the marriage ceremony performed by at least two leading liberal divines. She is strongly inclined in favour of Mr Ward Beecher and Mr Frothingham. She says she does not care so much about the mere ceremony, but she wishes to commit those influential men to a great principle. Orange Zee asked her stupidly whether she thought it likely she would ever change back again. Dollie, of course, told him to mind his own business. Orange Zee said he thought it was his business; but his mind is so little able to rise above the ordinary interests of everyday life that we never attend to what he says on these more profound questions. Whether I am the Smith from whom Dollie is going to be divorced, or the Smith to whom she is going to be married, is not a matter of the smallest interest to my readers. I may tell them what happens to us in Indiana and New York, or I may not, on some future occasion; but I cannot know till it is over whether it will be worth telling. Meantime, of this the public may rest assured, that Orange Zee, Dollie and I, all have the strongest possible affection, esteem and admiration for each other, and are all profoundly indifferent to anything the world may think of us.

MY CRUISE IN THE *ESPERANZA*.

[Maga, June 1932.]

I.

A TOWN with a seaport often shows a dirty face to such as approach it by sea; and the great seaport of X., on a foul day in a recent early spring, turned a deplorably dirty countenance to the leaden-coloured river which rolled turgidly towards the uplands of its origin. The tide was at flood. Unpleasing vistas of this, the town's main approach from the world at large, were offered down the ends of mean streets, abounding in greasy cobbles and liquid mud. At the end of one of these streets, and blocking the view, lay the good ship *Esperanza*. In a couple of hours there would be enough water on the sill of her dock to enable her to step across it and leave all this mess behind her.

As ships go, she was a little ship, carrying but a few score passengers, and possessing neither a swimming pool, nor squash racquet courts, nor a golf course. She belonged to the Port of X. and was a regular homing-bird, never commencing or finishing her voyages at any other port. Her main mission in life was that of a fruiter. She sailed to Madeira and the Canaries, where bananas and tomatoes grow, filled herself full to the brim with these and returned. But as bananas and tomatoes must travel in crates packed with straw, and as these islands are deficient in wood and straw, part of the *Esperanza's* outward cargo was bundles of battens and bales of straw for the making and packing of crates by the islanders.

I went, after settling into my cabin, to a large and comfortable room calling itself the lounge, and lounged in an easy-chair before a cheerful (electric) fire of logs. I fell asleep here. In the intervals of slumber there came sounds of passengers arriving in muddy taxis, and of the closing of hatches, and of a voice somewhere above my head bawling through a speaking trumpet. I saw greasy dock walls sliding past the porthole and shiny oilskinned men wrestling with wire ropes on the quay. I went off pretty sound at this point, and awoke to tremendous cheering. I slept again and awoke. We were now in mid-river, a longish way from the docks, and the shouting and cheering had grown more frantic. We seemed to be a very popular ship. I slept again, and on waking saw by the clock that we had been gone an hour or more. The cheering was now almost beastly in its frenzy. These shouters must have very powerful voices to be heard at a distance now to be reckoned in miles. I went to investigate. I found that the cheering came from much farther off than the port of X.—to wit, from Wembley, where a cup-tie final was in progress. A loud, a very loud, speaker was operating on the deck just below me and recording every incident in this gladiatorial show.

II.

"I've placed you on the Captain's right, sir."

It was the chief steward who spoke. I was looking for my place in the dining saloon. I explained to this well-intentioned fellow that I was not of the kidney nor yet of the calibre to sit in chief seats; that I did not agree with captains.

"But the Captain, sir," replied the steward, "is a very nice man. He likes pretty near anyone." Here the speaker looked at me as much as to say, "Even the likes of you."

The steward seemed such a kindly fellow, and to take it so much as a personal matter, that I gave way and sat on the Captain's right. I found him just as he had been described, and withal a very patient man. I heard him asked a good many questions during the next few weeks, and asked him a considerable number myself, and he must have been asked almost these very identical questions scores of times before, and yet he always replied to us as if we had asked him something rather new and original. When his ship was alluded to as a boat, he scarcely winced.

Opposite me sat an old lady largely covered with small black beads, and wearing as a chest protector a brooch in bas-relief which must have been executed by a modernist sculptor in an extremely futurist mood. I seldom question the accuracy with which Mr Punch represents people, but I have sometimes thought that his old ladies were a little too old and too futile. I was wrong and make my apologies. Mrs Bunce had stepped straight out of the pages of the London Charivari into the chair on the Captain's left. She was now, in a snug, cosy voice, taking grand-maternal charge of the Captain—kind, helpful and illuminating.

"But as I was remarking, Captain, so far as I can make out—though I'd never pretend to know better than you—the way to get to Lisbon" (our first port of call) "is to take the third turning to the left. Not the first, because that would bring you to Bristol; nor yet the second, because that goes up the Channel; and on no account to bear to the left after passing the Channel, because that would lead you nowhere practically. It's one of those deceptive turnings, but really a dead end and probably used for parking ships. But take the next again to the left, and there you are at Lisbon. But as I was saying, you've probably larger maps than mine. In my young days the 'World Wide' atlas was considered pretty reliable, and that's the one I always use and it's quite at your service, only you must really not forget to give it back to me. And I do like your ship, Captain; so well designed, such lovely sheds to walk under. It was pouring with rain when I came down to dinner, but I had a shed to walk under all the way and didn't get a scrap wet."

Next Gran'ma sat a stern-looking man with billows of iron-grey hair rolling over his head and partly submerging his forehead. He had a troubled brow and tired eyes. I placed him as a professor, on the eve of a breakdown, who had discovered just in time that much study was a weariness to his flesh and that he had better take a spell off. A very gentle-looking lady next him was certainly his wife. I conjectured that her professor might be rather nervy at times and that her rôle would be to harp the dark moods away and dodge javelins. The passenger list gave their name as Gwyn; a board-ship rumour provided him with a chair at a Welsh university. On board he was always addressed as Professor, and always received his title with a slight but sardonic smile.

The passenger list also disclosed the presence at our table of the Dysart-Thunder family—Mr, Mrs and the Misses Félicité and Aimée Dysart-Thunder. If mere names meant anything, this must be a family of great distinction and gentility. Mrs Thunder always addressed her husband as Dysart or Dy, from which one adduced that his Christian name had been roped or hyphened on to give the family a double name and yet greater distinction. Mr Thunder conveyed to me the impression of having once been a chemist or perhaps an undertaker. The two professions are very honourable ones and not unconnected. There was something very smooth and precise and urbane about his appearance that strongly suggested the exact making up of prescriptions or a tactful handling of bereavements, and a complete mastery of *pompes funèbres*. I was quite wrong. He had nothing to do with pharmacies or embalmings. Had the Misses Félicité and Aimée been sons, their parents would have alluded to them as boykins; but as they were not sons they were called girlies. Félicité called her sister Amy, and Amy called hers, in perfect Stratford atte Bowe French, Flicity. They were graceful, pretty girls. Mrs Thunder was one of those happy mothers who find their families wholly admirable, superlative and unsurpassed. She seemed to spend this, her first meal on board, not so much in eating her dinner, but in devouring her perfect husband and daughters. When she spoke it was in one of those very soft voices that suggest the one which breathed o'er Eden.

Three males completed the table. One of these there was no difficulty in placing. The passenger list had him down as Dr D. O'Flannigan. He was very, very Irish, quite recently lassoed off a bog ; speaking with a brogue seldom heard off the stage ; boisterous as March. In the lounge after dinner that first night, while we were all still in the shy and hostile stage, he did what only the most boisterous of bhoys could dare. He rose from his chair and gave a long recitation about Father O'Somebody ; and in the frozen silence that followed sang a rollicking song—in Erse, or strongly Ersified English—about Father O'Somebody Else. He meant well and was a good fellow, and we all liked him much better later on ; but on a first night at sea, and with a slightly undulatory floor under us, he was premature.

Next the O'Flannigan came J. Godwot of Biggar. I guessed him as having something to do with banks and figures. It was my only right guess. He proved to be a banker and also a factor to several small estates. If O'Flannigan was of a bog boggy, Godwot was of a native heath and very heathery.

The last member of the Captain's table was cited as P. Whyborn of Bexhill. An indeterminate man, possessing no feature, expression, or accent whereby my idle, curious self could gain a clue as to what he was. He drank Burgundy mingled with lemonade, which caused painful impressions but led me nowhere. And his trousers had a little pocket over the right haunch, with a flap, clearly designed for a foot-rule; but this led nowhere either, for he was certainly not a carpenter. Not that he disclosed his haunch-pocket at dinner. It was discovered later. He remained quite unidentified. I do not think he had an identity. But later on Flicity told me that he was frightfully sympathetic and colossally brainy; that he knew several languages so terribly well, that during the war he had served at Boulogne as an interpreter, and could never be spared except for leave to England. Evidently not quite clever enough, or perhaps too clever by half, to find his way into the trenches. But I did not say this to Flicity because she and P. Whyborn had by that time become rather matey. He did not pronounce his name Whin or Whorn, and to the end of our cruise it suggested a query to which his next-door neighbour, Godwot, gave an unhelpful answer.

III.

Let us pass over, obliterate and utterly forget the next thirty-six hours. Suffice it that the *Esperanza* adopted a rolling gait, and most of us realised that those pleasing posters recommending ocean cruises in search of sunshine told but the pleasant half of the tale. It was by no means all blue sea and sunshine, all cheerio and whoopee. Most of us were doing whoopee of a very different kind on our backs, with our eyes shut, in our bunks. As I lay in mine I recalled the words of a friend. He is named Henry Groper, and infests a sea-beach, leans against a boat, handles live lobsters with impunity and, I feel sure, goes to bed in his clothes. H. Groper, or, as visitors call him, Captain Groper, is a great authority on anything connected with the sea. He just says a thing is so, and it is accepted as *ex cathedrâ*. I do not think he has ever been farther from his beach than lobster-pot soundings. But there is nothing he does not know about seas and oceans. And he holds a theory about sea-sickness. He is always propounding it to hearten up visitors for a trip in his smelly old boat, *The Pine-Apple.* Says the Captain, "Sea-sickness ain't nowise caused by the motion of them billers" (stabbing at them with his pipe). "If you arsts me the true cause on it, I'll tell ye; and I speaks as one wot knows. It's not them billers as does it, but the 'eaving of the rind of the guts." It is no good asking the Captain what causes the rind to heave. He resents being questioned and will not discuss. All I can say is that during those thirty-six hours on the *Esperanza* there was a great rind-heaving. Personally I am of opinion that the billows had something to do with it.

Then the sun shone and the sea went down, and sun-bathers began to prick for soft planks to bathe on.

The sun-bathers on the *Esperanza,* though not following an exact ritual, yet observed certain rites. There was the careful choosing of a site, publicity being rather sought than avoided. And this was the more remarkable since a state nearly approaching that of complete nudity is part of the cult, and the act of worship was often performed by pairs of young persons of opposite sexes. There followed the spreading of the prayer carpet, which had to me sometimes the appearance of an inflatable mattress. Next came the exact ordering of the music, the service being fully choral. The music was rendered by loud-speaker or gramophone, the more nasal, raucous and obscene the better. Then came the act of prostration, and immediately after there began and continued the ceremony of the roasting spit.

At this point I would withdraw to as distant a spot as I could find, partly to avoid the choral part of the service (" Good night, little girl, good night," and suchlike), and partly because I do not care to see nice pink-and-white people slowly turning to the colour of boiled lobsters.

IV.

Following Gran'ma's instructions, the *Esperanza* took her proper turning and found herself at rather a jumpy Lisbon. The rebellion at Madeira was at this time in full bloom, and Lisbon was getting a whiff of it. The *Esperanza* was also feeling it, because a number of her cabins, which would otherwise have been occupied, were empty.

Of Lisbon I saw a great deal from the ship and very little from the shore. Possessing a singular ineptitude for sight-seeing, I penetrated to but one of Lisbon's streets. In its own way it was a remarkable street, for in it I saw more blue chins, and off it—in cellars—more barbers scraping at them, than can be seen in any other street in the wide world. Having looked on the chins and realised the inadequacy of the barbers, I felt I had done my duty by the Iberian Peninsula and went back to the quiet solitude of our decks.

My fellow passengers had all gone ashore to see sights and find adventures. The Thunder party at least seem to have succeeded in regard to both. Father Thunder—a little shaken by his experiences—told me all about them in the smoking-room immediately after his return to the ship. I must, however, preface the narrative by stating my belief that Thunder should be taken as a flawless exemplar of a sheltered and respectable English citizen; that for the fifty years of his blameless life he had lived according to that noble slogan 'Safety First.' I am certain that he had never slept under the stars, or anywhere but in a well-aired box-mattressed bed, and clad in proper sleeping garments; that he had always changed his socks when they were damp, and never ran any risks other than those of street traffic, which to be sure are now pretty considerable. Mr Thunder's description of what he saw that day in the Lisbon streets may, therefore, have borne the deeper impress, the richer colour engendered by novelty. His idea of carnage, for example, might not be quite what yours would be or mine. But let it pass. To Dysart-Thunder it was carnage. And this is what he saw, or thought he saw.

"I had made up a little party for a whip-round ashore—just the wife, our girlies, Whyborn and Godwot: the ladies wanted to do a little shopping. They had got wind of a wonderful hat shop and of a wonderful glove shop, and so forth. Well, things looked much as they do in a London street. I was beginning to regret a lack of local atmosphere. I had thought we should have had more colour, perhaps a sight of a bandit thrumming on a banjo—or is it a guitar?—under a window. Of course, the language was different. I couldn't make out a word of it, and that gave a zest to our little jaunt. And then the Portuguese policeman on point duty—really they are quite comic—the way they flailed the air instead of using the proper traffic signals. Yes, 'flailing' was the word Flicity used. 'Isn't it an absolute scream the way they flail, Dad?' were her exact words.

"Well, as I was saying, we were standing in the doorway of a hat shop. I was just remarking on a very drainy smell (and not the first either) which would never be permitted in London, when the people started running, and all one way. Two policemen ran faster than any of them. Now I'm a tolerably cool sort of fellow and don't imagine things, but I'm almost sure I heard a shot or two fired somewhere near. And then to my horror a brigade of cavalry came thundering in line down the street, fierce-looking, dark-browed bravos, absolutely merciless. With drawn sabres, sir, naked sabres, and brandishing them in a perfectly horrible manner. These men extended right across the street—on to the pavement, sir, and the police doing nothing about it. There were no police to do anything.

"Well, we men, of course, had to keep our heads, ladies being present, and we threw ourselves into a cordon round them. I set my teeth and prepared myself for anything.

So far as we could we shielded them from the sight of the carnage going on round us. As the cavalry swept onwards they passed so close to us as almost to touch us. Men fell right and left, cut down (probably in their prime) ruthlessly. They lay in swathes, sir. Literally.

"No sooner was the street clear than I at once saw that there was only one thing to do, and that was to go to Thomas Cook & Sons. Thomas Cook had got us into this mess, for we had booked our berths through them, and, by cripes, they'd have to get us out of it. I fancy I rather kept my head here. I could still think perfectly clearly. A man can't do that if he loses his head, you'll allow. I felt that the helpless ones under my care would look to me for sound leadership, and I knew I should not fail them. I should have a word or two to say to Thomas Cook, and not very pleasant ones either. But Godwot insisted that board-ship was the place for the ladies, and the ladies agreed with him. None of them seemed to realise the fearful risk of finding our way there alone, strangers as we were in this far country. They insisted on my coming with them to protect them. They refused to go without me. Of course I yielded. But I shall drop T. Cook a line, and I shan't mince matters either.

"And by extraordinary luck, here we are."

At this juncture Amy and her cavalier Godwot arrived for a cocktail. It was Amy's rôle to be audacious and to shock, especially her father. To have a cocktail was Amy's form of audacity, and to call it "knocking back a quick one" was more audacious still.

"Well," she said (after knocking), "has father been telling you of the rough-house we were in? No end of a lark. Simply colossal. But the way these Portuguese did their silly charge was simply septic. They never went out of a trot. And no one was cut down or run through. Only a few guys fell down. And father was in no end of a dither, weren't you, darling?"

It must have been rather a wide street to take a brigade (in line)—even supposing it did spread on to the pavements. At least 600 yards wide.

I think it was a Saint's Day, and during dinner that night there were certainly fireworks. The first rocket to go off in the street close to the ship fairly lifted the hair on Thunder's head and Thunder himself out of his chair. But he kept his head and hit it again—his chair, not his head. No doubt Messrs Thomas Cook and all his sons and grandsons would hear something about this too.

V.

We had left England with its mud and rain so recently behind us that we were the more able to appreciate the amenities of a perfectly smooth Atlantic, an unclouded sun that was almost too warm to sit in, and superlatively beautiful and starlit nights. Through all this we slid quietly along with muted engines, for having cut out Madeira, we had to kill time and not get to the Canaries too soon.

Gran'ma was enjoying things immensely. Full of beans and ozone, she began to assume the rôle of rather a rollicking old tar, bouncing about on the roof of her shed, treading on the sun-bathers and revelling in what she called her sea-blow. She told the Captain (who had rounded the Horn eight times in sail) what a lucky man he was to be a sailor. She told him this several times. Once is more than enough for elderly seamen as a rule, but he never even laid back his ears. On one occasion, however, he said to Gran'ma: "See all these things on the table, Mrs Bunce? Plates of soup, cutlery, glass and all the rest? Well, last voyage and just about where we are now, the whole lot, and a couple of stewards, lay in a heap in that corner yonder. One roll did it, and that sort of thing went on for three whole days."

"Well, I never!" said Gran'ma.

"As a matter of fact," said the Captain to us later, "it's too much sunshine and fair weather that makes Dagos. I'm not saying anything against them, mind you, nor will you when you see these stevedores working our cargo at the ports. They can work all right and live on the smell of an oiled rag. And in their own hugger-mugger way they're good seamen. But they haven't our guts. They're Dagos."

There is nothing but a boat harbour at Orotava, and the *Esperanza* anchored in an exposed roadstead. Shore boats laden with crates of bananas immediately surrounded us, and a noisy day was plainly in prospect.

The Gwyns and I made up one shore party, the Thunder family and two of the men of our table another. In rickety motors driven by rackety islanders, we spent some hours hurtling about the place, seeing the sights—chiefly banana gardens. The professor, during the drive, became less sombre and quite communicative. In the following words he destroyed our illusions about his professorship—

"You know," he said, "this calling me a professor is all bilge and bunkum. I don't know that I've ever seen a professor. I suppose I must look like one. And so I am a professor if it comes to that, though not the kind you mean. Every man's a professor who's an expert in any particular line."

"And what's your particular line?" I asked.

Upon this the professor winked at me and said—

"Oh, I work for the Home Office. Confidential stuff. Secret and confidential."

His wife corroborated this by saying that it was so very secret that she did not know herself what it was. The professor laughed very heartily at this. There appeared to be some subtle jest in the secret and confidential stuff which he was unwilling to share with any one.

The day was warm and he had taken off his coat. His shirt blew open and disclosed a most unprofessorial chest, tattooed all over with hearts and darts and tombstones and suchlike emblems of affection and sentiment. An immensely hairy chest withal.

"I've been a good many things in my day," he continued. "Planted tea in Ceylon, been a soldier and a sailor. I've been lost four days in the spinifex—if you know what that is. I've been one of a pearling outfit, and the only survivor after a hurricane which blew the whole of our crowd into the sea off the atoll and drowned the lot and sunk the schooner. I happened to be on the windward side of a rock and the wind simply flattened me against it—like a postage stamp—and there I stuck. Ah, and I felt like a postage stamp, and a well-licked one, after it blew over."

The professor had apparently been a rolling stone. He had gathered some moss, on his chest at least.

"You should write a book about your experiences," I said.

"Ah, and I *could* write a book, only I ain't—I'm not much of a hand with a pen." And here the professor completely shut up. It was as if he had suddenly found his tongue wagging too freely. He scarcely opened his mouth again till our two cars, ours and the Thunders', reached the coast again early that afternoon. We got out to stretch our legs, and it was Thunder who made the great discovery. The ship was not there.

"The boat's gawn, I do declare!" he exclaimed.

"Nonsense, Dysart. Boats don't go away and leave passengers on islands like Robinson Crusoes. Look again." Thus his wife.

"She's not there," said Amy. "Is she, Mr Whyborn?"

Whyborn being of Bexhill and, therefore, knowledgeable about ships, we all hung on his reply. For it was now patent to all that the *Esperanza* was not where we had left her.

"I expect she's swung away with the tide," replied Whyborn. "They do, you know."

"When's she going to swing back again then? And where's she swung to?" asked the professor rather truculently.

"Then again," continued Whyborn, paying no regard to this interruption, "it may be the visibility. . . ."

"Invisibility, you mean," said the professor.

"I was going to say," resumed Whyborn, getting a little rattled, "that the visibility may be bad. It often is, you know. Why, down our way at Bexhill I've known 'em disappear just like the *Esperanza*. One moment you saw them—the next——" and here he made a snapping gesture with thumb and middle finger, to show even the dullest of us that the next moment you did not.

"And so," said Flicity, "we are now to conclude that our trusty old boat is swinging about somewhere in the Invisibility. Isn't that so, chaps?"

The chaps did not seem at all certain about it. It was the professor's quiet little wife who made the sensible suggestion that we had better get into our cars and drive on down to the harbour and find out. When we got there we found all the boats drawn up, and rather an angry-looking sea, also several boatmen who, by their vehement speech and abundant gestures, seemed to be rehearsing to us their rough island story. We could make nothing of it. Mrs Gwyn again helped us by saying that she had seen from the ship a large hotel at the back of the town, that it must still be there and would contain a manager or someone who could speak English and explain things.

We did not follow up this line till Godwot had tried baby-language on the boatmen. But he cut no ice with "Big ship, puff-puff, where gone?" and other simple queries. Then away we drove to the hotel. Here the manager soon made everything plain and nothing pleasant. The anchorage off Orotava being an exposed one when a certain wind blew (it had begun to blow early that afternoon), captains did not like it, and on the smallest threat of bad conditions were in the habit of weighing anchor and departing to the better harbour of Santa Cruz. At 2 P.M. the *Esperanza* had begun sounding the recall, had booed in vain for an hour and had then steamed away. She would be found at Santa Cruz. In the manager's opinion passengers never read any but sweepstake-on-the-run notices; but it was the custom of all ships to have notices posted on board warning passengers that if they went ashore this sort of thing might happen. Meanwhile all we had to do was to book rooms at his excellent hotel, and to be forwarded next day, per hotel motors, to Santa Cruz. And how far off was Santa Cruz? we asked. Only a couple of hours' drive by a good road. "Good," said we. "Then we will start at once and be reunited to our tooth-brushes and other little comforts before nightfall." "Not so," said the manager. "Your ship will arrive at Santa Cruz towards midnight. She will anchor out in the harbour and not move alongside the quays till after daylight to-morrow. You might get off to her at some late hour to-night, or you might not. And the Santa Cruz boatmen are sharks." He therefore begged us to spend the night where we were, and held out as additional reason for our doing so: our freedom to wander in the beautiful hotel gardens and to hear the cicadas cheep and the tree-frogs warble (after dark), and to view the green ray at sunset.

The green ray is a speciality of Teneriffe. It is to be seen at sunset. The Captain had said so, and now the hotel manager said so. But truth compels me to state that though we looked for it we never saw it, and do not in the least know what it is.

The manager's arguments appearing to be unanswerable, we fell in with them. And it was at about this moment that a subtle change began to come over us. It grew while we had tea, it increased while we wandered amongst the scents of the garden and the smells of the little town, and by dinner-time at seven-thirty it culminated. Hitherto we had been mere board-ship acquaintances. Now our bosoms expanded under a common adversity. We became matey. Till now I had felt a certain aloofness from the Dysart-Thunder circle, who, I felt, moved in grades of society more genteel and of greater distinction than those I moved in. People with names like that must. Gwyn, the professor, had kept himself to himself, and Mrs Gwyn had had eyes for nobody but him. The two males, of Bexhill and Biggar, had rendered a certain conventional allegiance to the Dysart-Thunders, as table mates, but had other friends amongst other passengers. This was now all changed. It was changed by that marooned feeling. It entered into us, became a complex, permeated. We were comrades in adversity. We had arrived comfortably enough at a comfortable hotel. Yet we felt somehow like sole survivors who had floated ashore on hen-coops and been cast up on an inadequate beach. Though enjoying a tolerable dinner, it was yet to us in a manner of speaking a meal of bats, beetles, edible slugs and such fare as castaways seem to exist on.

Under these influences the bosom of the Thunder family expanded, and we nestled in it. All petty differences in social rank were sunk. The two unattached men had definitely by dinner-time assumed the rôle of swains to the two young ladies. The cloud cleared from the professor's brow. He now openly, as he had before privately to me, abjured his chair in a Welsh university. He again alluded to it as bilge. He became blithesome at the can, and told several steepish pearling and planting yarns. No one was in the least shocked and his wife only said, "Oh, Wilfrid!" Father Thunder, as comforter of the weaker vessel, said more than once to his wife, "My dear, depend upon it, we shall come well out of this, well out of it. We shall look back on our little contretemps as quite an adventure, quite an adventure." And Mrs Thunder smiled a little motherly, wifely, wan smile (as if her last) upon husband and daughters, perishing as it were before her very eyes of cold and exposure. Yet she made a good dinner, though looking resigned throughout.

But P. Whyborn, staunch to the idea that doublet and hose must show themselves courageous to petticoat, ordered himself a whisky and lemonade in the most abandoned fashion, and said he did not give a dam, and that for all he cared it might snow ink. No one had said that he had given anything; and the sky was serene and starlit. And when Godwot called out, "Language, Whyborn, language!" he replied, "Not at all, Goddo. A dam is or was a Greek coin, though I forget its exact value. I always remember when ladies are present." Flicity—Whyborn being her swain—said, "Besides, we shouldn't in the least mind if it hadn't been a Greek coin." Whyborn produced from his little haunch pocket a jack-knife, and made as if he were going to eat his dinner with it. And Flicity said, "What things you *do*, Mr Whyborn!" To which he replied that he always carried a weapon when "knocking about in strange places." In short, we were all very jolly and chummy.

Then Thunder, having cleared his throat, called for a bottle of champagne, and as no one else liked it he drank it all and called for another—a half-bottle this time. And Mrs Thunder said, "Dysart, be careful. You will react to this." But she said it too late, I think. It would have been perfectly all right if she had not insisted on carrying him off to bed immediately after dinner, and if the dining-room had not been so exceedingly large and empty and its floor so flat. If she had let her Thunder sit quiet after we had dined it would have passed off. He was only in the laughing stage and enormously amused at things. He now rose roaring with laughter, and then walked across the great expanse of perfectly naked parquet floor, stepping very high, over heather or even gooseberry bushes, apparently. He was, in fact, reacting. But though he stepped very high and laughed very loud, he walked fairly straight. Partly because his wife walked by him and inserted her left shoulder into his right oxter. The pair reminded one ludicrously of a couple of staid old polo ponies riding one another off at a walk. On reaching the doorway the male pony wanted to come back, but the old mare rode him into it. Here he jibbed, and with tears of mirth called back to us that he was a jolly old thoroughbred sea-horse, stepping over the waves to keep his trousers from getting splashed because they were not rolled up high enough; that he was now going to neigh and then gorrobed. He neighed and went.

"A pity Dad's so boisterous," said Flicity.

"Such a young heart!" said Whyborn. The parent of this angelic being could never be boisterous.

"He gets so keyed up," added Amy.

"Sheer *joie de vivre!*" said Godwot. The author of this being, fairest of her sex, could never be keyed up.

At this point the Gwyns went off to bed. Then Godwot carried Amy away to listen to the frogs.

Flicity was a pretty girl, not unskilled in the ogle of a roguish eye. But only one of the pair ogled. Its fellow, very, very slightly out of the true, kept looking round the corner, keeping *cave* as it were, for the rogue. One slim hand dangled invitingly within reach of Whyborn. It gave me the impression of a bell-push which would answer if pressed by him. So I said good night and left him to ring.

Mrs Thunder had told me all about her husband during dinner. He was in the Civil Service, in a Department; rather high up and very well thought of. A great organising brain. The name Thunder was really an English rendering of its Irish equivalent. In Irish he would be The Thunder, because he was chief of all the kings and princes of that name. The Thunder, not *Mr* Thunder. An immensely ancient name—The Thunder of Thunder Castle—in Irish. She had it written down somewhere; it began with an O, but she could not remember the rest.

Though the professions I had associated The Thunder with were very honourable and ancient, they are not exactly royal. So I did not say anything to The Thunderess about them.

VI.

We drove over to Santa Cruz next morning and without further adventure found our ship. She was carrying on just as if nothing untoward had happened to nine of her passengers. Eight of them immediately dashed off on another round of sight-seeing. I remained on board to watch the scene. There was a blazing hot sun, but a slashing breeze blew all day. It blew in from the open sea an endless succession of most picturesque sailing craft of all sizes and rigs. These all seemed to make a dead set at the *Esperanza*. When a new arrival failed to find a vacant place alongside of her, she dropped a ponderous anchor, and her crew, as picturesque as their craft and in perfect keeping with her, lay down and slept in the sun. From the quay on one side of us, and from those boats on the other, cargo poured into us. At siesta-time there was an interlude. Then at it again till the sun went down and stars came out, and throughout the night. Never were such strenuous, furious workers. Along the quay mule-waggons and lorries swayed and clattered and bumped; winches rumbled; tackles chirped; bundles of cinctured crates swung and creaked, sank into holds, were seized, dismembered and hustled away by stevedores.

In the afternoon our apprentices and a junior ship's officer went for a sail in our emergency boat. I watched the lowering of her and her start. First, the falls jammed and wanted a good deal of humouring. Then when she was brought along to the accommodation ladder, her rudder refused to be shipped: a file and other tools had to be fetched from a remote part of the ship. Then two of the rowlock holes proved to be too small for the pins, and this had to be remedied. At last she got away. Time taken (about) half an hour. I determined not to fall overboard.

Miss Daisy Bollinger, a passenger, went with them. She

was a dark horse was Daisy. She started as supercargo and returned in command; her crew no longer kindly condescending, but smartly jumping to her orders. I do not know exactly what happened, save what I saw through my glasses and over the sea wall, for they quickly sailed out of the harbour. The boat, however, appeared to be performing strange antics. The breeze seemed to be quite enough for her, and the long Atlantic swell, which occasionally hid her, rather more than enough. On their return Daisy brought her boat alongside with skill and dash. They were all very wet. After she had changed I interviewed her. She was brief. "Oh, they meant well enough, but they don't really know much about open-boat work. Gybing they called 'going about.' After twice of that and the boat half-full, I had to take charge. The boat's suffering from dry-rot, too."

At 3 A.M. the last of our cargo was in the hold and on the deck. Here it was piled twelve feet high and very cunningly built up, boxes and crates of bananas and tomatoes, with narrow alleyways left to allow passage along the decks. I felt that it behoved the *Esperanza* to keep on a level keel lest her deck cargo should start tumbling about.

VII.

Near us at Las Palmas lay a long sooty coal hulk. The Captain called my attention to her. Closer inspection revealed a blackened star on her bow, and above it an undecipherable motto. Into the blue waters of the harbour she thrust forward a ram bow, which still held in its outline a hint of insolence. This had once been Her Majesty's ship *Serapis*, one of the old Indian troopships, for many years a familiar sight anywhere between Portsmouth and Bombay. And in their day tall ships enough, barque-rigged, carrying Royal Navy crews, able at the chirping of a pipe to clothe their lofty masts completely and almost instantaneously in a cloud of white canvas; the Star of India at their bows and the motto "Heaven's Light our Guide."

This debauched-looking old hulk had once carried the Prince of Wales, later King Edward VII., to India. For his benefit a small smoking-room had been built on deck, a great luxury in those days; and this smoking-room distinguished the *Serapis* above her consorts, *Crocodile*, *Euphrates* and *Malabar*. They all passed out of the service during the 1890's.

As I looked at her, a certain smell came back to me—that of a bit of smouldering rope or slow-match kept in a perforated brass box affixed to the forward side of the wheelhouse on the poop. That was the only means for lighting a pipe or cigarette then permitted. The Prince probably disregarded the orders. No one else did.

Near the *Serapis* was a very ancient-looking sailing craft about eighteen feet long. She looked about as seaworthy as a basket. Yet she, too, had a claim on attention. She had recently been bought for twelve dollars at New York, had then been sailed single-handed to Las Palmas without misadventure, save that her owner, cooking his last remaining food when within two days' sail of land, had had to go on deck to attend to some urgent matter. On his return below, he found that his dog had finished the food. Here, had his breeze failed him, he might have lain for an inconvenient number of days—but the wind was kind, and blew him in with an empty stomach. A long-moustached, bronzed and very hard-bitten tough, who passed as we were looking at her, was said to be the man who had owned and sailed her over. His reason for crossing the Atlantic in this fashion was not a love of adventure or notoriety, but because it was the cheapest way to return to his native island. And, indeed, four dollars (for he sold her for four less than he had given for her) was not a big price to pay for the voyage of himself and dog.

To get away from the noise of cargo-working I went ashore and wandered into a hotel. Here in a vast and silent lounge I found two persons—a large, round, blonde male, and a small, flattish, dark female. He was doing nothing, but evidently on the look-out for prey. She was laid out on a sofa, under a shroud of what looked like ordnance maps upon her and a pencil sticking out of her mouth.

On my entry the large man surged upwards from his chair and bellowed, "Hullo, old man! Who'd have thought of meeting you here!" I broke it to him gently that this was our first and only meeting. But I was not to get out of it like that. He grew heartier than ever and replied, "What, not remember old Frankie Brown of the Loyal Scorbutics! Why, man, your regiment and mine lay together way back in the 'nineties. Many's the blood night we've had together, you and me! Come now!" "Are you old Frankie Brown?" I asked, not quite sure whether he was alluding to himself or another. He immediately took this to mean that I remembered but had not recognised old F. B. He seized both my hands and said, "There now, I knew you'd remember me. Changed a bit I must be, but not so much as all that, eh?" I need not go into the unseemly wrangle which ensued between myself and this total stranger, he asserting and I denying our ancient cronyship. He was a big man and determined, and I a small one and very anxious to oblige. I never stood a chance, really, and he finally clinched the matter beyond all dispute. I had sold him a pony once, name of Cheddar, a cheesy chestnut, not over sound and with a moustache. Although I had never owned a pony in my life, I could not stand up to this, and finally and unwisely allowed that I was the old and long lost friend of this Loyal and persistent old Scorbutic. I had only now to learn my name, and business could proceed. In the end I never learnt what my real name was, but only the one my intimates knew me by. For Brown immediately conveyed to the recumbent lady the glad news that 'old Blotto' had blown in. She flapped a languid hand at me with a "How do, Blot." To say this she had to blow her pencil out of her mouth, and the consequent heaving of her chest sent some of her cerements sliding off her. They were ordnance maps, for when I hastened to shroud her up again I laid her under two miles to the inch of Sussex. Frankie said, "Just shove Bradshaw and the A.B.C. on the top of her while you're about it. They'll keep the dam things from slipping off. She's busy with our Sussex itin'ries."

So here was I (old Blot) with Frankie and Posy—that was what he called her; and the two latter busy over the Sussex topography, here in the Canaries. The situation seemed to me to be full of murky possibilities. But the first thing to do was to interpret correctly the part of Blotto. I sensed at once that to have earned a name like that I must have once been one of your sweet-bloods, full of *bonhomie* and back-slappings, and yet withal a bit of a horse-coper; genial, winning and a little sly. I am none of these things. I am not a hearty fellow and I hope I am not sly. However, I must play my part. So I vamped up a genial, swashing and toss-pot manner and addressed my old gossip.

"Damn me, old bird, and what are *you* doing here?"

"Oh," replied the bird, "we're havin' a spell off house huntin'."

"Settling here?"

"No—house huntin' in England."

"Oh—I've been through all that. Been long at it?"

"Let me see—how long is it, Posy? When did we start huntin' the merry wigwam and chasin' wild geese and findin' mares' nests?"

Posy blew her pencil, Bradshaw slid off, but the rest held. She answered concisely, "1912." Frankie confirmed this, and continued at some length as to how the war, to which he alluded as a mere interlude to the serious business of house hunting, interrupted things.

"A most annoying interruption, but we got down to it

again in 1918. You must do these things on a system," said Frankie. "Without a system you're lost, absolutely bushed, up a tree, down a hole. Take my word for it, Blot" (and here he took me by a buttonhole), "do it on a system—like we do—don't we, Posy? Make a base in each county, work it thoroughly from the centre outwards and then on to the next. We've done all the west, and are now in Sussex, or shall be soon when we've had a bit of a stand-off. It's wearin'—very wearin'."

Rather a barren system it seemed to me, and I intimated as much to F. B. as one may to an old friend.

"Oh, I don't know about that," replied Frankie. "A month ago, for instance, we found quite a nice little place—right size, right number of rooms and all that. But the blinkin' house faced north, although the prospectus said it had a southern aspect. Well, I wrote to the blighter about it, and he said his house had four aspects and one of them looked south, and that I should have written and asked first whether the principal rooms had a south aspect. Smart that, but not smart enough for old F. B. What!"

There was a sound of a mappy avalanche as Posy rose and joined us. "Tell him, little one," she said, "about that other try-on, that house near Winchester."

"Yes," said Frankie. "There the system came in and saved us. It was a nice little house in every way. We both fell in love with it, and might have bought it had I not just glanced down my little list of 'Essentials.' There I saw the words, 'Canary—groundsel.' I had forgotten them, so had Posy. I said to the owner, 'Any groundsel here?' 'Not an atom,' he answered. So I said, 'Well, it won't suit us.'"

"Now, little one," interposed Posy, "you're missing the whole point. What you said to him was, and it was really rather witty, 'No groundsel, no sell ground'! The fellow didn't know what to say to that. He just opened his mouth and stared."

I had to ask the Browns to explain the point of this matter to me. Little one, kindly patient with his old Blot, did so.

"You see," said he, "neither Posy nor me are chickens. We couldn't wait to grow the stuff. We had to find it, sort of ready-made, on the premises—if you take me."

I did not take him. I had to ask him again. The flavour of even the most intense jest is apt to dwindle under questions. Posy finally let a blast of light on to the point, and I heard that she hoped one day to keep a canary (two perhaps), and that as groundsel is food for canaries, the Brown system had ruled out any property on which that succulent herb did not grow, or was said not to grow. The Browns now realised that years, or drink, had blunted the perceptions of old Blot; but they were patient with him, and Brown began to explain the exact meaning of his joke on groundsel-sell ground. But I said that I had seen that straight away and all the time.

"As I was sayin'," resumed F. B., "work it on a system. Don't be too particular. Don't expect to find everything under one roof. Go for the essentials."

As I dexterously straightened out the crook of F. B.'s forefinger and gently eased it from its holdfast on the third buttonhole from the top of my waistcoat, I replied, "Well, I shan't count groundsel an essential, anyway." With that, old Blot went off to wash his hands for lunch. But he never reappeared. He preferred to go without lunch. In assuming the name and part of Blotto, he had over-estimated his strength.

The Frankie Brown system will probably carry the pair all over Great Britain, and they will find none but a Heavenly Mansion. That kind never really means to buy a house. If any reader of these lines meets a large pink man, a combination of the ponderous and the arch, and if he has with him a small woman who calls him little one, let him be very careful.

VIII.

During the passage from Las Palmas to our home port, Thunder unlocked his bosom and released from its cupboard a little domestic skeleton, which he seemed to hope we would lay or otherwise deal with. Not that it was a rare thing for Thunder to unlock his bosom. Rather he was one of the kind that leaves its bosom unlocked so that it can the more readily be opened. But hitherto his confidence had been mainly concerning his own interior plumbing and general sanitary system. He was very interested in his inside, and must have made a very close study of it. He would speak of it as one might suppose a very young and enthusiastic sanitary engineer to rhapsodise over a sink or a hot and cold water system. Strangers who offered a sympathetic ear or a buttonhole to Thunder, in the hopes that he might extend his interest or a buttonhole to similar confidences for themselves, regretted it. He liked unlocking his own, but yawned when I began to open my bosom.

On this particular occasion it was Thunder's *amour propre* and personal authority that caused him to expatiate. The professor was the victim, but he being in one of his contradictious moods, Thunder's eye had started rolling and had unfortunately met mine. I had been immediately co-opted. I had been reading, but had become aware of the colloquy, and now looked up to hear it going on as under.

"As a married man yourself and probably a father, Mr. Gwyn, you will understand my difficulty."

"I'm not a father," replied Gwyn.

"Still, speaking as man to man," persisted Thunder, who was not going to be shaken off by irrelevant trivialities.

The professor would have denied Thunder's statement if he could, but Thunder was unquestionably a man and he himself another.

"Very well, then," continued Thunder. "Naturally, as head of a family I like to be supreme."

The professor at once disputed the assumption that a man in competition with three women would be supreme.

At this point Thunder's eye rolled and caught and co-opted me. He made as if his last statement had been directed to me. Instead of resuming my book, I unwisely said "Certainly," and took Gwyn's place as victim. He was free now to wait for openings and to be factious.

"At the same time," continued Thunder, now addressing me exclusively, "with me it is ever the case of the velvet glove worn over the steel gauntlet."

"The point is," interrupted Gwyn, "not who wears gloves or gauntlets, but who wears the breeches." He said this very pointedly.

"And now," continued Thunder, paying no regard to the professor, "we come to the matter which is worrying me. And that is my girl Flicity's mouth. To be more accurate, I should say her lips. When we came aboard two weeks or so ago, as you may have noticed, her lips were straight, like ordinary lips, like yours or mine. Now—and I will ask you to note this particularly—her lips have assumed the shape of—let me see—how shall I describe them? Say, the shape of a bracket. . . ."

Thunder here sketched a bracket in the air with his forefinger and continued, "Not a wooden bracket to support things, but the sort of bracket used to enclose words or figures—but hers is a horizontal bracket. Naturally a mouth *would* be horizontal."

The professor was too surprised to dispute this.

Always apt at the *mot juste* and delighted to learn that it was pretty Flicity's mouth I was hearing about and not about The Thunder's inside, I murmured, "A Cupid's bow."

"Well," said Thunder, "I prefer bracket myself—but let it pass. But now I ask you—how do straight lips become, in two weeks' time, Cupid's bow or bracket lips?"

The professor here let out a loud and coarse and offensive guffaw. "Lip-stick!" he shouted.

I added gently, to soften the blow, "Lips are worn like that now, Mr Thunder—or were till quite recently. My niece tells me that the bow is going out in favour of the rose-bud or pout."

"Worn like that?" gasped Thunder. "How worn like that? You can't change your lips like boots, or—or—socks!"

"*You* can't," sneered the professor. "*They* can."

"But," returned Thunder, "I won't have lip-sticks in my family! I forbid them. They're immoral."

There was a pause here. You might have heard a pin drop or the professor smile. But Thunder took a pull at himself and resumed—

"I flatter myself I move with the times. I was young myself once. Fashions are fashions and so on and so forth. A touch of rouge now and again I permit, or even on rare occasions a little powder on the nose—perhaps even a touch or two at the eyebrows. I flatter myself I *know woman*—I can stretch a point—I can smile at giddy foibles. But I am quite, quite firm about lip-sticks. I will not have nature's sacred conformations tampered with and, in a sense, altered."

"What about the padding your tailor put into the dinner-jacket you're wearing now? Besides, if the stuff's kiss-proof, what's the harm of it?" This from Gwyn.

Thunder was now so dazed and stricken that at first he thought that his tailor had been giving him kiss-proof shoulders. But when the full dreadfulness of Gwyn's innuendo dawned on him, I saw that he had not been called Thunder for nothing. Up till then I had always thought his was a singularly inappropriate name. But when I observed his trembling right hand move in a deadly manner towards the heavily weighted match-holder, I knew that there was going to be a jolly loud clap. I hastened to muffle or even prevent the peal, by remarking suavely—

"Probably Miss Thunder kisses you good night, Mr Thunder. Some of the preparations they sell are not at all fixed. I'm told that they come off like those transfers which you and I used to delight in long ago as boys. Now, when Miss Thunder kisses you good night, or kisses Mrs Thunder good night, it would never do for her to leave a pair of Cupid's bows or brackets on her parents' faces, eh?"

I spoke with infinite tact, as I should address a child about to go into convulsions, and presently Thunder's eyes ceased protruding and rolling, and his lower mandible reunited itself to its fellow. He withdrew his hand from the match-holder. By a superhuman effort he became master of himself, breathed less stertorously, and at last became calm. I observed his right hand slip under the left shoulder of his jacket, and then his left hand gather up and pinch a thumb and fingerful of the right shoulder of his jacket. He pretended to be scratching himself and murmured something about "These mosquitoes," but he was realising that he, too, had been altering nature's handiwork, or his tailor for him, and he found comfort in this. The professor and I between us had laid or otherwise dealt with that little skeleton. Flicity would come out top. And then Mrs Thunder poked her head in, put a sudden end to our beauty-parlour talk and took her Dysart off to bed.

The professor, who was certainly a man of coarse fibre, said after Mr Thunder had gone—

"Kiss-me-good-night-Dad-and-Mum be sugared!"

IX.

On how many ships is the subject of tips discussed on the last night of the voyage? This was going forward in the smoking-room of the *Esperanza* as she was passing the coastwise lights on her last night at sea. It was our twentieth day out; and it was a dapper, rosy-gilled little man who spoke. His was the only decided statement contributed to an otherwise sterile discussion. "Well," said he, "I haven't had a bath since I've been on board, so I shan't give the bathroom steward anything."

Next morning we arrived at the port of X., our starting-point. All was just as we had left it. Could it have been going on like that for three weeks without a pause? The thick, hopeless drizzle, the greasy cobble-stones, the mud squirting from under the wheels of vehicles, the grimy warehouses and mean street-vistas presenting their deplorably dirty faces to the river and shipping.

I went to say good-bye to the Captain. On my way I ran into Gran'ma in full shore-going rig, looking very different. Quite ancestral. She had young'd very much on board and had managed to impart a suggestion of the jolly tar into her dress and gait. She had now discarded the rubber boots she had worn on board, and instead of a shiny thing with ear-flaps which she called "my north-wester," she wore on her head a well-beaded bonnet which became her years better. She remarked that we had had a lovely sail, hadn't we? and that she had enjoyed it ever so, and so passed out of my life.

In a far corner of a dim lounge I caught a glimpse of Whyborn and Flicity looking very hard at one another and seeming to find the view pleasant but fraught with agony.

I passed but did not break in upon two other persons. They were leaning over a damp rail with their heads well out in the rain, because it was more private like that. Godwot had the air of one asking a favour and Amy of one giving the matter favourable consideration. Something might have come of this, but I saw the Irish doctor blunder into them.

Below me on the quay were the Gwyns getting into a taxi. He answered my wave with a scowl, but she smiled and waved back. And they, too, passed.

I saw also Mr Dysart-Thunder, whose velvet and steel gauntleted hands were being kept busy by his wife in final touches to the family suitcases. Of these there were eight. I wondered *en passant* which of them held the lip-sticks.

I met a stranger coming out of the Captain's cabin. He was chuckling very deeply. I heard the Captain exclaim as I entered, " And on my ship, too ! " He looked at me in a dazed way.

" Who's your chuckling friend, Captain ? "

" One of the owners. The youngest of the three : always a bit of a joker. But I don't think he was pulling my leg. And on my ship, too ! "

" What's wrong ? "

The Captain sat down. He gazed at the photograph of his wife and family, which every good captain keeps in his cabin, to keep him good. Then he spoke.

" You know that fellow we all called the professor, with a wife, at my table ? Well, of course we knew he wasn't a professor, but we never guessed and he never let on who he was. Criminal, I call it ; beastly, revolting, scandalous."

" Oh, so it wasn't his wife, then ? Who was she ? Had he murdered Mrs Gwyn ? "

" Worse than that. Much, much worse. The young owner you met as you came in said he really couldn't wait till I came along to the office, but hurried on board as soon as we were tied up. He wanted to tell me whom I had been shipmates with. And at my table, too ! He said that they had found out a few days ago at the office quite by accident ; a letter opened by some junior clerk, or a telegram or a trunk call or something. I'm too dazed to think clear."

" I suppose the police have been notified," I said. " That sort of criminal mustn't get away. Because I saw him and the woman—such a nice, lady-like person, too, but the clever ones are like that—get into a taxi as I came along and drive away. Did you say he had dismembered the body and left it in a cloakroom, or had burnt it bit by bit, or what ? Give these fellows enough rope and they're sure to hang eventually."

"What body?" said the Captain testily. "There's no question of a body or of police either. As to ropes and hanging, I expect he's been concerned with a few and will be again. I shouldn't wonder if he's gone straight from my ship to an execution now, the dirty swine!"

"If you would only be a little more explicit, Captain."

"Why, I've been explaining all along, haven't I, who that fellow Gwyn was, curse him."

"Certainly, up to a point, you have. But you've not yet told me who he is."

"He's the Public Hangman."

. . . .

I said good-bye to this sorely stricken man, my heart too full for words. I was badly shaken up myself. I had been probably using the same bath as a hangman. That was the idea that kept recurring. There were a great many baths on the *Esperanza*, but the chances were that we had used the same one sometimes.

Sanity, however, returned to me after a few hours' reflection. I no longer felt it a crying scandal that a useful servant of the Crown should go about garbed as other men. There was no reason why he should go about when off duty wearing a mask and tights, and carry a rope over his shoulder. Moreover, Jack Ketch is entitled to a holiday as well as another; and to take his holiday how and where he likes.

"All work and no play
Makes Jack a dull boy."

And now I knew what Jack's surname was.

A NIGHT WITH THE VOLUNTEERS OF STRATHKINAHAN.

BY L. W. M. LOCKHART.

[Maga, September 1869.]

I HAVE the highest respect for the Volunteer movement, and the highest admiration for Volunteers. I think the country owes them an immense debt of gratitude. Perhaps a professional soldier can estimate better than a civilian what the magnitude of the debt really is. He knows how irksome a business it is to reduce one's self to the condition of an automaton, to abandon one's personal identity, to become Number One, Two or Three in a squad, and to concentrate for hours one's whole intellectual faculties upon the task of instantly adjusting the anguished frame to certain angles, in obedience to the unmelodious shriek of the drill-sergeant.

I can recall no instances of nervous tension so protracted and intense as those under which I suffered as a recruit officer of her Majesty's Line; and remembering that ordeal of terror and suffering, I regard the volunteer—the self-immolator—with feelings of profound admiration, sympathy and astonishment. I look upon his existence as a death-blow to the cynical idea that patriotism has ceased to be; and if you tell me that the age of chivalry is gone, I point triumphantly to the perspiring legions who offer themselves as willing victims in the dog-days—from morn to noonday bright, from noon to dewy eve, dreeing their self-imposed weird in the grand field-days of Wimbledon Common or the

Brighton Downs. The professional soldier, of course, has tangible advantages to gain by submitting himself soul and body to the thraldom of military discipline.

But the Volunteers? for what purpose eat they thus the bread of toil? *Cui bono* this deliberate expense of tissue?

The only solution I can find is, that these men are patriots.

Of course we are all accustomed to admit this in a general honorary sort of way—indeed it has become one of those standing after-dinner axioms, like the bravery of the army, or the merits of the Royal Family, which no true Briton would dream of attempting to controvert.

But I regard their patriotism as genuine and remarkable, and therefore worthy of something more than a mere assenting and commonplace admiration; and I record my own admiration here specially, and I make these few remarks on this occasion, lest in the following pages I should be suspected of a wish to throw ridicule on an institution so honourable to its members, and so beneficial to the country, which is justly proud of it. It is not to be supposed that such an institution can flourish with equal vigour in every district where it has taken root; and as in certain localities the superior energy and intelligence of the inhabitants will be displayed in this as in everything else which they take in hand to do, so in others where there is no energy and no intelligence, the Volunteer movement will be stamped with the same backwardness and inefficiency which characterise all the other undertakings of the place.

And if a district happens to be steeped in whisky, as Strathkinahan was (I say *was*, for let us hope the Strath has long ago abjured the deleterious 'creature'), why, naturally, its Volunteers, in the infancy of the movement, would be apt to regard the movement as they regarded everything else—from a purely alcoholic point of view.

So much by way of apology or disclaimer. And now to my story.

One autumn day, a good many years ago, I was taking

mine ease in mine inn in Edinburgh, when it was announced to me that a visitor, by the name of Captain Cumming, was waiting below. I occupied the interval between the announcement and his appearance in the room in mentally calling the roll of my acquaintances, but failed to discover anyone answering to this description; nor could I tax myself with knowing any member of the clan. From the Red Comyn who was made 'siccar' end of in the olden time, to the Black Cumming who threatens us with the immediate end of Time itself, all the clan Cumming 'were to me like shadows.' The difficulty was (not immediately) solved by the entrance of Tom Finlayson, not a few years ago my friend and brother subaltern in the —th Hussars.

"Hulloa, Peter!" I exclaimed, using his regimental misnomer—which, written in full, was 'Blue Peter'—"I'm delighted to see you; and how are you? and what are you? and where are you? and what will you drink? Take a weed and bring yourself to an anchor; and, by the quality of mercy, let my hand alone and spare at least my trigger finger;" for Peter was strong in his friendly feelings, and expressed them strongly upon such occasions by collecting one's fingers into a sort of fascine and then squeezing them with the full power of his vice-like grasp. "But where is your friend?" I went on.

"What friend?" replied Peter.

"Why, Captain Cumming, of course; I suppose he came with you."

"Captain Cumming!" said Peter; "why, hang it!—I'm—you don't mean to say you don't—eh?"

Peter had never been a lucid expositor of his ideas, but there was a haziness about this which led my gaze to his nose, the tints on which had given rise to his sobriquet, and had undoubtedly derived their own origin from habits not unconnected with a rather hurried close of his military career.

Peter, still sensitive about his tints, read my eye like a

book and laid his fingers nervously on the many-coloured feature. "Hang it!" he cried, "don't stare so, and listen to the end of a fellow's sentence. I was going to say that you don't positively assert that you don't know who Captain Cumming is?"

"Yes, I do assert that I know nothing about him."

"Well, he is in this room."

"Oh! is he?" said I banteringly, now convinced of Peter's melancholy state, but determined to humour him for the sake of the furniture. "Of course—not so bad—ha! ha!—pray introduce me."

"Now then, look here," burst out Peter, "I'm Captain Cumming!"

"Oh! I understand now. All right, Peter; the rose by any other name, &c., and of course I'm safe; but you're not half disguised. Let me recommend a beard, a dark wig and a lick of flesh-coloured paint on the—you know; and what have you broken for? and where are you off to? in short, let me hear all about it;" and I drew two chairs to the fire, and prepared to receive in comfort a recital of my friend's pecuniary embarrassments and his scheme of flight from the Philistine.

"Tut, tut! there's no deception, no mystery; can't you understand? I've changed my name for good and all—got a property by my wife, and taken her name."

I congratulated him heartily on his good fortune, and added, "I suppose the 'Captain' is a little honorary prefix of your own invention built on the ruins of that cornetcy which——"

"No, it isn't."

"What! did you acquire that by your wife too?"

"No; I'll tell you. You see, though in right of my wife I'm a landed proprietor, the property in question does not yield a very large revenue, and, moreover, what there is of it is a good deal burdened; and so, when we went down to take up our abode there, we found it rather difficult to make the ends meet, and therefore, to supplement our income, and give me some occupation at the same time, I accepted the appointment of Adjutant of the 2d Administrative Battalion of Keltshire Volunteers. My property lies in that county, so it suits very well; and that's how I stand before you, transformed from ex-Cornet Tom Finlayson into Captain Cumming."

"And how do you like the work?" I inquired.

"Oh, very well; the colonel does very little, so I have the corps pretty much in my own hands, and can work out my own system."

This was said with some dignity, and I had much difficulty in repressing a grim smile as I thought of Tom's military antecedents and the system likely to spring from them.

"Nothing like system," he went on. "I carry out old Chalk's —th Hussar system as much as possible. I hated Chalk, and he hated me; but I recognise his military talent, and I have made use of him I can tell you; and, though I say it that shouldn't, you'll find few corps that can walk round the 2d Ad. Batt. of the Keltshire Volunteers. I took 'em over, sir, like a lump of clay, and my what-d'ye-call-it hand has moulded them into a—a—moulded them, sir! The worst of the business is that the fellows won't stick to it. You drill them up to the highest pitch of perfection and then they leave you. You never saw such a fickle, captious set of devils as I have to deal with. They're always taking offence—sometimes with their officers, sometimes with me, and very often with my system—and then they resign; so that though the corps is a crack corps, it is a very small one. Three companies have already been broken up, and if another goes, the 2d Ad Batt. of the Keltshire Volunteers will collapse—the adjutancy will collapse—and Captain Cumming will also collapse financially. Now another company is in a very shaky state, which makes me horribly anxious and uneasy. It (the shaky company, the Strathkinahan company) has lately been transferred from the Kippershire county corps to ours. Strathkinahan is in our county, but in a part of it which dovetails itself far into Kippershire, so that the men are in feeling rather Kippershire than Keltshire men, more especially that they are all on the property of Lord Worrycow, the great Strathkinahan proprietor. Well, these fellows don't like the transfer, and won't co-operate at all. They lost their captain some time before they joined us, and being ordered to select his successor from our county, they keep shilly-shallying and doing nothing, much provoked thereto (I understand) by their lieutenant and ensign—the one a fellow who distils whisky on a large scale, and the other a sheep-farmer who largely consumes it—both, I believe, so thoroughly inefficient, that either the corps will not select them for promotion or they themselves decline to be promoted. I'll be hanged if I know what they want! but the result of it will certainly be, that if they don't get a good captain to keep them together they will fade away like the other three companies, and then good-bye to my appointment.

"Well, I've done what I could by writing threats and remonstrances—all to no purpose; so now I am going down to beat up their quarters in person. I have a man in my eye who would make a first-rate captain for them; and if I can only get them to elect him, the company will be saved, and so will be my adjutancy; so I am determined that they *shall* elect him, by fair means or foul. Couldn't you make a run down with me, and then come on for a few days to my place and try your hand at grouse-driving? It's a glorious district—splendid scenery, and all that—and I'm sure the natives will amuse you; and then your diplomatic talents might be of immense assistance in helping an old friend out of a difficulty."

I had some ten days at my disposal at the time, so I readily agreed to Tom's proposal, and the next day saw us *en route* for Strathkinahan.

It will not do, for obvious reasons, to describe too accurately

the geographical position of Strathkinahan. Suffic
that it lies far away out of the beaten tracks of men, a
he who would behold it must undergo a varied yet t
journey, with perils by land and perils by water, and
equally important Highland element of whisky. Our journ
was performed by almost every possible form of conveyance
—railway, steamboat, stage-coach, row-boat, dog-cart and
post-chaise ; we employed them all, and I had thus an opportunity of studying, not without interest, the habits of the
Celt in a state of locomotion, and of observing how, under his
quaint handling, the most modern inventions put on an
irresistible air of travesty. On a Highland railway I saw a
solution of the long-vexed question, "How should the
guard communicate with the engine-driver ?" It was very
simple, and consisted in the former functionary pelting the
latter with large stones until he was fortunate enough to
hit him in some telling place, and work upon his mind through
the sufferings of his body. I saw the deficiencies of pressure
on the valves of a steamboat-engine supplied by the nethermen of the steerage passengers, who kindly volunteered to
perform in turns this interesting duty. And it was not
without a tremor that I observed our driver quietly take off
his left boot and improvise therefrom a supplement to the
drag by wedging it in between the wheel and the worn-out
buffer, prior to plunging, at sixteen miles an hour, down a
long and dreadfully steep mountain road into the darksome
abysses of the 'Devil's Glen.'

Everything, however—even a Highland journey—must
have an end, and at last, amid pelting rain and owling
wind, our jaded horses were pulled up in the da opposite
the 'Bodach-beg Inn and Hotel.'

"Here we are," said Tom ; "we are to p here, and
have our meeting with the corps in th n behind the
house. I wonder if the officers have c I asked them
to dine with us. How infernally da quiet it all is
Kick the door, driver, and rouse th

[on]slaught by the driver's hoofs on the door produced

"[Bre]ak the window," shouted Tom; and the driver, [havi]ng no other missile handy, again had recourse to his [. . .] boot, which he hurled through a lower pane. This [d]estruction of property at once had the desired effect.

Lights shone in the windows, dogs barked, and at last the door was half opened and a head showed itself warily in the aperture. It was the head of an angry man, and from it proceeded winged words of wrath.

"Gang on! gang on! this meenut; I've tell't ye a'ready there's nae mair whusky in the inns, and if there was, there's nane for a drucken auld carle like you. A Collector! a bonny Collector! I'll collect ye! and it'll be fower and saxpence for the peen o' glass, and if ye dinna pay it this meenut ye shall march hame on your hose, for deil a sicht o' yer damned auld brogue shall ye get this nicht without the siller."

"The man's a maniac," cried Tom, springing past me and pouncing on the orator like a tiger, whom throttling, he thrust back into the house. "What in the name of all the whiskies do you mean, you jabbering idiot? Whisky! I don't want any of the abomination. We want the dinner and the rooms and the beds we ordered. Don't you know me—Captain Cumming? I was here fishing last summer; and didn't you get my letter, you numskull?"

"Captain Cumming! is it you, sir? Wha wad have [e]xpeckit yer honour at siccan a time o' year? I made sure it [w]as the Collector; he's on the ramble this eight days past, drin[kin]g three days here till I pit him oot, and five up i' the bothy, [an]d noo he's hunting for drink heigh and laigh—ragin' li[ke a] bear; for he would toom the Spey in spate if it ran wi' Ta[lis]ker or Glenleevat."

"But my [let]ter, man, my letter? Did you not get it?"

"I got na[e let]ter, sir. Ye see, the postman gaed aff a week sin' to s[is]ter, sir. Ye see, the postman gaed aff a week sin' to s[ee his] freens up Appin way, and there's been nae chance tae [get] a letter without sending ance errand the fifteen mile. But come in, gentlemen; beds ye ha'e and rooms, but for the denner I dinna ken what to [illegible] but I'll speak to the wife." With which he ushered us int[illegible] room, fireless and cold, yet stuffy withal, and pregnant wit[illegible] the odours of departed peat and whisky long ago consumed. Leaving his candle, he retired hastily to consult the guidwife upon the serious crisis.

"Well, this is a nice state of things," said Tom; "but I wrote to the Volunteers a fortnight ago, so they must have had time to get their warning before the confounded postman went off for his holiday—fancy a single-handed postman daring to have a holiday!—so we're sure to have them here; and even if we have a bad dinner and unaired rooms, it's only for one night, for we'll get the business over this evening and be off home to-morrow morning."

The landlord shortly after returned and told us, with many apologies, that ham and eggs, a fowl and perhaps "a bit braxy" would be our dinner, assuring us at the same time that his statement as to the whisky, outside, was only a humane fiction devised for the Collector's own good, and that there was an abundance of the best Glenlivet down below. He added ruefully that "the bodach" (meaning the Collector) had been lurking about the premises, and had taken advantage of the temporary confusion consequent on our arrival to effect a lodgment in the kitchen, where he was again "makin' himself most ootrageous" and resisting all attempts at eviction—physically with his fists, and morally with the argument that he was there on military duty.

"Ye see," explained the landlord, "he's in [illegible]e Strathkinahan Volunteers, and bein' 'on the bee[illegible] ye may say, he's gotten it into his head that he [illegible] tryst here this night wi' his commandin' offisher—[illegible]arl, I'm thinkin'—which shows that the Collector i[illegible]ough; for when he's in his ordinary he cares fo[illegible]nd wad break tryst wi' the archangel Gabriel hi[illegible] had the chance."

A light seemed t[illegible] Tom (who, by-the-bye, ha[illegible] visited the corps since its incorporation with his [batt]alion). "Who is this Collector?" he inquired.

"Weel, sir, he's no exacklee a Collector himsel', but he [a]ye gets it as a kin' o' title; his faything aye got it, but I'm thinking it wad be his grandfaything was the Collector."

"And what is his name?"

"Shooliter."

"Shoeleather?"

"Shooliter."

"That's a queer name; I never heard it before."

"It's no exacklee his name jist, but a byname from the bit farm. 'Hamish Shooliter, the Collector,' that's him in full," said the landlord, as if summing up and closing the discussion.

"But he must have a name—a surname I mean," said Tom.

"Weel, I suppose he wull; it'll be Cawmill maist likely."

Tom hurriedly consulted his notebook. "By Jove! just as I expected," he exclaimed; "'Ensign James Campbell, Shooliter Farm, Glencroaky;' why, this beastly Collector is the ensign, and his tryst is to dine with us here to-night!"

"Aweel," said the landlord, "nensign's the word; for he's been aye croonin' to himsel' as if he was discoorsin' with some ither body. He's been aye sayin' in a fierce voice, 'Nensign! Nensign Hamish! Nensign Shooliter, you're drunk, sir! You're not fit for t' nensign! Shoulder arms and faal oot, Nensign Cawmil!' and then he answers himsel' in a quate fleeching way, 'Jist anither glass o' tuddy afore I fa[...] my lord; the tuddy's goot; it's easy to tak'. I'm a Collec[tor] and a nensign, and anither glass can hairm naither the tane [...] the tither.' And aye the fierce voice again, 'Shooliter! [...] to the right half face! to the devil with you, Shootion! quick march!' And syne he greets."

Tom now short[...]ained to the landlord the new position which he occupied [...] Volunteers of Strathkinahan—told him of the meeting a[...] for that evening, and that the officers were expected to [...] dinner. "The lieutenant," what are you to be? Not more than a general and a knight, I think, to begin with. We can easily promote you as public enthusiasm warms up. So come along, General Sir Hercules O'Halloran, K.C.B.—that ought to fetch them. You're a trifle young for a colonel even, but you're big and burly, and the Doctor's the only one who's the least likely to suspect, and I can tell him, if necessary, that the Queen insisted on your promotion for services at Court. Come on."

We had not been long in the sitting-room when a sound of approaching wheels was heard, and a confused murmur of many voices, and on looking out of the window, we beheld, by the dusky light of a torch, a gig which had drawn up at the door. It contained two human figures, and was surrounded by a crowd of indistinct forms, who had apparently arrived with it.

"The doctor and the lieutenant, of course," said Tom, "thank goodness; and these weird shapes must be the corps: well, they shall have a captain to-night; and now for dinner." He rang the bell, which the landlord answered. "Is that the lieutenant who arrived just now?" inquired Tom.

"It's Glensnorruk himsel', sir, and the doctor wi' him safe enough; and there's a drove o' billies come alang wi' them. Maist likely they'll ha'e been waitin' up at the bothy till he cam' by; between oorsel's, I'm thinkin' there's mair gangs on at that bothy than the gauger kens o', but it's no for the like o' me——"

"Oh, hang the bothy! ask the lieutenant and the doctor to come up."

In a few moments we heard a peculiar sound on the wooden stairs—a hurtling, griding, bumping sound—suggesting the idea that some heavy body was being propelled upwards by an agency not altogether successful in resisting the tendency of the said body to gravitate to the bottom of the stairs. Occasional crashes took place, when both appeared to be involved in a common downfall. These crashes were succeeded by guttural sounds of the human voice, which I conjectured to be profane swearing in Gaelic. The ascent was, however, achieved, and there was a repetition of the sounds along the passage leading to our room, alternated with quick whispers of entreaty, expostulation and wrath. A heavy bump against our door announced that the expedition, whatever it might be, had arrived. There was a pause. Tom and I looked at each other.

"What the deuce can it be?" he said.

"Somebody very drunk," I replied, "taking care of somebody rather worse; the Collector, for choice."

At this moment the door was slowly opened, and an arm, terminating in a very evil and claw-like hand, was extended into the room and commenced a sawing vertical action in the air, that might mean deprecation, but was probably the result of heavy leverage going on at some other part of its proprietor's unseen body.

"Come in," cried Tom, "come in"; but the saw only worked more vigorously, and the fingers were clinched as if in intense muscular exertion.

"Stay out then," shouted Tom, in a rage, whereupon the saw worked for a few strokes with terrific vehemence, and a shoulder and eventually a head made their appearance. The head was a bald head, decorated on either side with a high and tapering horn of black hair; the face was swarthy and dingy, pierced with a pair of Chinese-looking eyes, and corrugated with a wild assortment of smiles, or rather grins, which broke out independently all over the face, cancelling and neutralising the expression of each other in a most puzzling manner. The arm continued to saw, and the horned head was butted backwards and forwards as if in salutation.

"Mephistopheles!" I exclaimed involuntarily.

"Her name's M'Taveesh, sir—M'Taveesh of Glenschnorruk, sir; Rifled Lifteenant, sir," said the head.

"Oh! Mr M'Tavish," said Tom, "how do you do? I'm glad to see you; won't you come in, though?"

"How doo yew doo? and how are yew? and how doo yew doo?" went the head, as if mechanically repeating some formula.

"Very well, thanks; but come in," said Tom.

"Can't," replied the head.

"What?" said Tom.

"Not able," said the head.

"Why not?" said Tom.

The head tossed one of its horns back indicatively to the door and murmured, "The Collecthur."

"Where?" cried Tom.

"On her ither airm and leg," replied the head.

"Why, damme! he's a regular old man of the sea, this infernal Collector!" shouted Tom.

"Run him in, Mr M'Tavish, and let's see him; give a tug; pull away—all your strength—there!" and the head, followed by its body, shot comet-like into the room and subsided on the floor, leaving behind it, inside the door, and on the perpendicular, an Apparition.

"The Collector!" said M'Tavish, picking himself up and extending another claw, by way of introduction, in the direction of the new arrival. It was satisfactory to see this historical character at last.

He was a tallish elderly man, with a very red face, a fixed and flaming eye, and white hair, on the top of which was perched, somewhat defiantly, a round drum-shaped boy's cap with a tassel at the side—a head-dress evidently filched from the nursery below.

He wore tartan trousers and a black dress-coat, with what are called 'weepers' on the cuffs. On the whole, his appearance was not disappointing. We tried to keep our gravity, and Tom to be courteous.

"How do you do, Mr a—a—Collector?" he said.

The Collector spoke not a word, but elevated his arm with the gesture of a minister bespeaking attention for grace before meat, and remained in this attitude, like the lion rampant in the Scottish shield. I think he had some hazy notion of performing a military salute, but was deterred by considerations of equilibrium.

"Won't you sit down?" said Tom, trying to look as if the attitude of the lion rampant was perfectly normal and expected. There was no answer. The fixed eye had shifted its angle and glued itself to a bottle of sherry which stood on the table; and the mind, such as it was, that shone through that eye, was in that bottle and nowhere else.

"Hadn't he better sit down, Tom?" I interposed, treating the Collector as a lay figure.

"Certainly," said Tom.

"Well, then, here goes"; and I poured out a glass of sherry and advanced towards the Collector. "Take a glass of sherry, ensign?" I said. He shot out the paw to its full extent, and slid one foot forward in my direction. I took a step back, still holding out the shining bait. Out went the paw again, and another shuffling pace was effected; and so on and so on till we got opposite the sofa, when I turned upon him and decanted him into it, giving him the wine by way of reward.

This he devoured, and then letting the glass fall and break on the floor, again, as if nothing had happened, fastened his burning orbs on the bottle. It was evidently fruitless to attempt any conversation with the wretch, so we left him to his contemplation and Tom turned his attention to Mr M'Tavish.

This gentleman was, no doubt, according to the Strathkinahan standard, very sober. By comparison he certainly was, but I am inclined to think he was indebted for this happy state of things less to personal abstinence than to the quelling influence of two sober Sassenachs and a certain feeling of being on a superior moral elevation to the Collector. He stood up with his thumbs stuck into the arm-holes of his waistcoat, his head carried low, as if preparing to butt, and every particular square inch of his visage working with a spasmodic action.

His English was broken and almost unintelligible, and every sentence was preceded, accompanied and followed by a series of sputterings and hootings which, with the working of his face, I could refer to no mental emotion whatsoever.

Mephistopheles, the Black Dwarf, the Gorilla, Waterton's Nondescript, the laughing hyena, the horned screech-owl and the vampire, were a few of the ideas instantly suggested by the contemplation of this Highlandman.

"Well, Mr M'Tavish," said Tom, "so you got my letter all right; I suppose you warned the corps, and I hope we shall have a good meeting and get through our business?"

"Shess, captain—that's adjutant, shess, sir. Letter? shess, Corps come? shess. Business? tit, tit, tit! no business." Then after a pause, and with an insinuating assortment of puckers playing all over his face, "Bheil Gaelig a'gad?"

"What?" said Tom.

"Spoke Gaelic? tit hish!"

"No," said Tom.

"No spokes? act tit! no spoke Gaelic?"

"But we *have* business, Mr M'Tavish, and very important business too."

"Shess, sir, shess, to be certainly, captain, major, adjutant, but no spokes? none? not a few?"

"Devil a word," said Tom testily.

"To be surely, tevil a word, ach tit!"

"This is healthy," said Tom, forgetting his manners and looking round at me with a shrug. The lieutenant also looked at me, and, catching his eye, I thought I read in it symptoms that he might speak better and stick more to the point if he chose. The instant our eyes met he fired off his "bheil Gaelig a'gad?" at me.

"No," said Tom; "this is a general, and a great friend of the Queen's, and he couldn't think of speaking it."

"Ach! she's a Queen's freend? and no spokes? Queen spoke a few?"

"Not a single one," said Tom; "she'd be ashamed to do it."

"Tit, tit, tit! to be surely, Sassenach Queen—no spoke."

"But about business, Mr M'Tavish——" A diversion in his favour was, however, created by the entrance of the dinner and a sudden movement on the part of the Collector. He had sat perfectly motionless and staring at the bottle; but his line of vision being intersected by the waiter, he uttered a low moan, rose from the sofa, and, with a stride and a plunge, made the door and lurched out of the room.

In the depths of his drunken Celtic inner-consciousness, the fellow was probably offended

"Ensign Cawmil—jist a little peety, she's no greatly hersel' the nicht," said the lieutenant. "She's a pretty fellow, ferry pretty, a good offisher, a good ensign—in Gaelic; but the nicht she's no jist hersel'; no, sir, no jist hersel'. But we'll not be angry or quarrel her, no, no; tit, tit! hish!" The last was semi-interrogative, semi-deprecatory.

"Well," said Tom, "I can't say I think it creditable. Being drunk and speechless may make a very excellent officer in Gaelic, but in any other language he would be considered a disgrace to his commission; and when I was only to be here for one night, he might, I think, have contrived to be sober."

"To be surely," replied the lieutenant; "and she'd be trying for four days to do it."

"To do what?"

"To lay the whisky, to be sure."

"To lay it in, I suppose you mean—and he seems to have succeeded to a marvel."

"Ach! no, tit, tit! to lay it with bitters *and more*."

"Well, hang me if I ever heard such a recipe! more whisky, do you mean?"

"Most certaintlee, bitters and more," in the indignant tone of one who heard an infallible specific for the first time called in question.

The landlord here announced Dr M'Kinlay, and a little, meek, elderly and apparently somewhat sober man walked into the room.

"How do you do, doctor?" said Tom. "As I had invited the other officers to dine, I took the liberty of asking you to join us as the honorary assistant-surgeon, and I'm delighted to see you."

"Much obliged, sir, and very proud I am to come; it's an honour, sir, to me to make your acquaintance."

"Let me present you," continued Tom, "to Sir Hercules O'Halloran, who has come down to have a look at the Scotch Volunteers." Then, in a whispered aside, "A very eminent man, particular friend of the Queen's; might do you all a deal of service; he reports everything, sir, everything—medical service and all."

"God bless me!" said the unsuspecting doctor; "it's a great honour, Sir Hercules, to see you, and to dine with you makes me very proud indeed. I never expected such a distinction, I'm sure. May I make so bold, Sir Hercules, as to ask how you left her Majesty the Queen?"

Trying to combine the air of camps and courts, I replied with bland condescension that my royal mistress was, at the date of my last telegram from Windsor that forenoon, in the enjoyment of excellent health and spirits; had lunched in private; was to drive to Eton College for inspecting purposes in the afternoon, "and by this time," looking at my watch, "is entertaining, with her usual condescension, the Archbishop of Canterbury and the Pope's Legate at dinner."

"God bless me!" cried the doctor; "this is wonderful! And you heard all this to-day, Sir Hercules? here, far away in the Highlands? Excuse the freedom, but there's something awful in meeting the like of you, Sir Hercules."

"Oh! I'm a very humble person, doctor; don't imagine" (with great humility) "I'm anybody to be afraid of. Her Majesty is good enough to keep me posted up in her movements. Three telegrams a-day, that's all. There's so much I have to be consulted about, you see; you understand me? eh?"

"Unquestionably, Sir Hercules, of course. It must be a great comfort to her Majesty, although I say it to your face, sir, to have such a fine, affable, pleasant nobleman to consult with; and she'll miss you much, no doubt."

"Tut, tut, doctor, you flatter me and make a great man of a mere nobody—a poor soldier, sir, nothing more, who is glad to make your acquaintance, doctor."

I concluded with an access of condescension, extending my hand, which the doctor took in a tumult of delight and awe.

Tom warned me by a look not to go too far; but as he had given me my *rôle*, I was determined to play it for myself. Besides, indeed, the doctor was evidently prepared to swallow anything.

"Now let us sit down to dinner," said Tom. "Sir Hercules, will you kindly face me? Gentlemen, pray be seated. I'm afraid the dinner won't be very choice."

Nor, in truth, was it. He who hath bent his hungry head over dinner in a Highland inn, even in the tourists' season, may remember how much that meal is indebted to the keen mountain air and the appetite with which it is approached; and he may therefore form some idea of a similar banquet out of the season. Fowl there was, but such as reminded one of the feathered spectre which, on arriving at a dhâk bungalow in India, the traveller inevitably sees led shrieking to the slaughter, to serve as the *pièce de resistance* fifteen minutes after. Eggs were there, but such as 'Brother Sam' describes as having been "very nice little eggs six weeks ago"; and as for the ham, it painfully suggested the universal adaptability of the driver's boot.

Our guests, however, seemed to enjoy it thoroughly. The doctor, though perched, timid and bird-like, on the edge of his chair, contrived to play an excellent knife and fork; and the lieutenant, his head almost flush with the table, ate like a ghoul, albeit sorely impeded therein by an attempt to reconcile the normal position of his hands in the arm-holes of his waistcoat with their duties of wielding knife, fork and spoon.

I had taken a quiet opportunity of hinting to Tom my suspicion that the lieutenant was hiding his light under a bushel with a view to evading business; and that if the conversation was to be kept off it for a time, the scoundrel would be found comparatively fluent, especially under the immediate influence of meat and drink. In pursuit of these tactics, therefore, we contrived to make the conversation (if such it could be called) general.

We drew Glensnork on the subject of his farm—the merits of black-faced and white-faced, wool, heather, wintering, turnips and other congenial topics. He became comparatively lucid, and by degrees, as glass after glass of vitriolic sherry descended, there was no lack of a certain fluency. His English was execrable, but he had plenty of it. The doctor, though penetrated with awe, and sitting as it were on the threshold of royalty, nevertheless contrived to chat away pretty freely, and was of considerable service in acting as a sort of jackal to the lieutenant, laying him on to topics on which he had some ideas, and eventually, when the creature passed into the narrative and facetious stage, drawing him out in what he evidently considered his brilliant things. In this way we were favoured with a little episode in his military career which was clearly held to reflect much credit on the lieutenant's courage and wit.

"When the Queen had a reviews," he said (his use of singulars and plurals was remarkably vague and impartial), "in Edinburgh—— Ferry certaintlee you would be there, general?"

"Oh yes!" I replied; "and I think I remember your face there."

"Most notoriouslee you would be seeing me there. Well, sir, when the Queen had her reviews there, I went to it, with his lordship's regiment—eight hundred ferry beautiful fine fellows—and when we were making the march into the Cannygate, a French Spies keepit walkin' beside us and lookin' pretty surprised and frightened like. At last the Spies comes to me and says, 'Can these men fight?' says he. And I turned to him, mighty fierce, and says I to the Spies, 'Go away, you tamned ugly teef of a Spies!' says I; 'go and tell your King and your countree not to give them the Chance,' and she jist turned aboot and went away with a ferry white face. I put the fear of deeth on to that Spies." This gem he favoured us with three or four times, accompanying it with a great deal of weird laughter.

The doctor then turned the conversation to salmon-fishing; and on my asking how they were off for fish in the river there, he replied, that what with stake-nets at the mouth, and 'burning the water' up above, there was but poor sport to be had.

"Burning the water!" I said; "I thought that had been illegal for long."

"So it has, Sir Hercules; but it's done a good deal for all. Ask Glensnork, Sir Hercules," said the doctor, with a twinkle in his eye.

"'Deed, doctor, and it's a pretty small quantitee Glensnorruk kens aboot the wather; he never touches it"; a statement which in many senses was no doubt incontrovertible.

"Ah! but your shepherds, your shepherds? I'm afraid they're pretty guilty."

"Hoosh, doctor! not kilty at all; the shepherds be on the hills with the sheeps, and not able to be kilty with the fishes and swamonts in the wather."

"Well, Glensnorruk, there was Fraser you know——"

"Ach! to be certaintlee, Lauchy Fraser. But who made her kilty? Me, surr—Glensnorruk hersel'—spoke to the Shirra's man and made her kilty."

"Ah! how was that?" said the doctor.

"Well, Lauchy be always makin' his tamned ugly traffics into my house, and always coortin' and coortin' my servant lass for trams and brose, and kissin' and trash. I be findin' him pretty seldom oot o' the house, and quarrelled him. 'Mister Lauchy,' says I, 'be greatlee kind, and get trams and brose and servant lasses for yoursel', and don't be bringing yourself into my kitchings twice again, you nasty trooper!' says I, 'or maybe there'll be a little more said.' Ferry well, two days afterhin, I be going into my own kitchings to crack wi' Shennet, my own servant lass—shess, sir, my own servant Shennet—and there is my pretty shentleman Lauchy again, wi' a tram in his mooth and a big fishes beside him, coortin' and quarrellin' at Shennet to kettle the fishes for him. 'You plackgard!' says I, 'you vagabones! you are into here again!' 'Plackgard your nanesell, Glenschnorruk,' says he, giving me his peastly tongue. 'Where have you been, you *sloightear?*' says I. 'To the hills and to the sheeps,' says he. 'Did you find that big sawmonts on the hills among the sheeps?' says I. 'I met her there,' says he. 'Ach! you tamned *breugadair!*' says I; 'I will teach you to come coortin' at Shennet, you teef! you poacher! and to set fire to the wather against the law. Come to Donald, come to the Shirra's man, and get your fishes kettled.' So I handed them, him and his fishes, to the lockup, and *kettled him*; and it was 'Good-bye, Mr Lauchy; ye've saved Glenschnorruk six months' wage,' which he was awed."

"And where is he now?" I inquired.

"The tevil may ask the questions—in the chails, to be sure."

"And you never paid him ?"

"Not a hapnee, the teef! he would have paid the Shirra for the poachin', and been oot o' the chails coortin' again."

Glensnork was, of course, so much delighted with this splendid illustration of crime, law and justice, that he repeated it frequently; and the appreciation displayed by his audience bringing him into high good-humour, Tom seized the opportunity of turning the conversation into a business channel.

"Well, M'Tavish," he said, dinner being now some time over, "I'm very glad to have made your acquaintance in this pleasant sort of way. Here's to your very good health; and now I think it's time to discuss the *real business* of the evening."

"Goot life, captain! business already? You must be ferry heavy on the speerits, if you would be for beginning already," said the lieutenant. "No, surr; my thanks to you, but not a trop of tuddy till the wine settled herself. It was a mighty fine surprise for Mr Lauchy when she obsairved herself in the lock-up. 'It will be your fun, Glenschnorruk,' says she, 'that——'"

"I beg your pardon," interrupted Tom; "you misunderstood my meaning; what I wished to express was, that we should lose no time in looking at the concern which has brought us here to-night."

"Hoosh, captain! you would not be thinkin' of that. If the postboy cannot look at his own horses and his own concern, he must be a ferry poor cratur inteed, and the doctor's powney Callum, she looks at herself. 'It will be your fun, Glenschnorruk,' says Mr Lauchy, 'that you are putting on to my head.' 'My teer goot friend,' says I——"

"You misunderstand me again, Mr M'Tavish," said Tom firmly. "You must be aware that it is now six months since you lost your captain, and——"

"Six months, captain? will it be six months sin' the cratur died?"

"Six months," said Tom.

"Well, maybe, maybe; oich! oich! six months. Well, well, she was a nice bit cratury. 'Yes, Mr Lauchy,' says I, 'you are ferry right, and you will have——'"

"The devil seize Mr Lauchy!" thundered Tom in a fury. "I'll tell you what it is, Mr M'Tavish, I have come here to discuss business and not to waste time, and if you had the proper spirit——"

"Well, well, captain," said the irrepressible, in the tone of one yielding to excessive importunity, "if you must set to the speerits, goot life! let us yoke to them, but be ferry strict with Mr Stew-art to give them out of his own brown pig.[1] As the meenister says, 'Stew-art's pig is like the cask o' the weedy woman, with a last drop always into it.' You will ken the meenister, captain?"

Tom's wrath melted away at the peal of laughter with which I greeted the lieutenant's last flank movement; he joined in it, but denied all knowledge of the divine, and outmanœuvred M'Tavish by plunging *in medios res.*

"Now, Mr M'Tavish," he said, "have the goodness to listen without interrupting me. I have come here to-night to see that the corps *does* elect a captain, and I mean to see that it does, and I wish to know if you will support Sir William M'Vittie. The Lord-Lieutenant is anxious that he should be nominated, and what is more, so is the Queen. You must elect a Keltshire man; he is a Keltshire man, and the best, and indeed the only, man you can get in the district. Now I have said my say; let me hear yours, but let it be to the point. We have had quite enough of Mr Lauchy and his salmon, and I won't listen to another word except on business."

[1] An earthenware vessel called a 'grey-beard' in the Lowland dialect, and containing a gallon.

"Ferry well, to be certaintlee, Surr, ferry well; but you will likely be ringin' for Stew-art's pig first?"

"Certainly," said Tom, ringing the bell, "and now go on."

"Ferry well, I was just saying to me ownself and to the Collecthur lately, that it would be incaatious to be in a tremendeous hurry aboot the business. 'Collecthur,' says I, 'we cannot chump over crayt big hetches and titches withoot a look into them.' 'What you say is a true case,' says the Collecthur. 'You are a cliver man, Glenschnorruk,' says he; 'and we must not chump over a captain ferry hastily.'"

"Well," said Tom, "that's all very true; but I'll be hanged if six months isn't long enough to look at the biggest hedge or ditch that was ever jumped over, and in fact there *is* to be no more delay in the matter. I tell you I won't stand this humbug any longer, and you mistake your man if you think you can play the fool with me. Will you support Sir William or will you not? and if not, will you propose someone else, in opposition to the Queen's wishes, and the Lord-Lieutenant's and mine?" Tom added demurely.

"I am sure," said the doctor, on whom the fiery sherry was working its effect perceptibly—"I am sure such a statement would be sufficient for the corps; the Queen's wish and the Lord-Lieutenant's and yours, captain, and I may add yours, Sir Hercules (for of course your feeling will be her Majesty's), would weigh with them against any other suggestion; and I will say this, that if Glensnork were to set himself up in an opposition to these wishes of yours, he would pan himself, pan himself, Sir Hercules, I do assure you."

"I don't doubt it," I said, assuming that the process of 'panning' was equivalent to ostracism in Strathkinahan; "and serve him right too," I added rather fiercely.

"But he may be sure of this," continued the doctor, "that Strathkinahan will refuse to be panned with him."

"Hoosh, doctor!" said the lieutenant, whose normal attitude towards the doctor was that of an honoured patron evidently; "you are a ferry cliver man, but you are incaatious to speak when you are not asked to spoke. Ailsie M'Leod is in crayt trouble with her tooth-gums; you had petter" (with a dignified wave) "go and make them heal—tit, tit!"

"The opinion of a sober professional man," cried the doctor in high wrath, "is at least as valuable as that of a being who forgets himself daily with the bottle."

"Deed, doctor, he'll be a ferry smart man that forgets the pottle when you are into the room. Go away—go and sing a song to Ailsie's tooth-gums."

"Come, come, gentlemen," cried Tom, as the doctor was bursting out in huge wrath at this *tu quoque*, "we are forgetting ourselves; to business, business, business. What do you say, Mr M'Tavish—will you support Sir William?"

"Well, well, Sir William is a fine man, a ferry fine nice nobleman; but, for God's sake, captain, is Stew-art niver bringing his pig?"

"Oh yes! this will bring him" (ringing the bell); "and now go on, for heaven's sake!"

A diversion was, however, again created in the lieutenant's favour by the entrance of the landlord, who informed us that the corps had been for a considerable time awaiting us in the barn, and were beginning to get a "little troublesome"; and as it appeared to Tom and myself that perhaps more might be done by a direct appeal to the whole body than by fencing with their impracticable officer, we decided to descend at once.

A strange scene presented itself to our eyes as we entered the barn. It was dimly lighted by a few tallow candles stuck into bottles, and by a stable-lantern suspended from a crossbeam in the centre. A heavy cloud of tobacco-smoke brooded over all, through which were hazily revealed the figures of the Volunteers. We had a dim panorama of shaggy crests of hair, of red faces, of tobacco-pipes and of all manner of improvised drinking-vessels; while the hum of many voices, the puffing of many pipes and the glugging of lips that drank greedily, were the sounds that met our ears. When our entrance was observed, suddenly uprose from the mist the form of a tall man with an outstretched arm, and from his lips proceeded a sound much resembling an ill-executed sneeze—" Att-itshun ! " The form and the voice were those of the Collector, who seemed to have partially succeeded in 'laying the spirit,' and who now, in the exercise of his military function, was calling the room to 'attention.'

The men all rose, looking like the peaks of hills appearing above the morning mist.

" Saloot ! " cried the Collector, still favouring the attitude of the lion rampant ; whereupon the corps all began to make what looked like mesmeric passes with their right arms in the air. " Dooble saloot ! " shouted the Collector again ; and then each man employed his left arm also, which gave the pleasing general effect of about fifty men swimming for their lives in an ocean of tobacco-smoke. This movement had for me such a delightful novelty that I could not help remarking on it to the lieutenant, who explained with great pride that it was an invention of his own devised to meet a difficulty he had felt in receiving merely the same salute as the Collector. " So I doobled it for my nanesel' ; and if the craturs had more airms, they would use plenty more of them for the captain and yoursel'."

Tom now told the lieutenant that he would like to see the company fallen in in their ranks for a minute or two, just to get an idea of the general appearance of the men.

" Would you put the craturs into rangks withoot their sojer's clothes on, captain ? and withoot their guns ? Tit, tit ! begging your grace, that would be a ferry fulish-like trick, to be sure."

" I don't want to see their clothing or their rifles ; I want to see the men themselves. Have the goodness to fall them in," said Tom firmly, " and get them into single rank."

" Ferry goot, ferry well," said the lieutenant, with a shrug. " Shooliter, be craytly kind and put the craturs into a single rank." The Collector had, however, apparently succumbed to his old enemy again, for he only waved his arm feebly, and muttered, with a sort of imbecile snigger, "She kens naething aboot it."

"Very well," said Tom, "I'll do it myself; give me a sergeant."

"Is there a sergeant among ye?" cried M'Tavish.

"No," shouted the collective voice of Strathkinahan from the mist.

"Very well, a corporal will do," said Tom.

"Is Corporal M'Ildhu thereaboots?" inquired M'Tavish, peering into the haze.

"He's at the bothy," shouted a score of voices.

"Why did he not take heed to come doon?" said the lieutenant.

"He had words wi' the Collector," explained the chorus again.

"Well, well, that's a peety—a sore peety—and the captain here and all."

I understood the chorus to admit, by a sort of rumbling growl, that it *was* a pity.

"Well, never mind," said Tom; "give me a 'coverer' of some sort, and we'll get on."

"Deed, and it's a thing the corps never had, captain. There was a taak of sairvin' them oot at our own costs; and they would be ferry goot in the wat nichts if they were happenin' to be M'Intoshe's clothes, and cheap."

"Isn't this nice?" said Tom grimly, looking round at me. "Give me your right-hand man, then; I suppose the company has a right and a left?"

"Shess, sir! most notoriouslee, most certaintlee. Hand me oot the richt-hand man," he cried into the mist.

"She is not into here," replied the chorus.

"Who is she then, at all?" cried the lieutenant.

"Lauchy Fraser," shouted the chorus, with a roar of laughter.

"Ach! deed, and it is trooth," cried the lieutenant, heartily joining in the mirth; "she is on a veesit to the shirra"; whereupon there was another roar, which put Tom quite out of temper, and he pounced personally into the mist, and seizing the first man he found there, stood him up against the wall.

"This is the right-hand man," he said; "and now come on, all the rest of you, and fall in." And what with the doctor's assistance and mine, he at length contrived to get them into a row against the wall, all continuing to smoke their pipes and to retain their drinking-vessels in their hands. Tom winked at these delinquencies, however, for the purpose, as he explained to me after, of keeping them in good humour and carrying his point. "Now, Mr M'Tavish, take command of them; and if your ensign can stand, which seems doubtful, he may as well take his place—it may keep him out of mischief, at least."

"I am to command them, captain?"

"If you please, Mr M'Tavish."

The lieutenant waddled out in front of the line, his hands in the arm-holes of his waistcoat, his head low, and shooting backwards and forwards like a large gander waddling heavily to a pond, while from his lips came a sort of preliminary hissing also suggestive of that bird. The hissing gradually 'boiled up,' so to speak, till it bubbled into a cry of "Oarter arrums!" whereupon the men gave an apologetic plunge in their ranks, apparently to imply that if they had the means, the lieutenant's wish would be cheerfully complied with.

"Tut, tut! Mr M'Tavish," said Tom, struggling between laughter and indignation, "I don't mean that; take command in the regular way."

"Shoolter arrums!" shouted the bewildered lieutenant, and again the corps executed a sort of *pas d'extase*.

"Fall in on the right, Mr M'Tavish," said Tom, with a desperate effort to keep his countenance; "and, for the love of heaven, take your hands out of your waistcoat, and hold up your head, and try to look like a reasonable being for three minutes!" he added, as the lieutenant moved sulkily to his position.

The arrangements being at last completed, including the position of the Collector, who, by way of compromise, was accommodated with a stool on the left flank, Tom and I walked slowly down the rank and inspected the men. They were a fine set of fellows, certainly—tall, sinewy, broad-shouldered and athletic-looking. Many, indeed, bore very unequivocal traces of the manner in which they had occupied their time at 'the bothy'; but there was no disgraceful case like that of the Collector, the intermittent nature of whose inebriety made it difficult to deal with on any uniform system. The men, as a rule, stood steadily enough in the ranks, though in one or two exceptional cases an attempt was made to shake hands with the inspecting officer as he passed.

"Gentlemen," said Tom, when the inspection was completed, "I have to congratulate you on your fine, I may say your soldier-like, appearance. I had often heard of the fine *physique* you have in this district——" ("It could not have been the feesick of Dr M'Kinlay," interpolated M'Tavish, still rankling at his medical friend), "and I am not disappointed. A fine *physique*, and the mental intelligence which you evidently possess, are immense advantages; but they must be properly applied, and there are two things that can alone compass this end—drill and discipline. As it is with the regular, so it is with the volunteer soldier. I am sorry to find, with regard to the first, that you have been unfortunate in losing your drill-sergeant; but I am now making arrangements to supply his place. With regard to the second, the grand essential is, that the corps should be fully and efficiently officered; above all things, that there should be at its head a competent captain—a man of intelligence, energy, and, I may add, social position. A long period has elapsed since the death of your late captain, and no step has been taken to elect and nominate his successor to the Lord-Lieutenant. I have made frequent representations to your officers on this score, but without any result. I have therefore personally visited you for the double purpose of inspecting the corps and of impressing upon you all the necessity of at once proceeding to elect a captain. When I say that *I* am inspecting the corps, I do not speak correctly, for I am in reality on this occasion only the attendant of the distinguished General Sir Hercules O'Halloran, who, in his capacity of Inspector-General of Reserves, does you the honour of being present here to-night, and may not improbably feel himself called upon to address a few words of advice to you on the subject I have been insisting upon. When I mention that Sir Hercules, in addition to his great military distinction, is so highly honoured as to be the confidential adviser of our beloved Sovereign, you will, I am sure, concur with me in the propriety of at once giving three cheers for that eminent officer. Hip! hip! hip! hurrah!" The cheers were given with right goodwill, till roof and rafters rang; and then Tom gravely continued his oration: "The Lord-Lieutenant will not appoint a gentleman to that position without your nomination, and I must tell you that he is not a little surprised and disappointed at the delay which has taken place. It would not be right for me to conceal from you, and I have Sir Hercules's sanction to mention, that pain and surprise have also been excited in far more august quarters, by what he has felt himself compelled to stigmatise as 'this unseemly tardiness'; but to-night I am confident this stigma will be removed, and I now propose that we proceed at once to elect a gentleman to the vacant position. I will not trouble you to stand in the ranks while this goes on; but I earnestly request you to sit down in an orderly manner and discuss the matter in a business-like way. To the right face! Break off!" The men tumbled out of their ranks and reseated themselves on the benches; the Collector obeyed the order by turning a back somersault off his stool; and the lieutenant waddled back into civil life much relieved, to lay aside the crown of office. "Now," said Tom, "let us discuss the matter quietly. I say Sir William M'Vittie is our best man, and that we ought to elect him at once. Light your pipe, M'Tavish, and give us your opinion."

"Sir William is no doot a ferry fine, nice, parteecular, pretty fellow, captain," said the lieutenant, emphasising each epithet with a draw at his pipe, in which an inordinate amount of suctional power was employed; "but if a captain is to be aal the goot things that you have spoke into your bit speech, Sir William will not be our man."

"How d'ye mean?" inquired Tom.

"Angus M'Rioch, will you be craytly kind, and tell the captain whether Sir William is for the dipping or for the smearing of the sheeps?" said the lieutenant, in a voice of the deepest solemnity.

"Dipping!" bellowed the whole room as one man.

"Ferry well, captain, you will not, after that, again be speaking for Sir William," said M'Tavish, with an air of one who has got rid of the first of a series of difficulties, and proceeds to handle the next, confident of success.

"But I don't see what that has got to do with the question," urged Tom. "As he has neither got to dip nor smear the Volunteers, I don't think it matters what he does with his sheep."

"There niver was a yowe, there niver was a tupp, there niver was a wedder dipped yet at aal on to the holdings of my father's son; there niver will be a yowe, there niver will be a tupp, there niver will be a wedder dipped on to his holdings," said a lantern-jawed old fellow in a sort of chant; and the somewhat irrelevant statement was received with much applause, and evidently held to strengthen the case against Sir William.

"What would the old red man, Colin-with-the-crooked-nose, have said to all the dippings and the trash, Angus?" inquired another anti-Sir William-ite; but the Nestor only smoked with ineffable grimness. He had uttered, and that, he evidently thought, should settle the matter without further parley.

"There was once a pollis-offisher, by the name of M'Ardle, in the Strath," suggested another of the party, "but he is not into it now. Will somebody be ferry kind, and say who pit him oot?"

"Sir William!" cried a dozen voices.

"I suppose a pollis-offisher is to have no mouth in this Strath," observed a gentleman largely provided in respect of that feature, and with complexional indications that neither in eating nor in speaking was it principally employed.

"M'Ardle was not a drucken man," hiccoughed the Collector. "He tasted—at a time—like me; it was his dewty—Sir William pit him oot for—for his dewty. His name was Peter." And much honour was done to these decidedly hazy propositions.

"If Sir William is to be captain in the Strath, the Volunteers may ferry quickly put their mouths into the store wi' the guns, and not bring them oot again," suggested another satirist.

"After the shearin', when the ball was in the barn at Craig-Vittie, there was plenty of tea, but I did not obsairve anything for a manbody to drink," said another.

"If Sir William is to be captain, he will have to list the auld wives into the company. Betty M'Candlish will make a ferry parteecular fine lieutenant to him, and Ailsie M'Leod will be ensign instead of the Collector."

"Sir William is a temperanst man at his heart."

"And a temperanst man is a teirant."

"And we will have no teirants and no teiranny here."

Loud applause followed these heroic sentiments, and the lieutenant, turning to Tom, observed, "You see, captain, Sir William is a parteecular nice goot nobleman, but the Volunteers will not be for having a teirant for their captain."

"But there is no one else in the district you can elect, and as you must elect someone, why, you must elect Sir William. It's all nonsense about tyranny. Sir William is an excellent man, and no more a teetotaller than I am, though, of course, he doesn't think that every parade is to be turned into a drinking bout. When you know him better, when he is mixed up with you as your captain, you will find all these things you've been hearing about him are nonsense, and I hear he is going to reside regularly at Craig-Vittie."

"If I might make bold to say a word," said a diplomatist, whose opinion was evidently held in high esteem, "I would say this, that if we must elect a captain, we must elect him; but if there is no one into the Strath who is shootable for the poseetion, then, for Got's sake, let us not at aal forget that there is other places with shootable people into them. We will elect some ferry crayt man; we will elect the Prince of Whales. He will be captain to the company; but we will not be troubling him, and he will not be troubling himself to come down to the Strath for the dreels; and so we will have a captain and no teiranny."

This novel method of solving the difficulty found universal favour; and M'Tavish at once abandoned his Fabian policy and became clamorous for instant action as to the Prince's election.

Tom took me out of the room for consultation. "Did you ever see such an impracticable set of devils?" he said. "What's to be done?"

"Arguing won't mend matters, that's clear," I replied. "Give me some particulars about this Sir William and I'll see what I can do." Tom did so, and I learned that Sir William had quite recently succeeded to the property; that he had lived principally abroad in the diplomatic service, and was as yet almost unknown in the Strath; but that he was about to settle on his acres, and that his co-operation and assistance would be of the greatest importance in saving the Volunteer movement in the locality from death by alcoholic drowning. He was reported to be a very sensible man; and though neither the tyrant nor the ascetic he was alleged to be by the corps, he had, on a recent short visit to the Strath, been not a little startled and scandalised at the extraordinarily chronic state of fuddlement in which its inhabitants lived, and had expressed himself pretty broadly on the subject, and, in one or two instances, made a clearance of the most inveterate offenders. *Hinc illæ lacrymæ.* "In fact," Tom concluded, "he is just the man to keep these dipsomaniacs in order; and I know he will accept if he is elected."

"Very well," said I, "you had better let me speak to them. Just say that 'the General' will address a few observations to the corps."

When we returned to the meeting we found that they had just elected the Prince of Wales *nem. con.*, and were expecting with flaming eyes the arrival of the 'glasses round' with which the lieutenant had suggested they should celebrate the event 'at their own costs.'

Three cheers for "our captain, the Prince," were given somewhat defiantly on our entrance; and, on the whole, matters bore a decidedly unsatisfactory aspect.

"Gentlemen," cried Tom, "Lieutenant-General Sir Hercules O'Halloran, K.C.B., Inspector of the Reserve Forces, will address you"; and I stepped forward, desperately determined that if unscrupulous impudence could avert the collapse of the Keltshire 'Ad. Batt.' and the loss of my friend Tom's appointment, it should not be wanting to me on this occasion.

"Gentlemen," I said, "first of all I must express to you, as representing the Royal Family, my very sincere thanks for the honour which you have so loyally and so very properly bestowed upon us—I mean, upon the Prince of Wales. Gentlemen, you have done honour to yourselves in honouring him—(cheers)—and before I go further I beg that you will allow me, on behalf of the Queen, to defray the expense of the further honour which you propose to offer him in drinking his health." (Loud and protracted cheering, during which I tried to look as if the Privy purse was at that moment in my portmanteau upstairs.) "But having said thus much, it deeply grieves me to add that duty and my instructions compel me to decline, with every expression of gratitude, the honour which you have done to his Royal Highness." (Murmurs, soothed by the arrival of the liquor, during which I paused for a second or two.) "Yes, gentlemen," I resumed, "it is my painful duty to be obliged to decline. You must all be aware, of course, that the Prince, from his position and natural affability, is perpetually importuned to accept situations similar to that which you have offered him to-night. In such great numbers are they offered to him, indeed, that to fill one tithe of them, even in a nominal and honorary way, would strain and overtax his royal energies most insupportably. Under these circumstances we were obliged to come to a fixed determination; and I assure you that in coming to it I experienced the greatest hesitation and difficulty, but having been come to, it cannot be deviated from. It was this—that the Prince should only consent to take command of one corps at a time. What that corps should be it was of course left for me to decide; and after renewed hesitation, my choice fell upon—upon—upon the corps which—now enjoys that distinction.

"The Prince himself, with that self-abnegation which characterises him, has frequently implored me to reconsider the matter, and bring him into a wider connection with a movement which he honours and admires.

"Supported by her Majesty, I have, however, remained firm; and you must pardon me if I say that even the impression which you as a corps have made upon me to-night, and the *absorbing* interest which you clearly take in your duties, cannot make me waver.

"On Monday night, the night before I left London, I was dining in private with the Prince and the Duke of Cambridge; and his Royal Highness, understanding that I was about to proceed northward on my tour of inspection, again reverted to the subject. 'Are you still as obstinate as ever, Hercules?' said his Royal Highness. 'Please your Royal Highness, I am a rock,' I replied. 'As the Russians found at Inkerman,' remarked the Duke of Cambridge." ("Three cheers for Sir Hercules!" cried the doctor, which were rather quiveringly given, however.) "'Won't you give me a corps in each of the three kingdoms?' urged the Prince. 'It can't be done at any price, your Royal Highness,' I replied, firmly but respectfully. 'I like the Scotch,' continued the Prince. 'They are a noble race,' I replied; 'especially the Highlanders.' 'You should have seen them following me up the Alma Heights,' said the Duke. 'Give me a Scotch corps, General,' said the Prince—'there's a good fellow.' 'It cuts me to the heart to say "No," sir,' I replied. 'But what am I to say to all these fine fellows?' he inquired, pulling out a bundle of papers, which were requisitions from the Kirkintilloch, Kilbogie, Slamannan, Cowcaddens, and other corps. 'You can show your interest in them by nominating the gentleman you would wish to fill the post instead of your Royal Highness,' I replied. 'It is a happy thought,' said the Prince; 'but it is impossible for me to go down to Kilbogie and Cowcaddens at present, and I would not nominate a substitute without being sure of him, as, of course, where *I* nominate, the corps can't refuse to elect.' 'Leave it all to Sir Hercules,' said the Duke; 'his judgment in all military matters is simply the best in the country.' 'Your Highness does me infinite honour,' I replied. 'Pooh, pooh! only your due, O'Halloran,' said the Duke. 'Well, O'Halloran, would you mind going to these places for me,' said the Prince, 'to say that I thank the corps with all my heart, and that I leave you to act for me and nominate a substitute?' 'It is my duty and delight to do what your Royal Highness wishes,' I replied.

'But you must be very careful in your selection, General; you must be sure that the man is fit in every way—above all, that he is a district proprietor —and when you have made your choice you must be firm. Remember that for the moment you are the Prince of Wales; and if any other corps should elect me while you are in the north, pray go to them also and select a substitute for me. I am ashamed to give you so much trouble.' 'Don't mention it, Prince,' I replied; 'I will carry out your instructions to the letter.'

"Well, gentlemen, I have been to Kirkintilloch, I have been to Kilbogie, to Slamannan, and to Cowcaddens, and in each of these places I have made, I think, satisfactory appointments. In one instance the corps had set their hearts upon a gentleman I could not appoint; but I am bound to say, that the moment they became aware of the ground on which I stood, they evinced the patriotic and loyal self-denial which is characteristic of the volunteer, and at once accepted with enthusiasm the gentleman I had selected.

"Now, gentlemen, by your selection of the Prince to-night you have virtually thrown, as you must see, the appointment of your captain into my hands; for though, as a matter of form, I shall simply propose a gentleman to you, you will, as a matter of course, accept him; and standing in this position, I feel the grave responsibility which rests upon me. On the one hand, it is most unpleasant to me to run counter to your inclinations; but on the other, the duty I owe to the Prince is paramount.

"As far as my own convictions go, however, I have no hesitation in making my selection. In many districts where I might be called upon to act as I am to-night, I should require time for inquiry and consideration; but here, in Strathkinahan, I find ready to my hand the right man, and that in the person of one of my oldest and dearest friends, a man of great distinction, high character, probity and Presbyterian principles—a man, in fact, every inch a man and a soldier. I allude to my honourable friend Sir William M'Vittie of Craig-Vittie, Baronet."

A perfect howl of indignation rose from the party, upon whom this came like a thunderclap. It was necessary to take a high tone at once, so "Volunteers!" I cried, raising my voice sternly, "you forget in whose presence you virtually are. Situated as you are, this unseemly demonstration is very nearly approaching to a seditious cry, and I trust" (with grim emphasis) "that I shall never have to report or to punish sedition in Strathkinahan. I propose to you Sir William M'Vittie. I am sorry there is a prejudice against him, but I can't help it. How groundless it is I well know.

"His views upon certain practical matters, such as the dipping of sheep, may not be as healthy as I could wish, but a residence in Strathkinahan will correct them. As to his being a temperance man, *that* I repudiate, on behalf of my old friend, as a personal insult; and when I tell you that at Court, where he is known well, his singular power of consuming claret and other fluids has procured for him the nickname of 'Gallon' M'Vittie, you will, I think, acquit him of any such baseness." ("Hurrah! hurrah!" from the doctor and Tom, slightly joined in by a few converts.)

"I beg to propose him, then, as a fit and proper person to be Captain of the Strathkinahan Volunteers, and I *expect* the proposal to be seconded and carried unanimously."

"I second it, Sir Hercules!" cried the doctor at once.

"And it is carried *nem. con.*," I added hastily. "Get paper, pen and ink, and I will draw the requisition."

"I make so bold as to make a protest against it," said the diplomatist.

It was necessary to nip this sort of thing in the bud by a *coup d'état*, so I replied, with fierce energy, advancing and gobbling at the fellow, "Hold your tongue, sir! you ought to be ashamed of yourself, sir! All your brother volunteers blush for you, sir! Another word, and I shall turn you out of the corps, and out of the room, and send you to the lock-up, sir ! "

This quelled the fellow ; and the rest of them accepted me as apparently a sort of dictator, endowed with the fullest legislative and executive powers. No further difficulty was made ; and after I had ordered another round of liquor to the health of the Queen, another to the health of Sir William, and a third in honour of Tom and myself, certain hieroglyphs were dashingly appended to the requisition ; and the meeting broke up in the highest delight after singing "Auld Lang Syne" and dancing hand in hand round the prostrate and senseless form of the Collector.

Next morning we departed at daybreak, and posted the requisition at the first village. I confess I had many misgivings as to what the morning feelings of the Volunteers might be, and whether, in my wish to serve Tom, I might not have run him into a serious scrape. All, however, went well, and in three weeks I had the satisfaction of seeing Sir William gazetted. And I can assure my readers that the pious fraud has turned out to admiration.

The Strathkinahans are now a flourishing corps, and Sir William and Tom are still flourishing in their official connection with the once tottering 'Ad. Batt.'

For once, then, the efforts of a practical joker have been productive of beneficial results, for my friend Tom has much benefited therefrom, and thereby, in Strathkinahan, the Volunteer institution has been placed on a solid and satisfactory basis ; so that though the austere may decline to admit the Horatian "Dulce est desipere in loco," perhaps the blending in this case of the 'utile' with the 'dulce' may lead them to find extenuating circumstances in the outrageous audacity of my conduct. Tom has no doubt whatsoever on the subject. Looking over my shoulder as I write, he bawls out—

"Omne tulit punctum qui miscuit utile dulci." "You carried my point for me, old boy, and I'm for ever grateful."

THE WISE WOMAN OF OUR PARISH.

BY W. E. W. COLLINS.

[Maga, September 1907.]

I HAVE chosen this title for my old acquaintance Goody Barker because, the more I think of her the more firmly convinced I am that she was a good deal wiser than most, if not any, of her fair neighbours. Fair, I should say, is to be taken as an ornamental or complimentary epithet applicable to the sex rather than to individual members of it. We did not run much to good looks in our little village. Nor were we saddled with a superfluity of brain-power. Rather were we homely in word and deed and personal appearance.

Yet 'knowledge is power,' that unmitigated scoundrel Master Randall Leslie was fond of saying to himself. Probably he was right, even though too much knowledge of 'ways that were dark' upset his own coach at last. The converse of the proposition suggests, if my logic be sound, that some power is knowledge. And so I seem to arrive at the conclusion that the power displayed by Goody Barker of living on the fat of the land at her neighbour's expense for several years, and finally securing and maintaining to the end of the chapter a position from which a good many people seemed anxious to oust her, stamped her as a wise woman. Considering, too, her age and personal infirmities—for she could be deaf, dumb and blind on convenient occasions, not to say both asthmatic and rheumatic, and afflicted with a chronic cough which ran up the gamut and ended with a crow—she had, moreover, a truly remarkable power of grabbing a grandchild who chanced to tread on her toe or otherwise annoyed her, and of getting it properly spanked and turned right side up again before he or she could say Jack Robinson. The asthma, let me explain, was a spirit that could be only exorcised by the persuasions of a particular brand of virulent shag tobacco; the rheumatic attacks were especially reserved for those Sundays when there was nothing material to be gained by going to church; the cough was utilised as a species of defensive armour to ward off the assaults of strong-minded curates who were inclined to offer spiritual consolation only, and of district visitors who were apt to ask almost impertinent questions. 'Jack Robinson' also must only be regarded as a euphemism for what was really said later on by the victim of the strong hand. Imitation is the best form of flattery, and out of the mouths of even babes and sucklings in a labouring community are apt to issue forms of expression which might shock the ears of the uninitiated, though the meaning is probably more innocent than the form. There were not wanting, both in the foreground and the background, crumbs of consolation for the sufferer. For Grannie contrived, for all her quickness of temper, to retain some hold on the affections of the third generation by being even lavish in her distribution of lozenges of various types, proffered to her by district and other visitors who had the feminine craze for popularising their own pet nostrums. And in the background there was ever the enchanting prospect held out by a mother, who perhaps in her heart of hearts resented the interference with her own privileges in the way of spanking more keenly than she cared to show, that at no very distant date Grannie's burying should be celebrated on a scale of unprecedented magnificence.

And on the strength of the assurance of good things to come, children allowed the spankings to pass as so many regrettable but natural occurrences in the course of everyday life, and regarded their grandmother as a sort of goose that was likely to lay golden eggs when the time appointed came.

Cherished illusions die hard, especially in a simple-minded community those cherished illusions which have to do with other people's worldly possessions. And the baker's wife was not the only woman in the parish who for many days nursed to her soul the conviction that somewhere or other Goody Barker was keeping secreted a private hoard, either in the form of bank-notes or perhaps a stocking full of gold. To be sure, the village sage was among those who held a contrary opinion. But the sage is wont to share Cassandra's fate, and to be discredited, out of that spirit of sheer perversity which is an attribute of womankind. Tom Barker, or 'Muster Tummas' as he was commonly called, Goody's deceased husband, had been a small farmer and miller who, if he had not exactly lived in the odour of sanctity—for he was not over-particular about cleaning out his pig-stye—may to a certain extent be said to have died in it. For was it not prophesied by old John Ball that "t' owd chap, he'll best Petter one way or t' other, and 'll worm hisself in at t' back door while Petter's rummaging around i' t' front."

"You mark my words if he don't," was the conclusion; and in the absence of proof positive to the contrary, a good many of our villagers thought old John was quite as likely as not to be right. I suppose that I must have shown myself sceptical on the point, for the oracle seemed to take especial care to try to convince me.

"Now, look-ee here, Master Garge. Was there ever a woundier old varmint than Muster Tummas hatched? He were the woundiest, leastways, as ever I clapped eyes on in this world, and I reckons they'll find it hard to match him in t' kingdom come. T' Reverend, he reads out of prayer-book as folks don't bring nothing into this world, and ain't a-going to take nout out o't. Now I ain't a-saying, mind-ee, as Muster Tummas brought much wi' him, barring his woundiness, but all as he had he took along wi' him. Leastways.

he've not left none of it behind 'cept his missis, and t' owd tom-cat as nobody didn't seem to hanker arter. He've done them fair in this world as knowed him best, and you mark my words if he ain't done old Petter, as hadn't had no 'sperience of his artfulness."

Whatever might be the value of the prognostication of Muster Tummas's future career, the point which John Ball had touched upon, as to the wholesale disappearance of his worldly goods, remained a mystery for many a long day.

The quondam miller had been esteemed a warm man in our village when he finally sold his stock-in-trade, retired from business, and, exchanging the mill-house for a six-roomed cottage, settled down to keep his servant-girl, his breeding-sow and his poultry-yard, and to smoke his pipe like any other independent gentleman. He had taken plenty of good money in his time, had lived comfortably indeed—but to all outward appearance well within his means—and had never joined in the general plaint of the hardness of the times. And yet when his affairs came to be wound up, it was discovered that after the furniture had been sold there might be just sufficient money to discharge his liabilities to his son the baker, his son-in-law the butcher, and a matter of two or three pounds to the proprietor of the village shop. Visible surplus there was none, unless that may be called a surplus which consists of a multiplicity of potential heirs and heiresses. Of these, indeed, in our village there were enough and to spare; for the Barkers, one way with another, were a highly prolific family. One son had died in his infancy, but two other sons and six daughters had grown up to marry, settle in the parish and sensibly increase the population. If rumour asserted that the young ladies had brought their husbands little in the way of tocher beyond the clothes they wore on their backs, they had one and all made fair matches, as things go in a quiet country village, on the strength of their expectations.

During Muster Tummas's lifetime the will itself had been

a very valuable asset, almost as much so as the ace of trumps which is held up *in terrorem* by a lady whist-player. It is not often, perhaps, that a householder keeps the whole pot boiling for self and family, sow and chickens included, for a full year before his decease on the strength of good things to come after that event. Yet this, so Butcher Haines informed me with tears in his eyes—as he was rather a beery man tears came pretty easily—is what Muster Tummas had apparently done.

"Tell me this, Master Garge," said the tear-laden butcher, "what were I to do? T' owd man he were that artful as there weren't no holding of him, and I dunno as t' owd woman weren't artfuller. This is how it were time after time. Whiles I'd go to him, seeing as he'd give me an order for a leg of mutton or a line of pork, and I'd take it up in a basket, and I'd say, 'Well, fearther'—we all on us called him fearther, you see, Master Garge, just so as he'd no cause to forget that my missis was his darter—'Well, fearther,' I'd say, 'and about that there little bit of money as was owing to me? I've got it all wrote out on paper, so as you mayn't lose count on it. I ain't 'xactly what you'll call druv, not just to-day, I ain't, but——'"

"'Put down the pork, my lad, and let's look at un,' he'd say; and then he'd weigh un in his hand, and he'd smell un, and he'd poke his finger into un, and then he'd up and say quite smart-like, 'And whose d—d fule of a pig did-ee get that jint off, Enoch?' he'd say. 'You never was no jedge of pork, and no more you'll never be, not if you live so long as 'Thuselah.' Well, Master Garge, no man don't like his trade run down afore his face, and mebbe we'd start argy-fying about pigs and suchlike. And t' owd woman she'd sot and smoke her pipe in t' chimbly-corner, and wouldn't say nothing till all of a sudden she'd scretch out: 'Ha done wi't, I say. That there Enoch, he'd argyfy a dog's hind leg off. And you'm be just so bad, master. Just you take and leave t' pork on t' table, Enoch. It aren't worth eightpence, no, nor yet tuppence a pound; but seeing as you married my darter as might have done better for herself, and you says as you be druv, we'll make shift wi't, some ways. And leave the paper and all, what's wrote out that bad that as nobbudy wouldn't think as no gal of mine would ever have married so uneddicated a man. And, Tummas, you'll go into t' town to-morrow, and you'll draw out money at t' bank, and you'll pay Enoch, and you'll bring back t' will and all, so as me and you can look un over agin. You ain't got 'arf an ounce of 'bacca in your pocket, Enoch? 'Tain't likely, is it?' Well, what were a chap to do, Master Garge? I'd pull out my pouch, and she'd empty that, and in course I'd say as fearther weren't to trouble hisself to go to t' bank, seeing as I could make shift somehow. And fearther he'd grumble and growl to hisself, and mebbe fetch down t' Bible and gie I a nasty jar out o' Proverbs to take home along wi' me. But t' owd woman she'd be for smoothing on him down, and she'd walk down to garden gate wi' me. 'Good e'en to you, Enoch,' she'd say, 'and don't you be taking on too much of what the muster says. His bark is wuss nor his bite,' she'd say, 'and I'll see as there's no altering of wills, and suchlike fullishness. Mary-Hann she were allers my favourite darter, and you'll gie her my respecks, and you'll take two-pennorth of goodies home wi' you and gie it to the childer wi' a kiss from Grannie. I ain't got tuppence in my pocket, but you can put it on to t' paper. Tuppence for sweetbreads, eh, Enoch?' And home I'd go wi'out my money, and wi'out my pork, and wi'out my 'bacca, and wi'out my tuppence. For I'd have to go to t' shop on way home to buy some more bacca, and I'd buy the goodies and all."

True tale, I am afraid, and doubtless the baker could have corroborated it.

The will, when it was found necessary to produce it, was not a lengthy document:—

"I leave my property to my wife, the care of my wife and

the old tom-cat to my children, and I appoint Mr Thomas Campion, whom I believe to be honest, as my executor."

Had the original apple of discord itself been thrown into the middle of the assembly, it could hardly have created a greater commotion. The contention, indeed, for the possession of the presumed heiress waxed so sharp among her children, that the baker was challenged by his younger brother to have a quiet round outside the back door, while the female mourners bandied to and fro between each other the most highly personal and highly uncomplimentary remarks.

"They called one the t'other all t' old cats i' t' place, and danged if I don't think as if Muster Campion hadn't a-chanced to be there, they'd have set to clawing. That spiteful they was!"

My informant was John Ball, who was generally to be found to the fore at either a meeting of the foxhounds or a funeral, and was, taking all in all, a reliable and accurate reporter. Fortunately old Tom Campion, who, having apparently had some inkling of the honour in store for him, had for once in a way donned a black coat and put in an appearance at the funeral, acted as peacemaker. If it could be said of any man in our parish at that time that his word was law, the man was Tom Campion. He, who is known to be essentially a man of his word, and is reported of as being both ready and able, for all his years, to take on the cleverest man with his fists in the country-side, is, in his own village at least, a veritable 'king of men.' Tom at once allayed the warlike ardour of the chief belligerent by the remark that "we ain't a-going to have no fighting over a job like this, and if Bill Barker can't keep a civil tongue in his head, I'll take and stand him wrong end up in t' water-butt in t' back-yard. And when you wimmen-folk have given over your skirling, I'll see if us can't put two and two together."

And having thus secured comparative silence, he then,

in his capacity of executor, proceeded to issue his judgment, wisely standing up for the right of primogeniture.

"First come, first served," he said. "That's law all the world over. Sons come afore daughters, and that's law too. So as Abe Barker comed into the world afore Bill, he be the rightful man to have charge of t' owd lady, being if she's willing to bide along wi' him. And"—for Tom Campion had ever a dry sense of humour—"seeing as Bill be so set on being hospittable, so as he shan't have nothing to grumble about, he shall have t' owd tom-cat. And"—after a pause—"they can shift about arter a while, if so be as a change of air and of lodgers be agreeable to all parties. But the way as I said is the way as we'll start t' business. T' owd lady, she'll go along o' Abe, and Bill, he can take t' owd cat home along o' him. If"—no man of my acquaintance, with the exception of perhaps here and there a semi-blind parson, ever had a better knowledge of the Prayer-Book phraseology than Tom Campion—"anybody can show just cause or impediment agin all this, let him now speak, or for ever hold his peace. You'd best hold your peace quick-stick, Bill Barker, or, as I said afore, you'll find yourself stood wrong end up in t' water-butt."

This rather hastily added corollary to the original proposition was provoked by a *sotto-voce* remark emanating from the wholly dissatisfied Bill, which promised a short shrift and a watery grave for his new lodger.

For a moment a dead silence followed Tom Campion's announcement, even Bill thinking it better to reserve his comments till the executor was well out of hearing.

And then, in shrill, indignant, protest uprose the voice of the widow, who up to this point in the proceedings had maintained what might be called the masterly silence of gratified inactivity. She had not been so far bowed down with grief as to prevent her listening with a grim smile—"grinning like a dog showing his teeth, though she hain't got none to speak of," was John Ball's version—to the none too seemly competition for the possession of her body, and nodding approvingly at intervals when some more than usually high-spiced compliment or ornamental epithet had been applied by one daughter to another.

"Bolt upright in her chair she sat," said John Ball, "and took and gied tongue, and dressed 'em all down proper. I dunno as Muster Campion he weren't the worst on the whole biling; but all on us was bad, and by the time she were done there weren't a man nor yet a woman in the room as were left wi' a shred of character. She weren't a-going to be ordered about by no Tom Campion; she reckoned she could tell a thing or two about him if she'd a mind. No, she weren't a-going to do as she were bid by him, nor by nobbudy else neither. She weren't no parish constable, nor a pore-sperited farm gal. 'Tweren't likely as she were going to be chuckled about from one side o' t' street to t' ither. She weren't neither a shittlecock nor yet a ingey-rubber ball. Where she went, there she'd bide, and she'd take old tom-cat along wi' her. She didn't know as she wouldn't as lief go to Abe Barker as ony o' the rest on 'em, seeing as how he'd got a back parlour where she could sit and do her bit o' knitting wi'out being mullocked up wi' dough and childer, which one was well anigh as bad as t'other. I can't tell you one-half as she said, Master Garge, nor yet one-quarter. Seemed as though she were wound up like a hingin, and couldn't stop till she were run down."

The end of the matter was that, Bill Barker gladly waiving his claim to the cat, the baker carried off the honours of the day by consenting to give up the back parlour and one bedroom in his house to the two new lodgers.

"And what be I to get wi't, Master Campion?" he inquired, being thereto instigated by his wife.

"Can't say, my lad, till I'm through wi' the execciting," and with this enigmatical answer the baker, who scratched his head rather sadly, had to rest content.

So far as I was concerned, the first enlightenment came

from Tom Campion, with whom I forgathered on the following afternoon as he was feeding his collection of waterfowl in the Park meadow. I could not help noticing that our squire —for our squire he really was, though he never claimed the title—was looking rather preoccupied.

"Good afternoon, Mr Campion. You had rather a busy day yesterday, hadn't you?"

"Ah!" he said rather gloomily; "then you've heard tell, and all?" Then after a pause, "I reckon as you knows a mort o' things, don't you?"

"Well, I suppose most of us know something."

"You knows, then, I suppose, as there's no fool like an old fool. And now I'll tell you summat as you don't know, p'r'aps. There never was a man yet as were made such an old fool as this here Tom Campion. Now we've got straight, ain't we?"

"Well, yes, perhaps! But what's gone wrong, Mr Campion?"

"Well, seeing as you're a man, and not a woman, as never can keep their tongues from wagging, I'll tell you. Tom Barker made his will a goodish time back, and it have been locked up in my burro-drawer five years come Christmas, seeing as I'd promised to be his execciter. Well, there was just four things in't. There were the will itself, and that were short and sweet; and there were t' owd woman, who've got a temper as is more short nor sweet; and tom-cat, whose tail ain't neither short nor sweet; and then there be the property. Do you follow me, Master George?"

I nodded my head.

"Well, the property, that ain't 'xactly what you'd call short nor yet sweet neither. For barrin' tom-cat and t' owd sow, and what be in t' house and yard, there ain't nothing left to execcite. Tom-cat, he'll be execcited double-quick time if I catch him prowling round my coops again; but twould be waste of money t' execcite t' owd sow, seeing as she's in pig."

"But surely there's money in the bank, Mr Campion?"

"Drawed it all out, t' miller did, years ago. Took it in notes, he did, so as nobbudy shouldn't know what he'd done wi' it."

"Well, what are you going to do, Mr Campion?"

"Sell the stuff and pay the bills. Mind you," he added as an after-thought, "I ain't a-going to say that one way or another there won't be something just enough to keep t' owd lass going, but that's between ourselves, Master George."

And that was the last word I ever heard from Tom Campion on the subject.

What with the executor himself paying a rare high price for the old sow, and some of the furniture selling almost suspiciously well, the miller's creditors were paid off in full. And as for the space of a year and a half the widow received a weekly dole of six shillings from Tom Campion, of which sum all but sixpence went straight into the baker's pocket, the latter, what with the bed-clothing and other garnishments which he had annexed, may be held to have so far come pretty well out of the transaction. To be sure, five shillings a week for the old lady's and sixpence for the cat's board did not suggest a large surplus. But when a widow's trustee keeps his mouth religiously closed on the subject of the sources of her income, there is always some ground for speculation. And the mere fact that Goody Barker was known to be a close-fisted woman, and one capable of driving a hard bargain, intensified the general impression in our village that she had got a good deal more up her sleeve than she cared to show, and that one fine day there would be some fair pickings for the family. Many a crumb of bread, then, was cast upon the waters, and according to John Ball, whose tiny cottage lay almost within earshot of the baker's more pretentious dwelling, grandchildren from all parts of the parish spent half their play-time in trotting to and fro, bearing tribute in kind, or armed with inquiries for 'Grannie.' It was ever the old cobbler's custom to do his work, when the weather permitted, sitting in his open doorway, so that few things that went on in the main street escaped his observation. And as most of the small messengers stopped on their errands to pass the time of day to him, he was well posted with the contents of pretty nearly every dish and parcel, and the purport of every message, that went to the baker's house.

"'Twere t' carrier's lad this morning; he was wanting to know if Grannie 'd like a airing this arternoon in fearther's cart. 'Grannie she don't want no airings,' says Mrs Abe; 'and you go home and tell your mither, as if she did happen to want one, we've gotten a cart o' our own as carries good wholesome bread in it, and isn't mullocked up wi' dead things and suchlike.'" Or again, "'Twere butcher's lass this morning, and she'd brought a dish of sossages as comed off fearther's own pig. 'Well, I dunno,' says Mrs Abe, 'as his pig is no better nor anyone else's, seeing as it's like to be fed on offal and suchlike. But you can thank your mither kindly, Meg, and tell her as Grannie is that set on sossages.' One way or t' ither, Master Garge, I do reckon as t' baker and his wife they've gotten a softish job o' Grannie and t' cat and all. Not as t' owd lady she aren't got a tongue in her head, and sorts 'em proper betimes. But 'ard words breaks no bones, and best make hay while t' sun shines, is two good motters, all said and done. But you mark my words, Master Garge, when t' owd critter be dead and buried there'll be some wailings and gnashings o' teeth, arter if not afore, mind-ee!"

I had, to be sure, some grounds for fancying that John Ball was in this, as in many other matters, at least as wise as his neighbours; but neither of us had solid excuse for believing that Goody Barker's weekly income actually came out of Tom Campion's pocket.

For eighteen months or more the baker's wife sustained what she was pleased to speak of in private conversation as her 'cross' with tolerable complacency. For five shillings and sixpence a week, supplemented by a chronic if not continuous flow of sausages, pigs' trotters, black puddings, fresh eggs and other seasonable delicacies, could be accounted as a fairly good set-off against the widow's occupation of the back parlour, a few extra howlings on the part of the children and the acquisitive talents of the tom-cat. Yet the landlady would hardly have been a mortal woman if she had not occasionally grumbled to her neighbours, and declared that what between her mother-in-law's requirements and the thieving propensities of the cat she was being "druv to death," if she had not once in a way donned her armour of offence and embarked upon a wordy altercation with her permanent lodger. To provoke an encounter when the odds are largely in the other party's favour, argues more rashness than wisdom. The satisfaction of getting the last word is commonly the end in view when woman meets woman in a battle of tongues; and the most soundly logical syllogisms and carefully matured personalities are, as accessories to the meed of victory, but chaff before the wind in comparison with alternating puffs of smoke from an evil-smelling pipe and the noisy barkings of a well-manipulated cough.

With poor Tom Campion's rather unexpected death came the bursting of the bubble and the end of the illusion. That which I had only guessed at, and shrewd old John Ball had foretold, became the common property of the parish. Tom Campion had paid Goody Barker's allowance from start to finish entirely out of his own pocket.

"I'm not at all surprised, George," remarked the rector, inclined perhaps to be wise after the event. "It was just the sort of thing Tom Campion would have done. His right hand often gave without his left hand knowing it."

Under the circumstances it was not unnatural, perhaps, that the contributions in kind to the widow's support also came to an untimely end, and that the interest taken in

Grannie's health and Grannie's proceedings wholly evaporated. Not unnatural either that a week after Tom Campion's decease Mrs Abe Barker found her way to the rectory and there poured out her soul.

"Couldn't the rector do nothing? Trade was as bad as bad, and what between mother-in-law and the cat they were being fairly eaten out of home. Mother-in-law's temper was that short, and the cat the rombustiest animal as ever were. What with one smacking of the childer and the other scratching of them, there weren't a moment's peace in the house. And now, as times was hard, mother-in-law had took to going over to the baking-house, helping herself and the cat to whatever they fancied, and puffing 'bacca-smoke over the dough so as the bread tasted of it. What were 'The House' intended for if it weren't for such as she, who hadn't got no money nor conscience neither? And," wound up the plaintiff, "she ain't one as will take no 'ints. 'Twere only yesterday as I said to her, 'If you won't go out quiet, you'll be put out!' I says. That were a 'int, weren't it, sir?"

"Well, yes," said the rector with judicial gravity; "I should say that it partook of the nature of a hint, or at least a suggestion."

"And who's a-going to do the putting?" says she. Who indeed!

I was lunching at the rectory that day, having promised to go there to meet the curate, a young gentleman who was apt to get rather upon the rector's nerves in a *tête-à-tête* conversation. As I had met Mrs Barker coming down the rectory drive, I was not altogether surprised when, pending the curate's arrival, my host at once commenced to talk about old Goody.

But a word about our curate, the Reverend Edward Stroud. He had only been in the parish for about a month, but had already begun to teach us how things really ought to be done, being indeed a young man with very good points and that modest amount of self-assurance which might have tempted him to offer to command the royal yacht, or to play the part of Hamlet at the Lyceum. It was a strong point in his favour that he was brimful of energy; a weakness that in conversation he assumed a truly remarkable amount of all-round knowledge on the part of the person to whom he happened to be talking. As well attempt to divert the stars from their courses as to prevent the Rev. Edward Stroud from tacking on 'you know' to the tail of each proposition. Ours was, unfortunately, one of those parishes in which there is obviously rather too much work for one parson, and not quite enough for two. And we were predestined to be subjected to the ministrations of a succession of young curates, because, on the one hand, the rector declined to entertain applications from those whom he was wont to denominate 'elderly failures,' and on the other hand an active-minded young man soon began to pine for a larger sphere of work.

"There is something in what the woman says after all, George," concluded the rector. "A growing family and an old woman who keeps possession of the two best rooms in the house are two incompatible quantities, and, between ourselves, I should fancy that old Goody is not a very comfortable lodger. She would be quite well looked after in the workhouse, though she might have to leave her pipe and her cat behind her. I think I will ask Stroud to go and have a quiet talk with her. He has got quite what you might call a persuasive manner with the fair sex—eh, George?"

"He's got plenty of ch——" but at that moment the door opened and the gentleman himself was ushered in.

Never did a man tumble more readily to a suggestion than did our curate that day. He simply jumped at the prospect of bringing Goody Barker to an amenable frame of mind.

"I'll make a point of going this very afternoon, you know. I've promised to look in at the school, you know. And

I must see the clerk about the vestry door, you know. And I've got one or two people to visit at the other end of the village, you know. But I can work my way round to the baker's by about four o'clock, you know. And I'll soon talk the old lady round, you know."

"Well, I won't say that I do know, exactly," said the rector rather drily, "but I hope that you'll—eh—succeed in your mission."

Our curate had so far accurately timed his visit to the baker's house that it was somewhere between four and half-past when I found him hovering round the neighbourhood of the Red Lion with a hunted look on his face, an empty medicine-bottle in one hand and a small newspaper parcel in the other.

"I say," he began, coming up to me at once, "can you tell me how much gin I ought to get for fourpence? And where can I borrow a cork? I don't want them exactly for myself, you know. But I have to get them—somehow. It's the right sort of place to buy gin, isn't it? I'm rather ignorant about those matters, you know. And about the cork?"

"If you pay for the gin, I expect they'll give you a cork," I replied. "But isn't it a little derogatory to the dignity of the cloth for the parson to buy four pennyworth of gin in the middle of the afternoon? As you don't want the gin yourself, I suppose you want it for Goody Barker?"

"Yes, to rub on her joints, you know."

"Well, I don't know, and don't think either. But as I have no particular character to keep up, suppose you hand over the fourpence, and I'll manage the gin business for you. And you go on to my house, and we'll have a cup of tea presently. Hulloa!" as he hastily thrust parcel, medicine-bottle and four coppers into my hand, "is the parcel Mrs Barker's property too?"

"Oh yes, it's all hers! But, I say, thanks awfully, you know. If you really don't mind, it's awfully kind of you, you know. And I'll have a cup of tea with pleasure."

I duly discharged my commission, or rather the curate's commission, and carried the spoil to Goody Barker.

"Why, it's you, is it, Master George? Well, I never, now! I quite thought it would a been the curick. Nice civil-spoken young gemman he is, and all. If you was to see him, by any chance, Master George, tell him as I hopes he'll call again next week."

"Over gods forbode!" ejaculated the curate, when I delivered my message. "What a terrible old woman is that, you know! She's got a way of taking you up and ordering you about, you know, that is downright startling and peremptory, you know. Puts a fellow quite off his balance, you know."

And then, over a cup of tea, he expounded to me the story of his interview. Here it is, word for word as he gave it to me.

"Good afternoon to you, Mrs Barker; I am very glad to make your acquaintance. This is almost the first time I've had the pleasure of seeing you, you know."

"Them as wants to see me knows where to find me."

"Well, I hoped I might have seen you in church, you know. But I haven't seen you there the last two Sundays."

"And I ain't seed you, nuther."

"Well, but you know I was there, and you were not there, you know."

"You'm paid to go, and I beant."

Here the curate rather abruptly changed the subject.

"Your poor old neighbour, Mrs Brown, was only buried last week."

"Good job too, as she were took; she were a bad un!"

"Oh, I say, Mrs Barker, that won't do at all! Charity, you know! And, besides, 'de mortuis,' you know!"

"Don't know him—never heard tell of him, nuther," retorted the widow. "But charity! Talk of charity, you ain't got such a thing as a shilling in your pocket, has you? Ah, then," as he rather weakly produced the coin, "I reckons as your legs be younger than mine. So just step down t' street, my lad, and buy me two ounces o' 'bacca, same as I allers has, at t' shop, a ha'p'orth o' cough lozenges and two bull's-eyes. And then I'll have four penn'orth o' gin, my jints is that bad. There's bottle on mantelpiece, and you'll ha' to borrer a cork. I ain't got one just now."

And before the curate quite knew where he was, he found himself standing in the street with a medicine-bottle in his hand, and, I may add, with a little of his self-confidence abated.

The curate having proved a broken reed, the rector next entrusted that which was an essentially delicate mission to the able hands and willing heart of his well-proved lieutenant, Miss Sarah Tuggs, the grimmest and gauntest of our trio of district visitors. Grim of appearance only, for I believe that each one of those self-denying and ever-busy ladies was really and truly overflowing with the milk of human kindness. They were spinsters all, though I have no occasion to believe that they had taken vows of celibacy, such an action in their cases being indeed liable to be accounted as partaking of the nature of a work of supererogation. Now and again, perhaps, a too fervid zeal outran a less conspicious discretion; but taking it all in all, they did good work in the parish, ferreting out impostures and grievances that might otherwise have escaped detection. Miss Tuggs may be said to have looked her part better than either of her sisters in office. She stood, at a modest calculation, some five feet ten inches in her stocking-feet, and was bony and flat in wrong places. Moreover, she was in the habit of concealing what I think in Leah's case was called a weakness of eyes —with Miss Tuggs it took the form of a squint—by a pair of huge blue goggles, which imparted mingled dignity and ferocity to her countenance. An unfortunate inclination to stutter, especially in the presence of the dreaded men-tribe, had a truly disastrous effect, inasmuch as it caused two most worthy and kind-hearted individuals to go to their graves not indeed at enmity, but yet not altogether at peace with one another.

Miss Tuggs, as it happened, carrying in her hand a slipper which needed a few stitches, had made her way to John Ball's cottage, there to find the old cobbler sitting, as his custom was, in the open doorway and discoursing with Tom Campion. Poor, dear lady! She had never interchanged a word with Tom Campion in her life before, and yet—well, it seemed hardly neighbourly not to pass the time of day to him. But why, oh, most unfortunate of women, having once got safely over the all-sufficient "Good afternoon, Mr Campion," essay quite a superfluous remark about the weather, and pick out a B to begin it with?

"Good afternoon, Mr Campion. Isn't it a bub—bub—bub—bub——"

Small wonder, then, that worthy old Tom, what with innate bashfulness, sympathetic nervousness and laudable anxiety to spare the lady further contortions of countenance, was so far thrown off his balance that for the second recorded time in his life he employed a really strong swear-word.

"Yes, miss, I'm d—d if it ain't!" he blurted out heartily.

"And miss," said John Ball, "she guv one scretch, and then off she ran up t' lane same as if a tin kettle were tied to her tail."

Nothing after that could ever have persuaded the lady that Tom Campion was not a profane and vulgar swearer; while Tom himself, having had one sample of her facial and conversational powers, from that day forth avoided her like poison.

Such, then, was our second ambassador, and, to do her justice, she seemed to have got somewhere nearer the right mark than the Rev. Edward Stroud had done. At least she may be said to have worked the conversation round to the legitimate order of the day, or, in other words, to that which our euphemists generally spoke of as 'The House.'

But then? The rector, after hearing the outraged spinster's

tale of woe, came down to my house on purpose to have the pleasure of repeating it. Never mind either the preliminaries or the stammerings, except that one all-important "de—de—de—," to be pronounced French-wise.

"You've no idea how comfortable the old women are there, Mrs Barker."

"P'r'aps I ain't."

"Such nice warm fires and such cosy rooms!"

"Are 'em?"

"And so bright and happy they all looked!"

"Well, miss," very politely, "seeing as it's all that nice and that conformable, why don't you go there yourself? We'd try to make shift to get along wi'out you. 'Twould be 'ard, no doubt!"

"Oh! but you see, Mrs Barker, I'm quite young and active, and——"

"And that took up wi' t' young men and all!" interrupted the widow. "'Twere 'Arry Webb, weren't it, as I see you winking at i' t' church, three weeks ago come Sunday?"

In an instant the spinster was ablaze, indignation at the accusation fairly mastering her utterance.

"De—de—de—de—de——"

And she got no further, for—

"We don't want no swearing here, miss!" quoth the widow. "You'd pop out 'Yes,' wi'out no stuttering, if 'Arry Webb was to arst t' question."

Miss Sarah Tuggs's retreat was even more rapidly accomplished than the curate's.

"But hark! the cry is Astur."

As the great Clusian lord at last assailed that pass which had baffled less renowned warriors, so now our rector girded up his loins for the fray, and marched down to the baker's house in all the grandeur of frock-coat and tall hat, and armed with 'such divinity' as possibly to this day 'hedges a king,' and used in a more primitive age to hedge a rector of an outlying country parish.

"'Veni, vidi, vici!'—is that what you're going to tell me?" I inquired, as he looked into my house on the return journey.

"Well, not that exactly, George," he said very quietly. "Let me see, by the way. It was a shilling, wasn't it, that Stroud was charged for his—eh—parochial visit?"

"Yes."

"Ah!" rather pensively, "mine cost me half-a-crown. I did only mean to pay a shilling, but unfortunately I had not got one in my pocket. I'm afraid there'll be more to follow. However, I suppose the rector ought to pay a bit more than the curate. A funny world this, George! Come, I suppose you're dying to know what happened?"

"Well, yes," I admitted.

"Well, that half-crown, which I really did mean to be a shilling till I found that I had not got one, I think we must regard as entrance-money. I really couldn't sit down in that atmosphere of bad old woman and bad tobacco. Now don't put down your pipe, my dear fellow; I never mind your tobacco. Stroud, I suppose, paid for her stuff, and I paid half-a-crown for an open window and a temporary cessation of smoking; and I may have committed myself for something in the future. However, I did not come away quite empty-handed, as I've got more home-truths in my pocket than I have had for many a long day. For once in a way I had to listen to a sermon from one of my congregation instead of preaching one. I supplied the text myself—at least, I read it, and she pointed out the place in the Bible. I had only got through two verses when she pulled me up short. 'That's you!' she said; 'you'm the Pharisee what devours widders' houses and makes long prayers. Leastways, you offers to pray for folks, and then tries to turn 'em out o' their houses!' I wanted to argue the point, but she cut me short with, 'It's me as is pretching!' Then, George, I'm afraid that

I make the blind to go out of the way, 'leastways, out o' t' house,' and so forth. Finally, to cut a long story short, I am 'that meddlesome,' and to tell you the honest truth, I'm not so sure that she isn't in her rights there. Who am I, after all, George, to try and make laws for my neighbours, and to do Mrs Barker, junior's, dirty work for her? It is dirty work, if you look at it the right way, George, to deprive an old woman of that age of the only two things she really finds comfort in—her old cat and her, or rather Stroud's, tobacco. I'm afraid they wouldn't put up with either in the workhouse. And so, George, the long and short of it is, that I had a talk with the baker's wife afterwards, and we agreed to revert to the old arrangement—the mother-in-law to stop where she is, and six shillings a week to go into the house. I can probably get a half-crown a week, and perhaps a couple of loaves of bread to go against that sixpence for tobacco, out of the Board of Guardians, and the deficiency I'll make up myself."

The new arrangement did not last long. In the course of the winter the curate read the Burial Service over the old woman's grave, and on the very day after the funeral—for it's a poor heart that knows no rejoicing—the baker's children celebrated the tom-cat's obsequies in the baker's garden, and the baker himself baked a special cake for the occasion.

"Curious fancies old folk does get into their heads, Master George," remarked the baker, by no means a bad-hearted fellow, to me about a year later. "The very last words as my old mother said when she were a-dying was, ''T had ought to ha' been a jint,' says she, and half an hour later she was dead. Nobbudy never would ha' thought as she'd been a-wanting a jint just then, would-ee, Master George? She'd had beef-tea and grule, and sichlike. But if I'd knowed as she were 'ankering arter a jint, a jint she should 'ave 'ad. Not"—after a momentary reflection—"as there'd ha' been time to cook it."

And again—

"Curious fancies old folk do get into their heads, George," said to me dear old Mr Honeywood, the kindest and cheeriest of solicitors, when three years ago, at his urgent invitation, I ran down to spend a night in the old country. "Mine was to see you once again, my boy. But I think the most curious of all was an old fellow's years ago. He had made up his mind, when he was going on for seventy, that he'd got just seven years longer to live, and he sank all his money in a seven years' annuity on the strength of it. He had got a wife too, and I tried to persuade the old couple that, as one was pretty sure to outlive the other, they would both feel more comfortable if they bought a *joint* annuity for their lives. They took a night to think it over, and then they came back to say that they had talked it out together and had come to the conclusion that the plan I suggested would not give them enough to live upon 'conformably,' as they called it; that the old man was a year or so younger than his wife, and that seven years were their limit of expected life. So they got a few pounds more each year for their money, and the old man lived out his time and a few months to spare. I never heard what became of the old woman."

"Was the name Barker, by any chance, Mr Honeywood?"

"Bless my heart!" he exclaimed, "Barker was the name. Why, to be sure, George, now I come to think of it, they lived in your old parish!"

AN ADMIRALTY FARM.

With apologies to those officers at the Admiralty who, during the spring of 1916, spared no efforts to provide the ships of the White Sea Squadron with fresh meat.

BY H. A. LE F. H.

[Maga, March 1919.]

I.

It was nearly midnight by the clock, but it was still broad daylight, and if there had been no clouds and no hills to the Northerd, the sun would have still been visible skimming along the top of the horizon. The 'white nights,' as the Russians call them, are not conducive to sleep, although in the mornings the inclination is more marked. Anyhow, there was no apparent intention of going to bed displayed by the small group of officers who were sitting in a circle round a fire in the wardroom of one of H.M. ships: they were discussing what appeared to them at the time a most important question.

They were all dressed in naval uniform, representatives of various ranks from a commander to a clerk, but if the same group had been assembled in July 1914, very few would have been in uniform. One had returned post-haste from a farm in British Columbia, one had been a land-agent in England, one had come from the gold-mines in South Africa, several had been officers in various lines of Steamship Companies, and the Law and the Joint-Stock Banks had supplied one or two of the others with a means of livelihood.

The conversation had rather drifted away from the point under discussion, tending to become frivolous, and the Commander was beginning to look rather harassed and worried.

"It's all very well for you fellows to joke about it," he said, "but I wish to Heaven you would pull yourselves together and help me to make out some answer to this telegram. I got it yesterday morning, and it's high time I sent an answer. Several of you are supposed to be agricultural experts, and I don't believe you know the first thing about it, or, if you do, you conceal it wonderfully well."

"I've rather forgotten what the telegram said," remarked the Canadian. "Read it out again, Clerk, and we'll try and help to make up some sort of a reply; but I wish to repeat once more that I know nothing about either sheep or cattle——"

"I thought you owned a farm in B.C.," said one of the younger members of the R.N.R. in rather a surprised voice.

"Perhaps I do, but that doesn't say that I farm it. Maybe I was keeping it to sell to some young idiot from England who knew less about farming than I did," and the Canadian looked rather pointedly at the last speaker.

"I'll read out the telegram," said the Clerk. He took up the paper lying by his side and read as follows:—

"*From the Admiralty, dated two days ago. . . . My Number so-and-so.*

"Report by telegram whether there is suitable accommodation for pasturing live stock at Forsakenskie for the use of H.M. ships during the summer months. State whether sheep or cattle, or both, should be sent, and in what numbers, and whether hay can be purchased locally."

"Surely we ought to be able to make up an answer to that," said the land-agent, "and I call it a very reasonable and sensible telegram to get from their lordships: shows how we're progressing as a nation when the Admiralty know that cattle eat hay without first referring to the Board of Agriculture."

"The Admiralty are pretty hot stuff in these days," remarked the Chief. "I suppose you heard about their three-word telegram to the poor old *Nonsuch* last winter when they had opened about their last case of provisions, and telegraphed to say they had run out of fresh water altogether, and hadn't enough coal left to distil?"

"No, what was that, Chief?" said several voices.

The answer was, "Snow will melt."

"I wish to goodness you wouldn't start these interruptions, Chief," said the Commander irritably; "we shall never get on. Now let's take the telegram bit by bit and write down an answer to each part, and then we can form it up into an intelligible reply. First of all, is there suitable pasturage or not?"

"You ought to be able to say that without any hesitation," he said, glaring at the land-agent, "after dragging me all round the country this afternoon on that visit of inspection."

"My dear old chap," said the land-agent rather scornfully, "the less said about that walk to-day the better. Apart from the fact that there was at least six inches of snow still left on the ground, I couldn't induce you to move out of the first Lap house you came to, though what the attraction was I couldn't see."

"I was trying to buy furs," said the Commander, "and it was obviously useless to walk about looking for pasturage in all that snow. Anyhow we saw a lot of reindeer, and they must eat something, so write down, Clerk. Your Number so-and-so, mine so-and-so. There is ample pasturage for live stock in the summer: stop!"

"I wouldn't say ample," said the Canadian cautiously.

"I wouldn't say pasturage," said the land-agent. "Reindeer eat moss."

"I wouldn't say live stock," said the Chief; "that means sheep and cattle."

"I wouldn't say there is ample in the summer," said the Clerk. "I should say there will be."

I should say, "I hope there will be," remarked one of the more pessimistic of the R.N.R. lieutenants. "We don't know for certain that the snow will ever go, and it's June now."

"What the devil is the good of my suggesting anything if you are all going to pull it to pieces in this way?" said the Commander irritably. "Let's have a little more constructive, not destructive criticism—especially from you, Clerk," he added rather fiercely.

"I am sorry, sir," said the Clerk, "but shall I rewrite the sentence to fall in line with the suggestions these other officers have made?"

"Yes, go on," said the Commander.

After several minutes' delay the Clerk read out, "There will probably be food for animals in the autumn."

"Cross that out," said the Commander angrily. "I am not asked for an expression of opinion, but for a statement of fact. Write down, 'I am informed there is ample pasturage for stock in the summer.'"

"Who informed you?" demanded the land-agent rather anxiously. "Don't say I did and try and blame me when they all die of hunger."

"I told you, didn't I, that I was asking that Lap about it this afternoon when I was up in the village—or anyhow, if I didn't tell you, I was."

"I thought you were buying furs," remarked the Canadian.

The Commander treated this with contempt, and picking up the copy of the telegram, "Now as to sheep or cattle, or both—which do the experts advise?" he asked sarcastically.

"I prefer beef to mutton," said the Chief, "so I votes for cattle."

"We aren't discussing beef *versus* mutton, Chief," said the land-agent. "It is improbable they will ever be eaten unless they are killed before they land. You can't eat things which die a natural death," he added fatuously.

"Hunger isn't a natural death," said the Commander drily. "But as I probably have to look forward to landing the brutes, I want to ask for the animals that will give me the least trouble."

"How are you going to land them?" asked one of the trawler officers. "Make them swim?"

"I suppose so," said the Commander. "Now which swim best, cattle or sheep?"

"Sheep can't swim," said the Clerk hastily, anxious to show his knowledge in matters agricultural. "They cut their throats when they try, so that quite settles it. We must have cattle, which I am very glad of, as I hate mutton."

"Am I likely to be disembarkation officer, sir?" inquired one of the R.N.R. officers rather anxiously.

"Certainly you are," said the Commander. "Why, what has that got to do with it?"

"Only that I strongly advise sheep, sir," said the disembarkation officer. "They are much easier to handle, and they aren't nearly so strong, and they have no horns."

"Can sheep swim, or can't they? Can any of you experts tell me that? It must be a very easy thing to earn your living anyhow in these days if one can get hold of expert's jobs with such very little knowledge," said the Commander wearily.

"Yes, they can swim all right," said the land-agent, "and I expect you'll be asking to be taken on one day as my pupil after they retire you—which they are bound to do soon if you take as long as this answering a telegram."

"All right, we appear to be making some progress at last," said the Commander. "Now then, Clerk, cross out quadrupeds and put sheep, and read the telegram again."

"I didn't put quadrupeds, I put stock, sir," said the Clerk. "The Admiralty said live stock."

"Don't contradict, but read it out as I tell you, my good boy."

"The telegram now reads, 'I am informed there is ample pasturage for sheep in the summer,'" said the Clerk, with a note of forbearance in his voice.

"Now then add, 'Only sheep should be sent, number to commence with'—what do you think, Pay.?" asked the Commander.

"I don't know how much they'll weigh, sir," said the Paymaster thoughtfully. "I am only accustomed to dealing with them as mutton, not as sheep."

"How much do your sheep average?" asked the Chief, addressing the Canadian.

"I thought I had made it plain enough that I haven't got any sheep, and that I know nothing about them," said the Canadian irritably. "You'd better look it up in 'Chambers'."

"Get the Encyclopædia, Clerk," said the Commander, "and look up 'Sheep.'"

There was a lengthy pause while the right volume was got down from the shelf.

"It doesn't say anything about their weight," said the Clerk, "but apparently there are several sorts of breeds. I wonder whether we ought to specify the breed. It says they are a docile animal."

"I should estimate a sheep to weigh about 50 lbs.," said the land-agent. "They'll probably weigh nearly that when first landed, and as to breed I should specify those most suitable for a rocky island, where the only food is moss and mosquitoes. I am getting rather tired of this, and am off to bed very soon," he added. "I've got to be off to sea early in the morning."

"For God's sake, hang on now and get this thing finished," said the Commander. "We are really making a little headway now; come on, Paymaster, how many sheep will keep us all going for, say, a month?"

After some moments of anxious calculation, the Paymaster announced 400.

"Rot," said the Commander. "I said a month, not a year."

"Well, sir, 700 men will eat that number in a month, if you allow them fresh meat every day."

"Every day — certainly not," said the Commander. "Once a week is ample."

"Once a week is not enough," said the Doctor emphatically. "If we don't get it more often than that we shall have an outbreak of scurvy; I've been very anxious about it for the last three months."

"Will you take on disembarkation officer, Doc.?" asked the R.N.R. lieutenant anxiously. "Because if I'm to do it I hope you won't ask for more than a hundred, sir," he said, addressing the Commander.

"Heavens, no," said the Commander, "100 is ample to start off with. Now then, Clerk, write that down and read it out again."

The Clerk read out: "I am informed there is ample pasturage for sheep in the summer; only sheep should be sent, number to commence with 100."

"Add, 'No hay purchasable locally; enough should be sent to feed the brutes.' Lord, I am sick to death of these cursed sheep already."

"What do you want hay for if there is ample pasturage?" said the Canadian.

"To fatten the brutes," said the Commander irritably.

"You don't fatten animals on hay," said the land-agent in a tactful voice, "but I should ask for it in case there is no pasturage."

The Commander's brow was furrowed with thought for several minutes. "I think that does the trick now, doesn't it?" he said to the Clerk. "Cross out, 'I am informed,' and get the telegram coded and sent off."

"There's one thing I should like to say," said the Canadian, rising from his chair and walking to the door, "and that is, that if you turn out a hundred sheep and don't have some dogs to round them up, you'll never see them again; they'll spread all over Russia. Good-night."

"We've got eight dogs in the ship already," said the Commander, "and I wonder what the First Lord will say if I telegraph for sheep-dogs. He'll think I am pulling his leg."

"I really advise you to ask for some dogs," said the Chief, "or anyhow, one. The Admiralty will quite understand that every flock of sheep must have a dog."

"All right," said the Commander rather bitterly. "Add to the end of the telegram 'Request one sheep-dog may be sent.'"

"Now read it out, Clerk, and then let's go to bed."

The Clerk read out, "There is ample pasturage for sheep in the summer; only sheep should be sent, good climbers; number to commence with 100. Request one dog sheep may be sent."

"What the devil are you driving at, Clerk," said the Commander furiously. "Who said anything about climbing? and I said sheep-dog, not dog sheep. They'll probably send us out a ram if we put it like that."

"No, that's the proper way of expressing it," said the Chief decidedly. "I've kept stores for twenty years, and I assure you if you ask for a sheep-dog you'll get a ram for a certainty; whereas if you ask for a dog sheep you'll get a dog."

"God forbid we should get a ram," said the embarkation officer. "They're as fierce as the devil."

"Well, you'll probably have to take them all on charge in your store accounts, Chief, when they do arrive," said the Commander wearily, "and then transfer them to the Paymaster's account when they become mutton; so I suppose we'd better leave it as you say. I'm going to bed, and you can bring me the telegram first thing in the morning, Clerk.

Find some more official word than climbers to designate the breed. I hate the thought of mutton already; good night, everybody," and the meeting broke up.

At lunch next day the Chief asked the Commander if the telegram had gone off.

"Yes, it's gone," said the Commander; "but I cut out the dog altogether, and the Clerk put in something about breed suitable for mountainous country."

"Why did you cut out about the dog?" said the Chief.

"When I woke up I found myself repeating the lines out of the laws of the Navy: 'He does well who tears up in the morning the letter he wrote overnight,' and I wasn't certain if these two blooming experts, the land-agent and the Canadian, were not pulling my leg over that dog. I suppose they've gone out in their trawlers now, leaving me to bear the burden and heat of the day in here. Well, thank God my telegram can't bear fruit for at least three weeks."

In about three weeks, however, the Admiralty intimated that the first consignment of 100 sheep might be expected in a few days, mentioning that a Scotch mountain breed had been selected, and informing the S.N.O. that on no account were any to be killed until they had been shorn.

It happened that the two experts were in harbour when the telegram arrived, and a council of war was again called to consider this new complication.

"Things are getting ridiculous," said the Commander, "and I'm beginning to think the Admiralty are pulling my leg. I'm sorry I didn't ask for that dog now. How the devil am I going to arrange to shear 100 sheep?"

"I've put that notice up on the mess deck, sir," said the First Lieutenant, "but there has been no result, and the Master-at-Arms says he doesn't think there is a single man in the ship who has ever shorn a sheep, and even if there was, we haven't any shears."

"Can't you shear sheep?" said the Commander to the

land-agent; "and if you can't do it yourself, what do you suggest?"

"I think the Chief ought to be able to manage it," said the land-agent drily. "He's got a workshop full of all sorts of noisy beastly machinery, and surely he could devise something or other to cut wool off a sheep."

"It's no use talking rubbish of that sort," said the Chief. "Do you imagine I'm going to put one of my skilled artificers to work to cut wool off a struggling savage brute's back? Your trawlers keep me going night and day with all their repairs, without beginning a wild enterprise of that sort."

"What about the ship's butcher?" said the Canadian. "Surely he can shear sheep?"

"No, he can't," said the First Lieutenant emphatically. "He says he can kill them and skin them, but that is all."

"I'm not going to start an undignified altercation with the Admiralty on this matter," said the Commander, "and so I think the best thing to do is to take no notice of this last brain-wave of their lordships. We will just kill the sheep and skin them, and then use black-list men to clip wool off the skins with scissors."

"When are they due to arrive?" asked the land-agent.

"Any time in the next couple of days," said the Commander. "I suppose you'll be here to help to land them?"

"I'm afraid we're awfully busy just now," said the land-agent, glancing at the Canadian rather anxiously. "We shall have to be down sweeping off that bit of the coast where the mines were laid last year. If it wasn't for that we should love to help."

"I am taking my division out to-night," said the Canadian.

"You told me you would be in till to-morrow morning," said the Chief rather angrily, "and I've started on the *Fram's* boiler. She can't be ready till then."

"She'll have to follow," said the Canadian. "We think

we ought not to waste a minute longer than necessary in beginning this sweeping."

"I've a good mind to take the ship out, and go down to see if I can do anything to help the salvage of the *Carelyn*," said the Commander, "and leave the yacht to carry on S.N.O.—just for a few days only," he added cheerfully.

"If the ship has to go to sea now," said the Chief, "it means the trawler's repairs go to the devil. I can't think why you suddenly want to go and see the *Carelyn*, as we can't do anything more to her now the Russians have undertaken the salvage work."

"I think I can guess why he wants to go," said the land-agent, "but your duty as S.N.O. here, Commander, is to stick to the sheep, I mean ship!"

"I shall be in again at the end of the week, and look forward to lamb and mint sauce. So long, you fellows. I hope you'll enjoy it."

"These retired officers have no sense of duty," said the Commander. "Well, if you go and bump a mine during the next few days, I shall feel it is a judgment on you."

II.

About five days later the trawlers returned and secured alongside their mother cruiser just before dinner. Conversation during dinner was general, and no allusion was made to the sheep; but the land-agent could not help remarking to the Paymaster that he was looking particularly fit and well.

"So would you be looking fit and well if you'd stayed here and not shirked," said the Commander drily. "The younger officers of the ship are going in for training for sports just at present, and we are hoping you and the Canadian will be entering for one or two of the races."

"The two-mile is the one I'm hoping to win," said the Clerk. "I did it in record time this afternoon."

"That's about the length of the island you were turning into a farm, isn't it?" asked the Canadian; "and, by-the-bye, how are the sheep getting on? I see we are still on bully beef," he added, looking at the menu.

"I am given to understand that the sheep are very happy indeed," said the Commander. "They are eight dozen of the most agile brutes that ever lived, enjoying themselves to the top of their bent, and likely to continue to do so as far as I can see."

"I thought there were 100 coming," said the land-agent.

"Yes, there were," said the Paymaster, "but four died on the way out, and as far as I can make out they died every other day with suspicious regularity. The trip took eight days, and I said to the Captain that I was glad he wasn't delayed a few more days or some more might have died."

"The old ruffian only grinned, and said he thought it would have been highly probable, that they were very fine sheep, and the rate of mortality might even have risen."

"The yacht arrives in three days' time with the Commodore," said the Commander, "and we have got to have some sheep killed by then. It is really getting beyond a joke—the whole of the ship's officers and the accountant staff have been ashore all day, and they haven't managed to catch a single one."

"They are a wonderful lot of brutes," said the embarkation officer. "They swim like otters and climb and jump like monkeys, and can do the two miles from one end of the island to the other in about ten minutes. There is any amount of grass there now, and if it wasn't for mosquitoes it would be very pleasant ashore."

"This is five days since the sheep arrived, and we haven't even tasted one yet," said the Commander. "However, I am going to put a stop to it to-morrow all right."

"What are you going to do, Commander?" said the land-agent anxiously. "Poison them or trap them, or what?"

"No," said the Commander, "I'm going to land small-arm companies, skirmish across the island and corner them into an enclosure; and if we can't do that I am going to shoot them."

Next morning about sixty men fully equipped, and with a liberal amount of small-arm ammunition, landed on the island. They took their dinners, and were absent until late in the afternoon. Occasional bursts of rifle-firing were heard from the ship, but nothing much could be seen. After the landing party returned it transpired that they had achieved a moderate success, though at great sacrifice of energy and wind. The sheep had completely outwitted them, and they were eventually driven to killing them with rifles. One had been bayoneted in a valiant attempt to break through the line of hot and angry skirmishers.

However, the sheep were killed and eaten, and though by the time they arrived on board they seldom weighed more than 30 lbs., still they were a very excellent change and were much appreciated. The first skin was experimented with in the hopes of getting the wool off, but it was found to be such a laborious and difficult task that it was abandoned, and the skins were sent home with the wool attached. No comment was made by the home authorities.

Towards the end of the season a small Russian ship stranded on the coast in the vicinity, and the Canadian with other trawlers went to her assistance. He found the ship deserted and on fire, and clustered in the stern were three terrified sheep. He rescued the poor brutes, and two of the three were promptly despatched for the use of the two ships' companies of the trawlers.

The third sheep was carefully adorned with a large red rosette on her tail, and next day the Canadian could have been seen seated in a trawler's boat, with a sheep sitting by his side, making for the island on which the farm was situated.

The sheep was landed, and joined what was left of the general flock.

Shortly afterwards a general signal was made to all ships from the S.N.O., informing them that the sheep with the red tag on its tail was the personal property of the Canadian, and was on no account to be killed. It lived for several weeks, and eventually fell a victim to a combined attack by the whole of the Canadian's trawler crew, armed with every sort of weapon from a .303 rifle to a .380 revolver.

On board the cruiser it had been considered bad taste even to mention the word sheep for a long time, and the whole subject of the farm was taboo. It was felt by most of the people concerned that they had been made victims, owing to the stupidity of their messmates. On the few occasions when the subject was discussed, the Chief was always saying that if we had had cattle it would have been all right. The land-agent harped on the sheep-dog with irritating frequency. The Commander made bitter remarks on the inadequacy of his expert advisers and on the Clerk's wording as to the climbing capabilities of the sheep.

The Canadian had been sarcastically amused at the way the whole thing had been mismanaged, and made nasty comparison with the way things were done in the Colonies. The Paymaster, who by this time was gaunt and careworn, could not eat mutton at all on the rare occasions it appeared in the wardroom, and his feelings towards all who had been in any way mixed up in the farm were too bitter to permit of expression.

On the occasion of the death of the red-tailed sheep, which occurred late in the autumn, the last of the Admiralty sheep had also fallen a victim to a well-armed landing force ; and, though riddled with bullets, the Paymaster had been relieved to find that a small portion was still fit for human consumption. The general relief which was felt by all interested parties in the wardroom was so great that, after a glass or two of port, the subject was once more reopened.

The Commander gravely congratulated the Canadian on

his success as a stalker, and inquired whether his ancestors had been Border folk or not.

"I didn't steal it," said the Canadian. "I saved the poor brute from a terrible death in a burning ship, and we got it second shot. I turned the skin over to the butcher, Pay.," he added, turning to the Paymaster; "it may help to fill up some of the nasty hiatuses there must be in your farm accounts."

"Thanks," said the Paymaster, "it will certainly help me a little; but really I'm in despair as to how to account for these brutes. They weigh about 20 lbs. by the time they are killed or murdered, and half of it is not fit to eat."

"The only possible thing for you to do, Pay.," said the land-agent, "is to expend them, skins and all. I kept stores years ago when I was a navigator, and there were lots of ways of putting your accounts right. The Admiralty are very good about it as a rule—why, one fellow expended a gun eaten by rats, and nothing was said."

"Well, how do you suggest I should expend sheep?" said the Paymaster. "It sounds all right, but I've got to deal with a different department to the one you used to."

"I should put them down eaten by wolves," said the land-agent.

"Good idea," said the Chief. "Russia is full of wolves, you know, even in these days."

So wolves were decided upon.

HOW I STOOD FOR THE DREEP-DAILY BURGHS.

BY W. EDMONDSTOUNE AYTOUN.

[Maga, September 1847.]

CHAPTER I.

"My dear Dunshunner," said my friend Robert M'Corkindale as he entered my apartments one fine morning in June last, "do you happen to have seen the share-list? Things are looking in Liverpool as black as thunder. The bullion is all going out of the country, and the banks are refusing to discount."

Bob M'Corkindale might very safely have kept his information to himself. I was, to say the truth, most painfully aware of the facts which he unfeelingly obtruded upon my notice. Six weeks before, in the full confidence that the panic was subsiding, I had recklessly invested my whole capital in the shares of a certain railway company, which for the present shall be nameless; and each successive circular from my broker conveyed the doleful intelligence that the stock was going down to Erebus. Under these circumstances I certainly felt very far from being comfortable. I could not sell out except at a ruinous loss; and I could not well afford to hold on for any length of time, unless there was a reasonable prospect of a speedy amendment of the market. Let me confess it—I had of late come out rather too strong. When a man has made money easily, he is somewhat prone to launch into expense and to presume too largely upon his credit. I had been idiot enough to make my *debut* in the sporting world—had started a couple of horses upon the verdant turf of Paisley—and, as a matter of course, was remorselessly sold by my advisers. These and some other minor amusements had preyed deleteriously upon my purse. In fact, I had not the ready; and as every tradesman throughout Glasgow was quaking in his shoes at the panic, and inconveniently eager to realise, I began to feel the reverse of comfortable and was shy of showing myself in Buchanan Street. Several documents of a suspicious appearance—owing to the beastly practice of wafering, which is still adhered to by a certain class of correspondents—were lying upon my table at the moment when Bob entered. I could see that the villain comprehended their nature at a glance; but there was no use in attempting to mystify him. The Political Economist was, as I was well aware, in very much the same predicament as myself.

"To tell you the truth, M'Corkindale, I have not opened a share-list for a week. The faces of some of our friends are quite long enough to serve as a tolerable exponent of the market; and I saw Grabbie pass about five minutes ago with a yard of misery in his visage. But what's the news?"

"Everything that is bad! Total stoppage expected in a week, and the mills already put upon short time."

"You don't say so!"

"It is a fact. Dunshunner, this infernal tampering with the currency will be the ruin of every mother's son of us!"—and here Bob, in a fit of indignant enthusiasm, commenced a vivid harangue upon the principles of contraction and expansion, bullion, the metallic standard and the Bank reserves, which no doubt was extremely sound, but which I shall not recapitulate to the reader.

"That's all very well, Bob," said I—"very good in theory, but we should confine ourselves at present to practice.

The main question seems to me to be this: How are we to get out of our present fix? I presume you are not at present afflicted with a remarkable plethora of cash?"

"Every farthing I have in the world is locked up in a falling line."

"Any debts?"

"Not many; but quite enough to make me meditate a temporary retirement to Boulogne!"

"I believe you are better off than I am. I not only owe money, but am terribly bothered about some bills."

"That's awkward. Would it not be advisable to bolt?"

"I don't think so. You used to tell me, Bob, that credit was the next best thing to capital. Now, I don't despair of redeeming my capital yet, if I can only keep up my credit."

"Right, undoubtedly, as you generally are. Do you know, Dunshunner, you deserve credit for your notions on political economy. But how is that to be done? Everybody is realising; the banks won't discount; and when your bills become due, they will be, to a dead certainty, protested."

"Well—and what then?"

"*Squalor carceris*, et cetera."

"Hum—an unpleasant alternative, certainly. Come, Bob! put your wits to work. You used to be a capital hand for devices, and there must be some way or other of steering clear. Time is all we want."

"Ay, to be sure—time is the great thing. It would be very unpleasant to look out on the world through a grating during the summer months!"

"I perspire at the bare idea!"

"Not a soul in town—all your friends away in the Highlands boating, or fishing, or shooting grouse—and you pent up in a stifling apartment of eight feet square, with nobody to talk to save the turnkey and no prospect from the window except a deserted gooseberry stall!"

"Oh Bob, don't talk in that way! You make me perfectly miserable."

"And all this for a ministerial currency crotchet? 'Pon my soul, it's too bad! I wish those fellows in Parliament——"

"Well? Go on."

"By Jove! I've an idea at last!"

"You don't say so! My dear Bob—out with it!"

"Dunshunner, are you a man of pluck?"

"I should think I am."

"And ready to go the whole hog, if required?"

"The entire animal."

"Then I'll tell you what it is—the elections will be on immediately, and, by St Andrew, we'll put you up for Parliament!"

"Me!"

"You. Why not? There are hundreds of men there quite as hard up and not half so clever as yourself."

"And what good would that do me?"

"Don't you see? You need not care a farthing about your debts then, for the personal liberty of a member of the House of Commons is sacred. You can fire away right and left at the currency; and who knows, if you play your cards well, but you may get a comfortable place?"

"Well, you *are* a genius, Bob! But then, what sort of principles should I profess?"

"That is a matter which requires consideration. What are your own feelings on the subject?"

"Perfect indifference. I am pledged to no party and am free to exercise my independent judgment."

"Of course, of course! We shall take care to stick all that into the address; but you must positively come forward with some kind of tangible political views. The currency will do for one point, but as to the others I see a difficulty."

"Suppose I were to start as a Peelite?"

"Something may be said in favour of that view; but, on the whole, I should rather say not. That party may not look up for some little time, and then the currency is a stumbling-block in the way. No, Dunshunner, I do not think, upon my honour, that it would be wise for you to commit yourself in that quarter at the present moment."

"If it were possible, I should like to join the Conservatives. They must come uppermost soon, for they are men of pluck and ability. What do you say to that? It is an advantage to act with gentlemen."

"True; but at the same time, I see many objections. In a year or two these may disappear; but the press is at present against them, and I should like you to start with popularity on your side."

"Radical, then? What do you think of Annual Parliaments, Universal Suffrage, Vote by Ballot and separation of Church and State?"

"I am clear against that. These views are not popular with the electors, and even the mob would entertain a strong suspicion that you were humbugging them."

"What, then, on earth, am I to do?"

"I will tell you. Come out as a pure and transparent Whig. In the present position of parties, it is at least a safe course to pursue, and it is always the readiest step to the possession of the loaves and the fishes."

"Bob, I don't like the Whigs!"

"No more do I. They are a bad lot; but they are *in*, and that is everything. Yes, Augustus," continued Bob solemnly, "there is nothing else for it. You must start as a pure Whig, upon the Revolution principles of sixteen hundred and eighty-eight."

"It would be a great relief to my mind, Bob, if you would tell me what those principles really are?"

"I have not the remotest idea; but we have plenty time to look them up."

"Then, I suppose I must swallow the Dutchman and the Massacre of Glencoe?"

"Yes, and the Darien business into the bargain. These are the principles of your party, and of course you are bound to subscribe."

"Well! you know best; but I'd rather do anything else."

"Pooh! never fear; you and Whiggery will agree remarkably well. That matter, then, we may consider as settled. The next point to be thought of is the constituency."

"Ay, to be sure! what place am I to start for? I have got no interest, and if I had any, there are no nomination burghs in Scotland."

"Aren't there? That's all you know, my fine fellow! Hark ye, Dunshunner, more than half of the Scottish burghs are at this moment held by nominees!"

"You amaze me, Bob! The thing is impossible! The Reform Bill, that great charter of our liberties——"

"Bravo! There spoke the Whig! The Reform Bill, you think, put an end to nomination? It did nothing of the kind; it merely transferred it. Did you ever hear of such things as CLIQUES?"

"I have. But they are tremendously unpopular."

"Nevertheless, they hold the returning power. There is a Clique in almost every town throughout Scotland, which leads the electors as quietly, but as surely, as the blind man is conducted by his dog. These are modelled on the true Venetian principles of secrecy and terrorism. They control the whole constituency, put in the member, and in return monopolise the whole patronage of the place. If you have the Clique with you, you are almost sure of your election; if not, except in the larger towns, you have not a shadow of success. Now, what I want to impress upon you is this, that wherever you go, be sure that you communicate with the Clique."

"But how am I to find it out?"

"That is not always an easy matter, for nobody will acknowledge that he belongs to it. However, the thing is not impossible, and we shall certainly make the experiment. Come, then, I suppose you agree with me, that it is hopeless to attempt the larger towns?"

"Clearly: so far as I see, they are all provided already with candidates."

"And you may add, Cliques, Dunshunner. Well, then, let us search among the smaller places. What would you think of a dash at the Stirling District of Burghs?"

"Why, there are at least half a dozen candidates in the field."

"True, that would naturally lessen your chance. Depend upon it, some one of them has already found the key to the Clique. But there's the Dreepdaily District with nobody standing for it, except the Honourable Paul Pozzlethwaite; and I question whether he knows himself the nature or the texture of his politics. Really, Dunshunner, that's the very place for you; and if we look sharp after it, I bet the long odds that you will carry it in a canter."

"Do you really think so?"

"I do indeed; and the sooner you start the better. Let me see. I know Provost Binkie of Dreepdaily. He is a Railway bird, was an original Glenmutchkin shareholder, and fortunately sold out at a premium. He is a capital man to begin with, and I think will be favourable to you: besides, Dreepdaily is an old Whig burgh. I am not so sure of Kittleweem. It is a shade more respectable than Dreepdaily, and has always been rather Conservative. The third burgh, Drouthielaw, is a nest of Radicalism; but I think it may be won over, if we open the public-houses."

"But, about expenses, Bob—won't it be a serious matter?"

"Why, you must lay your account with spending some five or six hundred pounds upon the nail; and I advise you to sell stock to that amount at least. The remainder, should it cost you more, can stand over."

"Bob, five or six hundred pounds is a very serious sum!"

"Granted—but then look at the honour and the immunity you will enjoy. Recollect that yours is an awkward predicament. If you don't get into Parliament, I see nothing for it but a stoppage."

"That's true enough. Well—hang it, then, I will start!"

"There's a brave fellow! I should not in the least wonder to see you in the Cabinet yet. The sooner you set about preparing your address the better."

"What! without seeing Provost Binkie?"

"To be sure. What is the use of wading when you can plunge at once into deep water? Besides, let me tell you that you are a great deal more likely to get credit when it is understood that you are an actual candidate."

"There is something in that too. But I say, Bob—you really must help me with the address. I am a bad hand at these things, and shall never be able to tickle up the electors without your assistance."

"I'll do all I can. Just ring for a little brandy and water, and we'll set to work. I make no doubt that, between us, we can polish off a plausible placard."

Two hours afterwards, I forwarded, through the post-office, a missive, addressed to the editor of the *Dreepdaily Patriot,* with the following document enclosed. I am rather proud of it, as a manifesto of my political principles:—

"TO THE ELECTORS OF THE UNITED DISTRICT OF BURGHS OF DREEPDAILY, DROUTHIELAW AND KITTLEWEEM.

"GENTLEMEN,—I am induced, by a requisition, to which are appended the signatures of a large majority of your influential and patriotic body, to offer myself as a candidate for the high honour of your representation in the ensuing session of Parliament. Had I consulted my own inclination, I should have preferred the leisure of retirement and the pursuit of those studies so congenial to my taste, to the more stormy and agitating arena of politics. But a deep sense of public duty compels me to respond to your call.

"My views upon most subjects are so well known to many of you, that a lengthened explanation of them would probably be superfluous. Still, however, it may be right and proper for me to explain generally what they are.

"My principles are based upon the great and glorious Revolution settlement of 1688, which, by abolishing, or at least superseding, hereditary right, intrusted the guardianship of the Crown to an enlightened oligarchy, for the protection of an unparticipating people. That oligarchy is now most ably represented by her Majesty's present Ministers, to whom, unhesitatingly and uncompromisingly, except upon a very few matters, I give in my adhesion so long as they shall continue in office.

"Opposed to faction and an enemy to misrule, I am yet friendly to many changes of a sweeping and organic character. Without relaxing the ties which at present bind together Church and State in harmonious coalition and union, I would gradually confiscate the revenues of the one for the increasing necessities of the other. I never would become a party to an attack upon the House of Peers, so long as it remains subservient to the will of the Commons; nor would I alter or extend the franchise, except from cause shown, and the declared and universal wish of the non-electors.

"I highly approve of the policy which has been pursued towards Ireland, and of further concessions to a deep-rooted system of agitation. I approve of increased endowments to that much-neglected country; and I applaud that generosity which relieves it from all participation in the common burdens of the State. Such a line of policy cannot fail to elevate the moral tone, and to develop the internal resources of Ireland; and I never wish to see the day when the Scotsman and the Irishman may, in so far as taxation is concerned, be placed upon an equal footing. It appears to me a highly equitable adjustment that the savings of the first should be appropriated for the wants of the second.

"I am in favour of the centralising system, which, by drafting away the wealth and talent of the provinces, must augment the importance of London. I am strongly opposed to the maintenance of any local or Scottish institutions, which can merely serve to foster a spirit of decayed nationality; and I am of opinion that all boards and offices should be transferred to England, with the exception of those connected with the Dreepdaily district, which it is the bounden duty of the legislature to protect and preserve.

"I am a friend to the spread of education, but hostile to any system by means of which religion, especially Protestantism, may be taught.

"I am a supporter of free trade in all its branches. I cannot see any reason for the protection of native industry, and am ready to support any fundamental measure by means of which articles of foreign manufacture may be brought to compete in the home market with our own, without restriction and without reciprocity. It has always appeared to me that our imports are of far greater importance than our exports. I think that any lowering of price which may be the result of such a commercial policy, will be more than adequately compensated by a coercive measure which shall compel the artisan to augment the period of his labour. I am against any short hours' bill, and am of opinion that infant labour should be stringently and universally enforced.

"With regard to the currency, I feel that I may safely leave that matter in the hands of her Majesty's present Ministers, who have never shown any indisposition to oppose themselves to the popular wish.

"These, gentlemen, are my sentiments; and I think that, upon consideration, you will find them such as may entitle me to your cordial support. I need not say how highly I shall value the trust, or how zealously I shall endeavour to promote your local interests. These, probably, can be best advanced by a cautious regard to my own.

"On any other topics I shall be happy to give you the fullest and most satisfactory explanation. I shall merely add, as a summary of my opinions, that while ready on the one hand to coerce labour, so as to stimulate internal industry to the utmost, and to add largely to the amount of our population; I am, upon the other, a friend to the liberty of the subject, and to the promotion of such genial and sanatory measures as suit the tendency of our enlightened age, the diffusion of universal philanthropy and the spread of popular opinion. I remain, GENTLEMEN, with the deepest respect, your very obedient and humble servant,

"AUGUSTUS REGINALD DUNSHUNNER.

"ST MIRREN'S HOUSE,
"*June* 1847."

The editor of the *Dreepdaily Patriot*, wisely considering that this advertisement was the mere prelude to many more, was kind enough to dedicate a leading article to an exposition of my past services. I am not a vain man; so that I shall not here reprint the panegyric passed upon myself, or the ovation which my friend foresaw. Indeed, I am so far from vain, that I really began to think, while perusing the columns of the *Patriot*, that I had somewhat foolishly shut my eyes hitherto to the greatness of that talent and the brilliancy of those parts which were now proclaimed to the world. Yes! it was quite clear that I had hitherto been concealing my candle under a bushel—that I was cut out by nature for a legislator—and that I was the very man for the Dreepdaily electors. Under this conviction, I started upon my canvass, munimented with letters of introduction from M'Corkindale, who, much against his inclination, was compelled to remain at home.

CHAPTER II.

Dreepdaily is a beautiful little town, embosomed in an amphitheatre of hills which have such a winning way with the clouds that the summits are seldom visible. Dreepdaily, if situated in Arabia, would be deemed a paradise. All round it the vegetation is long, and lithe, and luxuriant; the trees keep their verdure late; and the rush of the nettles is amazing.

How the inhabitants contrive to live, is to me a matter of mystery. There is no particular trade or calling exercised in the place—no busy hum of artisans, or clanking of hammer or machinery. Round the suburbs, indeed, there are rows of mean-looking cottages, each with its strapping lass in the national short-gown at the door, from the interior of which resounds the boom of the weaver's shuttle. There is also one factory at a little distance; but when you reach the town itself, all is supereminently silent. In fine weather, crowds of urchins of both sexes are seen sunning themselves on the quaint-looking flights of steps by which the doors, usually on the second story, are approached; and as you survey the swarms of bare-legged and flaxen-haired infantry, you cannot help wondering in your heart what has become of the adult population. It is only towards evening that the seniors appear. Then you may find them either congregated on the bridge discussing politics and polemics, or lounging in the little square in affectionate vicinity to the public-house, or leaning over the windows in their shirt-sleeves in the tranquil enjoyment of a pipe. In short, the cares and the bustle of the world, even in this railroad age, seem to have fallen lightly on the pacific burghers of Dreepdaily. According to their own account, the town was once a peculiar favourite of royalty. It boasts of a charter from King David the First, and there is an old ruin in the neighbourhood which is said to have been a palace of that redoubted monarch.

It may be so, for there is no accounting for constitutions; but had I been King David, I certainly should have preferred a place where the younger branches of the family would have been less liable to the accident of catarrh.

Dreepdaily, in the olden time, was among the closest of all the burghs. Its representation had a fixed price, which was always rigorously exacted and punctually paid; and for half a year thereafter the corporation made merry thereon. The Reform Bill, therefore, was by no means popular in the council. A number of discontented Radicals and of small householders, who hitherto had been excluded from participation in the good things of the State, now got upon the roll and seemed determined for a time to carry matters with a high hand and to return a member of their own. And doubtless they would have succeeded, had not the same spirit been abroad in the sister burghs of Drouthielaw and Kittleweem; which, for some especial reason or other, known doubtless to Lord John Russell, but utterly unintelligible to the rest of mankind, were, though situated in different counties, associated with Dreepdaily in the return of their future member. Each of these places had a separate interest and started a separate man; so that, amidst this conflict of Liberalism, the old member for Dreepdaily, a Conservative, again slipped into his place. The consequence was, that the three burghs were involved in a desperate feud.

In those days there lived in Dreepdaily one Laurence Linklater, more commonly known by the name of Tod Lowrie, who exercised the respectable functions of a writer and a messenger-at-arms. Lowrie was a remarkably acute individual, of the Gilbert Glossin school, by no means scrupulous in his dealings, but of singular plausibility and courage. He had started in life as a Radical, but finding that that line did not pay well, he had prudently subsided into a Whig, and in that capacity had acquired a sort of local notoriety. He had contrived, moreover, to gain a tolerable footing in

Drouthielaw, and in the course of time became intimately acquainted with the circumstances of its inhabitants, and under the pretext of agency had contrived to worm the greater part of their title-deeds into his keeping.

It then occurred to Lowrie that, notwithstanding the discordant situation of the burghs, something might be done to effect a union under his own especial chieftainship. Not that he cared in his heart one farthing about the representation —Tyrian and Trojan were in reality the same to him—but he saw that the gain of these burghs would be of immense advantage to his party, and he determined that the advantage should be balanced by a corresponding profit to himself. Accordingly, he began quietly to look to the state of the neglected register; lodged objections to all claims given in by parties upon whom he could not depend; smuggled a sufficient number of his own clients and adherents upon the roll, and in the course of three years was able to intimate to an eminent Whig partisan that he, Laurence Linklater, held in his own hands the representation of the Dreepdaily Burghs, could turn the election either way he pleased, and was open to reasonable terms.

The result was, that Mr Linklater was promoted to a very lucrative county office, and moreover, that the whole patronage of the district was thereafter observed to flow through the Laurentian channel. Of course all those who could claim kith or kindred with Lowrie were provided for in the first instance; but there were stray crumbs still going, and in no one case could even a gaugership be obtained without the adhesion of an additional vote. Either the applicant must be ready to sell his independence, or, if that were done already, to pervert the politics of a relative. A Whig member was returned at the next election by an immense majority; and for some time Linklater reigned supreme in the government of Dreepdaily and Drouthielaw.

But death, which spares no governors, knocked at the

door of Linklater. A surfeit of mutton-pies, after the triumphant termination of a law-suit, threw the burghs into a state of anarchy. Lowrie was gathered unto his fathers, and there was no one to reign in his stead.

At least there was no apparent ruler. Everyone observed that the stream of patronage and of local jobbing still flowed on as copiously as before, but nobody could discover by what hands it was now directed. Suspicion fastened its eyes for some time upon Provost Binkie ; but the vehement denials of that gentleman, though not in themselves conclusive, at last gained credence from the fact that a situation which he had solicited from Government for his nephew was given to another person. Awful rumours began to circulate of the existence of a secret junta. Each man regarded his neighbour with intense suspicion and distrust, because, for anything he knew, that neighbour might be a member of the terrible tribunal by means of which all the affairs of the community were regulated, and a single ill-timed word might absolutely prove his ruin. Such, indeed, in one instance was the case. In an evil hour for himself, an independent town councillor thought fit to denounce the Clique as an unconstitutional and tyrannical body, and to table a motion for an inquiry as to its nature, members and proceedings. So strong was the general alarm that he could not even find a seconder. But the matter did not stop there. The rash meddler had drawn upon himself the vengeance of a remorseless foe. His business began to fall off ; rumours of the most malignant description were circulated regarding his character ; two of his relatives who held situations were dismissed without warning and without apology ; his credit was assailed in every quarter ; and in less than six months after he had made that most unfortunate harangue, the name of Thomas Gritt, baker in Dreepdaily, was seen to figure in the Gazette. So fell Gritt a martyr, and if anyone mourned for him, it was in secret and the profoundest awe.

Such was the political state of matters at the time when

I rode down the principal street of Dreepdaily. I need hardly say that I did not know a single soul in the burgh; in that respect, indeed, there was entire reciprocity on both sides, for the requisition referred to in my address was a felicitous fiction by M'Corkindale. I stopped before a substantial bluff-looking house, the lower part of which was occupied as a shop, and a scroll above informed me that the proprietor was Walter Binkie, grocer.

A short squat man, with an oleaginous face and remarkably bushy eyebrows, was in the act of weighing out a pennyworth of 'sweeties' to a little girl as I entered.

"Is the Provost of Dreepdaily within?" asked I.

"I'se warrant he's that," was the reply; "Hae, my dear, there's a sugar almond t'ye into the bargain. Gae your waus hame noo, and tell your mither that I've some grand new tea. Weel, sir, what was you wanting?"

"I wish particularly to speak to the Provost."

"Weel then, speak awa'," and he straightway squatted himself before his ledger.

"I beg your pardon, sir! Have I really the honour of addressing—"

"Walter Binkie, the Provost of this burgh. But if ye come on Council matters, ye're lang ahint the hour. I'm just steppin' up to denner, and I never do business after that."

"But perhaps you will allow me—"

"I will allow nae man, sir, to interrupt my leisure. If ye're wanting onything, gang to the Town-Clerk."

"Permit me one moment—my name is Dunshunner."

"Eh, what!" cried the Provost, bounding from his stool, "speak lower or the lad will hear ye. Are ye the gentleman that's stannin' for the burrows?"

"The same."

"Lord-sake! what for did ye no say that afore? Jims! I say, Jims! Look after the shop! Come this way, sir, up the stair, and take care ye dinna stumble on that toom cask o' saut."

I followed the Provost up a kind of corkscrew stair, until we emerged upon a landing-place in his own proper domicile. We entered the dining-room. It was showily furnished; with an enormous urn of paper roses in the grate, two stuffed parroquets upon the mantelpiece, a flamingo-coloured carpet, enormous worsted bell-pulls and a couple of portraits by some peripatetic follower of Vandyke, one of them representing the Provost in his civic costume, and the other bearing some likeness to a fat female in a turban, with a cairngorm brooch about the size of a platter on her breast, and no want of carmine on the space dedicated to the cheeks.

The Provost locked the door and then clapped his ear to the key-hole. He next approached the window, drew down the blinds so as effectually to prevent any opposite scrutiny and motioned me to a seat.

"And so ye're Mr Dunshunner?" said he. "Oh man, but I've been wearyin' to see you!"

"Indeed! you flatter me very much."

"Nae flattery, Mr Dunshunner—nane! I'm a plain honest man, that's a', and naebody can say that Wattie Binkie has blawn in their lug. And sae ye're comin' forrard for the burrows? It's a bauld thing, sir—a bauld thing, and a great honour ye seek. No that I think ye winna do honour to it, but it's a great trust for sae young a man; a heavy responsibility, as a body may say, to hang upon a callant's shouthers."

"I hope, Mr Binkie, that my future conduct may show that I can at least act up to my professions."

"Nae doubt, sir—I'm no misdoubtin' ye, and to say the truth ye profess weel. I've read yer address, sir, and I like yer principles—they're the stench auld Whig anes—keep a' we can to ourselves and haud a gudegrup. But wha's bringing ye forrard? Wha signed yer requisition? No the Kittleweem folk, I hope?—that wad be a sair thing against ye."

"Why, no—certainly not. The fact is, Mr Binkie, that I have not seen the requisition. Its contents were communicated by a third party, on whom I have the most perfect reliance; and as I understood there was some delicacy in the matter, I did not think it proper to insist upon a sight of the signatures."

The Provost gave a long whistle.

"I see it noo!" he said; "I see it! I ken't there was something gaun on forbye the common. Ye're a lucky man, Mr Dunshunner, and ye're election is as sure as won. Ye've been spoken to by them ye ken o'!"

"Upon my word, I do not understand—"

"Ay—ay! Ye're richt to be cautious. Weel I wat they are kittle cattle to ride the water on. But wha was't, sir—wha was't? Ye needna be feared of me. I ken how to keep a secret."

"Really, Mr Binkie, except through a third party, as I have told you already, I have had no communication with anyone."

"Weel—they *are* close—there's nae denyin' that. But ye surely maun hae some inkling o' the men—them that's ahint the screen, ye ken?"

"Indeed, I have not. But stay—if you allude to the Clique——"

"Wheest, sir, wheest!" cried the Provost, in an agitated tone of voice. "Gudesake, tak care what ye say—ye dinna ken wha may hear ye. Ye hae spoken a word that I havena heard this mony a day without shaking in my shoon. Aye speak ceevily o' the deil—ye dinna ken how weel ye may be acquaunt!"

"Surely, sir, there can be no harm in mentioning the——"

"No under that name, Mr Dunshunner—no under that name, and no here. I wadna ca' them that on the tap of Ben Nevis without a grue. Ay—and sae THEY are wi' ye, are they? Weel, they are a queer set!"

"You know the parties, then, Mr Binkie?"

"I ken nae mair aboot them than I ken whaur to find the caverns o' the east wind. Whether they are three, or thretty, or a hunder, surpasses my knowledge; but they hae got the secret o' the fern seed and walk about invisible. It is a'thegether a great mystery, but doubtless ye will obtain a glimpse. In the meantime, since ye come from that quarter, I am bound to obey."

"You are very kind, I am sure, Mr Binkie. May I ask, then, your opinion of matters as they stand at present?"

"Our present member, Mr Whistlerigg, will no stand again. He's got some place or ither up in London; and, my certie, he's worked weel for it! There's naebody else stannin' forbye that man Pozzlethwaite, and he disna verra weel ken what he is himsel'. If its a' richt yonder," continued the Provost, jerking his thumb over his left shoulder, "ye're as gude as elected."

As it would have been extremely impolitic for me under present circumstances to have disclaimed all connection with a body which exercised an influence so marked and decided, I allowed Provost Binkie to remain under the illusion that I was the chosen candidate of the Clique. In fact, I had made up my mind that I should become so at any cost, so soon as it vouchsafed to disclose itself and appear before my longing eyes. I therefore launched at once into practical details, in the discussion of which the Provost exhibited both shrewdness and goodwill. He professed his readiness at once to become chairman of my committee, drew out a list of the most influential persons in the burgh to whom I ought immediately apply, and gave me much information regarding the politics of the other places. From what he said, I gathered that, with the aid of the Clique, I was sure of Dreepdaily and Drouthielaw—as to the electors of Kittleweem, they were, in his opinion, "a wheen dirt," whom it would be useless to consult and hopeless to conciliate. I certainly had no previous idea that the bulk of the electors had so little to say in the choice of their own representative. When I ventured to hint at the remote possibility of a revolt, the Provost indignantly exclaimed—

"They daurna, sir—they daurna for the lives of them do it! Set them up indeed! Let me see ony man that wad venture to vote against the Town Council and the—and *them*, and I'll make a clean sweep of him out of Dreepdaily!"

Nothing, in short, could have been more satisfactory than this statement.

Whilst we were conversing together, I heard of a sudden a jingling in the next apartment, as if some very aged and decrepid harpsichord were being exorcised into the unusual effort of a tune. I glanced inquiringly to the door, but the Provost took no notice of my look. In a little time, however, there was a short preliminary cough, and a female voice of considerable compass took up the following strain. I remember the words not more from their singularity, than from the introduction to which they were the prelude:—

"I heard a wee bird singing clear,
In the tight, tight month o' June—
'What garr'd ye buy when stocks were high,
And sell when shares were doun?

'Gin ye hae play'd me fause, my luve,
In simmer 'mang the rain;
When siller's scant and scarce at Yule,
I'll pay ye back again!

'O bonny were the Midland Halves,
When credit was sae free!—
But wae betide the Southron loon
That sold they Halves to me!'"

I declare, upon the word of a Railway Director, that I was never more taken aback in my life. Attached as I have been from youth to the Scottish ballad poetry, I never yet had heard a ditty of this peculiar stamp, which struck me as a happy combination of tender fancy with the sterner realities of the Exchange. Provost Binkie smiled as he remarked my amazement.

"It's only my daughter Maggie, Mr Dunshunner," he said. "Puir thing! It's little she has here to amuse her, and sae she whiles writes thae kind o' sangs hersel'. She's weel up to the railroads; for ye ken I was an auld Glen-mutchkin holder."

"Indeed! Was that song Miss Binkie's own composition?" asked I, with considerable interest.

"Atweel it is that, and mair too. Maggie, haud your skirling!—ye're interrupting me and the gentleman."

"I beg, on no account, Mr Binkie, that I may be allowed to interfere with your daughter's amusement. Indeed, it is full time that I were betaking myself to the hotel, unless you will honour me so far as to introduce me to Miss Binkie."

"Deil a bit o' you gangs to the hotel to-night!" replied the hospitable Provost. "You bide where you are to denner and bed, and we'll hae a comfortable crack over matters in the evening. Maggie! come ben, lass, and speak to Mr Dunshunner."

Miss Binkie, who I am strongly of opinion was all the while conscious of the presence of a stranger, now entered from the adjoining room. She was really a pretty girl—tall, with lively sparkling eyes, and a profusion of dark hair, which she wore in the somewhat exploded shape of ringlets. I was not prepared for such an apparition, and I daresay stammered as I paid my compliments.

Margaret Binkie, however, had no sort of *mauvaise honte* about her. She had received her final polish in a Glasgow boarding-school, and did decided credit to the seminary in which the operation had been performed. At all events, she was the reverse of shy; for in less than a quarter of an hour we were rattling away as though we had been acquainted from childhood; and, to say the truth, I found myself getting into something like a strong flirtation. Old Binkie grinned a delighted smile, and went out to superintend the decanting of a bottle of port.

I need not, I think, expatiate upon the dinner which followed. The hotch-potch was unexceptionable, the salmon curdy, and the lamb roasted without a fault; and if the red-armed Hebe who attended was somewhat awkward in her motions, she was at least zealous to a degree. The Provost got into high feather, and kept plying me perpetually with wine. When the cloth was removed, he drank with all formality to my success ; and as Margaret Binkie, with a laugh, did due honour to the toast, I could not do less than indulge in a little flight of fancy as I proposed the ladies, and, in connection with them, the Flower of Dreepdaily—a sentiment which was acknowledged with a blush.

After Miss Binkie retired, the Provost grew more and more convivial. He would not enter into business, but regaled me with numerous anecdotes of his past exploits, and of the lives and conversation of his compatriots in the Town Council—some of whom appeared, from his description, to be very facetious individuals indeed. More particularly, he dwelt upon the good qualities and importance of a certain Mr Thomas Gills, better known to his friends and kinsfolk by the sobriquet of Toddy Tam, and recommended me by all means to cultivate the acquaintance of that personage. But however otherwise loquacious, nothing would persuade the Provost to launch out upon the subject of the Clique. He really seemed to entertain as profound a terror of that body as ever Huguenot did of the Inquisition, and he cut me short at last by ejaculating—

"Sae nae mair on't, Mr Dunshunner—sae nae mair on't! It's ill talking on thae things. Ye dinna ken what the Clique is, nor whaur it is. But this I ken, that they are everywhere, and a' aboot us ; they hear everything that passes in this house, and I whiles suspect that Mysie, the servant lass, is naething else than ane o' them in petticoats!"

More than this I could not elicit. After we had finished a considerable quantum of port, we adjourned to the drawing-room, and, tea over, Miss Binkie sang to me several of her own songs, whilst the Provost snored upon the sofa. Both the songs and the singer were clever, the situation was interesting, and, somehow or other, I found my fingers more than once in contact with Maggie's, as I turned over the leaves of the music.

At last the Provost rose, with a stertoracious grunt. I thought this might be the signal for retiring to rest; but such were not the habits of Dreepdaily. Salt herrings and finnan-haddocks were produced along with the hot water and accompaniments; and I presume it was rather late before my host conducted me to my chamber. If I dreamed at all that night, it must have been of Margaret Binkie.

CHAPTER III.

The next morning, whilst dressing, I heard a blithe voice carolling on the stair. It was the orison of Margaret Binkie as she descended to the breakfast-room. I listened and caught the following verses:—

> "O haud away frae me," she said,
> "I pray you let me be!
> Hae you the shares ye held, my lord,
> What time ye courted me?
>
> "'Tis woman's weird to luve and pine,
> And man's is to forget:
> Hold you the shares, Lord James," she said,
> "Or hae ye sold them yet?"
>
> "My York Extensions, bought at par,
> I sold at seven pund prem.—
> And, O my heart is sair to think
> I had nae mair of them!"

"That is really a remarkable girl!" thought I, as I stropped my razor. "Such genius, such animation and such a thorough knowledge of the market! She would make a splendid wife for a railway director."

"Come away, Mr Dunshunner," said the Provost, as I entered the parlour. "I hope ye are yaup, for ye have a lang day's wark before ye."

"I am sure it would be an agreeable one, sir, if accompanied with such sweet music as I heard this morning. Pardon me, Miss Binkie, but you really are a perfect Sappho."

"You are too good, I am sure, Mr Dunshunner. Will you take tea or coffee?"

"Maggie," said the Provost, "I maun put a stop to that skirling—it's well eneuch for the night, but the morning is the time for business. Mr Dunshunner, I've been thinking over this job of ours, and here is a bit listie of the maist influential persons in Dreepdaily, that you maun positeevely see this day. They wad be affronted if they kenned ye were here without calling on them. Noo, mark me—I dinna just say that ony o' them is the folk ye ken o', but it's no ava unlikely; sae ye maun even use yer ain discretion. Tak an auld man's word for it, and aye put your best fit foremost."

I acquiesced in the justice of the suggestion, although I was really unconscious which foot deserved the precedence. The Provost continued—

"Just ae word mair. Promising is a cheap thing, and ye needna be very sparing of it. If onybody speaks to ye about a gaugership, or a place in the Customs or the Post-office, just gie ye a bit wink, tak out your note-book and make a mark wi' the keelavine pen. It aye looks weel, and gangs as far as a downright promise. Deny or refuse naebody. Let them think that ye can do everything wi' the Ministry; and if there should happen to be a whaup in the rape, let them even find it out theirsells. Tell them that ye stand up for Dreepdaily, and its auld charter, and the Whig constitution, and liberal principles. Maist feck o' them disna ken what liberal principles is, but they like the word. I whiles think that liberal principles means saying muckle and doing naething, but you needna tell them that. The Whigs are lang-headed chiells, and they hae had the sense to claim a' the liberality for themsells, ever since the days o' the Reform Bill."

Such and suchlike were the valuable maxims which

Provost Binkie instilled into my mind during the progress of breakfast. I must say they made a strong impression upon me; and any candidate who may hereafter come forward for the representation of a Scottish burgh, on principles similar to my own, would do well to peruse and remember them.

At length I rose to go.

"Do I carry your good wishes along with me, Miss Binkie, on my canvass?"

"Most cordially, Mr Dunshunner; I shall be perfectly miserable until I learn your success. I can assure you of my support, and earnestly wish I was an elector."

"Enviable would be the Member of Parliament who could represent so charming a constituency!"

"Oh, Mr Dunshunner!"

Directed by the Provost's list, I set forth in search of my constituency. The first elector whose shop I entered was a draper of the name M'Auslan. I found him in the midst of his tartans.

"Mr M'Auslan, I presume?"

"Ay," was the curt response.

"Allow me to introduce myself, sir. My name is Dunshunner."

"Oh."

"You are probably aware, sir, that I am a candidate for the representation of these burghs?"

"Ay."

"I hope and trust, Mr M'Auslan, that my principles are such as meet with your approbation?"

"Maybe."

"I am a friend, sir, to civil and religious liberty—to Dreepdaily and its charter—to the old Whig constitution of 1688—and to the true interests of the people."

"Weel?"

"Confound the fellow!" thought I, "was there ever such an insensate block? I must bring him to the point at once. Mr M'Auslan," I continued in a very insinuating tone, "such being my sentiments, may I venture to calculate on your support?"

"There's twa words to that bargain," replied M'Auslan, departing from monosyllables.

"Any further explanation that may be required, I am sure will readily—"

"It's nae use."

"How?" said I, a good deal alarmed. "Is it possible you are already pledged?"

"No."

"Then what objection——"

"I made nane. I see ye dinna ken us here. The pear's no ripe yet."

"What pear?" asked I, astonished at this horticultural allusion.

"Hark ye," said M'Auslan, looking stealthily around him and for the first time exhibiting some marks of intelligence in his features—"Hark ye—hae ye seen Toddy Tam yet?"

"Mr Gills? Not yet. I am just going to wait upon him; but Provost Binkie has promised me his support."

"Wha cares for Provost Binkie! Gang to Toddy Tam."

Not one other word could I extract from the oracular M'Auslan; so, like a pilgrim, I turned my face towards Mecca and sallied forth in quest of this all-important personage. On my way, however, I entered the house of another voter, one Shanks, a member of the Town Council, from whom I received equally unsatisfactory replies. He, like M'Auslan, pointed steadily towards Toddy Tam. Now, who and what was the individual who, by the common consent of his townsmen, had earned so honourable an epithet?

Mr Thomas Gills had at one time been a clerk in the office of the departed Linklater. His function was not strictly legal, nor confined to the copying of processes: it had a broader and wider scope and was exercised in a more congenial manner. In short, Mr Gills was a kind of provider for the establishment. His duties were to hunt out business; which he achieved to a miracle by frequenting every possible public-house and wringing from them, amidst their cups, the stories of the wrongs of his compotators. Woe to the wight who sate down for an afternoon's conviviality with Toddy Tam! Before the mixing of the fourth tumbler, the ingenious Gills was sure to elicit some hardship or grievance for which benignant Themis could give redress; and rare, indeed, was the occurrence of the evening on which he did not capture some additional clients. He would even go the length of treating his victim, when inordinately shy, until the fatal mandate was given, and retraction utterly impossible.

Such decided business talents, of course, were not overlooked by the sagacious Laurence Linklater. Gills enjoyed a large salary, the greater moiety of which he consumed in alcoholic experiments; and shortly before the decease of his patron, he was promoted to the lucrative and easy office of some county registrarship. He now began to cultivate conviviality for its own especial sake. It was no longer dangerous to drink with him; for though, from habit, he continued to poke into grievances, he never, on the following morning, pursued the subject further. But what was most remarkable about Toddy Tam was his independence. He never truckled to dictation from any quarter; but, whilst Binkie and the rest were in fear and terror of the Clique, he openly defied that body and dared them to do their worst. He was the only man in Dreepdaily who ventured to say that Tom Gritt was right in the motion he had made; and he further added that if he, Thomas Gills, had been in the Town Council, the worthy and patriotic baker should not have wanted a seconder. This was considered a very daring speech, and one likely to draw down the vengeance of the unrelenting junta: but the thunder slept in the cloud, and Mr Gills enjoyed himself as before.

I found him in his back parlour, in company with a very rosy individual. Although it was not yet noon, a case-bottle and glasses were on the table, and the whole apartment stunk abominably with the fumes of whisky.

"Sit in, Mr Dunshunner, sit in!" said Toddy Tam, in a tone of great cordiality, after I had effected my introduction. "Ye'll no hae had your morning yet? Lass, bring in a clean glass for the gentleman."

"I hope you will excuse me, Mr Gills. I really never do—"

"Hoots—nonsense! Ye maun be neighbour-like, ye ken—we a' expect it at Dreepdaily." And so saying, Toddy Tam poured me out a full glass of spirits. I had as lieve have swallowed ink, but I was forced to constrain myself and bolt it.

"Ay, and so ye are coming round to us as a candidate, are ye? What d'ye think o' that, Mr Thamson—hae ye read Mr Dunshunner's address?"

The rubicund individual chuckled, leered and rose to go, but Toddy Tam laid a heavy hand upon his shoulder.

"Sit ye down man," he said; "I've naething to say to Mr Dunshunner that the hail warld may not hear, nor him to me neither, I hope."

"Certainly not," said I; "and I really should feel it as a great obligation if Mr Thomson would be kind enough to remain."

"That's right, lad!" shouted Gills. "Nae hole-and-corner work for me! A' fair and abune board, and the deil fly away with the Clique!"

Had Thomson been an ordinary man, he probably would have grown pale at this daring objurgation: as it was, he fidgeted in his chair and his face became a shade more crimson.

"Weel, now," continued Toddy Tam, "let us hear what Mr Dunshunner has got to say for himsel'. There's naething like hearing opinions before we put ony questions."

Thus adjured, I went through the whole of my political confession of faith, laying, of course, due stress upon the great and glorious Revolution of 1688, and my devotion to the cause of liberality. Toddy Tam and his companion heard me to the end without interruption.

"Gude—sae far gude, Mr Dunshunner," said Gills. "I see little to objeck to in your general principles; but for a' that I'm no going to pledge mysel' until I ken mair o' ye. I hope, sir, that ye're using nae underhand influence—that there has been nae communings with the Clique, a body that I perfeckly abominate? Dreepdaily shall never be made a pocket burrow, so long as Thomas Gills has any influence in it."

I assured Mr Gills, what was the naked truth, that I had no knowledge whatever of the Clique.

"Ye see, Mr Dunshunner," continued Toddy Tam, "we are a gey and independent sort of people here, and we want to be independently represented. My gude friend, Mr Thamson here, can tell you that I have had a sair fecht against secret influence, and I am amaist feared that some men like the Provost owe me a grudge for it. He's a pawkie loon, the Provost, and kens brawly how to play his cards."

"He's a' that!" ejaculated Thomson.

"But I dinna care a snuff of tobacco for the haill of the Town Council, or the Clique. Give me a man of perfeck independence, and I'll support him. I voted for the last member sair against my conscience, for he was put up by the Clique and never came near us: but I hope better things frae you, Mr Dunshunner, if you should happen to be returned. Mind, I don't say that I am going to support ye—I maun think about it: but if ye are a good man and a true, and no a nominee, I dare say that both my gude freend Thamson, and mysell, will no objeck to lend you a helping-hand."

This was all I could extract from Toddy Tam, and, though favourable, it was far from being satisfactory. There was a want, from some cause or another, of that cordial support which I had been led to anticipate ; and I almost felt half inclined to abandon the enterprise altogether. However, after having issued my address, this would have looked like cowardice. I therefore diligently prosecuted my canvass, and contrived, in the course of the day, to encounter a great portion of the electors. Very few pledged themselves. Some surly independents refused point-blank, alleging that they did not intend to vote at all : others declined to promise, until they should know how Toddy Tam and other magnates were likely to go. My only pledges were from the sworn retainers of the Provost.

"Well, Mr Dunshunner, what success?" cried Miss Margaret Binkie, as I returned rather jaded from my circuit. "I hope you have found all the Dreepdaily people quite favourable?"

"Why, no, Miss Binkie, not quite so much so as I could desire. Your townsmen here seem uncommonly slow in making up their minds to anything."

"Oh, that is always their way. I have heard Papa say that the same thing took place at last election, and that nobody declared for Mr Whistlerigg until the very evening before the nomination. So you see you must not lose heart."

"If my visit to Dreepdaily should have no other result, Miss Binkie, I shall always esteem it one of the most fortunate passages of my life, since it has given me the privilege of your acquaintance."

"Oh, Mr Dunshunner! How can you speak so? I am afraid you are a great flatterer!" replied Miss Binkie, pulling at the same time a sprig of geranium to pieces. "But you look tired—pray take a glass of wine."

"By no means, Miss Binkie. A word from you is a sufficient cordial. Happy geranium!" said I, picking up the petals.

Now I know very well that all this sort of thing is wrong, and that a man has no business to begin flirtations if he cannot see his way to the end of them. At the same time,

I hold the individual who dislikes flirtations to be a fool; and sometimes they are utterly irresistible.

"Now, Mr Dunshunner, I do beg you won't! Pray sit down on the sofa, for I am sure you are tired; and if you like to listen, I shall sing you a little ballad I have composed to-day."

"I would rather hear you sing than an angel," said I; "but pray do not debar me the privilege of standing by your side."

"Just as you please;" and Margaret began to rattle away on the harpsichord.

"O whaur hae ye been, Augustus, my son?
O whaur hae ye been, my winsome young man?
I hae been to the voters—Mither, mak my bed soon,
For I'm weary wi' canvassing, and fain wad lay me doun.

O whaur are your plumpers, Augustus, my son?
O whaur are your split votes, my winsome young man?
They are sold to the Clique—Mither, mak my bed soon,
For I'm weary wi' canvassing, and fain wad lay me doun.

O I fear ye are cheated, Augustus, my son,
O I fear ye are done for, my winsome young man!
'I hae been to my true love—'"

I could stand this no longer.

"Charming, cruel girl!" cried I, dropping on one knee—"why will you thus sport with my feelings? Where else should I seek for my true love but here?"

I do not know what might have been the sequel of the scene, had not my good genius, in the shape of Mysie the servant girl, at this moment burst into the apartment. Miss Binkie with great presence of mind dropped her handkerchief, which afforded me an excellent excuse for recovering my erect position.

Mysie was the bearer of a billet, addressed to myself, and marked 'private and particular.' I opened it and read as follows:—

"SIR,—Some of those who are well disposed towards you have arranged to meet this night, and are desirous of a private interview, at which full and mutual explanations may be given. It may be right to mention to you that the question of *the currency* will form the basis of any political arrangement; and it is expected that you will then be prepared to state explicitly your views with regard to *bullion.* Something *more than pledges* upon this subject will be required.

"As this meeting will be a strictly private one, the utmost secrecy must be observed. Be on the bridge at eleven o'clock this night, and you will be conducted to the appointed place. Do not fail, as you value your own interest.—Yours, &c. "SHELL OUT."

"Who brought this letter, Mysie?" said I, considerably flustered at its contents.

"A laddie. He said there was nae answer, and ran awa'."

"No bad news, I hope, Mr Dunshunner?" said Margaret timidly.

I looked at Miss Binkie. Her eye was still sparkling and her cheek flushed. She evidently was annoyed at the interruption, and expected a renewal of the conversation. But I felt that I had gone quite far enough, if not a little beyond the line of prudence. It is easy to make a declaration, but remarkably difficult to back out of it; and I began to think that, upon the whole, I had been a little too precipitate. On the plea, therefore, of business, I emerged into the open air; and, during a walk of a couple of miles, held secret communing with myself.

"Here you are again, Dunshunner, my fine fellow, putting your foot into it as usual! If it had not been for the arrival of the servant, you would have been an engaged man at this moment, and saddled with a father-in-law in the shape of a vender of molasses. Besides, it is my private opinion that you don't care sixpence about the girl. But it is the old story. This is the third time since Christmas that you have been on the point of committing matrimony; and if you don't look sharp after yourself, you will be sold an especial bargain! Now, frankly and fairly, do you not acknowledge yourself to be an idiot?"

I did. Men are generally very candid and open in their confessions to themselves; and the glaring absurdity of my conduct was admitted without any hesitation. I resolved to mend my ways accordingly, and to eschew for the future all *tête-à-têtes* with the too fascinating Maggie Binkie. That point disposed of, I returned to the mysterious missive. To say the truth, I did not much like it. Had these been the days of Burking, I should have entertained some slight personal apprehension; but as there was no such danger, I regarded it either as a hoax, or as some electioneering *ruse*, the purpose of which I could not fathom. However, as it is never wise to throw away any chance, I determined to keep the appointment; and, if a meeting really were held, to give the best explanations in my power to my correspondent, Mr Shell Out, and his friends. In this mood of mind I returned to the Provost's dwelling.

The dinner that day was not so joyous as before. Old Binkie questioned me very closely as to the result of my visits, and seemed chagrined that Toddy Tam had not been more definite in his promises of support.

"Ye maun hae Tam," said the Provost. "He disna like the Clique—I hope naebody's listening—nor the Clique him; but he stands weel wi' the Independents, and the Seceders will go wi' him to a man. We canna afford to lose Gills. I'll send ower for him and see if we canna talk him into reason. Haith, though, we'll need mair whisky, for Tam requires an unco deal of slockening!"

Tam, however, proved to be from home, and therefore the Provost and I were left to our accustomed duet. He complained grievously of my abstemiousness, which for divers reasons I thought it prudent to observe. An extra tumbler might again have made Miss Binkie a cherub in my eyes.

I am afraid that the young lady thought me a very changeable person. When the Provost fell asleep, she allowed the conversation to languish, until it reached that awful degree of pause which usually precedes the popping of the question. But this time I was on my guard, and held out with heroic stubbornness. I did not even launch out upon the subject of poetry, which Maggie rather cleverly introduced; for there is a decided affinity between the gay science and the tender passion, and it is difficult to preserve indifference when quoting from the "Loves of the Angels." I thought it safer to try metaphysics. It is not easy to extract an amorous avowal, even by implication, from a discourse upon the theory of consciousness; and I flatter myself that Kant, if he could have heard me that evening, would have returned home with some novel lights upon the subject. Miss Binkie seemed to think that I might have selected a more congenial theme; for she presently exhibited symptoms of pettishness, took up a book and applied herself diligently to the perusal of a popular treatise upon knitting.

Shortly afterwards, the Provost awoke, and his daughter took occasion to retire. She held out her hand to me with rather a reproachful look, but, though sorely tempted, I did not indulge in a squeeze.

"That's a fine lassie—a very fine lassie!" remarked the Provost, as he severed a Welsh rabbit into twain. "Ye are no a family man yet, Mr Dunshunner, and ye maybe canna comprehend what a comfort she has been to me. I'm auld now, and a thocht failing; but it is a great relief to me to ken that, when I am in my grave, Maggie winna be tocherless. I've laid up a braw nest-egg for her ower at the bank yonder."

I of course coincided in the praise of Miss Binkie, but showed so little curiosity as to the contents of the indicated egg that the Provost thought proper to enlighten me, and hinted at eight thousand pounds. It is my positive belief that the worthy man expected an immediate proposal: if so, he was pretty egregiously mistaken. I could not, however, afford, at this particular crisis, to offend him, and accordingly stuck to generals. As the hour of meeting was approaching, I thought it necessary to acquaint him with the message I had received, in order to account for my exit at so unseasonable a time.

"It's verra odd," said the Provost—"verra odd! A' Dreepdaily should be in their beds by this time, and I canna think there could be a meeting without me hearing of it. It's just the reverse o' constitutional to keep folk trailing aboot the toun at this time o' nicht, and the brig is a queer place for a tryst."

"You do not surely apprehend, Mr Binkie, that there is any danger?"

"No just that, but you'll no be the waur o' a stick. Ony gait, I'll send to Saunders Caup, the toun-officer, to be on the look-out. If ony body offers to harm ye, be sure ye cry out, and Saunders will be up in a crack. He's as stieve as steel, and an auld Waterloo man."

As a considerable number of years has elapsed since the last great European conflict, I confess that my confidence in the capabilities of Mr Caup, as an ally, was inferior to my belief in his prowess. I therefore declined the proposal, but accepted the weapon; and, after a valedictory tumbler with my host, emerged into the darkened street.

CHAPTER IV.

Francis Osbaldistone, when he encountered the famous Rob Roy by night, was in all probability, notwithstanding Sir Walter's assertion to the contrary, in a very tolerable state of trepidation. At least I know that I was, as I neared the bridge of Dreepdaily. It was a nasty night of wind and rain, and not a soul was stirring in the street—the surface of which did little credit to the industry of the paving department, judging from the number of dubs in which I found involuntary accommodation. As I floundered along through the mire, I breathed anything but benedictions on the mysterious Shell Out who was the cause of my midnight wandering.

Just as I reached the bridge, beneath which the river was roaring rather uncomfortably, a ragged-looking figure started out from an entry. A solitary lamp, suspended from above, gave me a full view of this personage, who resembled an animated scarecrow.

He stared me full in the face, and then muttered, with a wink and a leer—

"Was ye seekin' for ony body the nicht? Eh wow, man, but it's cauld!"

"Who may you be, my friend?" said I, edging off from my unpromising acquaintance.

"Wha may I be?" replied the other: "that's a gude ane! Gosh, d'ye no ken me? Au'm Geordie Dowie, the town bauldy, that's as weel kent as the Provost hissell!"

To say the truth, Geordie was a very truculent-looking character to be an innocent. However, imbeciles of this description are usually harmless.

"And what have you got to say to me, Geordie?"

> "If ye're the man I think ye are,
> And ye're name begins wi' a D,
> Just tak ye tae yer soople shanks,
> And tramp alang wi' me,"

quavered the idiot, who, like many others, had a natural turn for poetry.

"And where are we going to, Geordie, my man?" said I in a soothing voice.

"Ye'll find that when we get there," replied the bauldy.

> "Hey the bonnie gill-stoup!
> Ho the bonnie gill-stoup!
> Gie me walth o' barley bree,
> And leeze me on the gill-stoup!"

"But you can at least tell me who sent you here, Geordie?" said I, anxious for further information before intrusting myself to such erratic guidance.

He of the gill-stoups lifted up his voice and sang—

"Cam' ye by Tweedside,
Or cam' ye by Flodden?
Met ye the deil
On the braes o' Culloden?

"Three imps o' darkness
I saw in a neuk,
Riving the red-coats,
And roasting the Deuk.

"Quo' ane o' them—'Geordie,
Gae down to the brig,
I'm yaup for my supper,
And fetch us a Whig.'"

"Ha! ha! ha! Hoo d'ye like that, my man? Queer freends ye've gotten noo, and ye'll need a lang spoon to sup kail wi' them. But come awa'. I canna stand here the hail nicht listening to your havers."

Although the hint conveyed by Mr Dowie's ingenious verses was rather of an alarming nature, I made up my mind at once to run all risks and follow him. Geordie strode on, selecting apparently the most unfrequented lanes, and making, as I anxiously observed, for a remote part of the suburbs. Nor was his voice silent during our progress, for he kept regaling me with a series of snatches, which, being for the most part of a supernatural and diabolical tendency, did not much contribute towards the restoration of my equanimity. At length he paused before a small house, the access to which was by a downward flight of steps.

"Ay—this is the place!" he muttered. "I ken it weel. It's no just bad the whusky that they sell, but they needna put sae muckle water intil 't."

So saying, he descended the stair. I followed. There was no light in the passage, but the idiot went forward, stumbling and groping in the dark. I saw a bright ray streaming through a crevice, and three distinct knocks were given.

"Come in, whaever ye are!" said a bluff voice; and I entered a low apartment, in which the candles looked yellow through a fog of tobacco-smoke. Three men were seated at a deal table, covered with the implements of national conviviality; and to my intense astonishment none of the three were strangers to me. I at once recognised the features of the taciturn M'Auslan, the wary Shanks and the independent Mr Thomas Gills.

"There's the man ye wanted," said Geordie Dowie, slapping me familiarly on the shoulder—"Whaur's the dram ye promised me?"

> **"In Campbelltown my luve was born,**
> **Her mither in Glen Turrit!**
> **But Ferintosh is the place for me,**
> **For that's the strangest speerit!"**

"Haud yer clavering tongue, ye common village!" said Toddy Tam. "Wad ye bring in the neebourhood on us? M'Auslan, gie the body his dram, and then see him out of the door. We manna be interfered wi' in our cracks."

M'Auslan obeyed. A large glass of alcohol was given to my guide, who swallowed it with a sigh of pleasure.

"Eh, man! that's gude and strang! It's no ilka whusky that'll mak Geordie Dowie pech. Fair fa' yer face, my bonny M'Auslan! could you no just gi'e us anither?"

"Pit him out!" said the remorseless Gills. "It's just extraordinar how fond the creature is o' drink!" and Geordie was forcibly ejected, after an ineffectual clutch at the bottle.

"Sit ye down, Mr Dunshunner," said Toddy Tam, addressing himself to me; "sit ye down and mix yoursel' a tumbler. I daresay now ye was a little surprised at the note ye got this morning, eh?"

"Why, certainly, Mr Gills, I did not anticipate the pleasure——"

"Ay, I kenned ye wad wonder at it. But ilka place has its ain way o' doing business, and this is ours—quiet and cosy, ye see. Ise warrant, too, ye thocht M'Auslan a queer ane because he wadna speak out?"

I laughed dubiously towards M'Auslan, who responded with the austerest of possible grins.

"And Shanks, too," continued Toddy Tam; "Shanks wadna speak out neither. They're auld-farrant hands baith o' them, Mr Dunshunner, and they didna like to promise ony thing without me. We three aye gang thegither."

"I hope, then, Mr Gills, that I may calculate upon your support and that of your friends. My views upon the currency——"

"Ay! that's speaking out at ance. Hoo muckle?"

"Ay! hoo muckle?" interposed M'Auslan, with a glistening eye.

"I really do not understand you, gentlemen."

"Troth, then, ye're slow at the uptak," remarked Gills, after a meaning pause. "I see we maun be clear and conceese. Hark ye, Mr Dunshunner—wha do ye think we are?"

"Three most respectable gentlemen, for whom I have the highest possible regard."

"Hoots!—nonsense! D'ye no ken?"

"No," was my puzzled response.

"Weel, then," said Toddy Tam, advancing his lips to my ear and pouring forth an alcoholic whisper—"we three can do mair than ye think o'—It's huz that is THE CLIQUE!"

I recoiled in perfect amazement and gazed in succession upon the countenances of the three compatriots. Yes—there could be no doubt about it—I was in the presence of the tremendous junta of Dreepdaily; the veil of Isis had been lifted up, and the principal figure upon the pedestal was the magnanimous and independent Gills. Always a worshipper of genius, I began to entertain a feeling little short of veneration towards Toddy Tam. The admirable manner in which he had contrived to conceal his real power from the public—his assumed indignation and horror of the Clique—and his hold over all classes of the electors, demonstrated him at once to be a consummate master of the political art. Machiavelli could not have devised a subtler stratagem than Gills.

"That's just the plain truth o' the matter," observed Shanks, who had hitherto remained silent. "We three is the Clique, and we hae the representation o' the burrow in our hands. Now, to speak to the point, if we put our names down on your Committee, you carry the election, and we're ready to come to an understanding upon fair and liberal grounds."

And we did come to an understanding upon grounds which might be justly characterised as fair on the one side and certainly liberal on the other. There was of course some little discussion as to the lengths I was expected to go in financial matters ; and it was even hinted that, with regard to bullion, the Honourable Mr Pozzlethwaite might possibly entertain as enlarged views as myself. However, we fortunately succeeded in adjusting all our differences. I not only promised to give the weight of my name to a bill, but exhibited, upon the spot, a draft which met with the cordial approbation of my friends, and which indeed was so satisfactory that they did not offer to return it.

"That's a' right then," said Toddy Tam, inserting the last-mentioned document in a greasy pocket-book. "Our names go down on your Committy, and the election is as gude as won!"

An eldritch laugh at a little window, which communicated with the street, at this moment electrified the speaker. There was a glimpse of a human face seen through the dingy pane.

A loud oath burst from the lips of Toddy Thomas.

"Some deevil has been watching us!" he cried. "Rin, M'Auslan, rin for your life, and grip him afore he can turn the corner! I wad not for a thousand pund that this nicht's wark were to get wind!"

M'Auslan rushed, as desired; but all his efforts were ineffectual. The fugitive, whoever he was, had very prudently dived into the darkness, and the draper returned without his victim.

"What is to be done?" said I. "It strikes me, gentlemen, that this may turn out to be a very unpleasant business."

"Nae fears—nae fears!" said Toddy Tam, looking, however, the reverse of comfortable. "It will hae been some callant trying to fley us, that's a'. But, mind ye—no a word o' this to ony living human being, and aboon a' to Provost Binkie. I've keepit him for four years in the dark, and it never wad do to show the cat the road to the kirn!"

I acquiesced in the precautionary arrangement, and we parted; Toddy Tam and his friends having, by this time, disposed of all the surplus fluid. It was very late before I reached the Provost's dwelling.

I suppose that next morning I had overslept myself; for, when I awoke, I heard Miss Binkie in full operation at the piano. This time, however, she was not singing alone, for a male voice was audible in conjunction with hers.

"It would be an amazing consolation to me if somebody would carry off that girl!" thought I, as I proceeded with my toilet. "I made a deuced fool of myself to her yesterday; and, to say the truth, I don't very well know how to look her in the face!"

However, there was no help for it, so I proceeded downstairs. The first individual I recognised in the breakfast parlour was M'Corkindale. He was engaged in singing, along with Miss Binkie, some idiotical catch about a couple of albino mice.

"Bob!" cried I, "my dear Bob, I am delighted to see you—what on earth has brought you here?"

"A gig and a foundered mare," replied the matter-of-fact M'Corkindale. "The fact is, that I was anxious to hear about your canvass; and, as there was nothing to do in Glasgow—by the way, Dunshunner, the banks have put on the screw again—I resolved to satisfy my own curiosity in person. I arrived this morning, and Miss Binkie has been kind enough to ask me to stay breakfast."

"I am sure both papa and I are always happy to see Mr M'Corkindale," said Margaret impressively.

"I am afraid," said I, "that I have interrupted your music: I did not know, M'Corkindale, that you were so eminent a performer."

"I hold with Aristotle," replied Bob modestly, "that music and political economy are at the head of all the sciences. But it is very seldom that one can meet with so accomplished a partner as Miss Binkie."

"Oh, ho," thought I. But here the entrance of the Provost diverted the conversation, and we all sat down to breakfast. Old Binkie was evidently dying to know the result of my interview on the previous evening, but I was determined to keep him in the dark. Bob fed like an ogre, and made prodigious efforts to be polite.

After breakfast, on the pretext of business we went out for a walk. The economist lighted his cigar.

"Snug quarters these, Dunshunner, at the Provost's."

"Very. But, Bob, things are looking rather well here. I had a negotiation last night which has as good as settled the business."

"I am very glad to hear it.—Nice girl, Miss Binkie; very pretty eyes, and a good foot and ankle."

"An unexceptionable instep. What do you think!—I have actually discovered the Clique at last."

"You don't say so! Do you think old Binkie has saved money?"

"I am sure he has. I look upon Dreepdaily as pretty safe

now; and I propose going over this afternoon to Drouthielaw. What would you recommend?"

"I think you are quite right; but somebody should stay here to look after your interests. There is no depending upon these fellows. I'll tell you what—while you are at Drouthielaw I shall remain here and occupy your quarters. The Committee will require some man of business to drill them in, and I don't care if I spare you the time."

I highly applauded this generous resolution; at the same time I was not altogether blind to the motive. Bob, though an excellent fellow in the main, did not usually sacrifice himself to his friends; and I began to suspect that Maggie Binkie—with whom, by the way, he had some previous acquaintance—was somehow or other connected with his enthusiasm. As matters stood, I of course entertained no objection: on the contrary, I thought it no breach of confidence to repeat the history of the nest-egg.

Bob pricked up his ears.

"Indeed!" said he; "that is a fair figure as times go; and to judge from appearances, the stock-in-trade must be valuable."

"Cargoes of sugar," said I, "oceans of rum, and no end whatever of molasses!"

"A very creditable chairman, indeed, for your Committee, Dunshunner," replied Bob. "Then I presume you agree that I should stay here whilst you prosecute your canvass?"

I assented, and we returned to the house. In the course of the forenoon the list of my Committee was published, and, to the great joy of the Provost, the names of Thomas Gill, Alexander M'Auslan and Simon Shanks appeared. He could not, for the life of him, understand how they had all come forward so readily. A meeting of my friends was afterwards held, at which I delivered a short harangue upon the constitution of 1688, which seemed to give general satisfaction; and before I left the room, I had the pleasure of seeing the Committee organised, with Bob officiating as secretary. It was the opinion of everyone that Pozzlethwaite had not a chance. I then partook of a light luncheon, and after bidding farewell to Miss Binkie, who, on the whole, seemed to take matters very coolly, I drove off for Drouthielaw. I need not relate my adventures in that respectable burgh. They were devoid of anything like interest, and not quite so satisfactory in their result as I could have wished. However, the name of Gills was known even at that distance, and his views had considerable weight with some of the religious denominations. So far as I was concerned, I had no sinecure of it. It cost me three nights' hard drinking to conciliate the leaders of the Anabaptists, and at least three more before the chiefs of the Antinomians would surrender. As to the Old Light gentry, I gave them up in despair, for I could not hope to have survived the consequences of so serious a conflict.

CHAPTER V.

Parliament was at length dissolved; the new writs were issued and the day of nomination fixed for the Dreepdaily burghs. For a time it appeared to myself, and indeed to almost everyone else, that my return was perfectly secure. Provost Binkie was in great glory, and the faces of the unknown Clique were positively radiant with satisfaction. But a storm was brewing in another quarter, upon which we had not previously calculated.

The Honourable Mr Pozzlethwaite, my opponent, had fixed his headquarters in Drouthielaw, and to all appearance was making very little progress in Dreepdaily. Indeed, in no sense of the word could Pozzlethwaite be said to be popular. He was a middle-aged man, as blind as a bat, and, in order to cure the defect, he ornamented his visage with an immense pair of green spectacles, which, it may be easily conceived, did not add to the beauty of his appearance. In speech he was slow and verbose, in manner awkward, in matter almost wholly unintelligible. He professed principles which he said were precisely the same as those advocated by the late Jeremy Bentham; and certainly, if he was correct in this, I do not regret that my parents omitted to bring me up at the feet of the utilitarian Gamaliel. In short, Paul was prosy to a degree, had not an atom of animation in his whole composition and could no more have carried a crowd along with him than he could have supported Atlas upon his shoulders. A portion, however, of philosophic weavers, and a certain section of the Seceders, had declared in his favour; and, moreover, it was just possible that he might gain the suffrages of some of the Conservatives. Kittleweem, the Tory burgh, had hitherto preserved the appearance of strict neutrality. I had attempted to address the electors of that place, but I found that the hatred of Dreepdaily and of its Clique was more powerful than my eloquence; and, somehow or other, the benighted savages did not comprehend the merits of the Revolution Settlement of 1688, and were as violently national as the Celtic race before the invention of trews. Kittleweem had equipped half a regiment for Prince Charles in the Forty-five, and still piqued itself on its staunch Episcopacy. A Whig, therefore, could hardly expect to be popular in such a den of prejudice. By the advice of M'Corkindale, I abstained from any further efforts which might possibly have tended to exasperate the electors, and left Kittleweem to itself, in the hope that it would maintain an armed neutrality.

And so it probably might have done, but for an unexpected occurrence. Two days before the nomination, a new candidate appeared on the field. Sholto Douglas was the representative of one of the oldest branches of his distinguished name, and the race to which he more immediately belonged had ever been foremost in the ranks of Scottish chivalry and patriotism. In fact, no family had suffered more from their attachment to the cause of legitimacy than the Douglases of Inveriachan. Forfeiture after forfeiture had cut down their broad lands to a narrow estate, and but for an unexpected Indian legacy, the present heir would have been marching as a subaltern in a foot regiment. But a large importation of rupees had infused new life and spirit into the bosom of Sholto Douglas. Young, eager and enthusiastic, he determined to rescue himself from obscurity; and the present state of the Dreepdaily burghs appeared to offer a most tempting opportunity. Douglas was, of course, Conservative to the backbone; but, more than that, he openly proclaimed himself a friend of the people and a supporter of the rights of labour.

"Confound the fellow!" said Bob M'Corkindale to me, the morning after Sholto's address had been placarded through the burghs, "who would have thought of an attack of this kind from such a quarter? Have you seen his manifesto, Dunshunner?"

"Yes—here it is in the *Patriot*. The editor, however, gives him it soundly in the leading article. I like his dogmatic style and wholesale denunciation of the Tories."

"I'll tell you what it is, though—I look upon this as anything but a joke. Douglas is evidently not a man to stand upon old aristocratic pretensions. He has got the right sow by the ear this time, and, had he started a little earlier, might have roused the national spirit to a very unpleasant pitch. You observe what he says about Scotland, the neglect of her local interests, and the manner in which she has been treated, with reference to Ireland?"

"I do. And you will be pleased to recollect that but for yourself, something of the same kind would have appeared in my address."

"If you mean that as a reproach, Dunshunner, you are wrong. How was it possible to have started you as a Whig upon patriotic principles?"

"Well—that's true enough. At the same time, I cannot help wishing that we had said a word or two about the interests to the north of the Tweed."

"What is done cannot be undone. We must now stick by the Revolution settlement."

"Do you know, Bob, I think we have given them quite enough of that same settlement already. Those fellows at Kittleweem laughed in my face the last time that I talked about it, and I am rather afraid that it won't go down on the hustings."

"Try the sanitary condition of the towns, then, and universal conciliation to Ireland," replied the Economist. "I have given orders to hire two hundred Paddies, who have come over for the harvest, at a shilling a head, and of course you may depend upon their voices, and also their shillelahs, if needful. I think we should have a row. It would be a great matter to make Douglas unpopular; and, with a movement of my little finger, I could turn out a whole legion of navigators."

"No, Bob, you had better not. It is just possible they might make a mistake, and shy brickbats at the wrong candidate. It will be safer, I think, to leave the mob to itself: at the same time, we shall not be the worse for the Tipperary demonstration. And how looks the canvass?"

"Tolerably well, but not perfectly secure. The Clique has done its very best, but at the same time there is undeniably a growing feeling against it. Many people grumble about its dominion, and are fools enough to say that they have a right to think for themselves."

"Could you not circulate a report that Pozzlethwaite is the man of the Clique?"

"The idea is ingenious, but I fear it would hardly work. Dreepdaily is well known to be the headquarters of the confederation, and the name of Provost Binkie is inseparably connected with it."

"By the way, M'Corkindale, it struck me that you looked rather sweet upon Miss Binkie last evening."

"I did. In fact I popped the question," replied Robert calmly.

"Indeed! Were you accepted?"

"Conditionally. If we gain the election, she becomes Mrs M'Corkindale—if we lose, I suppose I shall have to return to Glasgow in a state of celibacy."

"A curious contract, certainly! Well, Bob, since your success is involved in mine, we must fight a desperate battle."

"I wish, though, that Mr Sholto Douglas had been kind enough to keep out of the way," observed M'Corkindale.

The morning of the day appointed for the nomination dawned upon the people of Dreepdaily with more than usual splendour. For once, there was no mist upon the surrounding hills, and the sky was clear as sapphire. I rose early to study my speech, which had received the finishing touches from M'Corkindale on the evening before; and I flatter myself it was as pretty a piece of Whig rhetoric as ever was spouted from a hustings. Toddy Tam, indeed, had objected, upon seeing a draft, that "there was nae banes intil't;" but the political economist was considered by the Committee a superior authority on such subjects to Gills. After having carefully conned it over, I went downstairs, where the whole party were already assembled. A large blue-and-yellow flag, with the inscription, 'DUNSHUNNER AND THE GOOD CAUSE!' was hung out from the window, to the intense delight of a gang of urchins, who testified to the popularity of the candidate by ceaseless vociferation to 'pour out.' The wall opposite, however, bore some memoranda of an opposite tendency, for I could see some large placards, newly pasted up, on which the words, 'ELECTORS OF DREEPDAILY! YOU ARE SOLD BY THE CLIQUE!' were conspicuous in enormous capitals. I heard, too, something like a ballad chanted, in which my name seemed to be coupled, irreverently, with that of the independent Gills.

Provost Binkie—who, in common with the rest of the company, wore upon his bosom an enormous blue-and-buff cockade, prepared by the fair hands of his daughter—saluted me with great cordiality. I ought to observe that the Provost had been kept as much as possible in the dark regarding the actual results of the canvass. He was to propose me, and it was thought that his nerves would be more steady if he came forward under the positive conviction of success.

"This is a great day, Mr Dunshunner—a grand day for Dreepdaily," he said. "A day, if I may sae speak, o' triumph and rejoicing! The news o' this will run frae one end o' the land to the ither—for the een o' a' Scotland is fixed on Dreepdaily, and the stench auld Whig principles is sure to prevail, even like a mighty river that rins down in spate to the sea!"

I justly concluded that this figure of speech formed part of the address to the electors which for the two last days had been simmering in the brain of the worthy magistrate, along with the fumes of the potations he had imbibed, as incentives to the extraordinary effort. Of course I took care to appear to participate in his enthusiasm. My mind, however, was very far from being thoroughly at ease.

As twelve o'clock, which was the hour of nomination, drew near, there was a great muster at my committee-room. The band of the Independent Teetotallers, who to a man were in my interest, was in attendance. They had been well primed with ginger cordial, and were obstreperous to a gratifying degree.

Toddy Tam came up to me with a face of the colour of carnation.

"I think it richt to tell ye, Mr Dunshunner, that there will be a bit o' a bleeze ower yonder at the hustings. The Kittleweem folk hae come through in squads, and Lord Hartside's tenantry have marched in a body, wi' Sholto Douglas's colours flying."

"And the Drouthielaw fellows—what has become of them?"

"Od, they're no wi' us either—they're just savage at the Clique! Gudesake, Mr Dunshunner, tak' care, and dinna say a word aboot huz. I intend mysel' to denounce the body, and maybe that will do us gude."

I highly approved of Mr Gills' determination, and as the time had now come, we formed in column and marched towards the hustings with the teetotal band in front, playing a very lugubrious imitation of "Glorious Apollo."

The other candidates had already taken their places. The moment I was visible to the audience, I was assailed by a volley of yells, among which cries of "Doun wi' the Clique!"—"Wha bought them?"—"Nae nominee!"—"We've had eneuch o' the Whigs!" et cetera, were distinctly audible. This was not at all the kind of reception I had bargained for; however, there was nothing for it but to put on a smiling face, and I reciprocated courtesies as well as I could with both of my honourable opponents.

During the reading of the writ and the Bribery Act, there was a deal of joking, which I presume was intended to be good-humoured. At the same time there could be no doubt that it was distinctly personal. I heard my name associated with epithets of anything but an endearing description, and, to say the truth, if choice had been granted, I would far rather have been at Jericho than in the front of the hustings at Dreepdaily. A man must be, indeed, intrepid, and conscious of a good cause, who can oppose himself without blenching to the objurgation of an excited mob.

The Honourable Paul Pozzlethwaite, on account of his having been the earliest candidate in the field, was first proposed by a town-councillor of Drouthielaw. This part of the ceremony appeared to excite but little interest, the hooting and cheering being pretty equally distributed.

It was now our turn.

"Gang forrard, Provost, and be sure ye speak oot!" said Toddy Tam; and Mr Binkie advanced accordingly.

Thereupon such a row commenced as I never had witnessed before. Yelling is a faint word to express the sound of that storm of extraordinary wrath which descended upon the head of the devoted Provost. "Clique! Clique!" resounded on every side, and myriads of eyes, ferocious as those of the wild cat, were bent scowlingly on my worthy proposer. In vain did he gesticulate—in vain implore. The voice of Demosthenes—nay, the deep bass of Stentor himself—could not have been heard amidst that infernal uproar; so that, after working his arms for a time like the limbs of a telegraph, and exerting himself until he became absolutely swart in the face, Binkie was fain to give it up, and retired amidst a whirlwind of abuse.

"May the deil fly awa' wi' the hail pack o' them!" said he, almost blubbering with excitement and indignation. "Wha wad ever hae thocht to have seen the like o' this? and huz, too, that gied them the Reform Bill! Try your hand at them, Tam, for my heart's amaist broken!"

The bluff independent character of Mr Gills, and his reputed purity from all taint of the Clique, operated considerably in his favour. He advanced amidst general cheering and cries of "Noo for Toddy Tam!" "Let's hear Mr Gills!" and the like; and as he tossed his hat aside and clenched his brawny fist, he really looked the incarnation of a sturdy and independent elector. His style, too, was decidedly popular—

"Listen tae me!" he said, "and let the brawlin', braggin', bletherin' idiwits frae Drouthielaw haud their lang clavering tongues, and no keep rowtin' like a herd o' senseless nowte! (Great cheering from Dreepdaily and Kittleweem—considerable disapprobation from Drouthielaw.) I ken them weel, the auld haverils! (cheers.) But you, my freends, that I have dwalt wi' for twenty years, is it possible that ye can believe for one moment that I wad submit to be dictated to by a Clique? (Cries of "No! no!" "It's no you, Tam!" and confusion.) No me? I dinna thank ye for that! Wull ony man daur to say to my face, that I ever colleagued wi' a pack that wad buy and seel the haill of us as readily as ye can deal wi' sheep's heads in the public market?

(Laughter.) Div ye think that if Mr Dunshunner was ony way mixed up wi' that gang, I wad be here this day tae second him? Div ye think——"

Here Mr Gills met with a singular interruption. A remarkable figure attired in a red coat and cocked-hat, at one time probably the property of a civic officer, and who had been observed for some time bobbing about in front of the hustings, was now elevated upon the shoulders of a yeoman, and displayed to the delighted spectators the features of Geordie Dowie.

"Ay, Toddy Tam, are ye there, man?" cried Geordie with a malignant grin. "What was you and the Clique doin' at Nanse Finlayson's on Friday nicht?"

"What was it, Geordie? What was it?" cried a hundred voices.

"Am I to be interrupted by a natural?" cried Gills, looking, however, considerably flushed in the face.

"What hae ye dune wi' the notes, Tam, that the lang chield up by there gied ye? And whaur's your freends, Shanks and M'Auslan? See that ye steek close the window neist time, ma man!" cried Geordie with demoniac ferocity.

This was quite enough for the mob, who seldom require any excuse for a display of their hereditary privileges. A perfect hurricane of hissing and of yelling arose, and Gills, though he fought like a hero, was at last forced to retire from the contest. Had Geordie Dowie's windpipe been within his grasp at that moment, I would not have insured for any amount the life of the perfidious spy.

Sholto Douglas was proposed and seconded amidst great cheering, and then Pozzlethwaite rose to speak. I do not very well recollect what he said, for I had quite enough to do in thinking about myself; and the Honourable Paul would have conferred a material obligation upon me if he had talked for an hour longer. At length my turn came.

"Electors of Dreepdaily!"—

That was the whole of my speech—at least the whole of it that was audible to any one human being. Humboldt, if I recollect right, talks in one of his travels of having somewhere encountered a mountain composed of millions of entangled snakes, whose hissing might have equalled that of the transformed legions of Pandemonium. I wish Humboldt, for the sake of scientific comparison, could have been upon the hustings that day! Certain I am, that the sibilation did not leave my ears for a fortnight afterwards, and even now, in my slumbers, I am haunted by a wilderness of asps! However, at the urgent entreaty of M'Corkindale, I went on for about ten minutes, though I was quivering in every limb and as pale as a ghost; and in order that the public might not lose the benefit of my sentiments, I concluded by handing a copy of my speech, interlarded with fictitious cheers, to the reporter for the *Dreepdaily Patriot*. That document may still be seen by the curious in the columns of that impartial newspaper.

I will state this for Sholto Douglas, that he behaved like a perfect gentleman. There was in his speech no triumph over the discomfiture which the other candidates had received; on the contrary, he rather rebuked the audience for not having listened to us with greater patience. He then went on with his oration. I need hardly say it was a national one, and it was most enthusiastically cheered.

All that I need mention about the show of hands is, that it was not by any means wholly in my favour.

That afternoon we were not quite so lively in the Committee-room as usual. The serenity of Messrs Gills, M'Auslan and Shanks—and, perhaps, I may add of myself—was a good deal shaken by the intelligence that a broadside with the tempting title of "*Full and Particular Account of an Interview between the Clique and Mr Dunshunner, held at Nanse Finlayson's Tavern, on Friday last, and how they came to terms. By an Eyewitness*," was circulating like wildfire through the streets. To have been beaten by a Douglas was nothing, but to have been so artfully entrapped by an imbecile!

Provost Binkie, too, was dull and dissatisfied. The reception he had met with in his native town was no doubt a severe mortification, but the feeling that he had been used as a catspaw and instrument of the Clique, was, I suspected, uppermost in his mind. Poor man! We had great difficulty that evening in bringing him to his sixth tumbler.

Even M'Corkindale was hipped. I own I was surprised at this, for I knew of old the indefatigable spirit and keen energy of my friend, and I thought that, with such a stake as he had in the contest, he would even have redoubled his exertions. Such, however, was not the case.

I pass over the proceedings at the poll. From a very early hour it became perfectly evident that my chance was utterly gone; and, indeed, had it been possible, I should have left Dreepdaily before the close. At four o'clock the numbers stood thus:—

	DREEP-DAILY.	DROUTHIE-LAW.	KITTLE-WEEM.
DOUGLAS . . .	94	63	192
POZZLETHWAITE . .	59	73	21
DUNSHUNNER . .	72	19	7
Majority for DOUGLAS . . .		196	

We had an affecting scene in the Committee-room. Gills, who had been drinking all day, shed copious floods of tears; Shanks was disconsolate; and M'Auslan refused to be comforted. Of course I gave the usual pledge, that on the very first opportunity I should come forward again to reassert the independence of the burghs, now infamously sacrificed to a Conservative; but the cheering at this announcement was of the very faintest description, and I doubt whether anyone believed me. Two hours afterwards I was miles away from Dreepdaily.

I have since had letters from that place, which inform me that the Clique is utterly discomfited; that for some days the component members of it might be seen wandering through the streets, and pouring their husky sorrows into the ears of every stray listener whom they could find, until they became a positive nuisance. My best champion, however, was the editor of the *Patriot*. That noble and dauntless individual continued for weeks afterwards to pour forth Jeremiads upon my defeat, and stigmatised my opponents and their supporters as knaves, miscreants and nincompoops. I was, he maintained, the victim of a base conspiracy, and the degraded town of Dreepdaily would never be able thereafter to rear its polluted head in the Convention of Royal Burghs.

Whilst these things were going on in Dreepdaily, I was closeted with M'Corkindale in Glasgow.

"So, then, you have lost your election," said he.

"And you have lost your wife."

"Neither of the two accidents appear to me irreparable," replied Robert.

"How so? Do you still think of Miss Binkie?"

"By no means. I made some little inquiry the day before the election, and discovered that a certain nest-egg was enormously exaggerated, if not altogether fictitious."

"Well, Bob, there is certainly nobody like yourself for getting information."

"I do my best. May I inquire into the nature of your future movements?"

"I have not yet made up my mind. These election matters put everything else out of one's head. Let me see—August is approaching, and I half promised the Captain of M'Alcohol to spend a few weeks with him at his shooting-quarters."

"Are you aware, Dunshunner, that one of your bills falls due at the Gorbals Bank upon Tuesday next?"

"Mercy upon me, Bob! I had forgotten all about it."

I did not go to the Highlands after all. The fatigue and exertion we had undergone rendered it quite indispensable that my friend Robert and I should relax a little. Accordingly we have both embarked for a short run upon the Continent.

BOULOGNE-SUR-MER,
12th August 1847.

THE GOLD STANDARD.

BY P. F. WALL.

[Maga, February 1933.]

I WAS working for a Corporation with extensive interests in mines and farms in the Orange Free State. It either owned or had options on some 500,000 acres. Much of this was fairly good, if decidedly arid, pastoral country; all of it was diamondiferous.

We had the option to prospect, and, should indications warrant it, to develop the mineral wealth on the farm of Mr August Kritzinger. Mr Kritzinger was typical of the back-veld Boer. He was tall, bewhiskered, somewhat unclean, deeply religious and God-fearing (as distinct from man-fearing), indolent, quite unambitious and perfectly happy. For most of the day he sat on the stoep of his house smoking, expectorating and drinking strong sweet coffee. In common with his kind, and not unlike the Irish peasant, he was courteous, and, considering his poverty, showed remarkable hospitality to every European irrespective of nationality.

He had inherited a farm of some 8000 acres, and considered it far too small for his requirements. He never appreciated the fact that the light rainfall, sandy soil and low quality of the herbage would always make it 'small,' until such time as ovines developed Marathon qualities and were able to travel at least twenty-six miles daily to get a bellyful of grass. That it more or less supported 300 sheep in low condition gave him the idea that 27 acres per sheep were insufficient, that things were very cramped. Mr Kritzinger never attempted to upset the balance of Nature, and jackals, allied with scab, insect pests and drought, kept the farm from becoming overstocked. Had it been possible to take a census of the other animals, in addition to a few horses and deplorably thin cattle, it would have included several thousand spring-hares and rather more meer-cats and ground squirrels, besides a goodly herd of springbok, many steinbok and an enormous quantity of feathered game.

The farm had been in the Kritzinger family since the time of the Voortrekkers. The floors of the house had become appreciably nearer the ceiling by liberal applications of cow-dung extending over many years. To stoke the fire one had only to dig up squares of it. The miserable bovines existing on a fibrous diet of wilted herbage incapable of digestion even by animals provided with several stomachs for the purpose, their droppings supplied a fuel equal to any peat-bog. There was a badly sited dam of enormous dimensions, but very little catchment area, invariably dry or little more than a muddy puddle ; a cart and waggon shed in the last stage of disrepair ; and one gaunt and solitary *eucalyptus viminalis*. Mr Kritzinger always pointed it out with pride as the sole survivor of fifty planted by his father many years ago.

Every twelve months or so Mr Kritzinger gathered together the survivors of his flock of sheep and deprived them of their valuable coats. It was hardly an organised mustering for shearing purposes. They were driven near the house by members of the numerous Kritzinger family, and, irrespective of size, sex or condition, caught by the hind-leg, thrown to the ground and shorn of their dusty or scabby wool by Morolong natives, who masqueraded under the self-bestowed title of 'shearers.' Mr Kritzinger did not take an active part in this strenuous work, but supervised from the stoep or the shade of the lone gum-tree. All but the more agile of the sheep were shorn, their fleeces dumped on the stoep, and thrown into bales with such items as the local fuel, sand, dust, grass and small bushes, ancient sacking and other matter. One could not call it false classification, as it was disposed of as sheep's wool in the grease.

I had been prospecting for the elusive diamond for the best part of a year. The *modus operandi* was a simple affair. Small shafts were sunk through the sand, lime and shale to about 30 feet; unless there had been a pronounced geological disturbance, one would come across yellow ground, should such exist, at this depth, which might or might not contain pure carbon. One frequently obtained yellow ground quite innocent of diamonds; on the other hand, it was impossible in this area to get diamonds without their being found in the yellow ground. If one struck yellow ground in a shaft, one sunk other shafts about it to prove the extent of the deposit. Often one would obtain a tiny blow-out or pocket extending laterally for a few yards only; on rarer occasions the halo of shafts around the original discovery might extend for a few hundred yards. Here, should there be diamonds in payable quantities, was the future mine. The deposit was carefully sorted for diamonds. In the washed deposit various stones would be found, such as agates and garnets. Diamonds and 'borts,' varying from the size of a pin's head to a large pea, might come to hand. On one occasion a 37 carat 'blue-white' was the first to catch my eye. Whether one struck yellow ground or not, all shafts were refilled until mining operations were seriously begun. One dare not leave the veld honeycombed with 6 by 6 by 20 to 30 feet holes where sheep valued at about 7s. 6d. each might fall down, to say nothing of horses and people.

By our agreement with Mr Kritzinger we had the option to acquire a portion of his farm not exceeding 900 acres "for the purpose of mining diamonds or other precious stones or minerals, also base minerals." (I imagine the latter clause was included as one unfortunate company prospecting for diamonds discovered a very valuable coal seam and were unable to operate, thus losing a concession sold later for

£100,000.) Should the option be taken up he was to receive the sum of £75,000 cash.

For years, except for the war years of 1899-1902, when the yield was nil, Mr Kritzinger's wool clip had averaged £75 per annum. He had, so he informed me, managed to live on this and raise a family of ten sons and daughters. Several of his and his wife's relations also lived on the place. Very little money passed through his hands. He delivered his clip at the local store kept by a Jew who had migrated from Riga. A mutual valuation was agreed upon; the store-keeper, although not mentioning it, knew the probable amount of 'foreign matter' in the baled wool, and would assess on a scoured basis. It took the best part of a day to arrive at this valuation, one over-estimating and the other under-estimating. When fixed, it was not a matter of handing over the agreed price. Mr Kritzinger might insist on £15 in cash, the balance of £60 to be taken in goods. Most of the goods consisted of groceries, such as 'Boer-meal,' sugar, coffee-beans, a few tins of condensed milk and other luxuries. There would be a sack of cut tobacco and a few dozen rolls of strong molasses-treated tobacco, various medicines, of which Beecham's Pills and Mother Siegel's Soothing Syrup formed the bulk, with a case of Epsom Salts as being equally good for sick sheep or ailing infants; clothing for himself, his wife and children, and the relatives. Often the value of the goods would greatly exceed £60, however; this was a charge against next year's clip, so Kritzinger was nearly always about a year in debt. Receiving £75 for his year's output probably put it into his head to ask £75,000 as appropriate compensation from those who desired to dig holes on his farm and eventually help themselves to some 900 acres of it.

I do not suppose the Kritzinger ménage had ever spent a farthing in their combined lives at a butcher's shop. The good Lord had always provided most of the perishable products deemed essential to nourish the human body. There was mutton, fresh, more or less fresh, and salted. Was there not a salt-pan at the far end of the farm? By the simple process of evaporating the brine in the sun one could obtain snow-white sodium chloride, except, of course, when a dust-storm blew up in the middle of the evaporating process and turned the salt red or a dirty brown. However, good clean dust never hurt anyone, if it was a bit trying to the eyes and lungs. Buck were there to be shot. Fresh it was delicious, salted it was not quite so delicious, but when turned into biltong it was more delicious than when fresh! Every winter Mr Kritzinger would shoot about a dozen of these antelopes. He was a good and extremely careful shot, careful, that is, in the economy of his kills; but not so careful of your person if you got within the line of fire. He had saved from the Anglo-Boer War, in which he took part until the end—being wounded several times but always evading capture—a few hundred cartridges of British manufacture and a rifle of the same origin. With an income of only £75, 'fancy' or sporting shots may be left to those who can afford them.

When a man and his numerous dependents live on 30s. per week, one might suppose that a proposal to pay him £75,000 for a bit of his farm would cause some little excitement. Not so. I informed him that we proposed exercising our option; he continued to smoke and expectorate, and called to Mrs Kritzinger to bring a cup of coffee. He always called for a cup of coffee when I went to interview him.

"Ja," was all he said to me.

His wife came out with the coffee. He said to her, "Those Jews are going to buy a portion of the farm."

"Ja," said his wife. "Don't you let them have the dam or the salt-pan."

Kritzinger turned to me. "I know you are not a Jew, but you work for them; perhaps you know what part of the farm they want."

"We don't want the dam, but the part we hope to mine does include the salt-pan," I replied.

"I told you not to let them dig holes all over the farm! Perhaps he can tell us where we are going to get salt now," said Mrs Kritzinger, who nearly always addressed remarks intended for me through her husband.

"Mrs Kritzinger," I replied, "for half the money these people will pay your husband you could buy all the salt-pans in the Free State."

"Tell him," she said, still treating me as though I did not understand her language, "that I have never spent a penny in my life on salt."

Within a week, the Secretary and the Legal Adviser of the Corporation arrived by car from Johannesburg. This event certainly caused no little excitement, but only as the first 'close up' of a motor-car. In those days there were very few cars in this portion of the Free State, and those that did come along usually got stuck in the sand or otherwise misbehaved themselves.

Kritzinger's English was more than limited, whilst the representatives of the Corporation had no knowledge whatever of Afrikaans. I was called aside by Kritzinger. He asked me if the visitors were Jews. I assured him that one was a Scot and the other an Australian.

"During the war I fought against both Scots and Australians; the English had everyone to help them, including niggers and Indians, to rob us of our country."

"When 'Uitlanders' want to pay you an enormous sum, it does not look as if they had robbed you of your land," I said. "Besides, what if these men were Jews? They have come to pay you; nationality can make no difference."

"You have to bargain with Jews," he informed me. "Don't I have to bargain all day with the Jew who buys my wool, and the 'Smouses' (itinerant pedlars, usually Jews) who come here several times every year?"

"This deal is for a fixed sum," I explained. "It is not a matter of trying to get more or their offering less."

"All right," he agreed, "I only wanted to know."

In the back-veld, deals of any nature are jobs for the patient. One must be prepared to listen to any amount of extraneous matter before the actual business is discussed, to say nothing of being shown the place where the floods of several years ago burst the wall of the dam.

The Legal Adviser, a very busy man never particularly noticeable for his tolerance or courtesy, told me to tell Kritzinger to get on with the job and inform Mrs Kritzinger that something worse than what happened to Lot's wife would be her fate if she kept harping on the subject of the salt-pan. What happened to Mrs Lot was put as, "We would tell the Board of Directors in Johannesburg of her difficulties, and perhaps—but, of course, we did not know their views—they might consider exchanging that portion of the farm for some other portion." This appeared to appease her, and she relapsed into silence.

In spite of my efforts it took the best part of another hour before Kritzinger would fully consider the object of their visit. Asking him to sign the agreement, I made it plain that 900 acres would be surveyed at our cost, that they would pass from his possession and become, as we all hoped, a productive diamond mine, complete with all manner of buildings and gear, and in time provide employment for several hundred Europeans and many thousand natives. That for all we knew another Kimberley—"I helped besiege Kimberley," he interrupted—might spring up, enabling him to dispose of the rest of his farm at township prices, "in fact, just as it all happened to Messrs Wessels and du Toit some fifty years ago."

"If all these natives are brought here my sheep will be stolen," he answered.

"Tell him," said the Secretary, "if he will sign along the dotted line and get two witnesses I will hand him the cheque."

I interpreted.

In the first place, Kritzinger said he could not write, all previous correspondence having been carried on by his eldest daughter; even if he could write he was not signing anything before consulting his father-in-law, an old man who looked more than a hundred, but was probably barely eighty. Oupa, as he was called, which means grandfather, knew all about agreements. Many years before, when he possessed a big farm of his own, had he not signed an agreement, receiving £300, and because he failed to pay the interest found that he was removed from the farm, which later was sold to another? It took me over three hours to convince him that the agreement was not a mortgage, but something in the nature of an outright sale.

Finally, Oupa agreed that it sounded different, and eventually advised his son-in-law to sign as soon as he got the money. He would guide his hand. He was no believer in marks or crosses—that was a 'nigger' method. Had he not guided his son-in-law's hand when he was courting his daughter? Of course he had. He wrote all his love letters, then getting on his horse had ridden over to his daughter, delivered them and guided her hand in reply. He knew all about writing, and could put down any person's name providing he knew what it was.

"That isn't legal," I explained. "You will have to witness his mark."

"Marks and crosses are things for Kafirs," he insisted.

I explained the position to the representatives.

The Legal Adviser said, "So long as the Law Society never hears of it, I don't give a damn how they sign, providing it is signed and I can get away."

Kritzinger was handed a fountain pen and called to Oupa to come along and help.

"That's right, sign and we'll hand you the cheque," I said, and a moment later would have given much had I remained silent.

"Cheque!" said Oupa; "we are not taking cheques."

"You do not expect," I said, "that men coming down from Johannesburg would bring £75,000 in notes with them."

"We do not," said Oupa; "we want and expect to be paid in gold."

"Gold!" I repeated. "£75,000 in gold would break the car; it must weigh the best part of a ton."

"We don't know what it weighs, but we want gold."

I interpreted their desire. My explanation that a wealthy Corporation dealing in millions was not in the habit of tendering dud cheques made not the slightest impression. Did not the Agreement, providing I had read it correctly, state that £75,000 was the agreed price?

"A cheque is exactly the same as gold or notes," I assured them.

"There's too much paper about the whole business," replied Oupa.

At the Secretary's suggestion I asked them to come into Bishoff, the nearest township, some twenty-five miles distant.

"We can all get in the car, find the bank manager, as the place will be closed long before we get there, and get him to convince you we are not a pack of robbers endeavouring to get your farm for nothing."

"We are not getting into one of those things and getting stuck in the sand," said Oupa, who by this time had taken charge of his side of the proceedings and probably suspected murder or kidnapping.

"Will you go by cart at once?" I asked.

"We'll come to-morrow," said Oupa.

We returned to my house some five miles away. I knew it was futile to go into Bishoff and expect them to arrive early next morning. At dawn I sent a native on one of my ponies and instructed him to wait for the inspanning of the cart. Immediately he saw it take the road to Bishoff he was to return and inform us. It was after 3 P.M. before he returned and said that half the Kritzinger family and their herd-boys had been looking for the horses since the early morning. It was about 2 P.M. when they found them. We followed on the dusty road as fast as the car was capable of travelling. After some ten miles we saw the inevitable cloud of dust and hoped it might be caused by Kritzinger's cart. Slowing down and just keeping the cloud of dust in view, we were greatly relieved on arrival to find Kritzinger and his father-in-law.

It was now nearly dark, and most of the villagers, not unlike the fowls in the backyards, were preparing to roost, whilst others sat up to enjoy the smelly illumination provided by a few candles made from the tallow of the fat-tailed sheep. We offered Kritzinger and Oupa the hospitality of the local hotel. They politely refused, explaining that they were accustomed to sleep beneath the cart, which they had outspanned on the Market Square, but they would be pleased to accept two sheaves of unthreshed oat straw for their horses.

Our efforts to find the bank manager and possibly get him to conduct important business after hours were fruitless. He was not to be found in the village, and nobody appeared to know his whereabouts.

At 9 A.M. the following morning he arrived, apologised for his absence and explained that he had spent the night on a farm some miles out.

We collected Kritzinger and Oupa and proceeded to the bank. The manager explained the function of a cheque and endeavoured to convince them that it was legal tender for any form of transaction. "Should Mr Kritzinger care to open an account with it he could draw on the account to the full value of the cheque."

"For God's sake," I said to the manager in English, "don't mention anything about the cost of cheques, ledger fees or other bank charges, or you'll lose a valuable depositor."

"If I take this bit of paper and give it to you, will you give me £75,000 in gold for it?" asked Kritzinger.

"Surely you must know," said the manager, "that a small branch like this does not keep such a large sum in gold locked in the safe; only very important branches in the cities have this amount available for immediate withdrawal."

"I told you they hadn't got it," said Oupa to his son-in-law.

The manager, who like ourselves had to confess that he could not negotiate with them, suggested we should all go into Kimberley by car; that he would wire and see the money was available as soon as we got there.

"Suggest it to them," I said. "So far they have turned down all my suggestions."

He did so, but neither would entertain the idea of leaving Bishoff, possibly looking upon the suggestion as an endeavour to get them as far away from home as possible and quietly murder them.

"If they have the money," said Oupa, "let them send for it; we'll wait until it comes."

We wired for the money, which arrived the next morning, distributed over three cars, each complete with an armed clerk.

For the first time in its history the bank opened some time before the usual hour. Seventy-five bags, each containing £1000, were laid on the counter.

"Here is your money," said the Secretary, "and I hope you appreciate the fact that you have delayed us several days over a very simple transaction. If you'll sign we shall return to Johannesburg at once."

"We'll sign when we've counted it," said Oupa.

"Lord, man, it will take you a month to count it," said the Legal Adviser. "Do you expect us to stay a month in this damned place?"

Coming to our aid, the bank manager said he would weigh the money for them, at the same time exhibiting the scales with various weights representing so many sovereigns.

"Wool, sugar, coffee-beans and many other things are weighed," said Oupa, "but money is counted."

"Count out fifty," said the manager, "and see if they agree with the number stamped on this weight."

"We'll count them all," said Oupa. "The Jew at the store and all the 'Smouses' count money; they never weigh it."

The money was removed into the manager's office and we left Kritzinger and Oupa to their task. Returning to the hotel, I was asked by the Secretary how long did I think it would take them. "I know nothing of the ability of Oupa as enumerator, but I do know that Kritzinger takes all day to count some 300 sheep, and invariably gets a different total after each effort."

"From that we shall be here for keeps," said the legal representative.

For five days we sat in the hotel reading 'The Outfitters' Guide,' 'The Farmers' Journal,' 'Commercial Advocate' and some ancient copies of other papers. The enumerators camped in the manager's office and all but smoked and expectorated him out of it. All day and most of the night they continued.

At the close of the fifth day Oupa came along and said they had counted the contents of the bags and found there were two sovereigns short. "But we'll count them again," he added.

"You'll do nothing of the sort," said the legal representative. "Probably one of the clerks lost 'em on the way out; or in Kimberley they don't count so well as you do. Here," he said, as he handed him £2, "let the Company make it up."

Eventually Oupa, grunting and breathing heavily, guided the hand of his daughter's husband more or less over the dotted line, and the representatives departed, probably confirmed racialists. My horse had been sent in, and I proposed returning early the following morning.

It was barely light when Oupa came to me. "We find," he said, "that the money weighs as much as three bales of wool or five bags of mealies. You said it weighed a ton, but it is only about a half-ton; it will break the cart if we put it in."

"It will," I agreed.

"What we want," continued Oupa, "is to get a trolley and four mules. Do you know where we could get one cheap?"

"I don't," I replied. "Now that you are men of wealth you will probably experience the pleasure of everyone attempting to overcharge you, but you might be able to get what you want for about £60."

"Almighty!" he exclaimed. "£60 for four bastard horses and a trolley!"

I heard later that he had to pay £70 to a coloured man for the conveyance.

Good as well as bad news travels extraordinarily rapidly. 'Smouses' of all types fell upon the Kritzinger household and endeavoured to sell them everything from enlarged photographs to patent cookers. It got so bad that Kritzinger came and saw me about it. Had I not spread the news of the sale, thus littering his house with every agent and canvasser in the Orange Free State? I informed him that it had been in every paper in the country, that one does not sell a portion of a farm for what the papers termed 'close upon six figures' and expect everyone to remain in complete ignorance of it.

"And the letters I get!" he said. "Every time I go to the post-office the postmaster hands me a bagful."

"You are," I said, "paying the price of notoriety."

"I'm paying nothing," he replied. "Now that you have taken 900 acres my sheep go hungry and I shall have to get another farm."

It was said that Kritzinger, when he returned to the farm with the half-ton of gold, buried it beneath the home-made double bed, and that if he was not occupying it his wife was. Man-like, he probably gave her the day-shift whilst he helped with the night-watch. So far as one could judge, the acquisition of so much wealth did not make the smallest difference to their mode of living. There may have been a little more sugar in the coffee, or perhaps an addition of condensed milk made it a little more palatable.

We brought huge quantities of building material and mining equipment from Kimberley and Bloemfontein by ox-waggon. As it sprang up all about him, Kritzinger still sat on the stoep, smoked and drank coffee. The rest of the family just sat in or about the house.

Within a year, and before we had got to the production stage, most of the buck had been chased away or poached. The sheep, in spite of good lambings and little disease, had decreased rather than increased. This worried Kritzinger, who now, for the first time in his life, suffered from living in an over-populated community possessed of thieving habits.

On one of our farms we 'farmed' some 3000 springbok and about 800 blesbok. Every winter five or six hundred would be shot and sent to the various markets. Kritzinger, whose heaven-presented buck had by now disappeared from his farm, came and asked my permission to shoot ten or a dozen for biltong. I told him at 12s. 6d. a head he could shoot up to twenty. He said he would shoot eight, and although not actually complaining, gave me to understand that I was grossly overcharging him.

Two years later, and just before the war of 1914-1918, we offered for sale one of our farms in the district. It comprised some 16,000 morgen or about 34,000 acres. As a pastoral property it was poor; as a diamond proposition it held out little hope of success.

Representing the Corporation I attended the sale and found a large crowd of farmers present, about two of whom appeared to be possible buyers. Others came, as they invariably do on such occasions in scattered districts, to watch the proceedings, meet friends and acquaintances and experience the joy of light refreshments provided gratis. When many buyers are present the light refreshments are moved up to the strong refreshments category, this being left to the discretion of the auctioneer. Free brandy, besides loosening the tongue, often loosens the purse-strings as well. However, the attendance hardly justified anything more than a little beer, with lashings of tea and coffee to follow, for the beer never lasts very long. Then, of course, there were the usual 'cookies,' a sort of over-sweet bun. The auctioneer's 'rostrum' was the top of an open waggon.

The conditions of the sale were read out, first in Afrikaans, then in English. It appeared that the highest bidder would be the purchaser; there was no reserve, and the farm was free of any restrictions, including the mining of such precious stones as diamonds, or coal, there being more than indications of both. I noted friend Kritzinger was giving all his attention to the conditions of sale. A buyer, I thought. The auctioneer, who did not know him, had to be informed, and there was little opportunity to tell him without being overheard. I hurriedly scribbled a note. "The tall dark man badly in need of a hair-cut and beard-trim standing immediately in front of me and to whom I will speak when you have read this note, is bursting with wealth and suffering from the nightmare effect of living in a crowded area. Push the price up to at least 20s. per morgen with safety. If it appears that he may go further, go on; but for goodness sake don't land it in the air, where most of the other bids will come from. His name is August Kritzinger. Yours, One who has a grudge against him."

I handed the note to the auctioneer, who read it and nodded to me. I then spoke to Kritzinger.

As expected, there were two bidders for the farm. Kritzinger started at 5s., and was pushed up by threepences, sixpences and sometimes ninepences by the other buyer, who dropped out at 10s. It was then that someone in the background surprised everyone by jumping it up to 12s. 6d. "Thank you, sir, that's the sort of bid I like," said the auctioneer. "Against you, Mr Kritzinger. Don't let a stranger to the district have a farm like this. Fifteen shillings, did you say, Mr Kritzinger? You didn't, Mr Kritzinger; my mistake. Oh, you did, Mr Kritzinger; again my mistake for missing a good bid." It was obvious that Kritzinger had said nothing, but was consulting with Oupa at the time. "Thank you, sir, another half-crown. Against you at 17s. 6d., Mr Kritzinger. Make it even money, Mr Kritzinger. What's a pound a morgen for a farm like this? Mr Kritzinger, it's against you." A pause. "For the second time, it's against you. You'll get it, sir. Mr Kritzinger can't afford to go higher. Thank you, Mr Kritzinger; a pound I'm offered. Now, sir," to the man at the back, whom apparently nobody but the auctioneer had seen bid, "don't let it go, sir. What, you shake your head! All right, you know best. Going at 20s.—going at 20s.—gone. Mr August Kritzinger, I congratulate you on getting it so cheaply."

No sooner was the farm sold than Kritzinger, Oupa and one of his sons deposited sixteen bags on the rostrum.

"Dar is die geld" (There is the money), said Kritzinger to the amazed auctioneer.

"What's in those bags?" he asked,

"Sixteen thousand pounds in gold," said Kritzinger.

"Come, come, Mr Kritzinger, I don't want that. Let me have your cheque, or, better still, drive into Bloemfontein to-morrow and arrange about transfer and payment."

"Dar is die geld," repeated Kritzinger.

If you have some two cwts. of the precious metal thrust upon you some eighty miles from home, and have only a somewhat capricious motor-car as a means of reaching that home, you have to be a gold hoarder to appreciate so much wealth.

Representing the sellers, and being some fifty miles nearer home than the unfortunate auctioneer, he turned to me and said, "Won't you take it with you?"

"I will not," I replied. "Some two years ago I handed him seventy-five of those bags, and it took me the best part of ten days to rid myself of them. They've never been mine, and I hate the sight of them. But you'll have to count them before you let him go."

"Count them," he repeated. "Who ever heard of anyone counting sixteen thousand quid on top of a waggon in the middle of nowhere ?"

"I have," I answered; "or rather Kritzinger and that old man spent five days and the best part of five nights counting nearly five times as many."

Twenty years later one wonders how much of the balance remains under the double bed of Mr and Mrs Kritzinger. Has he become modernised and banked it, or did he get the prevailing land hunger and purchase a lot of worthless land ?

Leaving in 1914 for the war I am now, like Kritzinger of old, counting my flocks and getting a different count each time. For a few hectic years profits varying between £15,000 and £35,000 per month were made from his infertile, in an agricultural sense, acres.

BUILDING IN PROVENCE.

BY THE HON. LADY FORTESCUE.

[Maga, October 1932.]

"*Madame! MADAME! MADAME!*"

A chorus of voices, French, Provençal and Italian, all yelling for me at once. What could be the matter *now?*

I had grown accustomed to these howls for help during the many weeks in which our army of workmen had been enlarging the little golden house we had bought—before the £ collapsed—in Provence. Hardly a day passed without a visit from one or other of them: the electrician with a finger cut by wire; a mason with a smashed thumb; various *blessés* with casualties greater or less, all howling for 'Madame' and *tincture d'iode*.

I hurried downstairs in the direction of the present howls, and found, outside the front door, a crowd of pale-faced workmen surrounding the prostrate form of a tall handsome boy who was lying in a pool of blood on the stone stairway leading to the terrace above.

At first I thought he had fallen from the scaffolding, and I felt sick with apprehension, but a few inquiries elicited the fact that it was merely a very bad nose hæmorrhage, and that the poor boy was subject to them. Of course, his *camarades* were, like workmen all the world over, paralysed by the sight of blood, and stood around gabbling excitedly but doing nothing. They turned on me, as one man, and informed me that *le pauvre malheureux* had lost at least two litres of good red blood in the *tourelle* before they could get him down.

With cold water applications I soon stopped the hæmorrhage, and after much coaxing persuaded him to enter my car and let me drive him to his home. He was terrified lest he might soil the new cushions, and only when enveloped in a bath-towel would he consent to get in!

All his comrades, of course, rushed to open the gate, falling over each other, shouting encouragement to the invalid and waving us farewell with every variety of gaudy coloured handkerchief. I knew that after our departure all work would remain in abeyance while *le pauvre malheureux* was discussed, and that not until they had comfortably interred him in imagination, with suitable *pompe funèbre,* would it be resumed.

I had grown to love these excitable emotional men of the South and to regard them as my children—for they were little more. They were perfectly maddening, entirely without initiative and quite irresponsible, but they were most lovable. And I wonder what woman could resist the unconscious way an Italian peasant makes love to her with his eyes while he is taking her orders?

For I found that I had to give orders. In Provence it is always Madame who conducts all business. In England the Contractor does everything, but we learned early that in Provence the *Entrepreneur* is only responsible for his masonry and his masons. It was my pleasing job to find carpenter, painter, plumber, electrician and iron-worker, and, after that, to make these men work together.

The old bald-headed *Entrepreneur* was splendid at his job, having grown old in his profession. He supplied the practical suggestions, and, being an Italian with a great artistic sense, he understood at once my love of line and of dignified simplicity and my passion for the apsidal ending and the Provençal arch. So we dispensed with the services of an architect and got on famously together. When I asked if such and such a thing were possible, he would stand silent for a while, his old bald head bent in thought and a gnarled forefinger curled round his nose. Then, the problem solved in his fertile brain, he would shoot up his head, his black eyes twinkling under shaggy brows, throw up his hands to Heaven and exclaim, "*Mais—DIABLE! OUI, Madame!*" and waddle off to instruct his masons, enthusiastic as a boy.

He was childishly pleased with praise of his men's work, though they never got a word of it from him. His old eyes would fill with tears when I told him that not one fruit or flower had been taken from our garden; or when I described the beautiful courtesy of his workmen who rushed to help me in every conceivable way, seizing baskets and bundles from my arms to carry them for me, and standing cap in hand in the hot sun when I spoke to them until I begged them, "*Couvrez-vous, je vous prie.*" Yet he seemed to spend his life in scolding and driving them whenever he appeared. His masons seldom obeyed him silently. Generally they argued with him for a quarter of an hour before they went off, grumbling, to the tasks he set them. But although he always got his way in the end, he could not make his men work harmoniously with the craftsmen of other professions. That was Madame's task, and to accomplish it she had to be among the workmen all day and every day.

My knowledge of technical French was *nil* when the building operations began, but I found my natural gift for dancing more valuable than anything else. If one only danced energetically enough, things got done, and, with violent gesture and childish drawings, I managed to convey my wishes and ideas. Once I had won the men's hearts—so easily done with a joke, a compliment and little acts of consideration for their welfare—I found that the word *blessée* did all the rest. If Madame were 'wounded' about something left undone that ought to have been done, that thing was immediately accomplished. If she appeared, grave-eyed and sorrowful, in the

whom I called *'Monsieur le Chef,'* because when he was not stirring his eternal puddings of mortar outside our front door he was heating up the tin mugs of vegetable soup for his fellow-workmen, still strove to mix his cement with water which froze as he mixed. He looked so pitifully frail and thin, his creaky laugh wheezing faintly as he tried to hearten his congealed companions, that I wrapped him from head to toe in a heavy peasant's cloak. In this he still laboured valiantly, looking like a very ancient hooded crow.

But always, after half an hour's effort, we heard the foreman's ominous 'cease work' whistle, and the whole army of workmen would drift off, gibbering with cold and blowing upon their frozen hands. Even their vocal chords seemed to be affected by frost and the eternal stream of chatter to be frozen in their throats. They trudged and shuffled silently away. . . . More delay—then—snow!

From our windows we looked out upon an enchanted land. The grey waves of olive foliage which surge and billow over valleys and mountains to the blue Mediterranean were powdered with fine snow and sparkled under an azure sky. Here and there tall cypresses, planted in pairs near each old Provençal homestead, one for *La Paix* and one for *La Prospérité,* stood out like black pointed rocks in the glittering sea. On the old golden-grey terrace walls and stairways late pink roses and pansy faces peeped through the snow, and even the hideous heaps of excavated earth in our garden were transformed into miniature ranges of snow-mountains.

Our little merry-eyed Italian *bonne* spent most of her time rushing out-of-doors to pick up handfuls of snow, toss it in the air, taste it and press it into snowballs, which she was much too polite to throw at the workmen. "*Madame! la neige! la belle neige! Regardez les oliviers qu'ils sont beaux sous la neige!*" A new and thrilling phenomenon for her, coming as she does from the hot sunshine of Southern Italy.

It was all very pretty and amusing to watch, but the

housework suffered, the garden suffered and our poor building operations suffered.

The old *Entrepreneur* had promised us that all should be finished by December 20th, 1931, and I, rashly believing him, gave him a month's margin and ordered our furniture and possessions, stored in London till the house should be ready to receive them, to be sent over in mid-January. Time was slipping on, and not even my husband's long gallery on the ground floor was finished yet. The unusual weather provided an excellent excuse for the delay in the building, and we were getting desperate.

However, at last came the blessed thaw and once more the work progressed, though slowly still. No doubtful point could be decided under half an hour, because it appeared to be essential and usual for every expert of each separate trade to down tools and rush to the debate whatever it might be. Each man had, of course, entirely different views, which he defended with vigour and violence, and, as it always fell to Madame to make the final decision, she found that building in Provence was anxious work. However, it was only necessary to make the men laugh and all was well.

Consideration for our comfort was genuinely the chief object of them all, though their opinions as to how this was to be assured might differ. When it came to the choosing of fittings for our bathroom, the head-plumber was most urgent that the bath should be deep enough so that the water should cover '*l'estomac de Monsieur*' (such a little one, too), and that a certain useful seat should be of good mahogany and "*bien arrondi pour le confort de Madame,*" who fled on the excuse that she heard a phantom telephone bell.

And so at last we had at any rate a bathroom actually finished, though its completion was delayed, as usual, by rain. When the fittings did not appear on the day appointed for their arrival, I telephoned to the plumber to inquire the cause. He replied that he could not possibly risk damage to the beautiful *appareil* in such weather. (Damage to a *bath*, a *basin*, &c., by WATER!) The fittings would be sent "*demain, ou après-demain.*" Of course they would.

Although the continued delays were very expensive and caused us great anxiety and much irritation of spirit, still I loved watching the men at their tasks. There was Big Jean, a huge dour-faced mason, who shovelled stones from the foundations and threw them into a narrow wooden trough fourteen feet above his head without ever dropping one. When I spoke admiringly of his skill to my little *bonne*, she at once gave me every detail of his life-story, and I learned that every day he had to leave an invalid wife, whom he adored, alone in bed, for he must earn bread for them both. That evening I picked a gay bouquet of flowers and slipped it into his great hands to cheer her sad solitude. To my consternation the granite face broke up and two big tears rolled down his dusty cheeks. From that moment he became my very devoted slave, competing with *Monsieur le Chef* for the first daily handshake.

The hand-shaking in Provence is most exhausting. My hand was shaken at least sixty times a day, shaken in greeting, in parting and on every possible pretext, by every variety of hand in every possible condition of dirt. The old veteran, posing black-and-white tiles in the hall like a jig-saw puzzle, would pause in his work to shake hands; the foreman, plastering huge boulders over an overflow pipe so that the water should burst through the perforated stones in a series of tiny cascades in my rose-garden, would proffer a slimy hand directly I appeared. Another artist, building up the big arched Provençal open fireplace of narrow rose-coloured bricks in the gallery, dropped his trowel so to salute me; and the phlegmatic-looking mason hollowing out a niche over the door in my little blue *salon* to hold a tiny Madonna, bent from his ladder with paw outstretched. And so it went on all day. We kept a supply of pumice-stone, turpentine and patent cleansers ever ready in the bathroom to remove the traces of our workmen's warmth of heart and hand.

We grew very fond of them all, and the trouble was that they returned our affection and were therefore unwilling to put an end to a pleasant experience. Love was being mixed with the mortar, we knew, but love can be leisurely, and at last I had to dance more and more energetically to hustle the old *Entrepreneur*.

After that, *camions* (lorries) came thick and fast, crashing down our little approach, slicing Hilaire's cherished grass, damaging his neat drive and discharging their loads of gravel and lime in a cloud of choking dust. Planks and boards arrived in a cart drawn by a vicious mule, who employed the time of unloading by kicking up the paths and munching Hilaire's precious pansies. My life was further complicated by the need of pacifying a frantic gardener.

Hilaire did not love the workmen. To him the old *Entrepreneur* was the arch-demon and his horde of masons a legion of devils who trampled upon his choice plants, broke off branches from his fruit trees and covered his vines with clouds of cement dust. Above all, he hated *Monsieur le Chef*. He it was who smothered the scarlet geraniums with lime, who sullied the clear water of the little fountain when cleaning his horrible shovel, who scorched the finest peach-tree on the lower terrace by making his little hell of lighted olive twigs and fir cones just beneath it to perform his cooking operations. Between Hilaire and *Monsieur le Chef* raged constant war, and, in spite of his eighty-four years and his toothlessness, it was amazing to hear the cataract of sarcastic retaliation the old mason poured over Hilaire's furious protests. I had rather a special weakness for the gallant old man, and once he even made mischief on this score between Hilaire and me, saying that Madame never scolded him, Madame always shook him by the hand first of all and so on. On that occasion it was quite difficult to make my peace.

No accident nor misfortune that happened to any one of the workmen drew the slightest sympathy from Hilaire. It was either the man's own silly fault, or a just visitation from *le bon Dieu*, or else a case of malingering. When I inquired after the welfare of my poor young mason who had the severe nasal hæmorrhage, to my amazement Hilaire only grinned, tapped his old nose significantly and assured me, "*Ce n'est rien, Madame, ce n'est rien!*" And when I indignantly protested that the poor boy had had a very serious hæmorrhage, Hilaire replied knowingly, "*Jeune marié! Jeune marié! Il faut aller doucement! Il faut aller doucement!*"

When Hilaire becomes Rabelaisian I am fain to flee.

I had been warned by a resident that when the roof went on to the little Provençal tower which surmounts the new building, *La Cabade* would be celebrated, and we should be lucky if there was a flower or a branch left in our garden. The workmen, I was told, would decorate their work and expect a half-holiday and bottles of wine to drink to the health of the house. What would happen with Hilaire then? I foresaw that unless I could prevail upon him to drink at least three bottles of wine, this feast was likely to become a second Passover and our lintel splashed with blood.

I begged the old *Entrepreneur* to give me fair warning when this celebration would take place, and asked how I should know when to buy my wine and make my preparations. He only put his old hands on his thighs, bent his knees and laughed soundlessly at some secret joke of his own. Then, when I pressed for an answer, he looked at me with twinkling eyes and wagging head, and assured me that I could not possibly miss it when the moment came.

But when *would* that moment come? we wondered apprehensively. Our furniture was due to arrive in less than a month, and so far no room was ready to receive it. The *Entrepreneur* swore that at any rate he would have the old part of the house habitable by then, and we hoped that the long gallery in the new building would be completed also, because that was large enough to store all the surplus furniture for the new rooms.

But when the dread day came and we got a telephone message to say that the two vans of furniture had arrived at Nice and would be transported to us that day, the gallery was ceiled but not floored, and the bedrooms above were floored but not ceiled! How were we to fit all our mass of stuff into a tiny hall, a diminutive salon and four wee bedrooms, which was all the accommodation that the old part of the house contained?

We left the flat where we were living during the building operations and started for our mountain, two kilometres away, with heavy hearts. It was a bitterly cold day and freezing hard, but having no garage ready we were obliged to leave our new car in the only place wide enough for two cars to pass in the lane leading to our house—a rocky ravine near a waterfall. Not the ideal place in which to leave a new car with a stiff engine on a wintry day, but we had no choice. Would she ever start again at night? For our agonies would not abate till darkness fell, of that I felt sure. However—sufficient unto the day—and that day we had more than enough to worry about. So we muffled the bonnet with rugs and went ahead on foot.

Suddenly we both stopped simultaneously and looked at each other with a wild surmise as a roar as of many waters in spate met our ears. The first van! It could be nothing else.

We hurried on in the direction of the roar, which suddenly ceased and was succeeded by mixed noises resembling those in a menagerie at feeding-time. As we drew nearer I distinguished a babel of voices, the minor howl of the Provençal peasant, the nasal Niçois twang, the bass bubbling of agitated Italians and the shrill exclamations of the French. Something had gone wrong. What could it be?

We rounded a bend in the lane and came upon—the van! There it stood in all its awful majesty, a Leviathan among vans, the most gigantic thing on wheels that I had ever seen. Round it surged a mixed mob of peasants and removal-men all pointing skywards and all yelling at once.

And then I realised the cause of the hubbub. A huge olive branch barred the way of this Monster of Transport invading the lovely peace of the mountains. I sympathised deeply with the protest of the old olive-tree—but I wanted my furniture. So I hurried forward to the scene of inaction.

Hilaire—of course Hilaire was in the centre of the crowd—saw me coming and rushed forward to give the first explanation, which was so painfully obvious, and the Niçois removal-men all turned upon me indignantly as though I had placed the bough there on purpose to obstruct their work. I ignored them, and suggested to Hilaire that the branch should be cut off. His eyes goggled, his mouth dropped open, and to his shocked protest was added a chorus of dissent from the crowd of collected peasants.

Cut off the branch of a sacred olive-tree! A fine branch laden with fruit? Of course, Madame was English and new to Provence, and had evidently not yet had time to learn that the olives were precious to the peasant.

I cut all this short by ordering Hilaire to go and find the proprietor of the olive yard and get his permission, offering to pay him compensation for the damage to his tree.

Hilaire lumbered off down the mountain leaving us to be lectured by the excited crowd. He returned after a short time to inform us that it was a *fête* day and the owner of the tree was not at home. *Impasse.* More conversation. And then suddenly Monsieur, generally a very patient man, grew desperate. Eyeglass fixed in a very fierce eye, he strode into the midst of the group, and towering over the men commanded that the branch should be cut off AT ONCE.

"Get a saw," ordered Monsieur curtly, turning upon Hilaire, who fled towards the house to do his bidding, returning with many saws, ropes and tackle.

Then a discussion arose as to who should cut off the branch; and suddenly they all became as eager to cut it off as they had been anxious to save it. Fourteen men rushed at the tree and began scrambling up it, shouting and squabbling as they climbed.

At this juncture we decided to crawl round or under the van and go on to the house, there to prepare for the arrival of the Monster which presumably would be freed in an hour's time.

After two hours the tractor appeared round the bend of the lane dragging the enormous van, and, at this thrilling sight, every workman in the building hurled down his tools and rushed to the edge of the scaffolding platforms to watch its arrival. Cries of

"*Mon Dieu!*"

"*Diable!*"

"*Sapristi!*"

"*Sacré nom d'un nom!*"

"*Quel horreur!*"

"*Madonna mia!*"

rent the air, and our little *bonne* tied on a huge apron and began rolling up her sleeves, murmuring "*Dieu d'Amour!*" with sparkling eyes.

For though she thoroughly enjoyed a crisis, she positively loved a catastrophe; and when the van, released from its tractor, rushed down to the front door by its own momentum and leaned wearily against the porch, thereby completely blocking the main entrance to the house, it looked very like a catastrophe. The united efforts of the removal-men assisted by the whole army of our workmen (delighted to do any other work than their own) failed to move it; and there we were, stuck once more. The only alternative was to unload the van and carry its contents up two stone stairways to another entrance on the terrace above.

The Niçois, tired and furious, of course protested violently, but we were firm. Enough time had been wasted, and the second van was yet to come. I reminded them of this, and was informed, consolingly, that the second van contained all the *heavy* furniture, and that 'The Son of a Pig' could not start till the tractor went back to fetch it. That, anyhow, was some small comfort. I felt that I could perhaps cope with one pig at a time.

We found that the Nice firm only undertook to dump our goods at their destination, but, as they insisted upon taking with them all empty crates and packing materials, we must unpack every single one of the gigantic cases of crockery and glass ourselves.

Well, somehow my husband and I accomplished this tremendous task, aided only by Hilaire and our little *bonne*, who had evidently never enjoyed an experience so much in their lives. The unpacking was somewhat delayed because they wanted to examine, stroke and praise all *les belles choses* as they emerged from their wrappings.

At intervals I rushed out-of-doors to instruct the removal-men as to where things were to be dumped. To do them justice they worked with fury once they had begun, though with ill-will. They ought to have been very grateful for all the voluntary assistance given to them by the masons, plumbers, painters, electricians and iron-workers who had permanently deserted their own work to join in the fun—but nothing seemed to please them.

At length the first van was actually depleted, the empty cases packed into it, the tractor attached once more and the horrible Monster thundered off down the drive. The struggle was over for a time; *Monsieur le Chef* appeared with his mugs of onion soup, and the workmen all squatted down among the shavings and *débris* to discuss the exciting events of the morning. For our part, we sank exhausted upon a few stray cushions and ate our sandwiches in apprehensive silence, knowing that 'The Son of a Pig' would soon be grunting on his way from Nice.

"What a morning!" exclaimed Madame.

"With a hell of an afternoon ahead!" ejaculated Monsieur.

And the little *bonne*, looking from one to the other with

dancing eyes, suddenly banged down the coffee she had contrived to make amid the wreckage in the kitchen, held her little fat sides and laughed and laughed and laughed.

"*Dieu d'Amour !*" she gasped when she could speak. After which we all felt better.

Our coffee was interrupted by a deputation of enraged men. The second van had, it appeared, arrived, but was sunk in our mountain lane half a kilometre away from the house. The 'Son of a Pig' had, we were informed, crushed a wall, and was in danger of rushing down the mountain like his Gadarene ancestors. Of course, it was *our* fault, as had been the mishap of the morning. Only the mad English would send such fantastic vans to climb the mountains of France, to spoil the valuable olive-trees and crush walls laboriously made by the poor peasants. Now, the Niçois supposed, we should expect *them* to unload the van in the lane and carry huge masses of heavy furniture to the house—work for giants and not for mere men whose families relied upon them for bread. If we insisted upon such work we might have murder upon our souls, and widows and fatherless children upon our consciences for the rest of our mortal lives.

The workmen, roused from their slumbers by the arrival of the men, had risen from their curious recumbent attitudes, heads on buckets, legs curled round a branch, and were listening intently. Big Jean suggested scornfully that a jack might be found and the van levered out of the road. Various masons volunteered to prop up the falling wall, "*Diable ! ce n'etait rien !*" And the whole band of them, enchanted once more to leave their own jobs and join in the fray, hustled off the Niçois to the scene of the disaster.

The van was eventually levered out and the wall shored up, and then the tractor dragging the huge van came crashing down the mountain, rushed through our entrance, carrying away a gatepost, slicing once more Hilaire's precious grass and smashing a young cherry-tree ; and the two, van and tractor, locked together by the force of impact, came to rest near our garage.

Then, of course, they had to be disentangled and dismantled before the doors of the van could be opened. However, with forty people assisting, this did not take very long, and soon the work proceeded.

Working with sulky removal-men, who obviously held us responsible for every difficulty that had to be surmounted, was not very heartening. But suddenly a very little thing changed their whole attitude. The first object to be unpacked from the second van was a gnarled oak root, transformed into a thing of beauty by the artist who fashioned the Elfin Oak in Kensington Gardens for the children of London. As I unwrapped it and the Niçois beheld the forms of fairies, gnomes, pixies, lizards, mice, an owl, a frog and a rat, found in the natural contortions of the wood, moulded further and then painted, they grouped around me silent and fascinated. English workmen would have picked up the root and dumped it in a room with other junk, unremarked. Not so these impressionable Southerners.

Seizing my opportunity I told them the story of the wonderful Elfin Oak of Kensington Gardens, describing the seventy-five figures of birds, beasts and The Little People the artist had found in it. The men listened enthralled; they had naturally never seen anything like it before. They stroked the little beasts with grimy forefingers and noticed their gleaming eyes.

My husband grew impatient, not realising the importance of the incident, but I finished my story, and then, with great sighs as though waking from a dream, they walked back to the van. But the fairies had bewitched them with their magic and transformed them from surly brutes into laughing, willing workers. They heaved heavy furniture on to their heads, and, puny as they looked, carried huge objects up steep terraces and stairways until, as dusk fell, the second van was empty and lumbered away. The battle was over, silence fell over the little domain, and only the battlefield strewn with shavings and old newspapers told the tale of our struggles.

There was as yet no electric light in the house and we had no candles. It was impossible to sleep in the house that night, so we decided to instal Hilaire as guardian. We fixed up a mattress on the floor, and I found three satin eiderdowns and a brocade cushion for his old bald head; and there he lay with his double-barrelled fowling-piece beside him, unable to sleep for fear that *voleurs* would come, murder him first, and then make off with all *les belles choses* of Monsieur and Madame. So he told us next day, and I had reached the stage when I really wished they *had*, so gigantic seemed the task of getting the house into order.

For, at the end of the day, having no more room to store anything indoors, out-houses being stacked from floor to ceiling, we had been driven in desperation to use the empty dog-kennels, hen-runs and rabbit-houses. These were now filled with odd objects of all sorts which must be sorted and placed elsewhere.

The very last straw which finally broke our patient backs was when, worn out with fatigue, we discovered that our car would not start. We tried everything, but the oil in the engine seemed to have frozen hard. Wrapped in rugs we wandered up and down in the darkness while our little *bonne*, who knew the locality, went in search of a house with a telephone on which she could summon aid from a garage.

After an Arctic interval, succour came; the engine was made to work and we all drove back to the flat. So ended one of the most terrific days of our lives.

In two days we were actually installed in part of our house, where we lived in a cloud of cement dust to the accompaniment of the music of masons and carpenters for many exhausting weeks. The work began to go on more quickly after our installation, and one morning, on going out into the garden, I was startled to see the new building decorated with a mass of flags of all nations, the English predominating; branches of trees were tied to the scaffolding; bosses of ivy hung from poles; two little pine-trees adorned with huge bows of flame-coloured ribbon (a gift, as I afterwards learned, from the old *Entrepreneur* himself) flanked the entrance to the Gallery, and a complete pine-tree was lashed to the spike of the Provençal tower.

La Cabade was upon us! The roof was ON! Then I knew what was expected of us. Workmen's eager faces beamed at me from every hole in the building, and I climbed up and shook them each and all by the hand and thanked them for their lovely decorations.

My husband and I unearthed some blue curtains with which we decorated the inside of the garage, and rigged up a long trestle table. This I covered with blue cloths and decorated with bowls of violets, vases of carnations and every cut-glass tumbler and wine-glass that I could find. We threw down blue garden cushions on plank benches, and then I drove down to the town and came back laden with bottles of red wine, tins of 'fancy' biscuits which I arranged in little silver cardboard shells on my table, packets of cigarettes and tobacco, and those wicked-looking slim black cheroots, beloved of all Italian workmen.

I put on a red chiffon frock with red shoes, tucked red carnations in my hair (to look Carnivalish) and went downstairs to receive my guests.

I turned on a gay waltz on the gramophone, and then my husband had an inspiration. He blew a loud blast on our puppy-whistle in imitation of the 'cease work' signal which had sounded so often and sometimes so ominously in our ears. The foreman's indignant face instantly peered out of a window to see who was usurping his authority, but when he saw my husband twinkling at him from below, he rocked with laughter and came scrambling down the scaffolding followed by his thirty masons, who burst from every aperture chattering and laughing like a crowd of excited children.

We shook each by the hand (once more) and led them to the garage. The old *Entrepreneur* resplendent in his best broadcloth had arrived with his chauffeur son, and he had the tact to invite Hilaire to sit in the place of honour on his right hand. Then Monsieur and Madame poured out wine, proposed toasts, listened to good wishes and served out biscuits and cigars for two solid hours. Everyone got very flushed; everyone talked and laughed at once; everyone (except the host and hostess) sang a solo, and all enjoyed themselves hugely.

And, nicest of all, everyone helped to take down the curtains and to carry cushions, wine-glasses, &c., into the house after the feast before they all drove off in a *camion*, singing into the night.

But the great moment of my day came when I gave the giant carpenter his tip in an envelope (for everyone gets a tip in an envelope at parting on these occasions). He and I happened to be alone with Monsieur in the salon when I gave it, and, to our immense astonishment (and my delight) he bent his beautiful head and very reverently kissed me on both cheeks, murmuring his thanks as though he were singing under water.

My enjoyment would have been greater had my mind not been clouded by apprehension lest all the other workmen should salute me in like manner, none of them very clean and all very prickly with a week's growth of beard (*La Cabade* fell on a Saturday), but happily only my beautiful clean-shaven giant did me that honour.

It was wonderful to know that the roof was really ON, and that soon our army of workmen would depart. We should miss them in more ways than one, but we longed for peace and privacy. But at last they did leave us, shaking